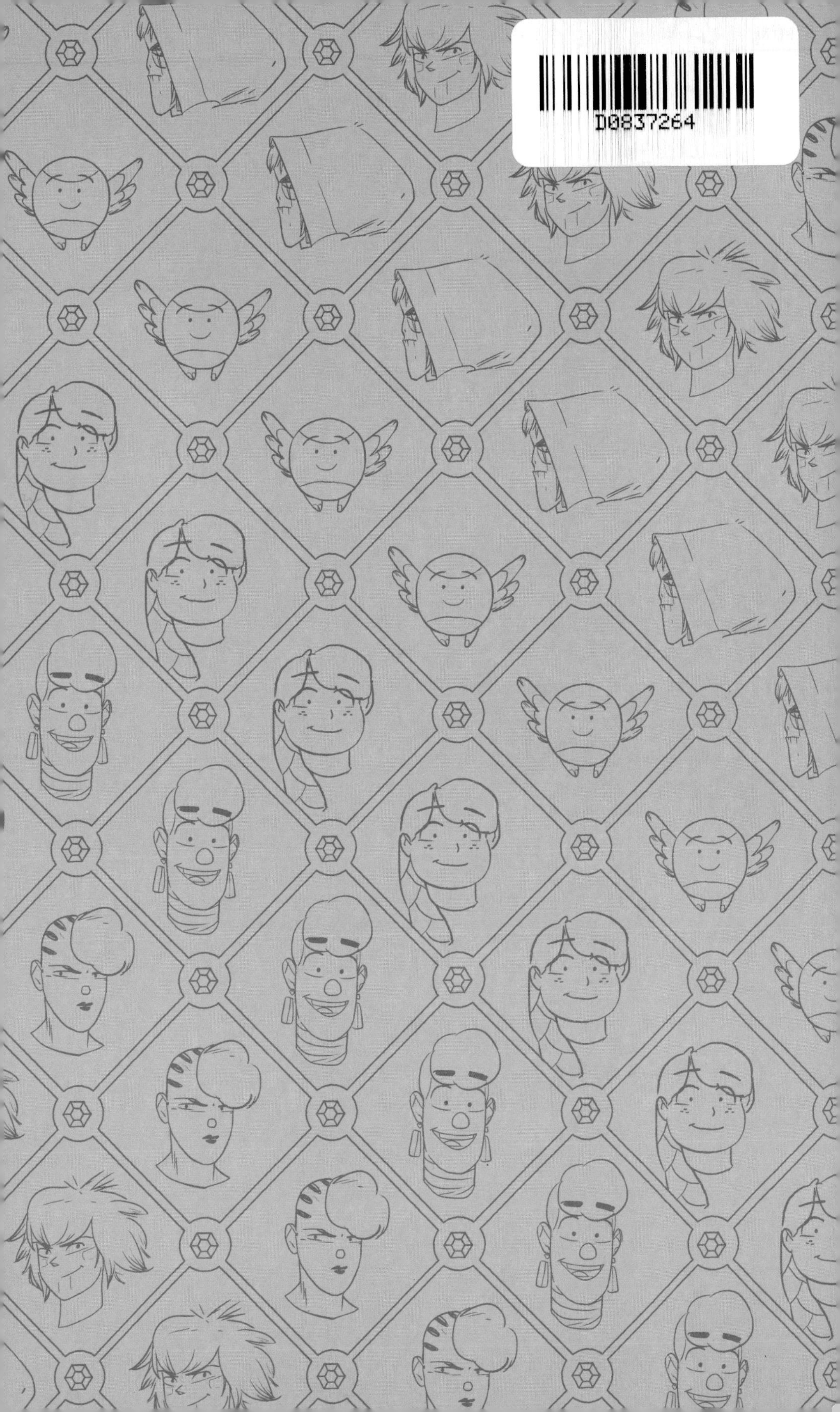

TKO STUDIOS

SALVATORE SIMEONE - CEO & PUBLISHER

TZE CHUN - PRESIDENT & PUBLISHER

JATIN THAKKER - CHIEF OPERATING OFFICER

SEBASTIAN GIRNER - EDITOR-IN-CHIEF

SCALES & SCOUNDRELS BOOK 1: WHERE DRAGONS WANDER

Published by TKO Studios, LLC.
Office of Publication: 1325 Franklin Avenue, Suite 545, Garden City, NY 11530.

ISBN: 978-1-952203-22-0

TKOPRESENTS.COM

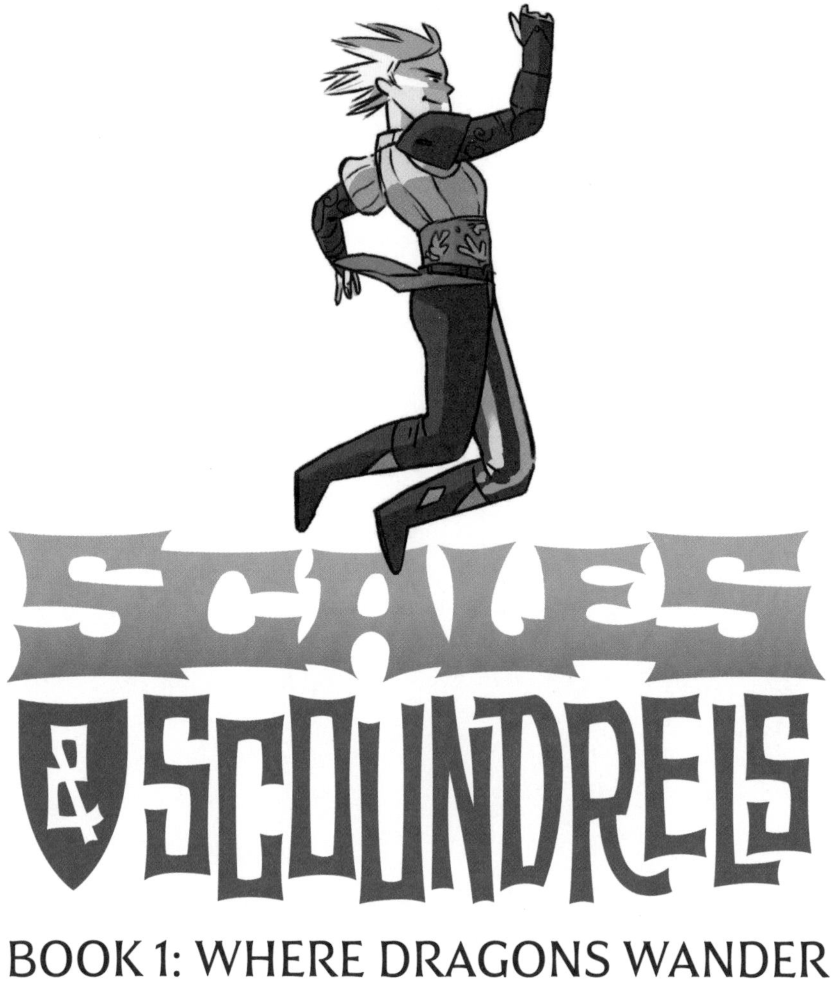

SCALES & SCOUNDRELS

BOOK 1: WHERE DRAGONS WANDER

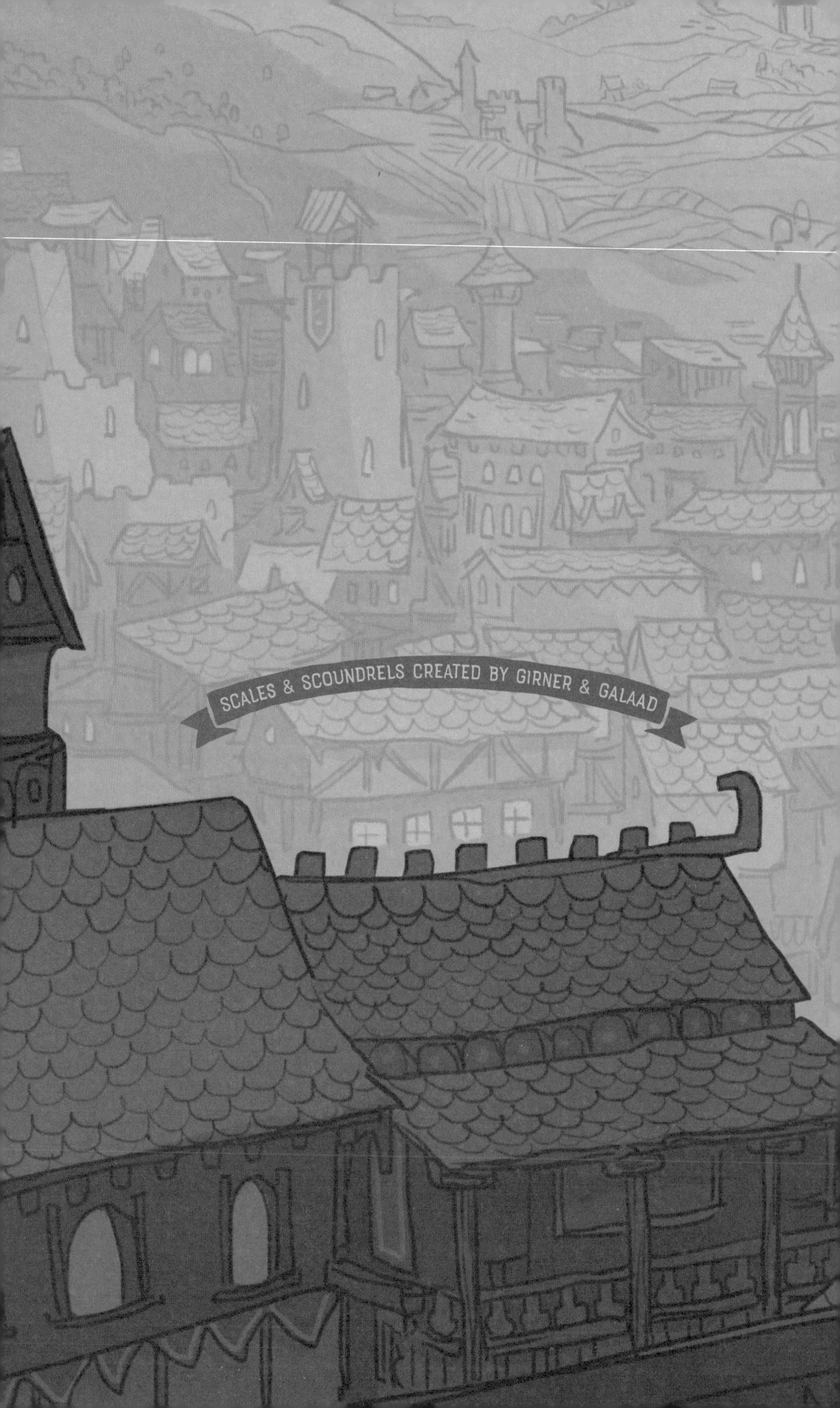
SCALES & SCOUNDRELS CREATED BY GIRNER & GALAAD

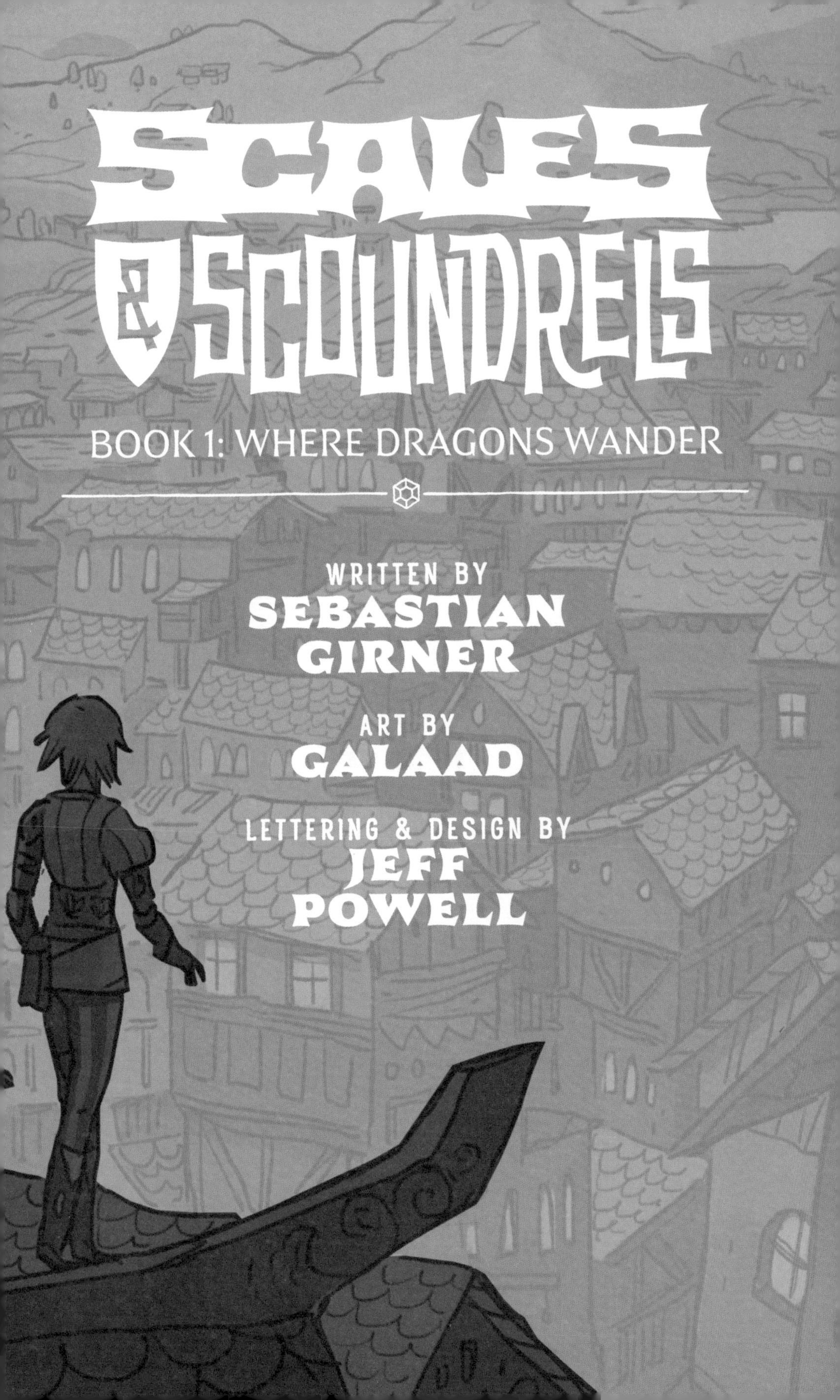

SCALES & SCOUNDRELS

BOOK 1: WHERE DRAGONS WANDER

WRITTEN BY
SEBASTIAN GIRNER

ART BY
GALAAD

LETTERING & DESIGN BY
JEFF POWELL

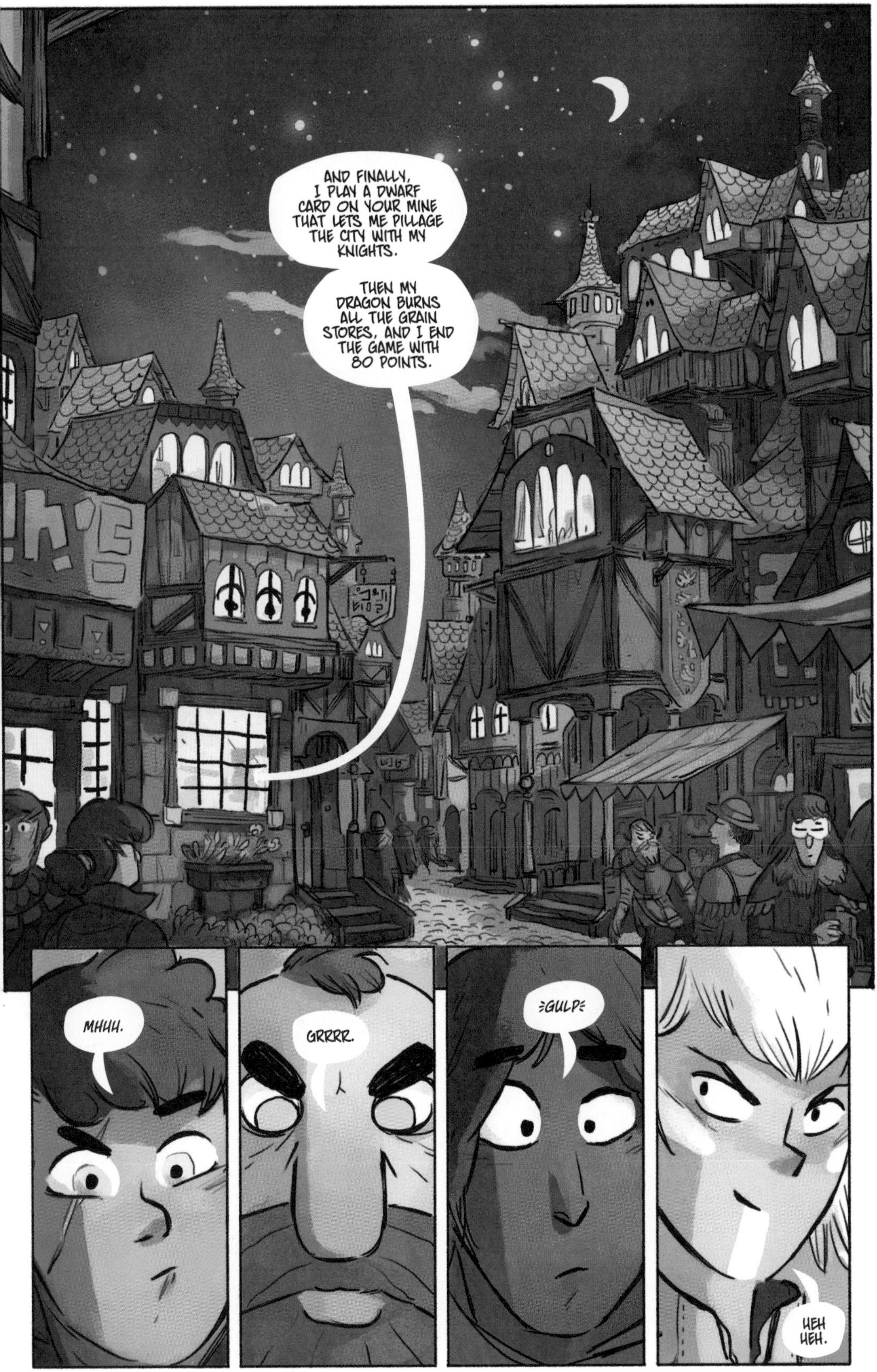
AND FINALLY, I PLAY A DWARF CARD ON YOUR MINE THAT LETS ME PILLAGE THE CITY WITH MY KNIGHTS.
THEN MY DRAGON BURNS ALL THE GRAIN STORES, AND I END THE GAME WITH 80 POINTS.
MHHH.
GRRRR.
GULP
HEH HEH.

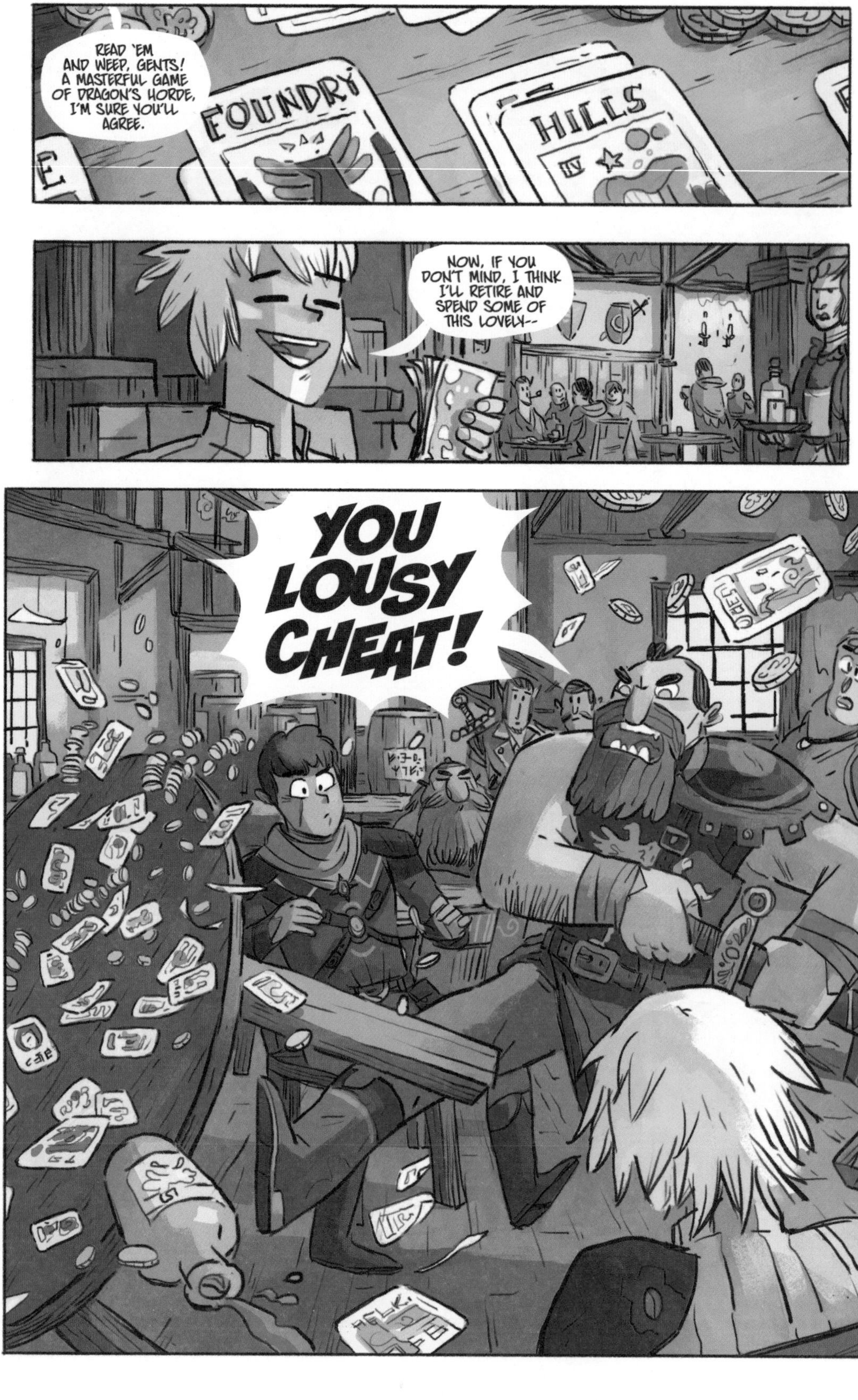

READ 'EM AND WEEP, GENTS! A MASTERFUL GAME OF DRAGON'S HORDE, I'M SURE YOU'LL AGREE.
FOUNDRY
HILLS
NOW, IF YOU DON'T MIND, I THINK I'LL RETIRE AND SPEND SOME OF THIS LOVELY--
YOU LOUSY CHEAT!

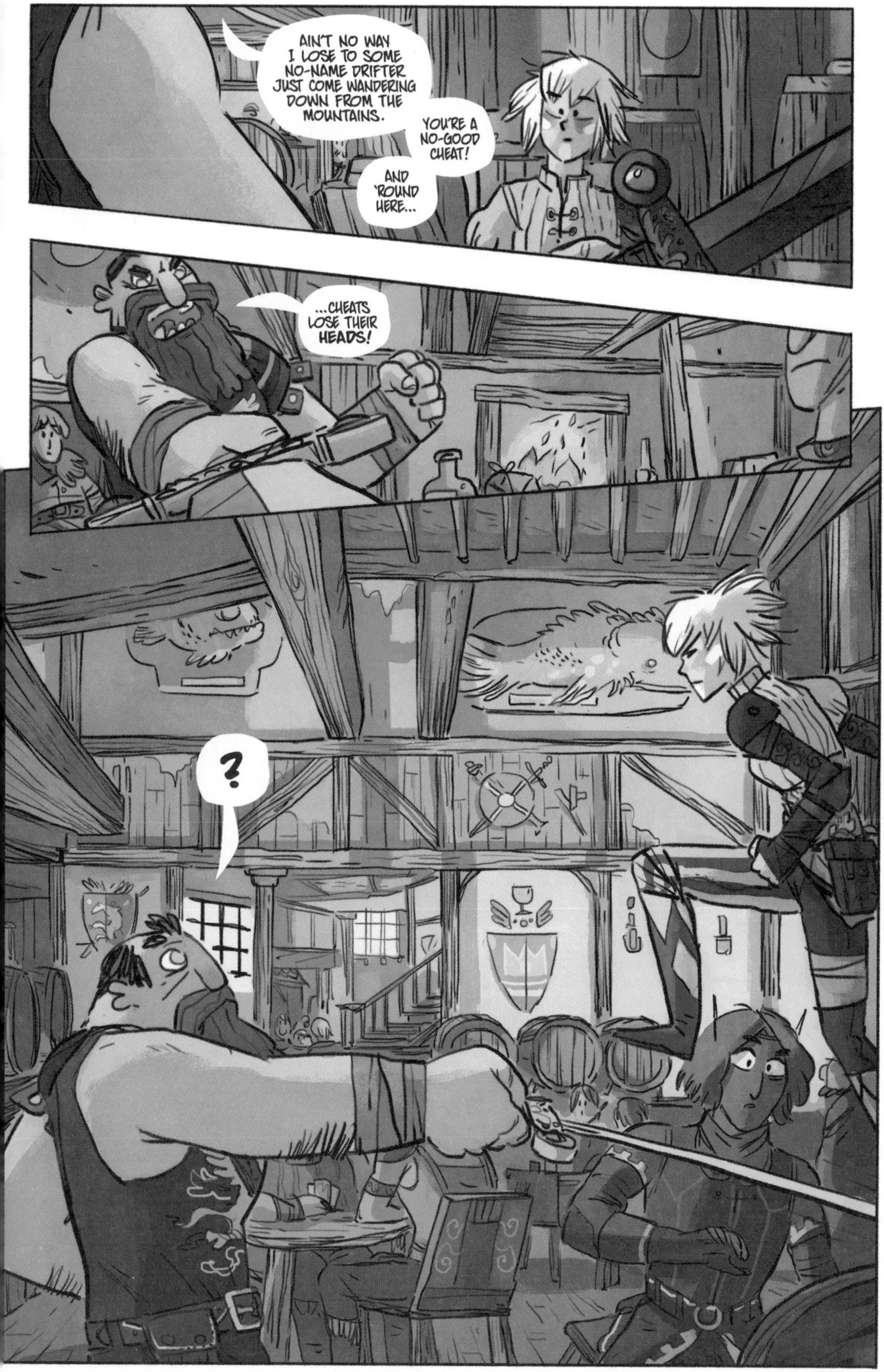
AIN'T NO WAY I LOSE TO SOME NO-NAME DRIFTER JUST COME WANDERING DOWN FROM THE MOUNTAINS.
YOU'RE A NO-GOOD CHEAT!
AND 'ROUND HERE...
...CHEATS LOSE THEIR HEADS!
?

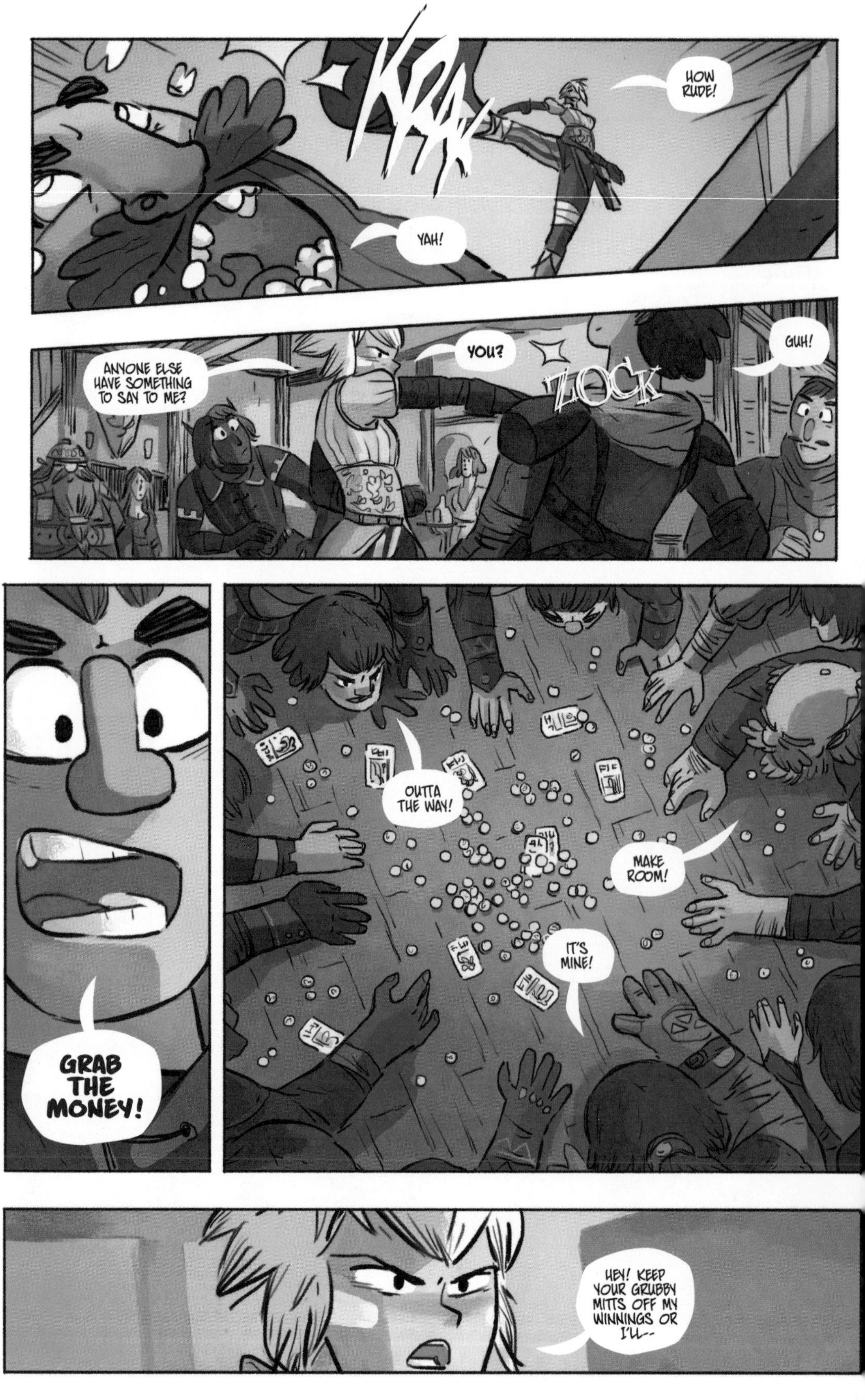
KRAK
HOW RUDE!
YAH!
ANYONE ELSE HAVE SOMETHING TO SAY TO ME?
YOU?
ZOCK
GUH!
GRAB THE MONEY!
OUTTA THE WAY!
MAKE ROOM!
IT'S MINE!
HEY! KEEP YOUR GRUBBY MITTS OFF MY WINNINGS OR I'LL--

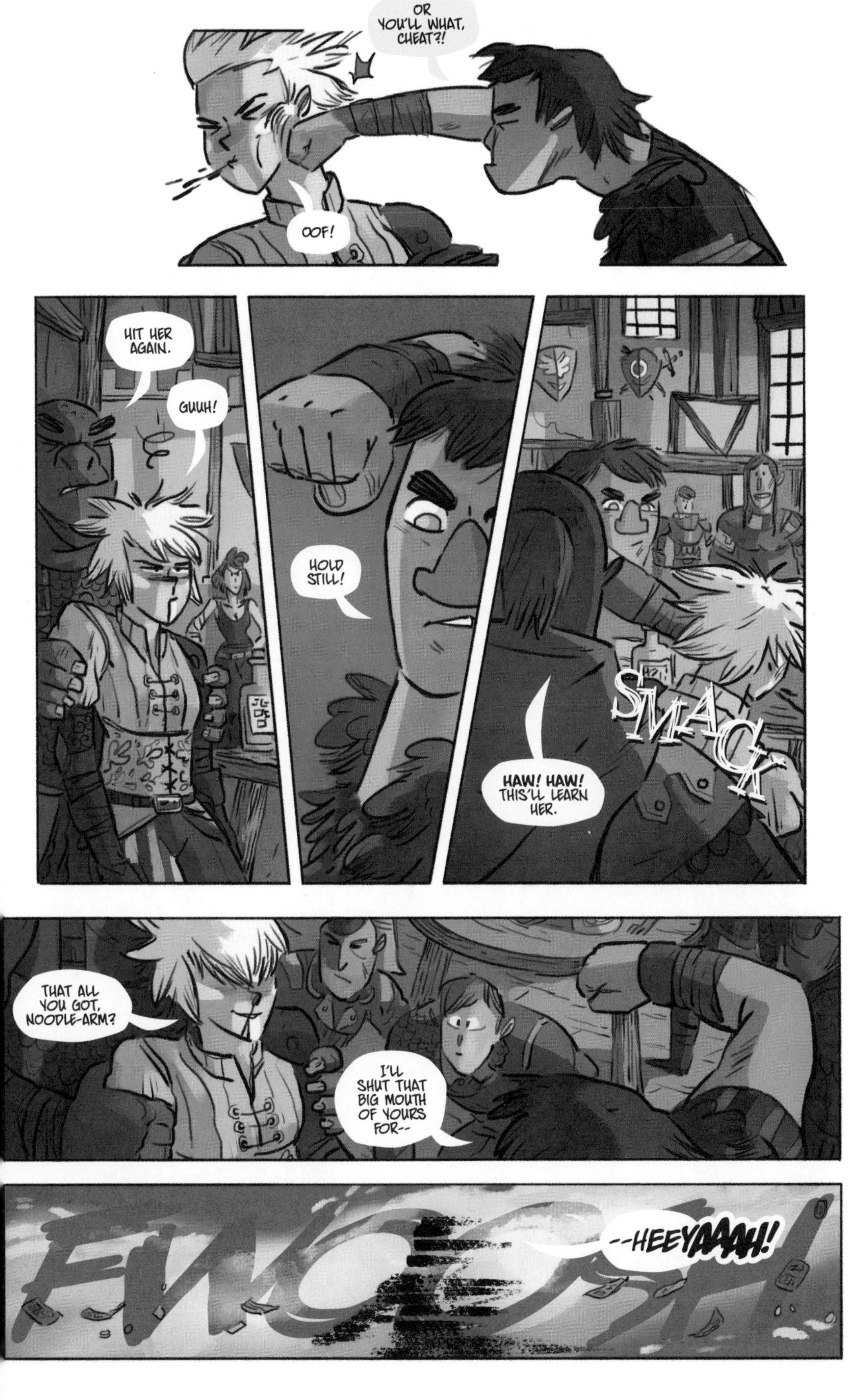

OR YOU'LL WHAT, CHEAT?!
OOF!
HIT HER AGAIN.
GUUH!
HOLD STILL!
SMACK
HAW! HAW! THIS'LL LEARN HER.
THAT ALL YOU GOT, NOODLE-ARM?
I'LL SHUT THAT BIG MOUTH OF YOURS FOR--
FWOOSH!
--HEEYAAAH!

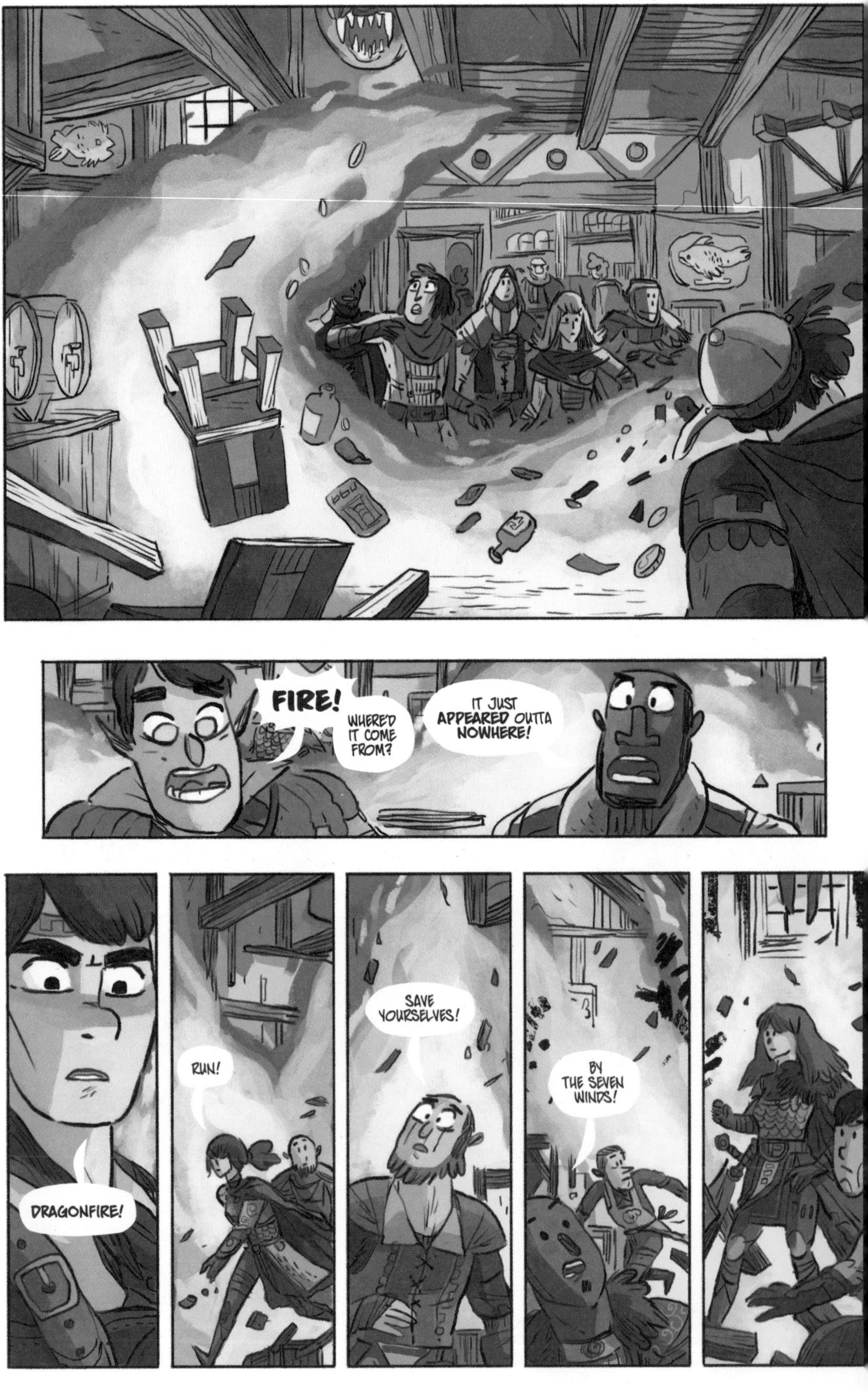
FIRE!
WHERE'D IT COME FROM?
IT JUST APPEARED OUTTA NOWHERE!
DRAGONFIRE!
RUN!
SAVE YOURSELVES!
BY THE SEVEN WINDS!

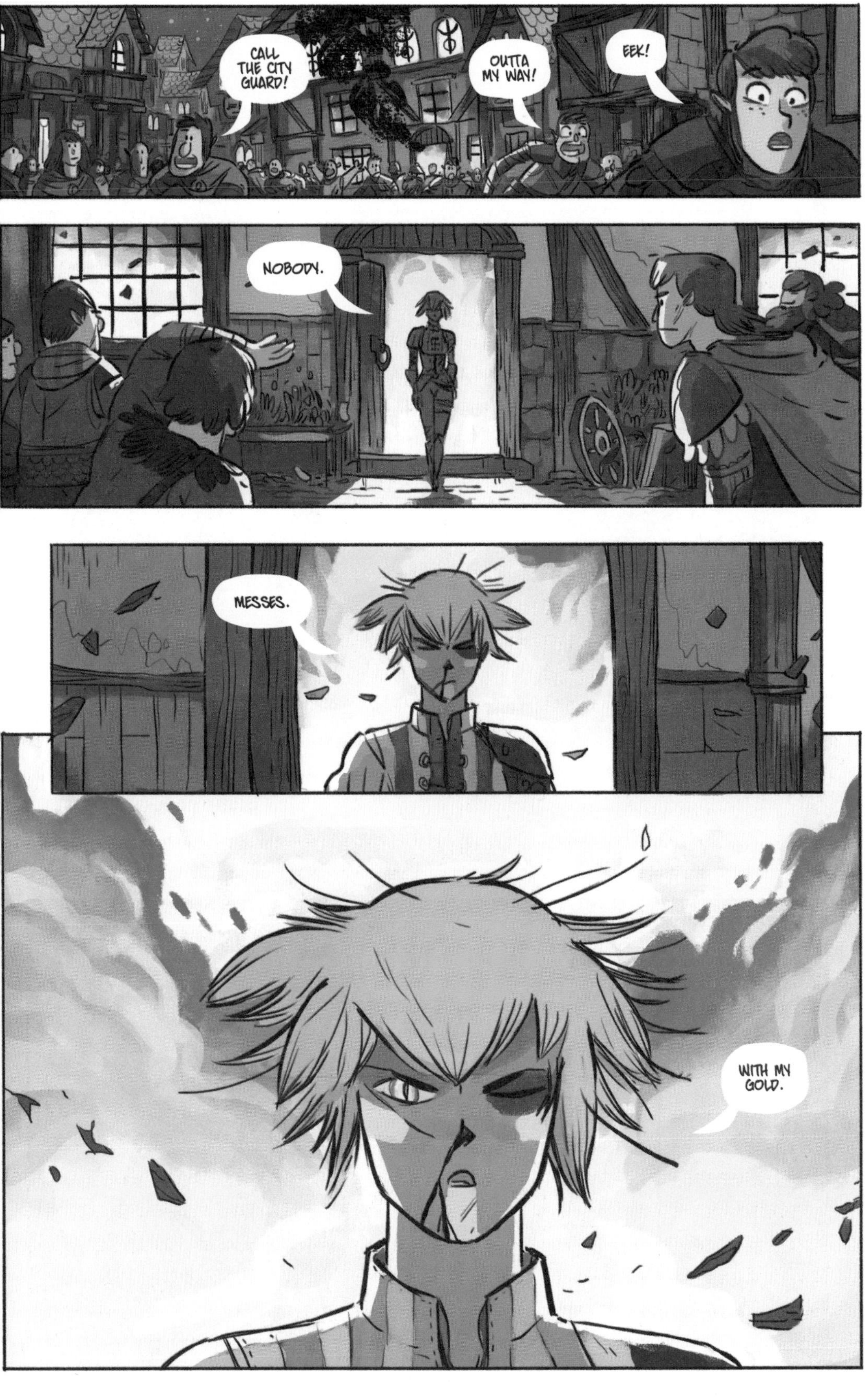
CALL THE CITY GUARD!
OUTTA MY WAY!
EEK!
NOBODY.
MESSES.
WITH MY GOLD.

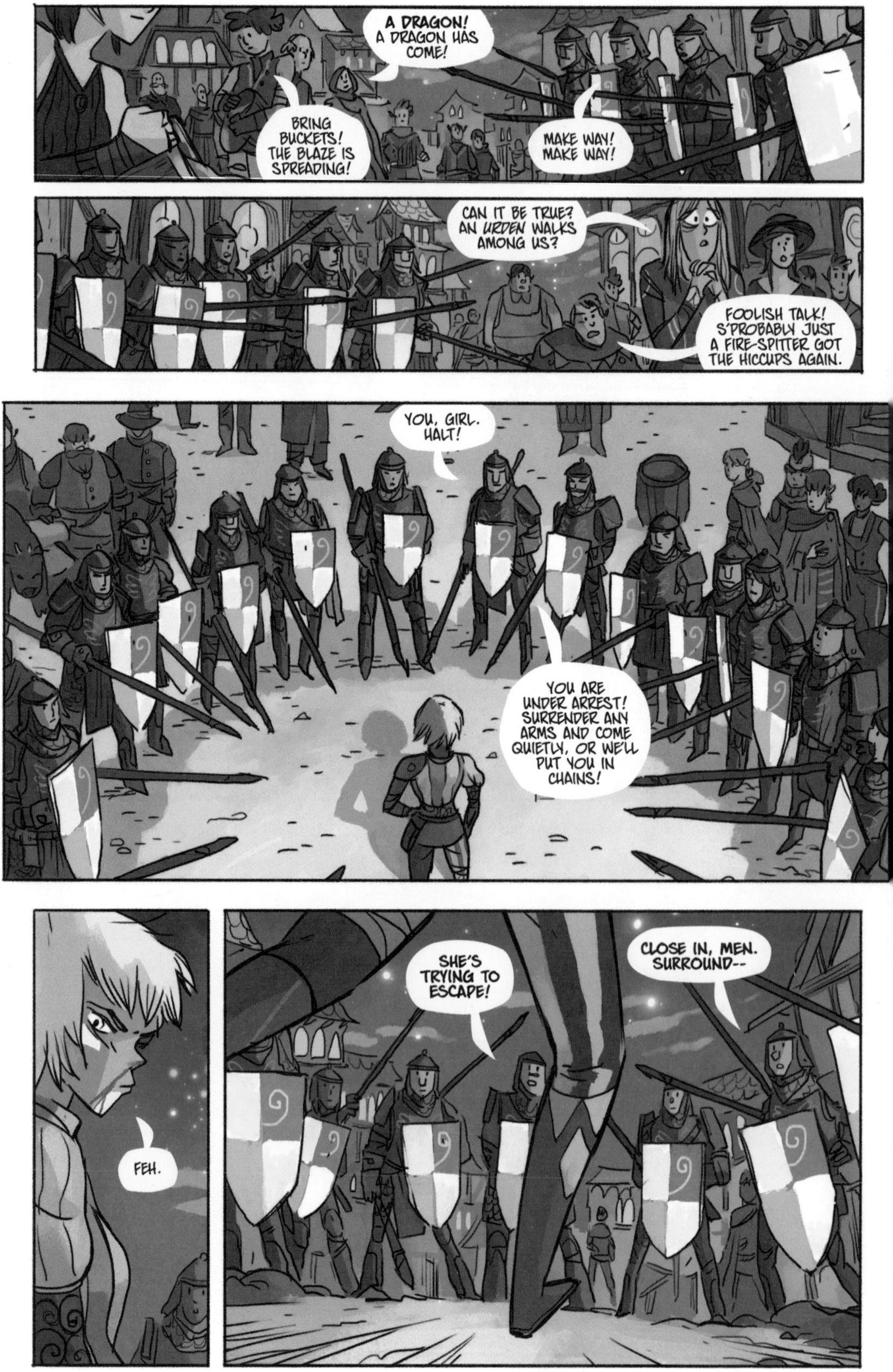
A DRAGON! A DRAGON HAS COME!
BRING BUCKETS! THE BLAZE IS SPREADING!
MAKE WAY! MAKE WAY!
CAN IT BE TRUE? AN URDEN WALKS AMONG US?
FOOLISH TALK! S'PROBABLY JUST A FIRE-SPITTER GOT THE HICCUPS AGAIN.
YOU, GIRL. HALT!
YOU ARE UNDER ARREST! SURRENDER ANY ARMS AND COME QUIETLY, OR WE'LL PUT YOU IN CHAINS!
FEH.
SHE'S TRYING TO ESCAPE!
CLOSE IN, MEN. SURROUND--

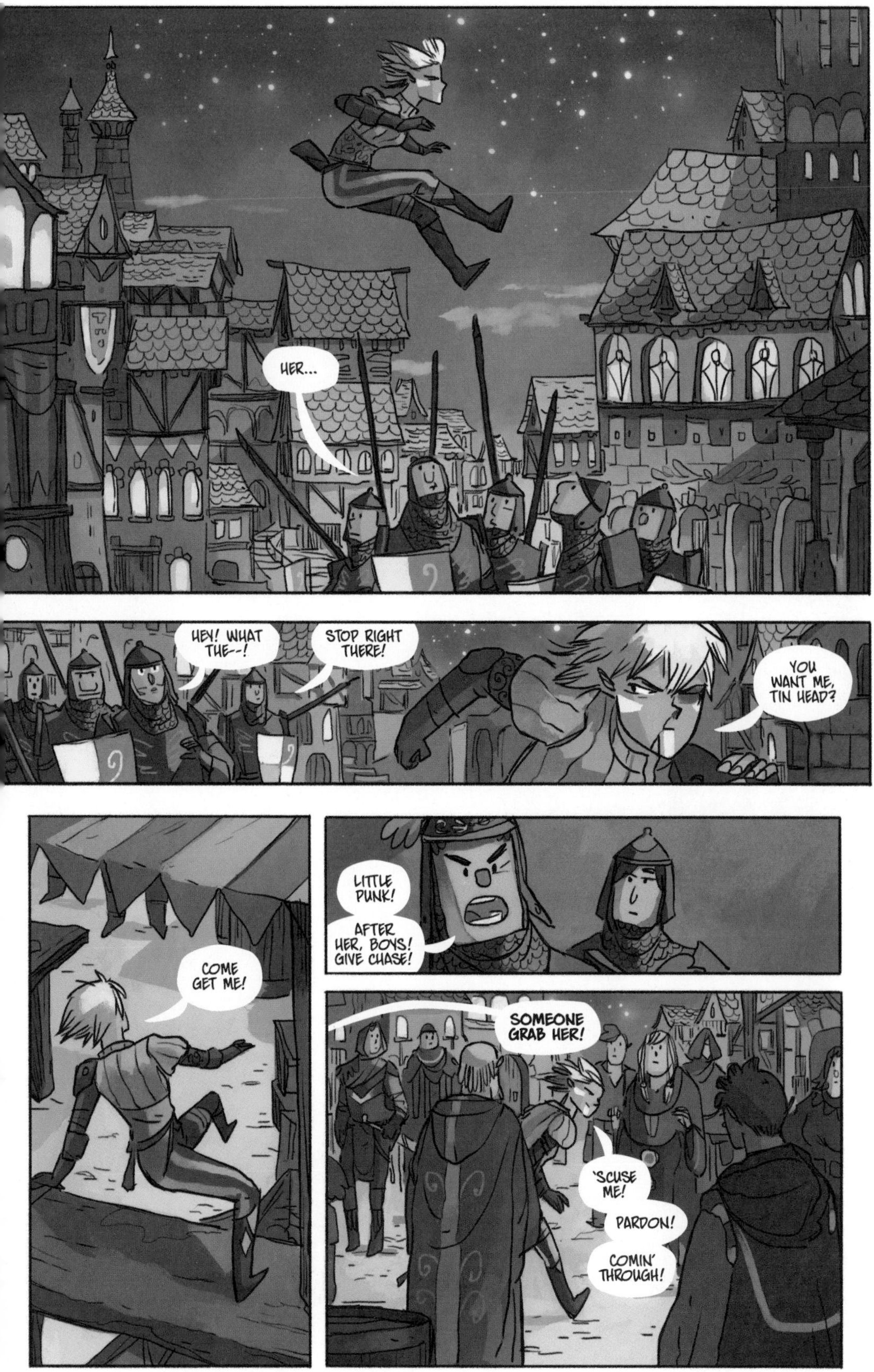
HER...
HEY! WHAT THE--!
STOP RIGHT THERE!
YOU WANT ME, TIN HEAD?
COME GET ME!
LITTLE PUNK!
AFTER HER, BOYS! GIVE CHASE!
SOMEONE GRAB HER!
'SCUSE ME!
PARDON!
COMIN' THROUGH!

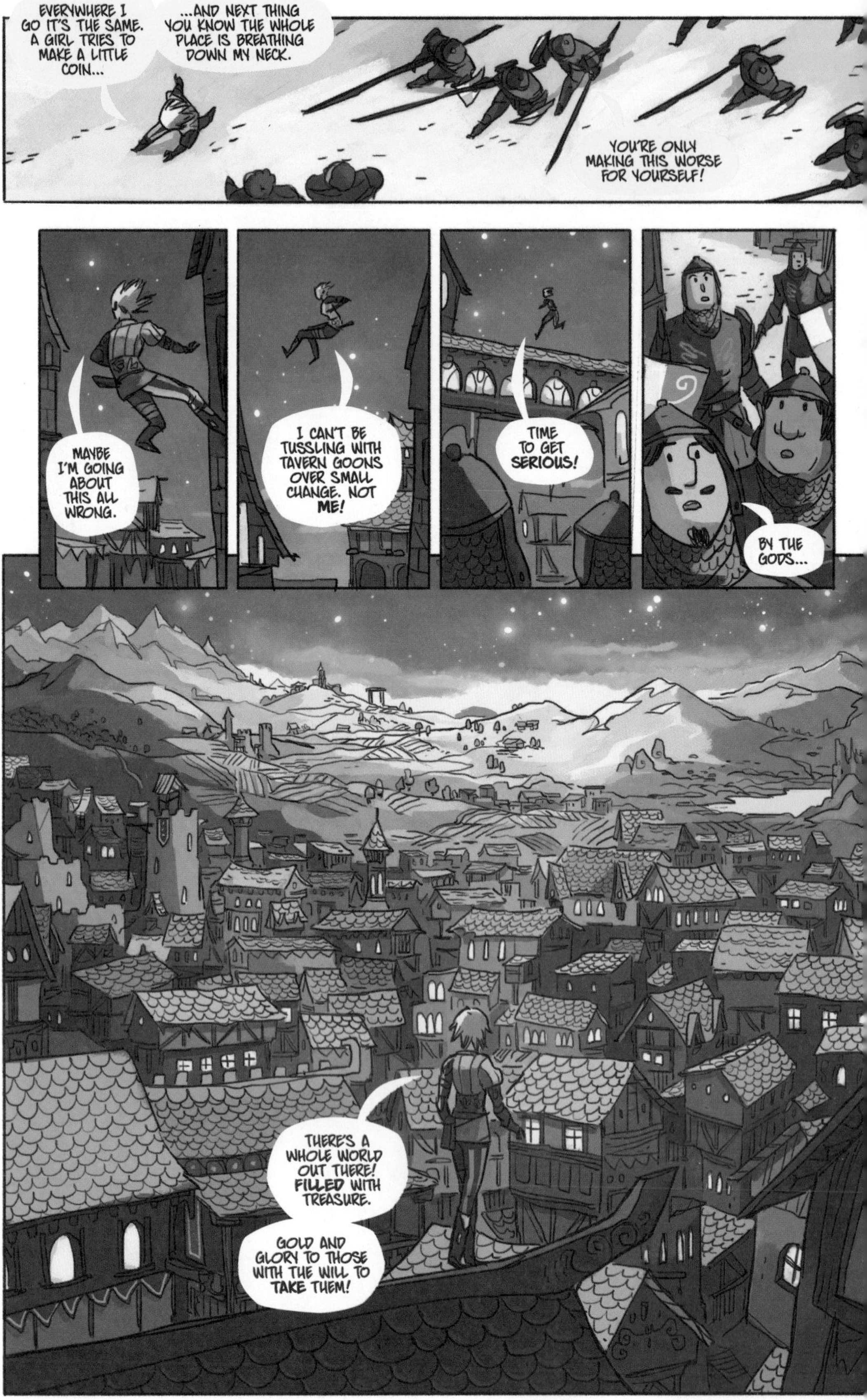
EVERYWHERE I GO IT'S THE SAME. A GIRL TRIES TO MAKE A LITTLE COIN...
...AND NEXT THING YOU KNOW THE WHOLE PLACE IS BREATHING DOWN MY NECK.
YOU'RE ONLY MAKING THIS WORSE FOR YOURSELF!
MAYBE I'M GOING ABOUT THIS ALL WRONG.
I CAN'T BE TUSSLING WITH TAVERN GOONS OVER SMALL CHANGE. NOT ME!
TIME TO GET SERIOUS!
BY THE GODS...
THERE'S A WHOLE WORLD OUT THERE! FILLED WITH TREASURE.
GOLD AND GLORY TO THOSE WITH THE WILL TO TAKE THEM!

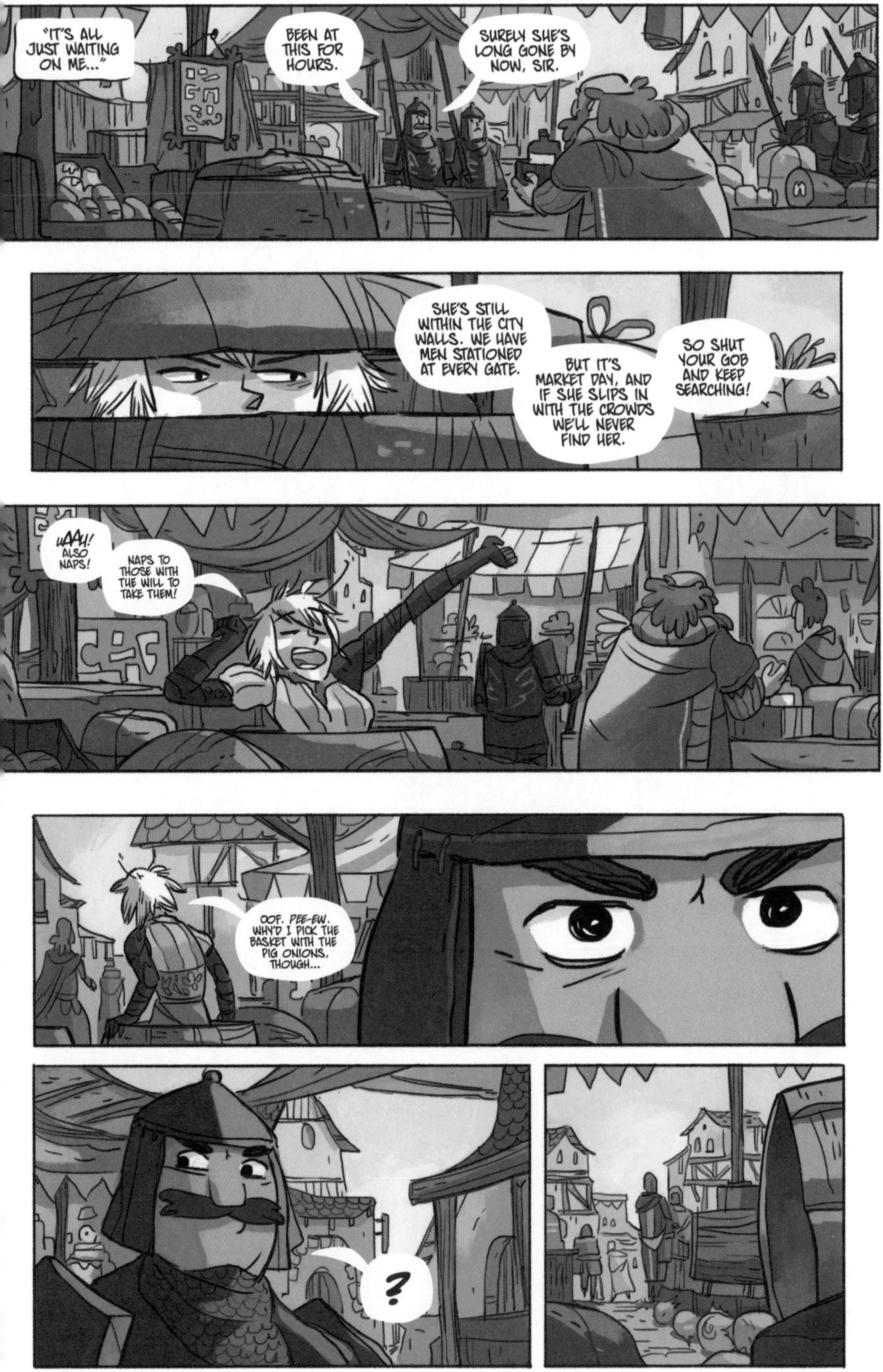
"IT'S ALL JUST WAITING ON ME..."
BEEN AT THIS FOR HOURS.
SURELY SHE'S LONG GONE BY NOW, SIR.
SHE'S STILL WITHIN THE CITY WALLS. WE HAVE MEN STATIONED AT EVERY GATE.
BUT IT'S MARKET DAY, AND IF SHE SLIPS IN WITH THE CROWDS WE'LL NEVER FIND HER.
SO SHUT YOUR GOB AND KEEP SEARCHING!
UAAH! ALSO NAPS!
NAPS TO THOSE WITH THE WILL TO TAKE THEM!
OOF. PEE-EW. WHY'D I PICK THE BASKET WITH THE PIG ONIONS, THOUGH...
?

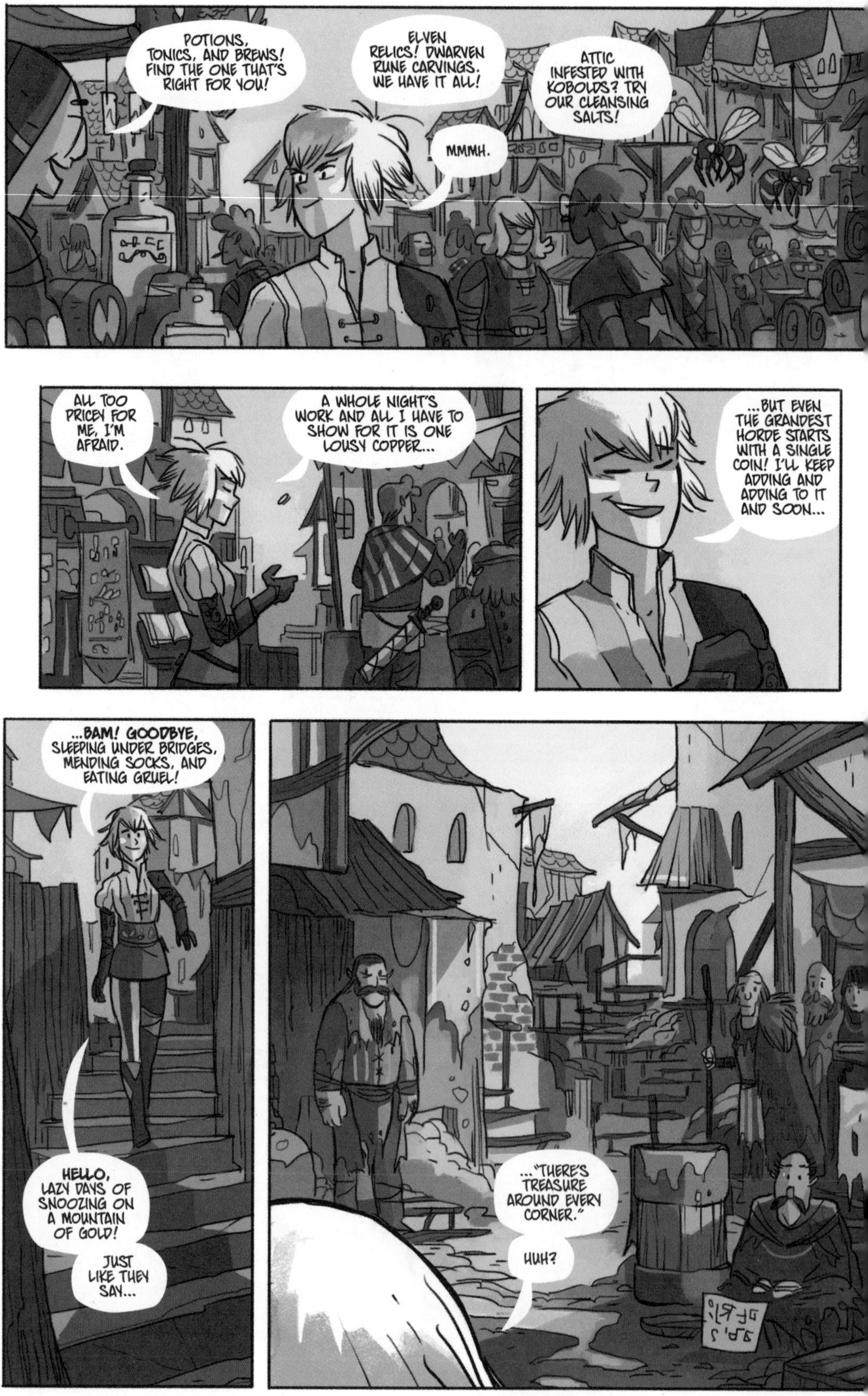

POTIONS, TONICS, AND BREWS! FIND THE ONE THAT'S RIGHT FOR YOU!
ELVEN RELICS! DWARVEN RUNE CARVINGS. WE HAVE IT ALL!
ATTIC INFESTED WITH KOBOLDS? TRY OUR CLEANSING SALTS!
MMMH.
ALL TOO PRICEY FOR ME, I'M AFRAID.
A WHOLE NIGHT'S WORK AND ALL I HAVE TO SHOW FOR IT IS ONE LOUSY COPPER...
...BUT EVEN THE GRANDEST HORDE STARTS WITH A SINGLE COIN! I'LL KEEP ADDING AND ADDING TO IT AND SOON...
...BAM! GOODBYE, SLEEPING UNDER BRIDGES, MENDING SOCKS, AND EATING GRUEL!
HELLO, LAZY DAYS OF SNOOZING ON A MOUNTAIN OF GOLD!
JUST LIKE THEY SAY...
..."THERE'S TREASURE AROUND EVERY CORNER."
HUH?

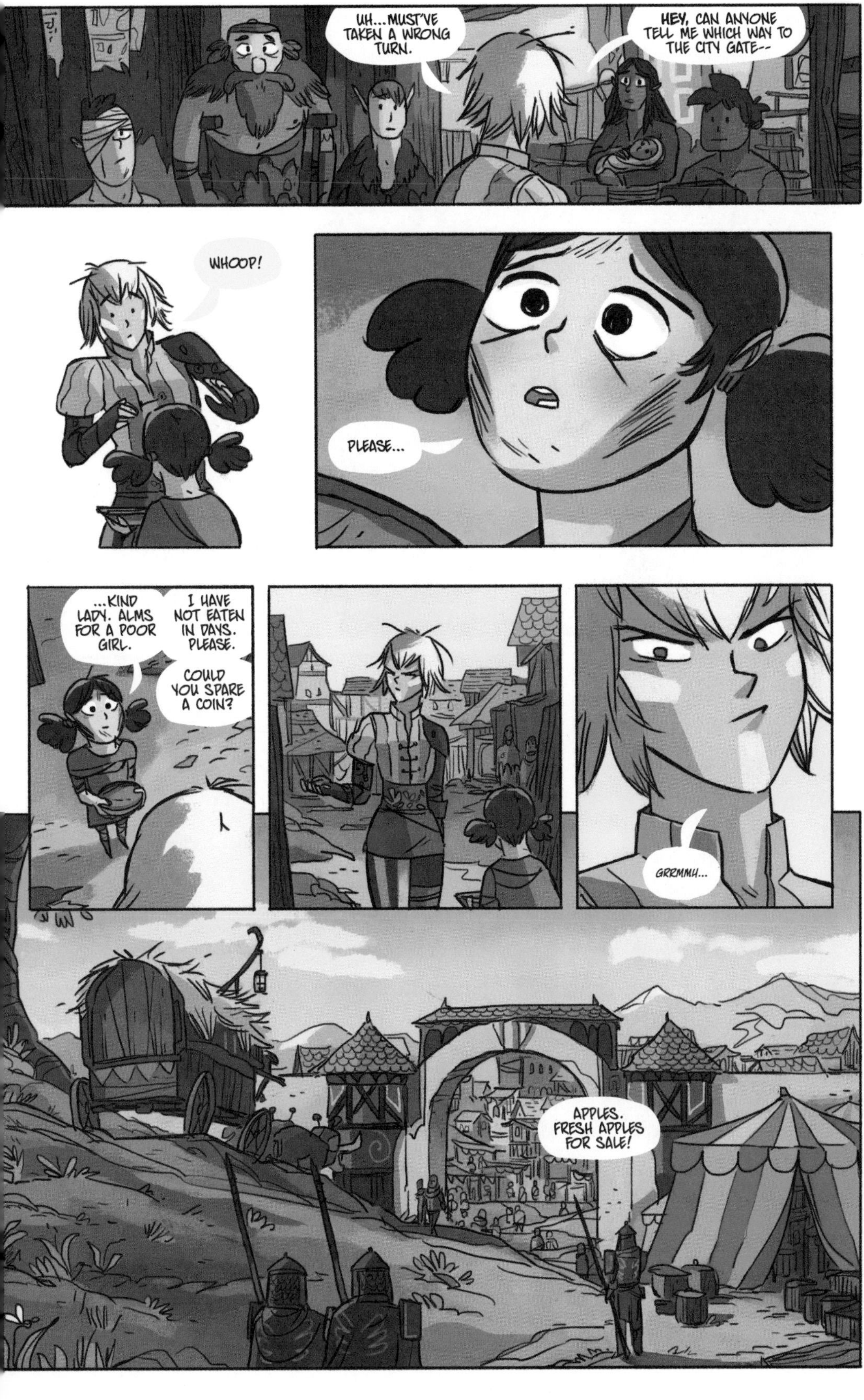
UH...MUST'VE TAKEN A WRONG TURN.
HEY, CAN ANYONE TELL ME WHICH WAY TO THE CITY GATE--
WHOOP!
PLEASE...
...KIND LADY. ALMS FOR A POOR GIRL.
I HAVE NOT EATEN IN DAYS. PLEASE.
COULD YOU SPARE A COIN?
GRRMMH...
APPLES. FRESH APPLES FOR SALE!

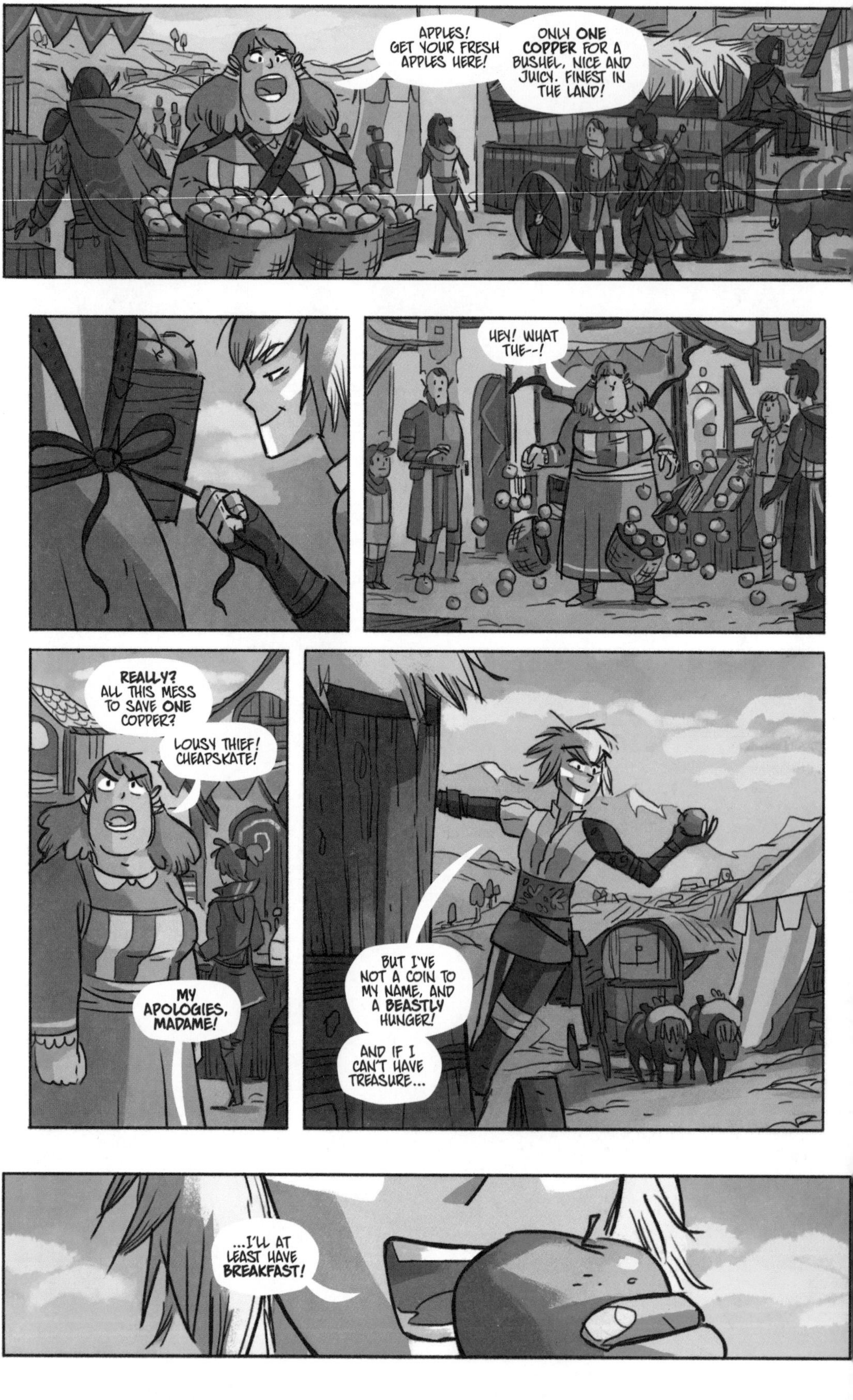
APPLES! GET YOUR FRESH APPLES HERE!
ONLY ONE COPPER FOR A BUSHEL, NICE AND JUICY. FINEST IN THE LAND!
HEY! WHAT THE--!
REALLY? ALL THIS MESS TO SAVE ONE COPPER?
LOUSY THIEF! CHEAPSKATE!
MY APOLOGIES, MADAME!
BUT I'VE NOT A COIN TO MY NAME, AND A BEASTLY HUNGER!
AND IF I CAN'T HAVE TREASURE...
...I'LL AT LEAST HAVE BREAKFAST!

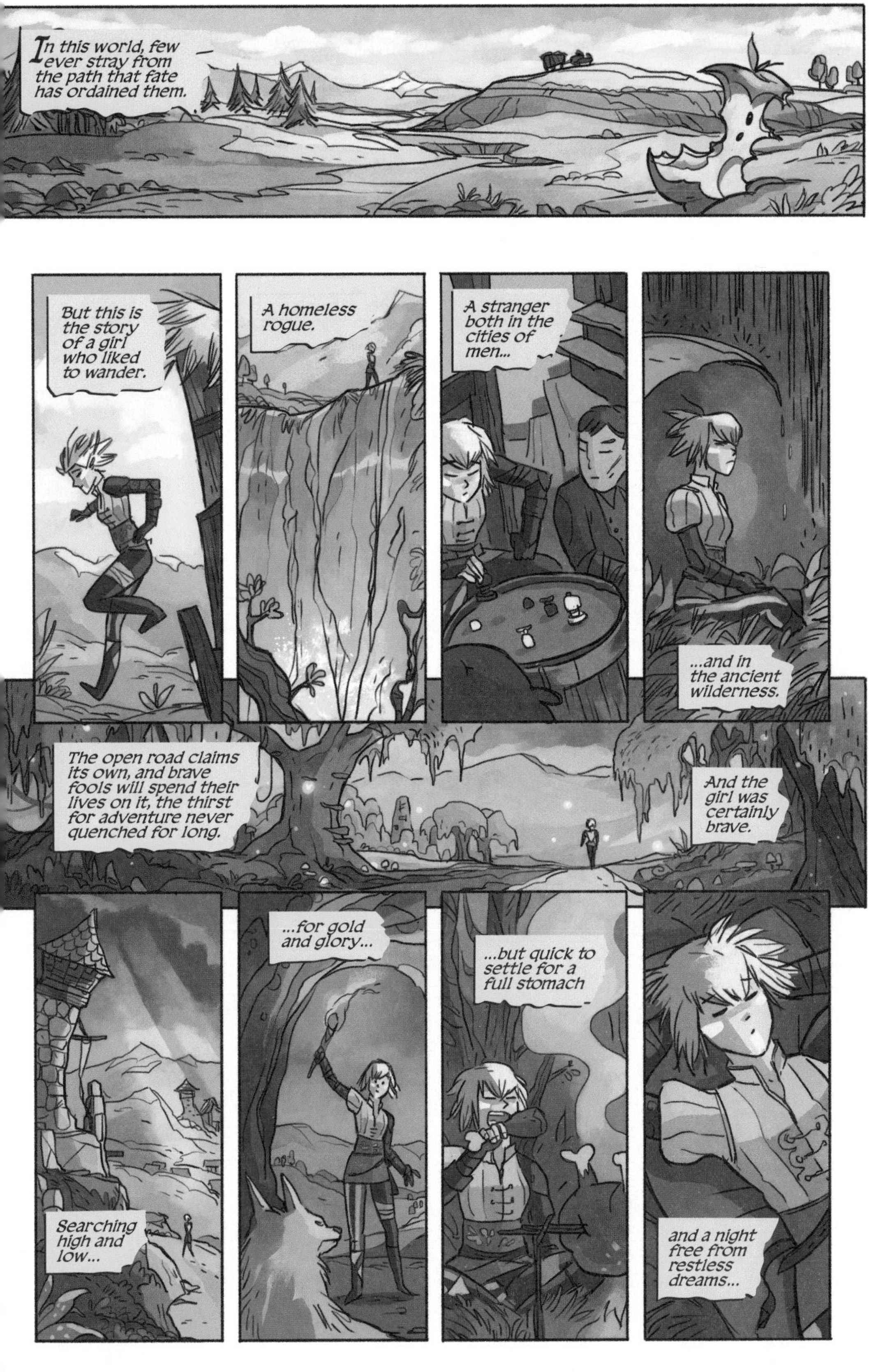

In this world, few ever stray from the path that fate has ordained them.
But this is the story of a girl who liked to wander.
A homeless rogue.
A stranger both in the cities of men...
...and in the ancient wilderness.
The open road claims its own, and brave fools will spend their lives on it, the thirst for adventure never quenched for long.
And the girl was certainly brave.
Searching high and low...
...for gold and glory...
...but quick to settle for a full stomach
and a night free from restless dreams...

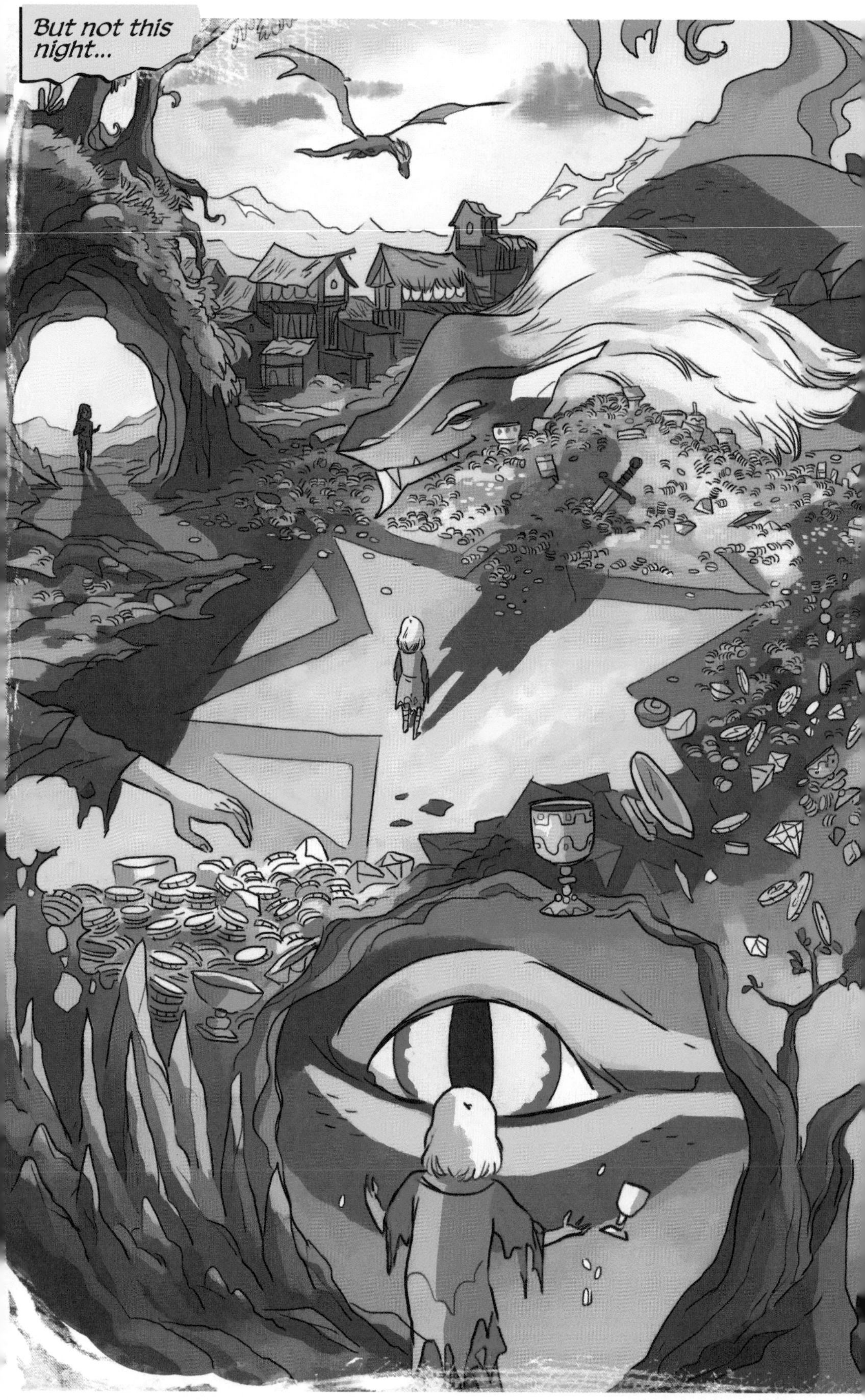
But not this night...

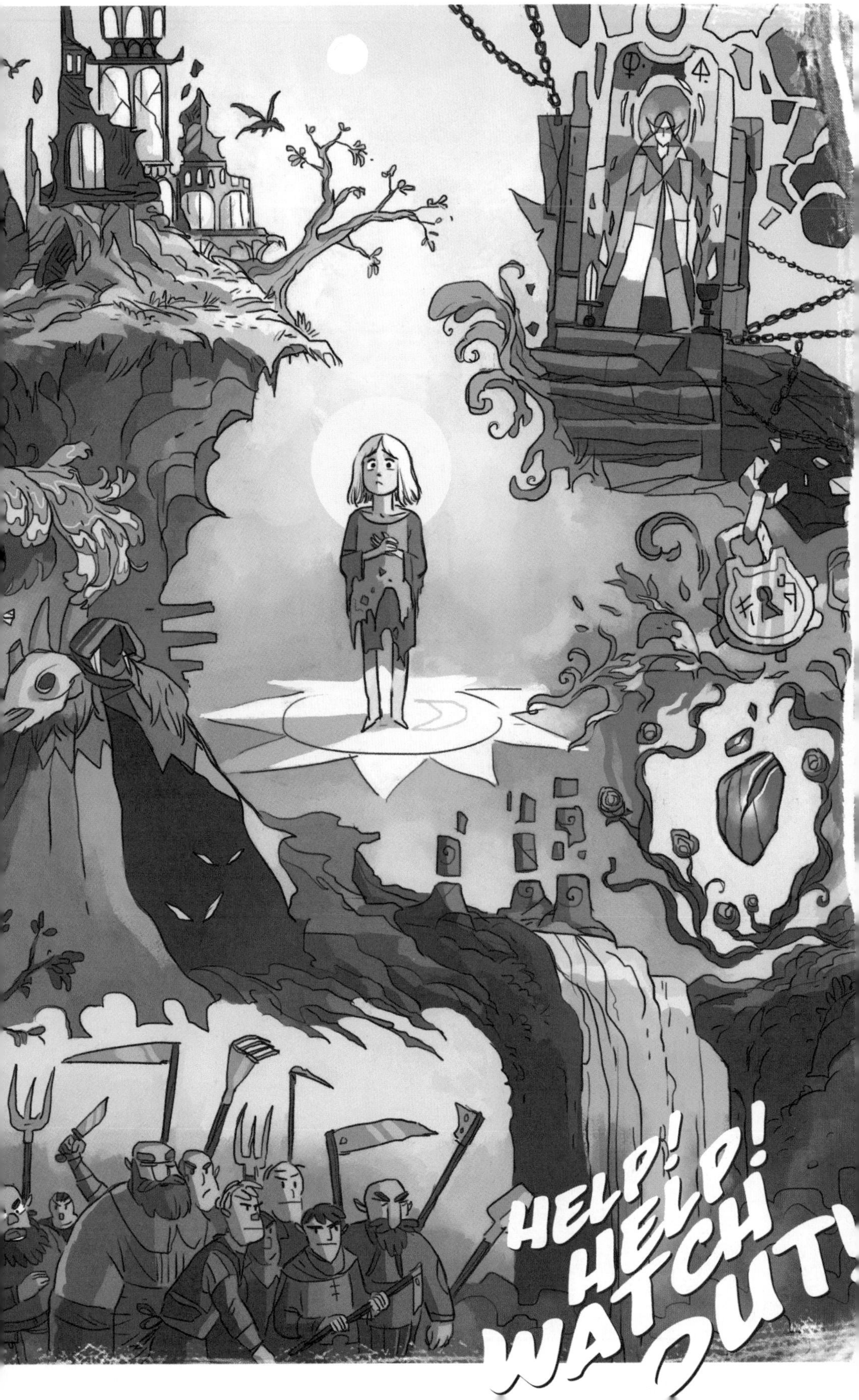
HELP!
HELP!
WATCH
OUT!

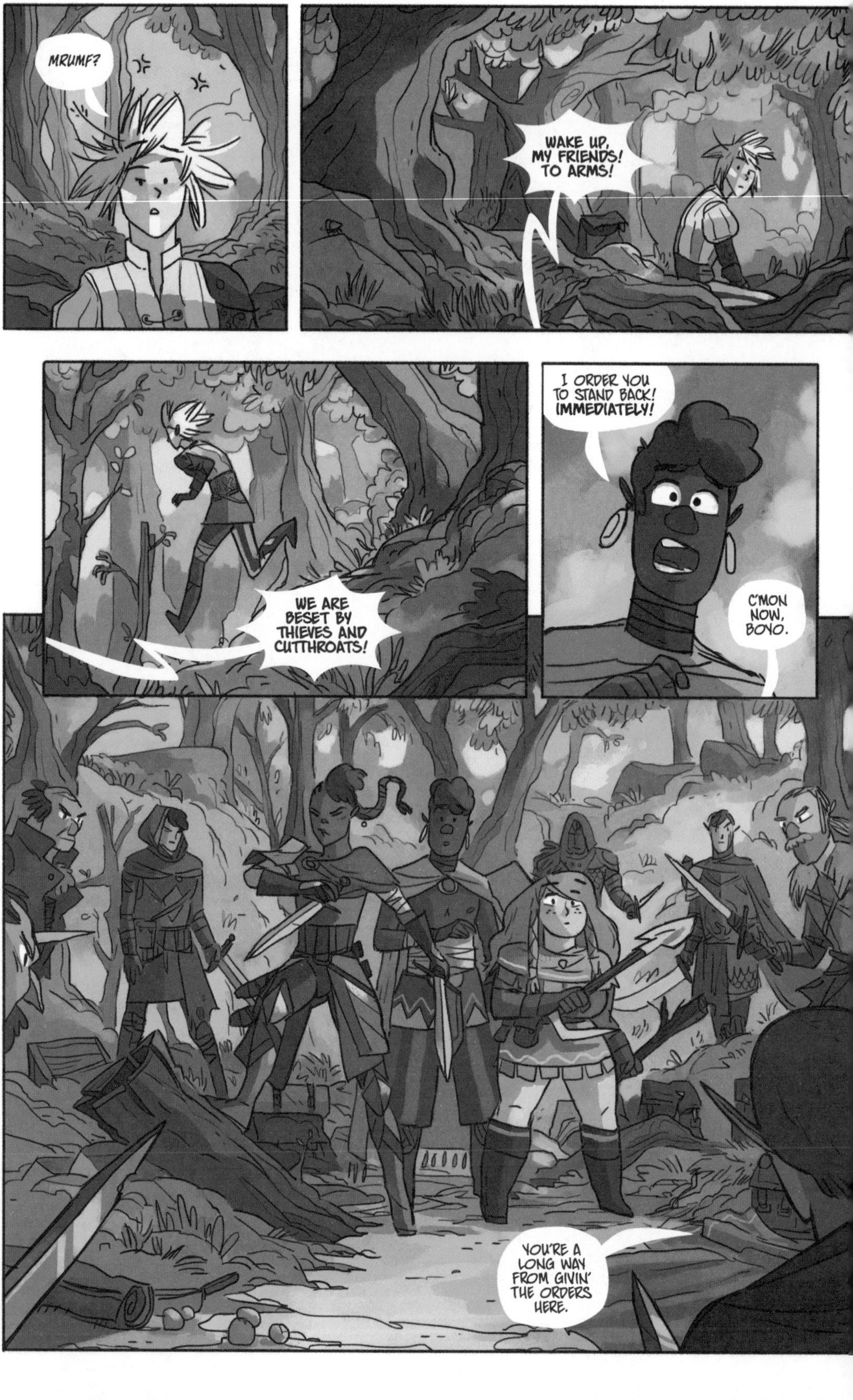
MRUMF?
WAKE UP, MY FRIENDS! TO ARMS!
WE ARE BESET BY THIEVES AND CUTTHROATS!
I ORDER YOU TO STAND BACK! IMMEDIATELY!
C'MON NOW, BOYO.
YOU'RE A LONG WAY FROM GIVIN' THE ORDERS HERE.

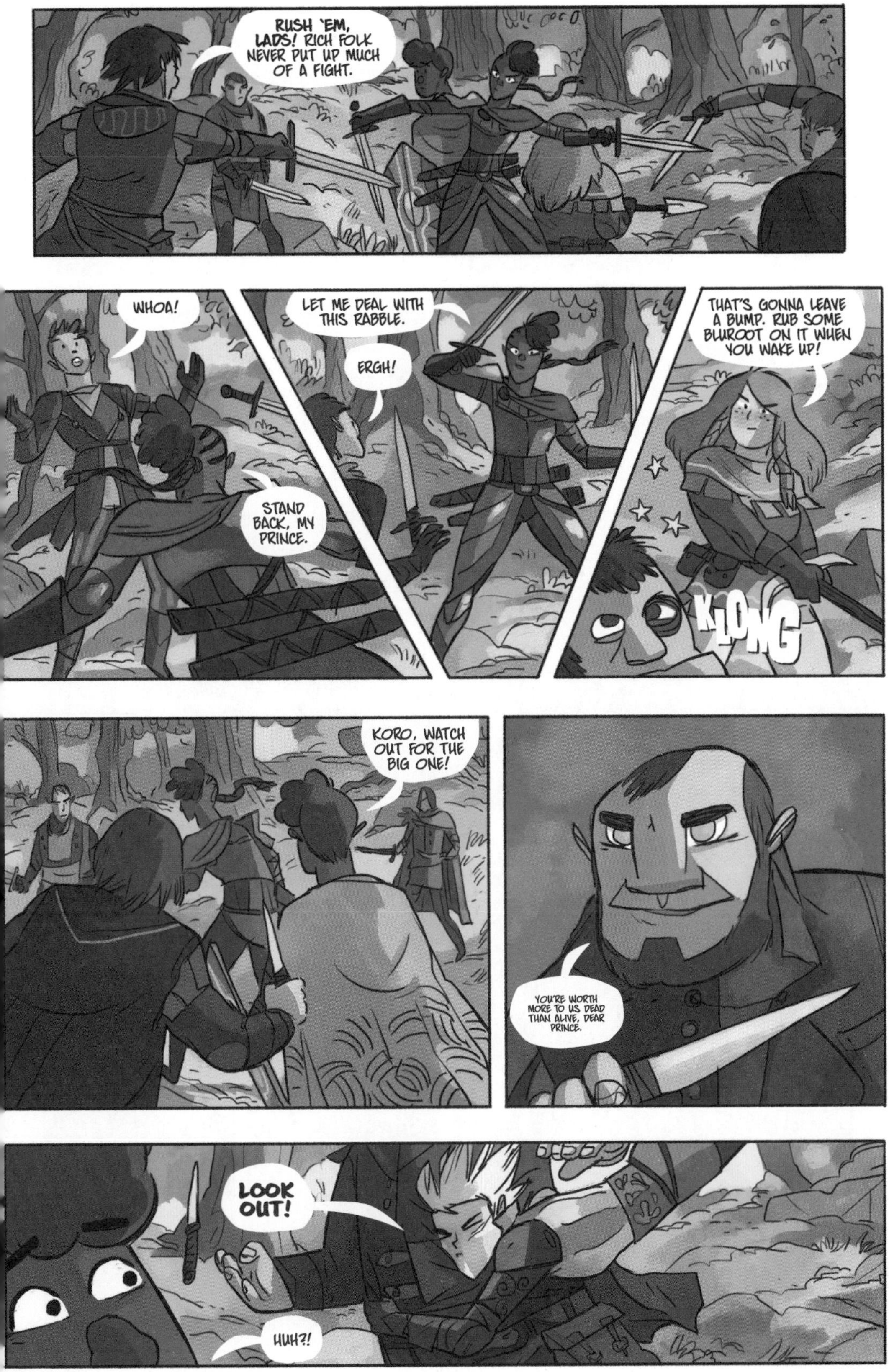

RUSH 'EM, LADS! RICH FOLK NEVER PUT UP MUCH OF A FIGHT.
WHOA!
STAND BACK, MY PRINCE.
LET ME DEAL WITH THIS RABBLE.
ERGH!
THAT'S GONNA LEAVE A BUMP. RUB SOME BLUROOT ON IT WHEN YOU WAKE UP!
KLONG
KORO, WATCH OUT FOR THE BIG ONE!
YOU'RE WORTH MORE TO US DEAD THAN ALIVE, DEAR PRINCE.
LOOK OUT!
HUH?!

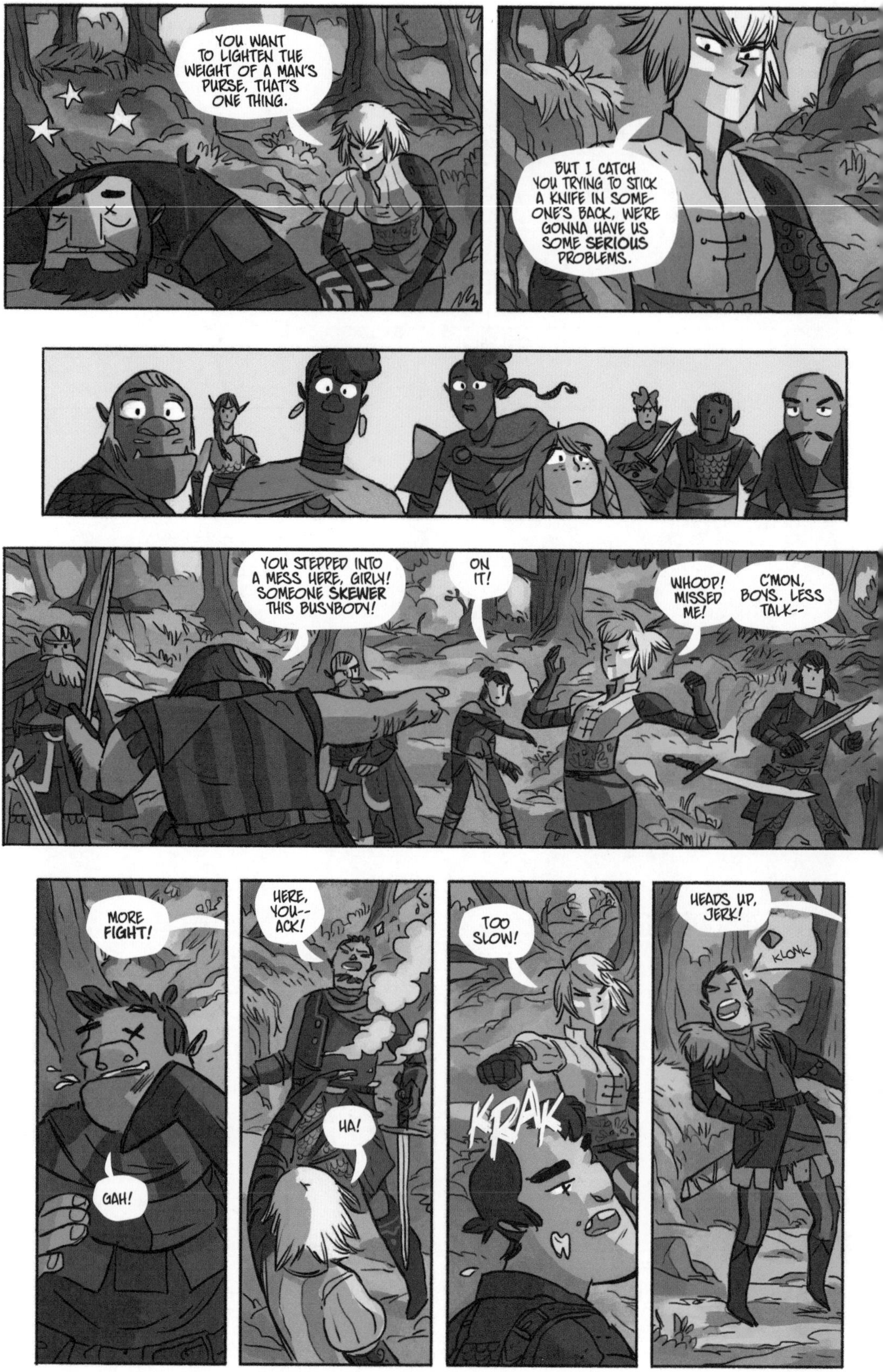

YOU WANT TO LIGHTEN THE WEIGHT OF A MAN'S PURSE, THAT'S ONE THING.
BUT I CATCH YOU TRYING TO STICK A KNIFE IN SOME-ONE'S BACK, WE'RE GONNA HAVE US SOME SERIOUS PROBLEMS.
YOU STEPPED INTO A MESS HERE, GIRLY! SOMEONE SKEWER THIS BUSYBODY!
ON IT!
WHOOP! MISSED ME!
C'MON, BOYS. LESS TALK--
MORE FIGHT!
GAH!
HERE, YOU-- ACK!
HA!
TOO SLOW!
KRAK
HEADS UP, JERK!
KLONK

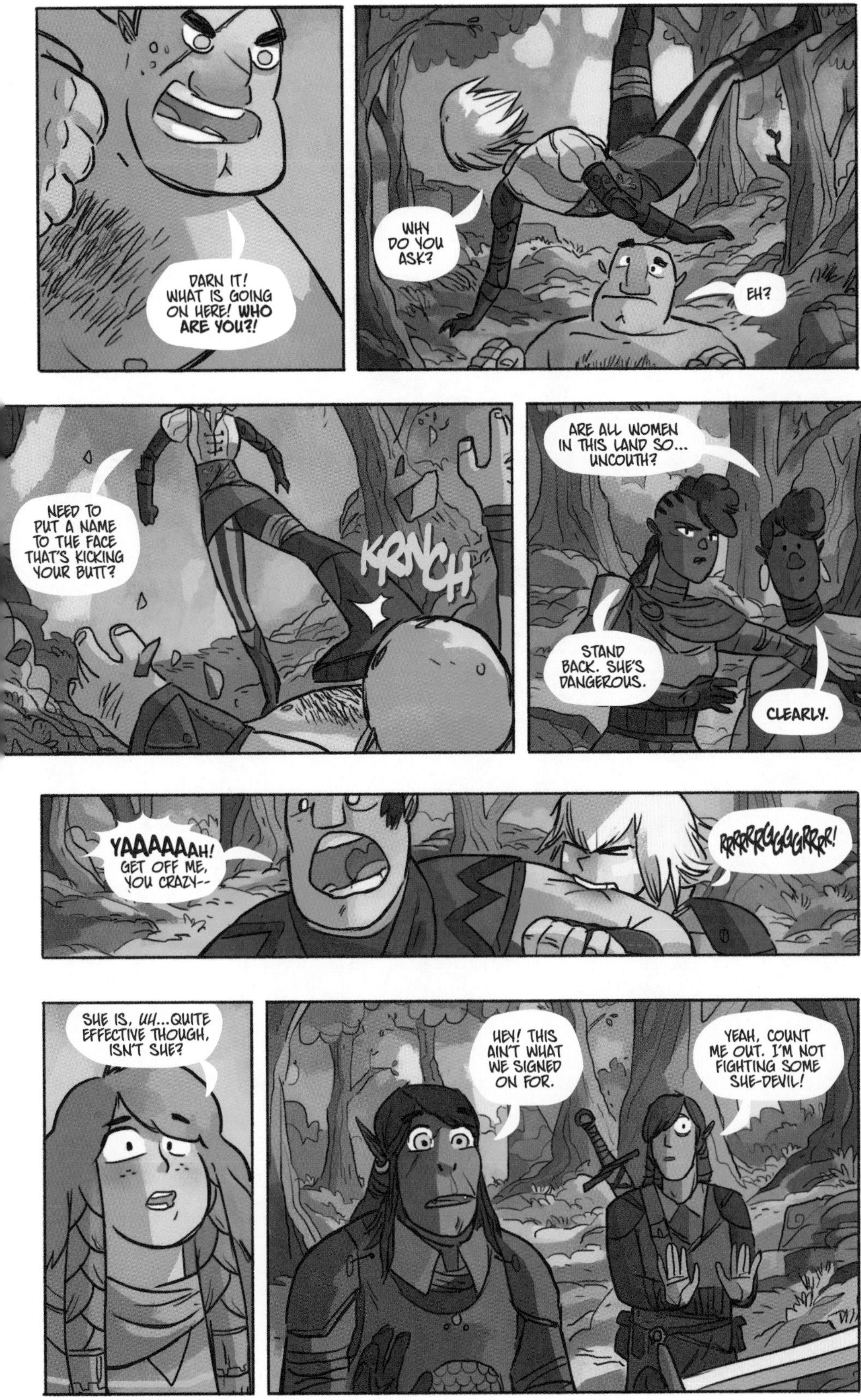
DARN IT! WHAT IS GOING ON HERE! WHO ARE YOU?!
WHY DO YOU ASK?
EH?
NEED TO PUT A NAME TO THE FACE THAT'S KICKING YOUR BUTT?
KRNCH
ARE ALL WOMEN IN THIS LAND SO... UNCOUTH?
STAND BACK. SHE'S DANGEROUS.
CLEARLY.
YAAAAAAH! GET OFF ME, YOU CRAZY--
RRRRRGGGRRRR!
SHE IS, UH...QUITE EFFECTIVE THOUGH, ISN'T SHE?
HEY! THIS AIN'T WHAT WE SIGNED ON FOR.
YEAH, COUNT ME OUT. I'M NOT FIGHTING SOME SHE-DEVIL!

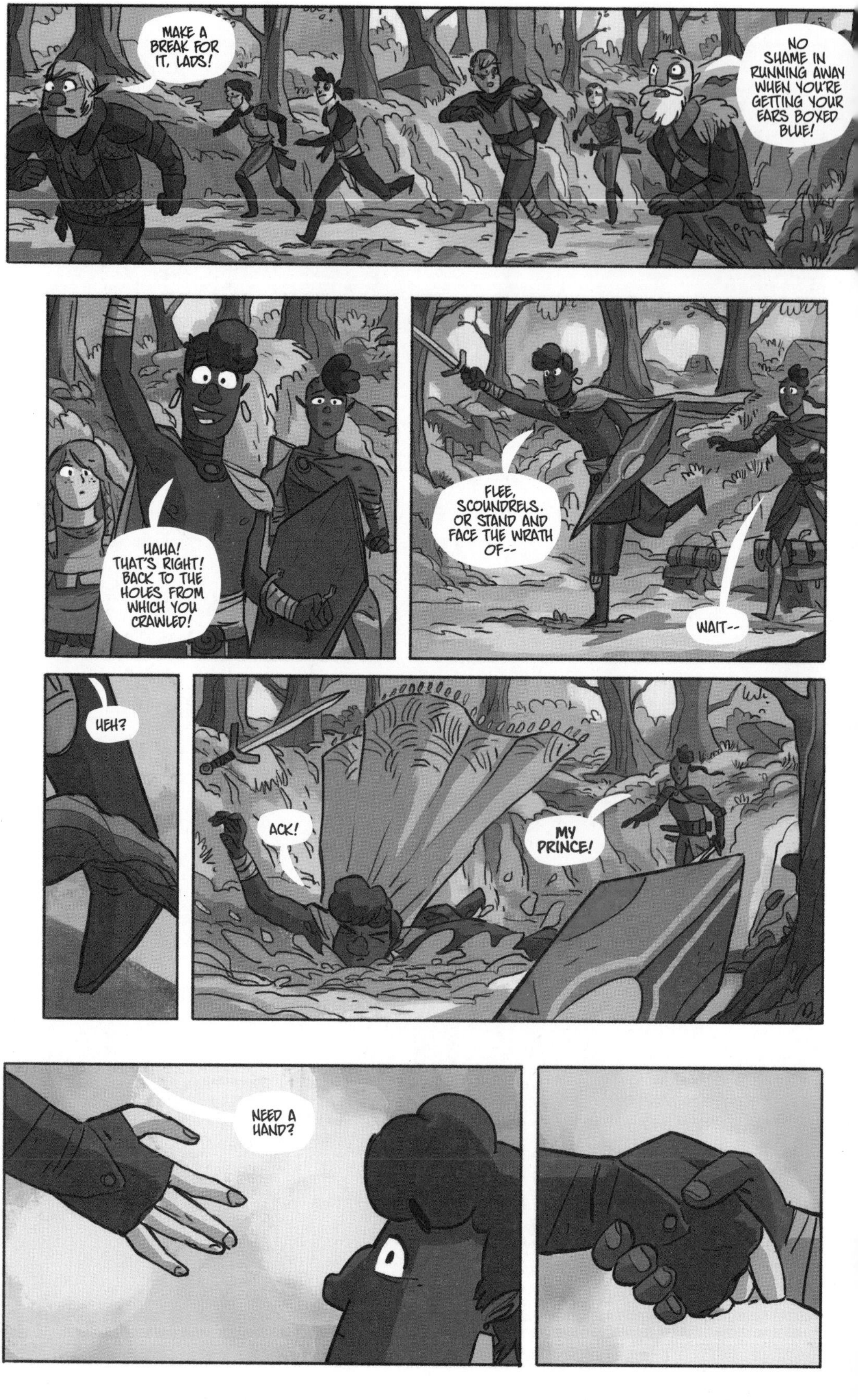
MAKE A BREAK FOR IT, LADS!
NO SHAME IN RUNNING AWAY WHEN YOU'RE GETTING YOUR EARS BOXED BLUE!
HAHA! THAT'S RIGHT! BACK TO THE HOLES FROM WHICH YOU CRAWLED!
FLEE, SCOUNDRELS. OR STAND AND FACE THE WRATH OF--
WAIT--
HEH?
ACK!
MY PRINCE!
NEED A HAND?

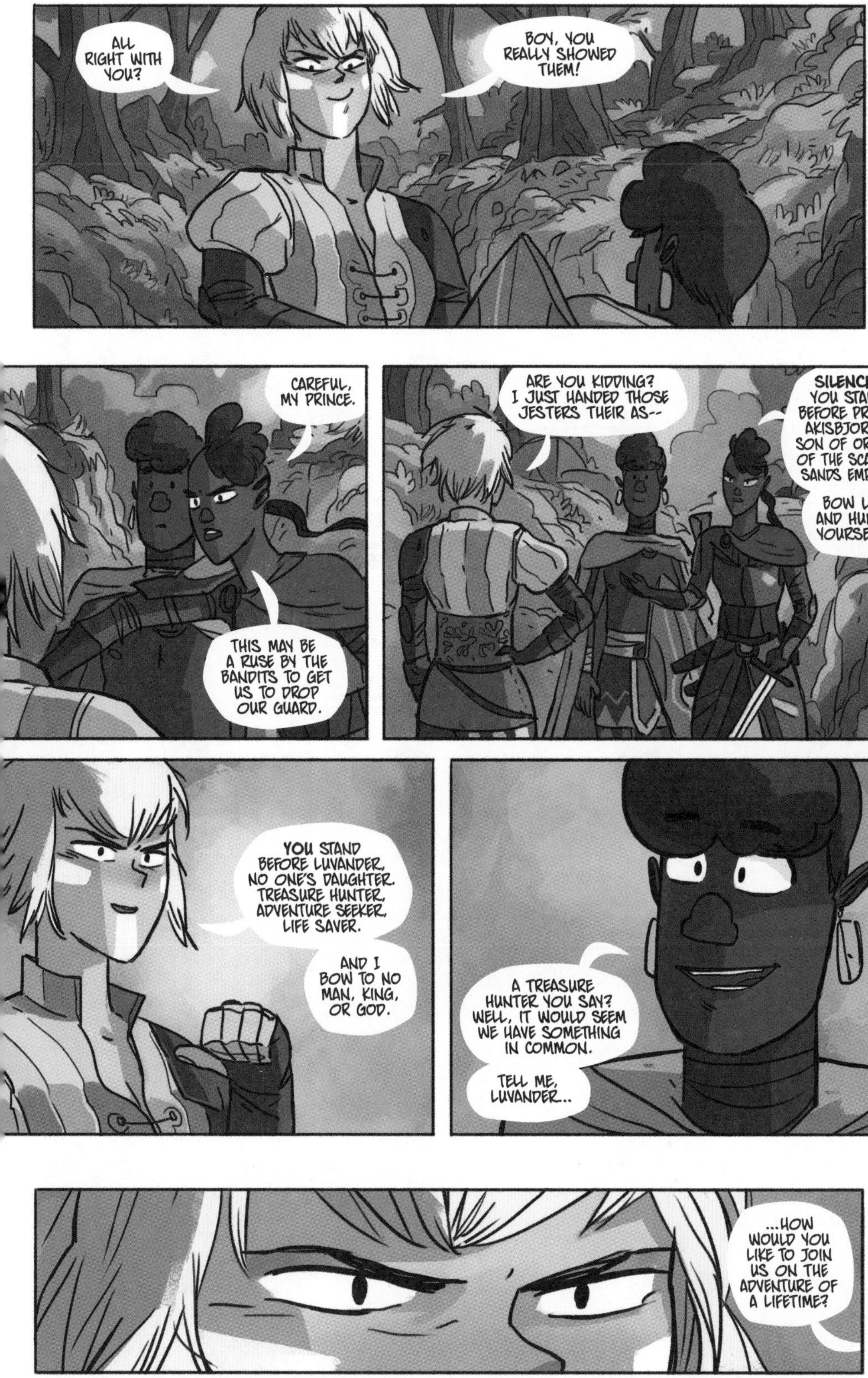

ALL RIGHT WITH YOU?
BOY, YOU REALLY SHOWED THEM!
CAREFUL, MY PRINCE.
THIS MAY BE A RUSE BY THE BANDITS TO GET US TO DROP OUR GUARD.
ARE YOU KIDDING? I JUST HANDED THOSE JESTERS THEIR AS--
SILENCE! YOU STAND BEFORE PRINCE AKISBJORNE, SON OF ORKAS, OF THE SCARLET SANDS EMPIRE.
BOW LOW AND HUMBLE YOURSELF!!
YOU STAND BEFORE LUVANDER, NO ONE'S DAUGHTER. TREASURE HUNTER, ADVENTURE SEEKER, LIFE SAVER.
AND I BOW TO NO MAN, KING, OR GOD.
A TREASURE HUNTER YOU SAY? WELL, IT WOULD SEEM WE HAVE SOMETHING IN COMMON.
TELL ME, LUVANDER...
...HOW WOULD YOU LIKE TO JOIN US ON THE ADVENTURE OF A LIFETIME?

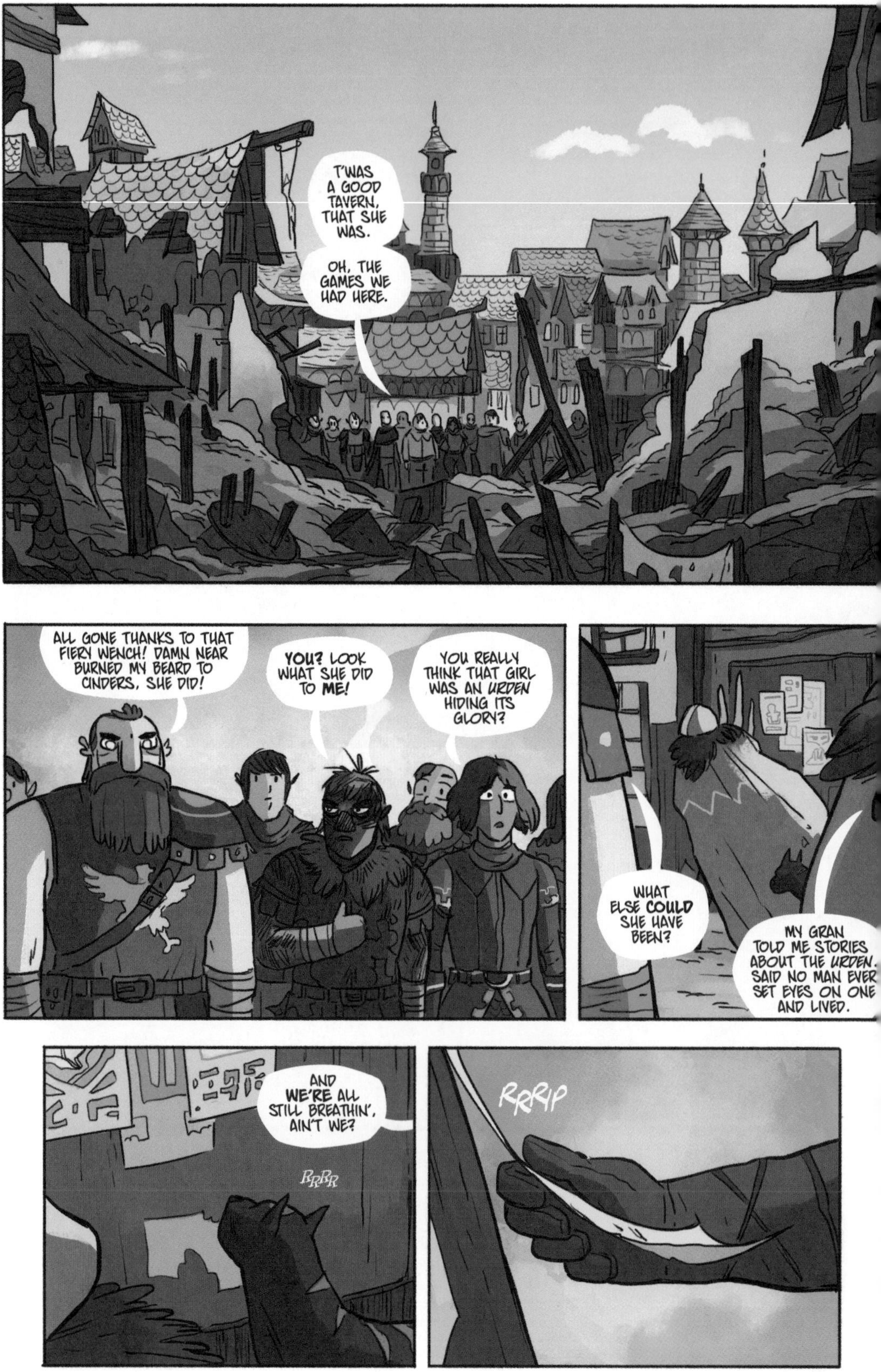
T'WAS A GOOD TAVERN, THAT SHE WAS.
OH, THE GAMES WE HAD HERE.
ALL GONE THANKS TO THAT FIERY WENCH! DAMN NEAR BURNED MY BEARD TO CINDERS, SHE DID!
YOU? LOOK WHAT SHE DID TO ME!
YOU REALLY THINK THAT GIRL WAS AN URDEN HIDING ITS GLORY?
WHAT ELSE COULD SHE HAVE BEEN?
MY GRAN TOLD ME STORIES ABOUT THE URDEN. SAID NO MAN EVER SET EYES ON ONE AND LIVED.
AND WE'RE ALL STILL BREATHIN', AIN'T WE?
RRRR
RRRIP

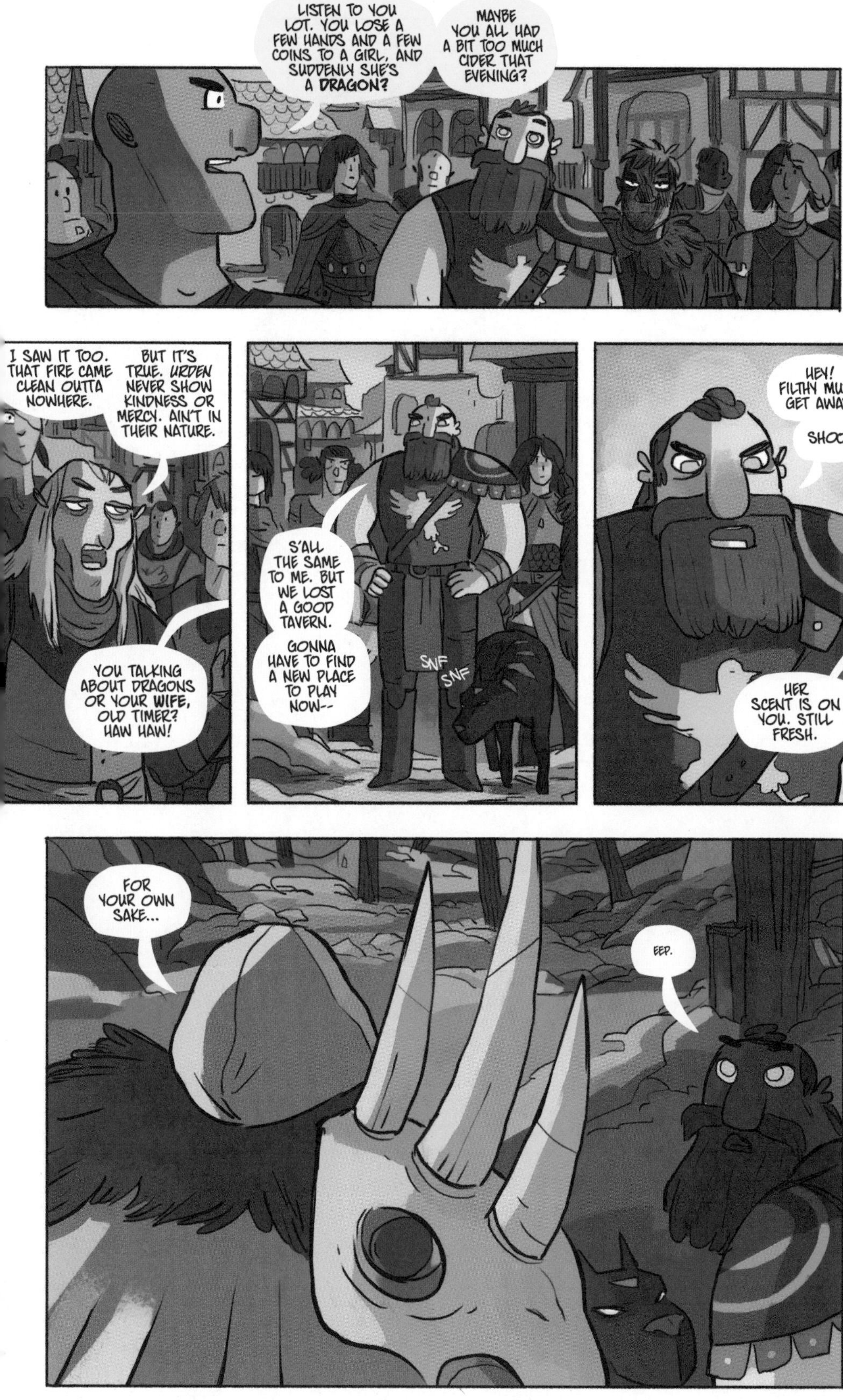

LISTEN TO YOU LOT. YOU LOSE A FEW HANDS AND A FEW COINS TO A GIRL, AND SUDDENLY SHE'S A **DRAGON?**
MAYBE YOU ALL HAD A BIT TOO MUCH CIDER THAT EVENING?
I SAW IT TOO. THAT FIRE CAME CLEAN OUTTA NOWHERE.
BUT IT'S TRUE. *URDEN* NEVER SHOW KINDNESS OR MERCY. AIN'T IN THEIR NATURE.
YOU TALKING ABOUT DRAGONS OR YOUR WIFE, OLD TIMER? HAW HAW!
S'ALL THE SAME TO ME. BUT WE LOST A GOOD TAVERN.
GONNA HAVE TO FIND A NEW PLACE TO PLAY NOW--
SNF SNF
HEY! FILTHY MUTT, GET AWAY.
SHOO!
HER SCENT IS ON YOU. STILL FRESH.
FOR YOUR OWN SAKE...
EEP.

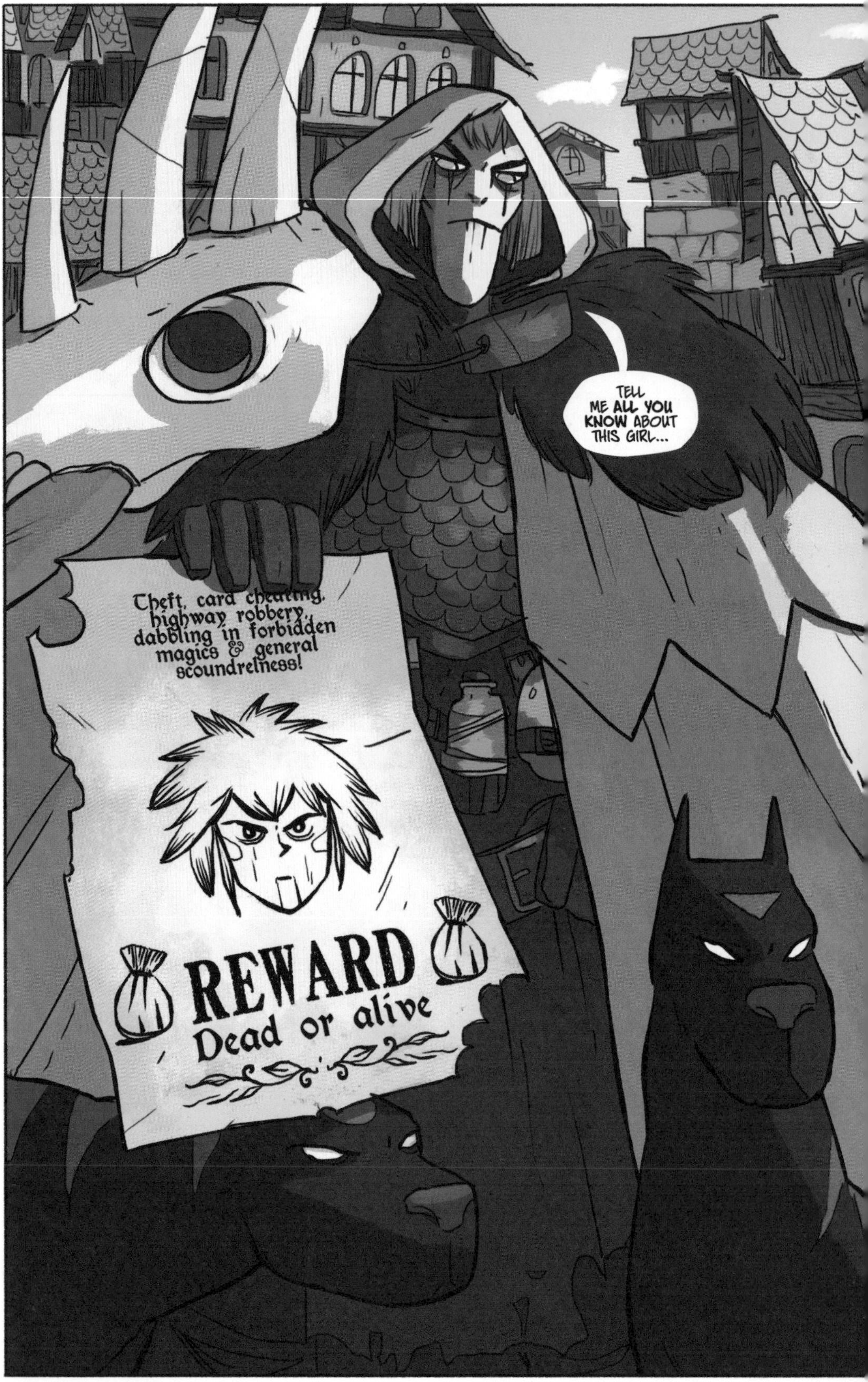
TELL ME ALL YOU KNOW ABOUT THIS GIRL...
Theft, card cheating, highway robbery, dabbling in forbidden magics & general scoundrelness!
REWARD
Dead or alive

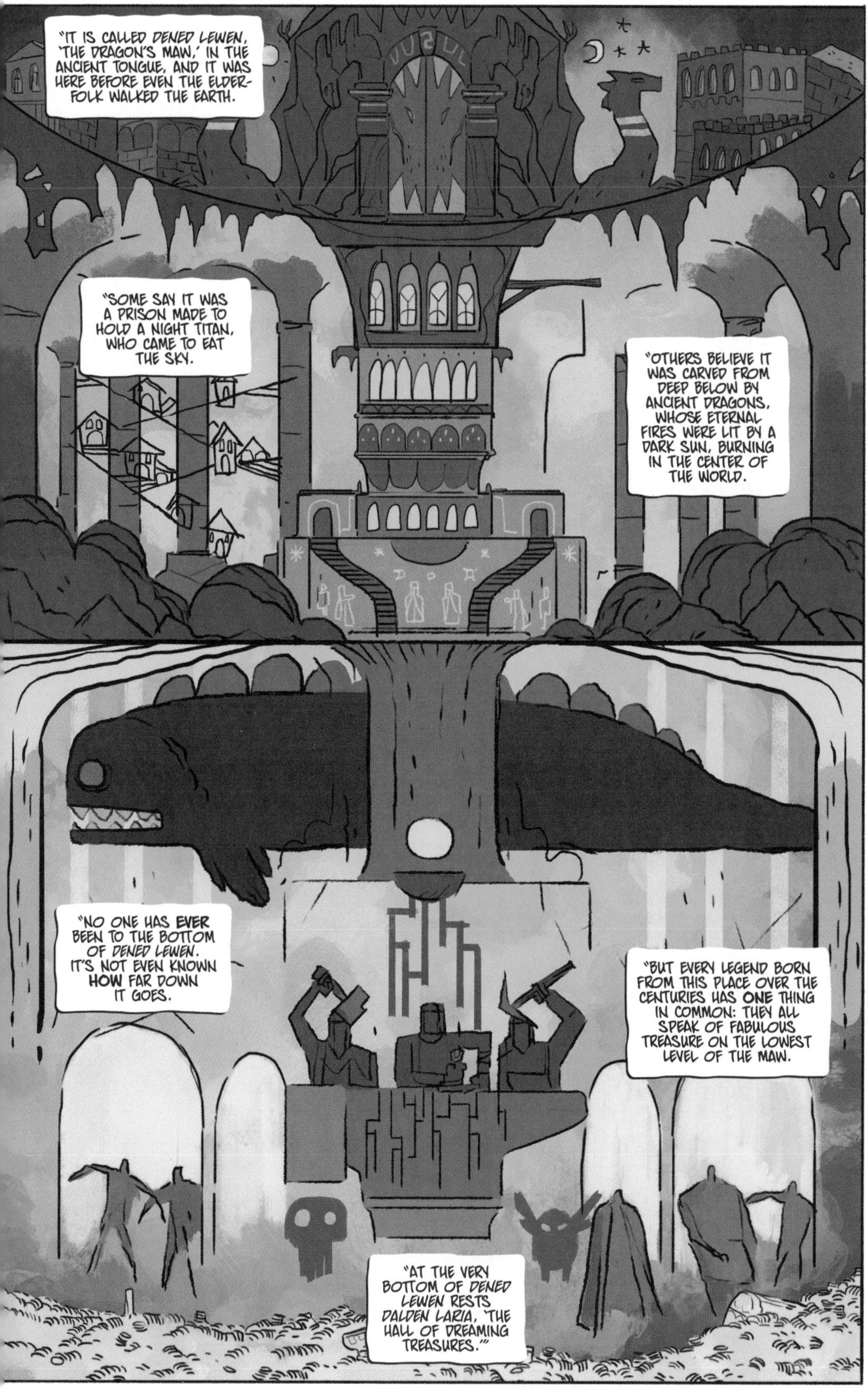
"IT IS CALLED DENED LEWEN, 'THE DRAGON'S MAW,' IN THE ANCIENT TONGUE, AND IT WAS HERE BEFORE EVEN THE ELDER-FOLK WALKED THE EARTH.
"SOME SAY IT WAS A PRISON MADE TO HOLD A NIGHT TITAN, WHO CAME TO EAT THE SKY.
"OTHERS BELIEVE IT WAS CARVED FROM DEEP BELOW BY ANCIENT DRAGONS, WHOSE ETERNAL FIRES WERE LIT BY A DARK SUN, BURNING IN THE CENTER OF THE WORLD.
"NO ONE HAS EVER BEEN TO THE BOTTOM OF DENED LEWEN. IT'S NOT EVEN KNOWN HOW FAR DOWN IT GOES.
"BUT EVERY LEGEND BORN FROM THIS PLACE OVER THE CENTURIES HAS ONE THING IN COMMON: THEY ALL SPEAK OF FABULOUS TREASURE ON THE LOWEST LEVEL OF THE MAW.
"AT THE VERY BOTTOM OF DENED LEWEN RESTS DALDEN LARIA, 'THE HALL OF DREAMING TREASURES.'"

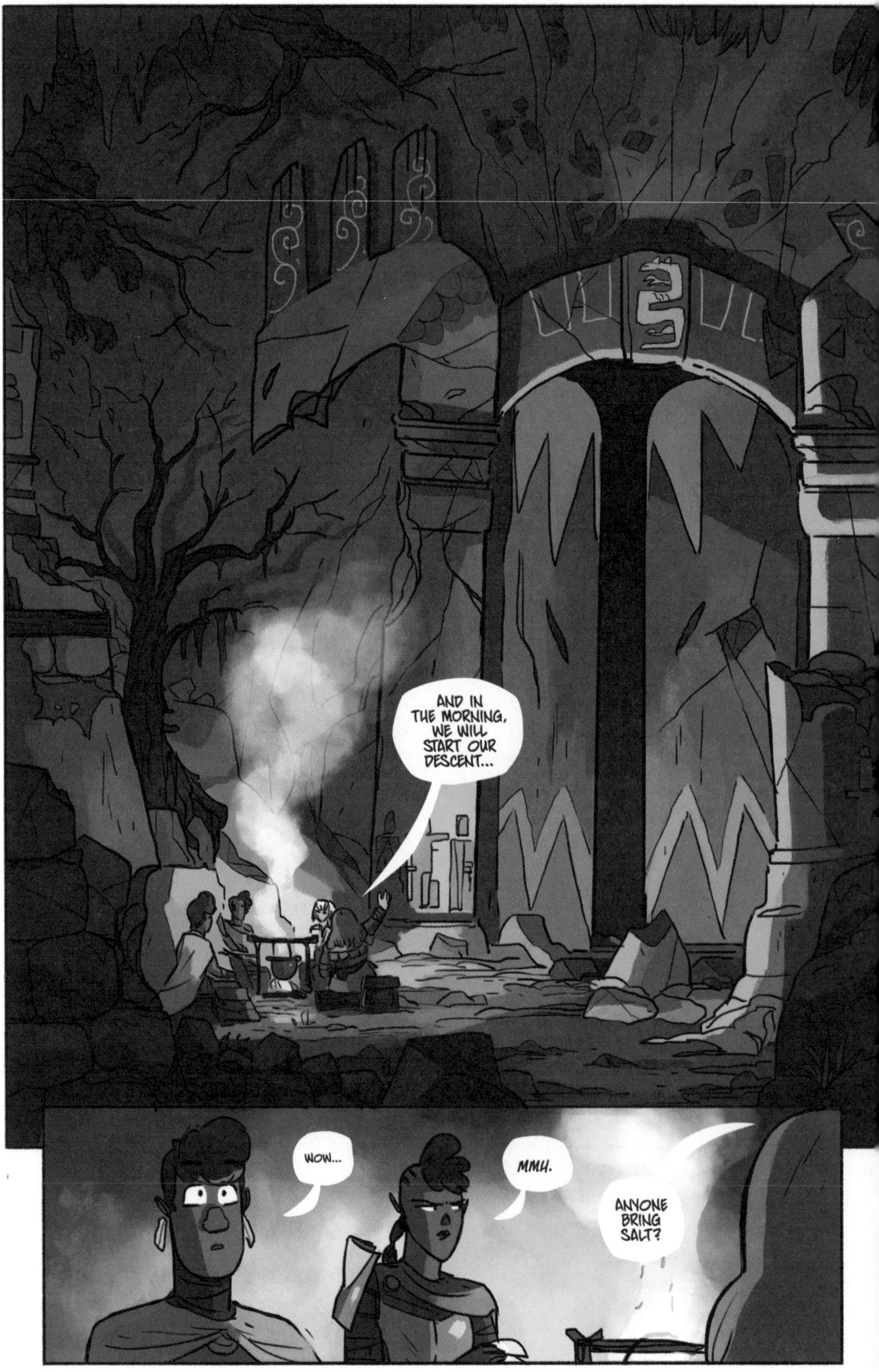
AND IN THE MORNING, WE WILL START OUR DESCENT...
WOW...
MMH.
ANYONE BRING SALT?

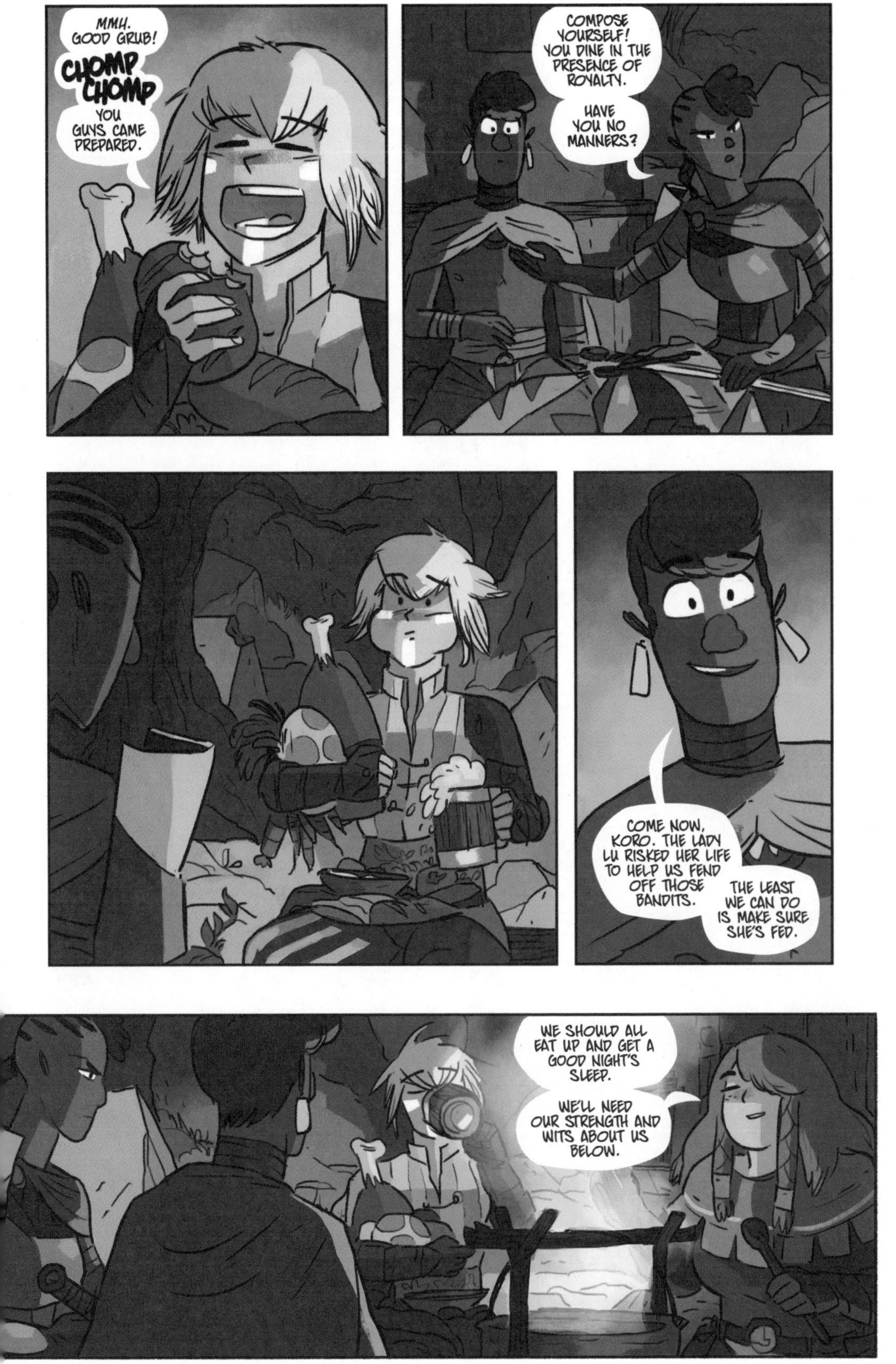

MMH. GOOD GRUB!
CHOMP CHOMP
YOU GUYS CAME PREPARED.
COMPOSE YOURSELF! YOU DINE IN THE PRESENCE OF ROYALTY.
HAVE YOU NO MANNERS?
COME NOW, KORO. THE LADY LU RISKED HER LIFE TO HELP US FEND OFF THOSE BANDITS.
THE LEAST WE CAN DO IS MAKE SURE SHE'S FED.
WE SHOULD ALL EAT UP AND GET A GOOD NIGHT'S SLEEP.
WE'LL NEED OUR STRENGTH AND WITS ABOUT US BELOW.

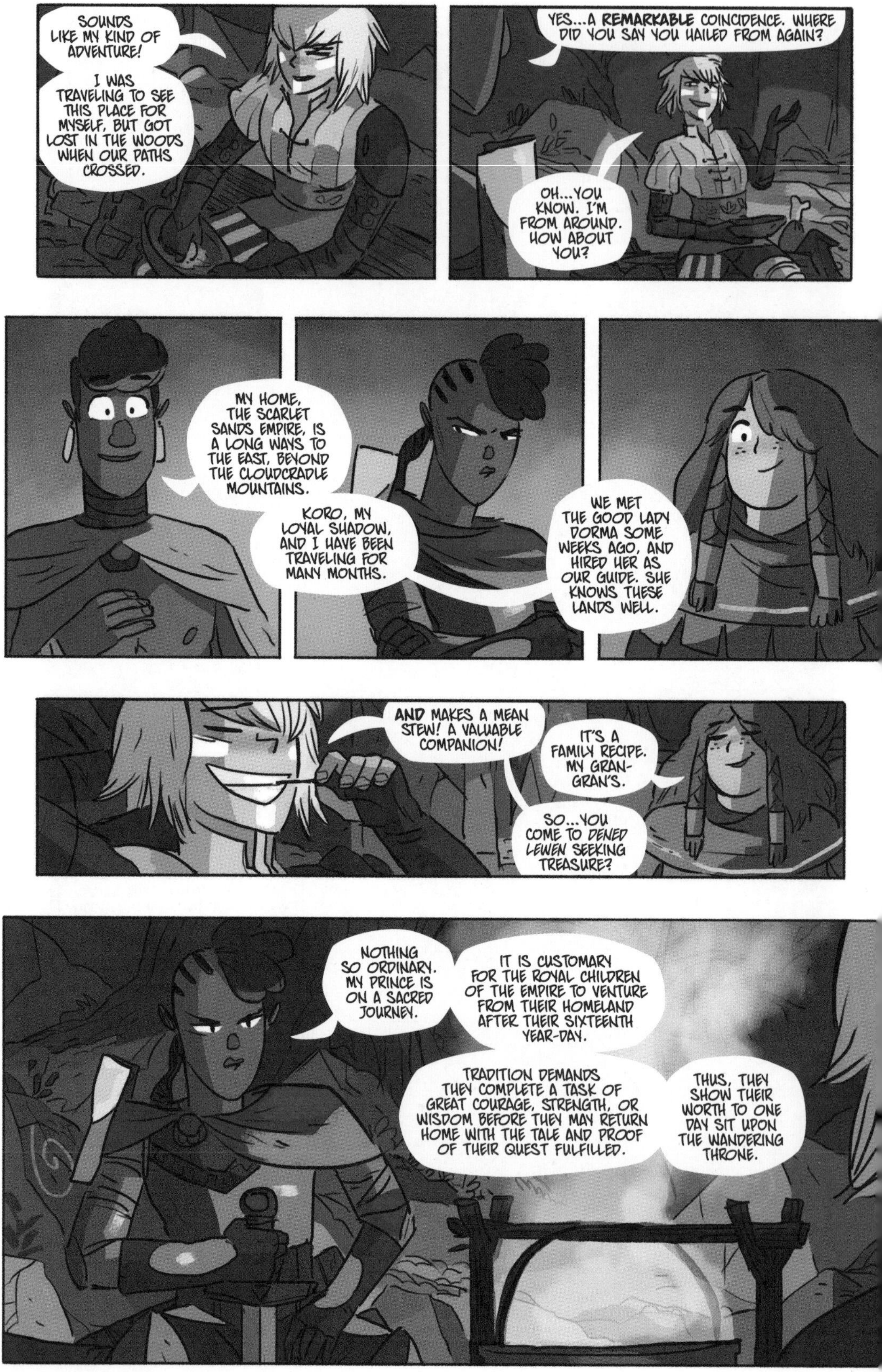
SOUNDS LIKE MY KIND OF ADVENTURE!
I WAS TRAVELING TO SEE THIS PLACE FOR MYSELF, BUT GOT LOST IN THE WOODS WHEN OUR PATHS CROSSED.
YES...A **REMARKABLE** COINCIDENCE. WHERE DID YOU SAY YOU HAILED FROM AGAIN?
OH...YOU KNOW. I'M FROM AROUND. HOW ABOUT YOU?
MY HOME, THE SCARLET SANDS EMPIRE, IS A LONG WAYS TO THE EAST, BEYOND THE CLOUDCRADLE MOUNTAINS.
KORO, MY LOYAL SHADOW, AND I HAVE BEEN TRAVELING FOR MANY MONTHS.
WE MET THE GOOD LADY DORMA SOME WEEKS AGO, AND HIRED HER AS OUR GUIDE. SHE KNOWS THESE LANDS WELL.
AND MAKES A MEAN STEW! A VALUABLE COMPANION!
IT'S A FAMILY RECIPE. MY GRAN-GRAN'S.
SO...YOU COME TO DENED LEWEN SEEKING TREASURE?
NOTHING SO ORDINARY. MY PRINCE IS ON A SACRED JOURNEY.
IT IS CUSTOMARY FOR THE ROYAL CHILDREN OF THE EMPIRE TO VENTURE FROM THEIR HOMELAND AFTER THEIR SIXTEENTH YEAR-DAY.
TRADITION DEMANDS THEY COMPLETE A TASK OF GREAT COURAGE, STRENGTH, OR WISDOM BEFORE THEY MAY RETURN HOME WITH THE TALE AND PROOF OF THEIR QUEST FULFILLED.
THUS, THEY SHOW THEIR WORTH TO ONE DAY SIT UPON THE WANDERING THRONE.

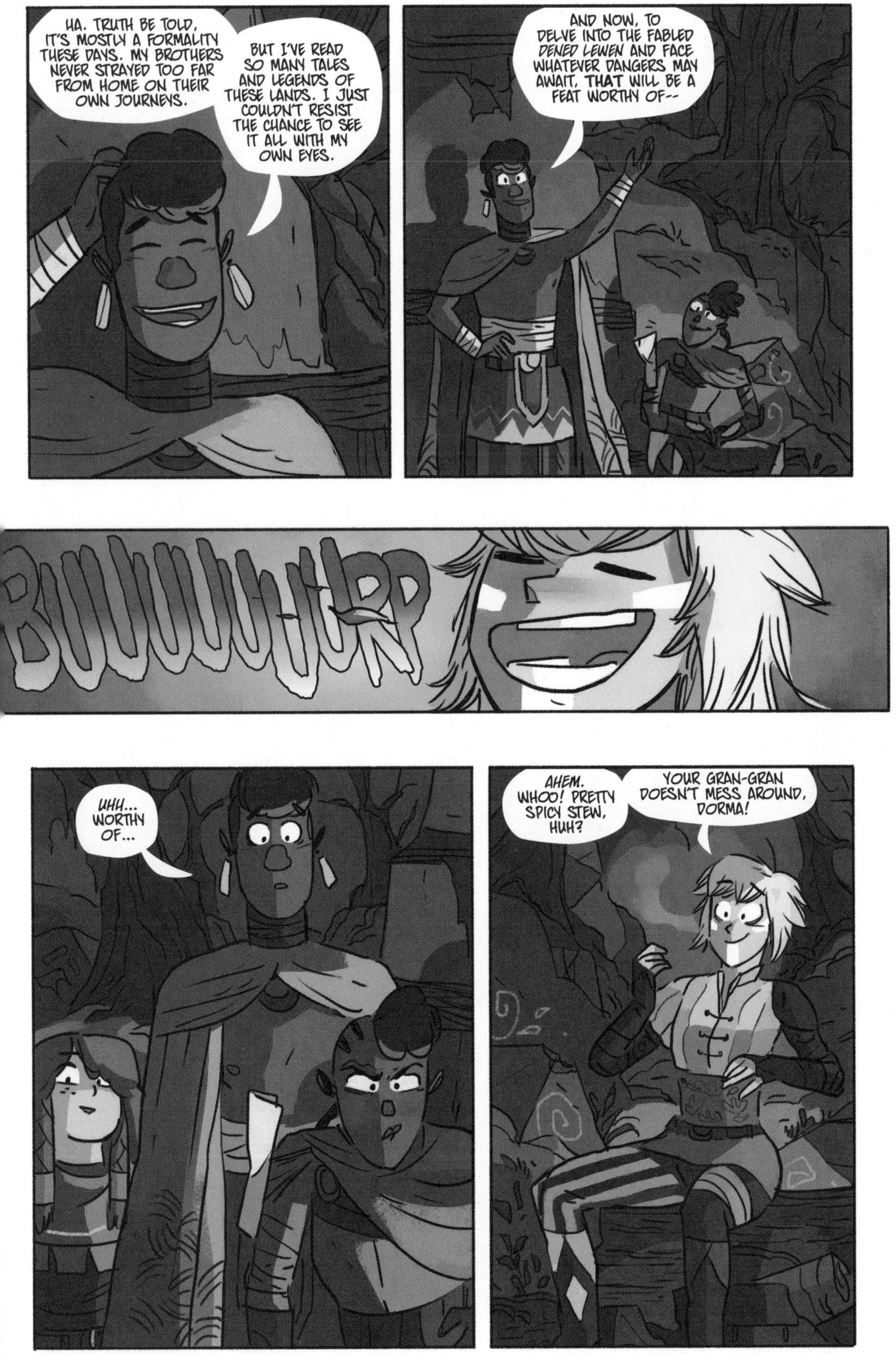
HA. TRUTH BE TOLD, IT'S MOSTLY A FORMALITY THESE DAYS. MY BROTHERS NEVER STRAYED TOO FAR FROM HOME ON THEIR OWN JOURNEYS.
BUT I'VE READ SO MANY TALES AND LEGENDS OF THESE LANDS. I JUST COULDN'T RESIST THE CHANCE TO SEE IT ALL WITH MY OWN EYES.
AND NOW, TO DELVE INTO THE FABLED DENED LEWEN AND FACE WHATEVER DANGERS MAY AWAIT, THAT WILL BE A FEAT WORTHY OF--
BUUUUUURP
UHH... WORTHY OF...
AHEM. WHOO! PRETTY SPICY STEW, HUH?
YOUR GRAN-GRAN DOESN'T MESS AROUND, DORMA!

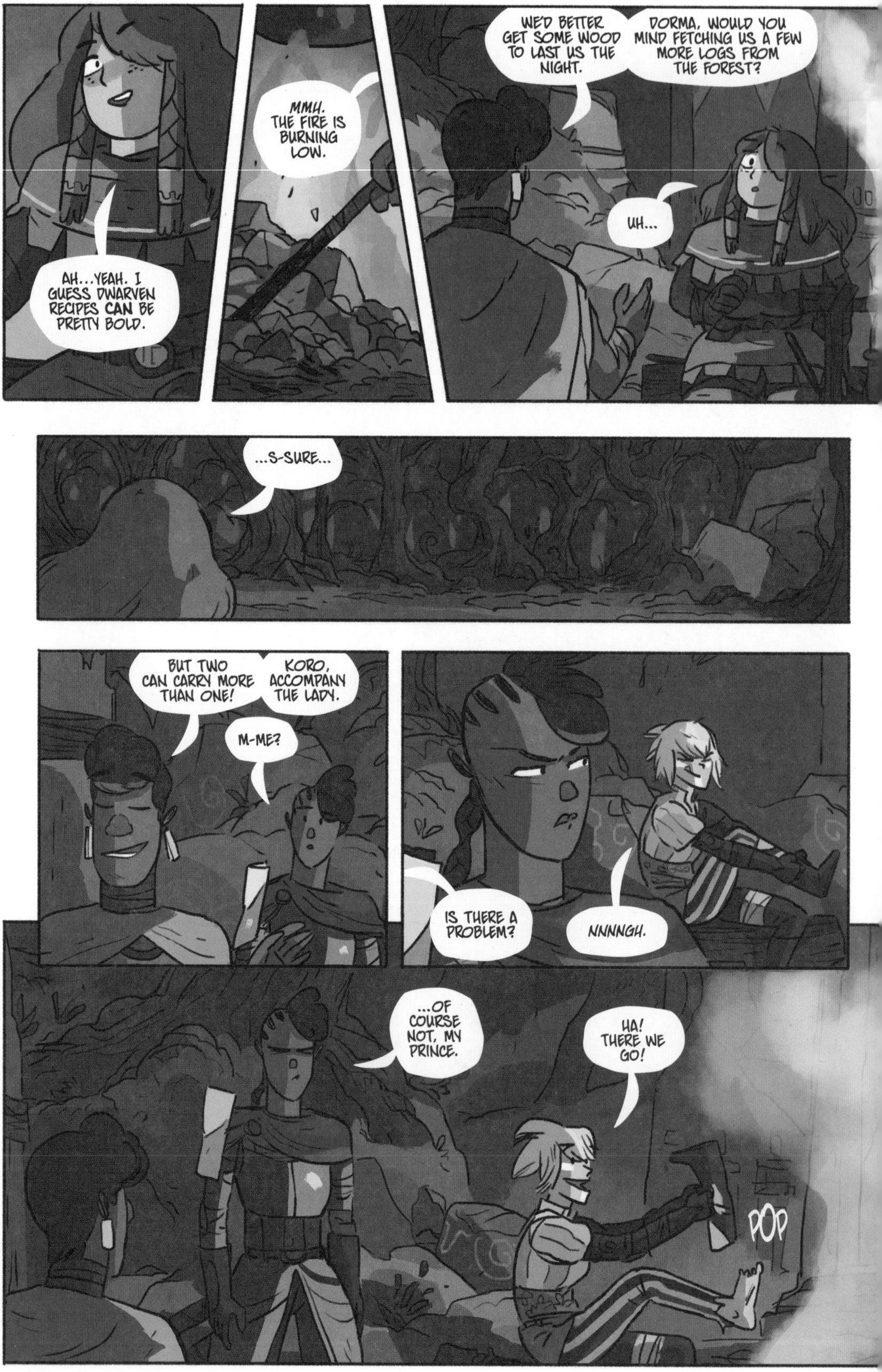

AH...YEAH. I GUESS DWARVEN RECIPES CAN BE PRETTY BOLD.
MMH. THE FIRE IS BURNING LOW.
WE'D BETTER GET SOME WOOD TO LAST US THE NIGHT.
DORMA, WOULD YOU MIND FETCHING US A FEW MORE LOGS FROM THE FOREST?
UH...
...S-SURE...
BUT TWO CAN CARRY MORE THAN ONE!
KORO, ACCOMPANY THE LADY.
M-ME?
IS THERE A PROBLEM?
NNNNGH.
...OF COURSE NOT, MY PRINCE.
HA! THERE WE GO!
POP

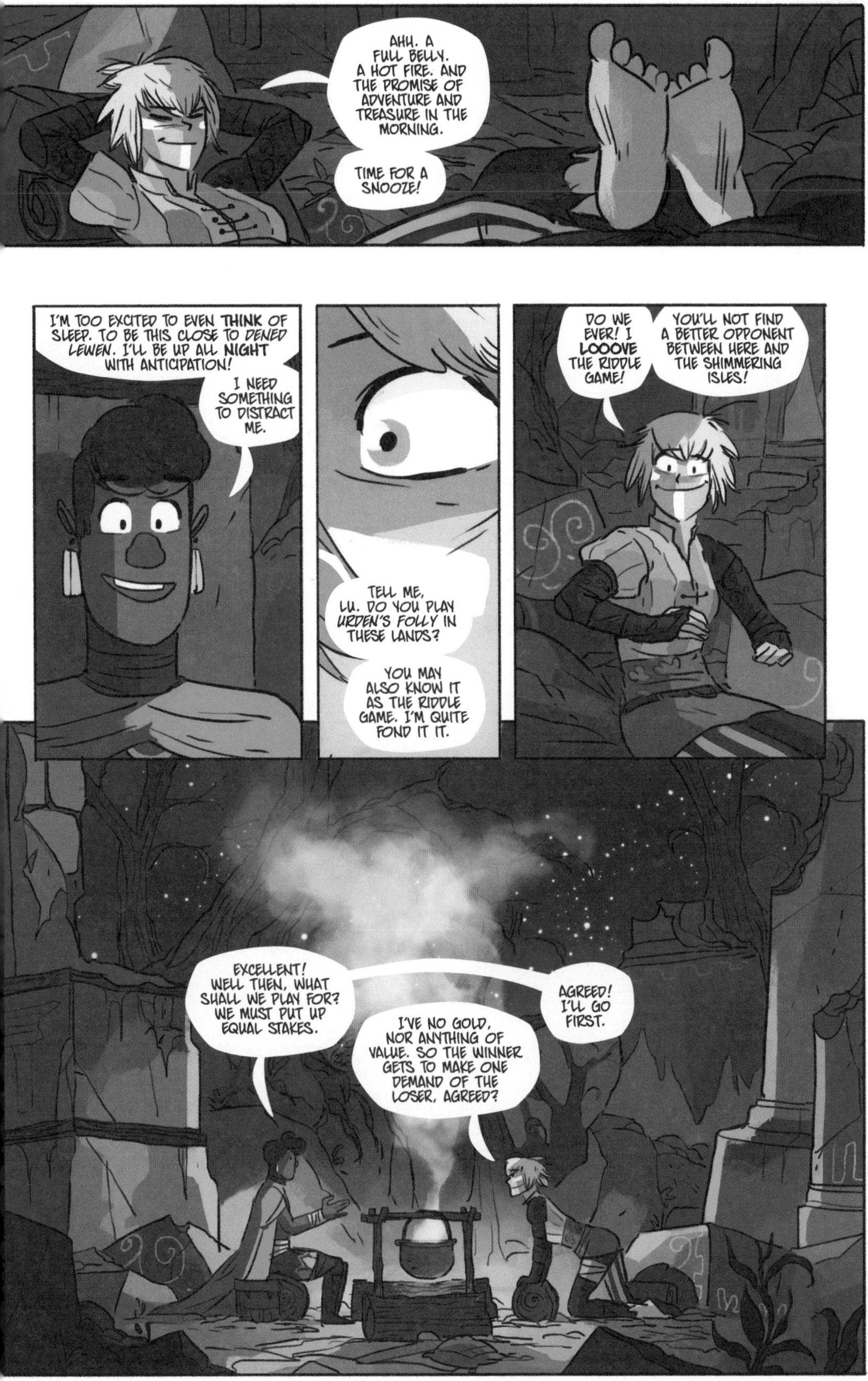
AHH. A FULL BELLY. A HOT FIRE. AND THE PROMISE OF ADVENTURE AND TREASURE IN THE MORNING.
TIME FOR A SNOOZE!
I'M TOO EXCITED TO EVEN THINK OF SLEEP. TO BE THIS CLOSE TO DENED LEWEN. I'LL BE UP ALL NIGHT WITH ANTICIPATION!
I NEED SOMETHING TO DISTRACT ME.
TELL ME, LU. DO YOU PLAY URDEN'S FOLLY IN THESE LANDS?
YOU MAY ALSO KNOW IT AS THE RIDDLE GAME. I'M QUITE FOND IT IT.
DO WE EVER! I LOOOVE THE RIDDLE GAME!
YOU'LL NOT FIND A BETTER OPPONENT BETWEEN HERE AND THE SHIMMERING ISLES!
EXCELLENT! WELL THEN, WHAT SHALL WE PLAY FOR? WE MUST PUT UP EQUAL STAKES.
I'VE NO GOLD, NOR ANYTHING OF VALUE. SO THE WINNER GETS TO MAKE ONE DEMAND OF THE LOSER, AGREED?
AGREED! I'LL GO FIRST.

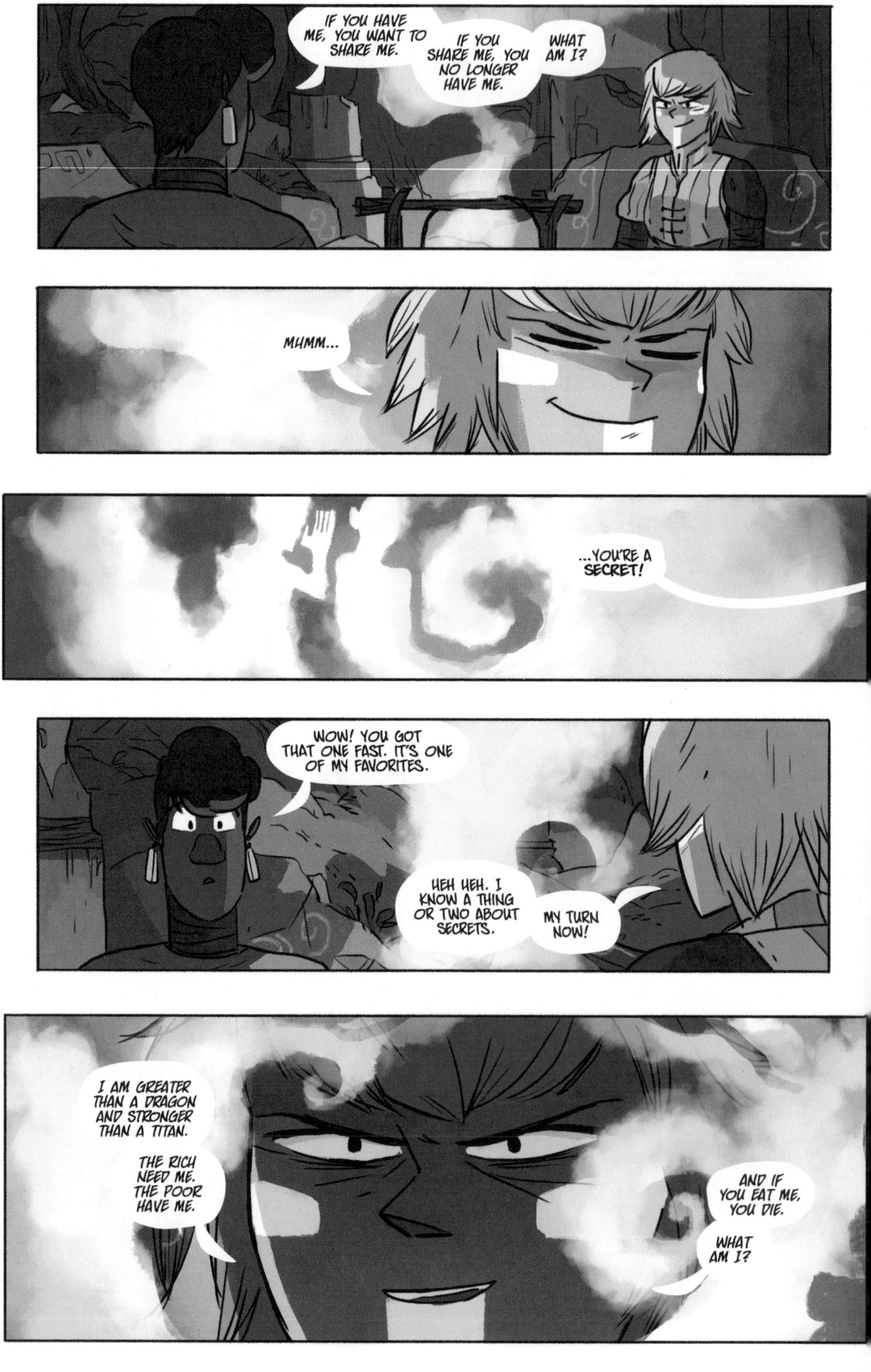
IF YOU HAVE ME, YOU WANT TO SHARE ME.
IF YOU SHARE ME, YOU NO LONGER HAVE ME.
WHAT AM I?
MUMM...
...YOU'RE A SECRET!
WOW! YOU GOT THAT ONE FAST. IT'S ONE OF MY FAVORITES.
HEH HEH. I KNOW A THING OR TWO ABOUT SECRETS.
MY TURN NOW!
I AM GREATER THAN A DRAGON AND STRONGER THAN A TITAN.
THE RICH NEED ME. THE POOR HAVE ME.
AND IF YOU EAT ME, YOU DIE.
WHAT AM I?

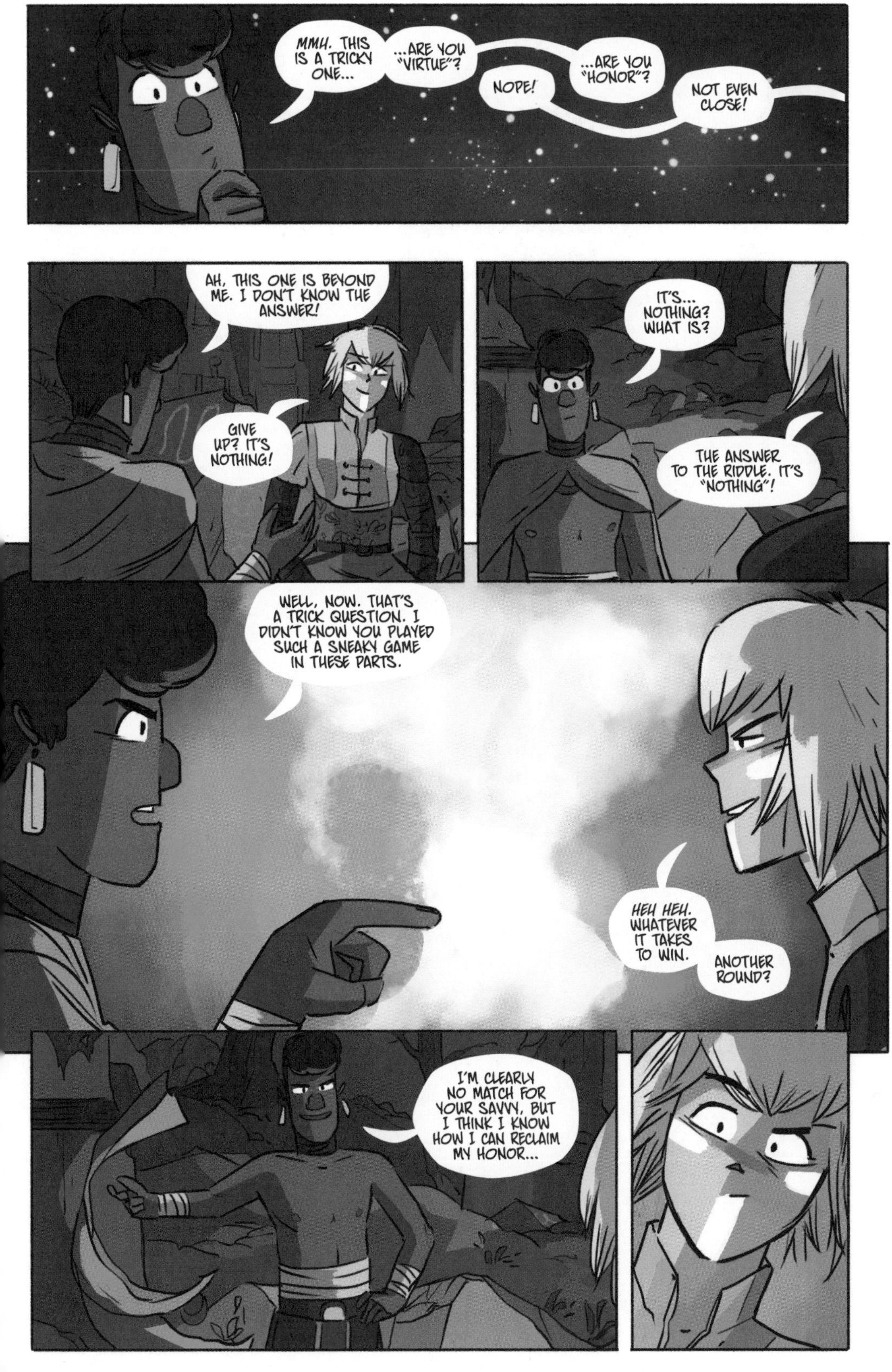
MMH. THIS IS A TRICKY ONE...
...ARE YOU "VIRTUE"?
NOPE!
...ARE YOU "HONOR"?
NOT EVEN CLOSE!
AH, THIS ONE IS BEYOND ME. I DON'T KNOW THE ANSWER!
GIVE UP? IT'S NOTHING!
IT'S... NOTHING? WHAT IS?
THE ANSWER TO THE RIDDLE. IT'S "NOTHING"!
WELL, NOW. THAT'S A TRICK QUESTION. I DIDN'T KNOW YOU PLAYED SUCH A SNEAKY GAME IN THESE PARTS.
HEH HEH. WHATEVER IT TAKES TO WIN.
ANOTHER ROUND?
I'M CLEARLY NO MATCH FOR YOUR SAVVY, BUT I THINK I KNOW HOW I CAN RECLAIM MY HONOR...

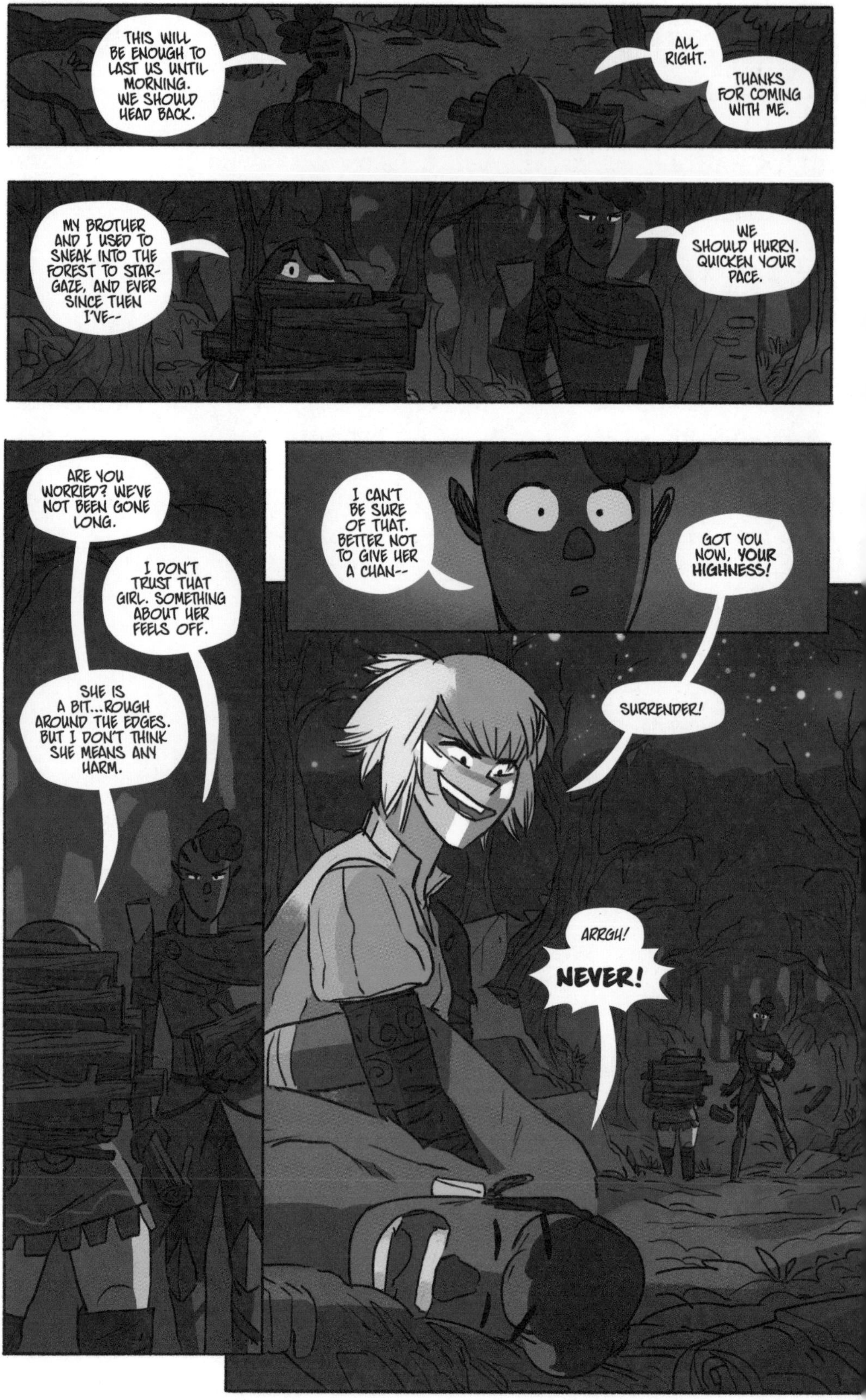

THIS WILL BE ENOUGH TO LAST US UNTIL MORNING. WE SHOULD HEAD BACK.
ALL RIGHT.
THANKS FOR COMING WITH ME.
MY BROTHER AND I USED TO SNEAK INTO THE FOREST TO STAR-GAZE, AND EVER SINCE THEN I'VE--
WE SHOULD HURRY. QUICKEN YOUR PACE.
ARE YOU WORRIED? WE'VE NOT BEEN GONE LONG.
I DON'T TRUST THAT GIRL. SOMETHING ABOUT HER FEELS OFF.
SHE IS A BIT...ROUGH AROUND THE EDGES. BUT I DON'T THINK SHE MEANS ANY HARM.
I CAN'T BE SURE OF THAT. BETTER NOT TO GIVE HER A CHAN--
GOT YOU NOW, YOUR HIGHNESS!
SURRENDER!
ARRGH!
NEVER!

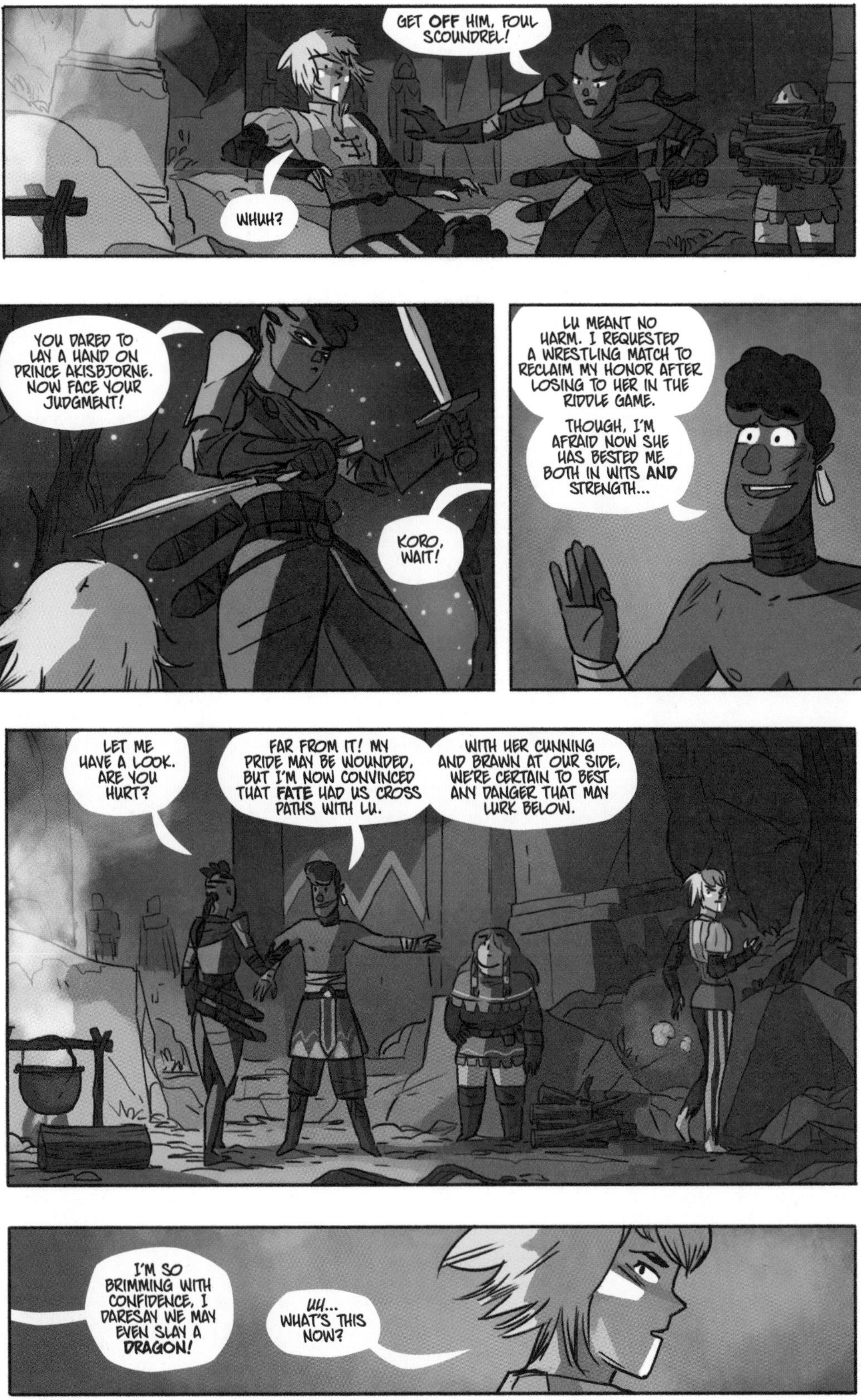

GET OFF HIM, FOUL SCOUNDREL!
WHUH?
YOU DARED TO LAY A HAND ON PRINCE AKISBJORNE. NOW FACE YOUR JUDGMENT!
KORO, WAIT!
LU MEANT NO HARM. I REQUESTED A WRESTLING MATCH TO RECLAIM MY HONOR AFTER LOSING TO HER IN THE RIDDLE GAME.
THOUGH, I'M AFRAID NOW SHE HAS BESTED ME BOTH IN WITS AND STRENGTH...
LET ME HAVE A LOOK. ARE YOU HURT?
FAR FROM IT! MY PRIDE MAY BE WOUNDED, BUT I'M NOW CONVINCED THAT FATE HAD US CROSS PATHS WITH LU.
WITH HER CUNNING AND BRAWN AT OUR SIDE, WE'RE CERTAIN TO BEST ANY DANGER THAT MAY LURK BELOW.
I'M SO BRIMMING WITH CONFIDENCE, I DARESAY WE MAY EVEN SLAY A DRAGON!
UH... WHAT'S THIS NOW?

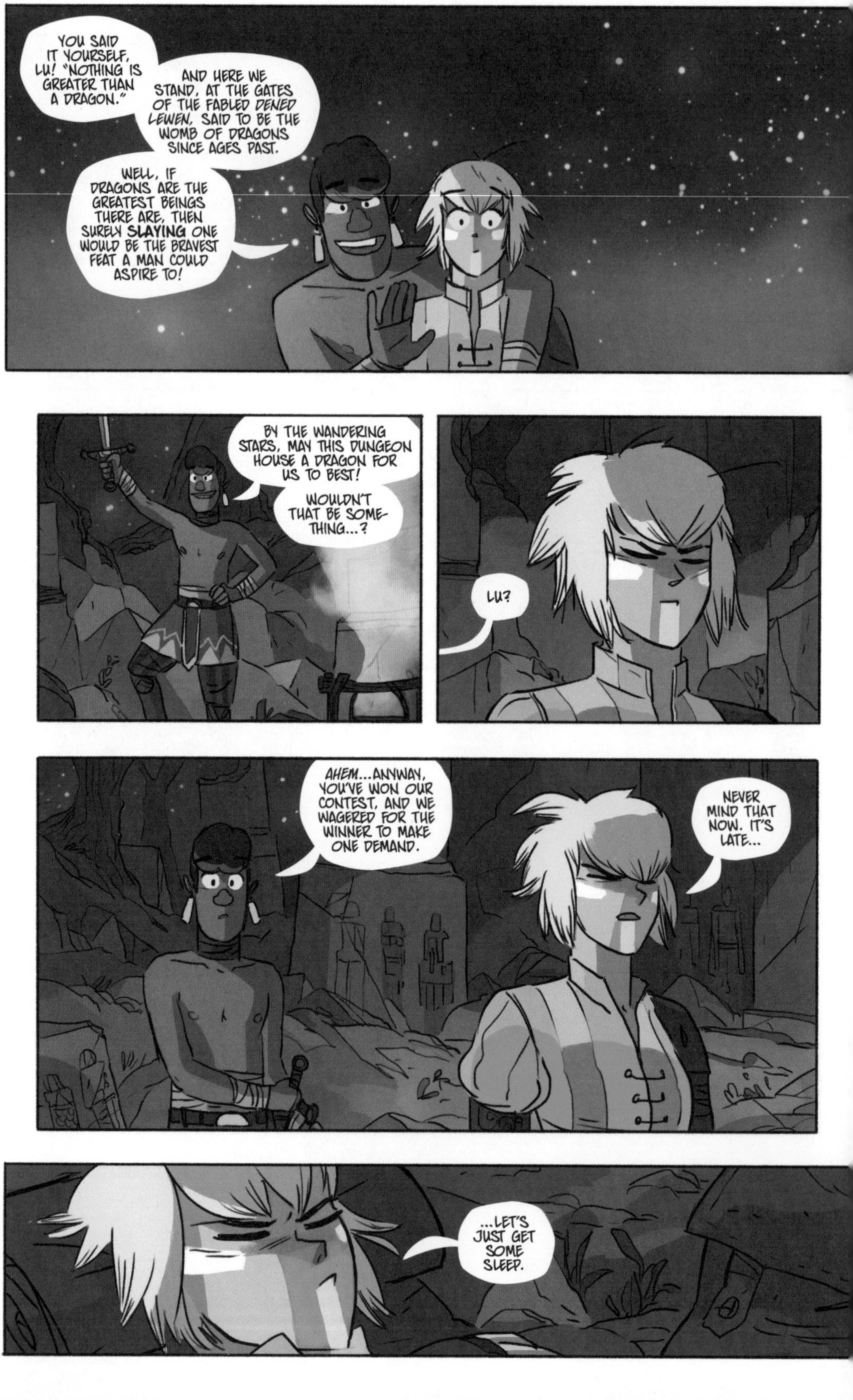
YOU SAID IT YOURSELF, LU! "NOTHING IS GREATER THAN A DRAGON."
AND HERE WE STAND, AT THE GATES OF THE FABLED DENED LEWEN, SAID TO BE THE WOMB OF DRAGONS SINCE AGES PAST.
WELL, IF DRAGONS ARE THE GREATEST BEINGS THERE ARE, THEN SURELY **SLAYING** ONE WOULD BE THE BRAVEST FEAT A MAN COULD ASPIRE TO!
BY THE WANDERING STARS, MAY THIS DUNGEON HOUSE A DRAGON FOR US TO BEST!
WOULDN'T THAT BE SOME-THING...?
LU?
AHEM...ANYWAY, YOU'VE WON OUR CONTEST, AND WE WAGERED FOR THE WINNER TO MAKE ONE DEMAND.
NEVER MIND THAT NOW. IT'S LATE...
...LET'S JUST GET SOME SLEEP.

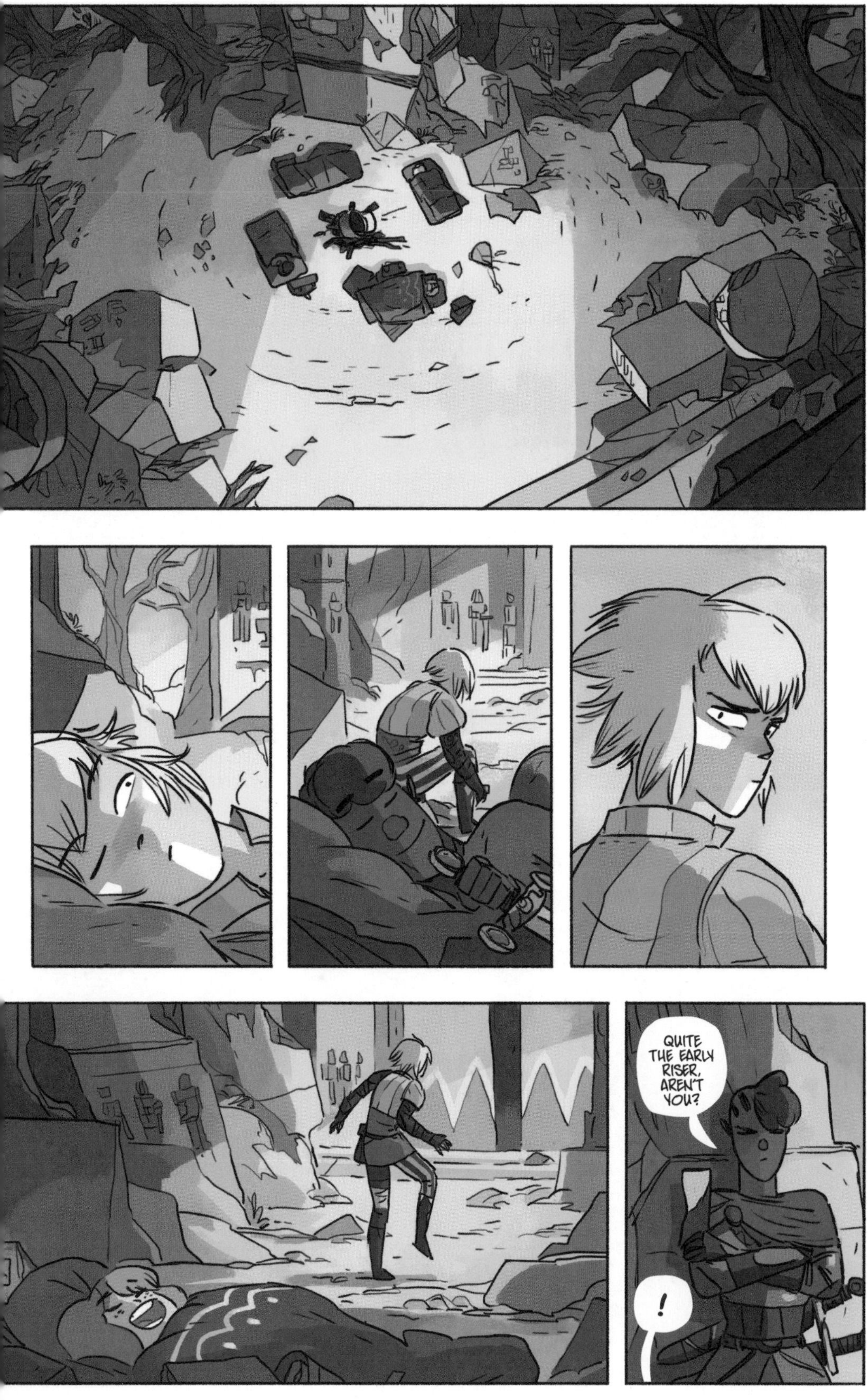
QUITE THE EARLY RISER, AREN'T YOU?
!

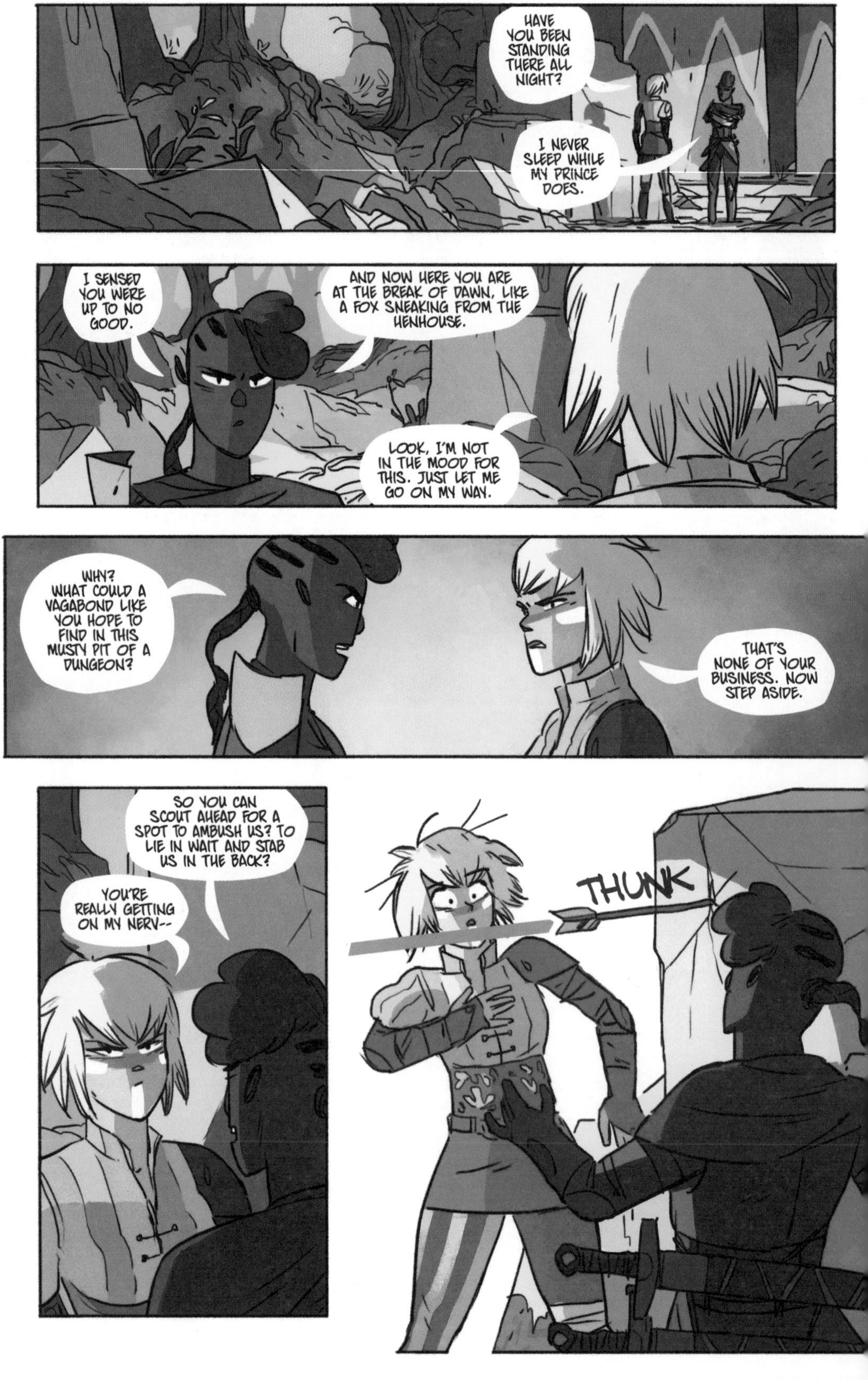
HAVE YOU BEEN STANDING THERE ALL NIGHT?
I NEVER SLEEP WHILE MY PRINCE DOES.
I SENSED YOU WERE UP TO NO GOOD.
AND NOW HERE YOU ARE AT THE BREAK OF DAWN, LIKE A FOX SNEAKING FROM THE HENHOUSE.
LOOK, I'M NOT IN THE MOOD FOR THIS. JUST LET ME GO ON MY WAY.
WHY? WHAT COULD A VAGABOND LIKE YOU HOPE TO FIND IN THIS MUSTY PIT OF A DUNGEON?
THAT'S NONE OF YOUR BUSINESS. NOW STEP ASIDE.
SO YOU CAN SCOUT AHEAD FOR A SPOT TO AMBUSH US? TO LIE IN WAIT AND STAB US IN THE BACK?
YOU'RE REALLY GETTING ON MY NERV--
THUNK

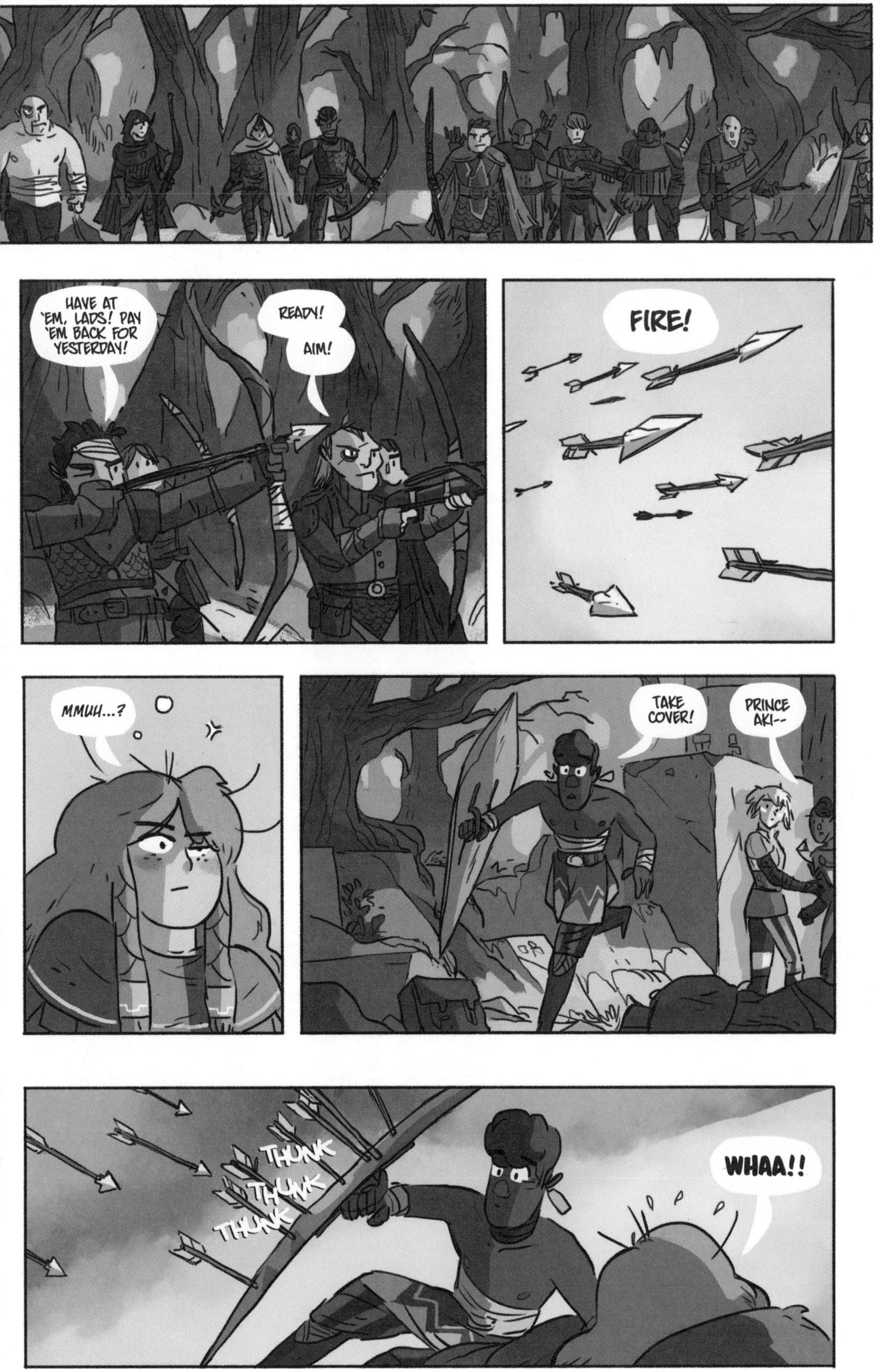
HAVE AT 'EM, LADS! PAY 'EM BACK FOR YESTERDAY!
READY!
AIM!
FIRE!
MMUH...?
TAKE COVER!
PRINCE AKI--
THUNK
THUNK
THUNK
WHAA!!

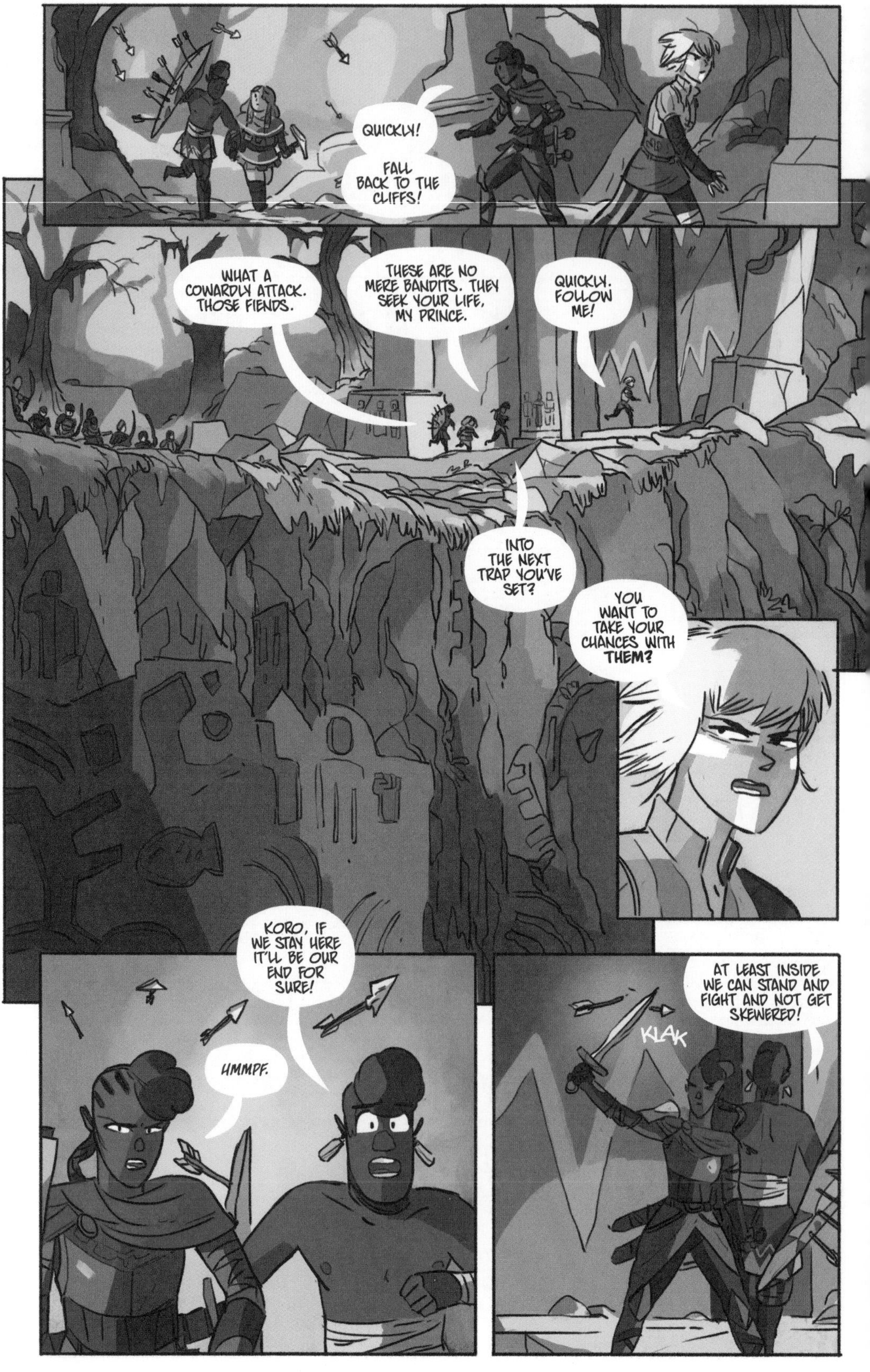
QUICKLY!
FALL BACK TO THE CLIFFS!
WHAT A COWARDLY ATTACK. THOSE FIENDS.
THESE ARE NO MERE BANDITS. THEY SEEK YOUR LIFE, MY PRINCE.
QUICKLY. FOLLOW ME!
INTO THE NEXT TRAP YOU'VE SET?
YOU WANT TO TAKE YOUR CHANCES WITH THEM?
KORO, IF WE STAY HERE IT'LL BE OUR END FOR SURE!
UMMPF.
KLAK
AT LEAST INSIDE WE CAN STAND AND FIGHT AND NOT GET SKEWERED!

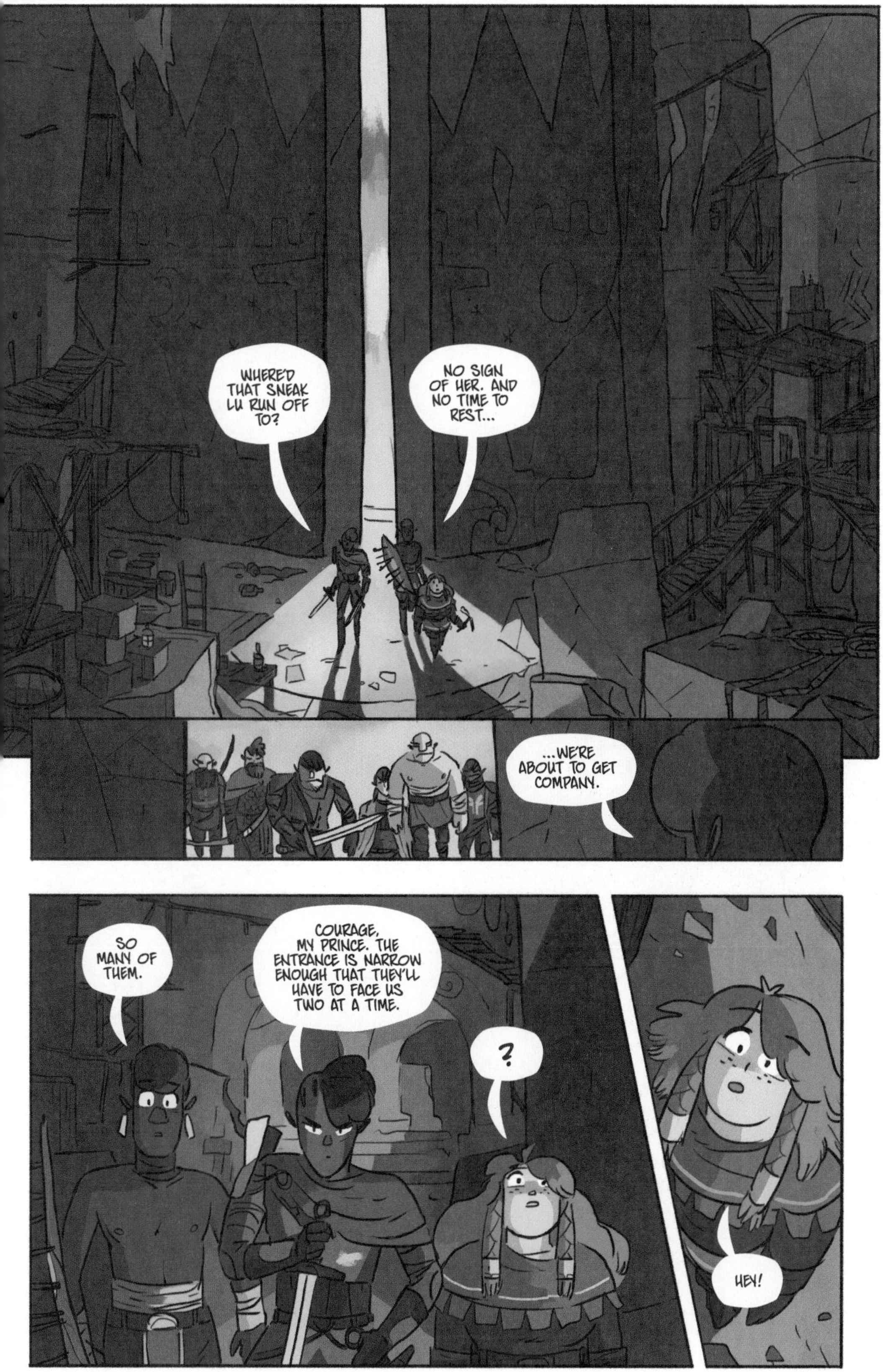
WHERE'D THAT SNEAK LU RUN OFF TO?
NO SIGN OF HER. AND NO TIME TO REST...
...WE'RE ABOUT TO GET COMPANY.
SO MANY OF THEM.
COURAGE, MY PRINCE. THE ENTRANCE IS NARROW ENOUGH THAT THEY'LL HAVE TO FACE US TWO AT A TIME.
?
HEY!

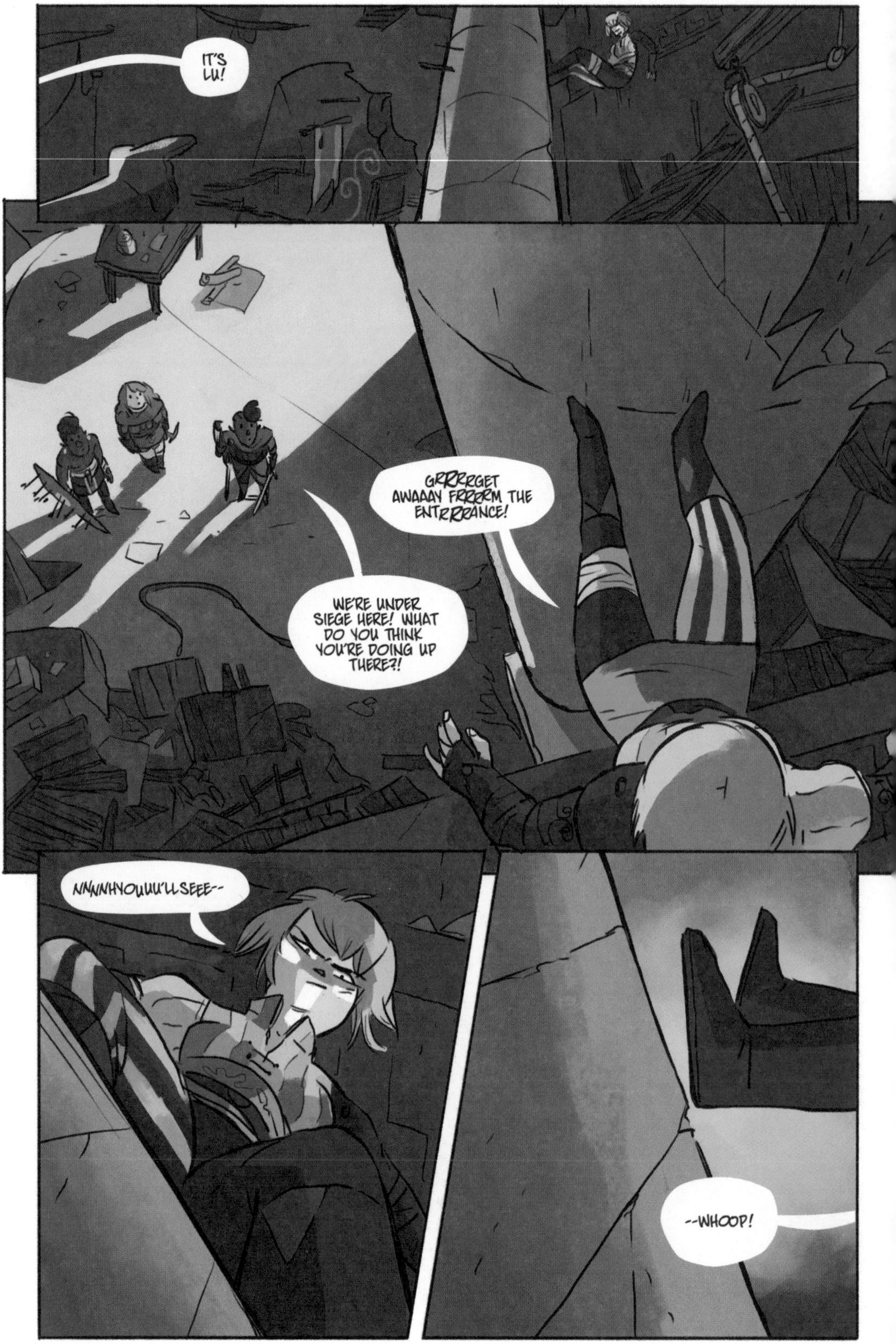
IT'S LU!
GRRRRGET AWAAAY FRRRRM THE ENTRRRANCE!
WE'RE UNDER SIEGE HERE! WHAT DO YOU THINK YOU'RE DOING UP THERE?!
NNNNHYOUUU'LLSEEE--
--WHOOP!

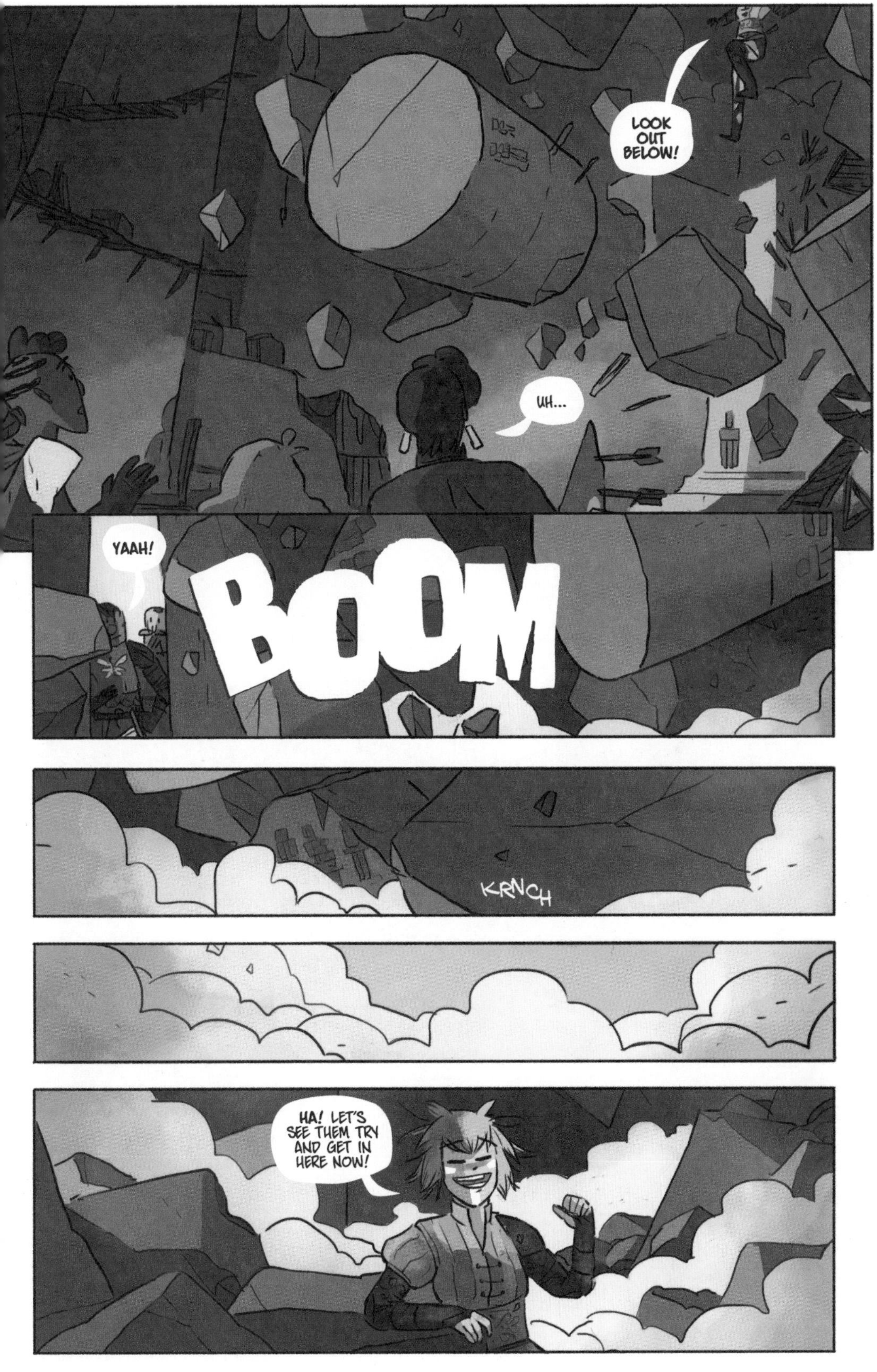
LOOK OUT BELOW!
UH...
YAAH!
BOOM
KRNCH
HA! LET'S SEE THEM TRY AND GET IN HERE NOW!

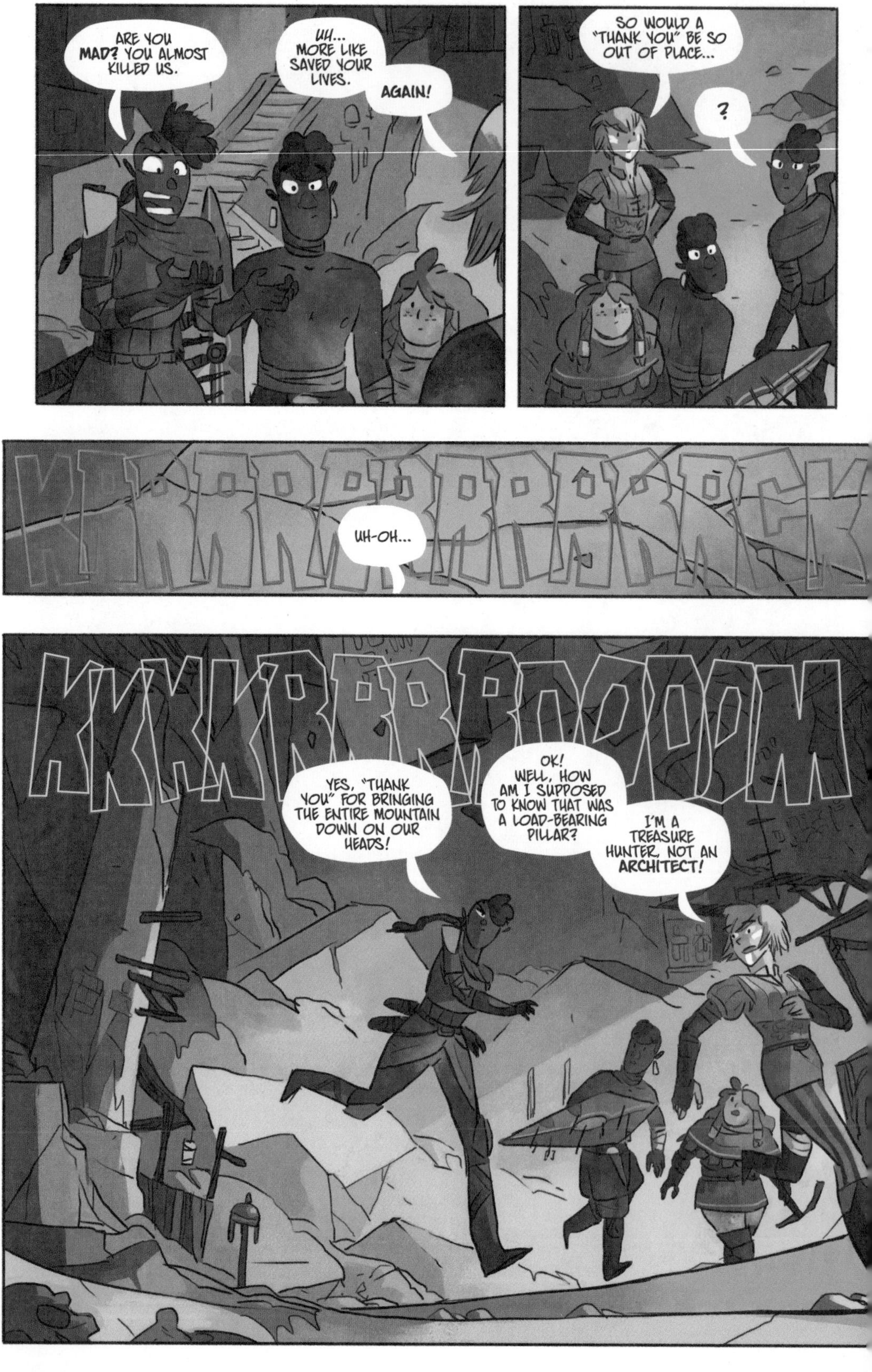
ARE YOU MAD? YOU ALMOST KILLED US.
UH... MORE LIKE SAVED YOUR LIVES.
AGAIN!
SO WOULD A "THANK YOU" BE SO OUT OF PLACE...
?
KRRRRRRRRACK
UH-OH...
KKKKRRRROOOOM
YES, "THANK YOU" FOR BRINGING THE ENTIRE MOUNTAIN DOWN ON OUR HEADS!
OK! WELL, HOW AM I SUPPOSED TO KNOW THAT WAS A LOAD-BEARING PILLAR?
I'M A TREASURE HUNTER, NOT AN ARCHITECT!

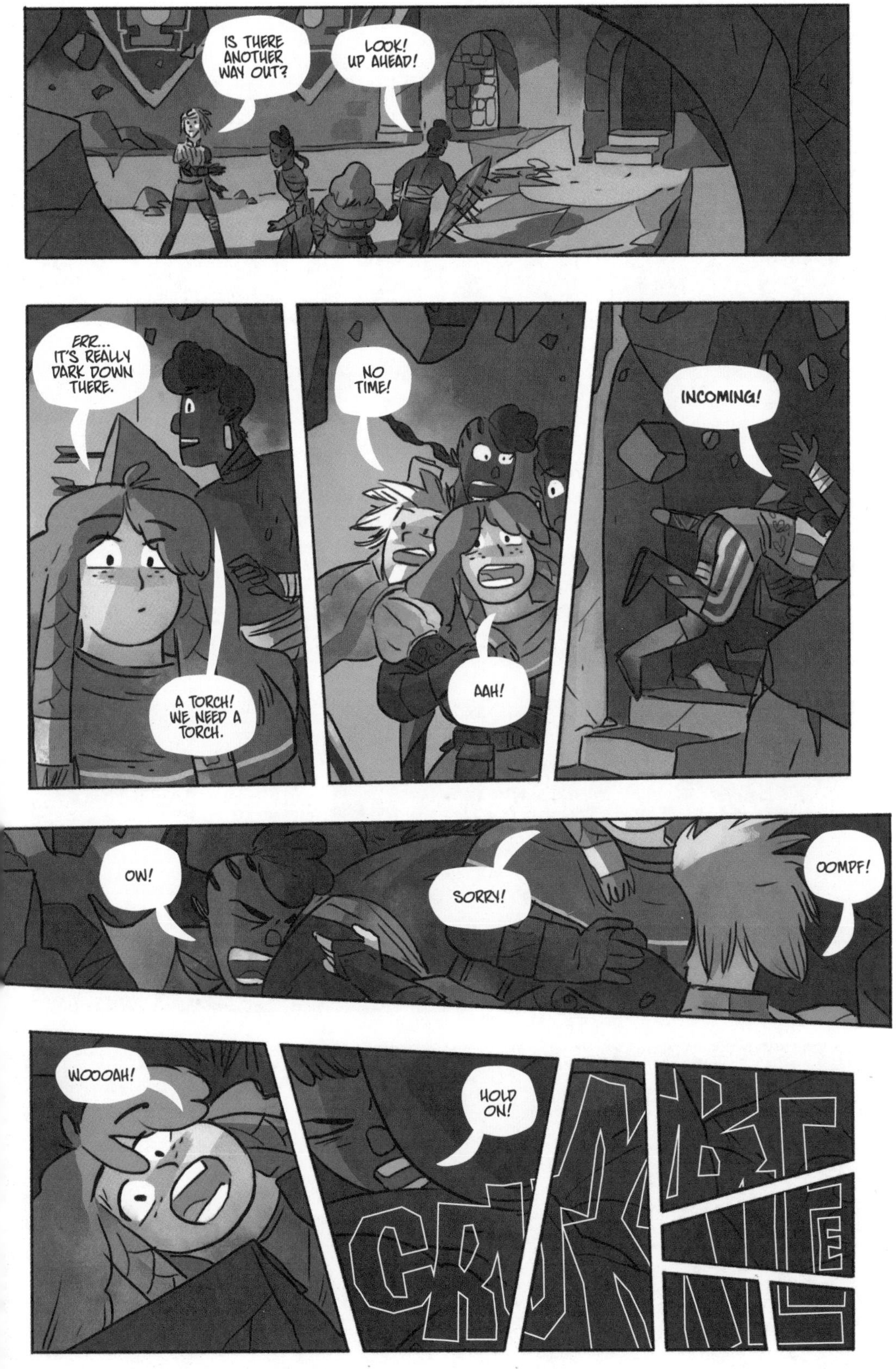
IS THERE ANOTHER WAY OUT?
LOOK! UP AHEAD!
ERR... IT'S REALLY DARK DOWN THERE.
A TORCH! WE NEED A TORCH.
NO TIME!
AAH!
INCOMING!
OW!
SORRY!
OOMPF!
WOOOAH!
HOLD ON!

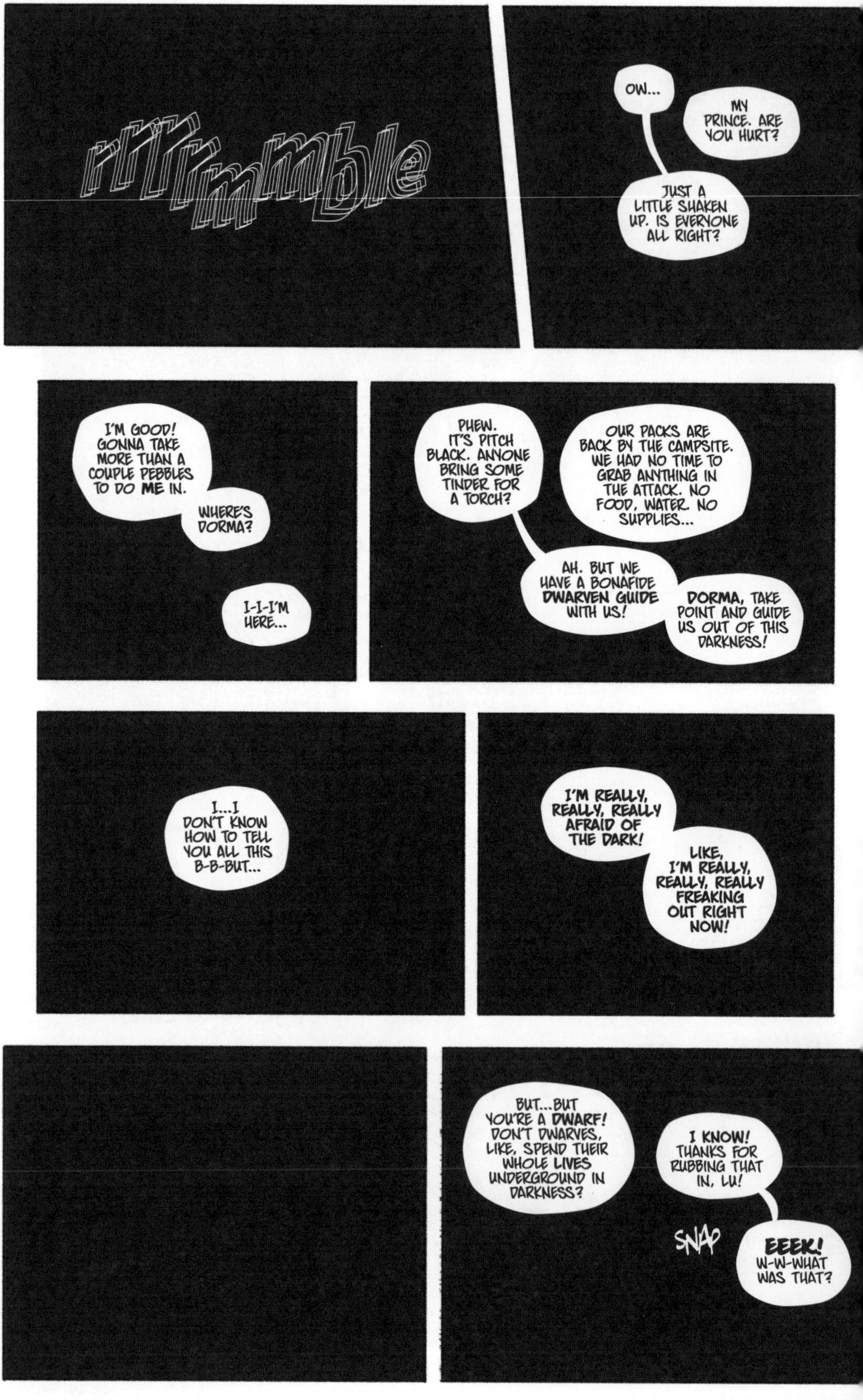
rrrrmmmble
OW...
MY PRINCE. ARE YOU HURT?
JUST A LITTLE SHAKEN UP. IS EVERYONE ALL RIGHT?
I'M GOOD! GONNA TAKE MORE THAN A COUPLE PEBBLES TO DO ME IN.
WHERE'S DORMA?
I-I-I'M HERE...
PHEW. IT'S PITCH BLACK. ANYONE BRING SOME TINDER FOR A TORCH?
OUR PACKS ARE BACK BY THE CAMPSITE. WE HAD NO TIME TO GRAB ANYTHING IN THE ATTACK. NO FOOD, WATER. NO SUPPLIES...
AH. BUT WE HAVE A BONAFIDE DWARVEN GUIDE WITH US!
DORMA, TAKE POINT AND GUIDE US OUT OF THIS DARKNESS!
I...I DON'T KNOW HOW TO TELL YOU ALL THIS B-B-BUT...
I'M REALLY, REALLY, REALLY AFRAID OF THE DARK!
LIKE, I'M REALLY, REALLY, REALLY FREAKING OUT RIGHT NOW!
BUT...BUT YOU'RE A DWARF! DON'T DWARVES, LIKE, SPEND THEIR WHOLE LIVES UNDERGROUND IN DARKNESS?
I KNOW! THANKS FOR RUBBING THAT IN, LU!
SNAP
EEEK! W-W-WHAT WAS THAT?

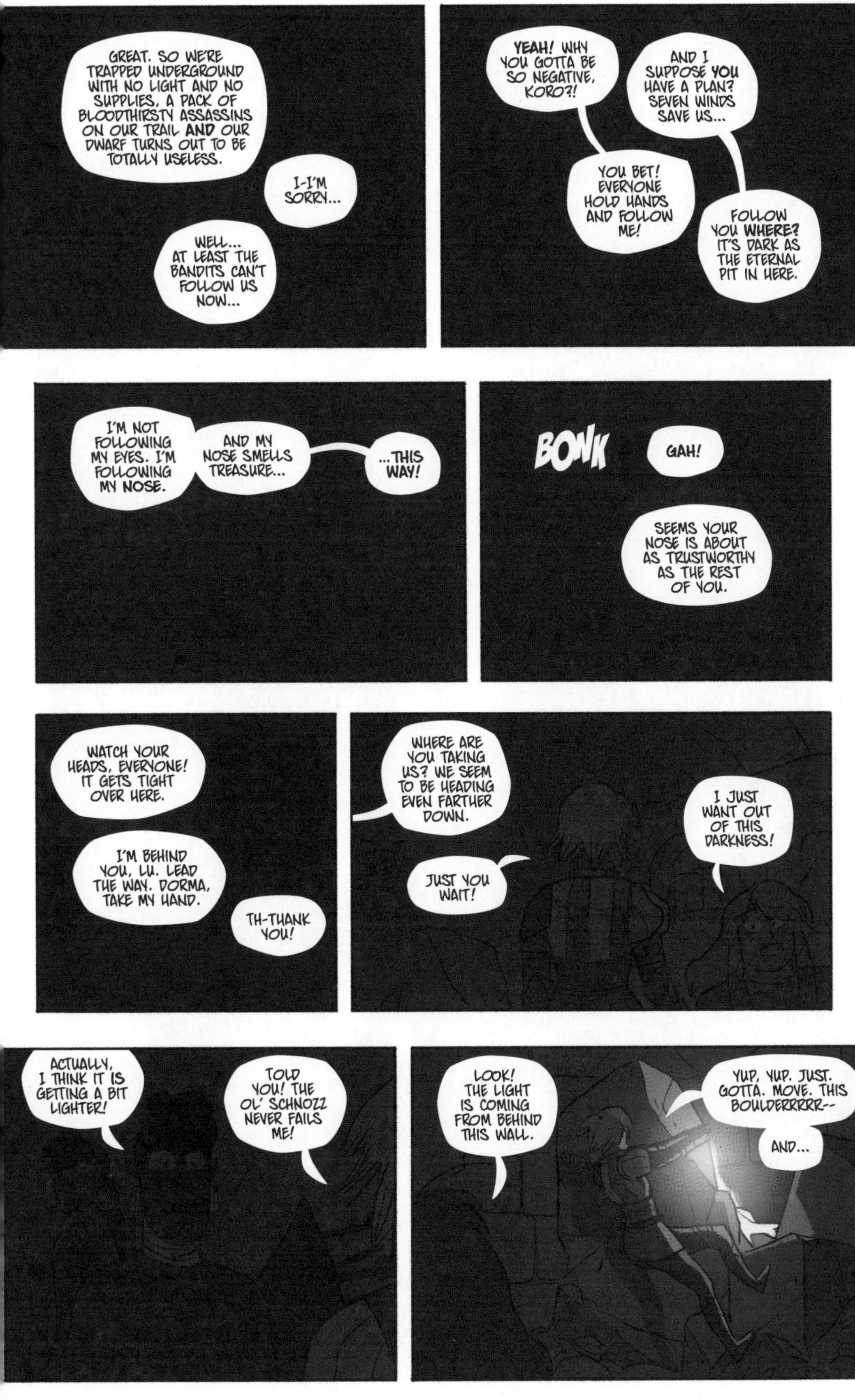
GREAT. SO WE'RE TRAPPED UNDERGROUND WITH NO LIGHT AND NO SUPPLIES, A PACK OF BLOODTHIRSTY ASSASSINS ON OUR TRAIL AND OUR DWARF TURNS OUT TO BE TOTALLY USELESS.
I-I'M SORRY...
WELL... AT LEAST THE BANDITS CAN'T FOLLOW US NOW...
YEAH! WHY YOU GOTTA BE SO NEGATIVE, KORO?!
YOU BET! EVERYONE HOLD HANDS AND FOLLOW ME!
AND I SUPPOSE YOU HAVE A PLAN? SEVEN WINDS SAVE US...
FOLLOW YOU WHERE? IT'S DARK AS THE ETERNAL PIT IN HERE.
I'M NOT FOLLOWING MY EYES. I'M FOLLOWING MY NOSE.
AND MY NOSE SMELLS TREASURE...
...THIS WAY!
BONK
GAH!
SEEMS YOUR NOSE IS ABOUT AS TRUSTWORTHY AS THE REST OF YOU.
WATCH YOUR HEADS, EVERYONE! IT GETS TIGHT OVER HERE.
I'M BEHIND YOU, LU. LEAD THE WAY. DORMA, TAKE MY HAND.
TH-THANK YOU!
WHERE ARE YOU TAKING US? WE SEEM TO BE HEADING EVEN FARTHER DOWN.
JUST YOU WAIT!
I JUST WANT OUT OF THIS DARKNESS!
ACTUALLY, I THINK IT IS GETTING A BIT LIGHTER!
TOLD YOU! THE OL' SCHNOZZ NEVER FAILS ME!
LOOK! THE LIGHT IS COMING FROM BEHIND THIS WALL.
YUP, YUP. JUST. GOTTA. MOVE. THIS BOULDERRRRR--
AND...

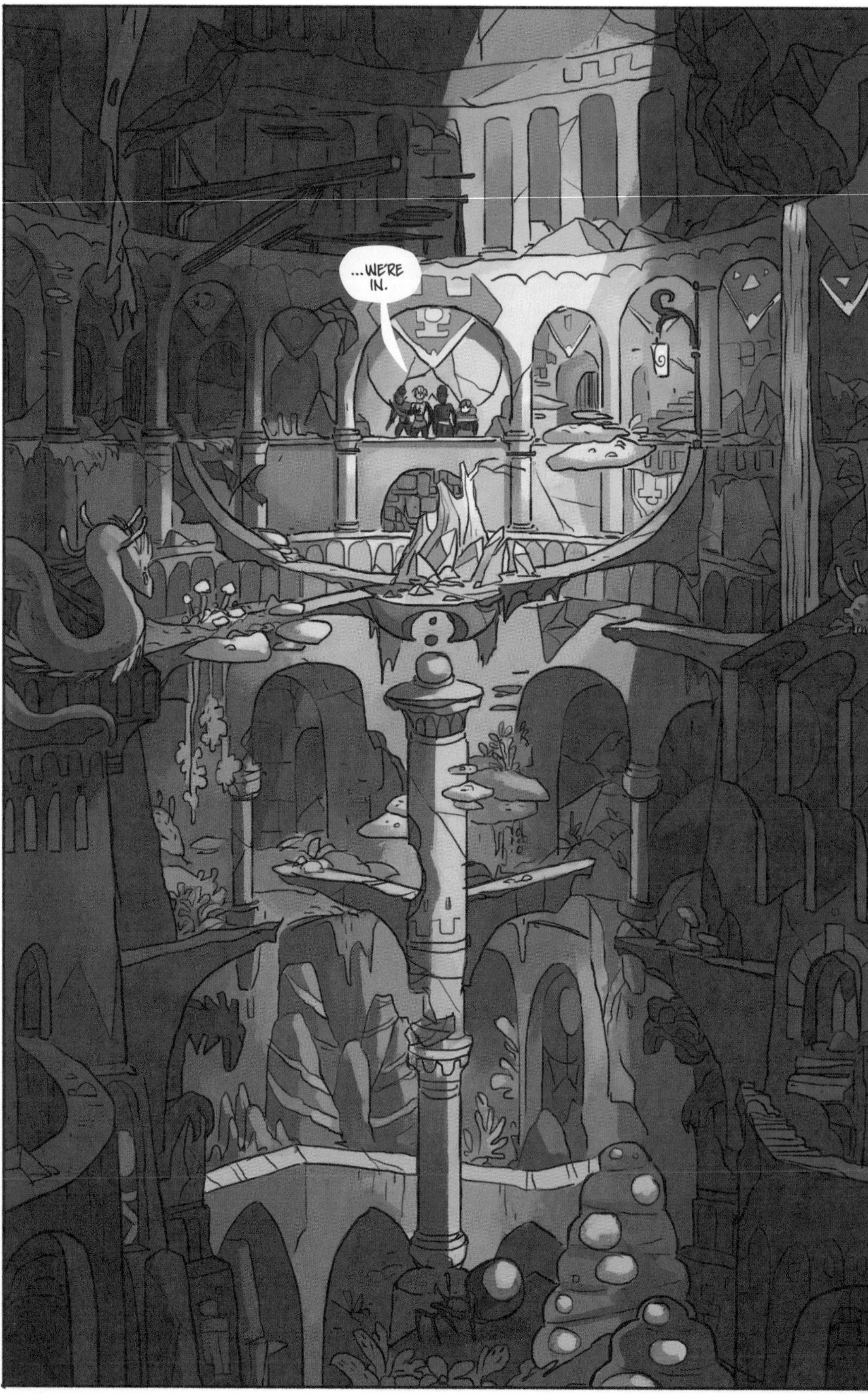
...WE'RE IN.

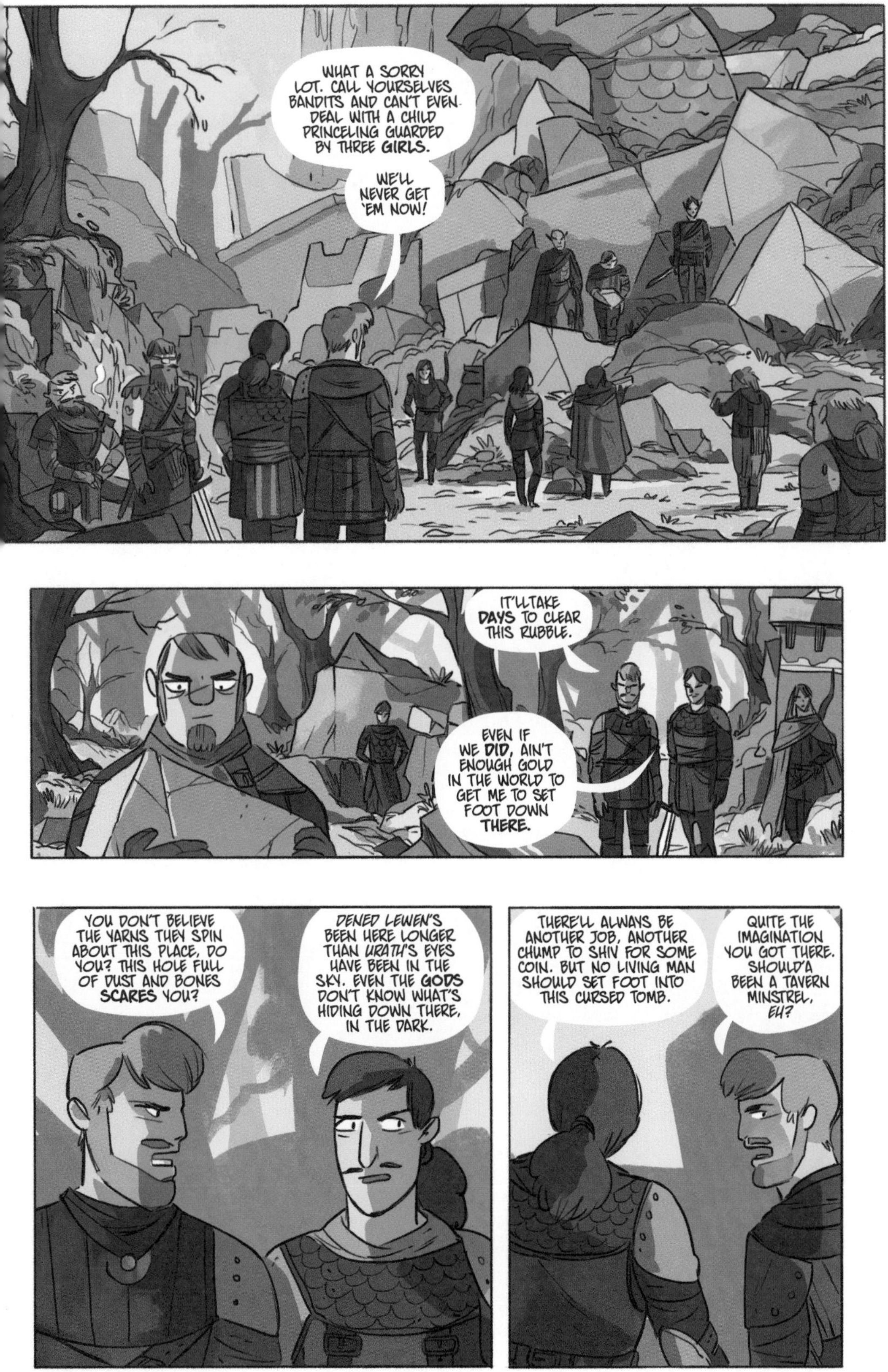
WHAT A SORRY LOT. CALL YOURSELVES BANDITS AND CAN'T EVEN DEAL WITH A CHILD PRINCELING GUARDED BY THREE **GIRLS**.
WE'LL NEVER GET 'EM NOW!
IT'LLTAKE **DAYS** TO CLEAR THIS RUBBLE.
EVEN IF WE **DID**, AIN'T ENOUGH GOLD IN THE WORLD TO GET ME TO SET FOOT DOWN **THERE**.
YOU DON'T BELIEVE THE YARNS THEY SPIN ABOUT THIS PLACE, DO YOU? THIS HOLE FULL OF DUST AND BONES **SCARES** YOU?
DENED LEWEN'S BEEN HERE LONGER THAN *URATH'S* EYES HAVE BEEN IN THE SKY. EVEN THE **GODS** DON'T KNOW WHAT'S HIDING DOWN THERE, IN THE DARK.
THERE'LL ALWAYS BE ANOTHER JOB, ANOTHER CHUMP TO SHIV FOR SOME COIN. BUT NO LIVING MAN SHOULD SET FOOT INTO THIS CURSED TOMB.
QUITE THE IMAGINATION YOU GOT THERE. SHOULD'A BEEN A TAVERN MINSTREL, EH?

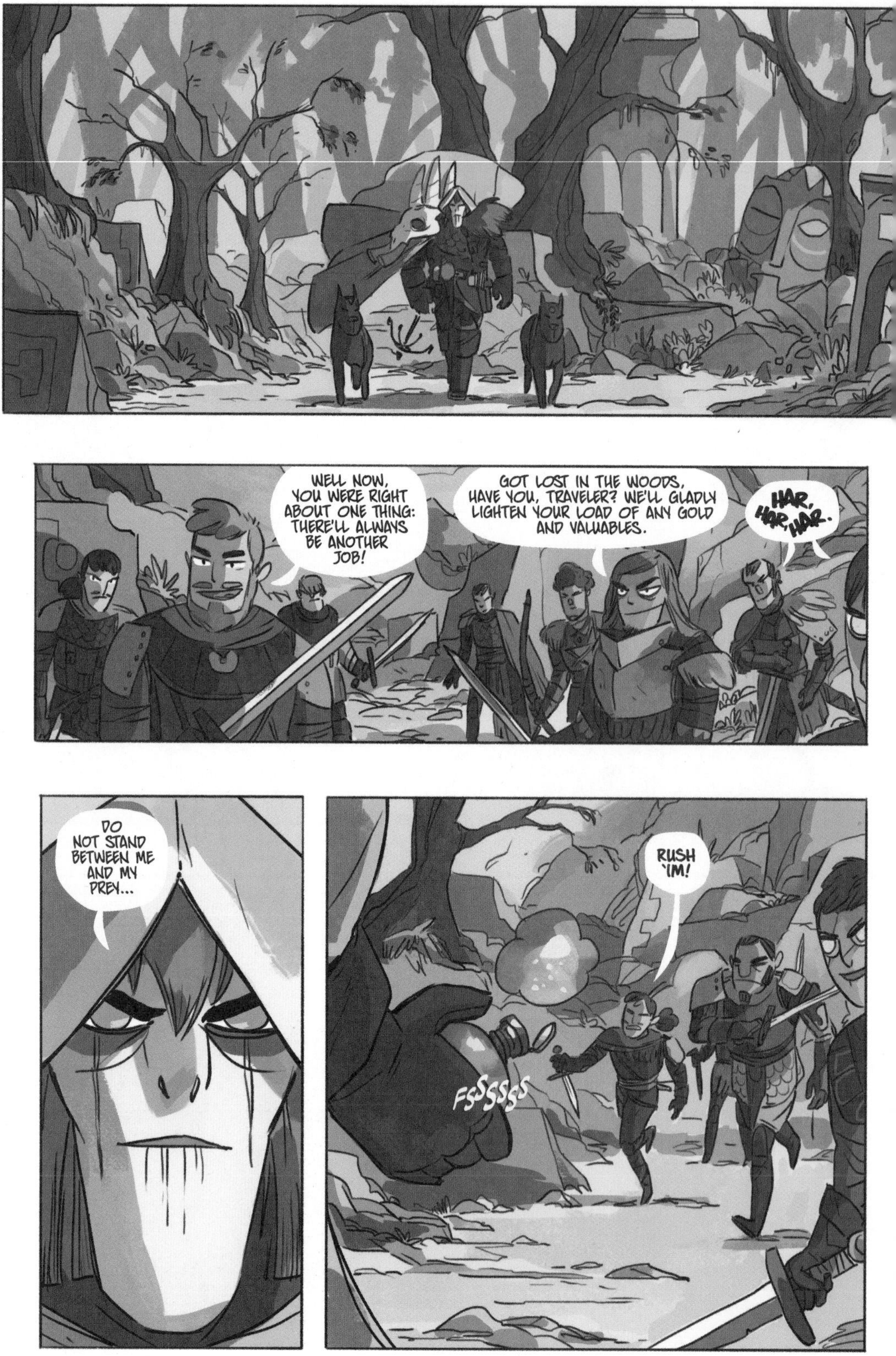
WELL NOW, YOU WERE RIGHT ABOUT ONE THING: THERE'LL ALWAYS BE ANOTHER JOB!
GOT LOST IN THE WOODS, HAVE YOU, TRAVELER? WE'LL GLADLY LIGHTEN YOUR LOAD OF ANY GOLD AND VALUABLES.
HAR, HAR, HAR.
DO NOT STAND BETWEEN ME AND MY PREY...
RUSH 'IM!
FSSSSSS

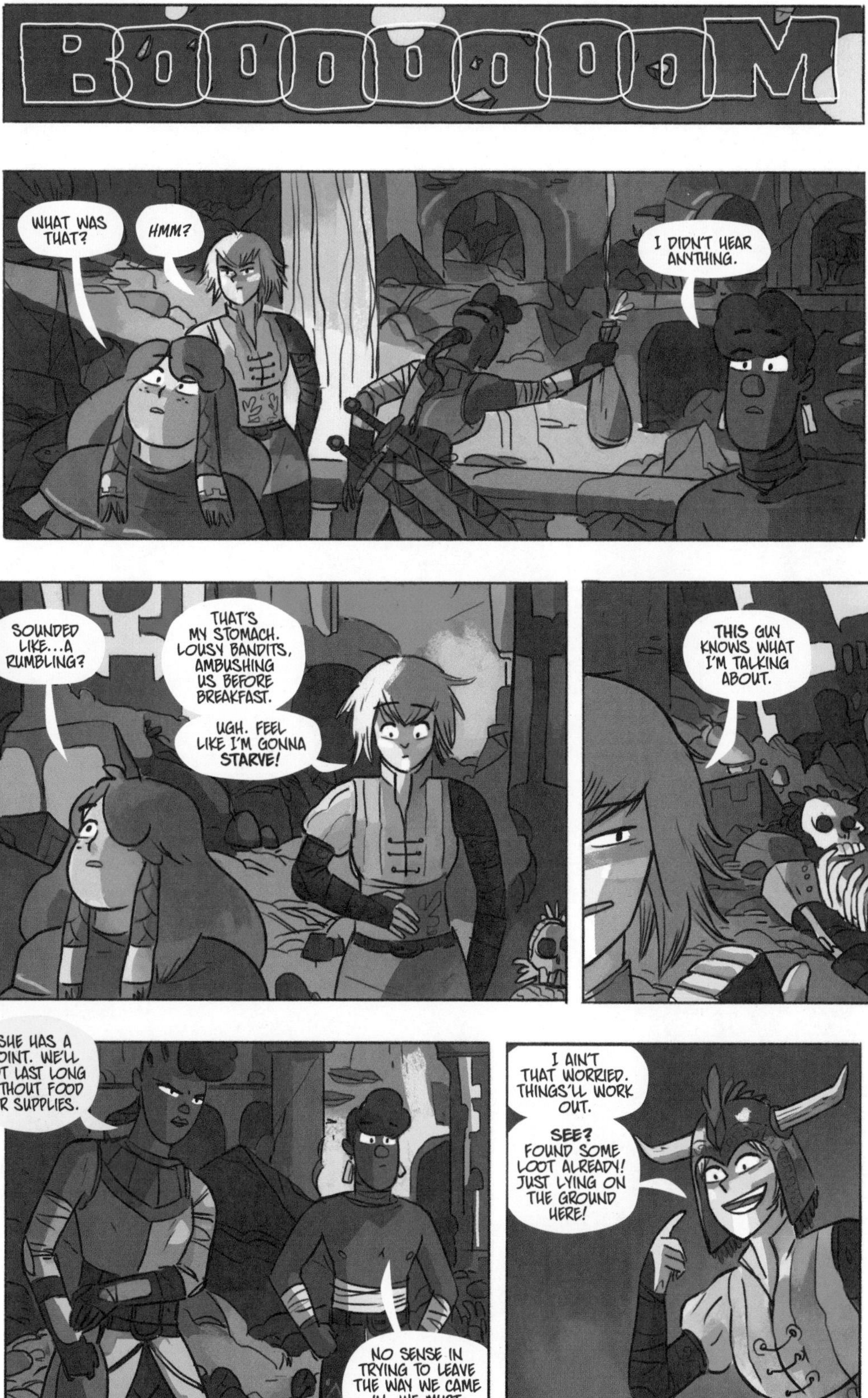
BOOOOOOOM
WHAT WAS THAT?
HMM?
I DIDN'T HEAR ANYTHING.
SOUNDED LIKE...A RUMBLING?
THAT'S MY STOMACH. LOUSY BANDITS, AMBUSHING US BEFORE BREAKFAST.
UGH. FEEL LIKE I'M GONNA STARVE!
THIS GUY KNOWS WHAT I'M TALKING ABOUT.
SHE HAS A POINT. WE'LL NOT LAST LONG WITHOUT FOOD OR SUPPLIES.
NO SENSE IN TRYING TO LEAVE THE WAY WE CAME IN. WE MUST PRESS ONWARD.
I AIN'T THAT WORRIED. THINGS'LL WORK OUT.
SEE? FOUND SOME LOOT ALREADY! JUST LYING ON THE GROUND HERE!

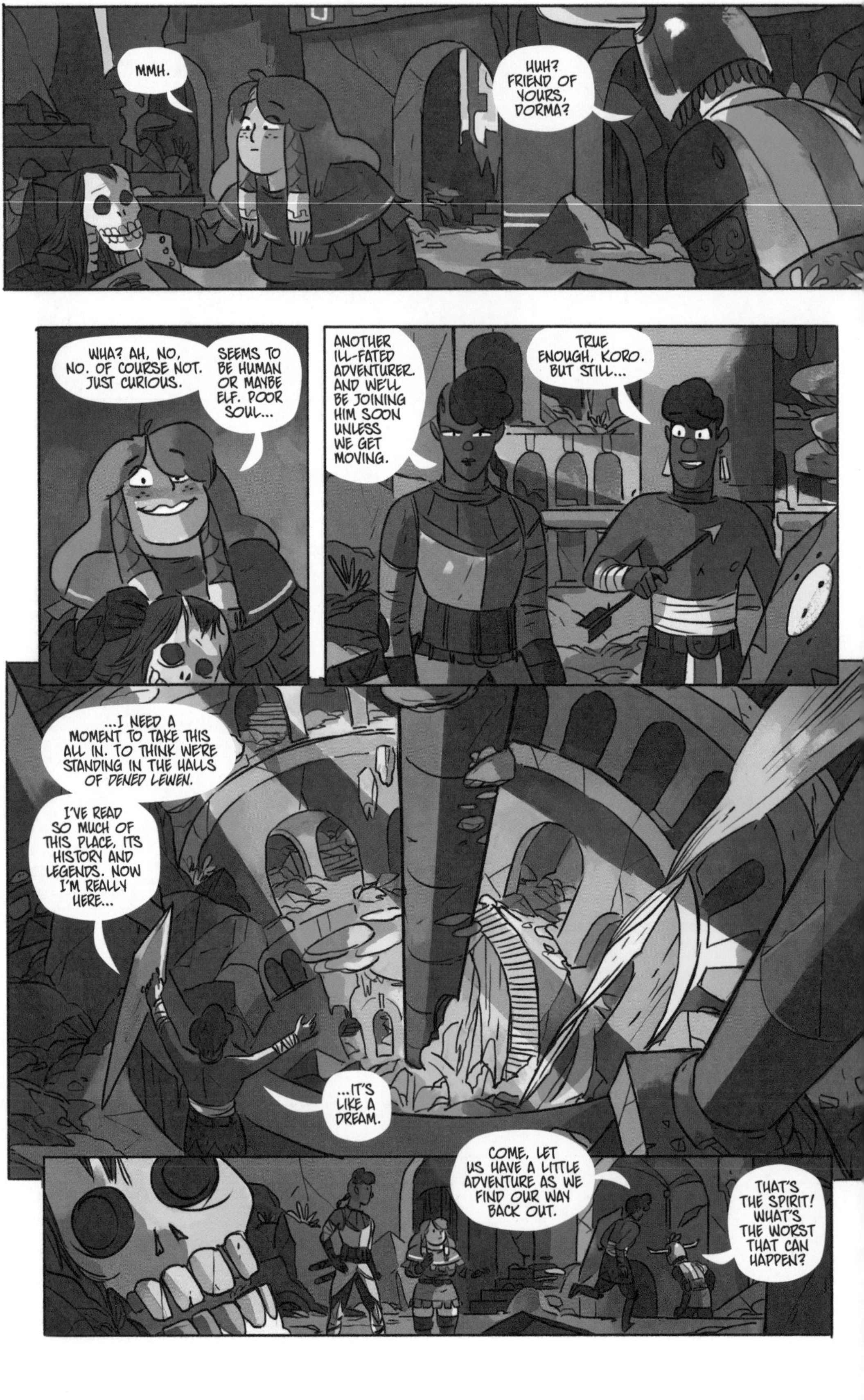
MMH.
HUH? FRIEND OF YOURS, DORMA?
WHA? AH, NO, NO. OF COURSE NOT. JUST CURIOUS.
SEEMS TO BE HUMAN OR MAYBE ELF. POOR SOUL...
ANOTHER ILL-FATED ADVENTURER. AND WE'LL BE JOINING HIM SOON UNLESS WE GET MOVING.
TRUE ENOUGH, KORO. BUT STILL...
...I NEED A MOMENT TO TAKE THIS ALL IN. TO THINK WE'RE STANDING IN THE HALLS OF DENED LEWEN.
I'VE READ SO MUCH OF THIS PLACE, ITS HISTORY AND LEGENDS. NOW I'M REALLY HERE...
...IT'S LIKE A DREAM.
COME, LET US HAVE A LITTLE ADVENTURE AS WE FIND OUR WAY BACK OUT.
THAT'S THE SPIRIT! WHAT'S THE WORST THAT CAN HAPPEN?

DID YOUR STUDIES HAPPEN TO MENTION ANOTHER GATE THE INHABITANTS MAY HAVE USED, MY PRINCE?

YEAH, OR WHERE THEY KEPT ALL THEIR GOLD AND STUFF?

SADLY, NOT. BUT UNLESS I'M MISTAKEN, WE ARE IN ONE OF THE BURGS OF THE LATE BURROW LORDS.

THIRD OR FOURTH DYNASTY PERHAPS?

MY GRAN-GRAN TOLD ME STORIES ABOUT THE UNDERKINGS. THE GREAT DWARVEN CITIES, CARVED FROM LIVING ROCK.

GOTTA BE A WHOLE **OCEAN** OF TREASURE DOWN HERE THEN. KINGS ARE ALMOST AS GREEDY AS DRAGONS.

HERE, DORMA. MY DWARVISH IS WOEFULLY LACKING. CAN YOU READ THIS?

ONLY A BIT. IT'S A STRANGE DIALECT...

..."WE DIG AND DIG UNTIL OUR PICKS RUST...BUT THE BOTTOM OF THE WORLD IS ONLY... THE BEGINNING."

AND HERE, THIS PART IS STRANGE:

"IS...DALDEN LARIA REAL...OR JUST A TALE? AN URDEN CURSE PLACED ON US MORTALS TO KEEP US...DIGGING FOREVER...

...SEARCHING FOREVER."

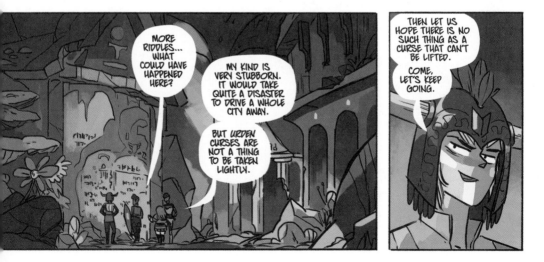

MORE RIDDLES... WHAT COULD HAVE HAPPENED HERE?

MY KIND IS VERY STUBBORN. IT WOULD TAKE QUITE A DISASTER TO DRIVE A WHOLE CITY AWAY.

BUT *URDEN* CURSES ARE NOT A THING TO BE TAKEN LIGHTLY.

THEN LET US HOPE THERE IS NO SUCH THING AS A CURSE THAT CAN'T BE LIFTED.

COME, LET'S KEEP GOING.

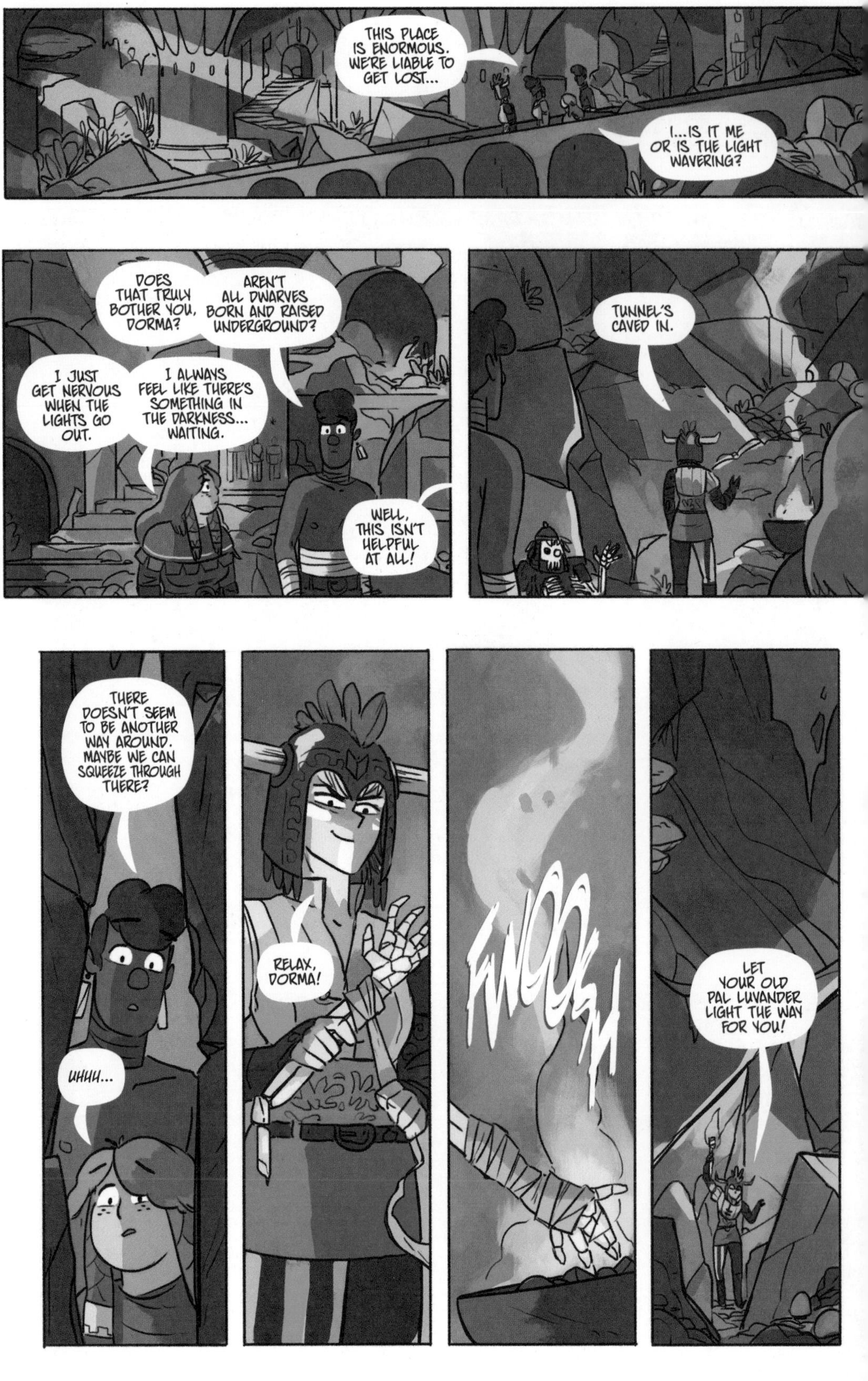
THIS PLACE IS ENORMOUS. WE'RE LIABLE TO GET LOST...
I...IS IT ME OR IS THE LIGHT WAVERING?
DOES THAT TRULY BOTHER YOU, DORMA?
AREN'T ALL DWARVES BORN AND RAISED UNDERGROUND?
I JUST GET NERVOUS WHEN THE LIGHTS GO OUT.
I ALWAYS FEEL LIKE THERE'S SOMETHING IN THE DARKNESS... WAITING.
WELL, THIS ISN'T HELPFUL AT ALL!
TUNNEL'S CAVED IN.
THERE DOESN'T SEEM TO BE ANOTHER WAY AROUND. MAYBE WE CAN SQUEEZE THROUGH THERE?
UHHH...
RELAX, DORMA!
FWOOSH
LET YOUR OLD PAL LUVANDER LIGHT THE WAY FOR YOU!

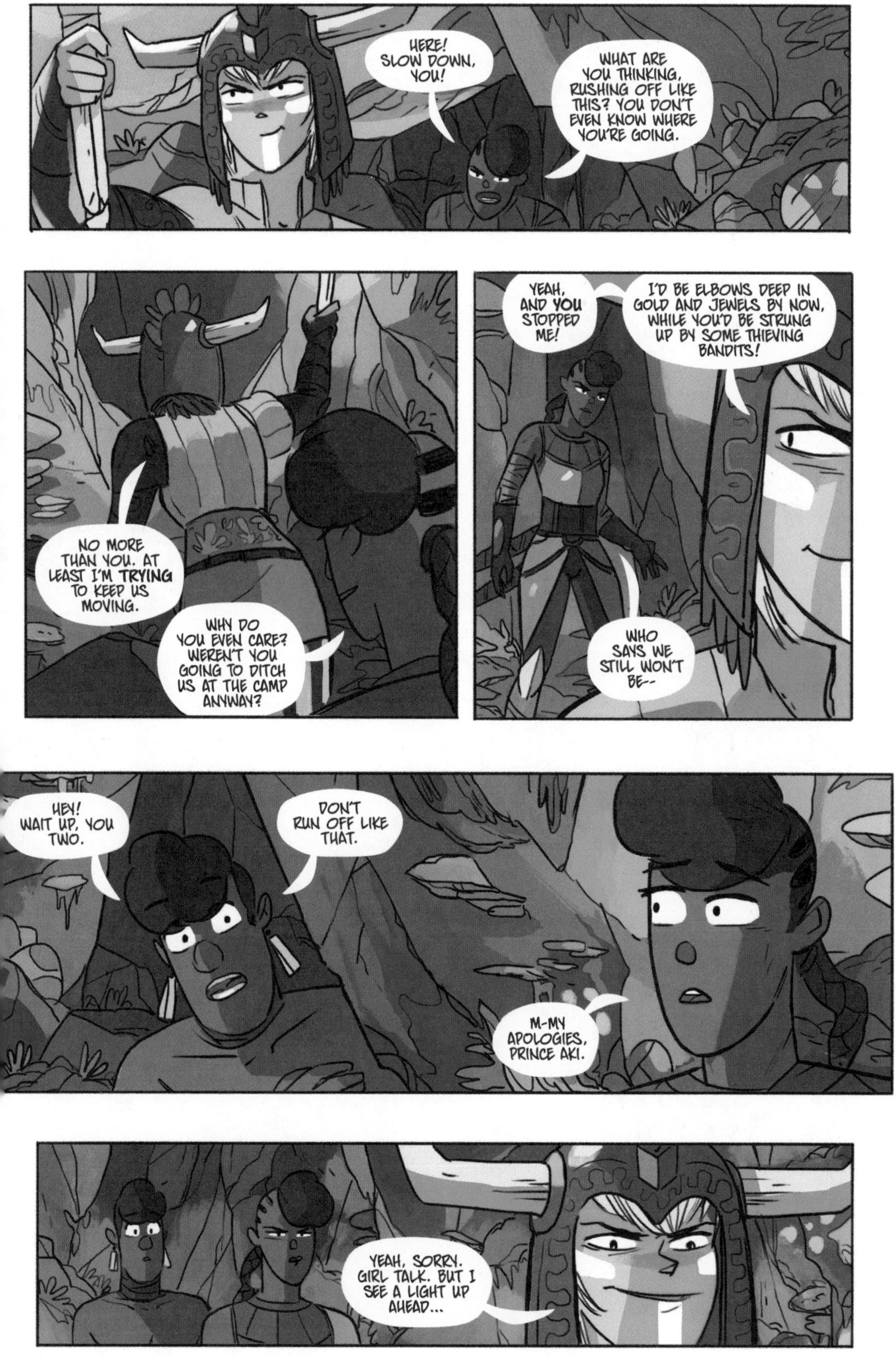
HERE! SLOW DOWN, YOU!
WHAT ARE YOU THINKING, RUSHING OFF LIKE THIS? YOU DON'T EVEN KNOW WHERE YOU'RE GOING.
NO MORE THAN YOU. AT LEAST I'M TRYING TO KEEP US MOVING.
WHY DO YOU EVEN CARE? WEREN'T YOU GOING TO DITCH US AT THE CAMP ANYWAY?
YEAH, AND YOU STOPPED ME!
I'D BE ELBOWS DEEP IN GOLD AND JEWELS BY NOW, WHILE YOU'D BE STRUNG UP BY SOME THIEVING BANDITS!
WHO SAYS WE STILL WON'T BE--
HEY! WAIT UP, YOU TWO.
DON'T RUN OFF LIKE THAT.
M-MY APOLOGIES, PRINCE AKI.
YEAH, SORRY. GIRL TALK. BUT I SEE A LIGHT UP AHEAD...

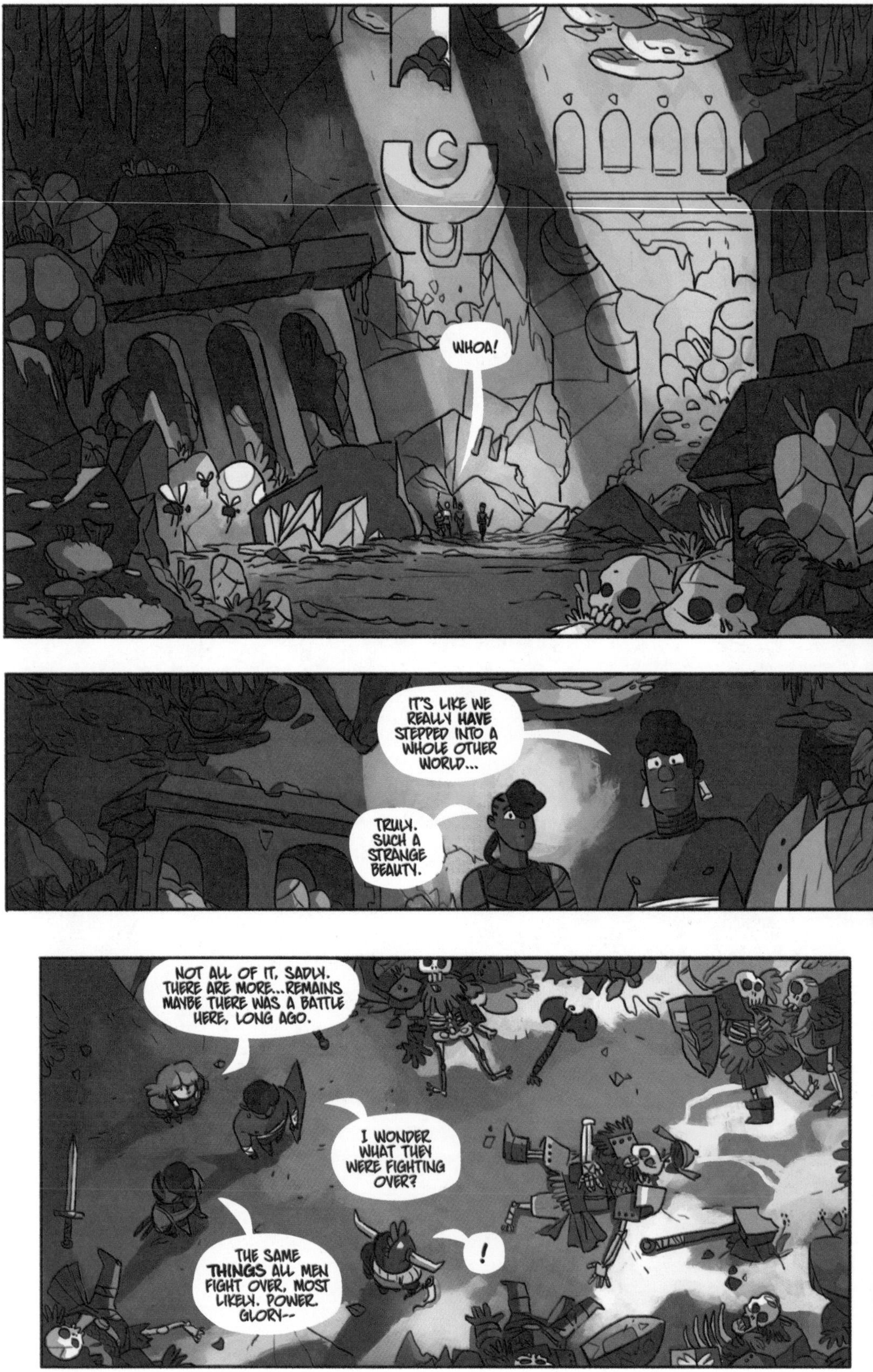
WHOA!
IT'S LIKE WE REALLY HAVE STEPPED INTO A WHOLE OTHER WORLD...
TRULY. SUCH A STRANGE BEAUTY.
NOT ALL OF IT, SADLY. THERE ARE MORE...REMAINS MAYBE THERE WAS A BATTLE HERE, LONG AGO.
I WONDER WHAT THEY WERE FIGHTING OVER?
THE SAME THINGS ALL MEN FIGHT OVER, MOST LIKELY. POWER. GLORY--
!

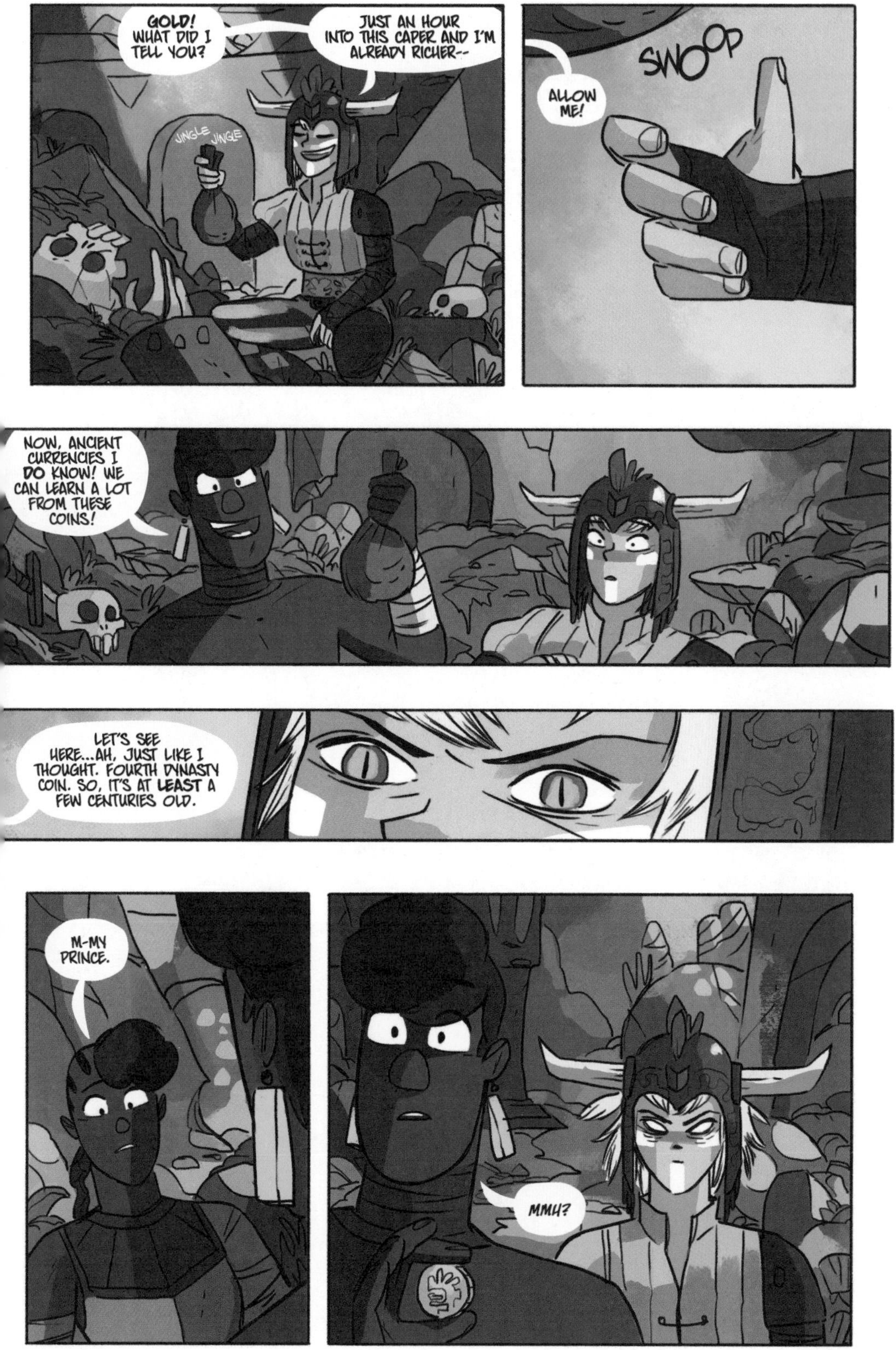
GOLD! WHAT DID I TELL YOU?
JINGLE JINGLE
JUST AN HOUR INTO THIS CAPER AND I'M ALREADY RICHER--
SWOOP
ALLOW ME!
NOW, ANCIENT CURRENCIES I DO KNOW! WE CAN LEARN A LOT FROM THESE COINS!
LET'S SEE HERE...AH, JUST LIKE I THOUGHT. FOURTH DYNASTY COIN. SO, IT'S AT LEAST A FEW CENTURIES OLD.
M-MY PRINCE.
MMH?

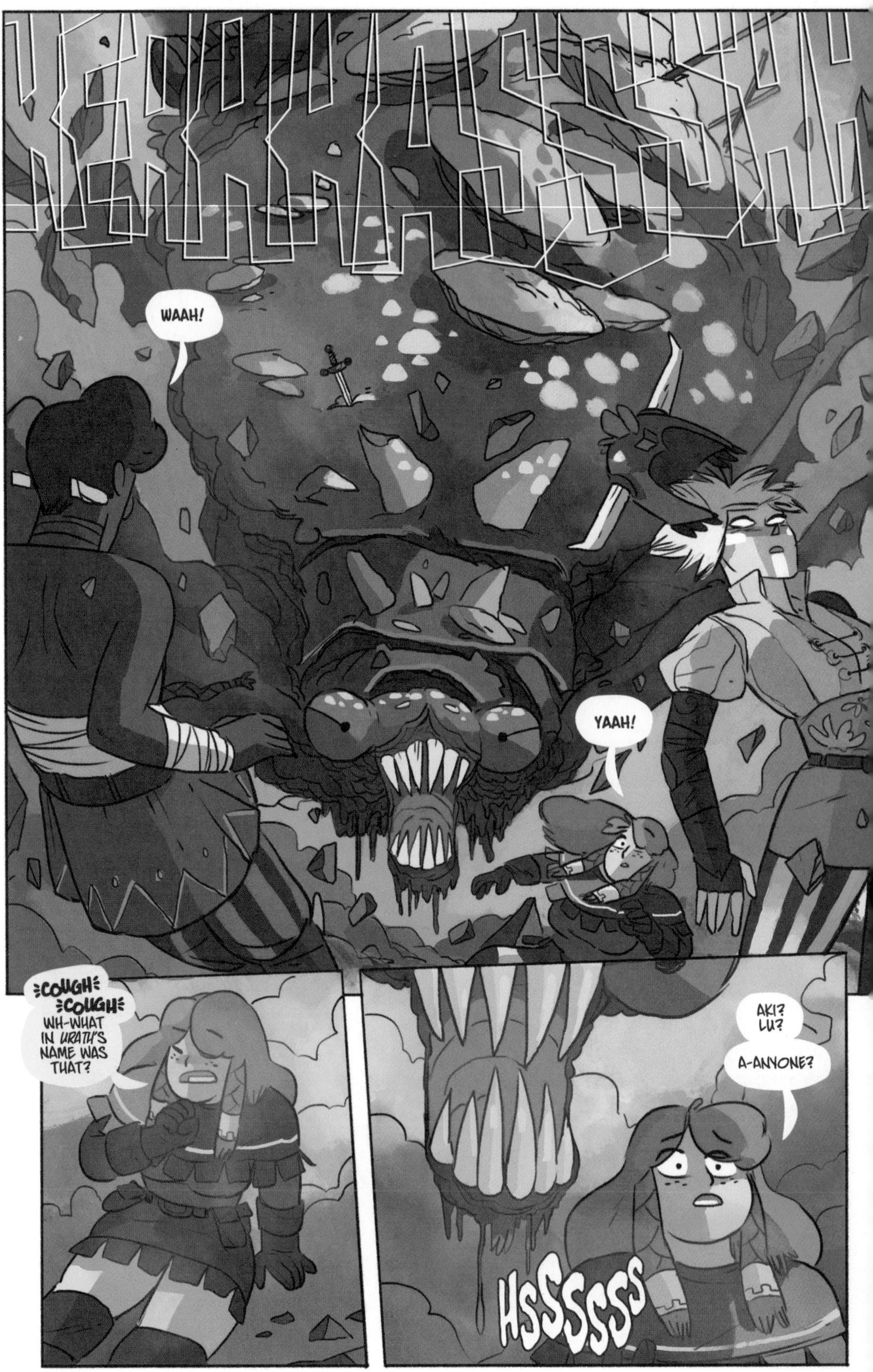
WAAH!
YAAH!
COUGH
COUGH
WH-WHAT IN URATH'S NAME WAS THAT?
AKI? LU?
A-ANYONE?
HSSSSSS

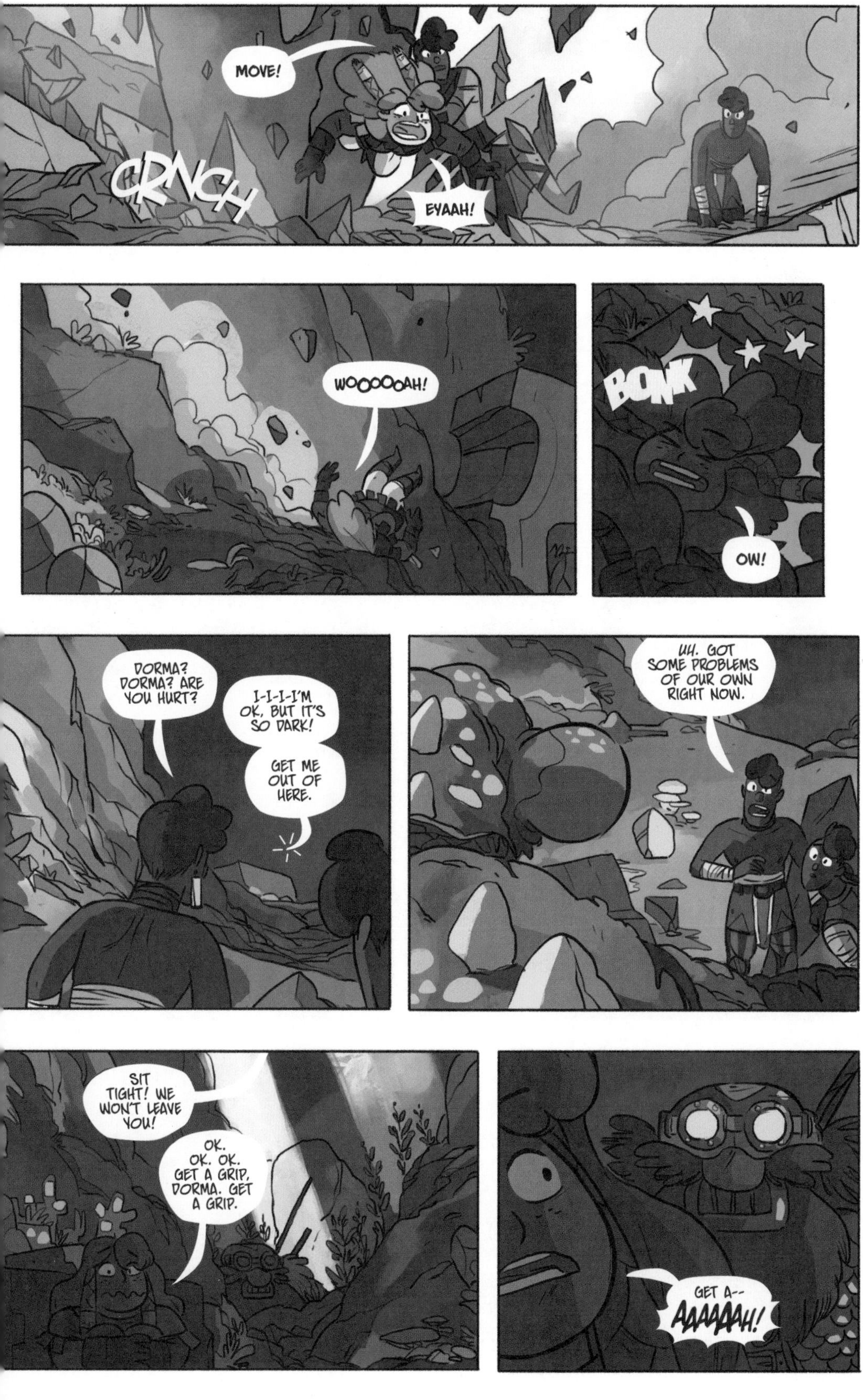
MOVE!
CRNCH
EYAAH!
WOOOOOAH!
BONK
OW!
DORMA? DORMA? ARE YOU HURT?
I-I-I-I'M OK, BUT IT'S SO DARK!
GET ME OUT OF HERE.
UH. GOT SOME PROBLEMS OF OUR OWN RIGHT NOW.
SIT TIGHT! WE WON'T LEAVE YOU!
OK. OK. OK. GET A GRIP, DORMA. GET A GRIP.
GET A--
AAAAAAH!

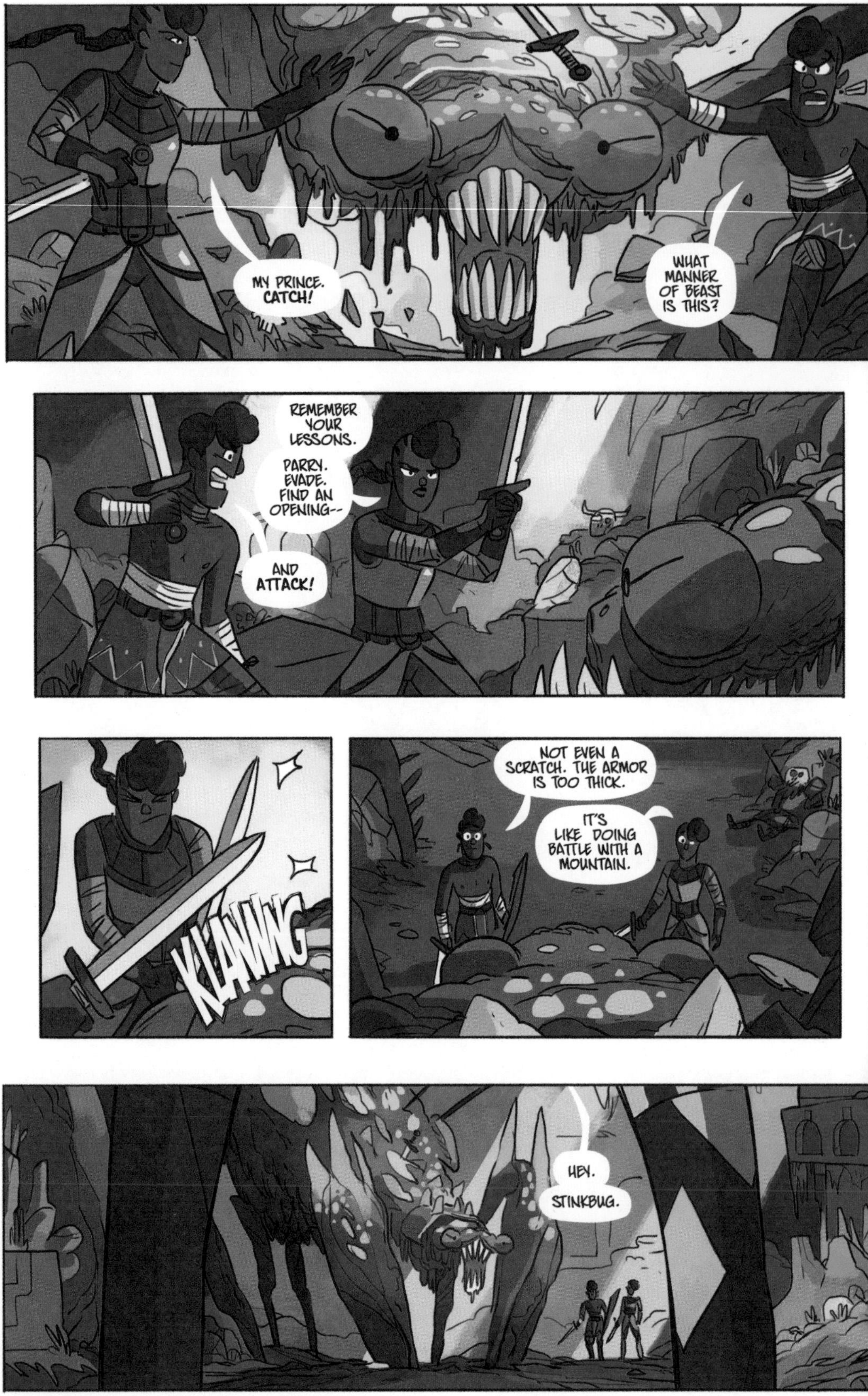
MY PRINCE. CATCH!
WHAT MANNER OF BEAST IS THIS?
REMEMBER YOUR LESSONS.
PARRY. EVADE. FIND AN OPENING--
AND ATTACK!
KLANNNG
NOT EVEN A SCRATCH. THE ARMOR IS TOO THICK.
IT'S LIKE DOING BATTLE WITH A MOUNTAIN.
HEY.
STINKBUG.

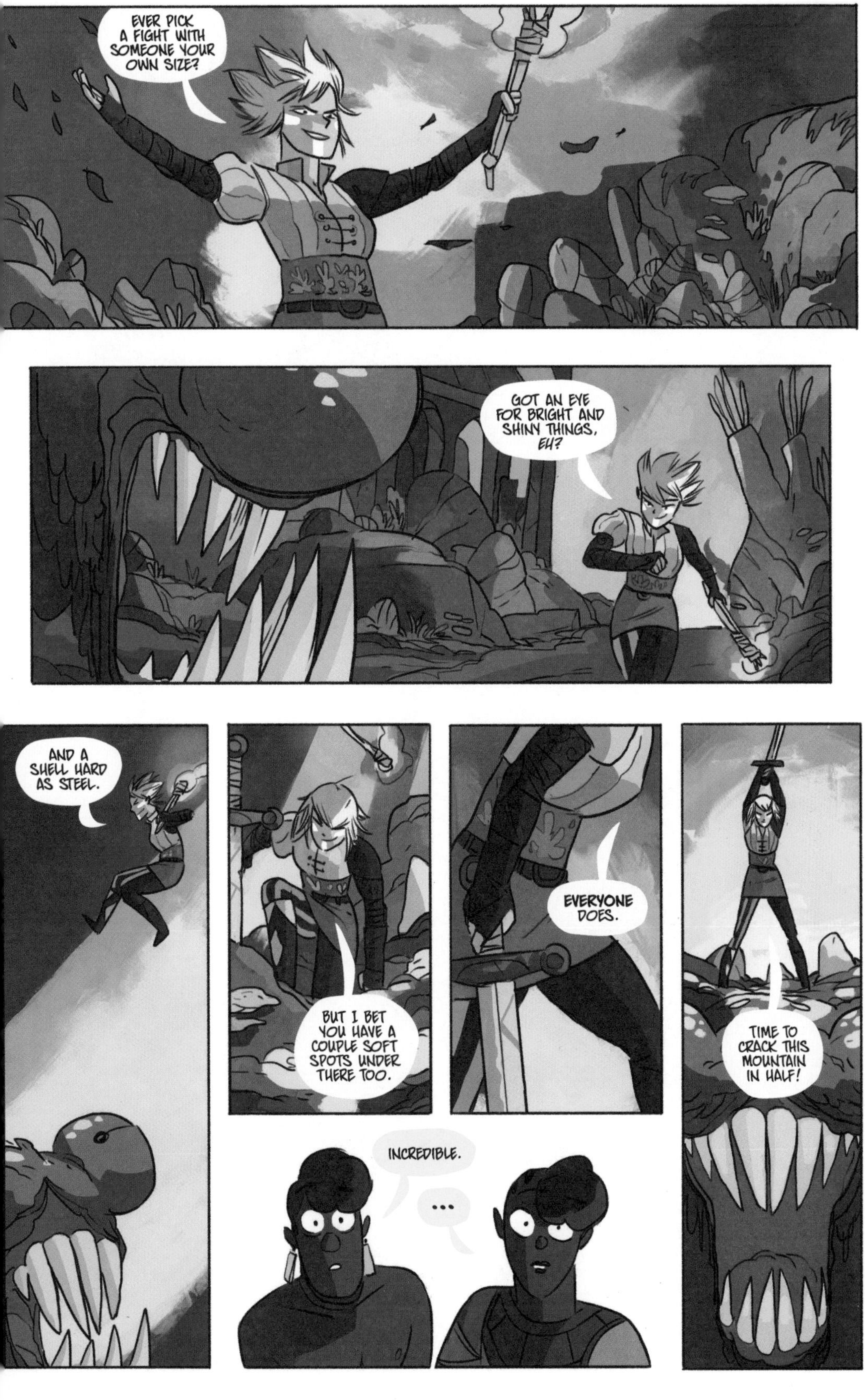
EVER PICK A FIGHT WITH SOMEONE YOUR OWN SIZE?
GOT AN EYE FOR BRIGHT AND SHINY THINGS, EH?
AND A SHELL HARD AS STEEL.
BUT I BET YOU HAVE A COUPLE SOFT SPOTS UNDER THERE TOO.
EVERYONE DOES.
TIME TO CRACK THIS MOUNTAIN IN HALF!
INCREDIBLE.
...

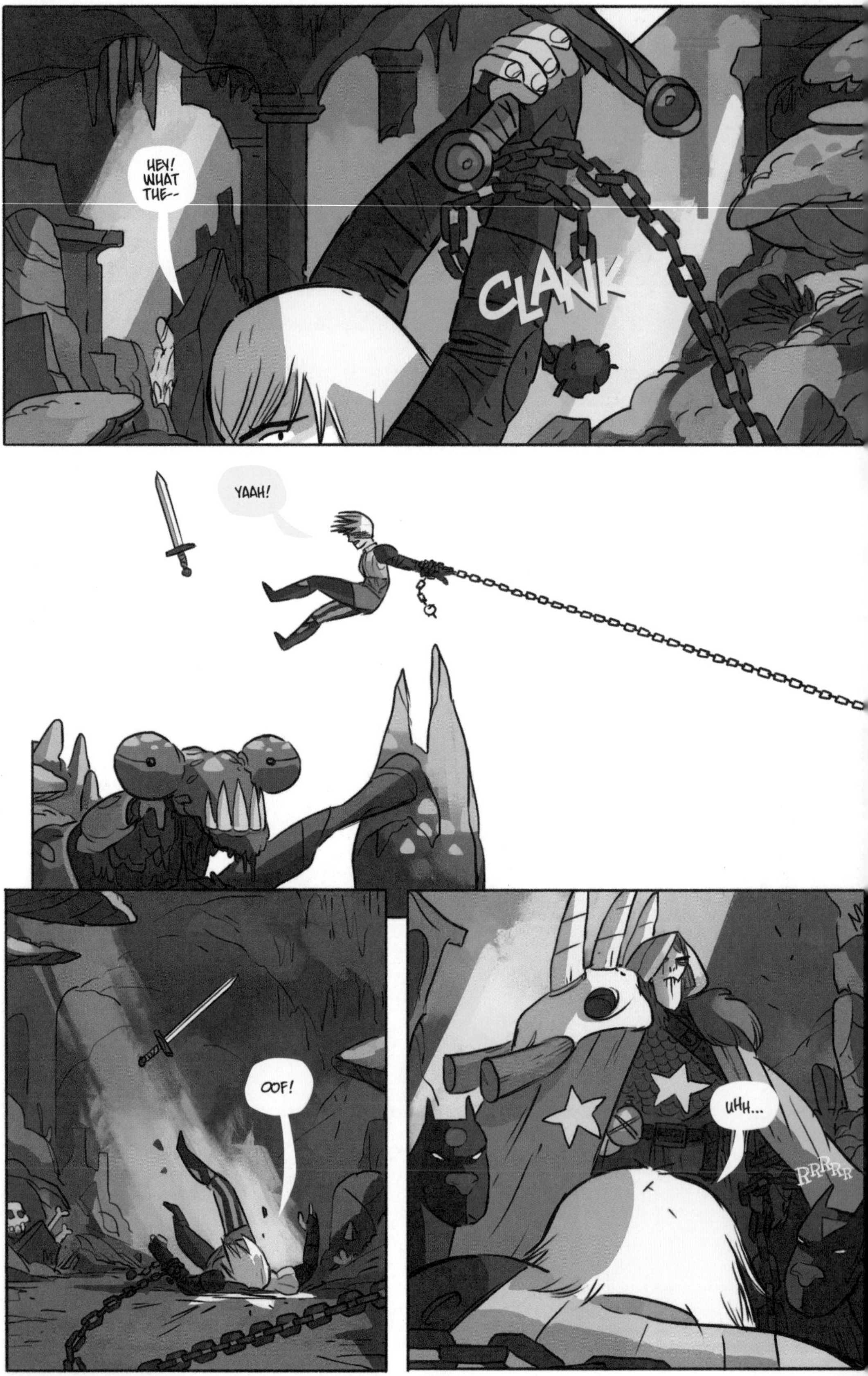
HEY! WHAT THE--
CLANK
YAAH!
OOF!
UHH...
RRRRR

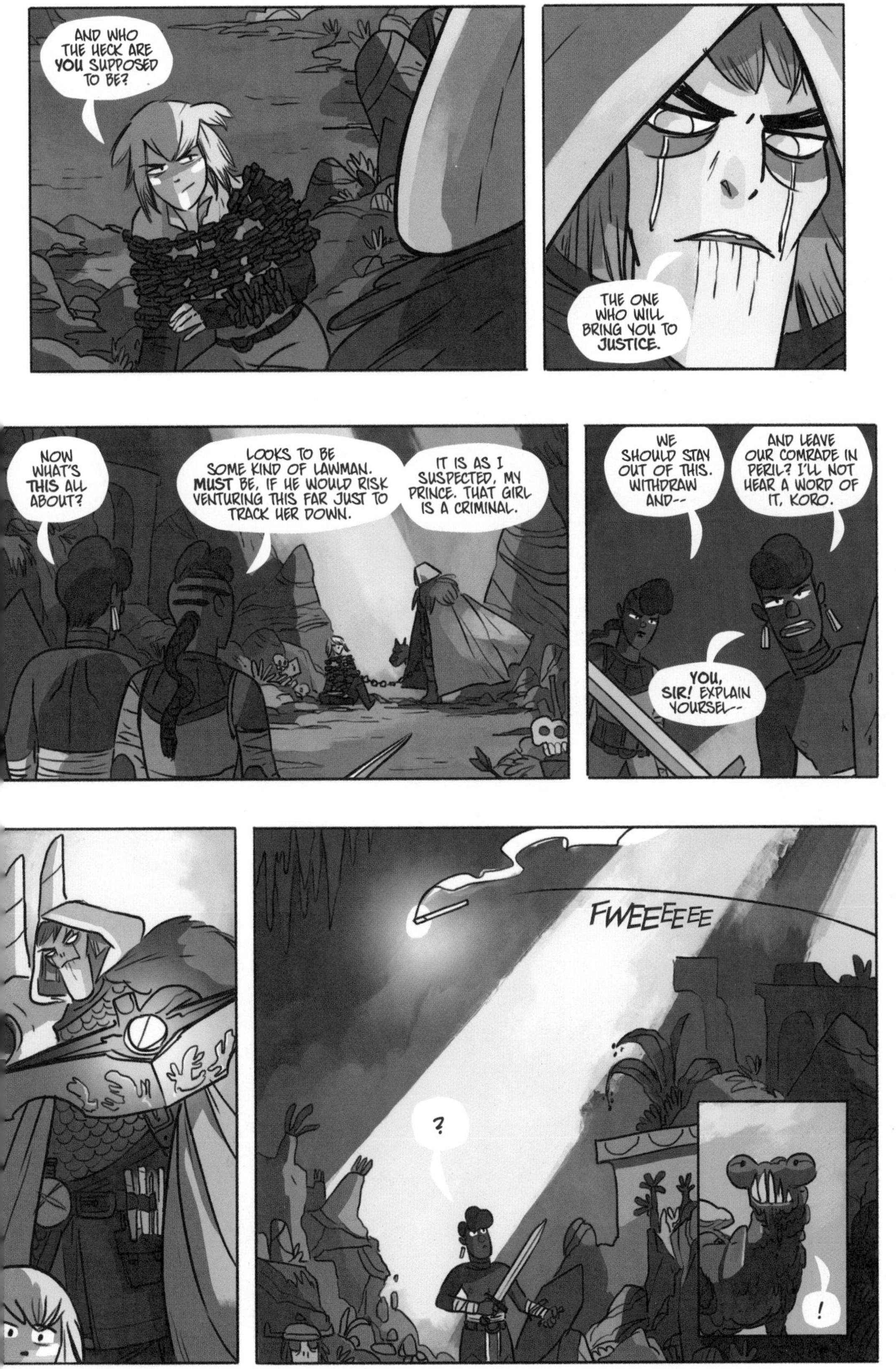
AND WHO THE HECK ARE YOU SUPPOSED TO BE?
THE ONE WHO WILL BRING YOU TO JUSTICE.
NOW WHAT'S THIS ALL ABOUT?
LOOKS TO BE SOME KIND OF LAWMAN. MUST BE, IF HE WOULD RISK VENTURING THIS FAR JUST TO TRACK HER DOWN.
IT IS AS I SUSPECTED, MY PRINCE. THAT GIRL IS A CRIMINAL.
WE SHOULD STAY OUT OF THIS. WITHDRAW AND--
AND LEAVE OUR COMRADE IN PERIL? I'LL NOT HEAR A WORD OF IT, KORO.
YOU, SIR! EXPLAIN YOURSEL--
FWEEEEEE
?
!

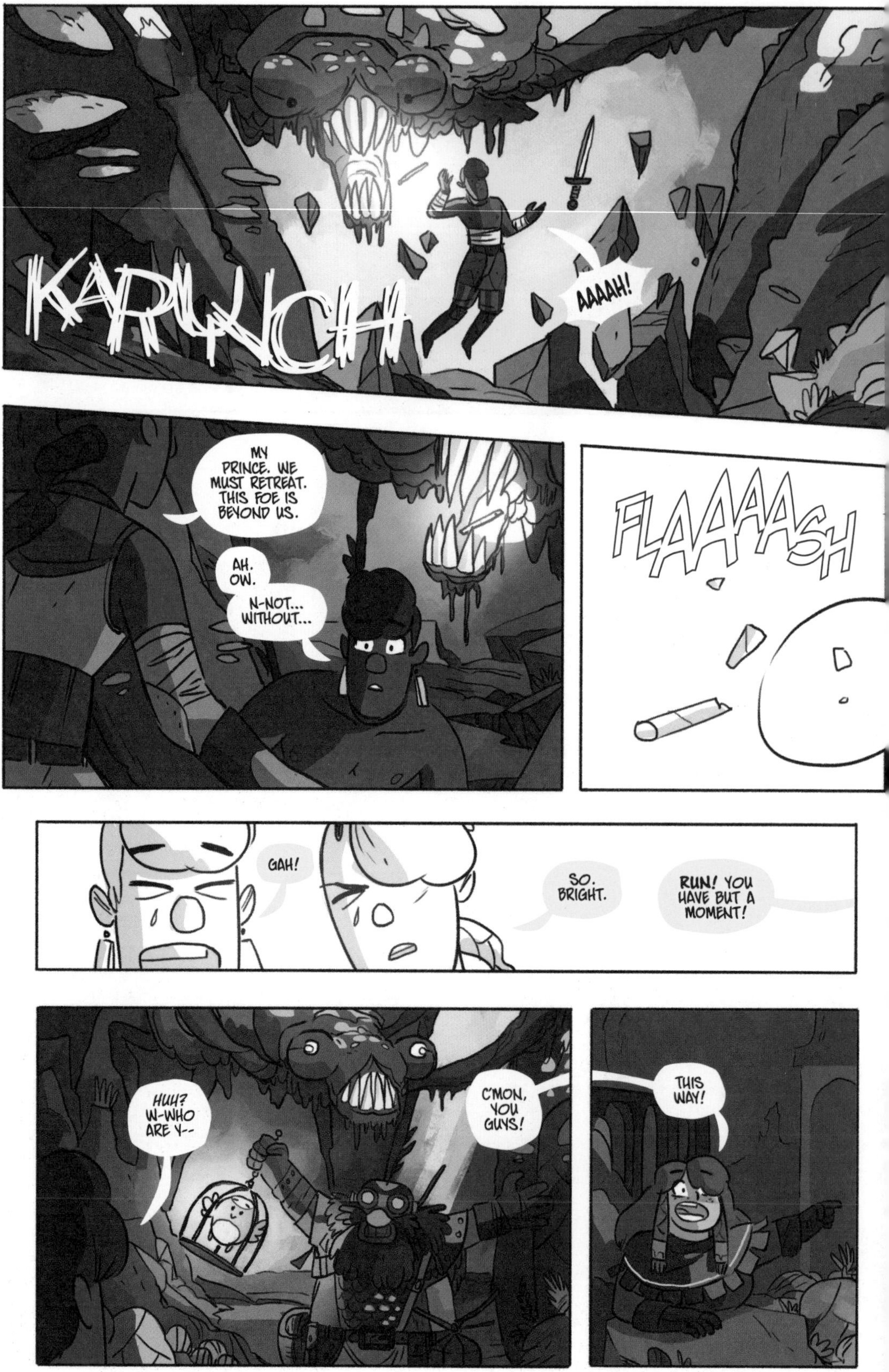
KARUNCH
AAAAH!
MY PRINCE. WE MUST RETREAT. THIS FOE IS BEYOND US.
AH. OW.
N-NOT... WITHOUT...
FLAAAAASH
GAH!
SO. BRIGHT.
RUN! YOU HAVE BUT A MOMENT!
HUH? W-WHO ARE Y--
C'MON, YOU GUYS!
THIS WAY!

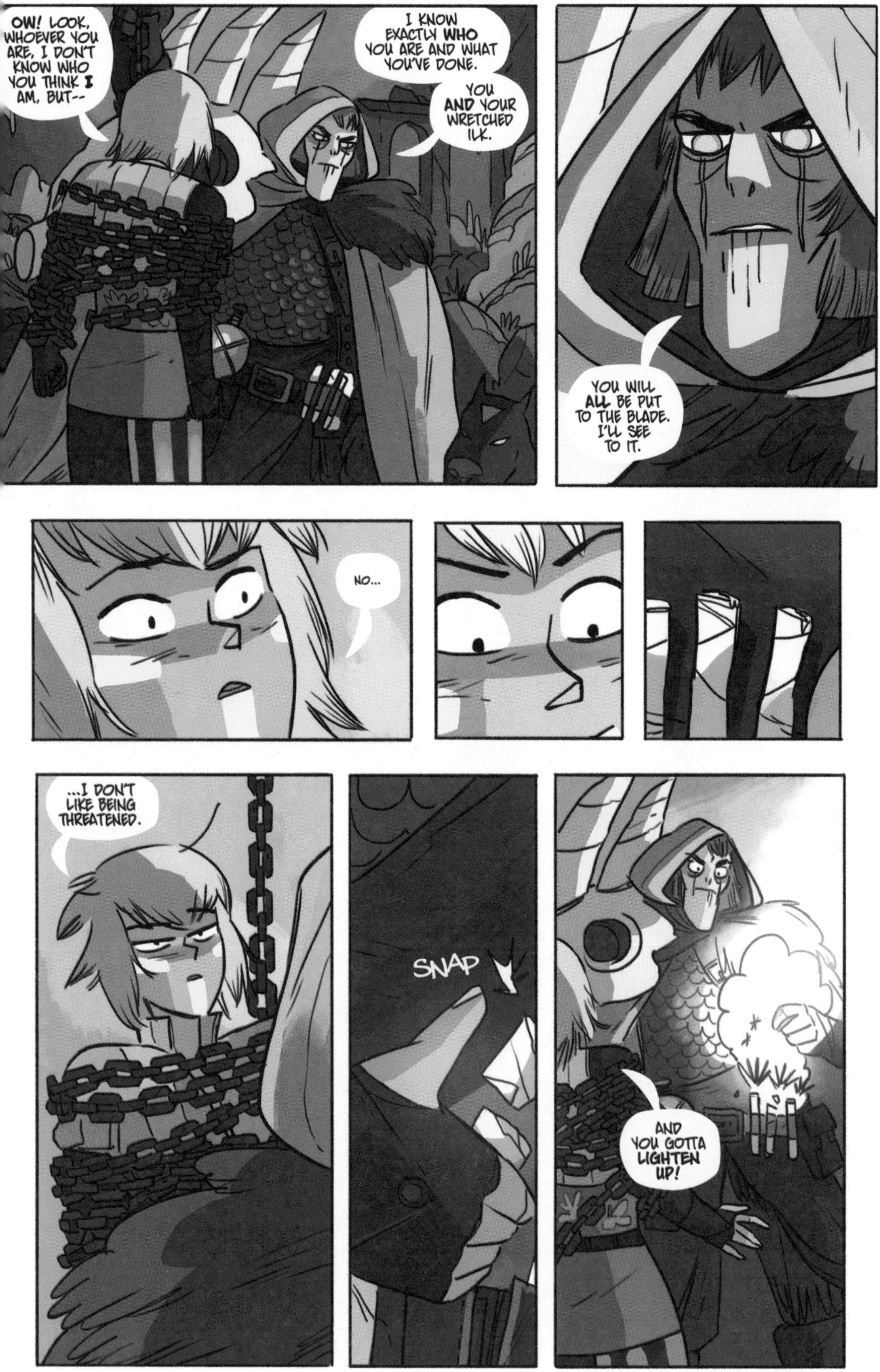
OW! LOOK, WHOEVER YOU ARE, I DON'T KNOW WHO YOU THINK I AM, BUT--
I KNOW EXACTLY WHO YOU ARE AND WHAT YOU'VE DONE.
YOU AND YOUR WRETCHED ILK.
YOU WILL ALL BE PUT TO THE BLADE. I'LL SEE TO IT.
NO...
...I DON'T LIKE BEING THREATENED.
SNAP
AND YOU GOTTA LIGHTEN UP!

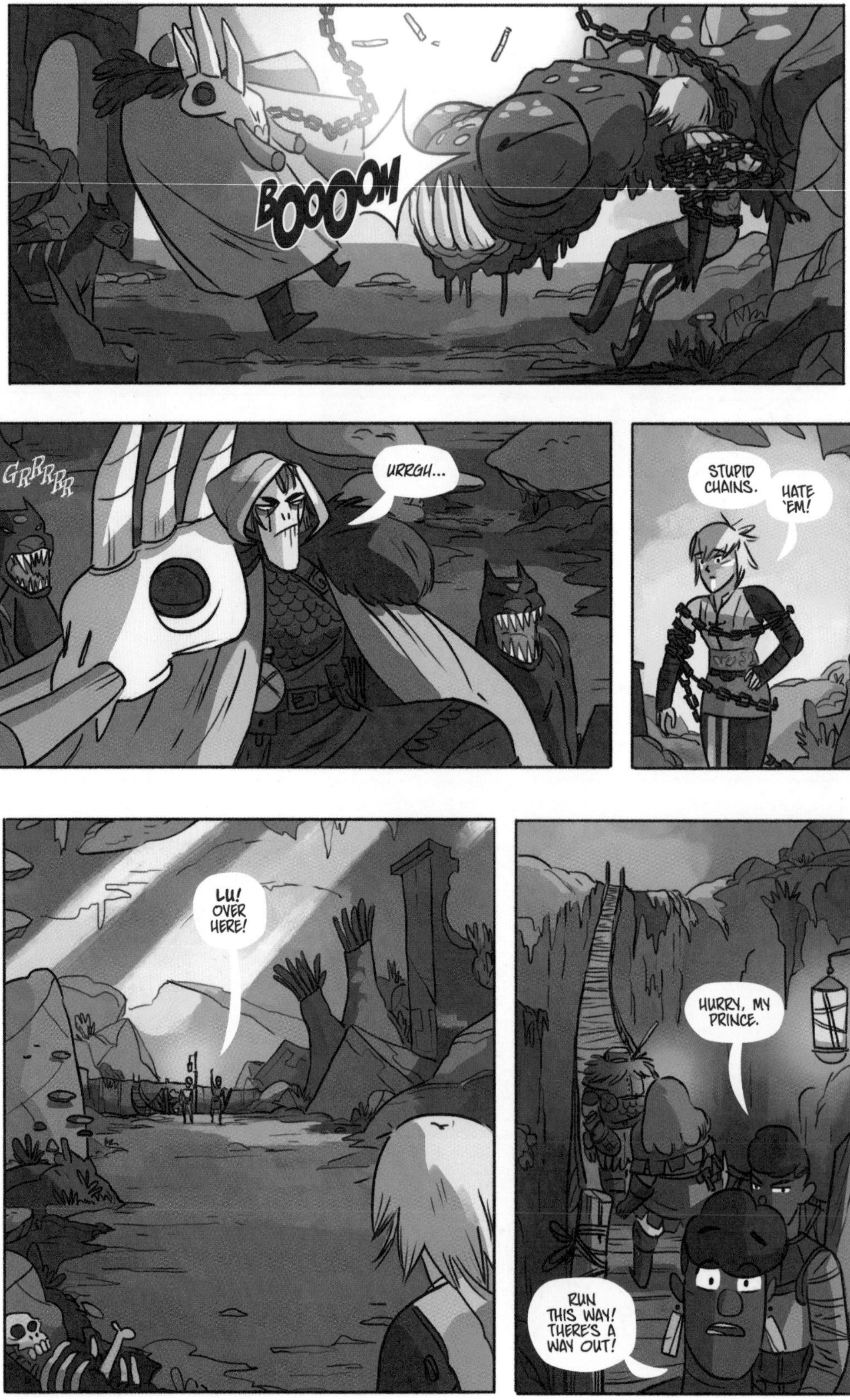
BOOOOM
GRRRRRR
URRGH...
STUPID CHAINS.
HATE 'EM!
LU! OVER HERE!
HURRY, MY PRINCE.
RUN THIS WAY! THERE'S A WAY OUT!

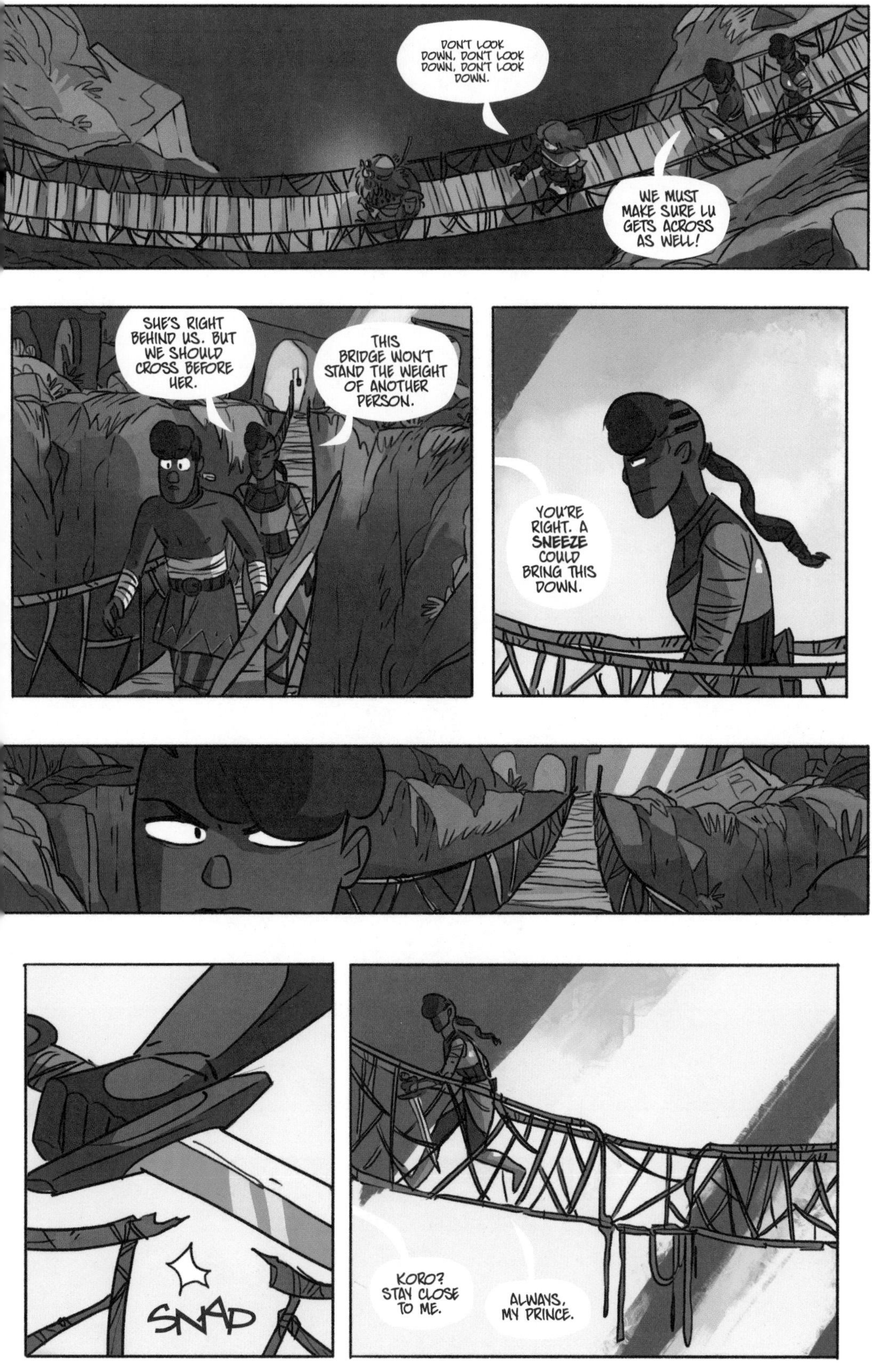
DON'T LOOK DOWN, DON'T LOOK DOWN, DON'T LOOK DOWN.
WE MUST MAKE SURE LU GETS ACROSS AS WELL!
SHE'S RIGHT BEHIND US. BUT WE SHOULD CROSS BEFORE HER.
THIS BRIDGE WON'T STAND THE WEIGHT OF ANOTHER PERSON.
YOU'RE RIGHT. A SNEEZE COULD BRING THIS DOWN.
SNAP
KORO? STAY CLOSE TO ME.
ALWAYS, MY PRINCE.

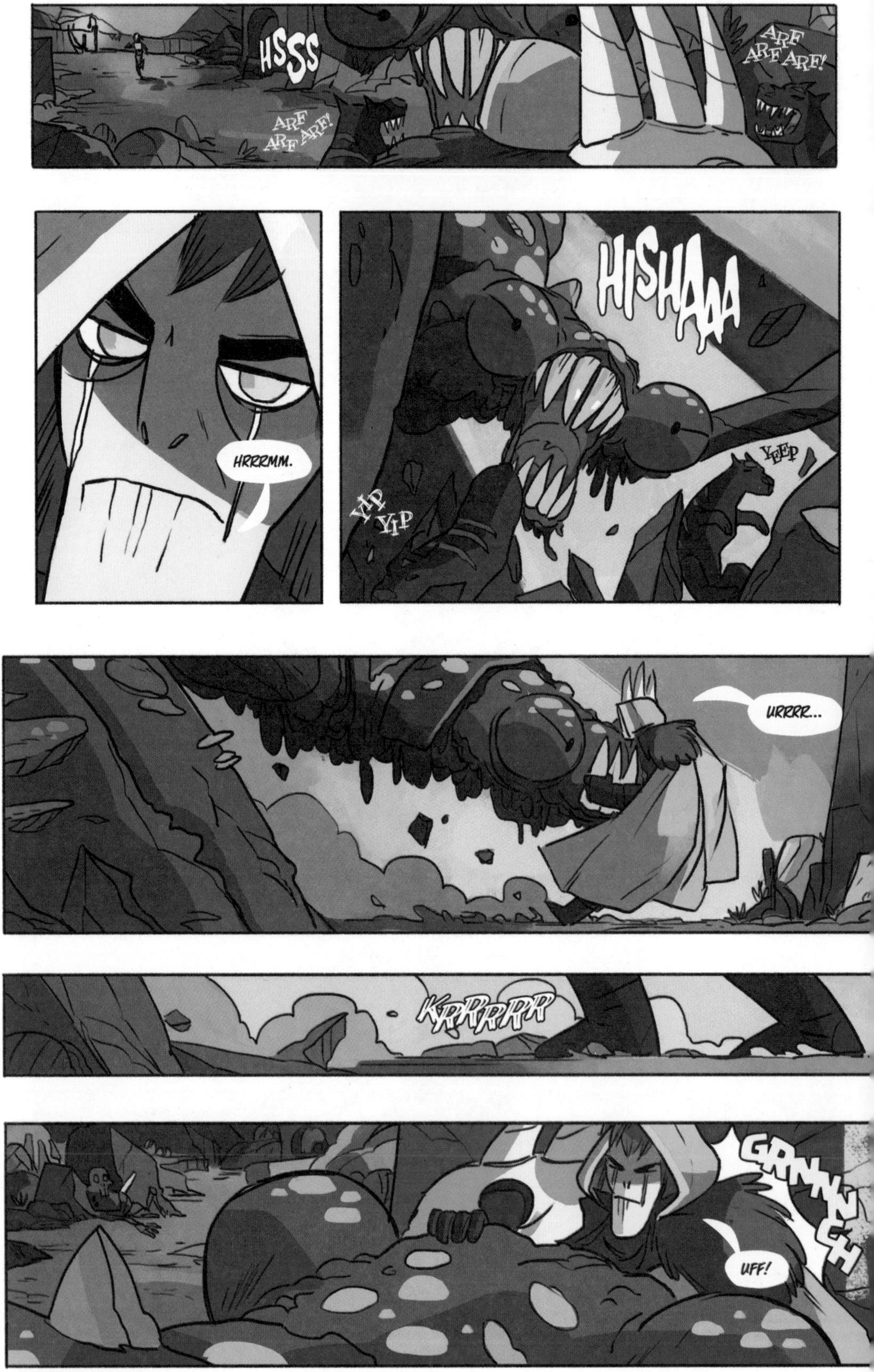
HSSS
ARF ARF ARF!
ARF ARF ARF!
HRRRMM.
HISHAAA
YIP YIP
YEEP
URRRR...
KRRRRRR
GRNNNGH
UFF!

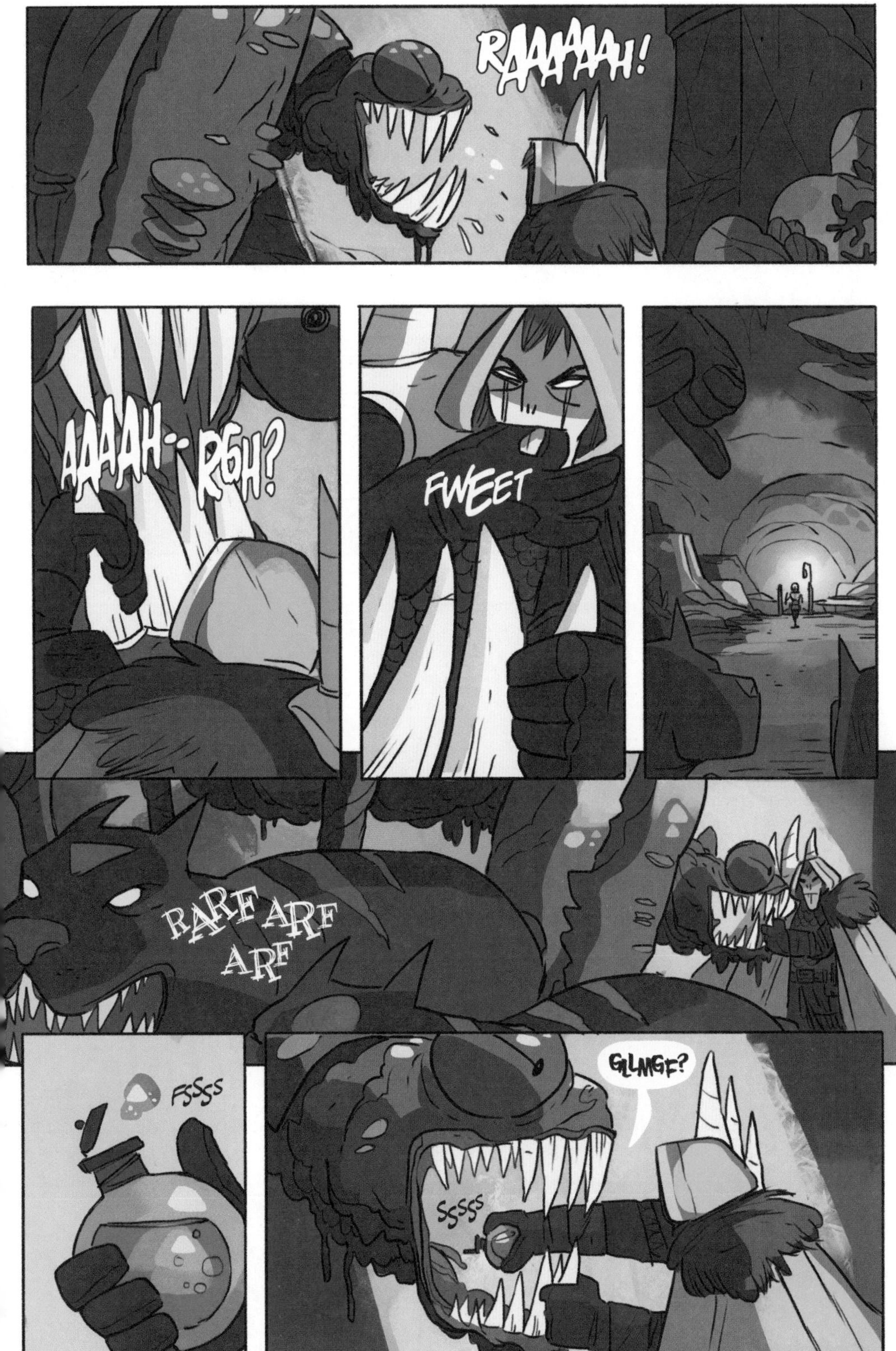
RAAAAAAH!
AAAAH-- RGH?
FWEET
RARF ARF ARF
ARF
FSSSS
GLLMGF?
SSSSS

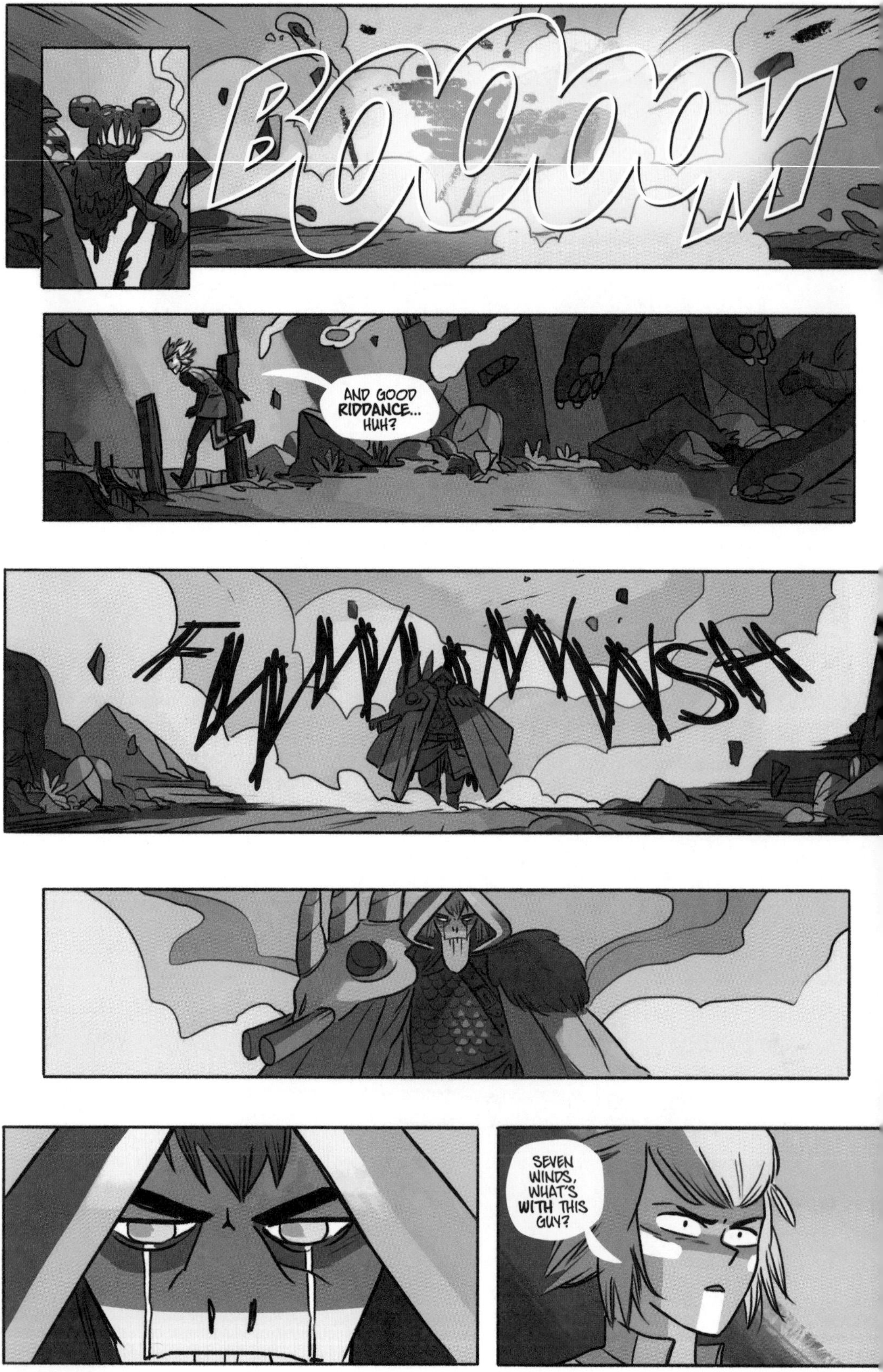
BOOOOOM
AND GOOD RIDDANCE... HUH?
FWWWWWWSH
SEVEN WINDS, WHAT'S WITH THIS GUY?

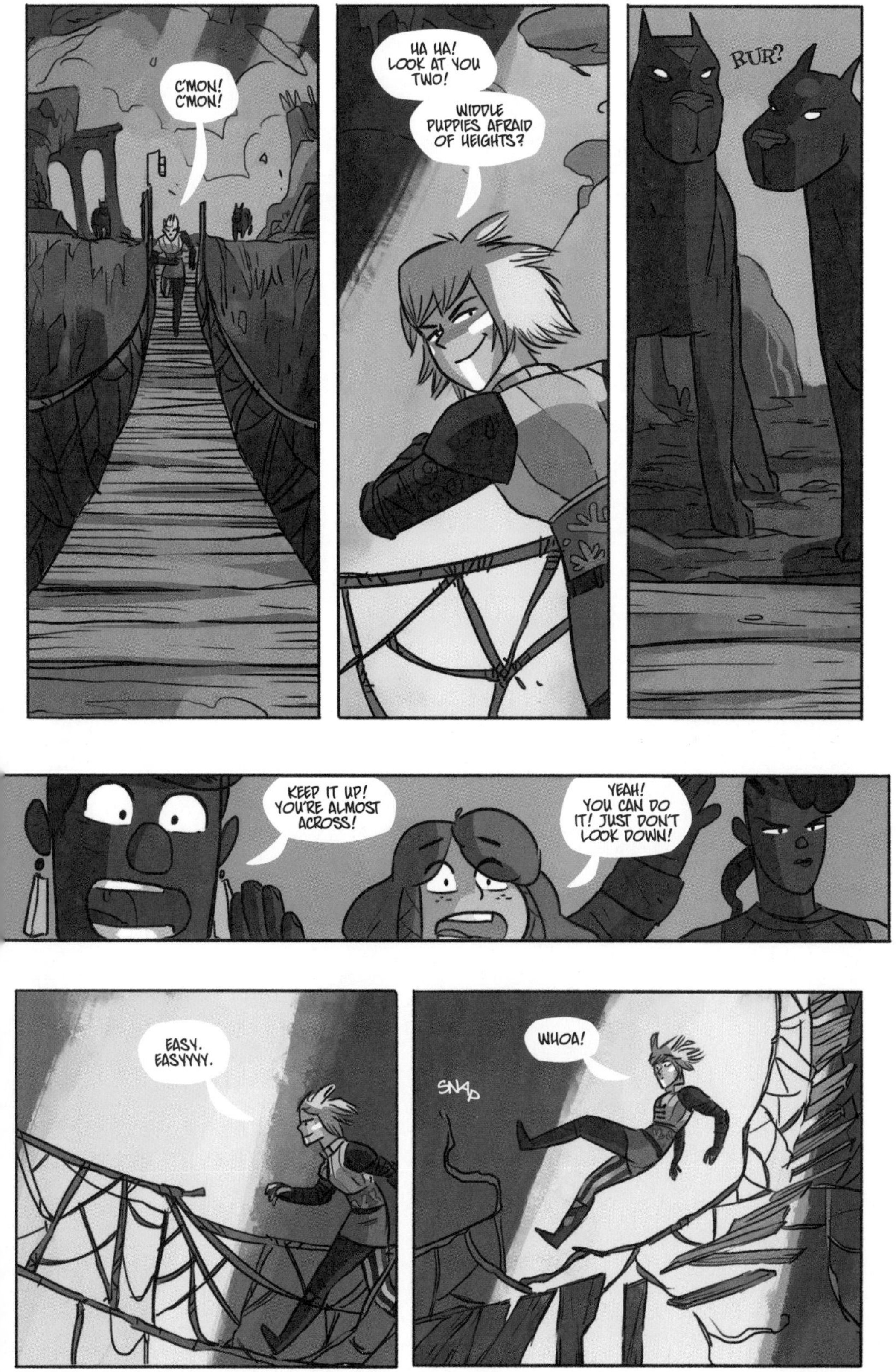
C'MON! C'MON!
HA HA! LOOK AT YOU TWO!
WIDDLE PUPPIES AFRAID OF HEIGHTS?
RUR?
KEEP IT UP! YOU'RE ALMOST ACROSS!
YEAH! YOU CAN DO IT! JUST DON'T LOOK DOWN!
EASY. EASYYYY.
SNAP
WHOA!

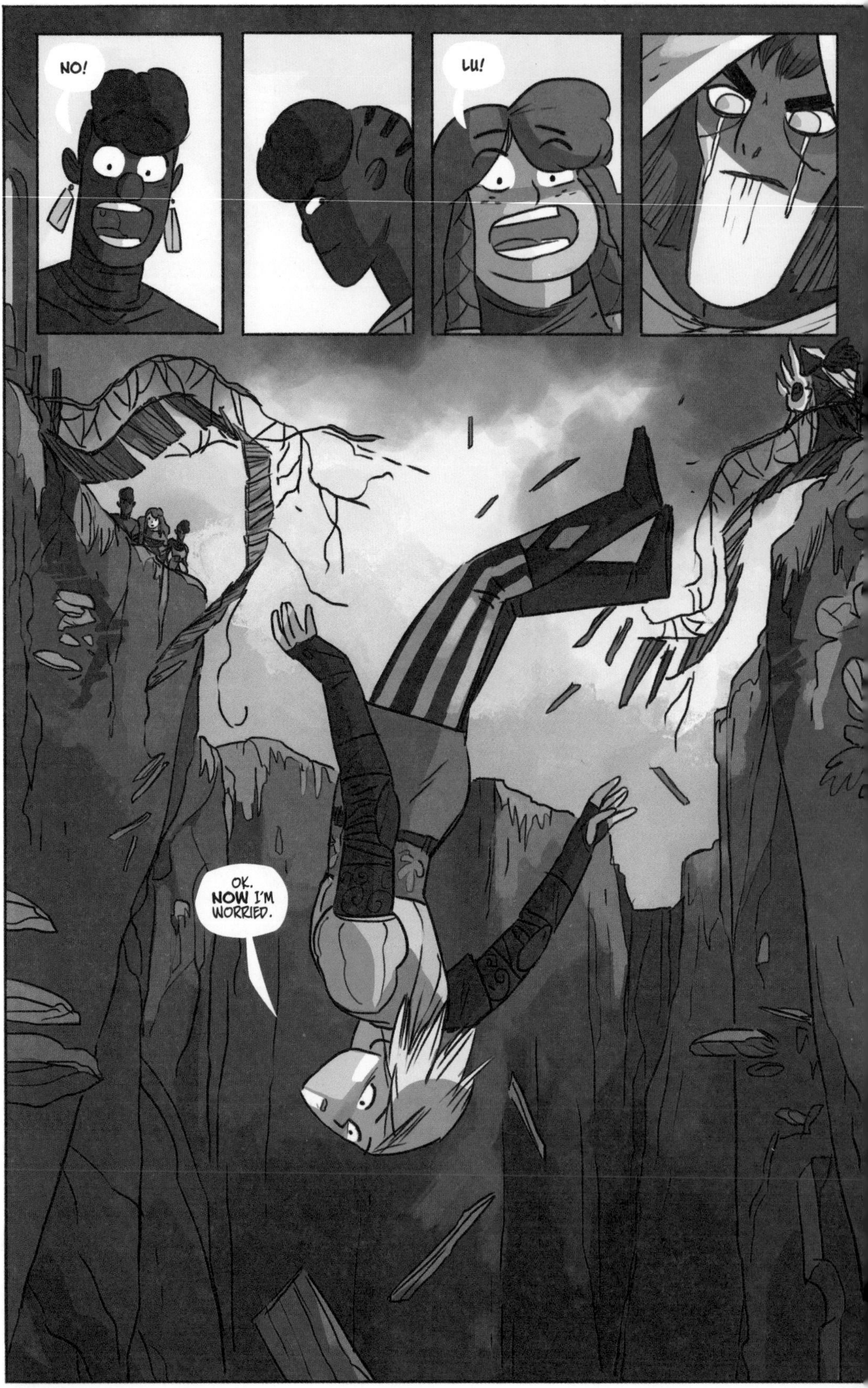
NO!
LU!
OK. NOW I'M WORRIED.

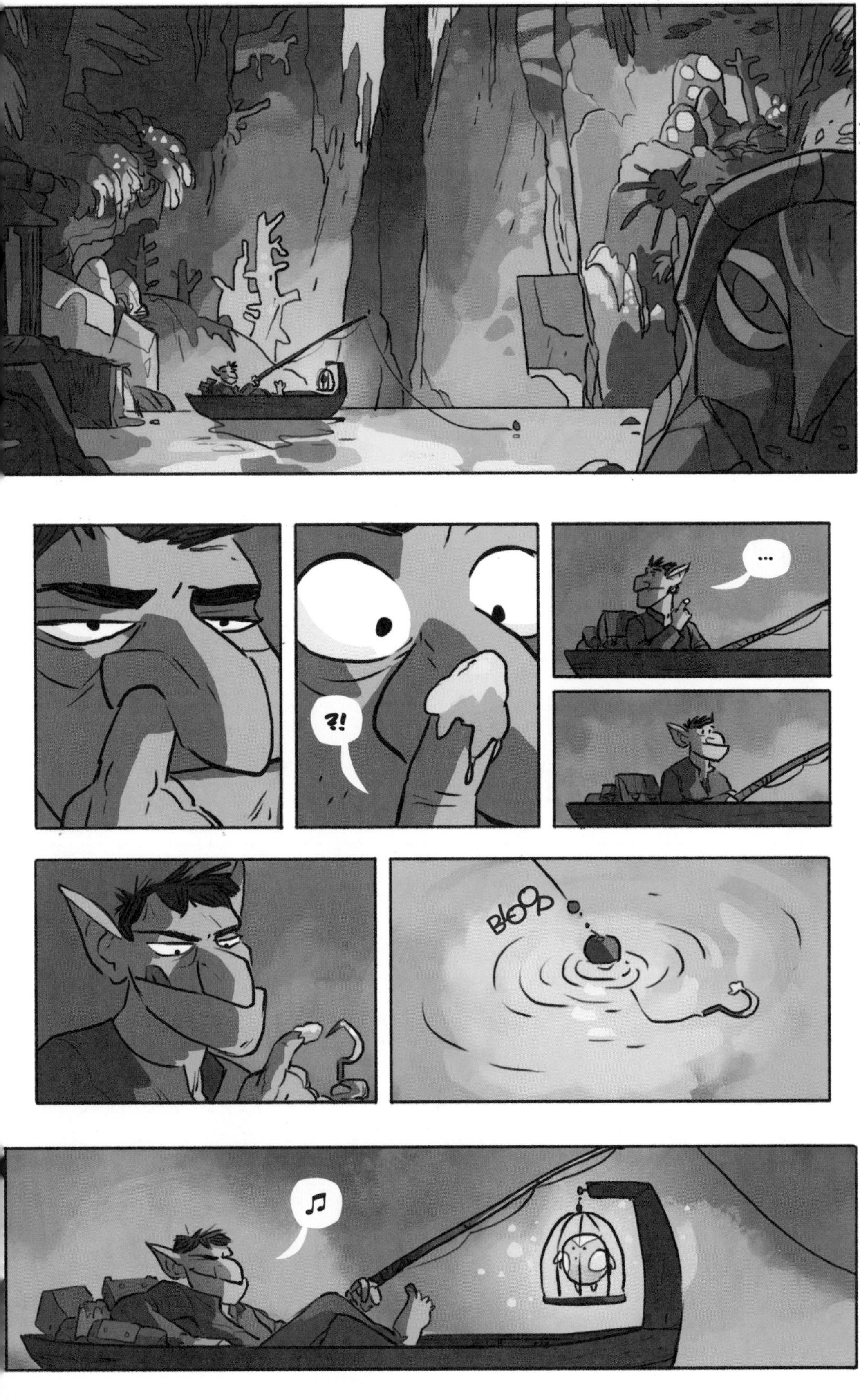
?!
...
BLOOP
♫

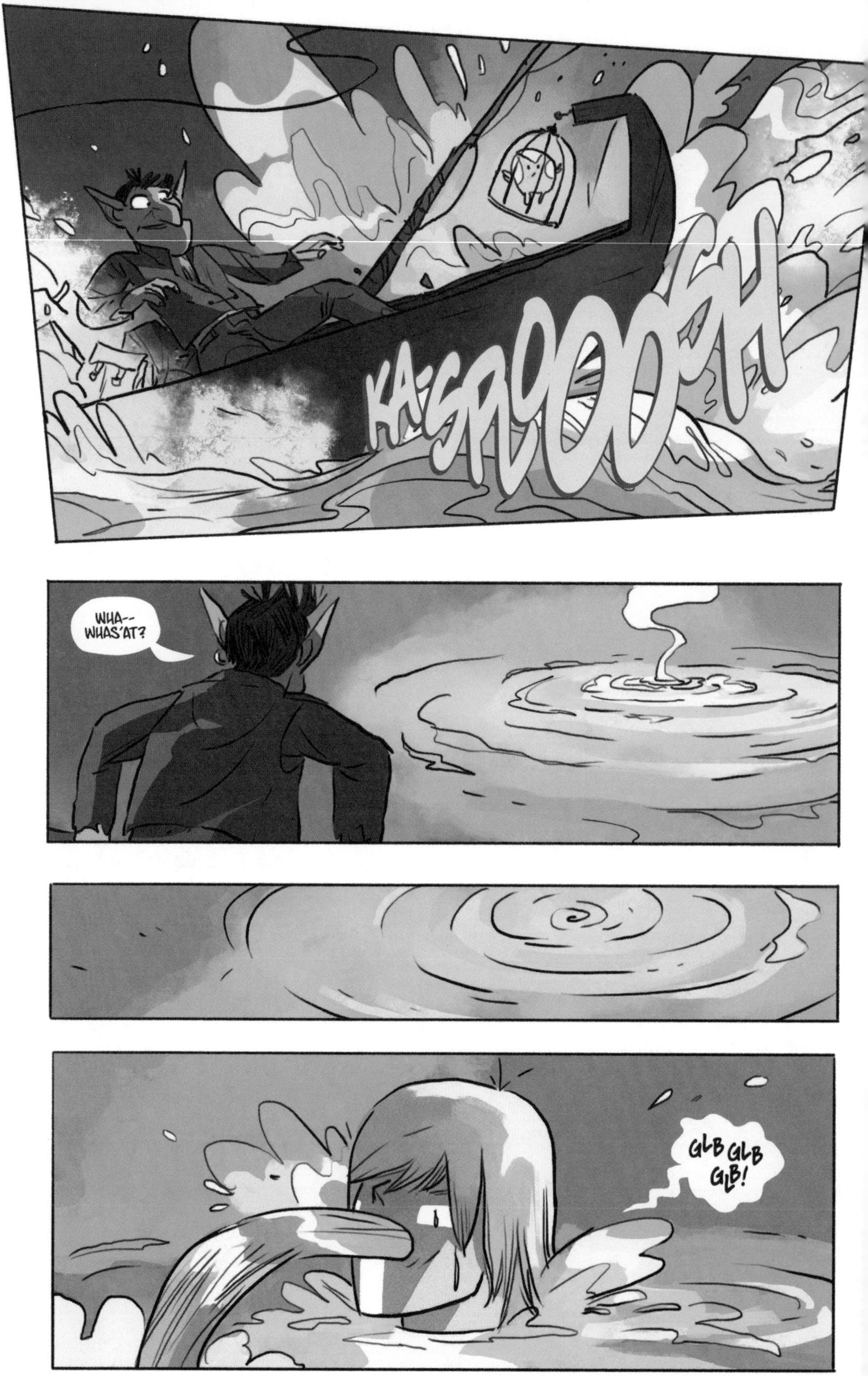
KA-SPLOOOSH
WHA-- WHAS'AT?
GLB GLB GLB!

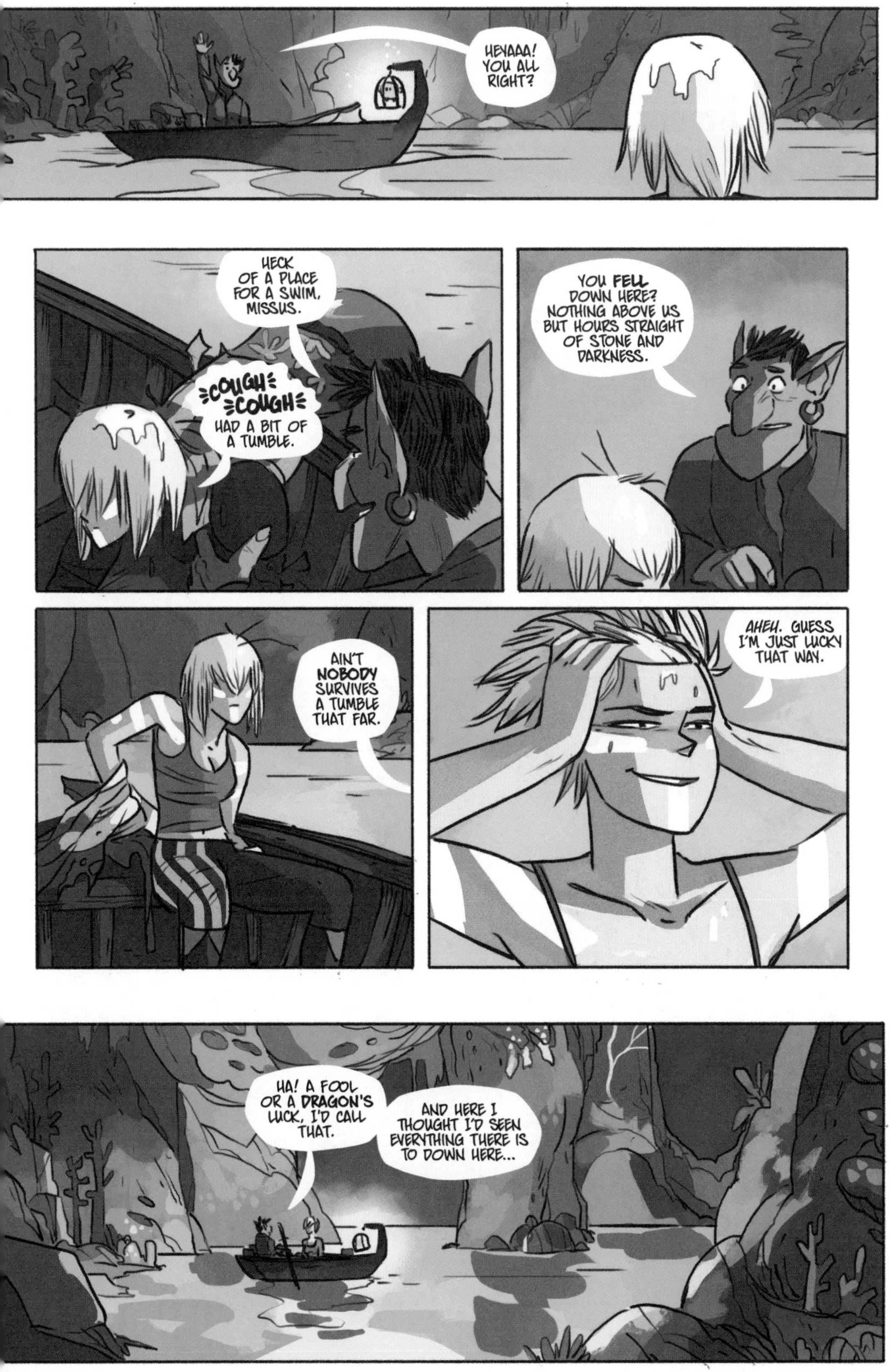
HEYAAA! YOU ALL RIGHT?
HECK OF A PLACE FOR A SWIM, MISSUS.
COUGH COUGH
HAD A BIT OF A TUMBLE.
YOU FELL DOWN HERE? NOTHING ABOVE US BUT HOURS STRAIGHT OF STONE AND DARKNESS.
AIN'T NOBODY SURVIVES A TUMBLE THAT FAR.
AHEH. GUESS I'M JUST LUCKY THAT WAY.
HA! A FOOL OR A DRAGON'S LUCK, I'D CALL THAT.
AND HERE I THOUGHT I'D SEEN EVERYTHING THERE IS TO DOWN HERE...

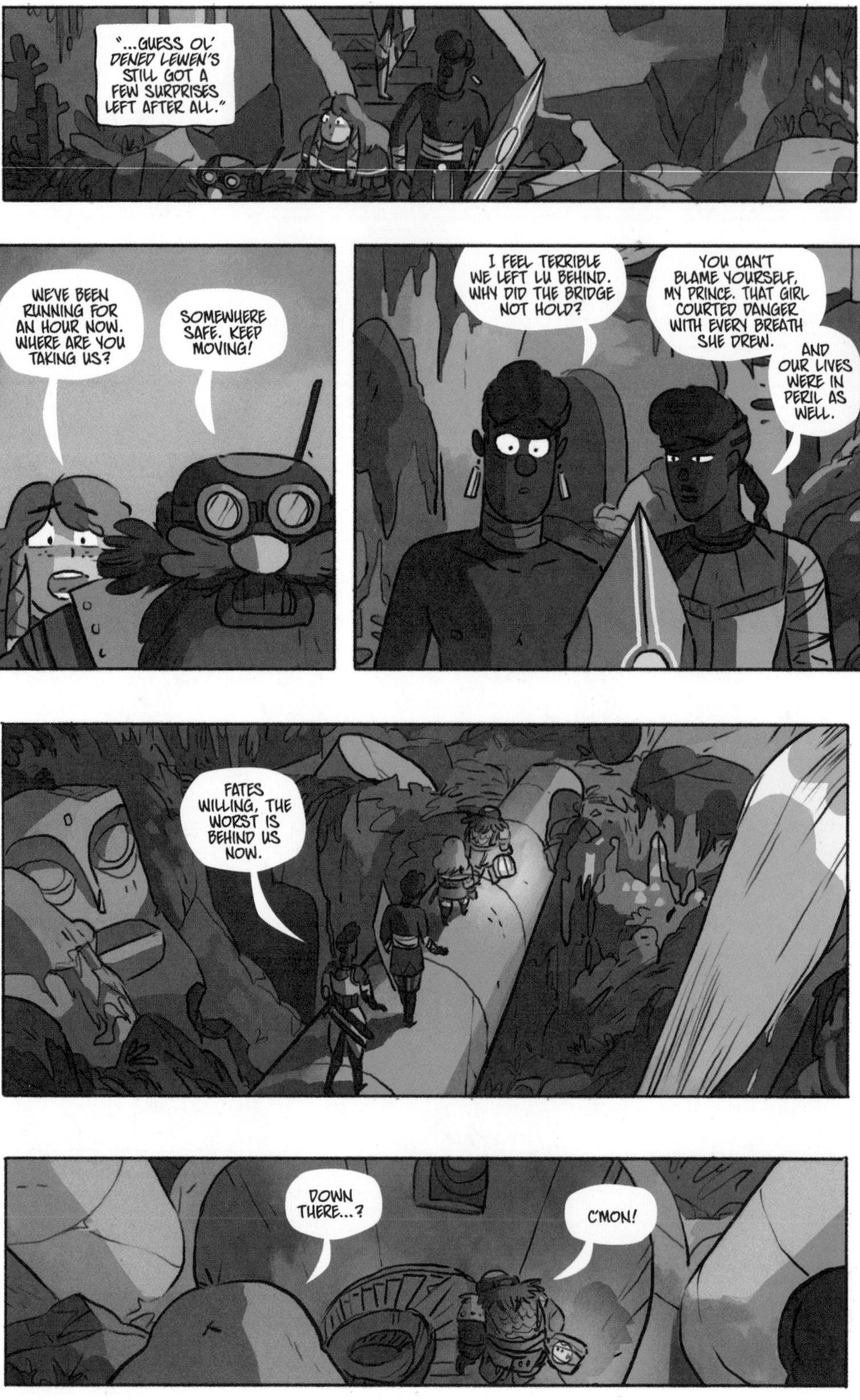
"...GUESS OL' DENED LEWEN'S STILL GOT A FEW SURPRISES LEFT AFTER ALL."
WE'VE BEEN RUNNING FOR AN HOUR NOW. WHERE ARE YOU TAKING US?
SOMEWHERE SAFE. KEEP MOVING!
I FEEL TERRIBLE WE LEFT LU BEHIND. WHY DID THE BRIDGE NOT HOLD?
YOU CAN'T BLAME YOURSELF, MY PRINCE. THAT GIRL COURTED DANGER WITH EVERY BREATH SHE DREW.
AND OUR LIVES WERE IN PERIL AS WELL.
FATES WILLING, THE WORST IS BEHIND US NOW.
DOWN THERE...?
C'MON!

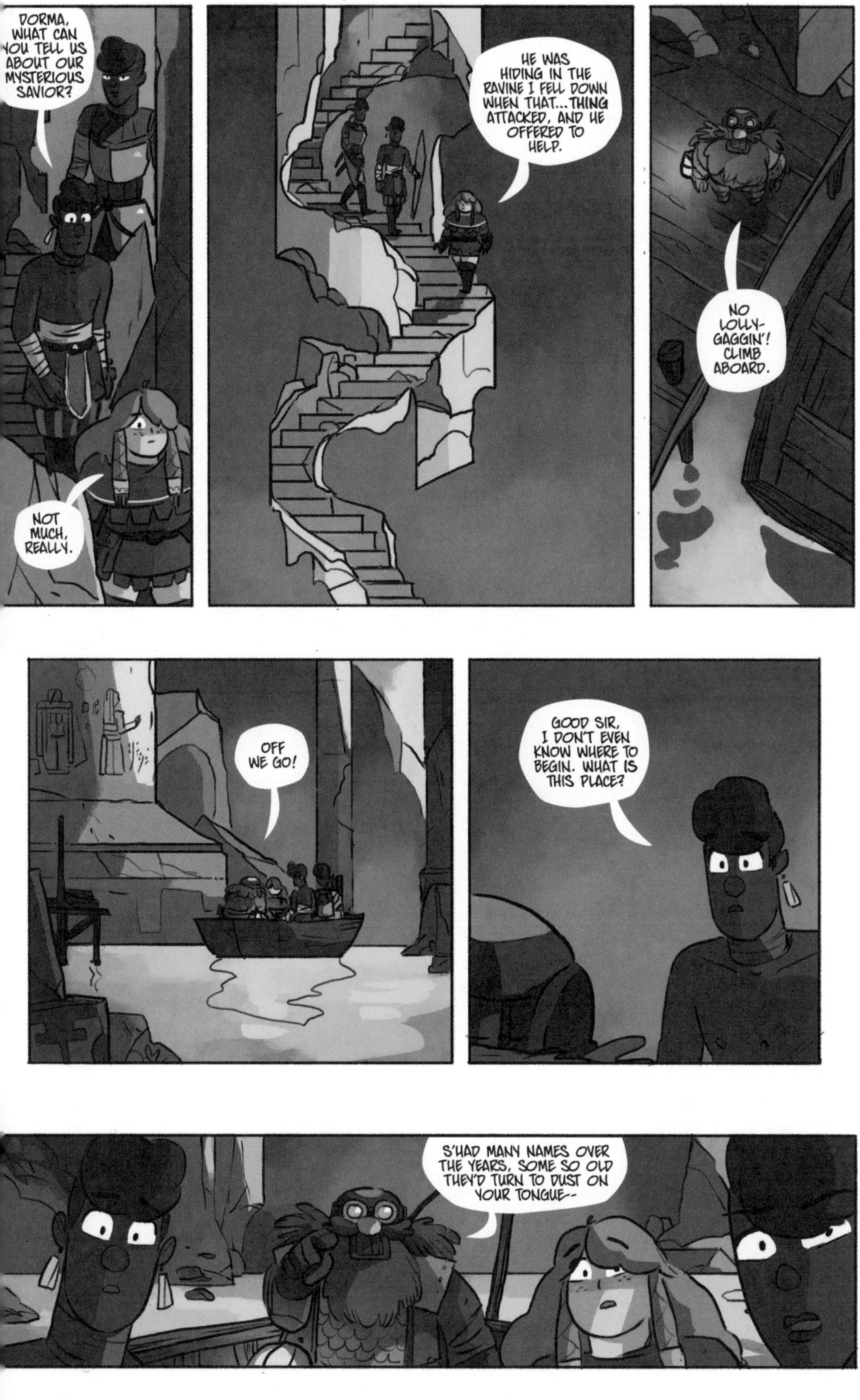
DORMA, WHAT CAN YOU TELL US ABOUT OUR MYSTERIOUS SAVIOR?
NOT MUCH, REALLY.
HE WAS HIDING IN THE RAVINE I FELL DOWN WHEN THAT...THING ATTACKED, AND HE OFFERED TO HELP.
NO LOLLY-GAGGIN'! CLIMB ABOARD.
OFF WE GO!
GOOD SIR, I DON'T EVEN KNOW WHERE TO BEGIN. WHAT IS THIS PLACE?
S'HAD MANY NAMES OVER THE YEARS, SOME SO OLD THEY'D TURN TO DUST ON YOUR TONGUE--

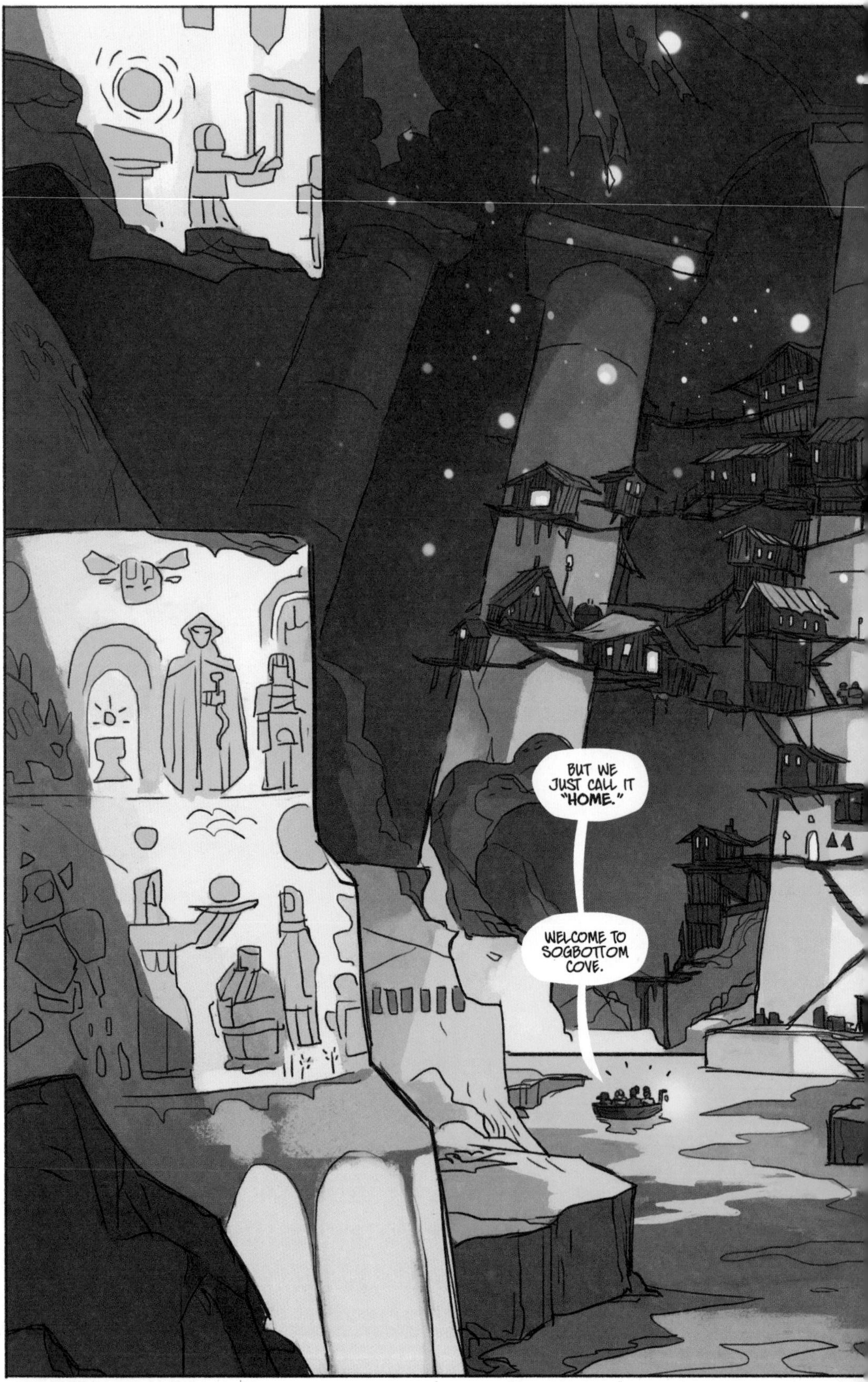
BUT WE JUST CALL IT "HOME."
WELCOME TO SOGBOTTOM COVE.

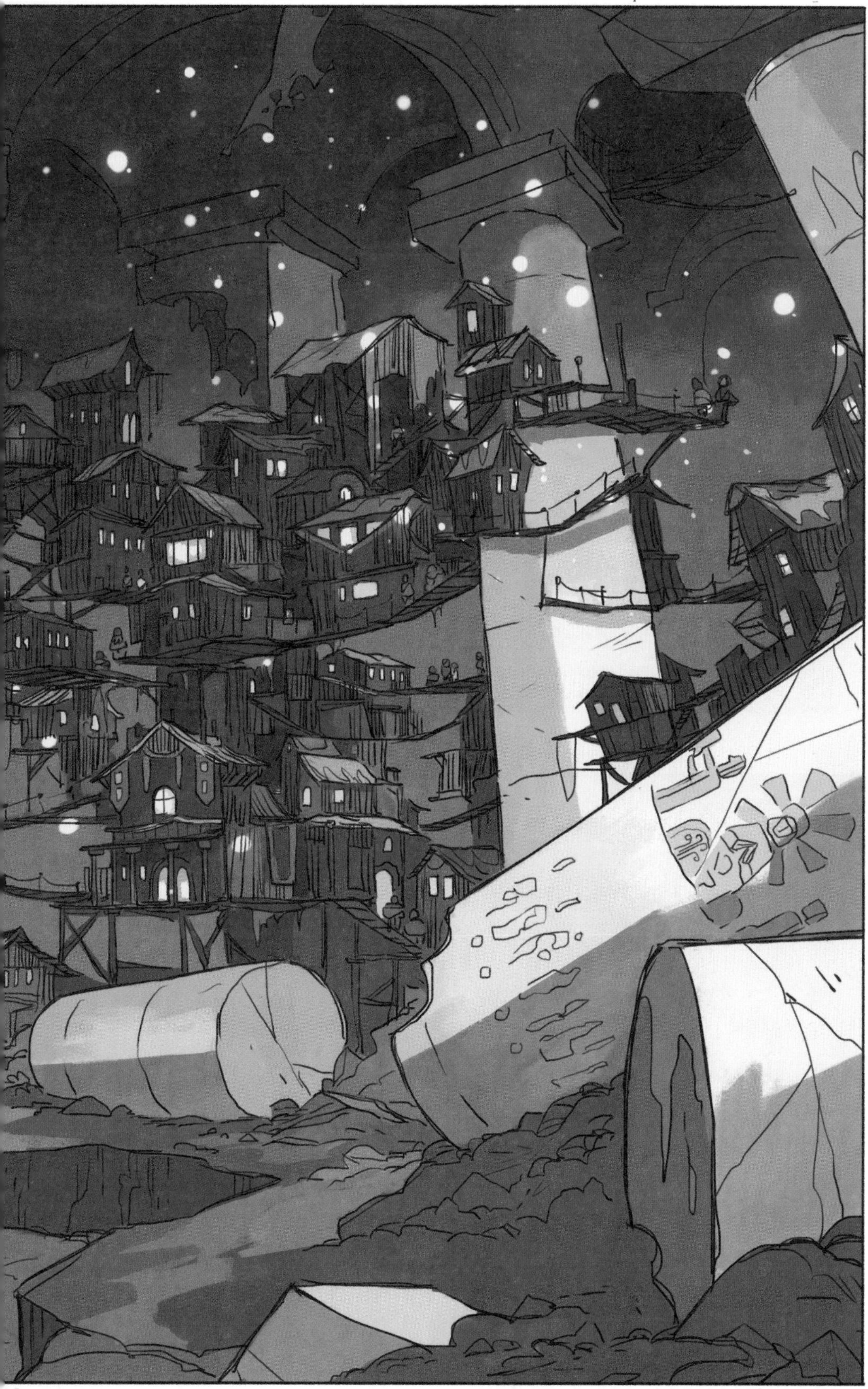

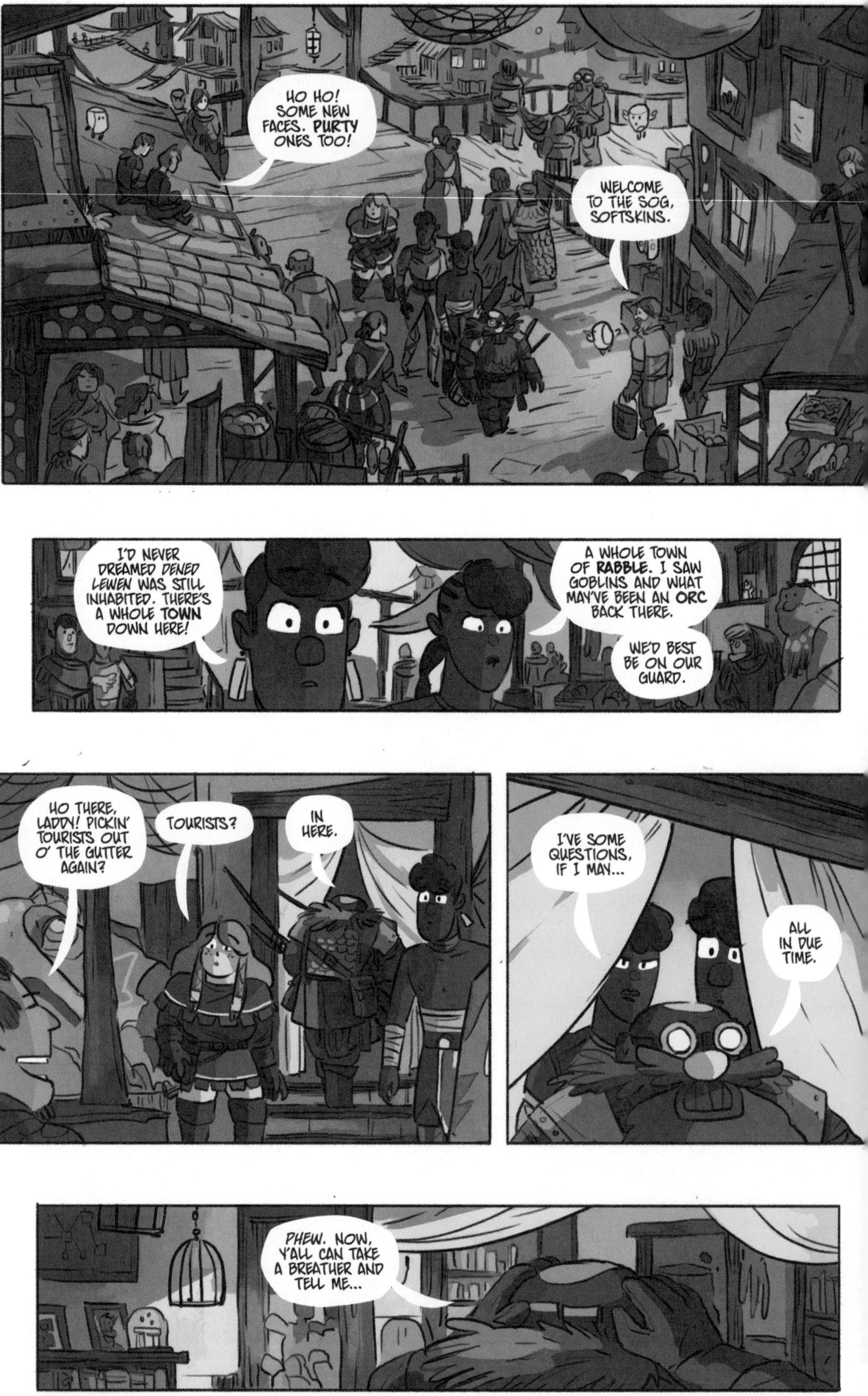
HO HO! SOME NEW FACES. PURTY ONES TOO!
WELCOME TO THE SOG, SOFTSKINS.
I'D NEVER DREAMED DENED LEWEN WAS STILL INHABITED. THERE'S A WHOLE TOWN DOWN HERE!
A WHOLE TOWN OF RABBLE. I SAW GOBLINS AND WHAT MAY'VE BEEN AN ORC BACK THERE.
WE'D BEST BE ON OUR GUARD.
HO THERE, LADDY! PICKIN' TOURISTS OUT O' THE GUTTER AGAIN?
TOURISTS?
IN HERE.
I'VE SOME QUESTIONS, IF I MAY...
ALL IN DUE TIME.
PHEW. NOW, Y'ALL CAN TAKE A BREATHER AND TELL ME...

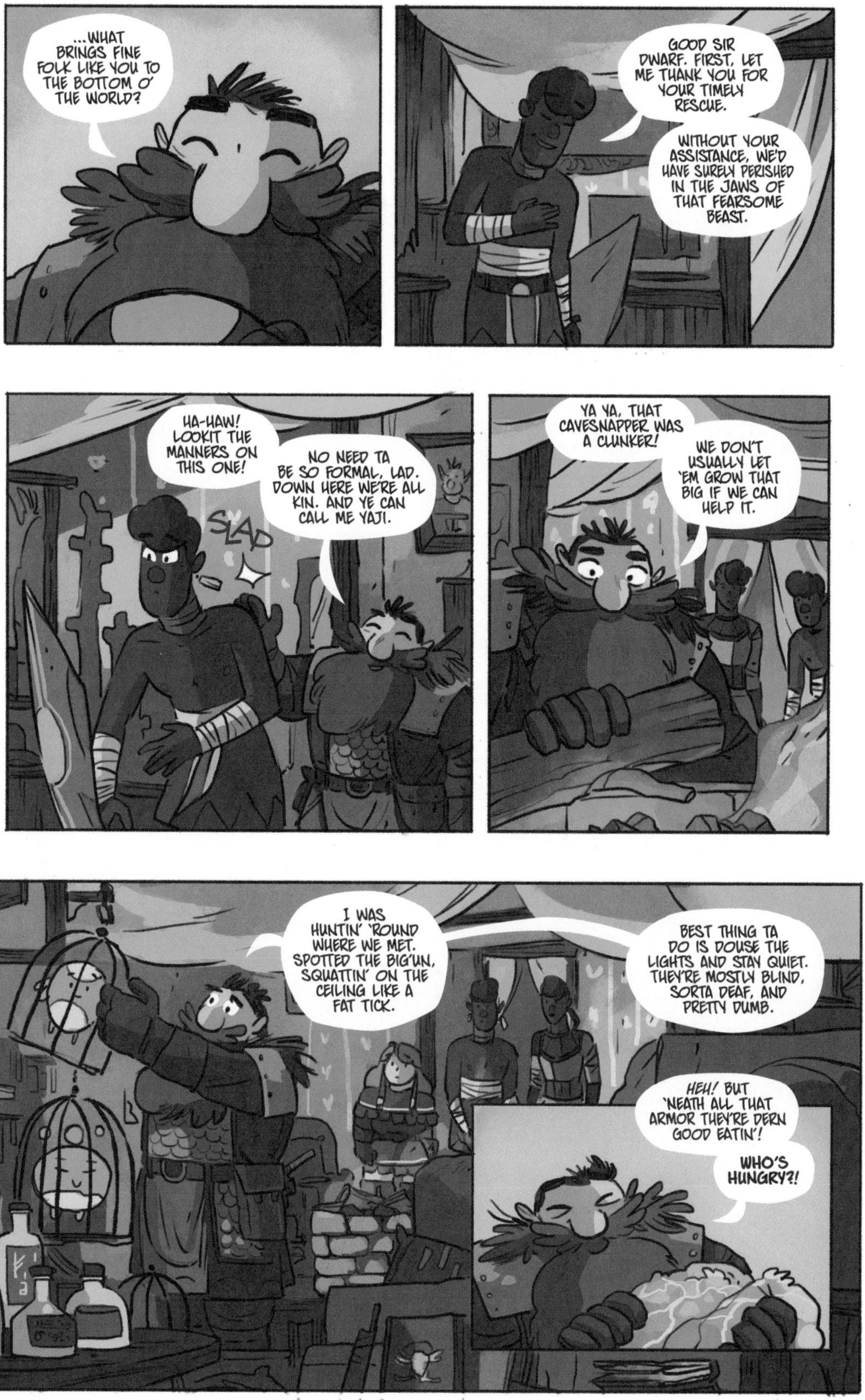
...WHAT BRINGS FINE FOLK LIKE YOU TO THE BOTTOM O' THE WORLD?
GOOD SIR DWARF. FIRST, LET ME THANK YOU FOR YOUR TIMELY RESCUE.
WITHOUT YOUR ASSISTANCE, WE'D HAVE SURELY PERISHED IN THE JAWS OF THAT FEARSOME BEAST.
HA-HAW! LOOKIT THE MANNERS ON THIS ONE!
SLAP
NO NEED TA BE SO FORMAL, LAD. DOWN HERE WE'RE ALL KIN. AND YE CAN CALL ME YAJI.
YA YA, THAT CAVESNAPPER WAS A CLUNKER!
WE DON'T USUALLY LET 'EM GROW THAT BIG IF WE CAN HELP IT.
I WAS HUNTIN' 'ROUND WHERE WE MET. SPOTTED THE BIG'UN, SQUATTIN' ON THE CEILING LIKE A FAT TICK.
BEST THING TA DO IS DOUSE THE LIGHTS AND STAY QUIET. THEY'RE MOSTLY BLIND, SORTA DEAF, AND PRETTY DUMB.
HEH! BUT 'NEATH ALL THAT ARMOR THEY'RE DERN GOOD EATIN'!
WHO'S HUNGRY?!

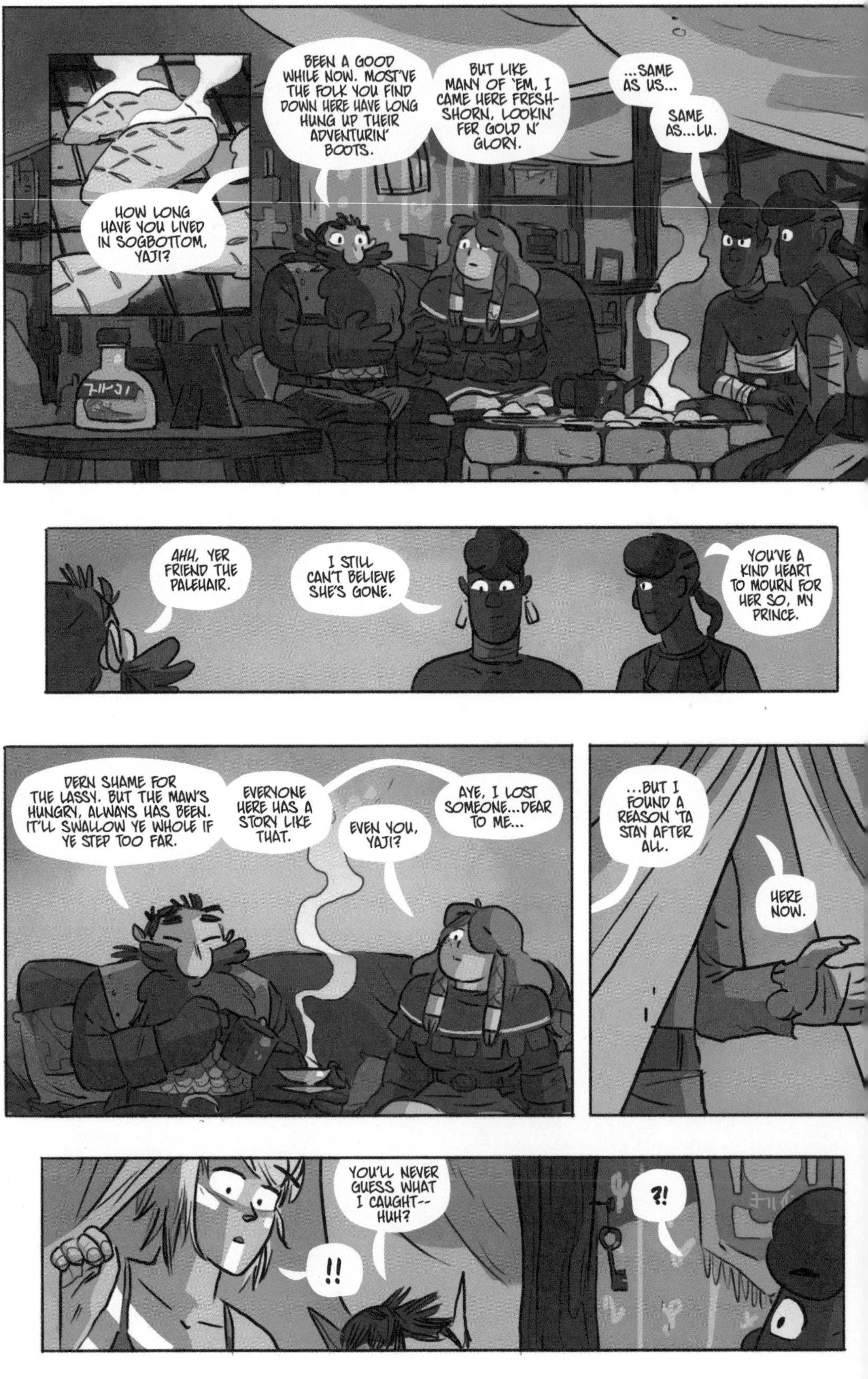
HOW LONG HAVE YOU LIVED IN SOGBOTTOM, YAJI?
BEEN A GOOD WHILE NOW. MOST'VE THE FOLK YOU FIND DOWN HERE HAVE LONG HUNG UP THEIR ADVENTURIN' BOOTS.
BUT LIKE MANY OF 'EM, I CAME HERE FRESH-SHORN, LOOKIN' FER GOLD N' GLORY.
...SAME AS US...
SAME AS...LU.
AHH, YER FRIEND THE PALEHAIR.
I STILL CAN'T BELIEVE SHE'S GONE.
YOU'VE A KIND HEART TO MOURN FOR HER SO, MY PRINCE.
DERN SHAME FOR THE LASSY. BUT THE MAW'S HUNGRY, ALWAYS HAS BEEN. IT'LL SWALLOW YE WHOLE IF YE STEP TOO FAR.
EVERYONE HERE HAS A STORY LIKE THAT.
EVEN YOU, YAJI?
AYE, I LOST SOMEONE...DEAR TO ME...
...BUT I FOUND A REASON 'TA STAY AFTER ALL.
HERE NOW.
YOU'LL NEVER GUESS WHAT I CAUGHT-- HUH?
!!
?!

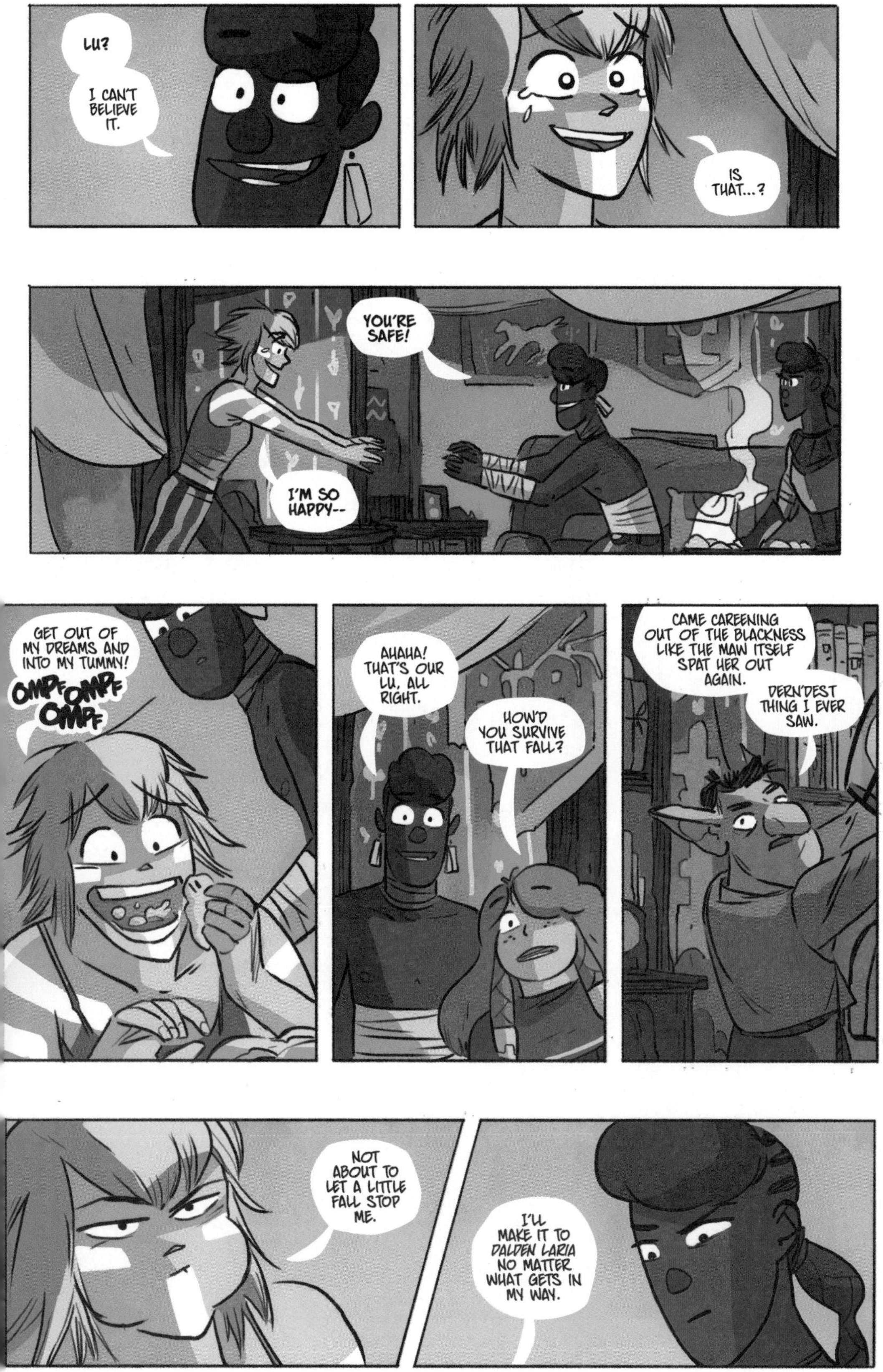
LU?
I CAN'T BELIEVE IT.
IS THAT...?
YOU'RE SAFE!
I'M SO HAPPY--
GET OUT OF MY DREAMS AND INTO MY TUMMY!
OMPF OMPF OMPF
AHAHA! THAT'S OUR LU, ALL RIGHT.
HOW'D YOU SURVIVE THAT FALL?
CAME CAREENING OUT OF THE BLACKNESS LIKE THE MAW ITSELF SPAT HER OUT AGAIN.
DERN'DEST THING I EVER SAW.
NOT ABOUT TO LET A LITTLE FALL STOP ME.
I'LL MAKE IT TO DALDEN LARIA NO MATTER WHAT GETS IN MY WAY.

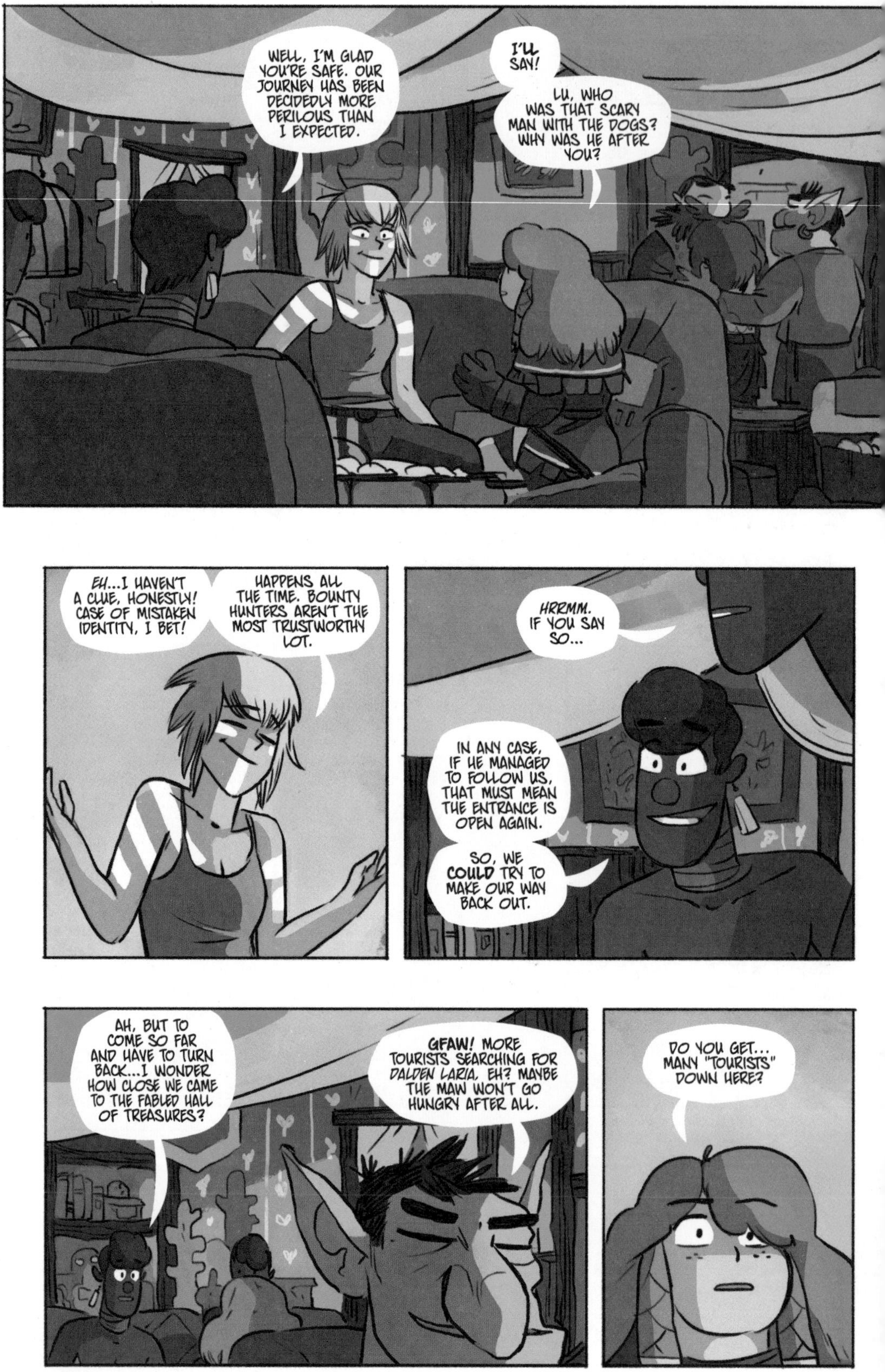

WELL, I'M GLAD YOU'RE SAFE. OUR JOURNEY HAS BEEN DECIDEDLY MORE PERILOUS THAN I EXPECTED.
I'LL SAY!
LU, WHO WAS THAT SCARY MAN WITH THE DOGS? WHY WAS HE AFTER YOU?
EH...I HAVEN'T A CLUE, HONESTLY! CASE OF MISTAKEN IDENTITY, I BET!
HAPPENS ALL THE TIME. BOUNTY HUNTERS AREN'T THE MOST TRUSTWORTHY LOT.
HRRMM. IF YOU SAY SO...
IN ANY CASE, IF HE MANAGED TO FOLLOW US, THAT MUST MEAN THE ENTRANCE IS OPEN AGAIN.
SO, WE COULD TRY TO MAKE OUR WAY BACK OUT.
AH, BUT TO COME SO FAR AND HAVE TO TURN BACK...I WONDER HOW CLOSE WE CAME TO THE FABLED HALL OF TREASURES?
GFAW! MORE TOURISTS SEARCHING FOR DALDEN LARIA, EH? MAYBE THE MAW WON'T GO HUNGRY AFTER ALL.
DO YOU GET... MANY "TOURISTS" DOWN HERE?

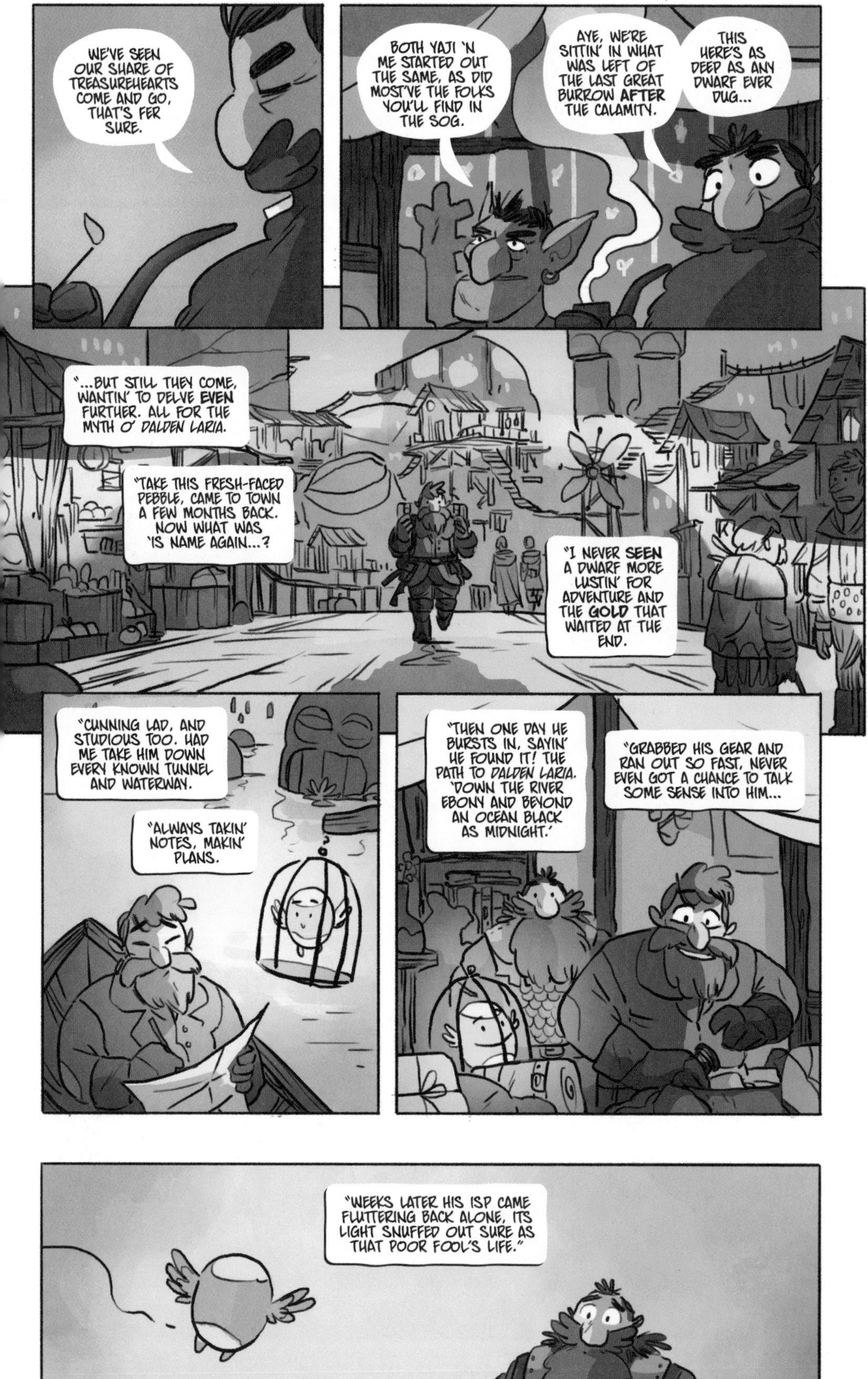

WE'VE SEEN OUR SHARE OF TREASUREHEARTS COME AND GO, THAT'S FER SURE.
BOTH YAJI 'N ME STARTED OUT THE SAME, AS DID MOST'VE THE FOLKS YOU'LL FIND IN THE SOG.
AYE, WE'RE SITTIN' IN WHAT WAS LEFT OF THE LAST GREAT BURROW **AFTER** THE CALAMITY.
THIS HERE'S AS DEEP AS ANY DWARF EVER DUG...
"...BUT STILL THEY COME, WANTIN' TO DELVE **EVEN** FURTHER. ALL FOR THE MYTH O' *DALDEN LARIA*.
"TAKE THIS FRESH-FACED PEBBLE, CAME TO TOWN A FEW MONTHS BACK. NOW WHAT WAS 'IS NAME AGAIN...?
"I NEVER **SEEN** A DWARF MORE LUSTIN' FOR ADVENTURE AND THE **GOLD** THAT WAITED AT THE END.
"CUNNING LAD, AND STUDIOUS TOO. HAD ME TAKE HIM DOWN EVERY KNOWN TUNNEL AND WATERWAY.
"ALWAYS TAKIN' NOTES, MAKIN' PLANS.
?
"THEN ONE DAY HE BURSTS IN, SAYIN' HE FOUND IT! THE PATH TO *DALDEN LARIA*. 'DOWN THE RIVER EBONY AND BEYOND AN OCEAN BLACK AS MIDNIGHT.'
"GRABBED HIS GEAR AND RAN OUT SO FAST, NEVER EVEN GOT A CHANCE TO TALK SOME SENSE INTO HIM...
"WEEKS LATER HIS ISP CAME FLUTTERING BACK ALONE, ITS LIGHT SNUFFED OUT SURE AS THAT POOR FOOL'S LIFE."

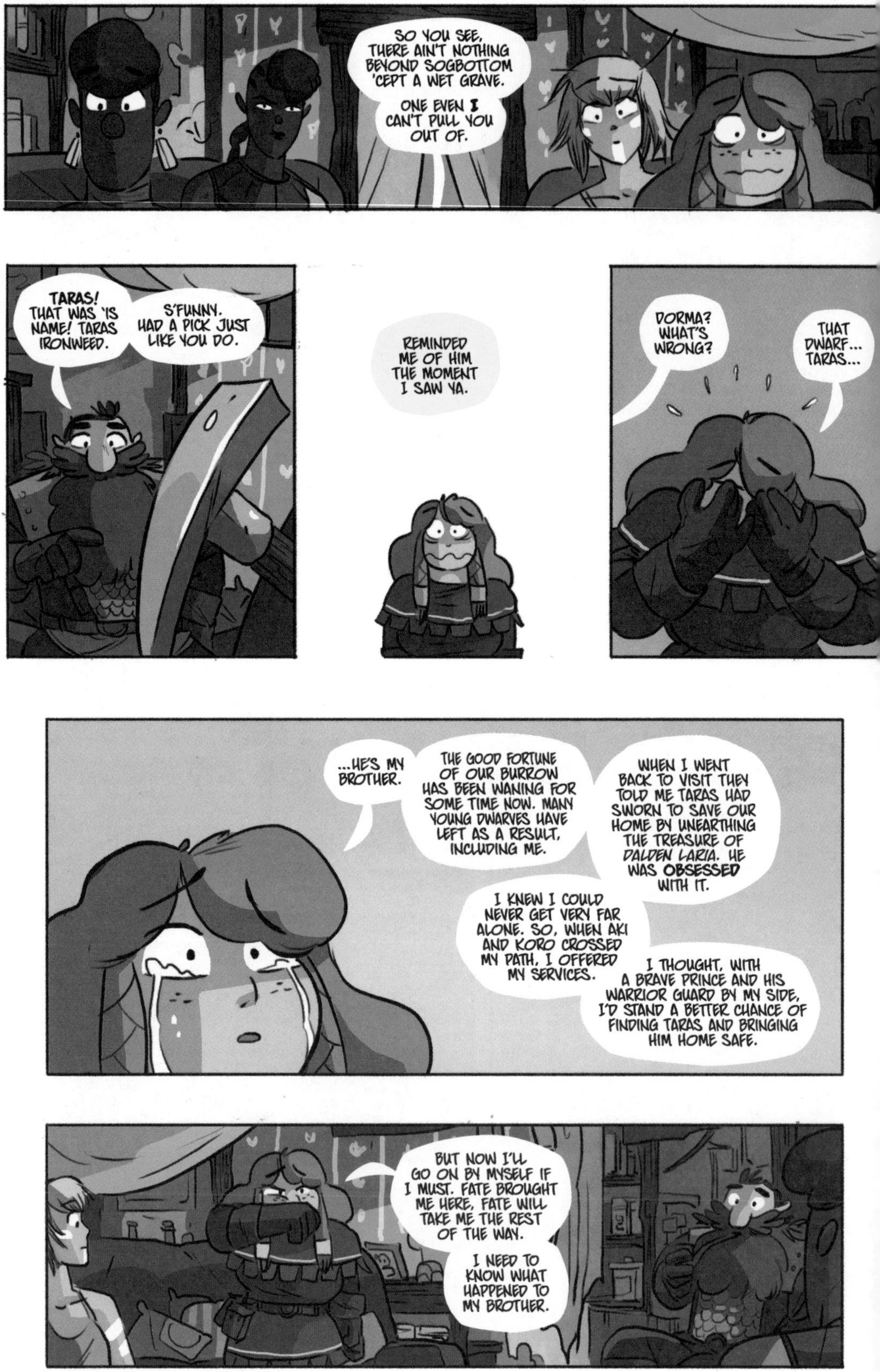
SO YOU SEE, THERE AIN'T NOTHING BEYOND SOGBOTTOM 'CEPT A WET GRAVE.
ONE EVEN I CAN'T PULL YOU OUT OF.
TARAS! THAT WAS 'IS NAME! TARAS IRONWEED.
S'FUNNY. HAD A PICK JUST LIKE YOU DO.
REMINDED ME OF HIM THE MOMENT I SAW YA.
DORMA? WHAT'S WRONG?
THAT DWARF... TARAS...
...HE'S MY BROTHER.
THE GOOD FORTUNE OF OUR BURROW HAS BEEN WANING FOR SOME TIME NOW. MANY YOUNG DWARVES HAVE LEFT AS A RESULT, INCLUDING ME.
WHEN I WENT BACK TO VISIT THEY TOLD ME TARAS HAD SWORN TO SAVE OUR HOME BY UNEARTHING THE TREASURE OF DALDEN LARIA. HE WAS OBSESSED WITH IT.
I KNEW I COULD NEVER GET VERY FAR ALONE. SO, WHEN AKI AND KORO CROSSED MY PATH, I OFFERED MY SERVICES.
I THOUGHT, WITH A BRAVE PRINCE AND HIS WARRIOR GUARD BY MY SIDE, I'D STAND A BETTER CHANCE OF FINDING TARAS AND BRINGING HIM HOME SAFE.
BUT NOW I'LL GO ON BY MYSELF IF I MUST. FATE BROUGHT ME HERE, FATE WILL TAKE ME THE REST OF THE WAY.
I NEED TO KNOW WHAT HAPPENED TO MY BROTHER.

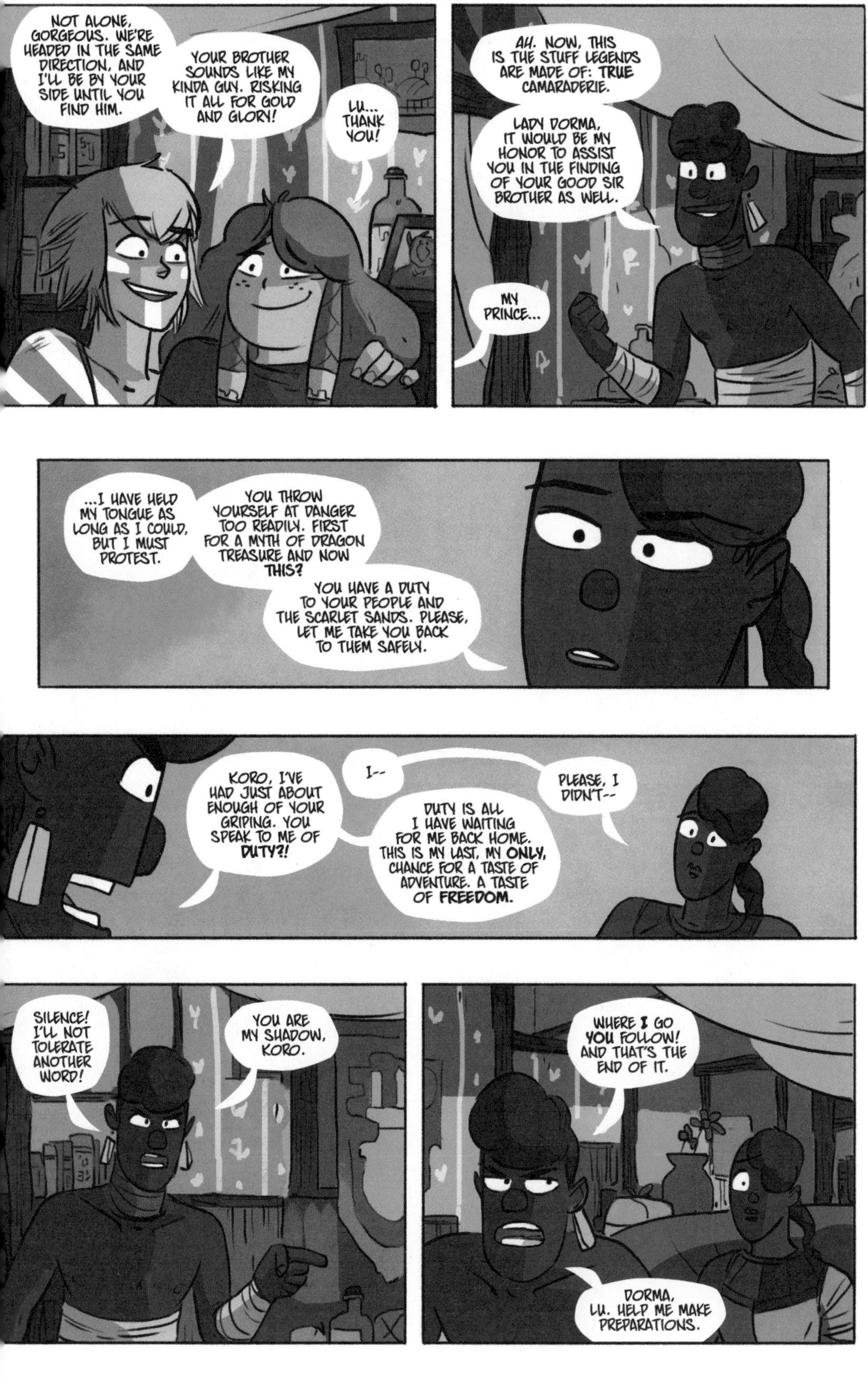
NOT ALONE, GORGEOUS. WE'RE HEADED IN THE SAME DIRECTION, AND I'LL BE BY YOUR SIDE UNTIL YOU FIND HIM.
YOUR BROTHER SOUNDS LIKE MY KINDA GUY. RISKING IT ALL FOR GOLD AND GLORY!
LU... THANK YOU!
AH. NOW, THIS IS THE STUFF LEGENDS ARE MADE OF: TRUE CAMARADERIE.
LADY DORMA, IT WOULD BE MY HONOR TO ASSIST YOU IN THE FINDING OF YOUR GOOD SIR BROTHER AS WELL.
MY PRINCE...
...I HAVE HELD MY TONGUE AS LONG AS I COULD, BUT I MUST PROTEST.
YOU THROW YOURSELF AT DANGER TOO READILY. FIRST FOR A MYTH OF DRAGON TREASURE AND NOW THIS?
YOU HAVE A DUTY TO YOUR PEOPLE AND THE SCARLET SANDS. PLEASE, LET ME TAKE YOU BACK TO THEM SAFELY.
KORO, I'VE HAD JUST ABOUT ENOUGH OF YOUR GRIPING. YOU SPEAK TO ME OF DUTY?!
I--
DUTY IS ALL I HAVE WAITING FOR ME BACK HOME. THIS IS MY LAST, MY ONLY, CHANCE FOR A TASTE OF ADVENTURE. A TASTE OF FREEDOM.
PLEASE, I DIDN'T--
SILENCE! I'LL NOT TOLERATE ANOTHER WORD!
YOU ARE MY SHADOW, KORO.
WHERE I GO YOU FOLLOW! AND THAT'S THE END OF IT.
DORMA, LU. HELP ME MAKE PREPARATIONS.

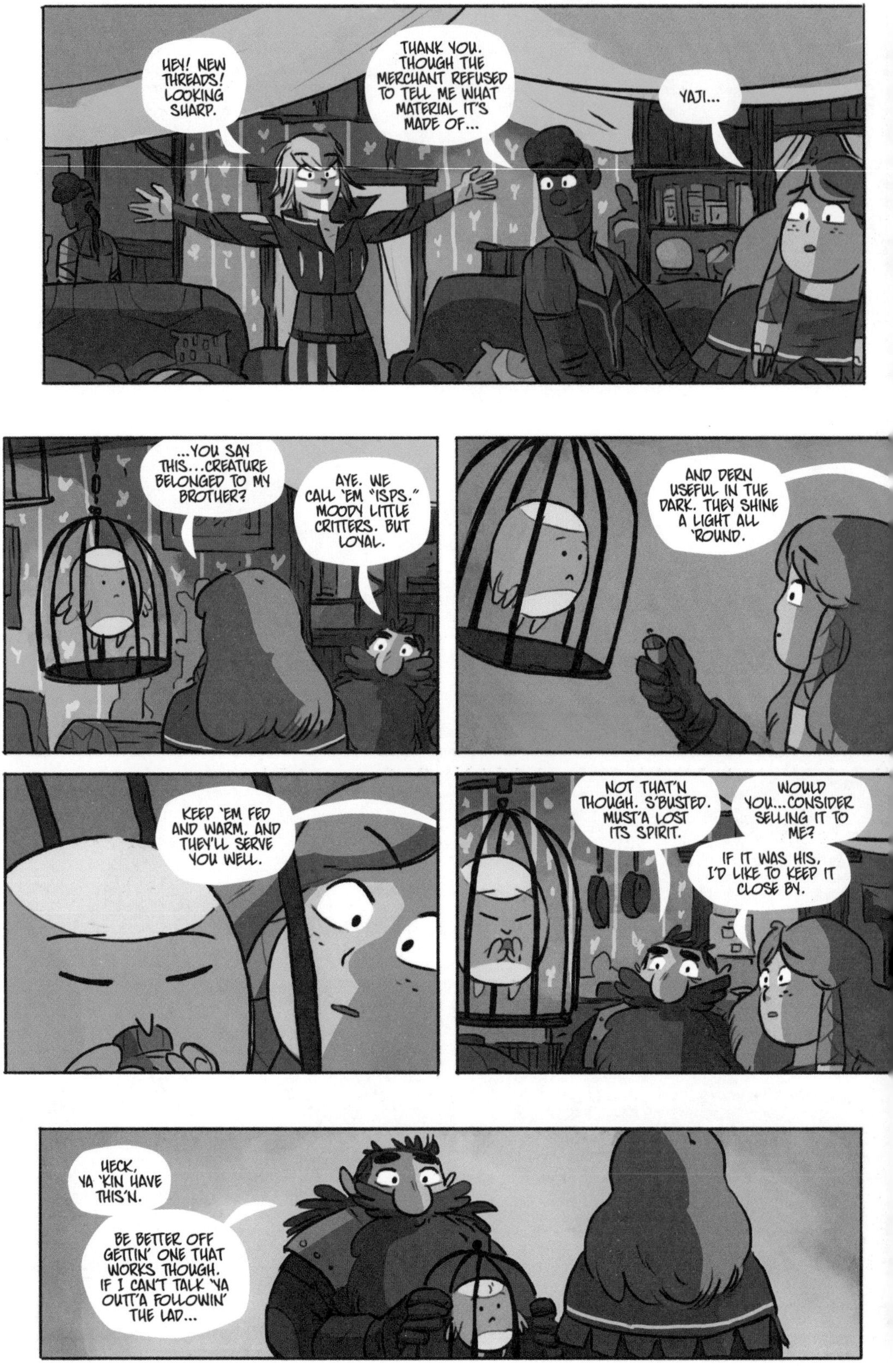
HEY! NEW THREADS! LOOKING SHARP.
THANK YOU. THOUGH THE MERCHANT REFUSED TO TELL ME WHAT MATERIAL IT'S MADE OF...
YAJI...
...YOU SAY THIS...CREATURE BELONGED TO MY BROTHER?
AYE. WE CALL 'EM "ISPS." MOODY LITTLE CRITTERS. BUT LOYAL.
AND DERN USEFUL IN THE DARK. THEY SHINE A LIGHT ALL 'ROUND.
KEEP 'EM FED AND WARM, AND THEY'LL SERVE YOU WELL.
NOT THAT'N THOUGH. S'BUSTED. MUST'A LOST ITS SPIRIT.
WOULD YOU...CONSIDER SELLING IT TO ME?
IF IT WAS HIS, I'D LIKE TO KEEP IT CLOSE BY.
HECK, YA 'KIN HAVE THIS'N.
BE BETTER OFF GETTIN' ONE THAT WORKS THOUGH. IF I CAN'T TALK 'YA OUTT'A FOLLOWIN' THE LAD...

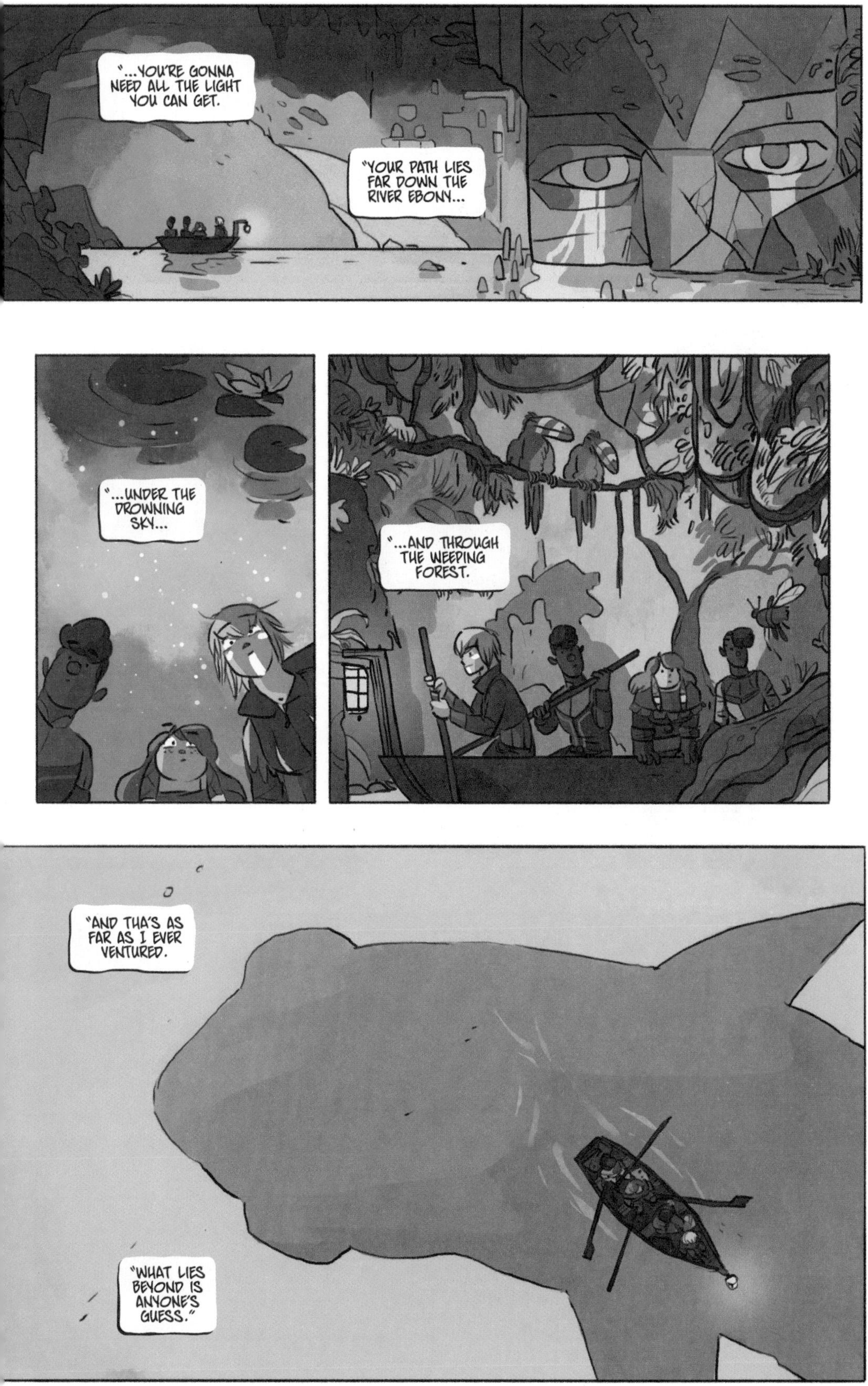
"...YOU'RE GONNA NEED ALL THE LIGHT YOU CAN GET.
"YOUR PATH LIES FAR DOWN THE RIVER EBONY...
"...UNDER THE DROWNING SKY...
"...AND THROUGH THE WEEPING FOREST.
"AND THA'S AS FAR AS I EVER VENTURED.
"WHAT LIES BEYOND IS ANYONE'S GUESS."

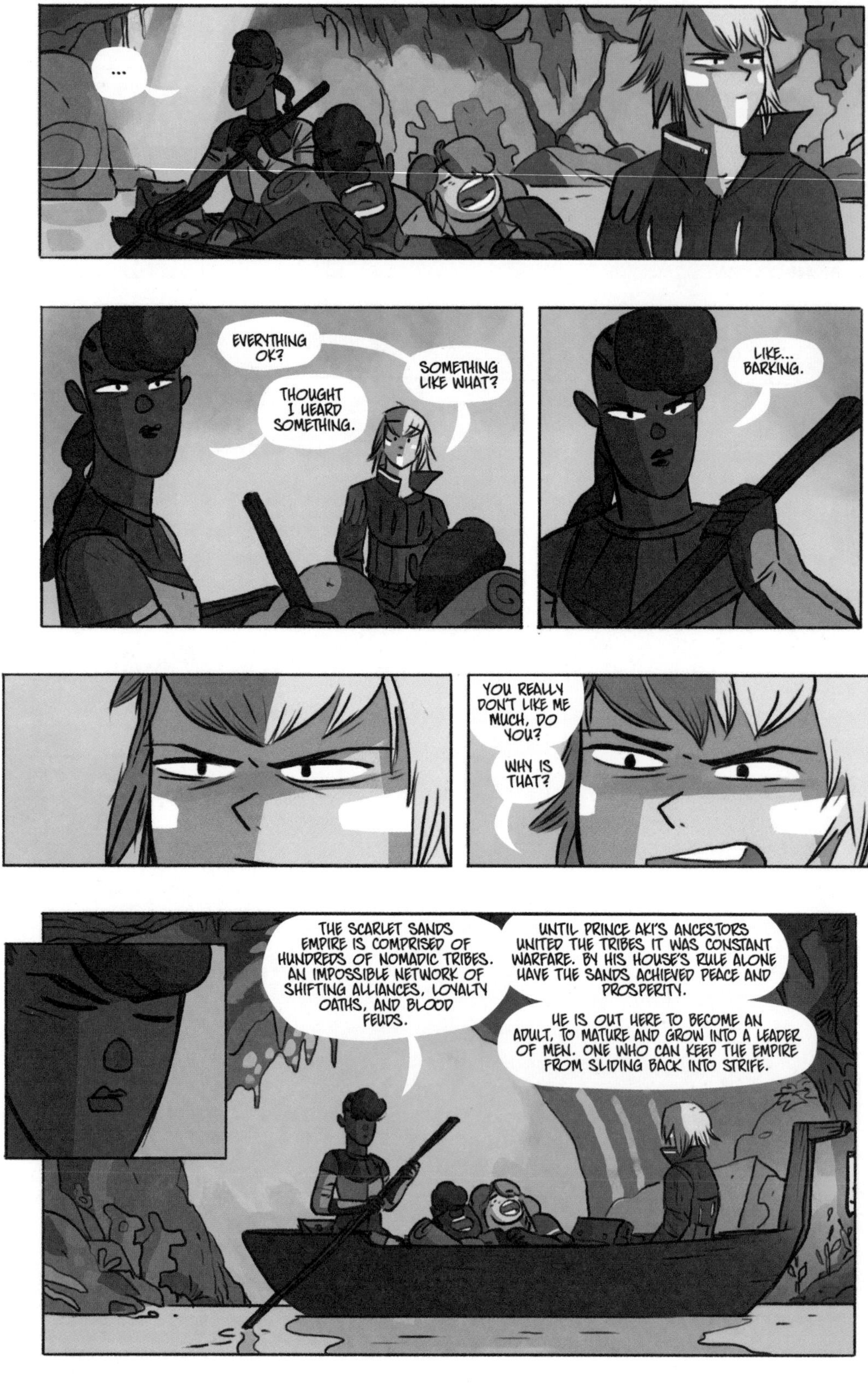
...
EVERYTHING OK?
THOUGHT I HEARD SOMETHING.
SOMETHING LIKE WHAT?
LIKE... BARKING.
YOU REALLY DON'T LIKE ME MUCH, DO YOU?
WHY IS THAT?
THE SCARLET SANDS EMPIRE IS COMPRISED OF HUNDREDS OF NOMADIC TRIBES. AN IMPOSSIBLE NETWORK OF SHIFTING ALLIANCES, LOYALTY OATHS, AND BLOOD FEUDS.
UNTIL PRINCE AKI'S ANCESTORS UNITED THE TRIBES IT WAS CONSTANT WARFARE. BY HIS HOUSE'S RULE ALONE HAVE THE SANDS ACHIEVED PEACE AND PROSPERITY.
HE IS OUT HERE TO BECOME AN ADULT, TO MATURE AND GROW INTO A LEADER OF MEN. ONE WHO CAN KEEP THE EMPIRE FROM SLIDING BACK INTO STRIFE.

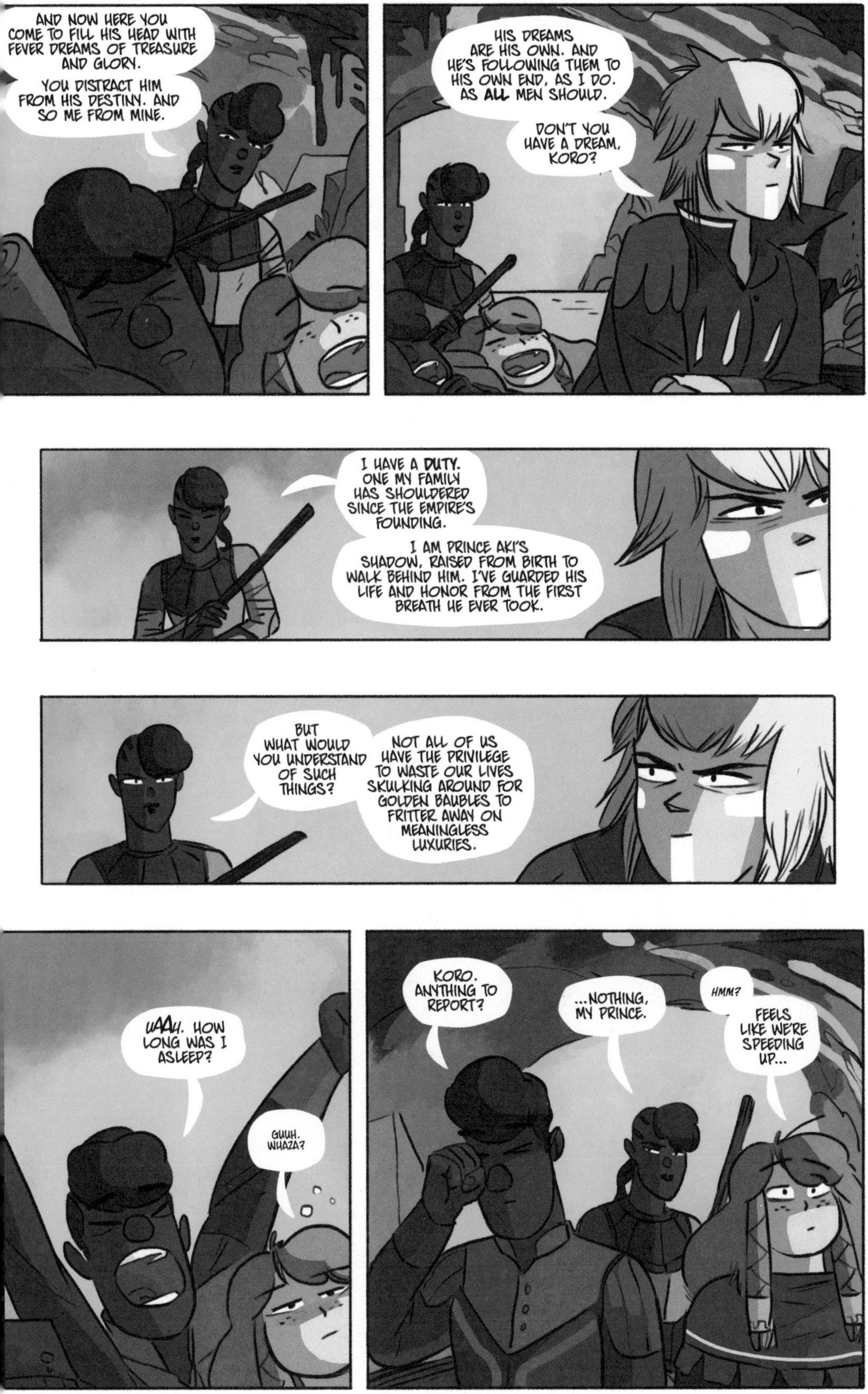
AND NOW HERE YOU COME TO FILL HIS HEAD WITH FEVER DREAMS OF TREASURE AND GLORY.
YOU DISTRACT HIM FROM HIS DESTINY. AND SO ME FROM MINE.
HIS DREAMS ARE HIS OWN. AND HE'S FOLLOWING THEM TO HIS OWN END, AS I DO. AS **ALL** MEN SHOULD.
DON'T YOU HAVE A DREAM, KORO?
I HAVE A **DUTY**. ONE MY FAMILY HAS SHOULDERED SINCE THE EMPIRE'S FOUNDING.
I AM PRINCE AKI'S SHADOW, RAISED FROM BIRTH TO WALK BEHIND HIM. I'VE GUARDED HIS LIFE AND HONOR FROM THE FIRST BREATH HE EVER TOOK.
BUT WHAT WOULD YOU UNDERSTAND OF SUCH THINGS?
NOT ALL OF US HAVE THE PRIVILEGE TO WASTE OUR LIVES SKULKING AROUND FOR GOLDEN BAUBLES TO FRITTER AWAY ON MEANINGLESS LUXURIES.
UAAH. HOW LONG WAS I ASLEEP?
GUUH. WHAZA?
KORO. ANYTHING TO REPORT?
...NOTHING, MY PRINCE.
HMM?
FEELS LIKE WE'RE SPEEDING UP...

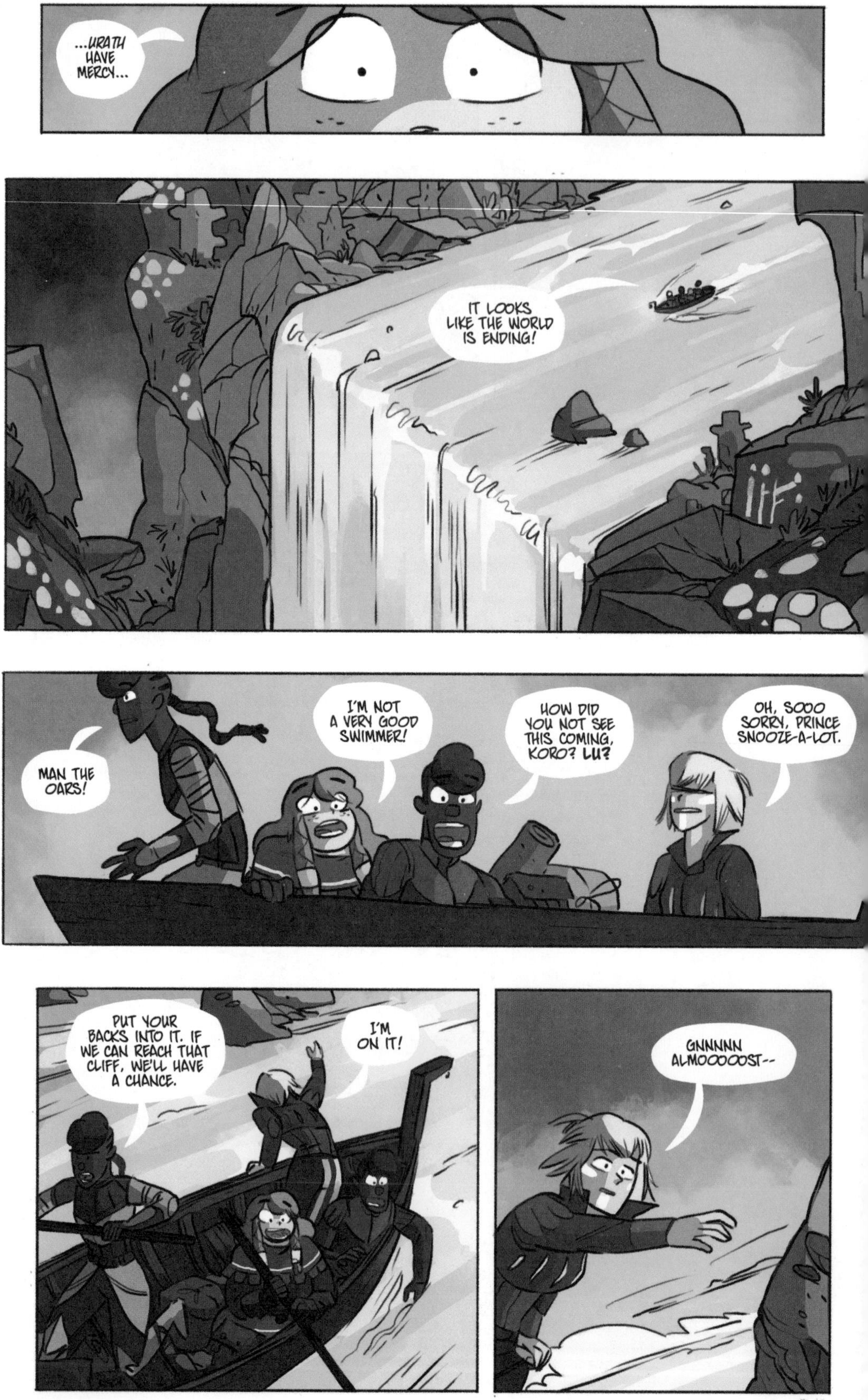
...WRATH HAVE MERCY...
IT LOOKS LIKE THE WORLD IS ENDING!
MAN THE OARS!
I'M NOT A VERY GOOD SWIMMER!
HOW DID YOU NOT SEE THIS COMING, KORO? LU?
OH, SOOO SORRY, PRINCE SNOOZE-A-LOT.
PUT YOUR BACKS INTO IT. IF WE CAN REACH THAT CLIFF, WE'LL HAVE A CHANCE.
I'M ON IT!
GNNNNN ALMOOOOOST--

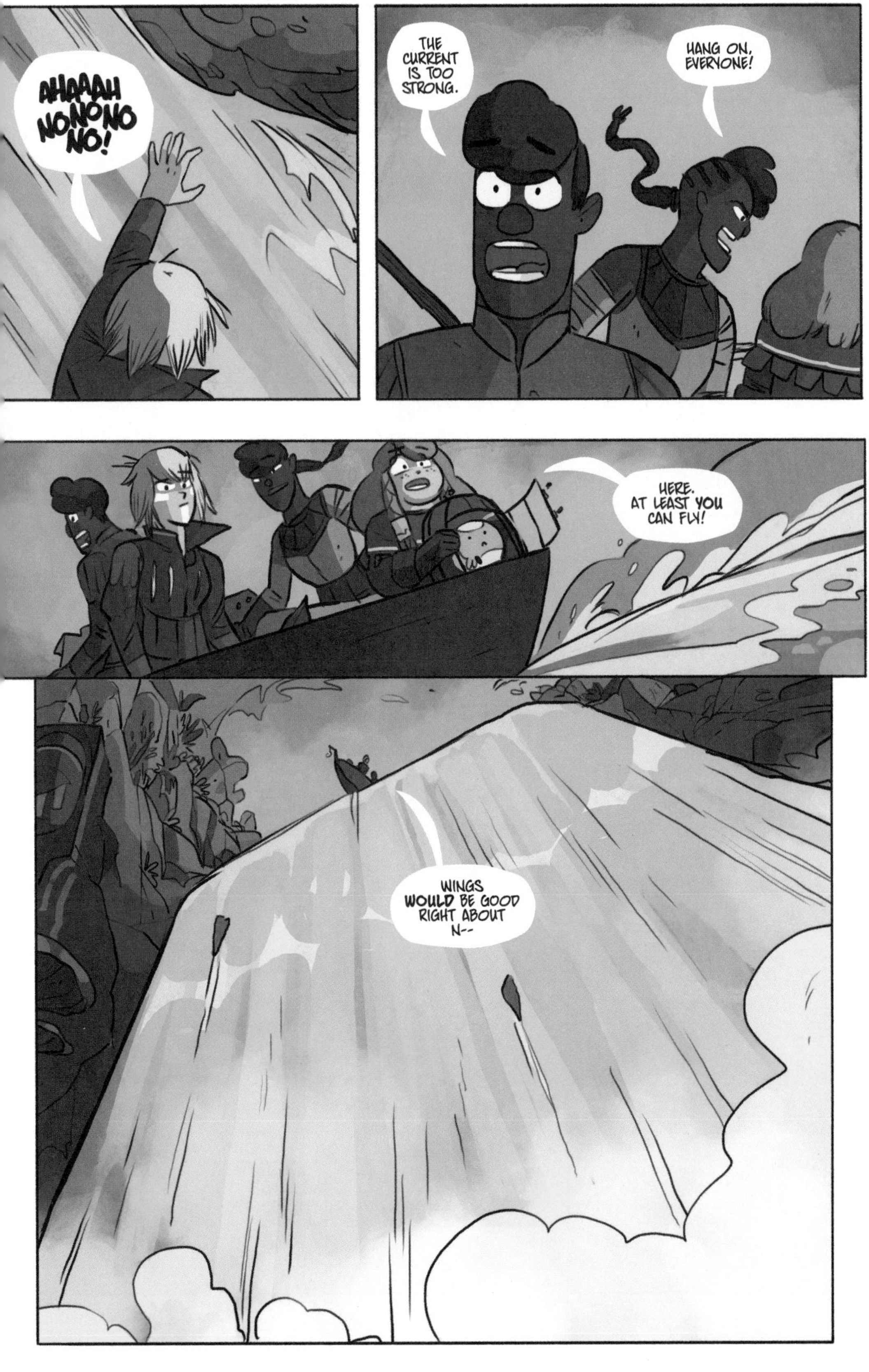
AHAAAH NONONO NO!
THE CURRENT IS TOO STRONG.
HANG ON, EVERYONE!
HERE. AT LEAST YOU CAN FLY!
WINGS WOULD BE GOOD RIGHT ABOUT N--

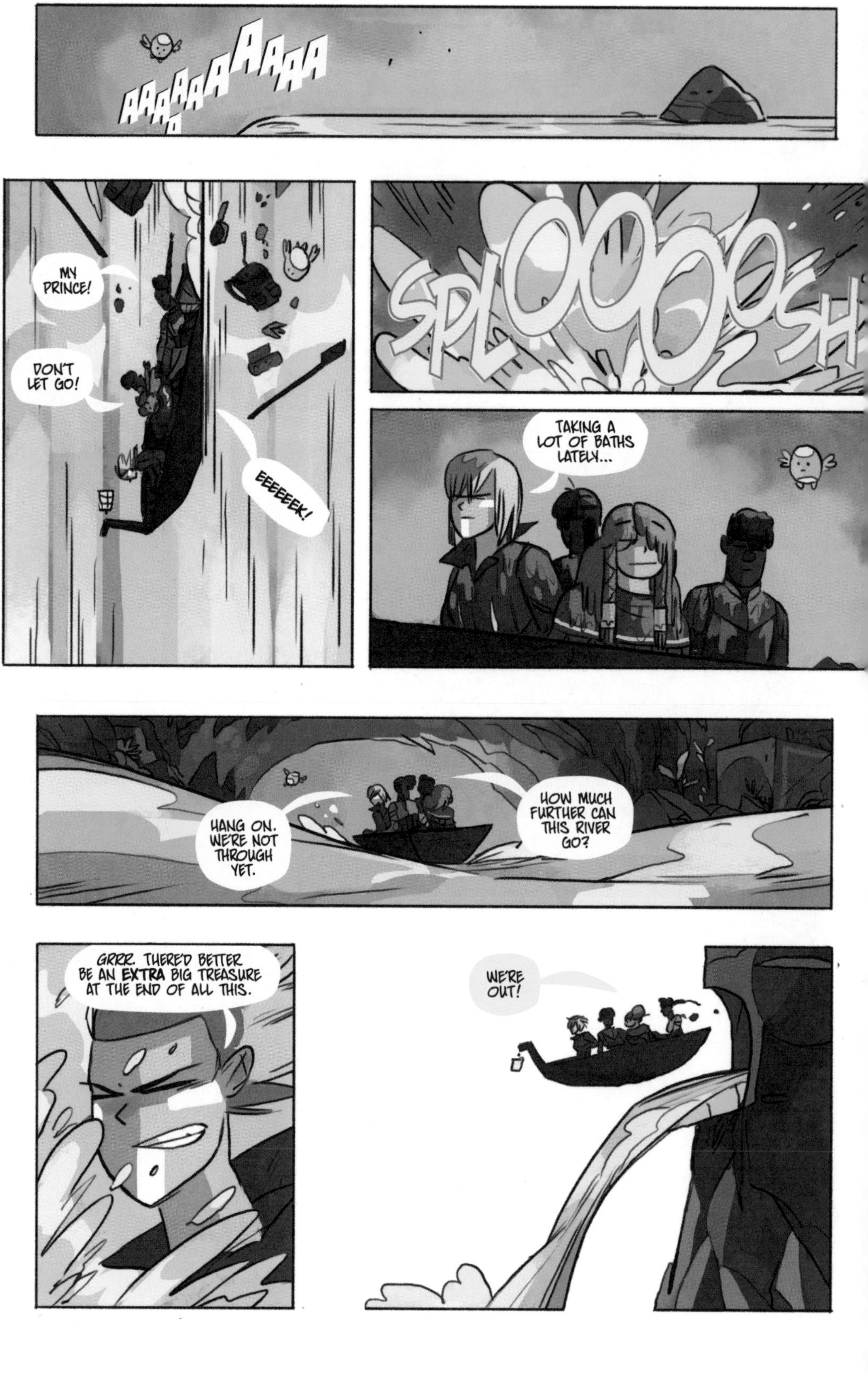
AAAAAAAAAAAA
MY PRINCE!
DON'T LET GO!
EEEEEEK!
SPLOOOOOSH
TAKING A LOT OF BATHS LATELY...
HANG ON. WE'RE NOT THROUGH YET.
HOW MUCH FURTHER CAN THIS RIVER GO?
GRRR. THERE'D BETTER BE AN **EXTRA** BIG TREASURE AT THE END OF ALL THIS.
WE'RE OUT!

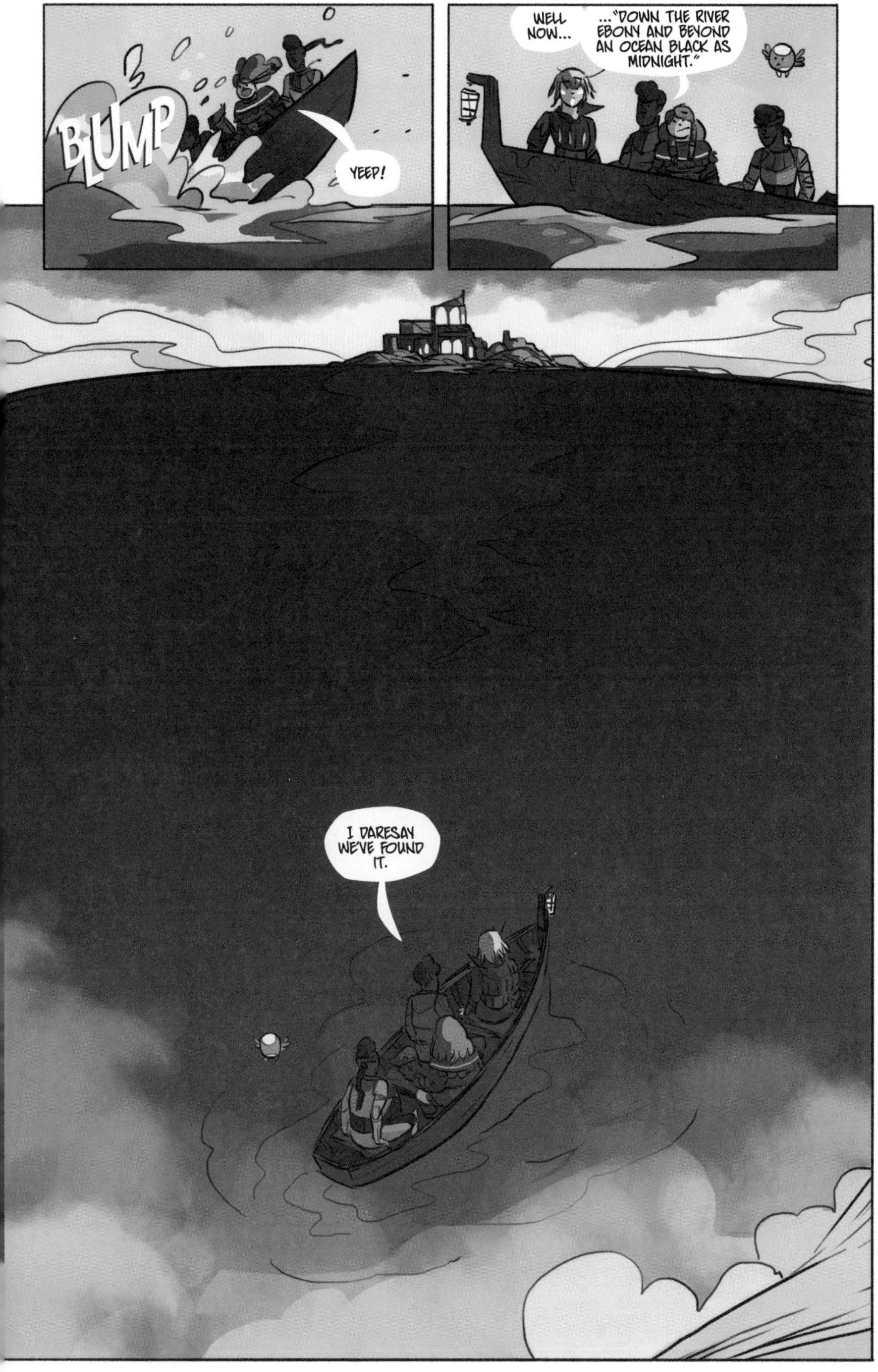
BLUMP
YEEP!
WELL NOW...
..."DOWN THE RIVER EBONY AND BEYOND AN OCEAN BLACK AS MIDNIGHT."
I DARESAY WE'VE FOUND IT.

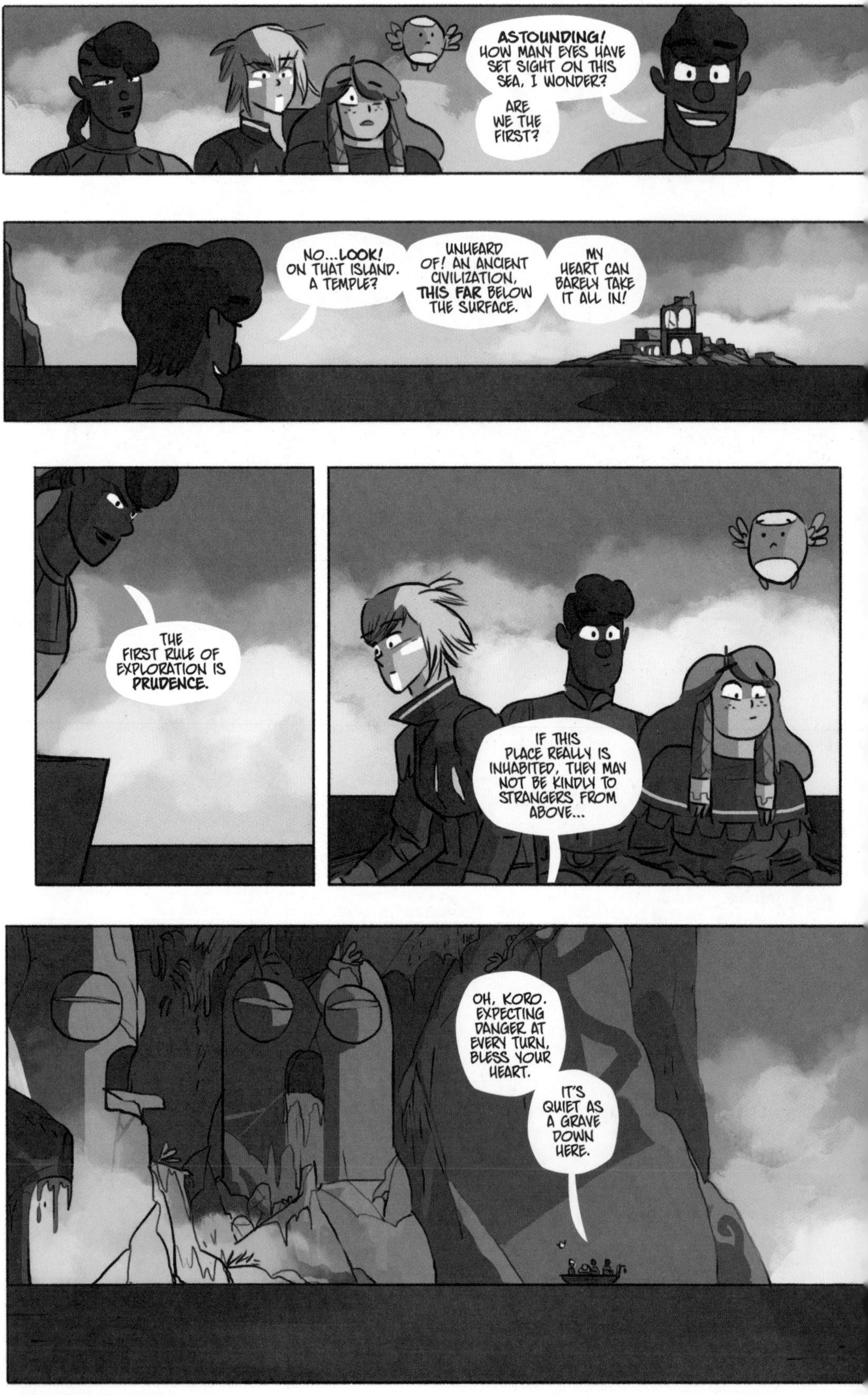

ASTOUNDING! HOW MANY EYES HAVE SET SIGHT ON THIS SEA, I WONDER?
ARE WE THE FIRST?
NO...LOOK! ON THAT ISLAND. A TEMPLE?
UNHEARD OF! AN ANCIENT CIVILIZATION, THIS FAR BELOW THE SURFACE.
MY HEART CAN BARELY TAKE IT ALL IN!
THE FIRST RULE OF EXPLORATION IS PRUDENCE.
IF THIS PLACE REALLY IS INHABITED, THEY MAY NOT BE KINDLY TO STRANGERS FROM ABOVE...
OH, KORO. EXPECTING DANGER AT EVERY TURN, BLESS YOUR HEART.
IT'S QUIET AS A GRAVE DOWN HERE.

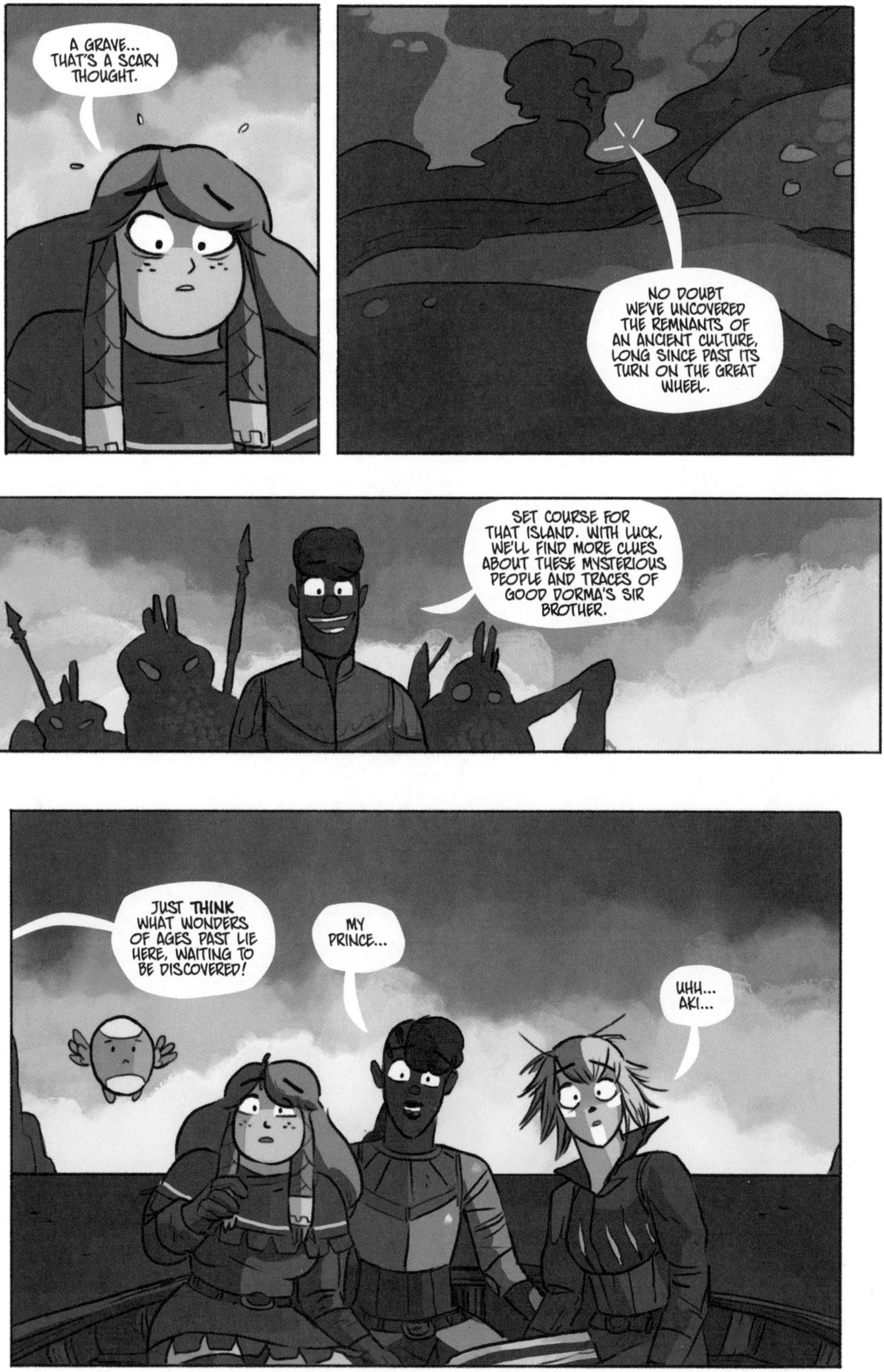
A GRAVE... THAT'S A SCARY THOUGHT.
NO DOUBT WE'VE UNCOVERED THE REMNANTS OF AN ANCIENT CULTURE, LONG SINCE PAST ITS TURN ON THE GREAT WHEEL.
SET COURSE FOR THAT ISLAND. WITH LUCK, WE'LL FIND MORE CLUES ABOUT THESE MYSTERIOUS PEOPLE AND TRACES OF GOOD DORMA'S SIR BROTHER.
JUST **THINK** WHAT WONDERS OF AGES PAST LIE HERE, WAITING TO BE DISCOVERED!
MY PRINCE...
UHH... AKI...

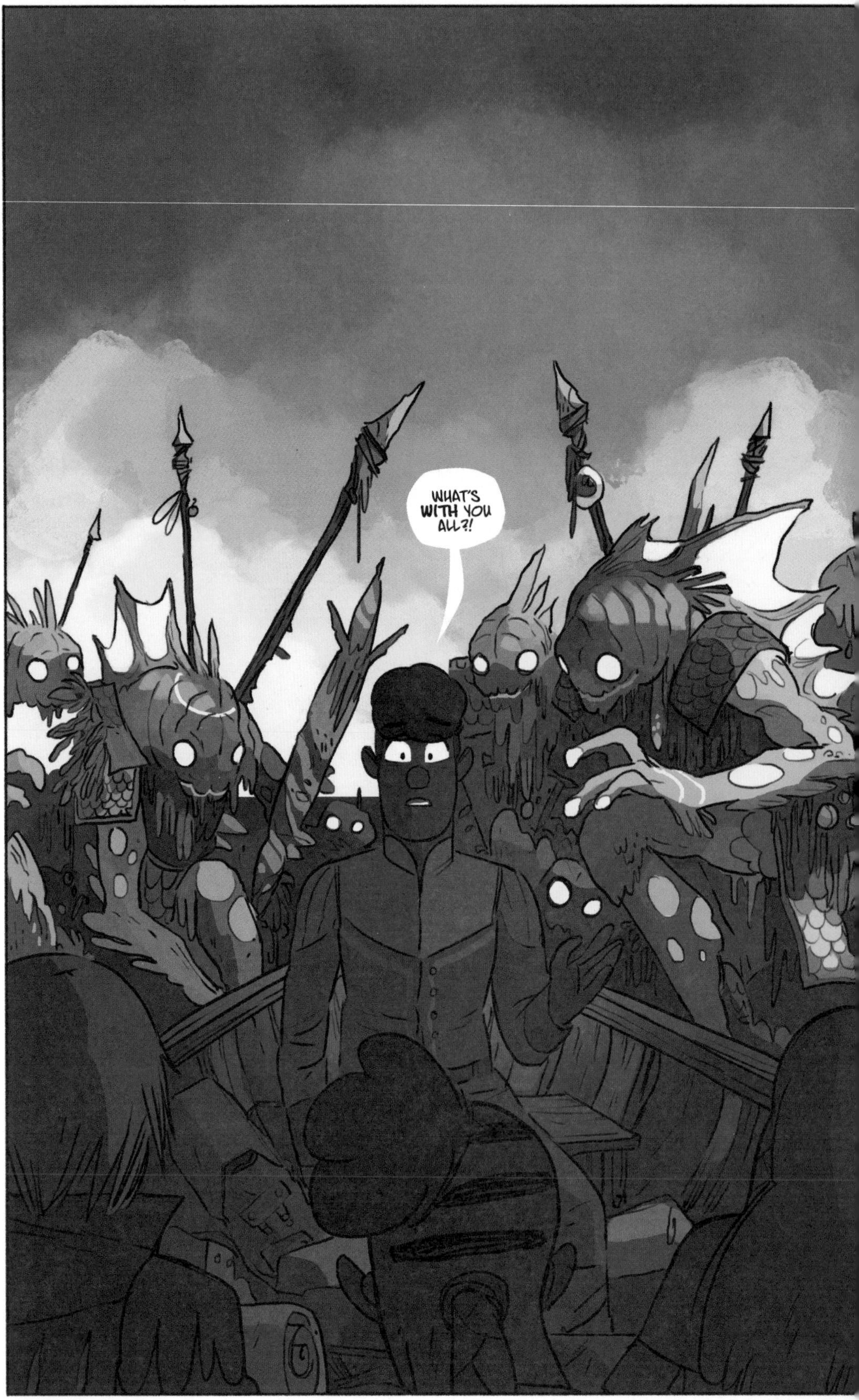
WHAT'S WITH YOU ALL?!

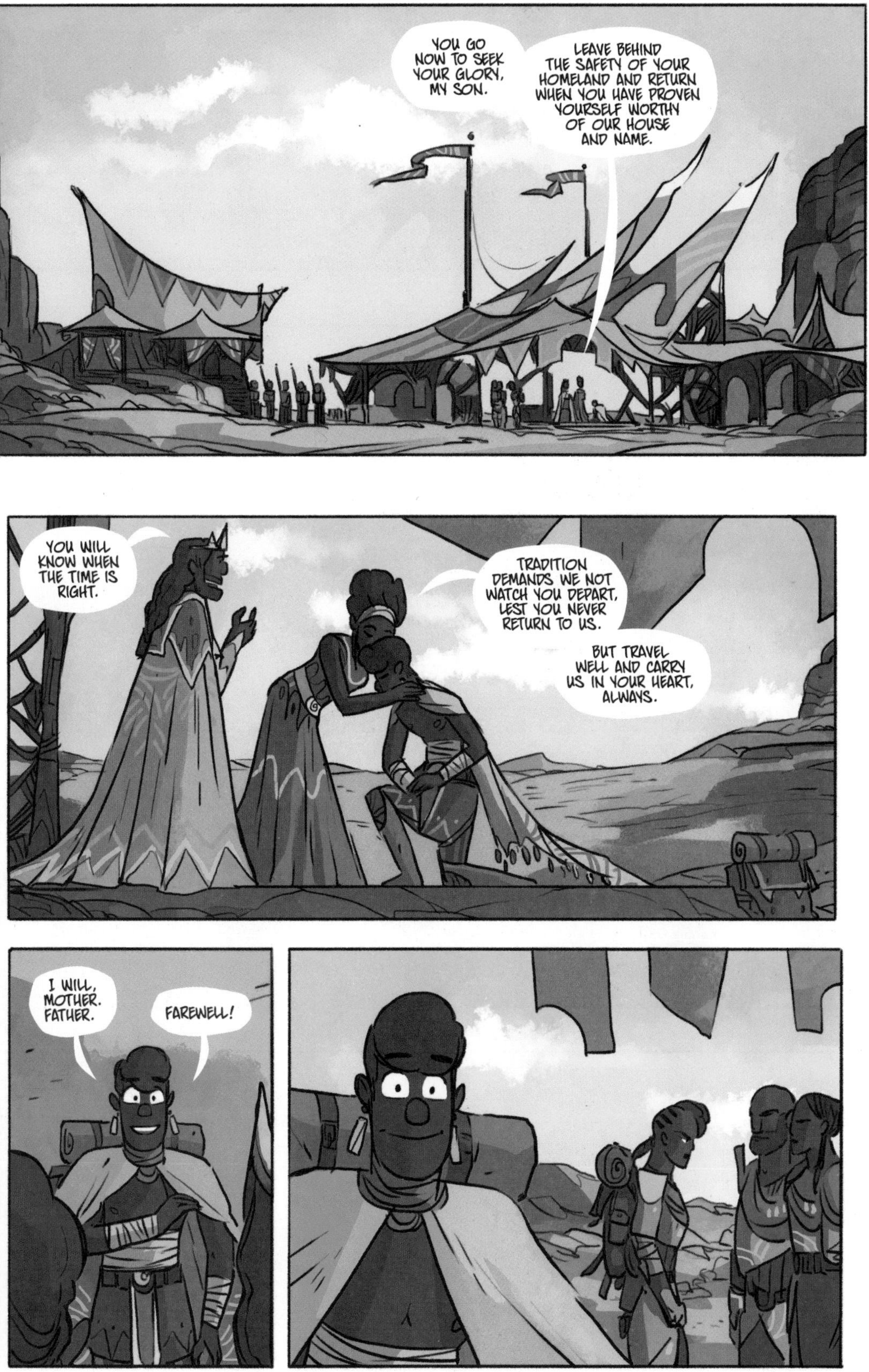
YOU GO NOW TO SEEK YOUR GLORY, MY SON.
LEAVE BEHIND THE SAFETY OF YOUR HOMELAND AND RETURN WHEN YOU HAVE PROVEN YOURSELF WORTHY OF OUR HOUSE AND NAME.
YOU WILL KNOW WHEN THE TIME IS RIGHT.
TRADITION DEMANDS WE NOT WATCH YOU DEPART, LEST YOU NEVER RETURN TO US.
BUT TRAVEL WELL AND CARRY US IN YOUR HEART, ALWAYS.
I WILL, MOTHER. FATHER.
FAREWELL!

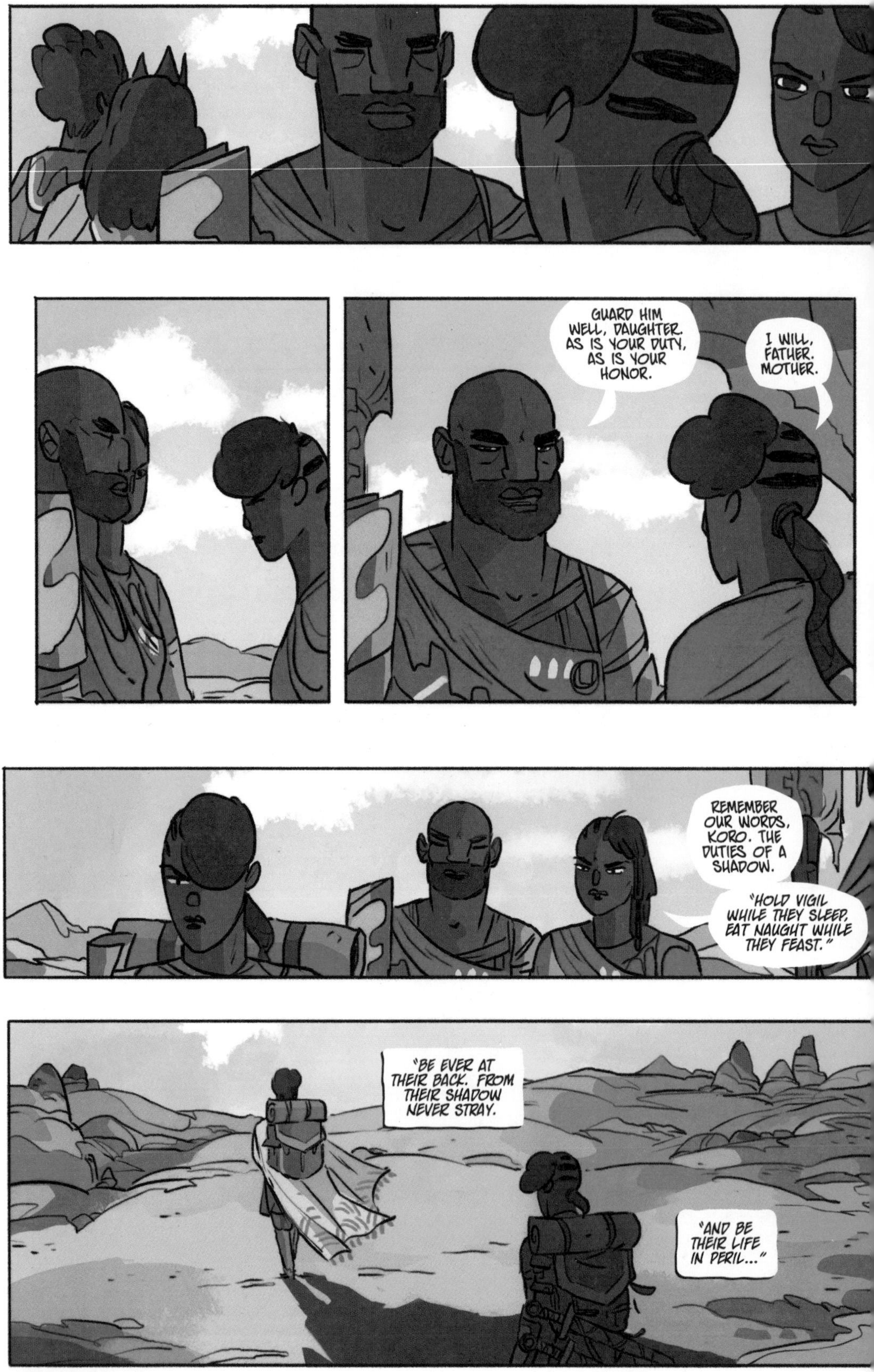
GUARD HIM WELL, DAUGHTER. AS IS YOUR DUTY, AS IS YOUR HONOR.
I WILL, FATHER. MOTHER.
REMEMBER OUR WORDS, KORO. THE DUTIES OF A SHADOW.
"HOLD VIGIL WHILE THEY SLEEP, EAT NAUGHT WHILE THEY FEAST."
"BE EVER AT THEIR BACK. FROM THEIR SHADOW NEVER STRAY.
"AND BE THEIR LIFE IN PERIL..."

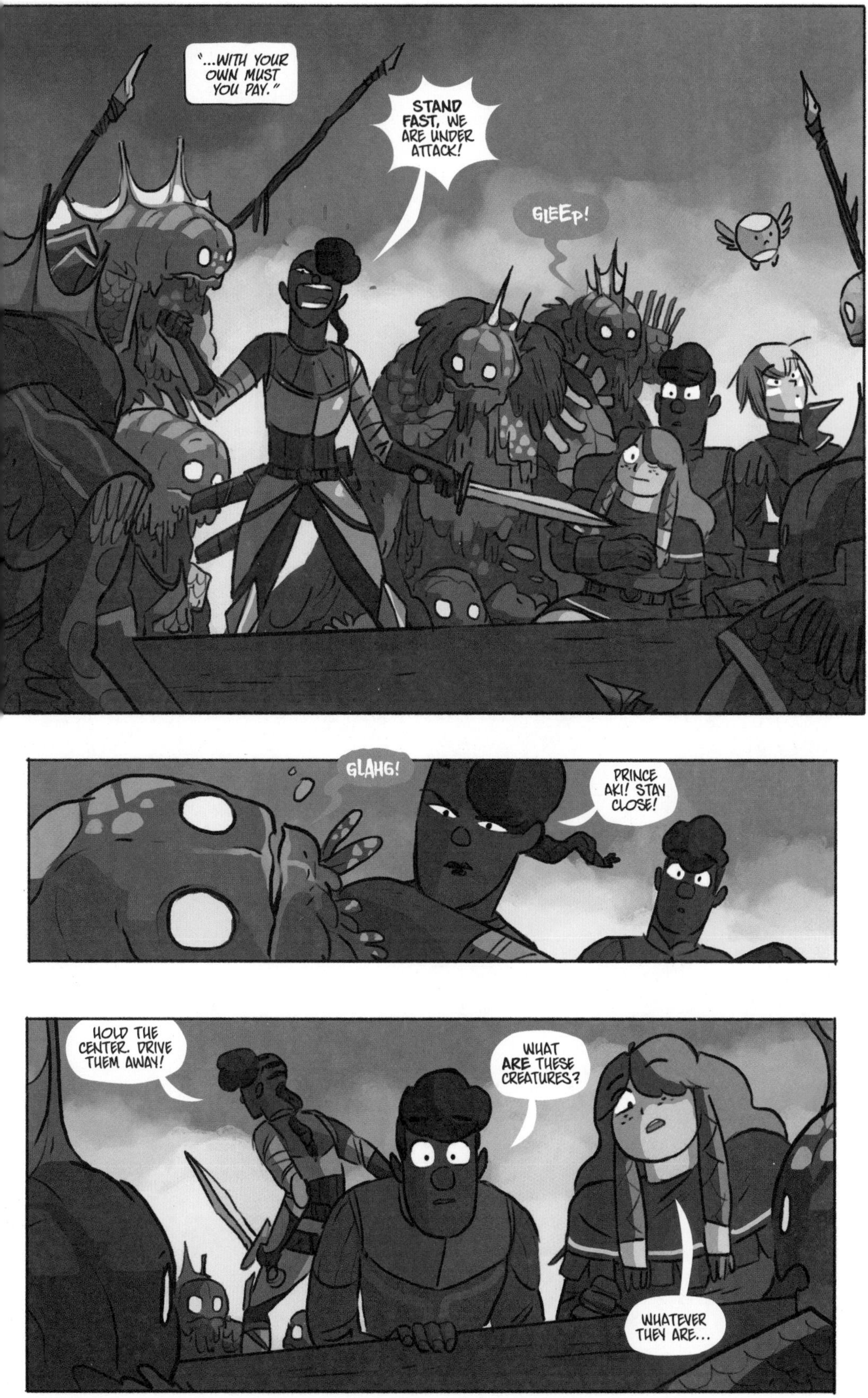
"...WITH YOUR OWN MUST YOU PAY."
STAND FAST, WE ARE UNDER ATTACK!
GLEEp!
GLAHG!
PRINCE AKI! STAY CLOSE!
HOLD THE CENTER. DRIVE THEM AWAY!
WHAT ARE THESE CREATURES?
WHATEVER THEY ARE...

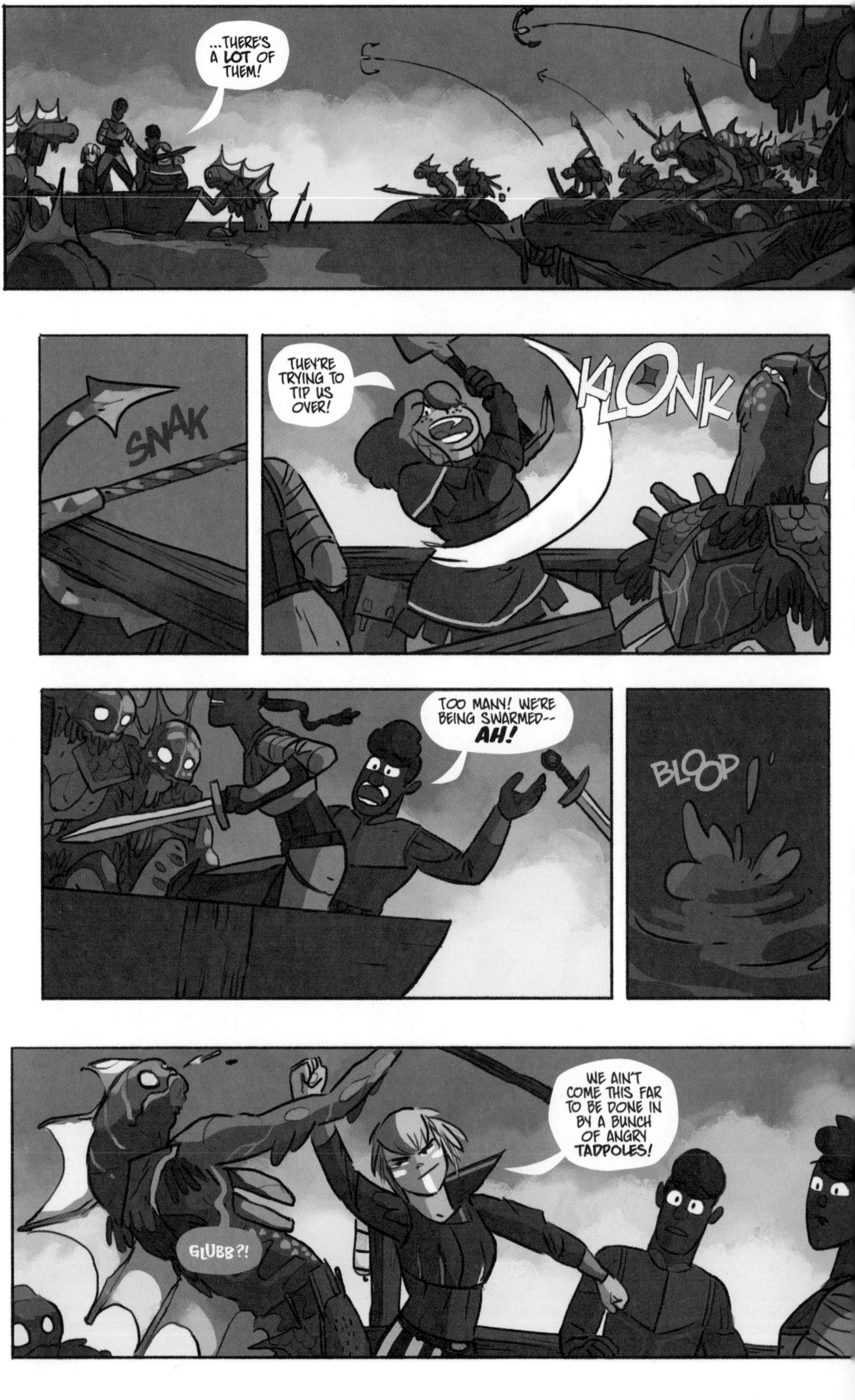
...THERE'S A LOT OF THEM!
SNAK
THEY'RE TRYING TO TIP US OVER!
KLONK
TOO MANY! WE'RE BEING SWARMED-- AH!
BLOOP
WE AIN'T COME THIS FAR TO BE DONE IN BY A BUNCH OF ANGRY TADPOLES!
GLUBB?!

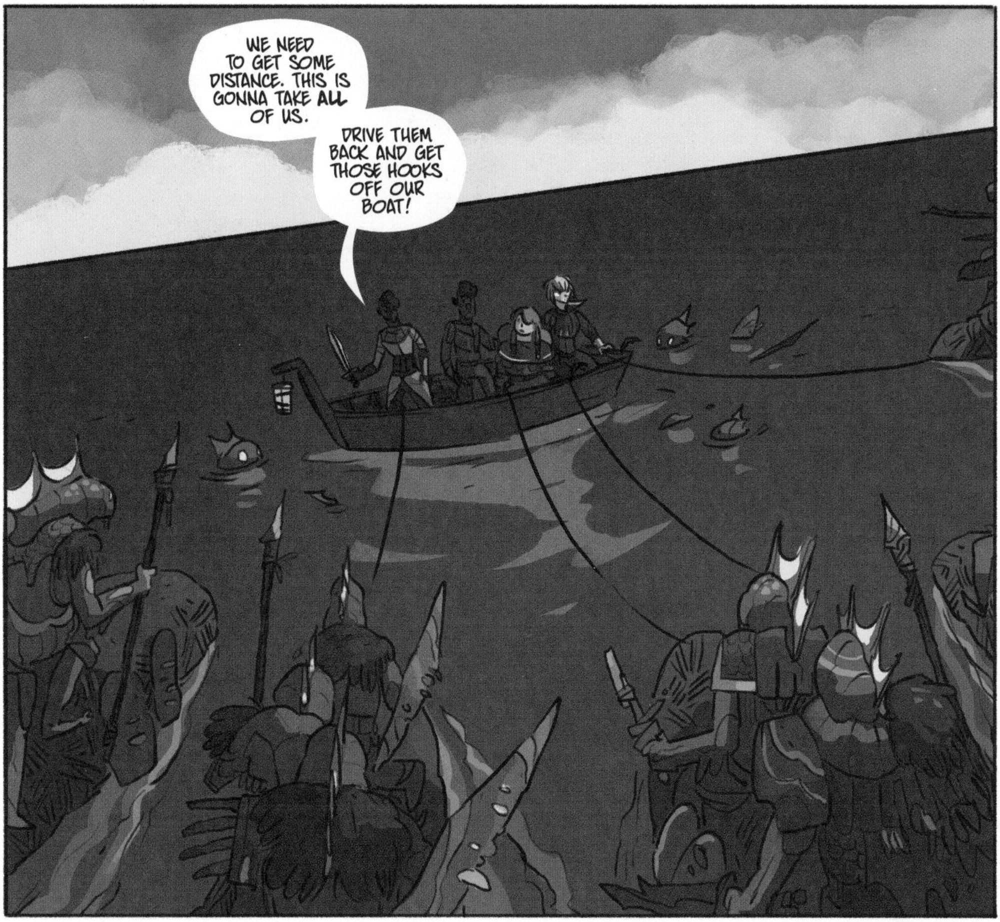
WE NEED TO GET SOME DISTANCE. THIS IS GONNA TAKE ALL OF US.
DRIVE THEM BACK AND GET THOSE HOOKS OFF OUR BOAT!

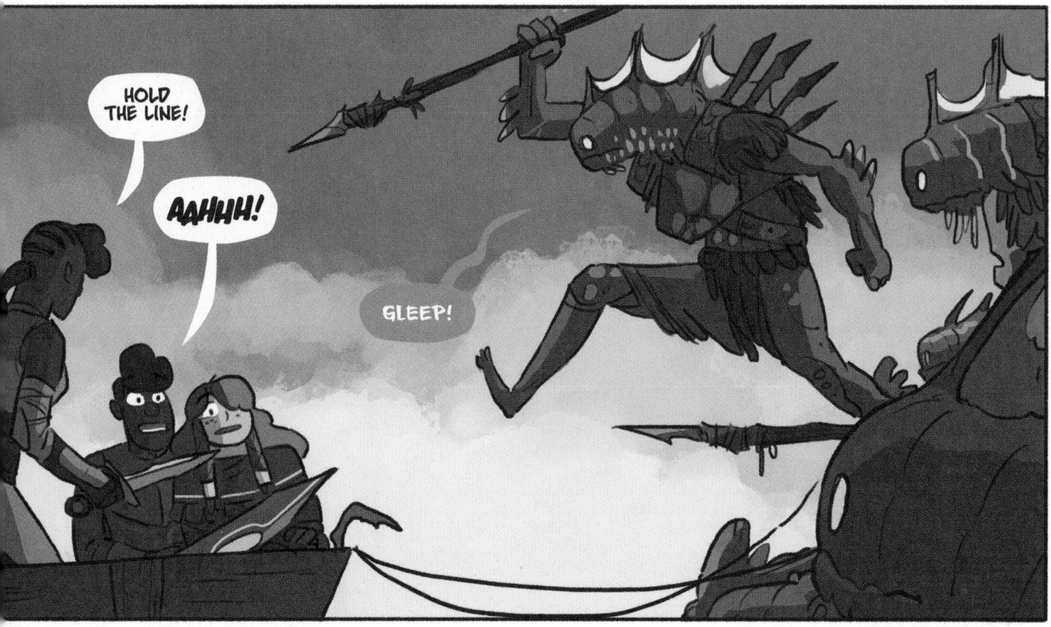
HOLD THE LINE!
AAHHH!
GLEEP!

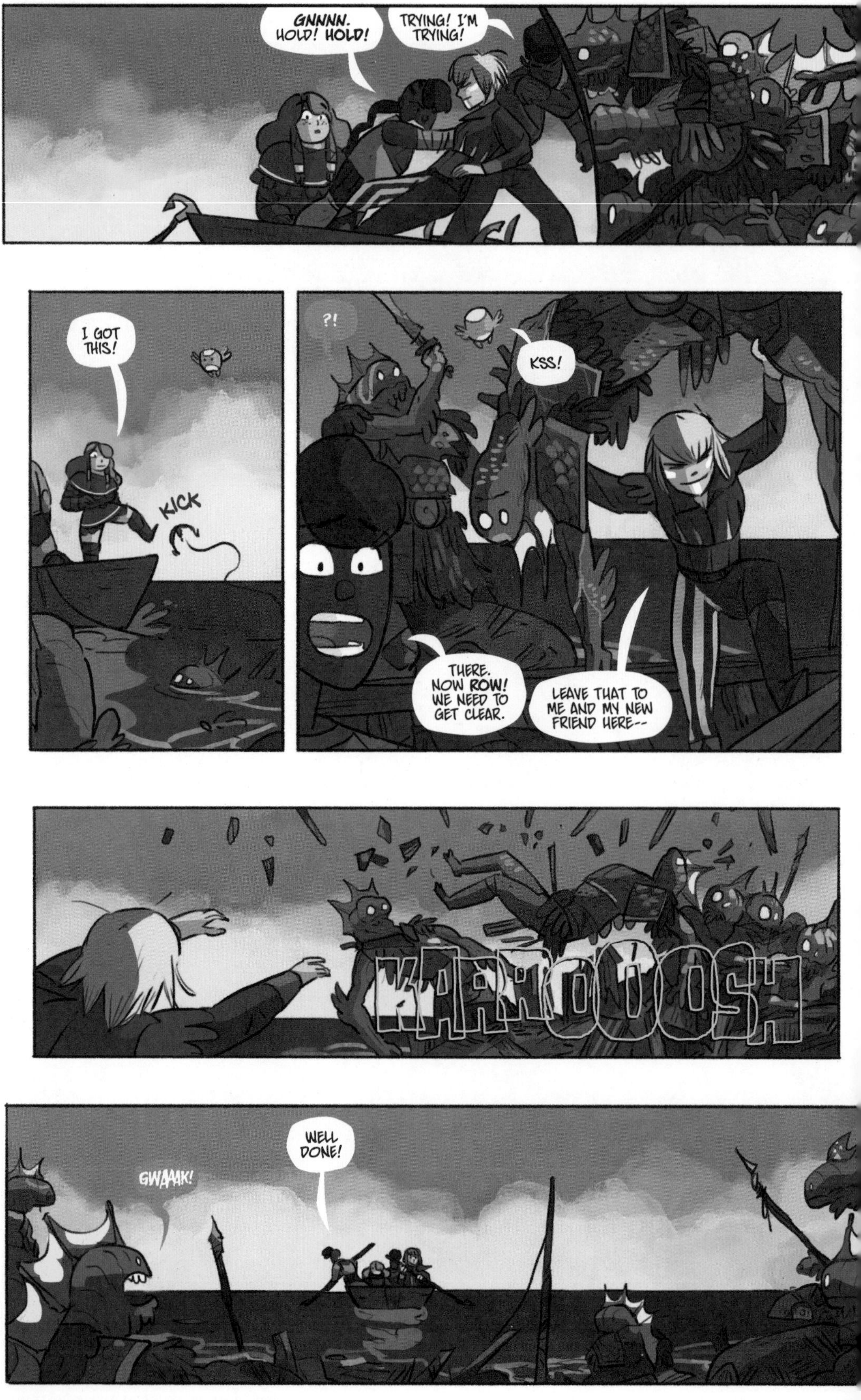
GNNNN. HOLD! HOLD!
TRYING! I'M TRYING!
I GOT THIS!
KICK
?!
KSS!
THERE. NOW ROW! WE NEED TO GET CLEAR.
LEAVE THAT TO ME AND MY NEW FRIEND HERE--
KARHOOOSH
GWAAAK!
WELL DONE!

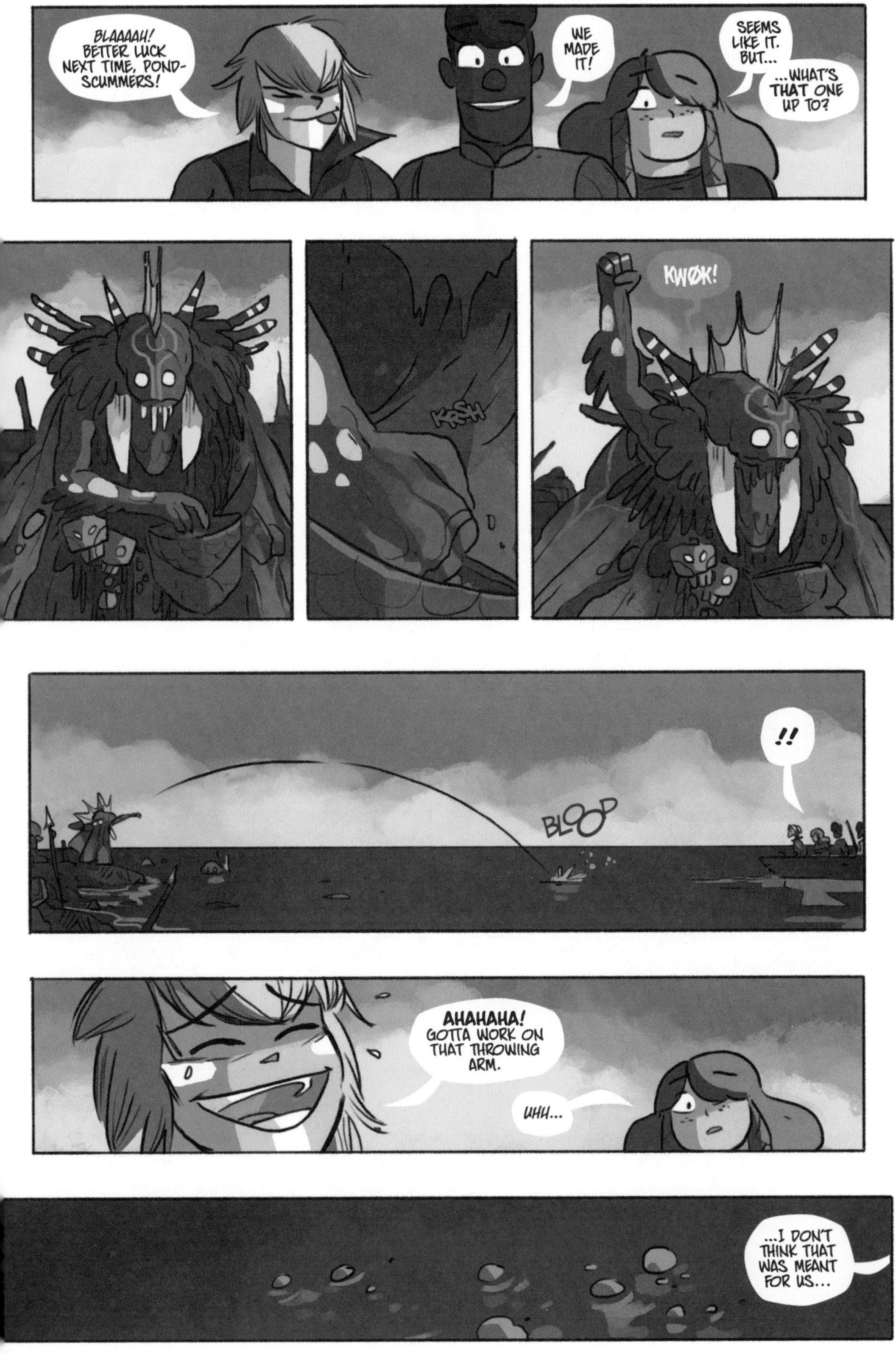
BLAAAAH! BETTER LUCK NEXT TIME, POND-SCUMMERS!
WE MADE IT!
SEEMS LIKE IT. BUT...
...WHAT'S THAT ONE UP TO?
KRSH
KWØK!
!!
BLOOP
AHAHAHA! GOTTA WORK ON THAT THROWING ARM.
UHH...
...I DON'T THINK THAT WAS MEANT FOR US...

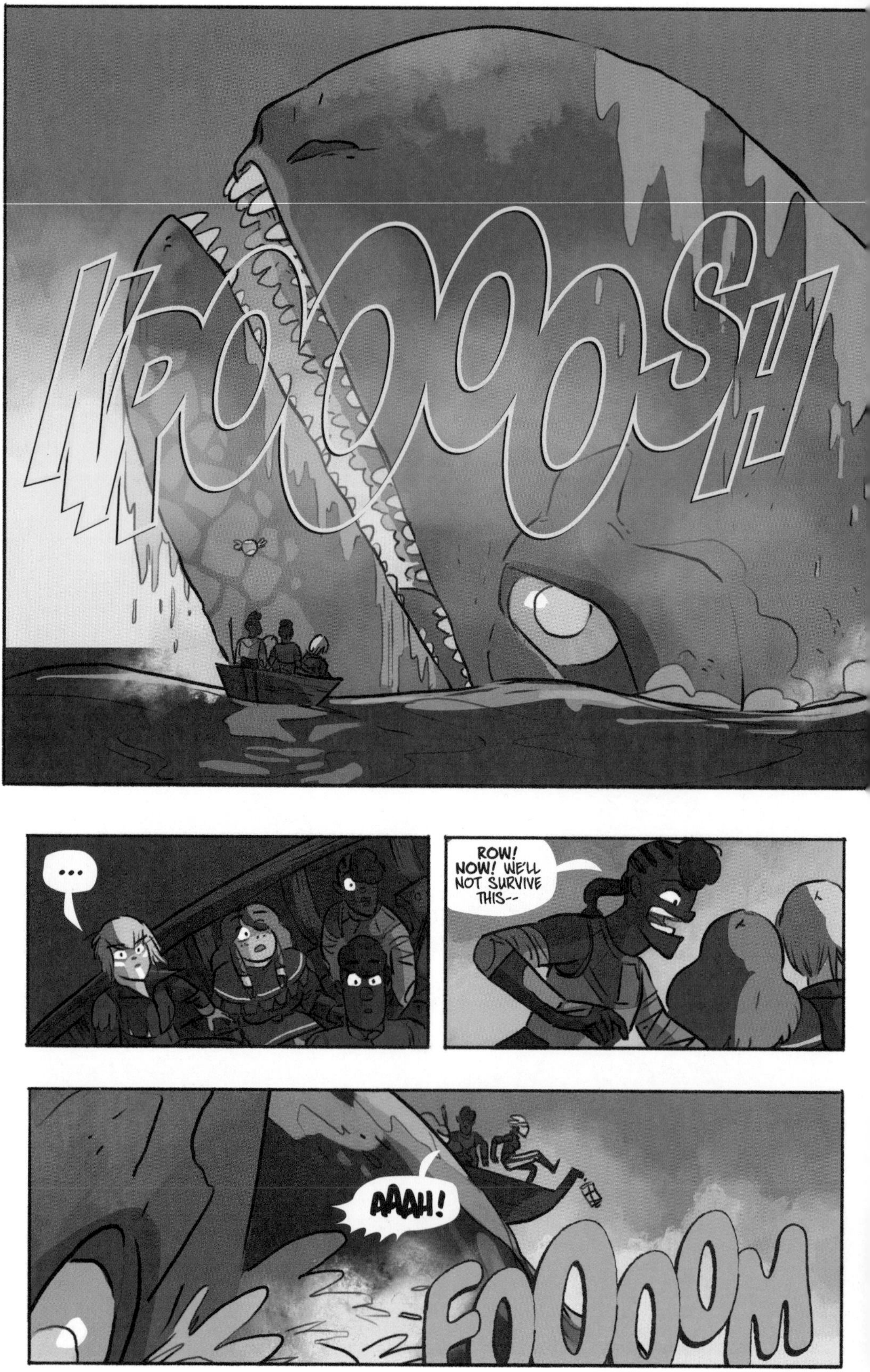

KROOOOOSH
...
ROW! NOW! WE'LL NOT SURVIVE THIS--
AAAH!
FOOOOM

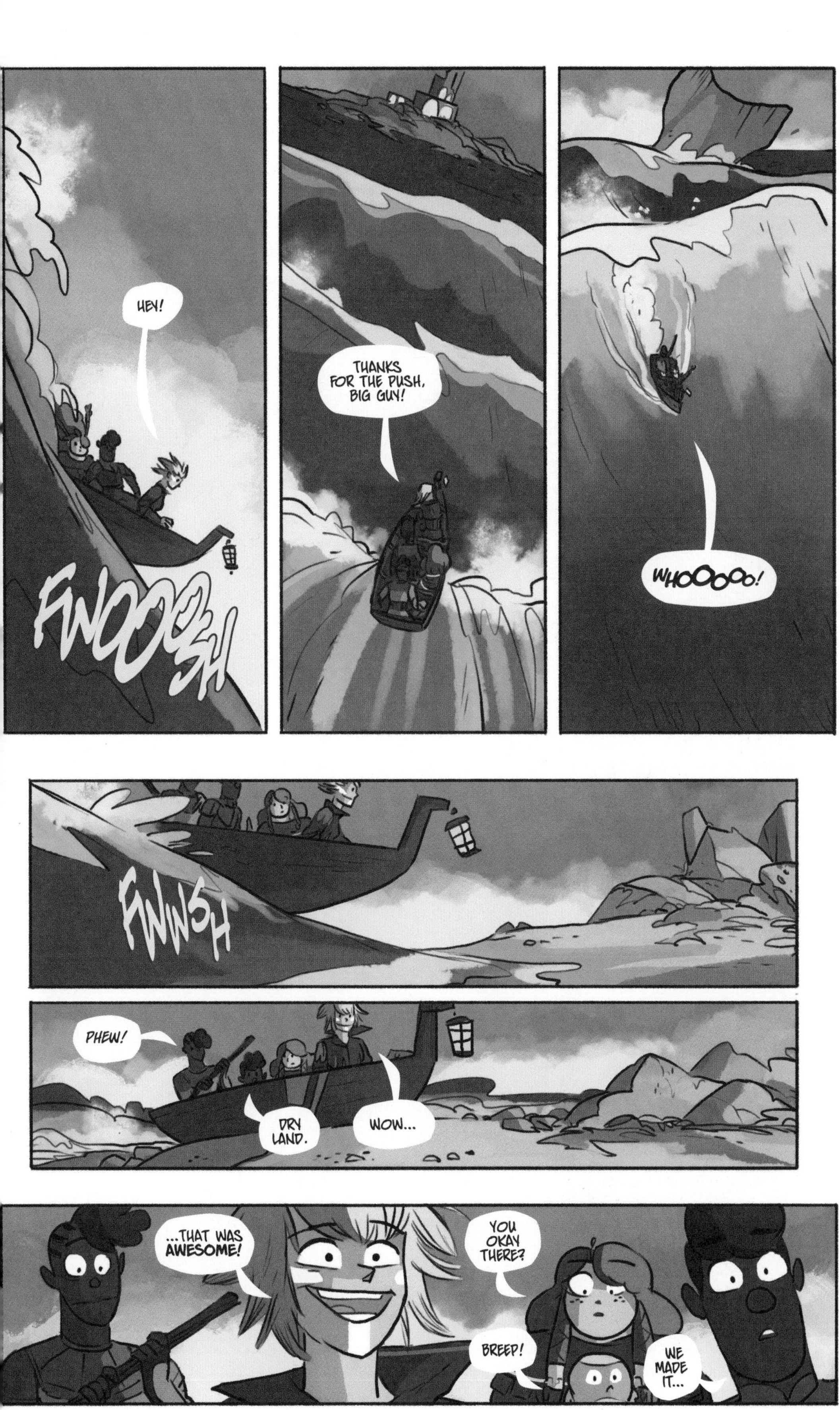
HEY!
FWOOOSH
THANKS FOR THE PUSH, BIG GUY!
WHOOOOOO!
FWNSH
PHEW!
DRY LAND.
WOW...
...THAT WAS AWESOME!
YOU OKAY THERE?
BREEP!
WE MADE IT...

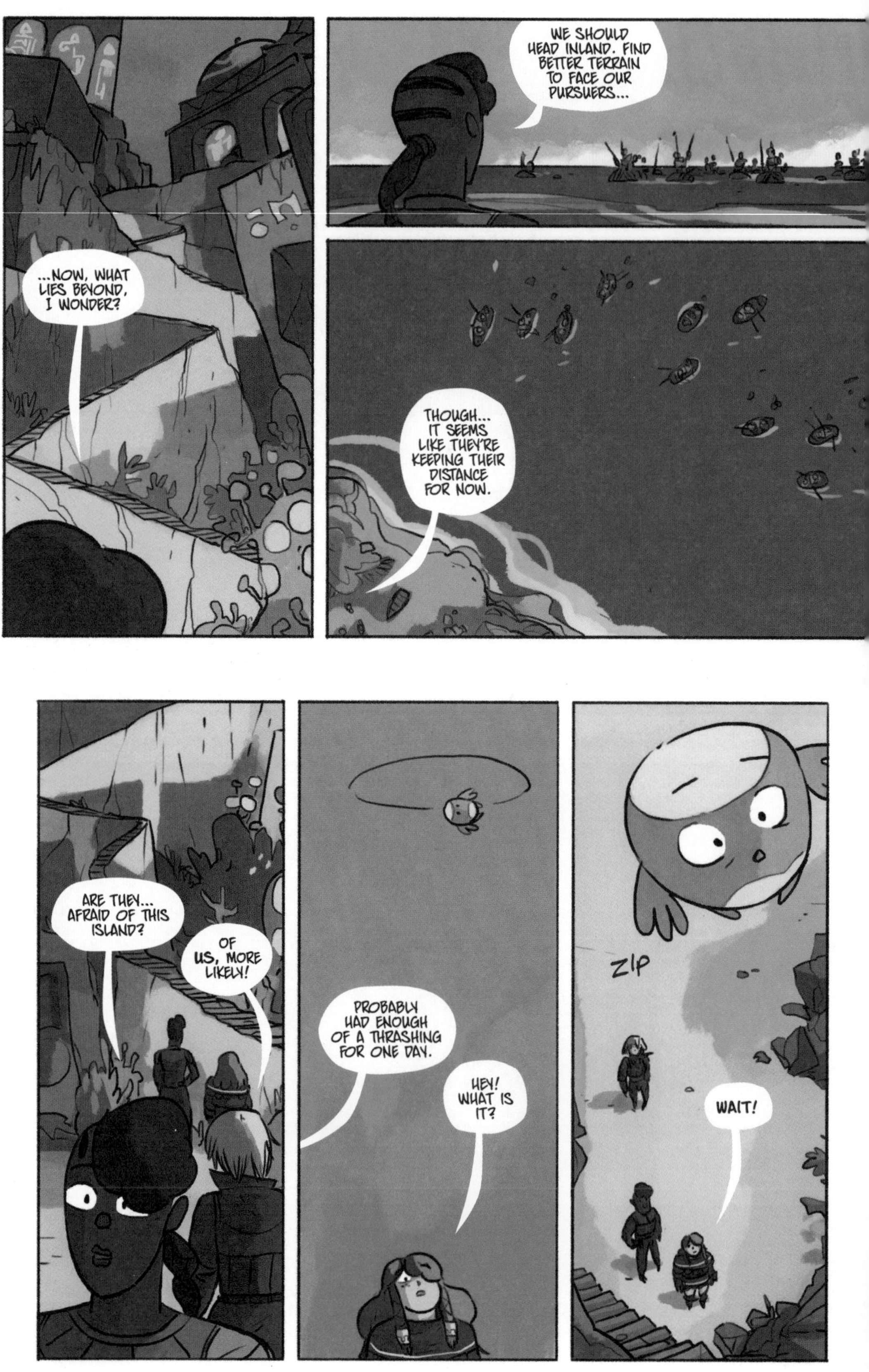
WE SHOULD HEAD INLAND. FIND BETTER TERRAIN TO FACE OUR PURSUERS...
...NOW, WHAT LIES BEYOND, I WONDER?
THOUGH... IT SEEMS LIKE THEY'RE KEEPING THEIR DISTANCE FOR NOW.
ARE THEY... AFRAID OF THIS ISLAND?
OF US, MORE LIKELY!
PROBABLY HAD ENOUGH OF A THRASHING FOR ONE DAY.
HEY! WHAT IS IT?
ZIP
WAIT!

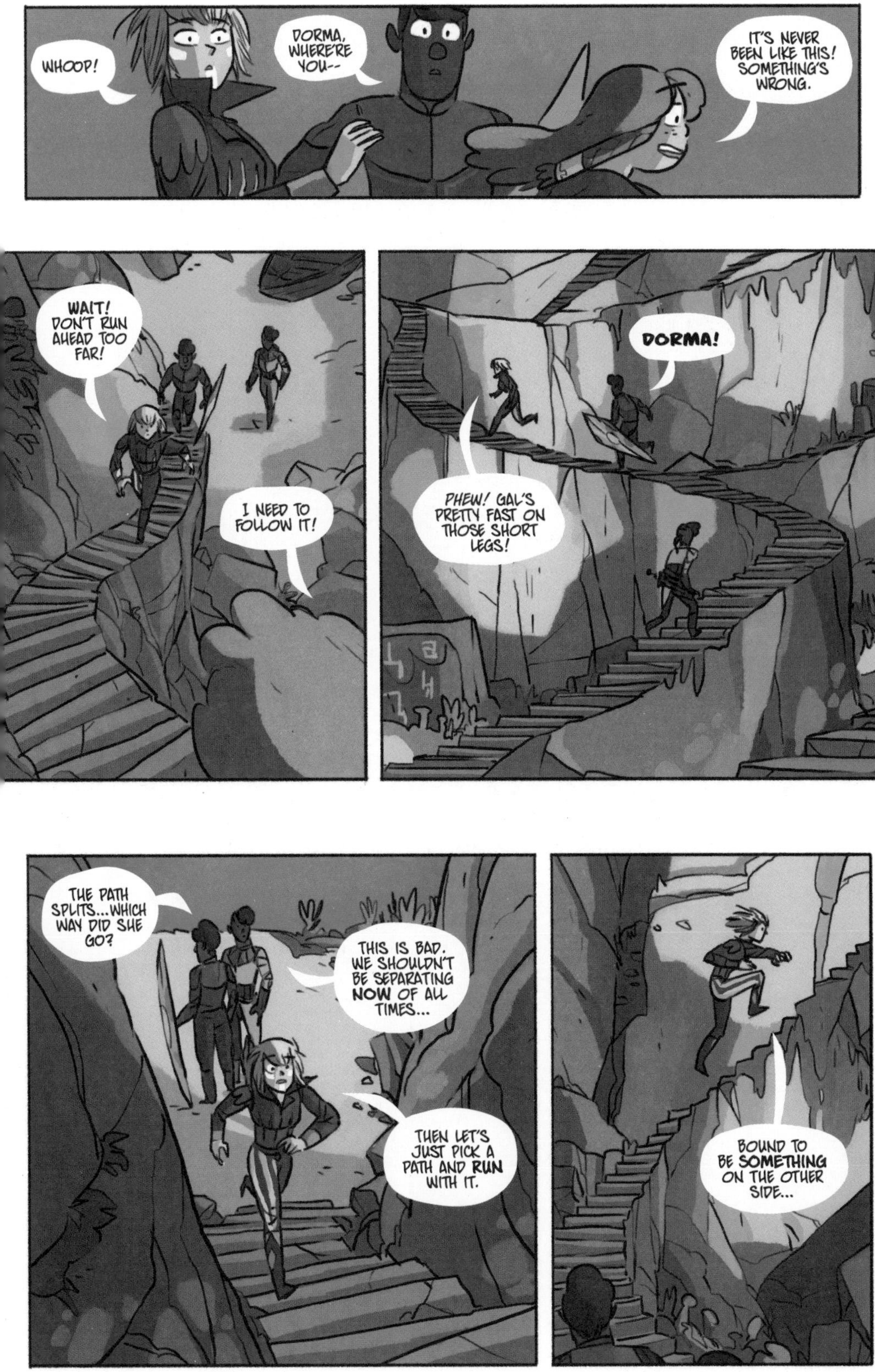

WHOOP!
DORMA, WHERE'RE YOU--
IT'S NEVER BEEN LIKE THIS! SOMETHING'S WRONG.
WAIT! DON'T RUN AHEAD TOO FAR!
I NEED TO FOLLOW IT!
DORMA!
PHEW! GAL'S PRETTY FAST ON THOSE SHORT LEGS!
THE PATH SPLITS...WHICH WAY DID SHE GO?
THIS IS BAD. WE SHOULDN'T BE SEPARATING NOW OF ALL TIMES...
THEN LET'S JUST PICK A PATH AND RUN WITH IT.
BOUND TO BE SOMETHING ON THE OTHER SIDE...

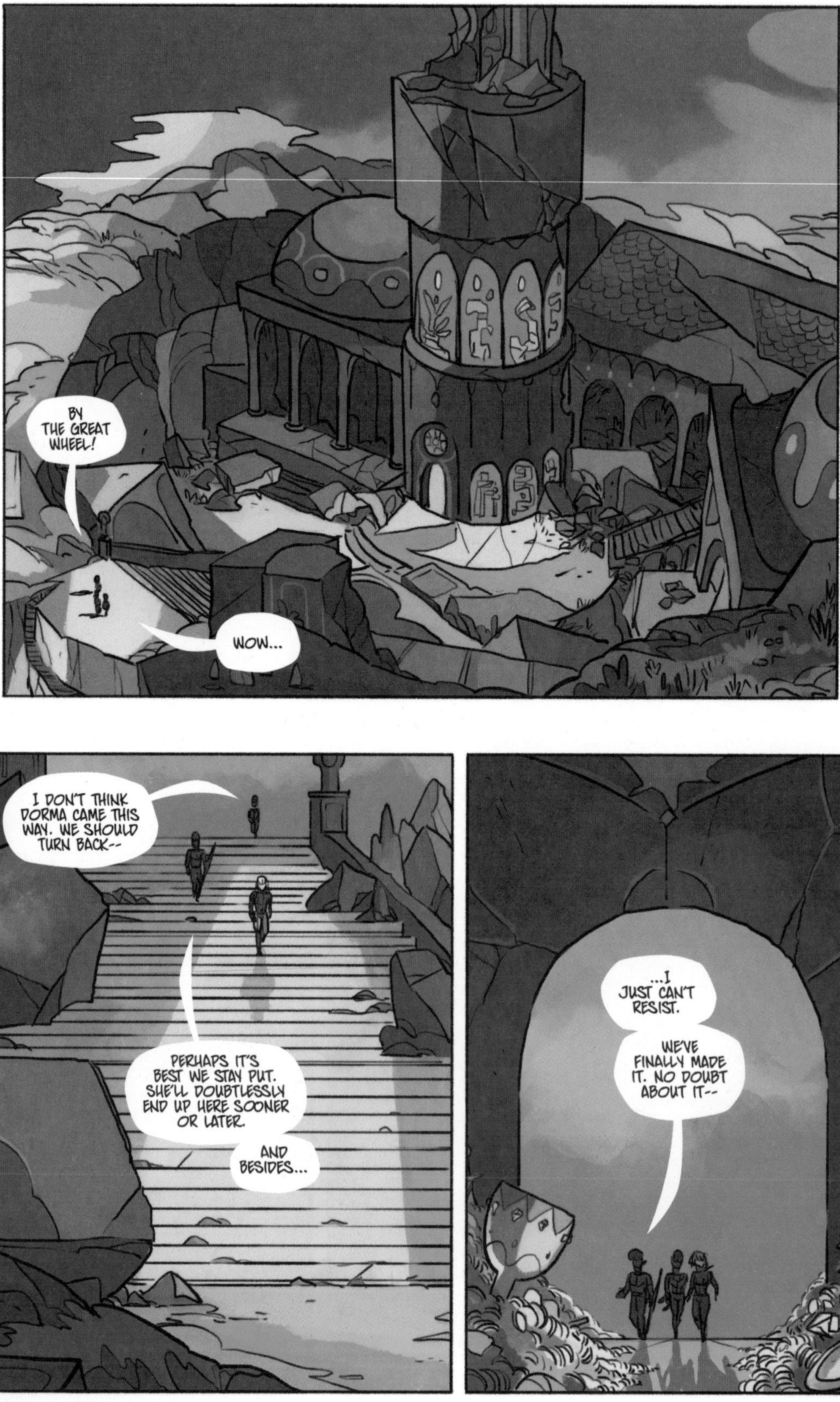
BY THE GREAT WHEEL!
WOW...
I DON'T THINK DORMA CAME THIS WAY. WE SHOULD TURN BACK--
PERHAPS IT'S BEST WE STAY PUT. SHE'LL DOUBTLESSLY END UP HERE SOONER OR LATER.
AND BESIDES...
...I JUST CAN'T RESIST.
WE'VE FINALLY MADE IT. NO DOUBT ABOUT IT--

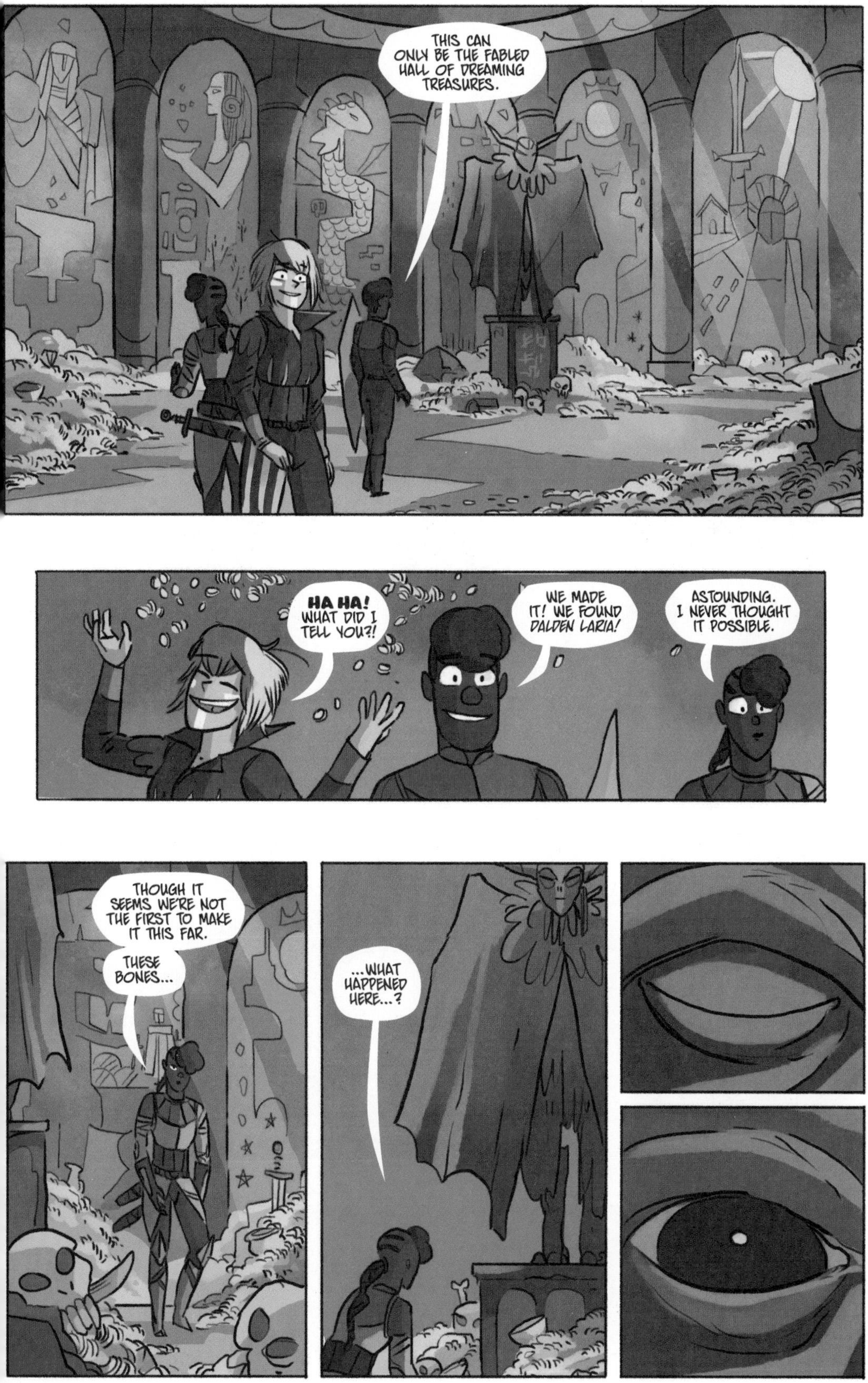

THIS CAN ONLY BE THE FABLED HALL OF DREAMING TREASURES.
HA HA! WHAT DID I TELL YOU?!
WE MADE IT! WE FOUND DALDEN LARIA!
ASTOUNDING. I NEVER THOUGHT IT POSSIBLE.
THOUGH IT SEEMS WE'RE NOT THE FIRST TO MAKE IT THIS FAR.
THESE BONES...
...WHAT HAPPENED HERE...?

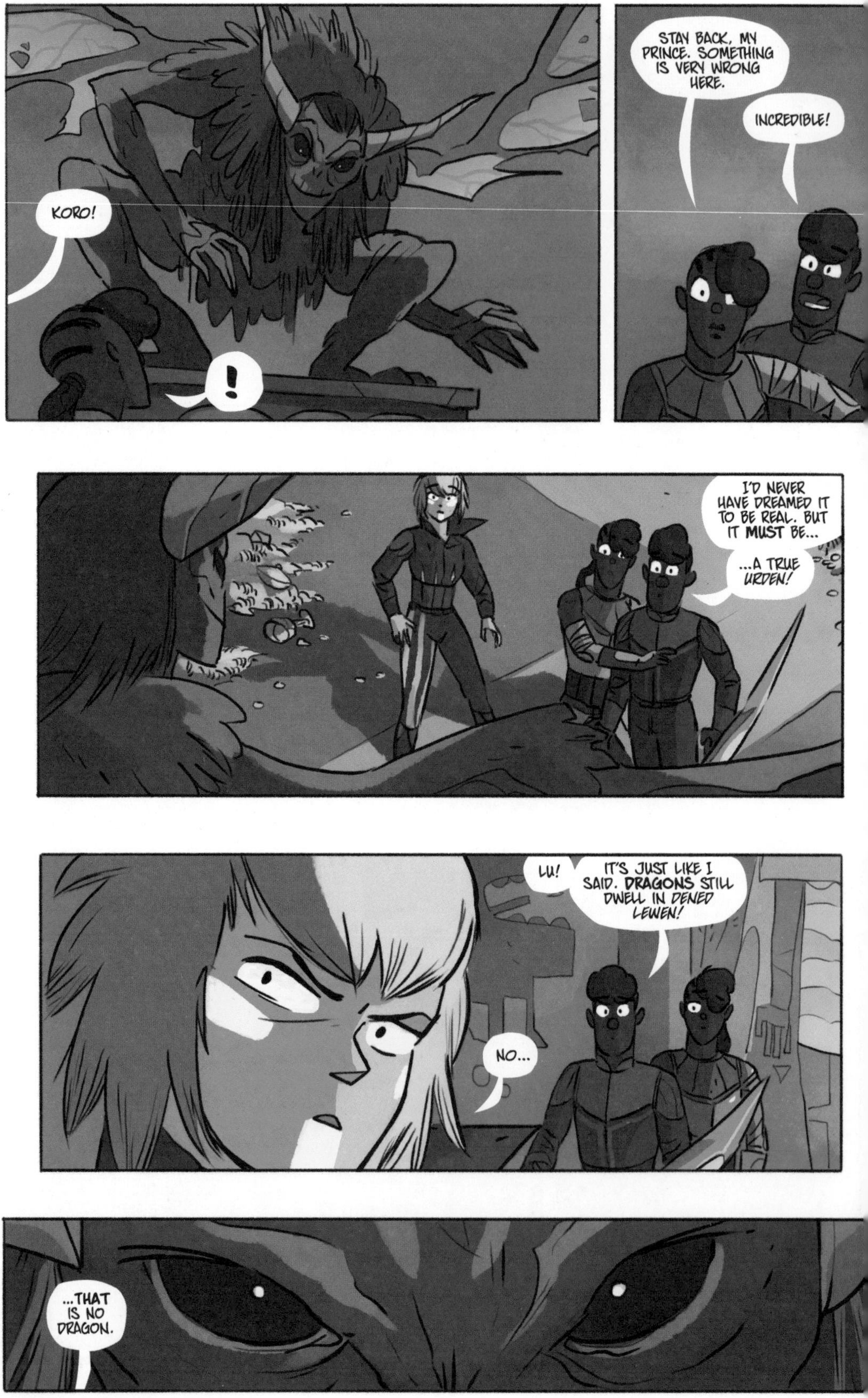
KORO!
!
STAY BACK, MY PRINCE. SOMETHING IS VERY WRONG HERE.
INCREDIBLE!
I'D NEVER HAVE DREAMED IT TO BE REAL. BUT IT MUST BE...
...A TRUE URDEN!
LU!
IT'S JUST LIKE I SAID. DRAGONS STILL DWELL IN DENED LEWEN!
NO...
...THAT IS NO DRAGON.

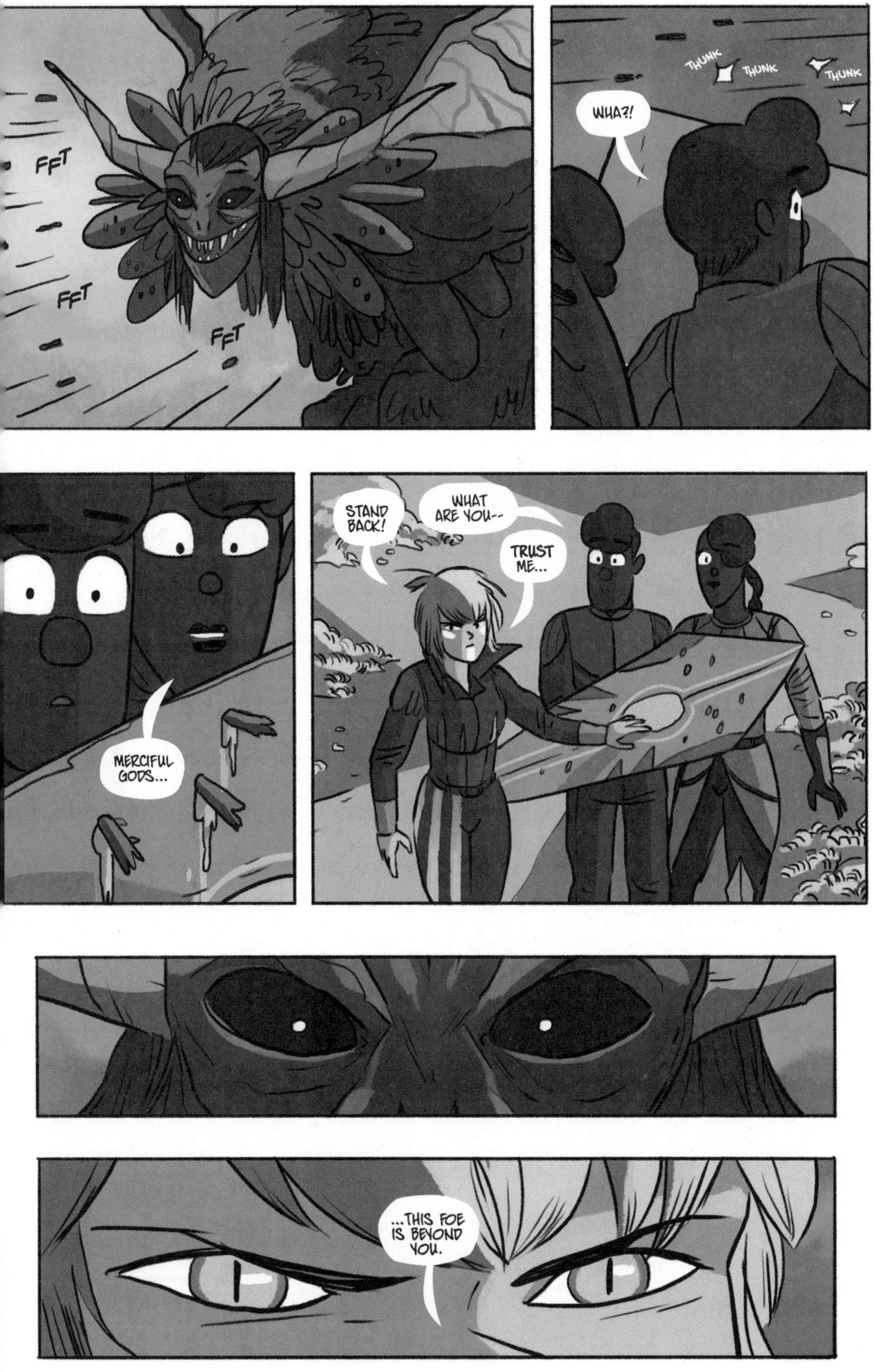
FFT
FFT
FFT
THUNK
THUNK
THUNK
WHA?!
MERCIFUL GODS...
STAND BACK!
WHAT ARE YOU--
TRUST ME...
...THIS FOE IS BEYOND YOU.

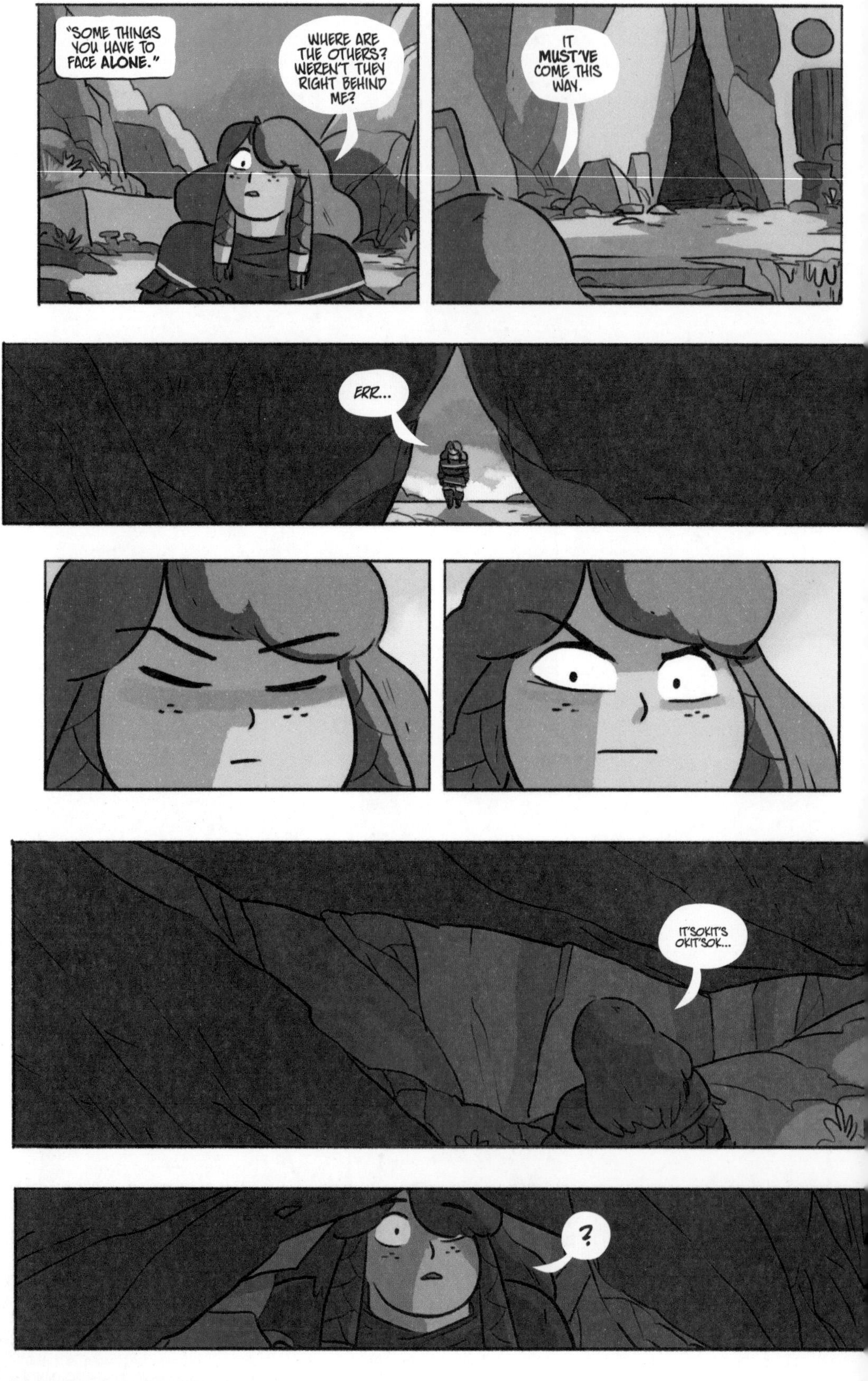
"SOME THINGS YOU HAVE TO FACE ALONE."
WHERE ARE THE OTHERS? WEREN'T THEY RIGHT BEHIND ME?
IT MUST'VE COME THIS WAY.
ERR...
IT'SOKIT'S OKIT'SOK...
?

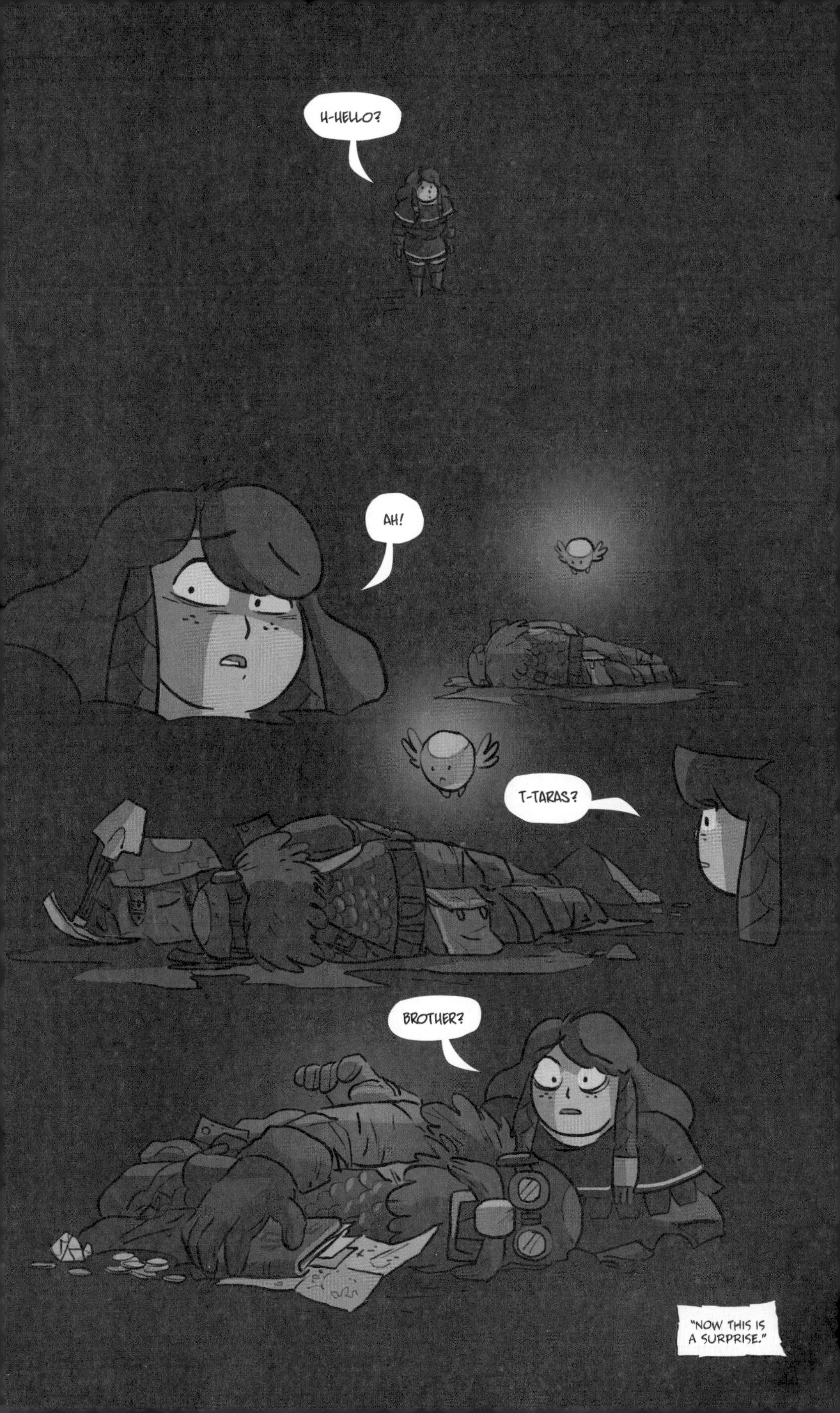
H-HELLO?
AH!
T-TARAS?
BROTHER?
"NOW THIS IS A SURPRISE."

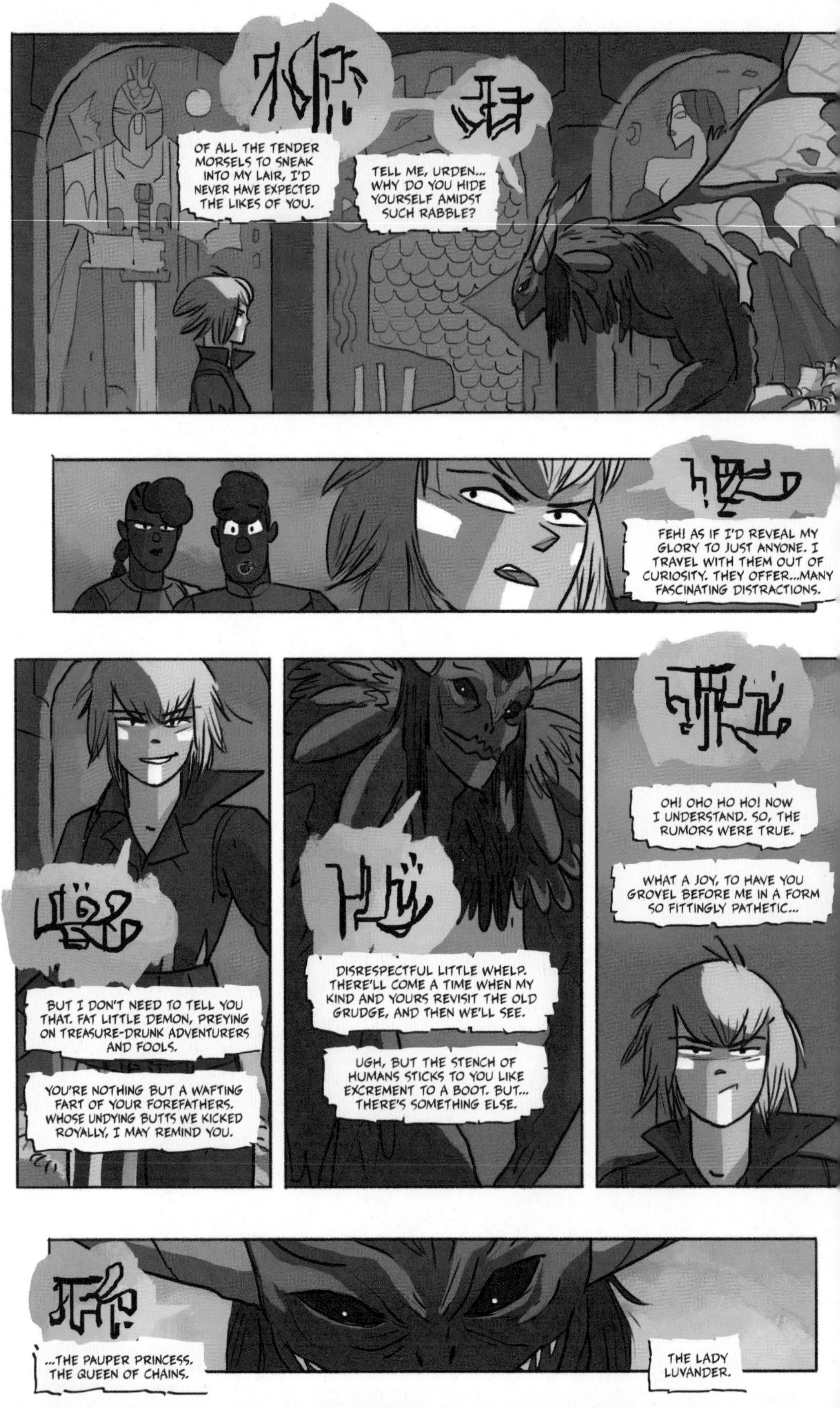

OF ALL THE TENDER MORSELS TO SNEAK INTO MY LAIR, I'D NEVER HAVE EXPECTED THE LIKES OF YOU.
TELL ME, URDEN... WHY DO YOU HIDE YOURSELF AMIDST SUCH RABBLE?
FEH! AS IF I'D REVEAL MY GLORY TO JUST ANYONE. I TRAVEL WITH THEM OUT OF CURIOSITY. THEY OFFER...MANY FASCINATING DISTRACTIONS.
BUT I DON'T NEED TO TELL YOU THAT. FAT LITTLE DEMON, PREYING ON TREASURE-DRUNK ADVENTURERS AND FOOLS.
YOU'RE NOTHING BUT A WAFTING FART OF YOUR FOREFATHERS. WHOSE UNDYING BUTTS WE KICKED ROYALLY, I MAY REMIND YOU.
DISRESPECTFUL LITTLE WHELP. THERE'LL COME A TIME WHEN MY KIND AND YOURS REVISIT THE OLD GRUDGE, AND THEN WE'LL SEE.
UGH, BUT THE STENCH OF HUMANS STICKS TO YOU LIKE EXCREMENT TO A BOOT. BUT... THERE'S SOMETHING ELSE.
OH! OHO HO HO! NOW I UNDERSTAND. SO, THE RUMORS WERE TRUE.
WHAT A JOY, TO HAVE YOU GROVEL BEFORE ME IN A FORM SO FITTINGLY PATHETIC...
...THE PAUPER PRINCESS. THE QUEEN OF CHAINS.
THE LADY LUVANDER.

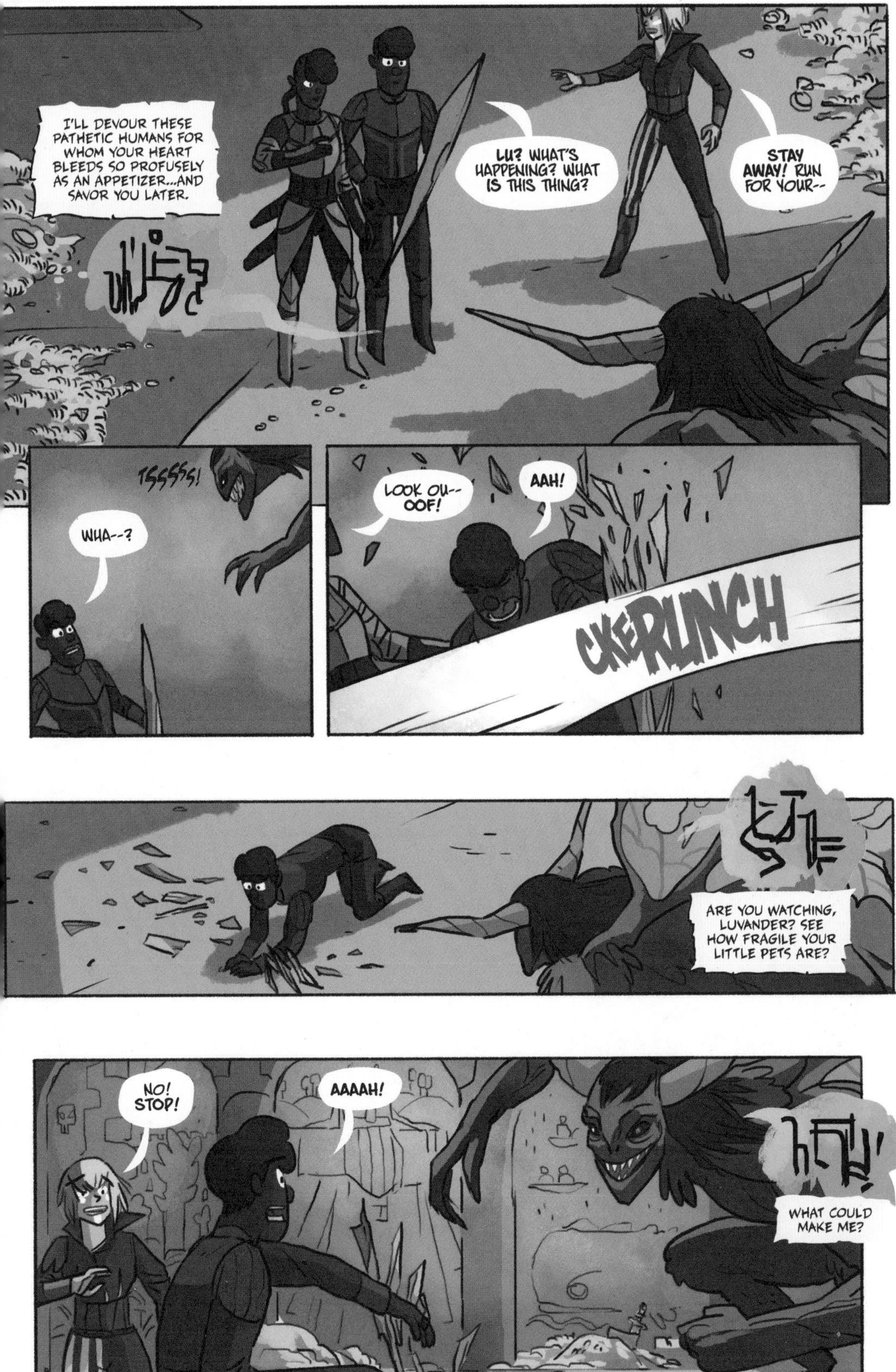
I'LL DEVOUR THESE PATHETIC HUMANS FOR WHOM YOUR HEART BLEEDS SO PROFUSELY AS AN APPETIZER...AND SAVOR YOU LATER.
LU? WHAT'S HAPPENING? WHAT IS THIS THING?
STAY AWAY! RUN FOR YOUR--
TSSSSS!
WHA--?
LOOK OU-- OOF!
AAH!
CKERUNCH
ARE YOU WATCHING, LUVANDER? SEE HOW FRAGILE YOUR LITTLE PETS ARE?
NO! STOP!
AAAAH!
WHAT COULD MAKE ME?

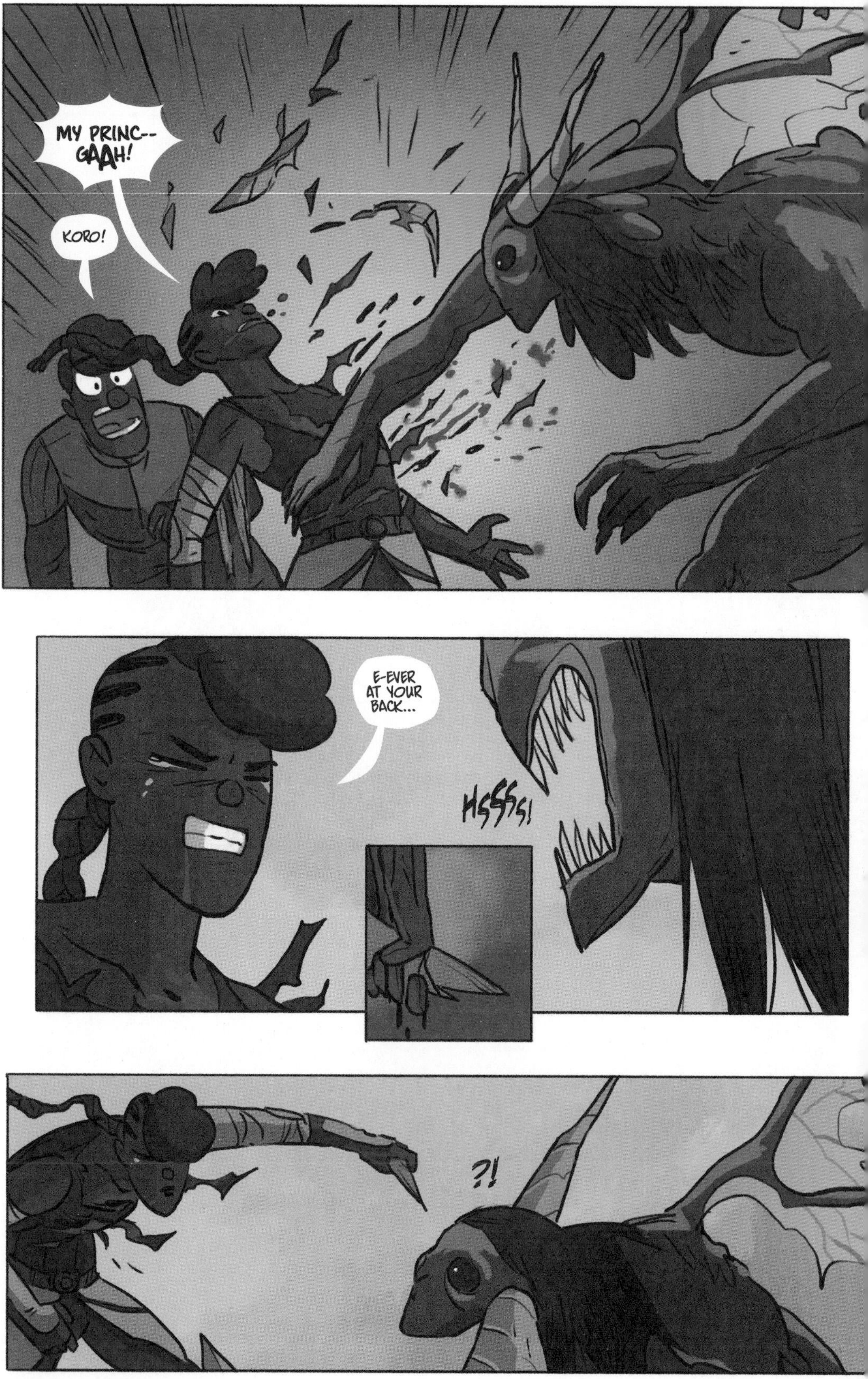
MY PRINC--
GAAH!
KORO!
E-EVER AT YOUR BACK...
HSSSS!
?!

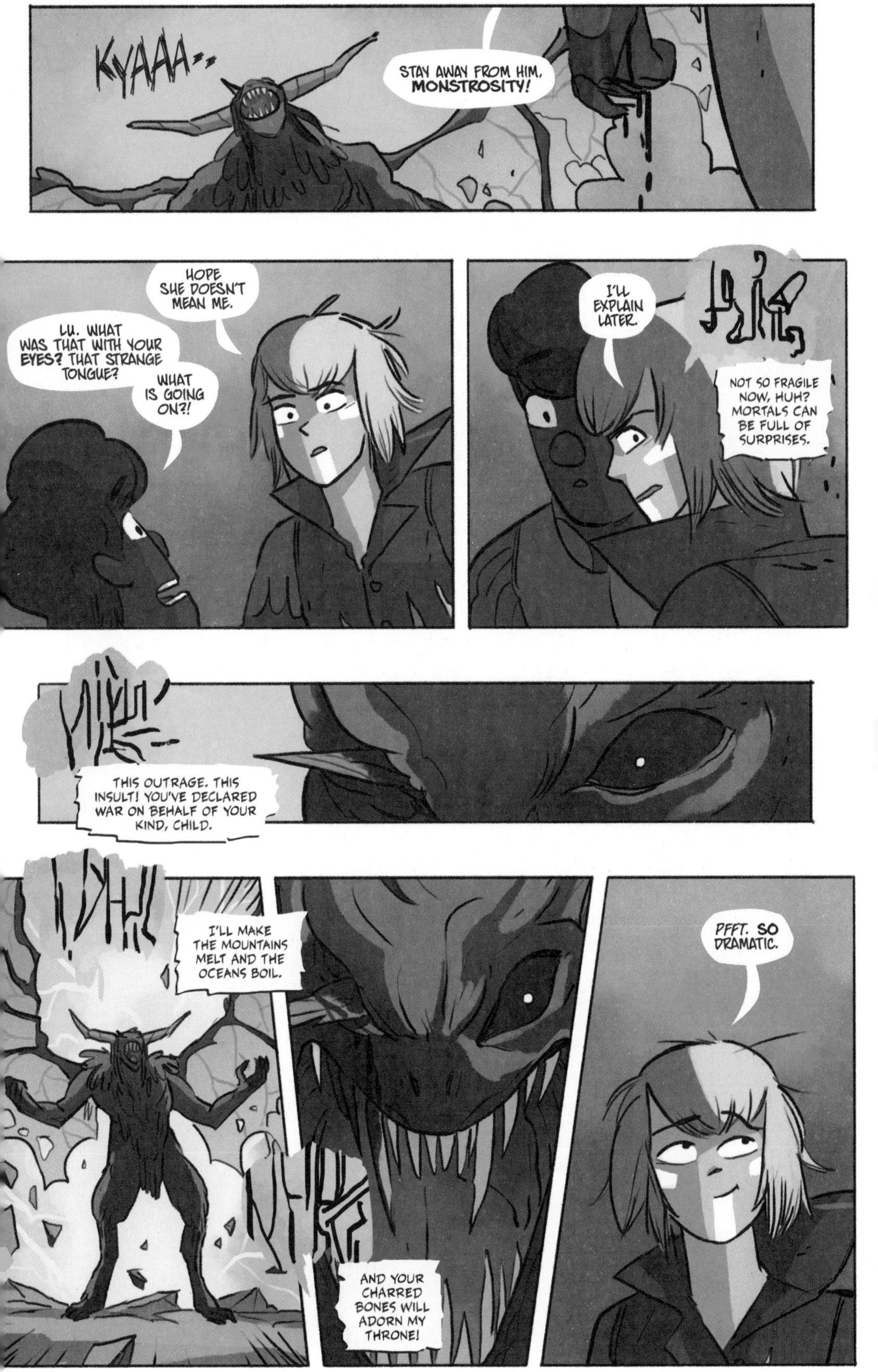
KYAAA-
STAY AWAY FROM HIM, MONSTROSITY!
HOPE SHE DOESN'T MEAN ME.
LU. WHAT WAS THAT WITH YOUR EYES? THAT STRANGE TONGUE?
WHAT IS GOING ON?!
I'LL EXPLAIN LATER.
NOT SO FRAGILE NOW, HUH? MORTALS CAN BE FULL OF SURPRISES.
THIS OUTRAGE. THIS INSULT! YOU'VE DECLARED WAR ON BEHALF OF YOUR KIND, CHILD.
I'LL MAKE THE MOUNTAINS MELT AND THE OCEANS BOIL.
AND YOUR CHARRED BONES WILL ADORN MY THRONE!
PFFT. SO DRAMATIC.

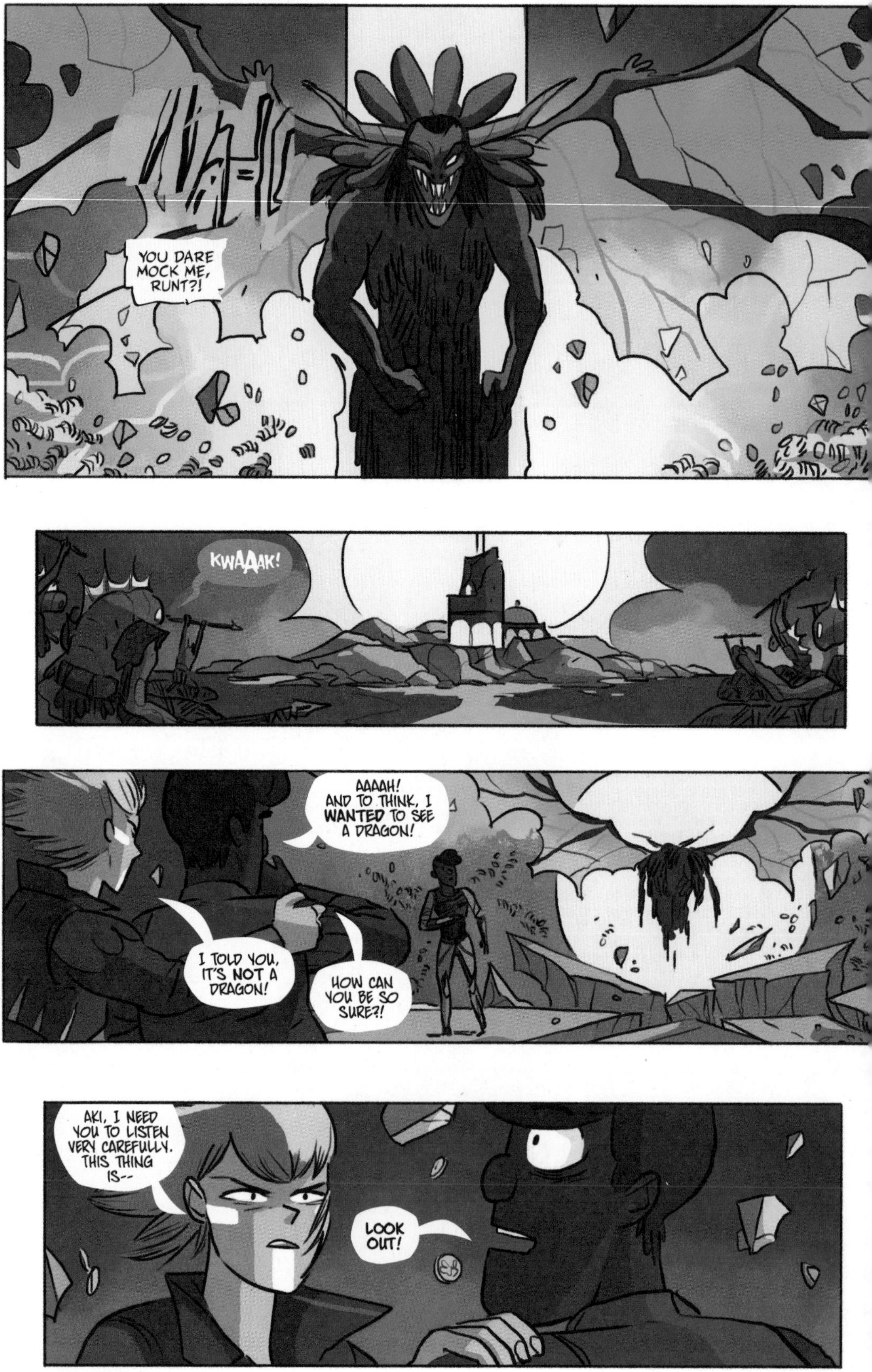
YOU DARE MOCK ME, RUNT?!
KWAAAAK!
AAAAH! AND TO THINK, I WANTED TO SEE A DRAGON!
I TOLD YOU, IT'S NOT A DRAGON!
HOW CAN YOU BE SO SURE?!
AKI, I NEED YOU TO LISTEN VERY CAREFULLY. THIS THING IS--
LOOK OUT!

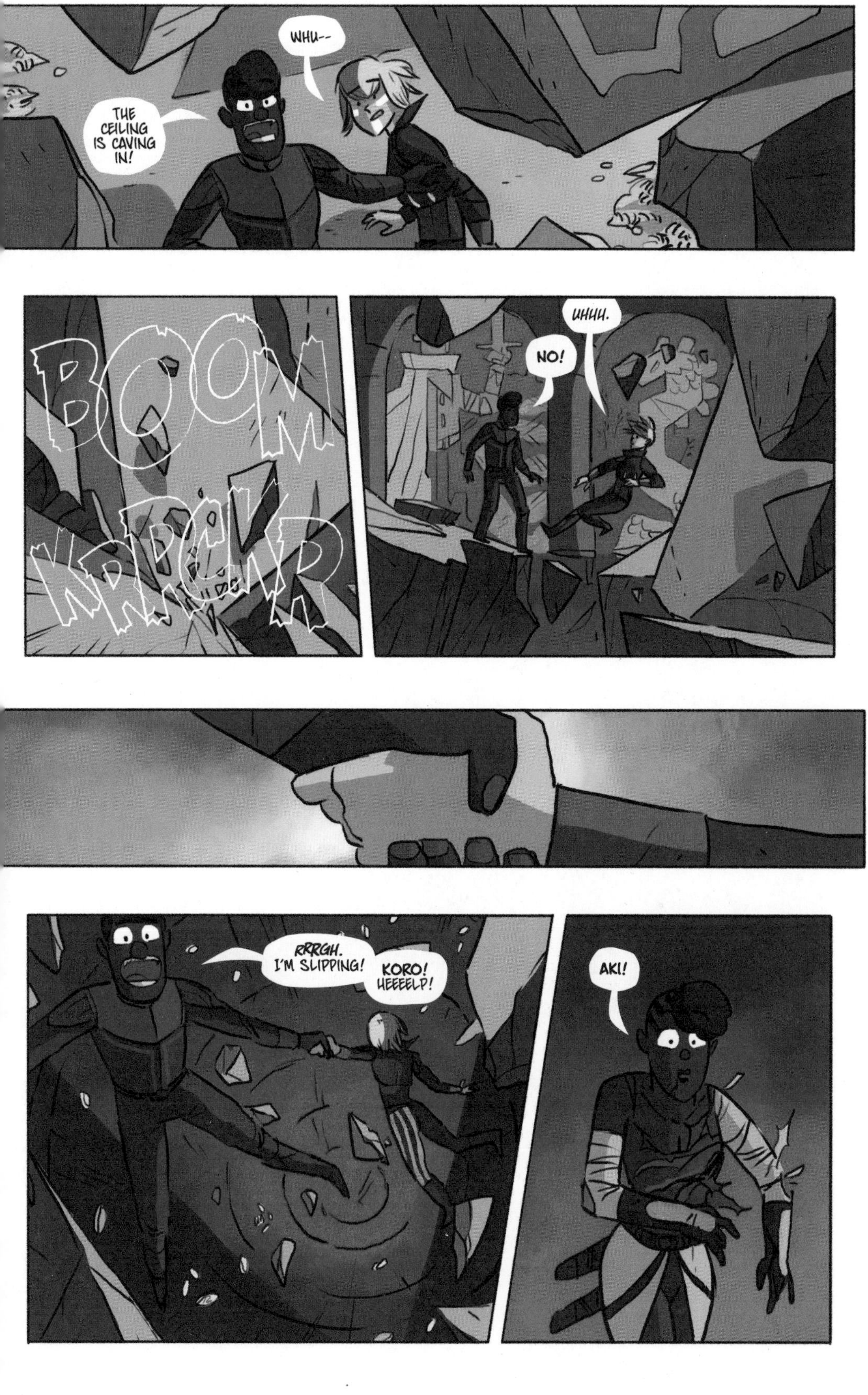
WHU--
THE CEILING IS CAVING IN!
BOOM
KRRCHK
NO!
UHHH.
RRRGH. I'M SLIPPING!
KORO! HEEEELP!
AKI!

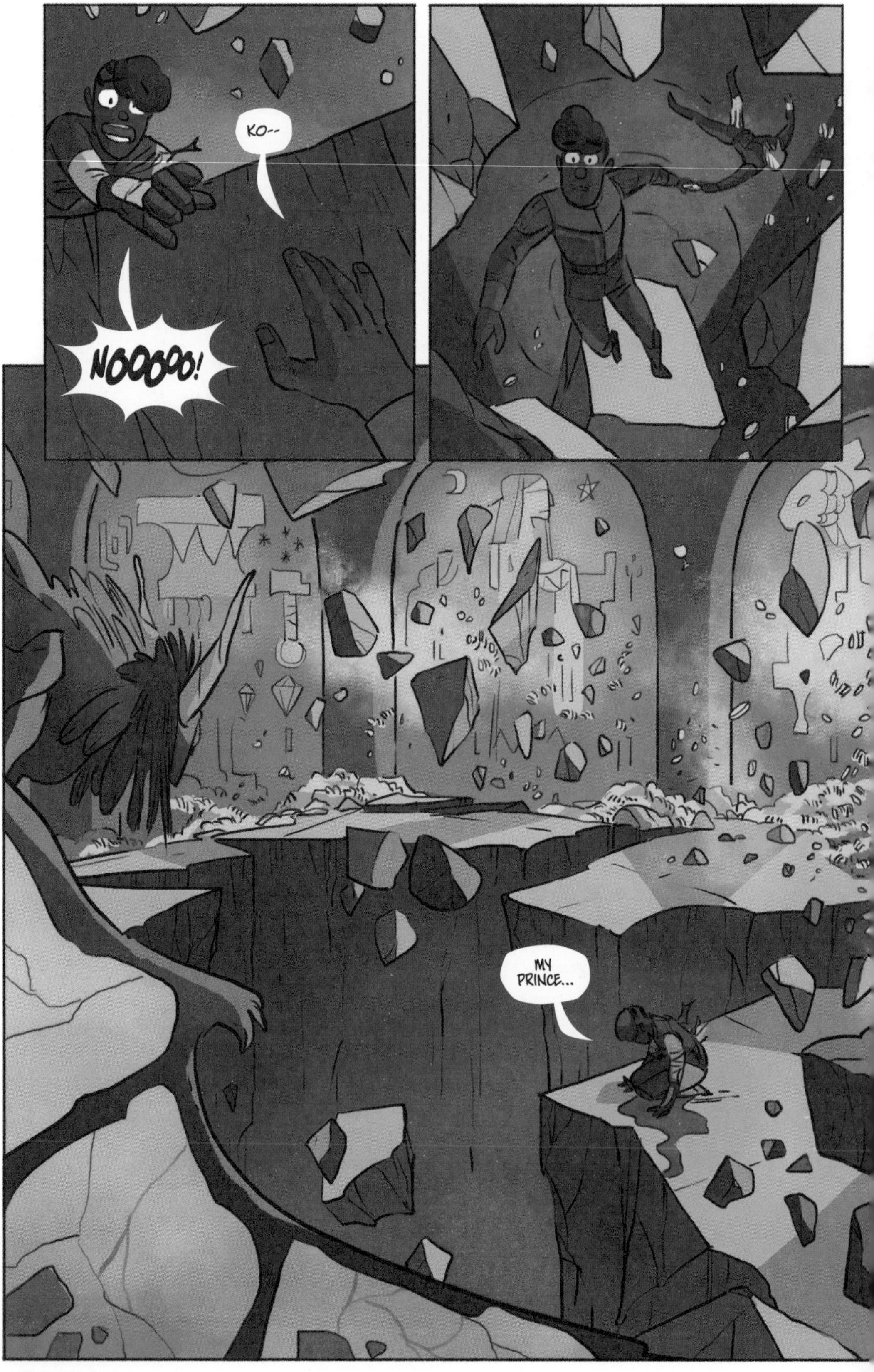
KO--
NOOOOO!
MY PRINCE...

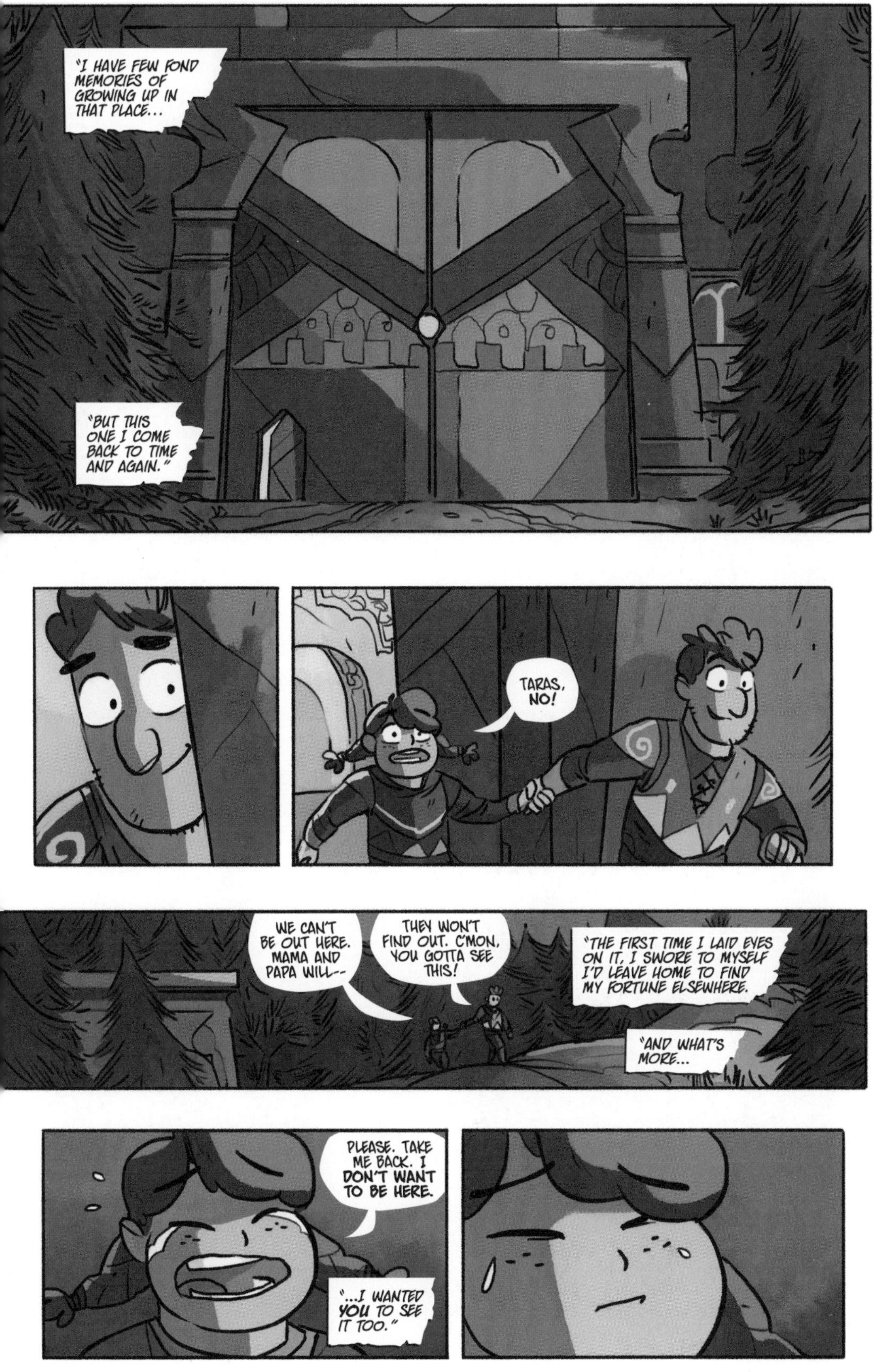
"I HAVE FEW FOND MEMORIES OF GROWING UP IN THAT PLACE...
"BUT THIS ONE I COME BACK TO TIME AND AGAIN."
TARAS, NO!
WE CAN'T BE OUT HERE. MAMA AND PAPA WILL--
THEY WON'T FIND OUT. C'MON, YOU GOTTA SEE THIS!
"THE FIRST TIME I LAID EYES ON IT, I SWORE TO MYSELF I'D LEAVE HOME TO FIND MY FORTUNE ELSEWHERE.
"AND WHAT'S MORE...
PLEASE. TAKE ME BACK. I DON'T WANT TO BE HERE.
"...I WANTED YOU TO SEE IT TOO."

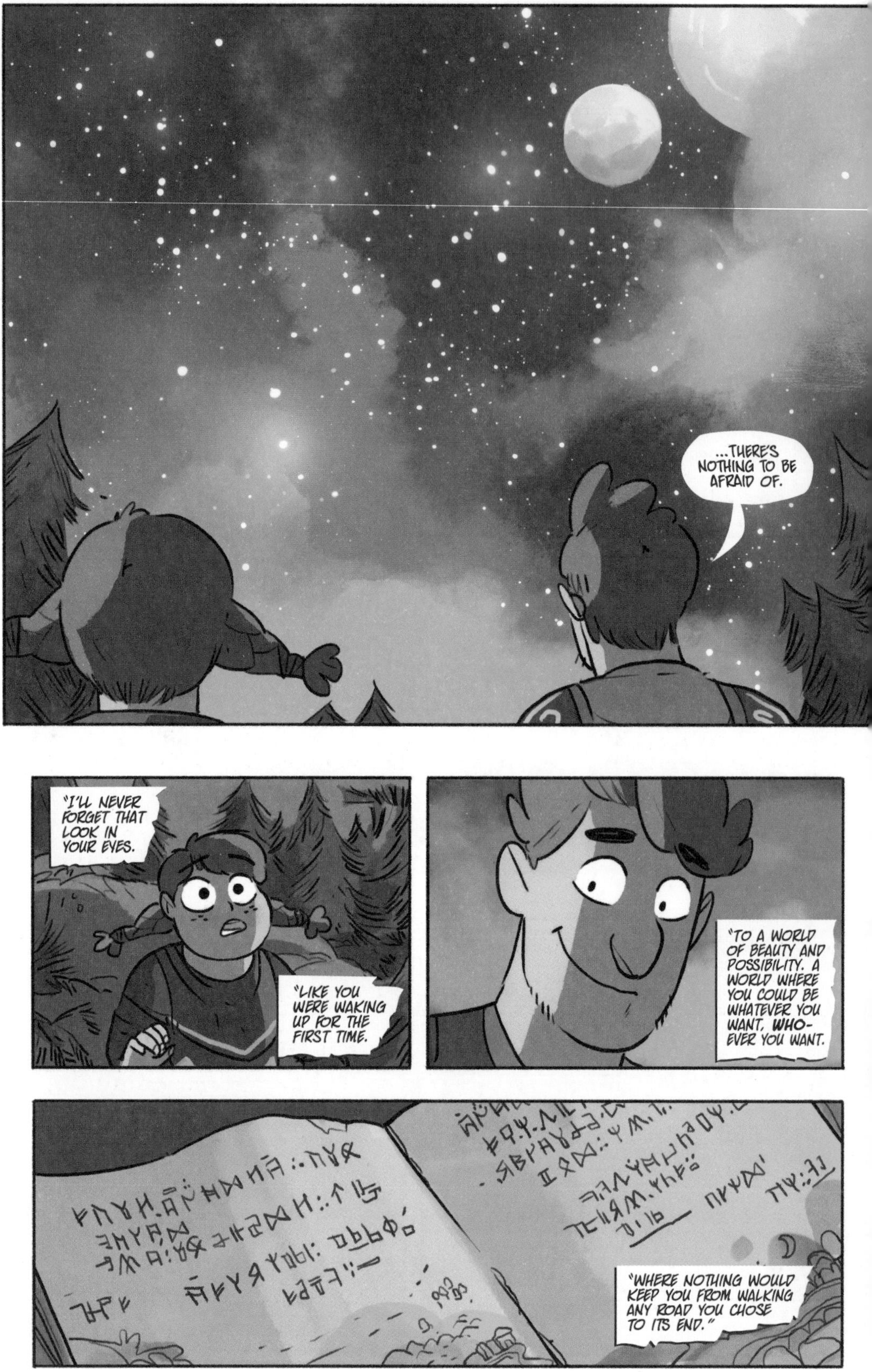
...THERE'S NOTHING TO BE AFRAID OF.
"I'LL NEVER FORGET THAT LOOK IN YOUR EYES.
"LIKE YOU WERE WAKING UP FOR THE FIRST TIME.
"TO A WORLD OF BEAUTY AND POSSIBILITY. A WORLD WHERE YOU COULD BE WHATEVER YOU WANT, WHO-EVER YOU WANT.
"WHERE NOTHING WOULD KEEP YOU FROM WALKING ANY ROAD YOU CHOSE TO ITS END."

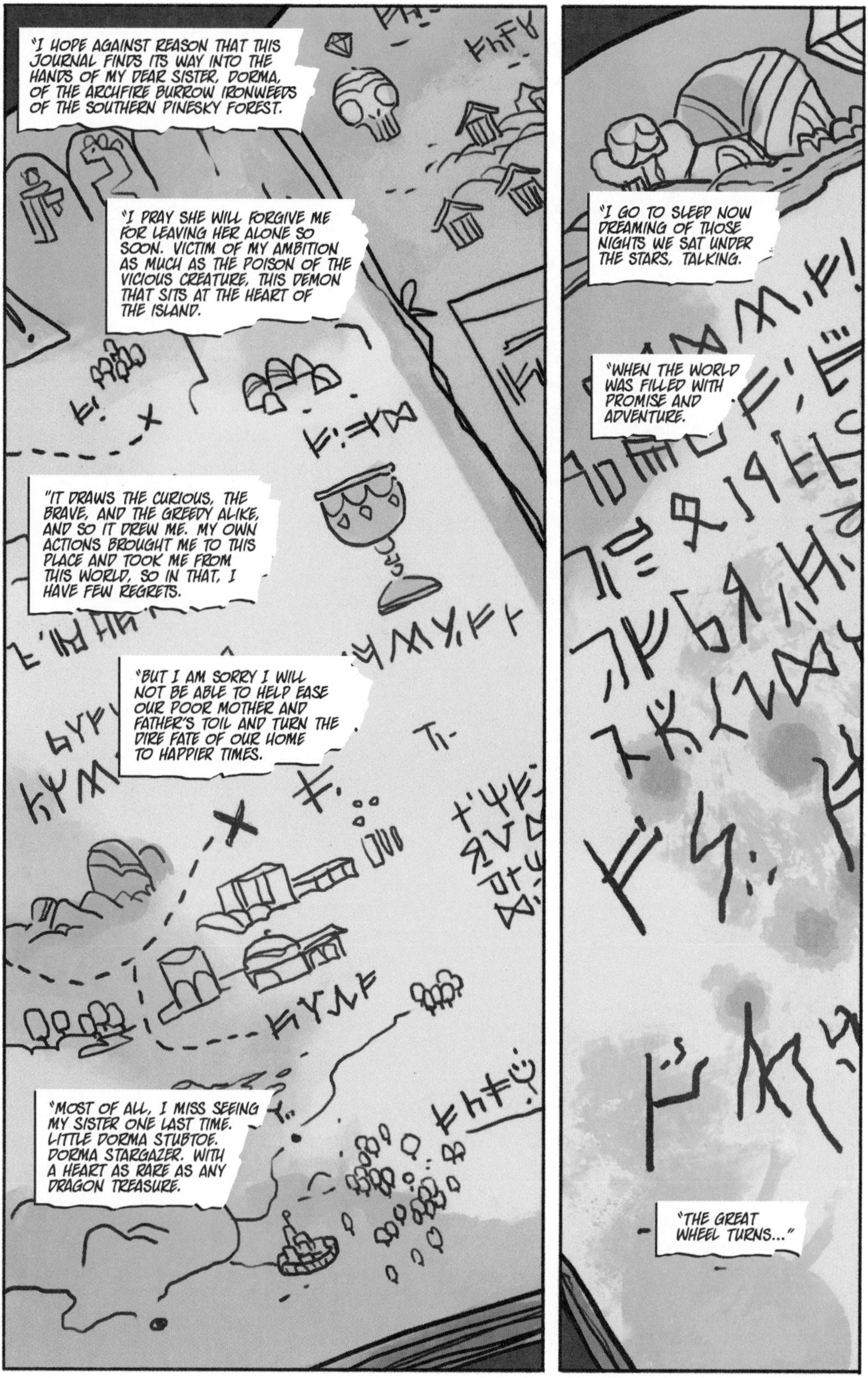
"I HOPE AGAINST REASON THAT THIS JOURNAL FINDS ITS WAY INTO THE HANDS OF MY DEAR SISTER, DORMA, OF THE ARCHFIRE BURROW IRONWEEDS OF THE SOUTHERN PINESKY FOREST.
"I PRAY SHE WILL FORGIVE ME FOR LEAVING HER ALONE SO SOON. VICTIM OF MY AMBITION AS MUCH AS THE POISON OF THE VICIOUS CREATURE, THIS DEMON THAT SITS AT THE HEART OF THE ISLAND.
"IT DRAWS THE CURIOUS, THE BRAVE, AND THE GREEDY ALIKE, AND SO IT DREW ME. MY OWN ACTIONS BROUGHT ME TO THIS PLACE AND TOOK ME FROM THIS WORLD, SO IN THAT, I HAVE FEW REGRETS.
"BUT I AM SORRY I WILL NOT BE ABLE TO HELP EASE OUR POOR MOTHER AND FATHER'S TOIL AND TURN THE DIRE FATE OF OUR HOME TO HAPPIER TIMES.
"MOST OF ALL, I MISS SEEING MY SISTER ONE LAST TIME. LITTLE DORMA STUBTOE. DORMA STARGAZER. WITH A HEART AS RARE AS ANY DRAGON TREASURE.
"I GO TO SLEEP NOW DREAMING OF THOSE NIGHTS WE SAT UNDER THE STARS, TALKING.
"WHEN THE WORLD WAS FILLED WITH PROMISE AND ADVENTURE.
"THE GREAT WHEEL TURNS..."

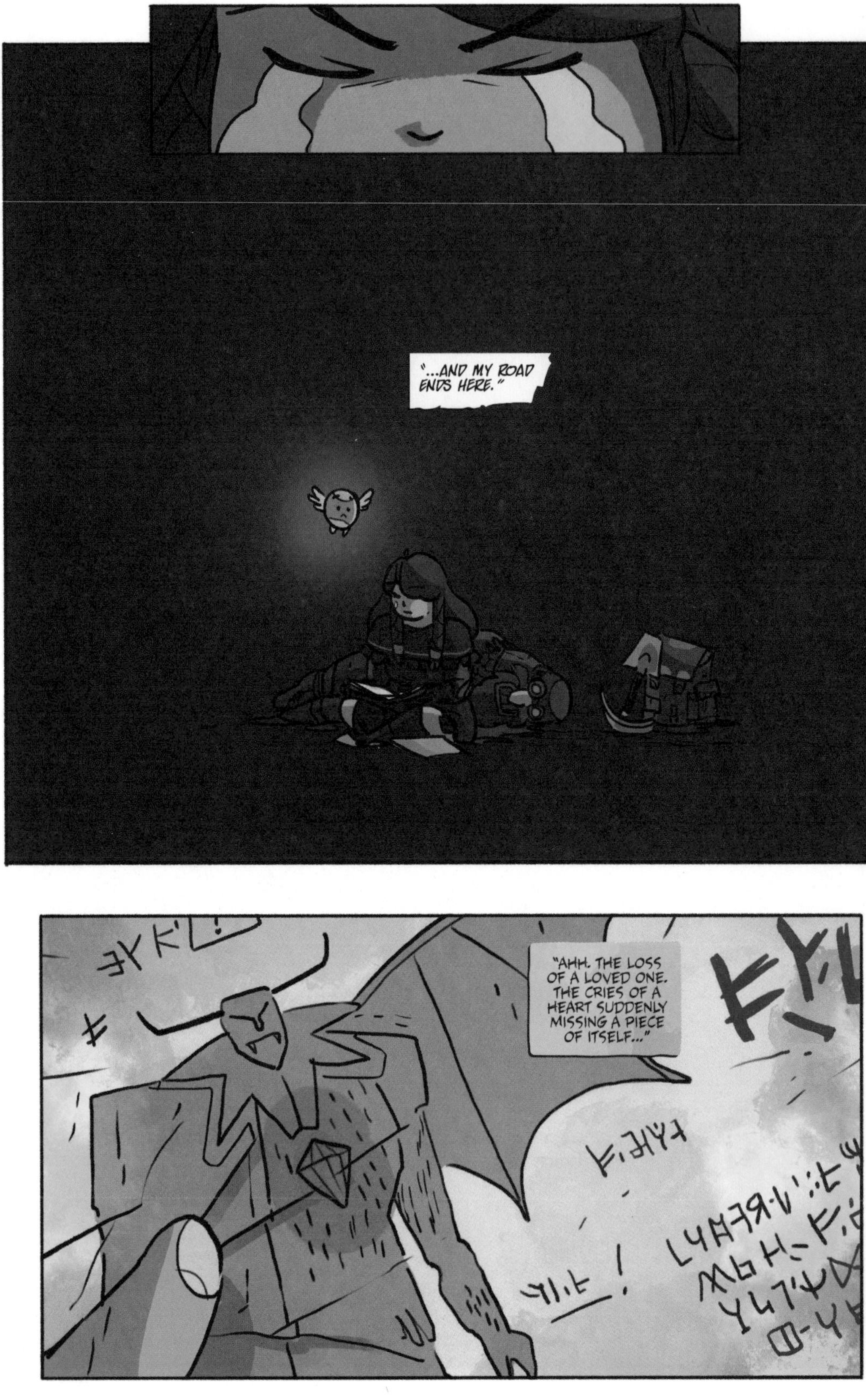
"...AND MY ROAD ENDS HERE."
"AHH. THE LOSS OF A LOVED ONE. THE CRIES OF A HEART SUDDENLY MISSING A PIECE OF ITSELF..."

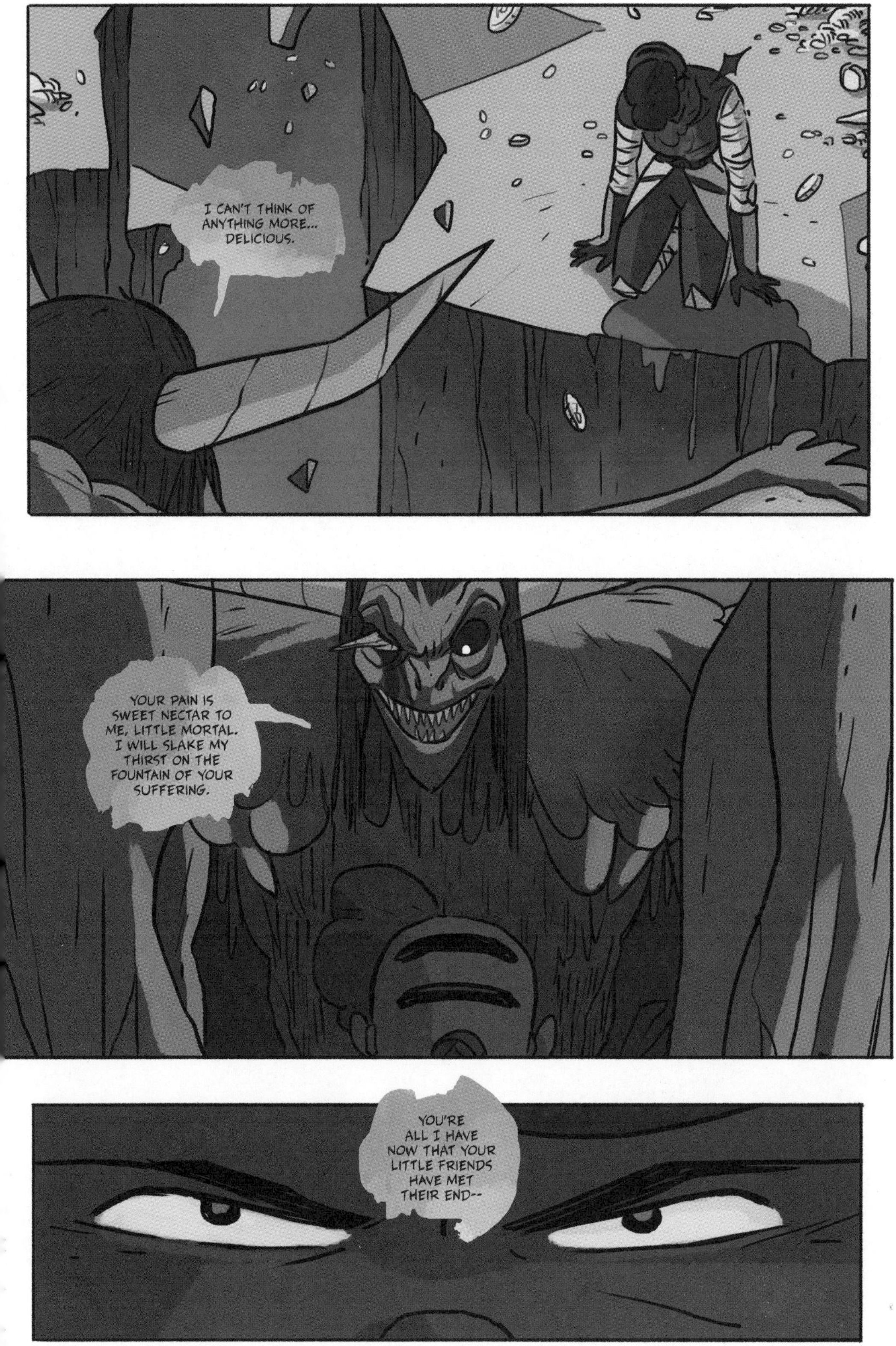
I CAN'T THINK OF ANYTHING MORE... DELICIOUS.
YOUR PAIN IS SWEET NECTAR TO ME, LITTLE MORTAL. I WILL SLAKE MY THIRST ON THE FOUNTAIN OF YOUR SUFFERING.
YOU'RE ALL I HAVE NOW THAT YOUR LITTLE FRIENDS HAVE MET THEIR END--

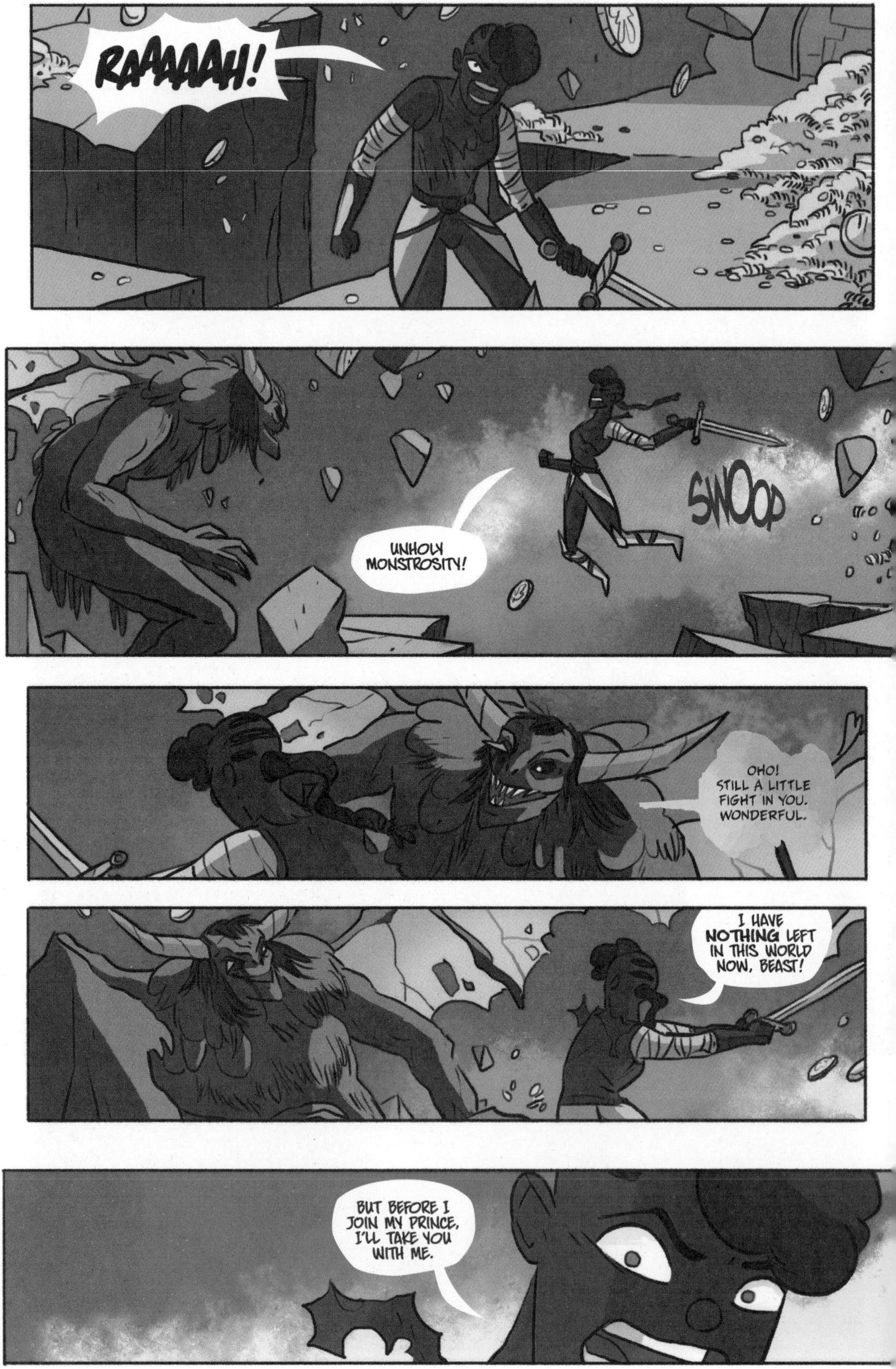
RAAAAAH!
UNHOLY MONSTROSITY!
SWOOP
OHO! STILL A LITTLE FIGHT IN YOU. WONDERFUL.
I HAVE **NOTHING** LEFT IN THIS WORLD NOW, BEAST!
BUT BEFORE I JOIN MY PRINCE, I'LL TAKE YOU WITH ME.

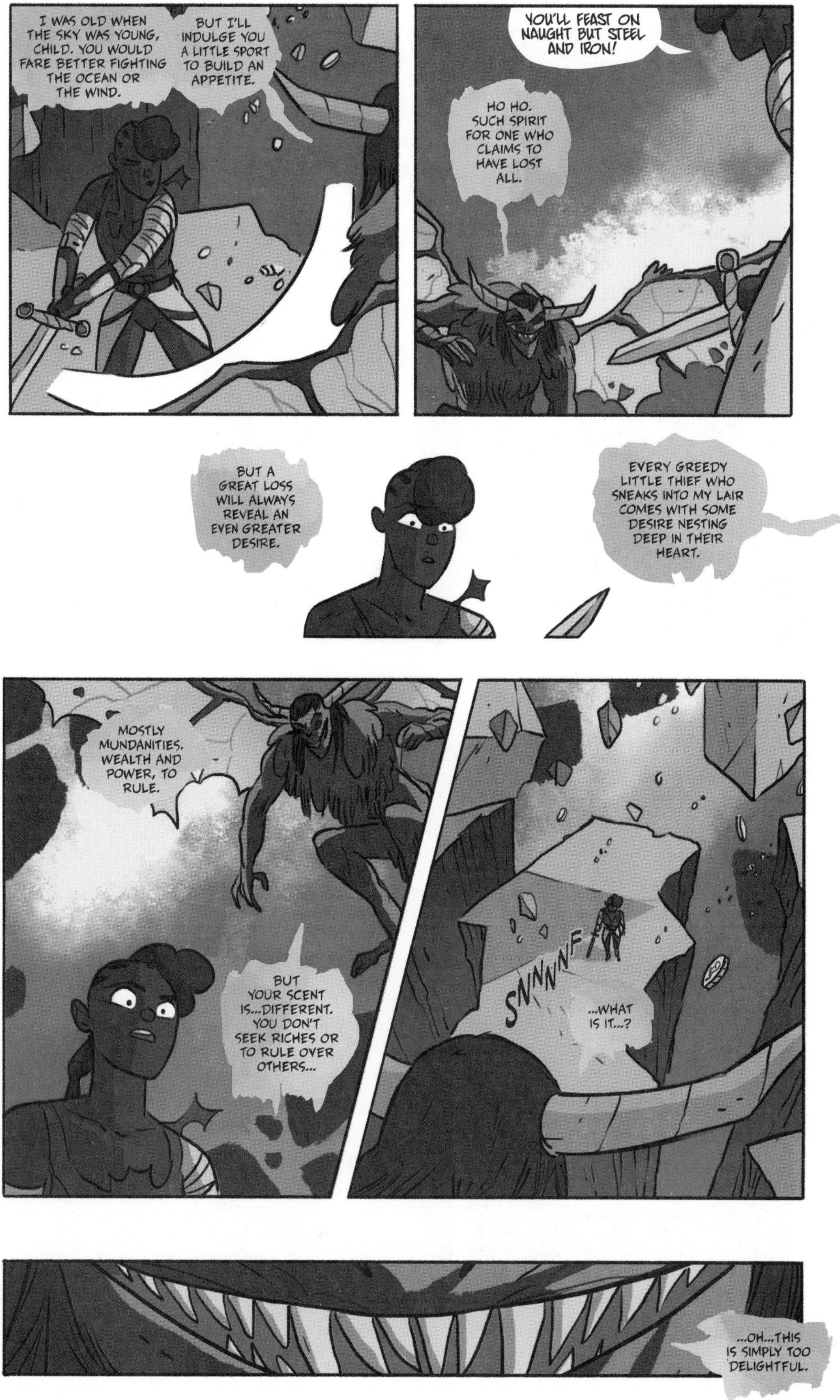
I WAS OLD WHEN THE SKY WAS YOUNG, CHILD. YOU WOULD FARE BETTER FIGHTING THE OCEAN OR THE WIND.
BUT I'LL INDULGE YOU A LITTLE SPORT TO BUILD AN APPETITE.
YOU'LL FEAST ON NAUGHT BUT STEEL AND IRON!
HO HO. SUCH SPIRIT FOR ONE WHO CLAIMS TO HAVE LOST ALL.
BUT A GREAT LOSS WILL ALWAYS REVEAL AN EVEN GREATER DESIRE.
EVERY GREEDY LITTLE THIEF WHO SNEAKS INTO MY LAIR COMES WITH SOME DESIRE NESTING DEEP IN THEIR HEART.
MOSTLY MUNDANITIES. WEALTH AND POWER, TO RULE.
BUT YOUR SCENT IS...DIFFERENT. YOU DON'T SEEK RICHES OR TO RULE OVER OTHERS...
SNNNNF
...WHAT IS IT...?
...OH...THIS IS SIMPLY TOO DELIGHTFUL.

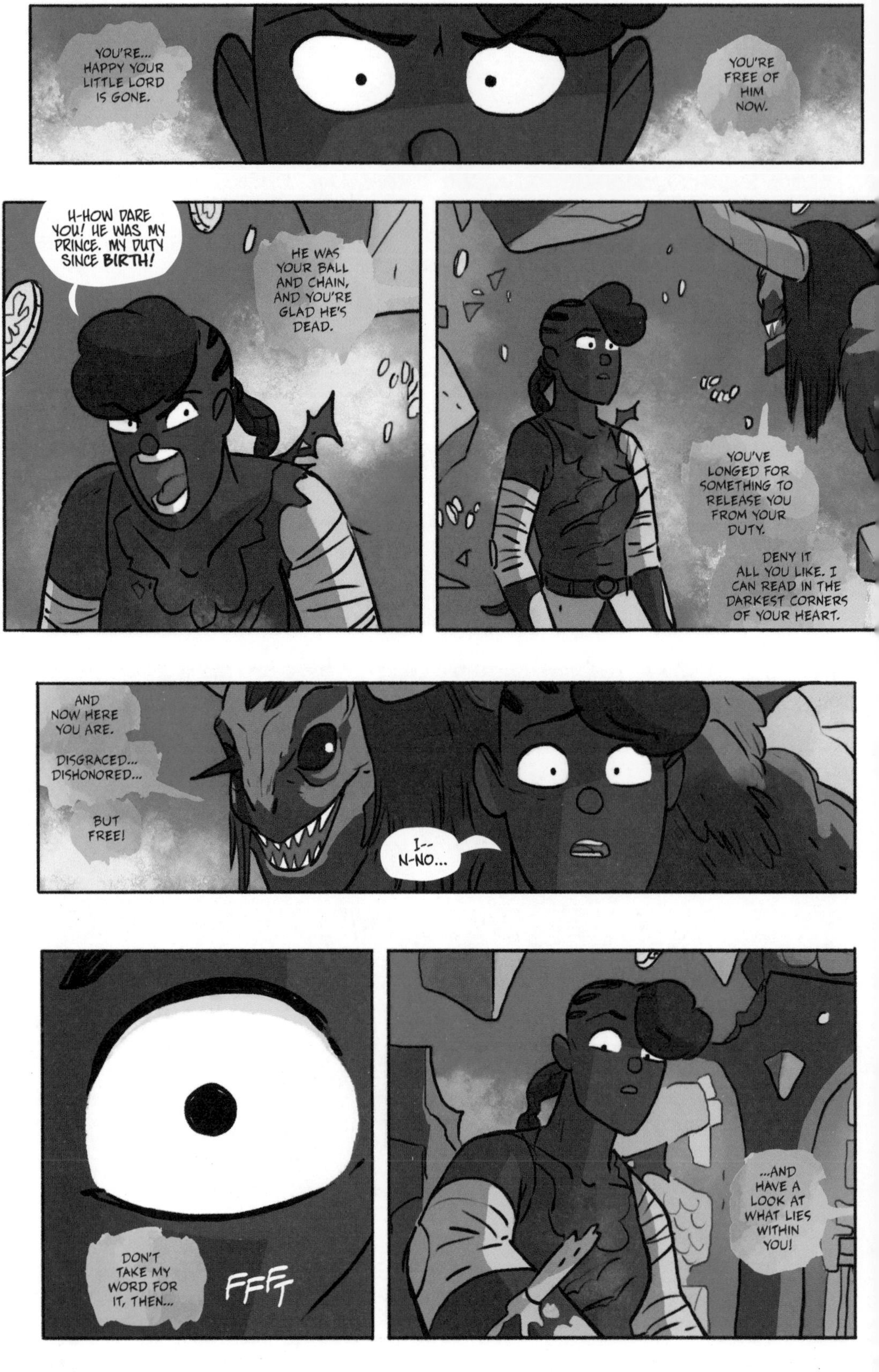

YOU'RE... HAPPY YOUR LITTLE LORD IS GONE.
YOU'RE FREE OF HIM NOW.
H-HOW DARE YOU! HE WAS MY PRINCE. MY DUTY SINCE **BIRTH!**
HE WAS YOUR BALL AND CHAIN, AND YOU'RE GLAD HE'S DEAD.
YOU'VE LONGED FOR SOMETHING TO RELEASE YOU FROM YOUR DUTY.
DENY IT ALL YOU LIKE. I CAN READ IN THE DARKEST CORNERS OF YOUR HEART.
AND NOW HERE YOU ARE.
DISGRACED... DISHONORED...
BUT FREE!
I-- N-NO...
DON'T TAKE MY WORD FOR IT, THEN...
FFFT
...AND HAVE A LOOK AT WHAT LIES WITHIN YOU!

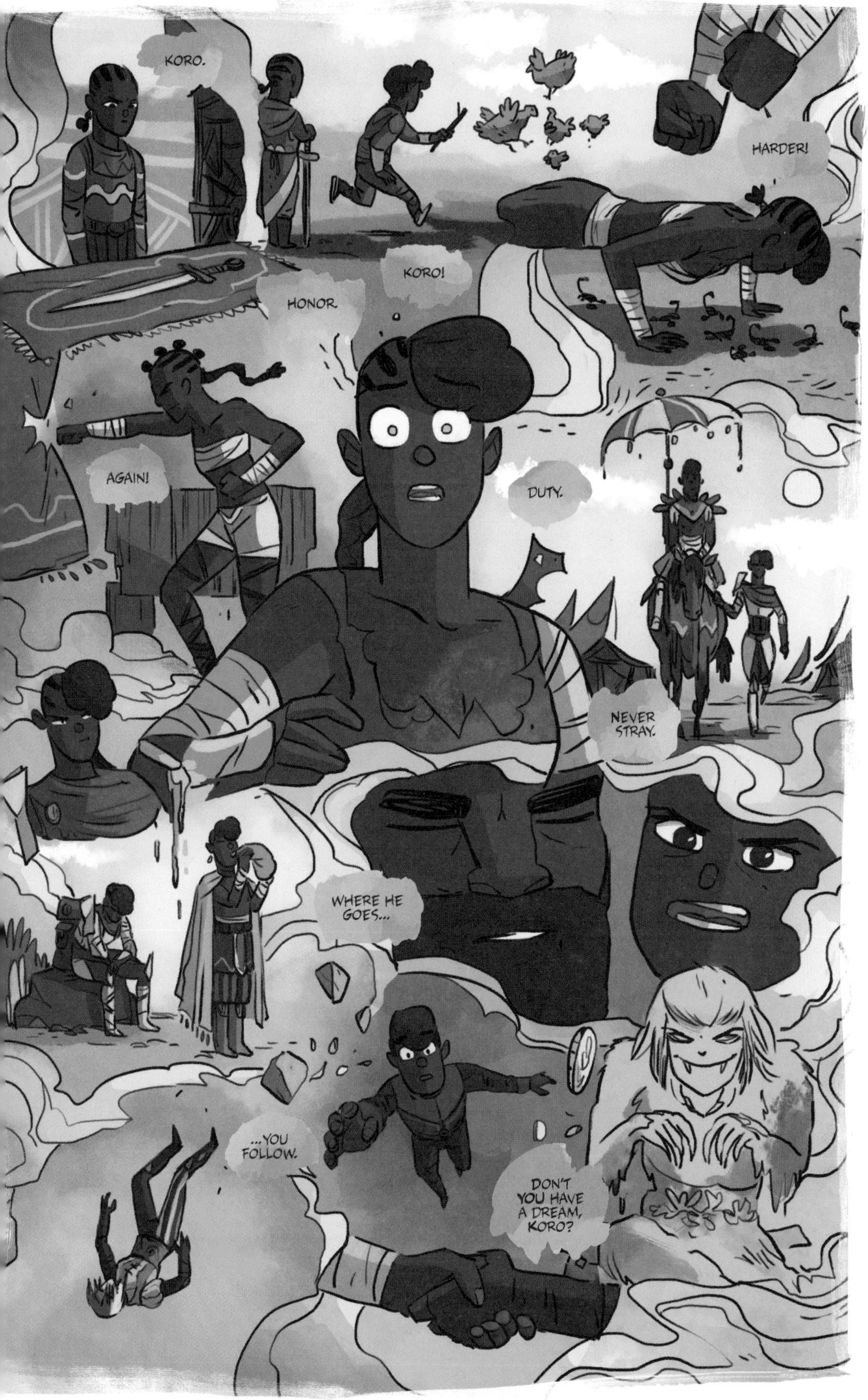
KORO.
HARDER!
KORO!
HONOR.
AGAIN!
DUTY.
NEVER STRAY.
WHERE HE GOES...
...YOU FOLLOW.
DON'T YOU HAVE A DREAM, KORO?

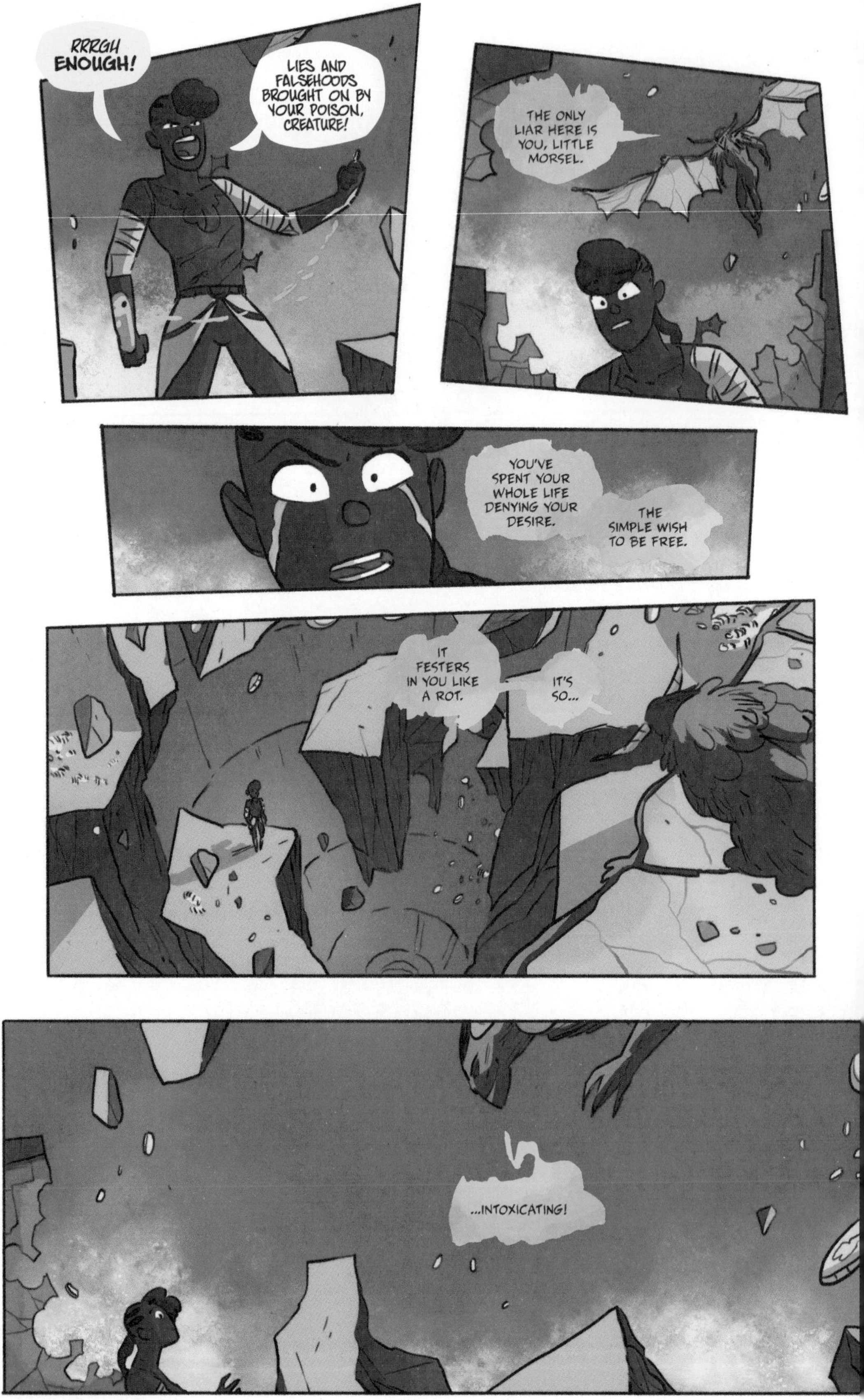
RRRGH ENOUGH!
LIES AND FALSEHOODS BROUGHT ON BY YOUR POISON, CREATURE!
THE ONLY LIAR HERE IS YOU, LITTLE MORSEL.
YOU'VE SPENT YOUR WHOLE LIFE DENYING YOUR DESIRE.
THE SIMPLE WISH TO BE FREE.
IT FESTERS IN YOU LIKE A ROT.
IT'S SO...
...INTOXICATING!

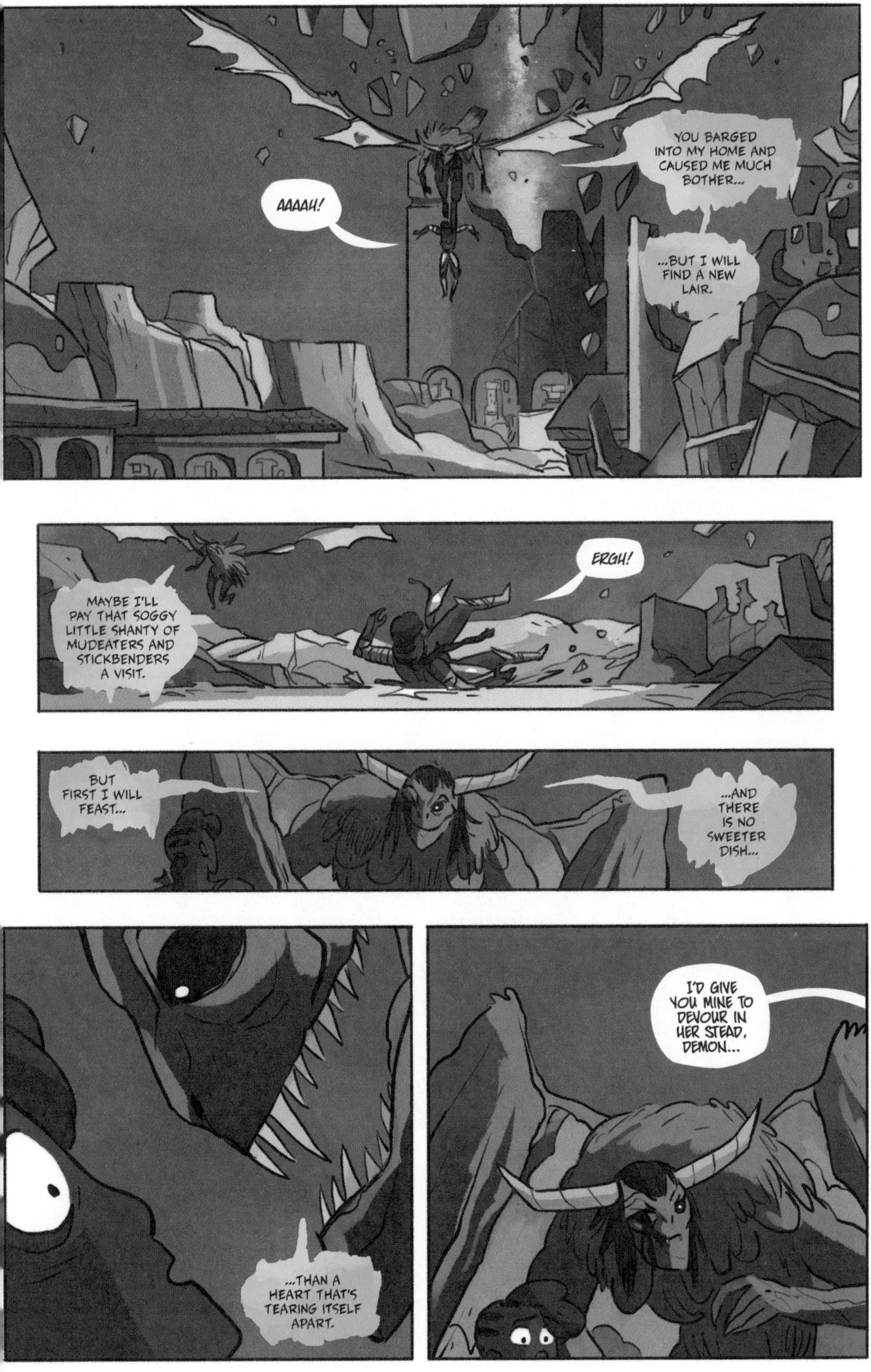
YOU BARGED INTO MY HOME AND CAUSED ME MUCH BOTHER...
AAAAH!
...BUT I WILL FIND A NEW LAIR.
MAYBE I'LL PAY THAT SOGGY LITTLE SHANTY OF MUDEATERS AND STICKBENDERS A VISIT.
ERGH!
BUT FIRST I WILL FEAST...
...AND THERE IS NO SWEETER DISH...
...THAN A HEART THAT'S TEARING ITSELF APART.
I'D GIVE YOU MINE TO DEVOUR IN HER STEAD, DEMON...

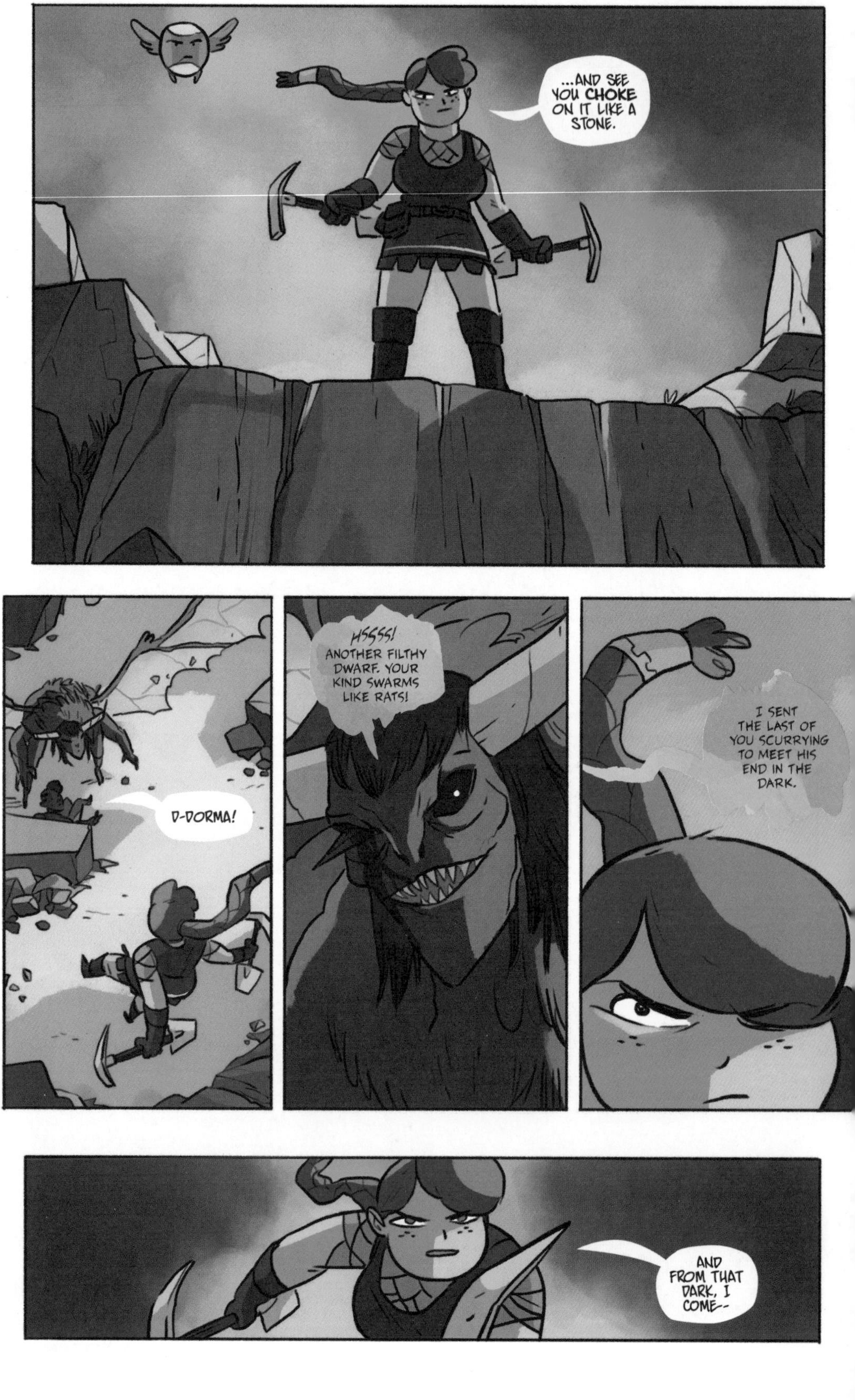
...AND SEE YOU CHOKE ON IT LIKE A STONE.
D-DORMA!
HSSSS! ANOTHER FILTHY DWARF. YOUR KIND SWARMS LIKE RATS!
I SENT THE LAST OF YOU SCURRYING TO MEET HIS END IN THE DARK.
AND FROM THAT DARK, I COME-

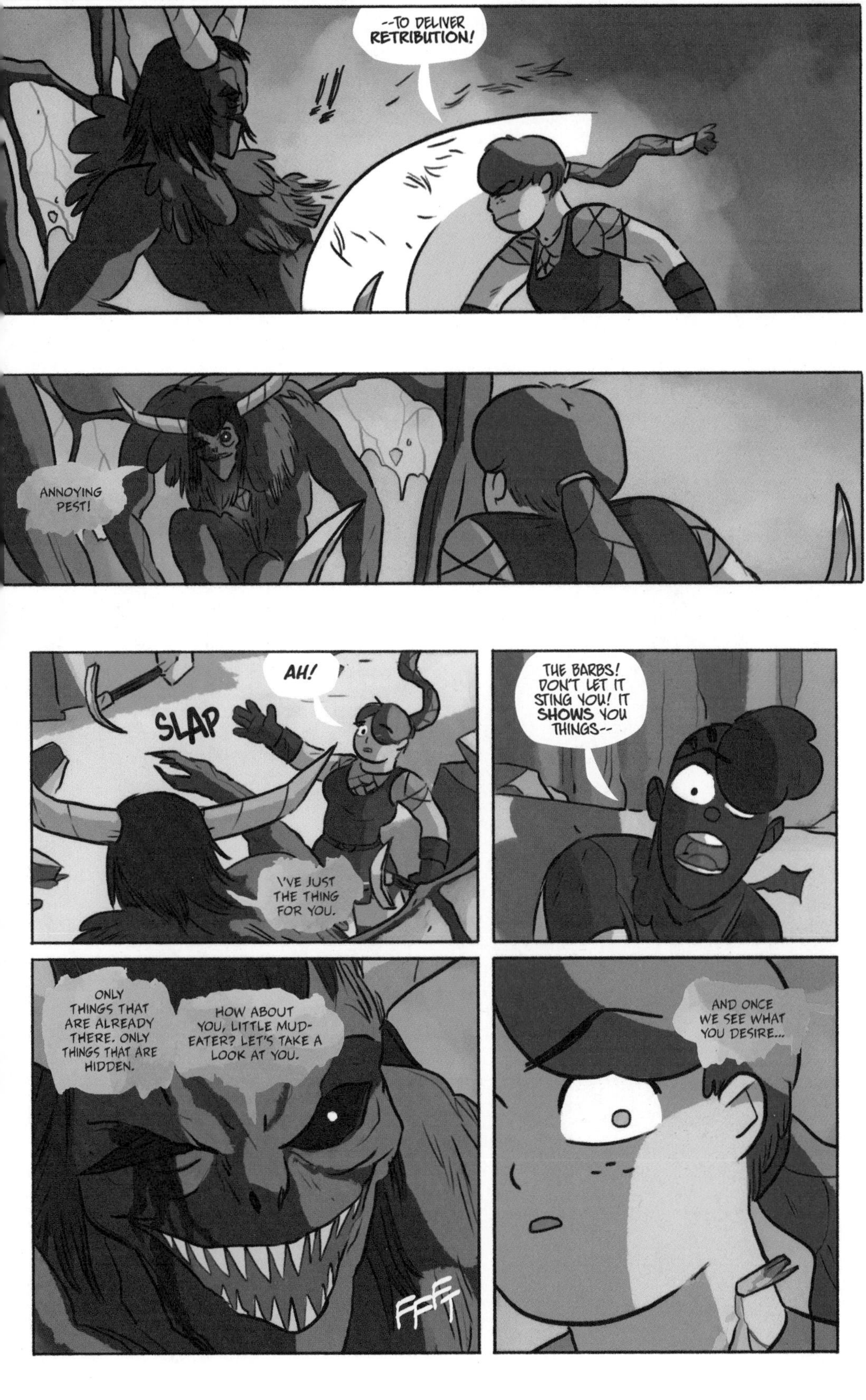
--TO DELIVER RETRIBUTION!
!!
ANNOYING PEST!
AH!
SLAP
I'VE JUST THE THING FOR YOU.
THE BARBS! DON'T LET IT STING YOU! IT SHOWS YOU THINGS--
ONLY THINGS THAT ARE ALREADY THERE. ONLY THINGS THAT ARE HIDDEN.
HOW ABOUT YOU, LITTLE MUD-EATER? LET'S TAKE A LOOK AT YOU.
FFFT
AND ONCE WE SEE WHAT YOU DESIRE...

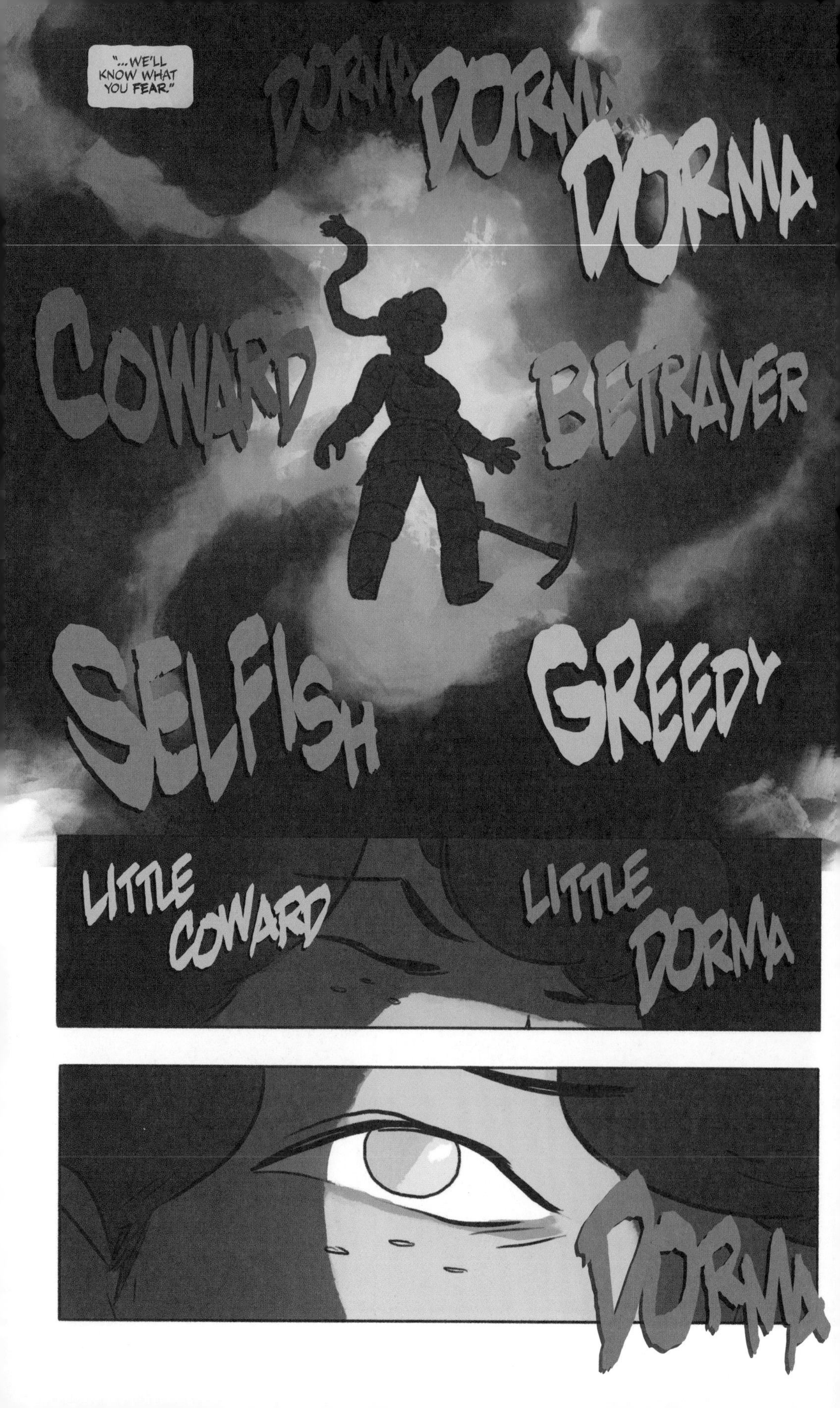
"...WE'LL KNOW WHAT YOU FEAR."
DORMA
DORMA
DORMA
COWARD
BETRAYER
SELFISH
GREEDY
LITTLE COWARD
LITTLE DORMA
DORMA

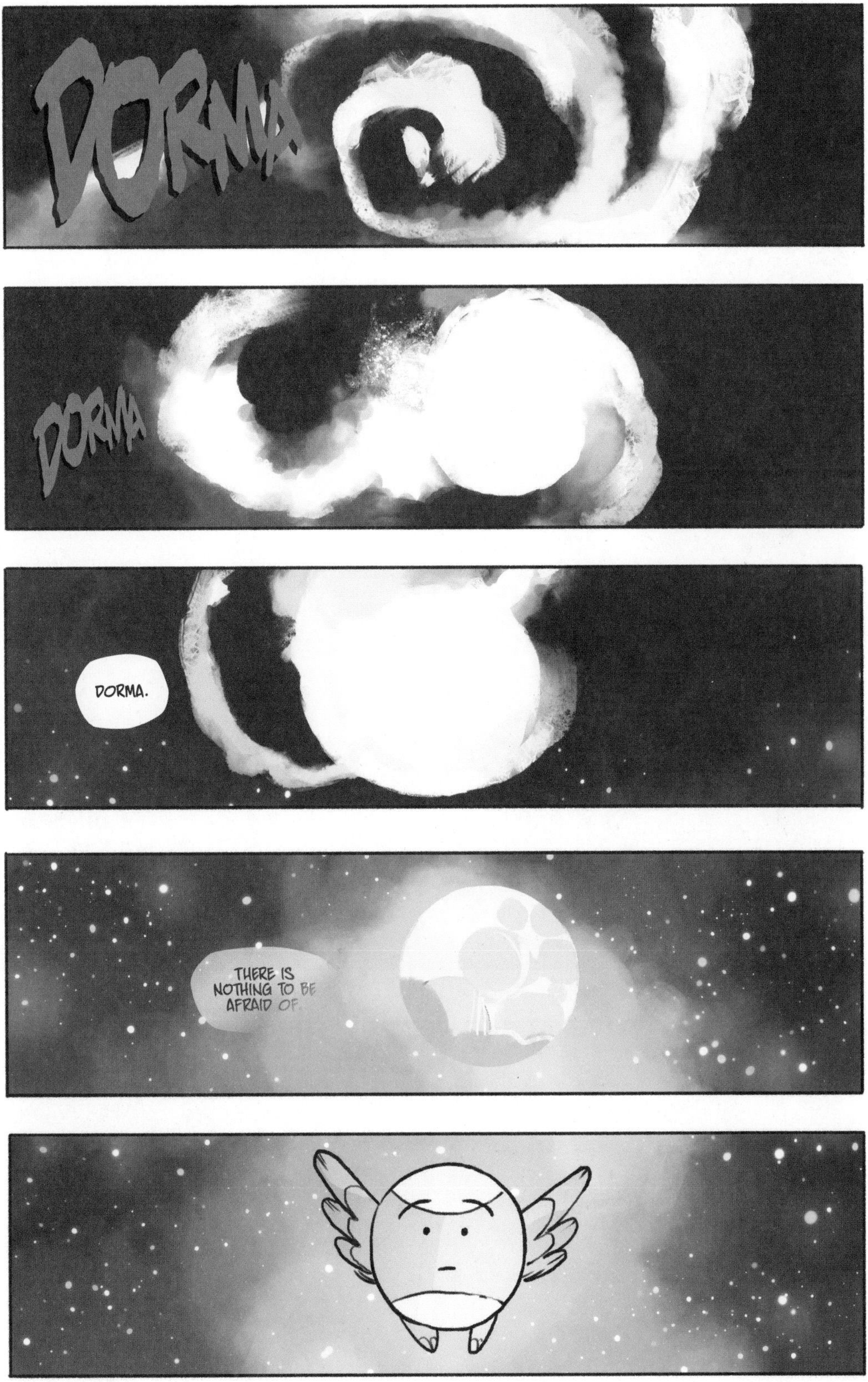
DORMA
DORMA
DORMA.
THERE IS NOTHING TO BE AFRAID OF.

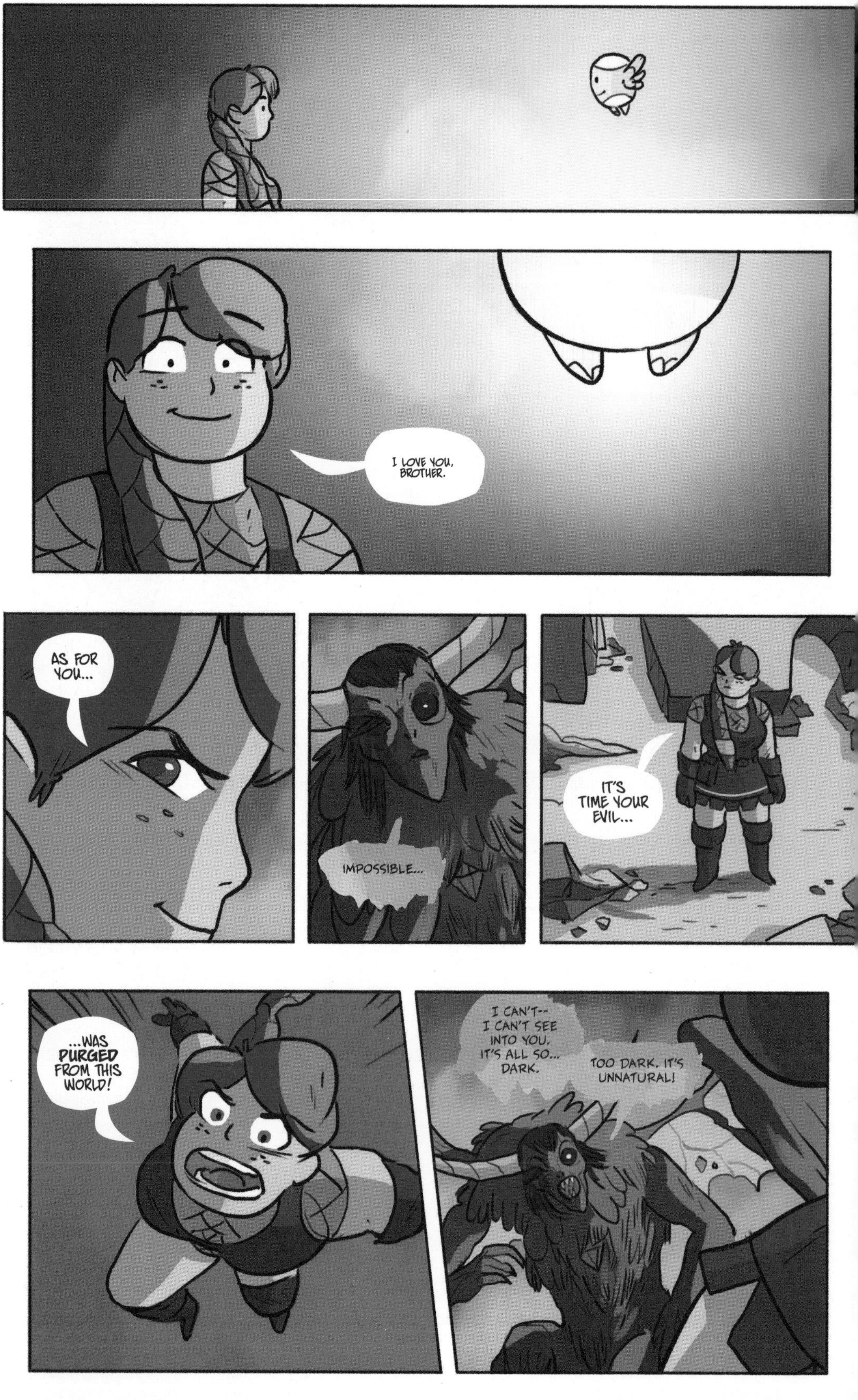
I LOVE YOU, BROTHER.
AS FOR YOU...
IMPOSSIBLE...
IT'S TIME YOUR EVIL...
...WAS PURGED FROM THIS WORLD!
I CAN'T-- I CAN'T SEE INTO YOU. IT'S ALL SO... DARK.
TOO DARK. IT'S UNNATURAL!

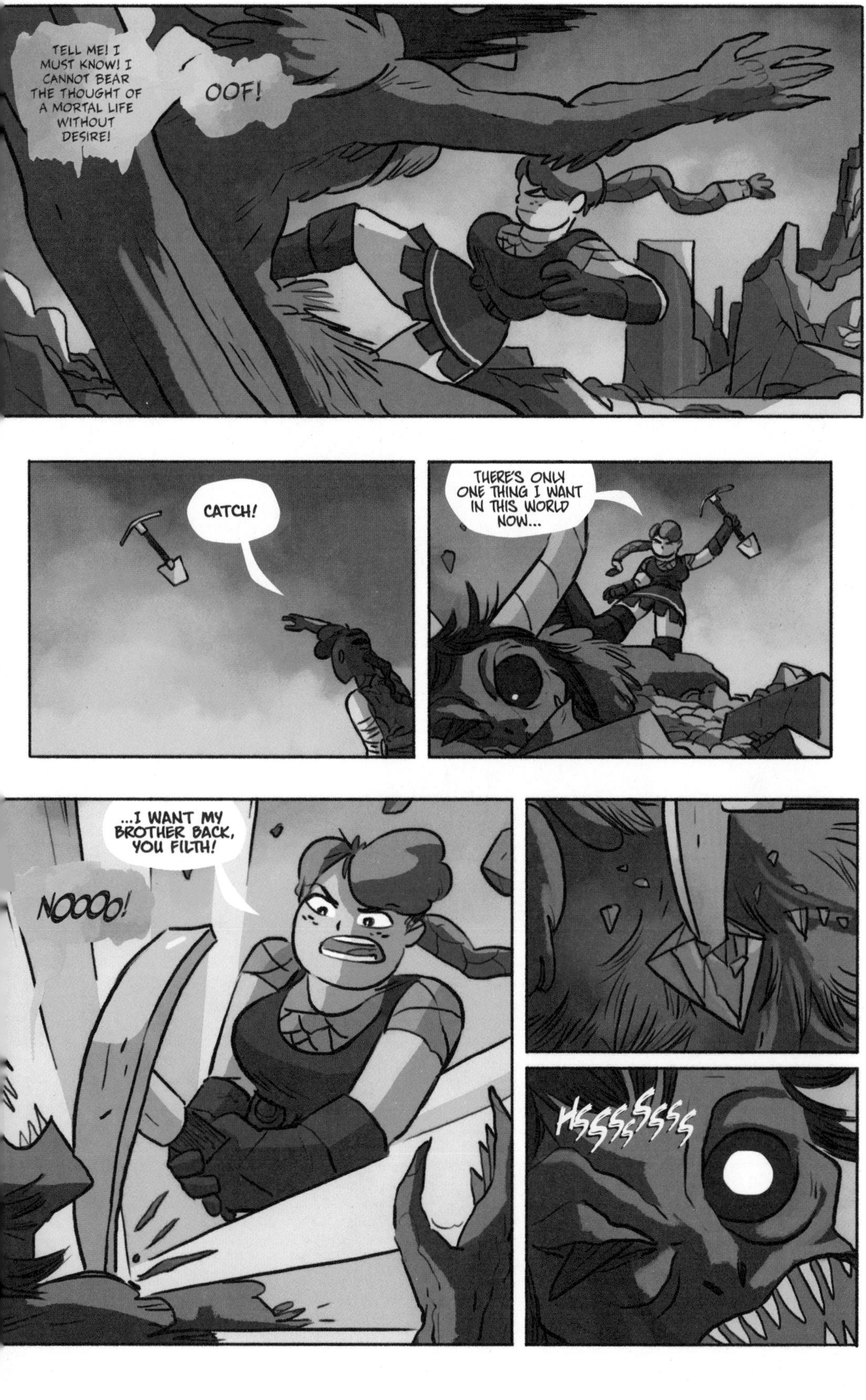
TELL ME! I MUST KNOW! I CANNOT BEAR THE THOUGHT OF A MORTAL LIFE WITHOUT DESIRE!
OOF!
CATCH!
THERE'S ONLY ONE THING I WANT IN THIS WORLD NOW...
...I WANT MY BROTHER BACK, YOU FILTH!
NOOOO!
HSSSSSSSS

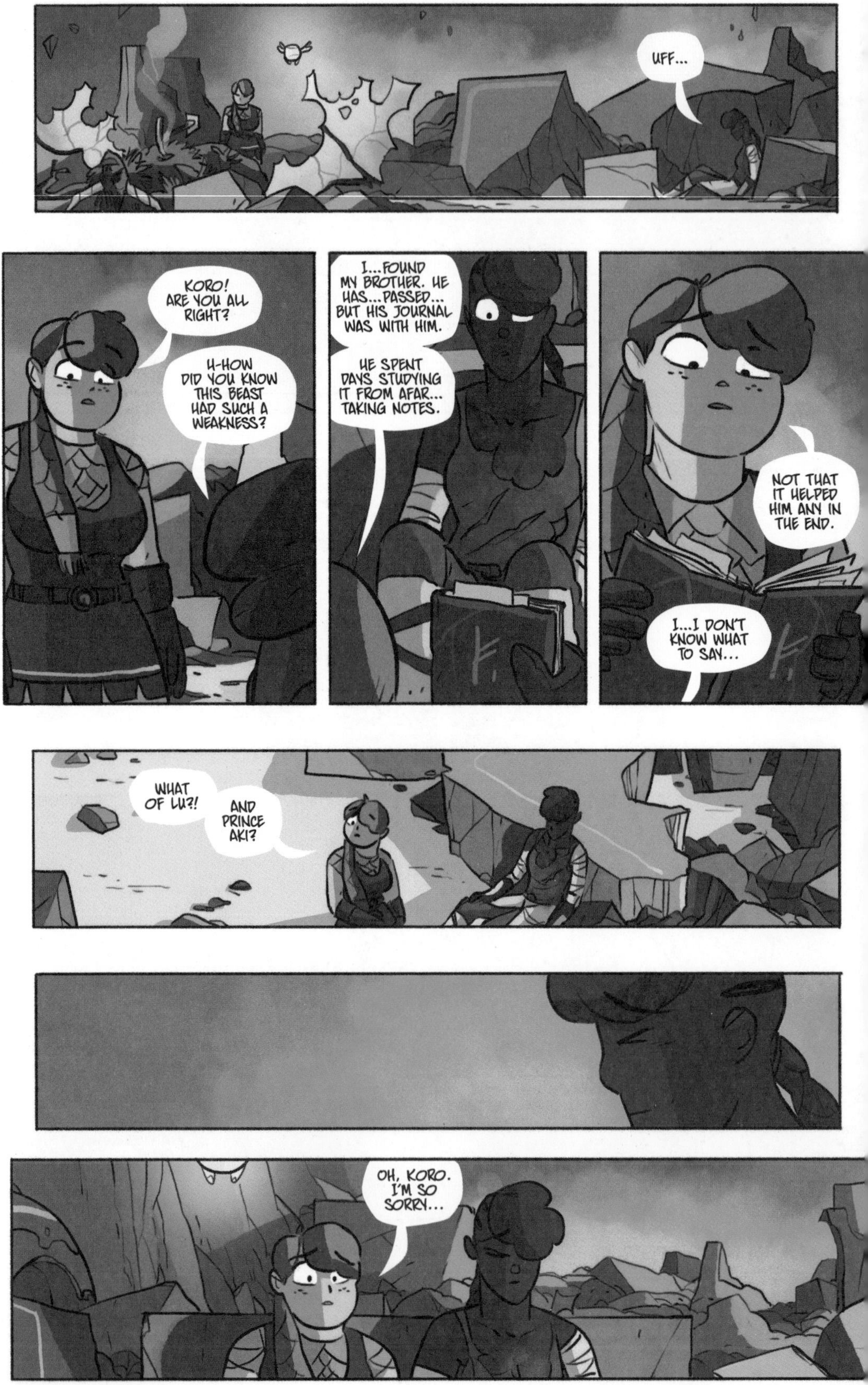

UFF...
KORO! ARE YOU ALL RIGHT?
H-HOW DID YOU KNOW THIS BEAST HAD SUCH A WEAKNESS?
I...FOUND MY BROTHER. HE HAS...PASSED... BUT HIS JOURNAL WAS WITH HIM.
HE SPENT DAYS STUDYING IT FROM AFAR... TAKING NOTES.
NOT THAT IT HELPED HIM ANY IN THE END.
I...I DON'T KNOW WHAT TO SAY...
WHAT OF LU?!
AND PRINCE AKI?
OH, KORO. I'M SO SORRY...

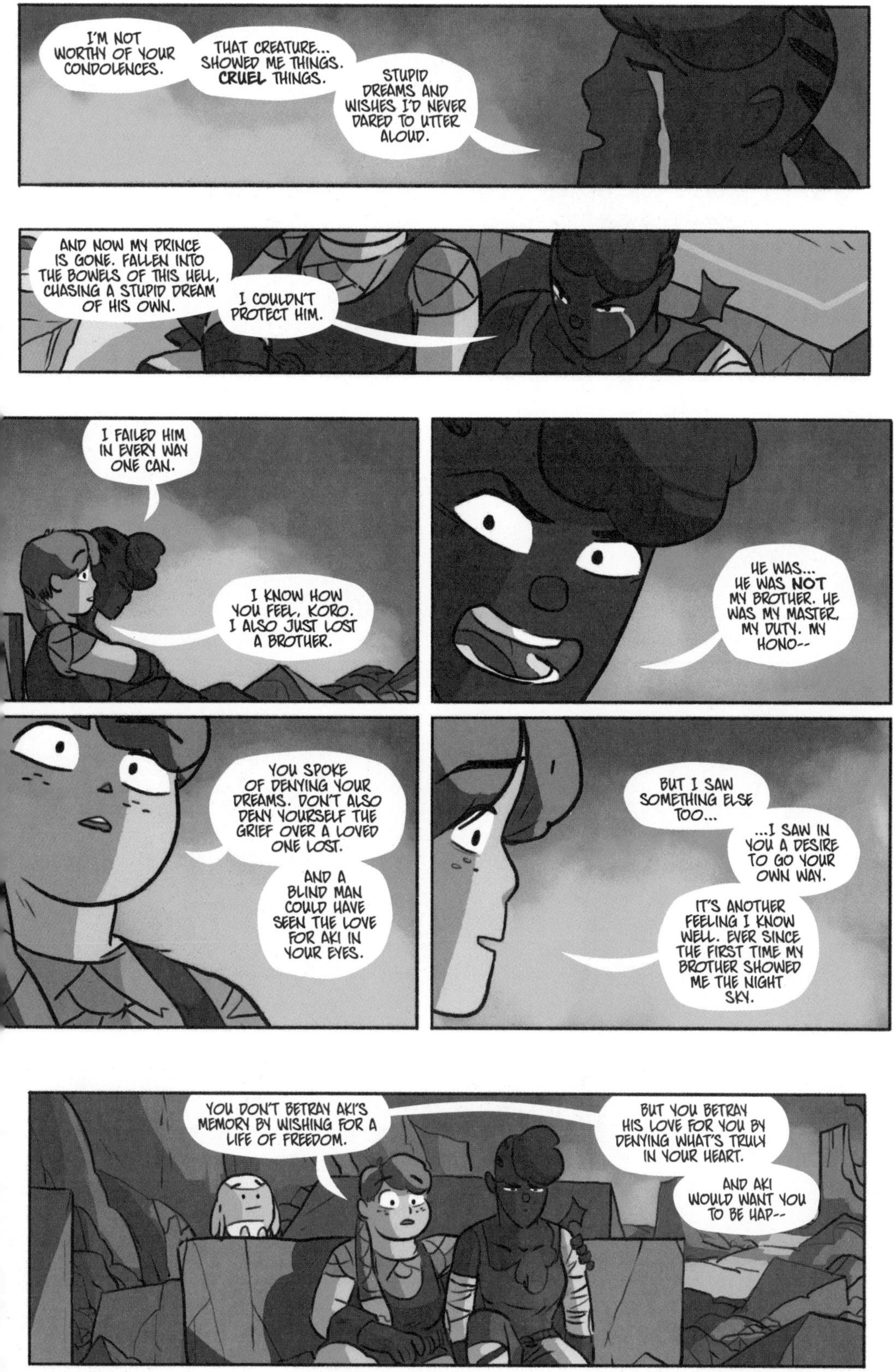
I'M NOT WORTHY OF YOUR CONDOLENCES.
THAT CREATURE... SHOWED ME THINGS. **CRUEL** THINGS.
STUPID DREAMS AND WISHES I'D NEVER DARED TO UTTER ALOUD.
AND NOW MY PRINCE IS GONE. FALLEN INTO THE BOWELS OF THIS HELL, CHASING A STUPID DREAM OF HIS OWN.
I COULDN'T PROTECT HIM.
I FAILED HIM IN EVERY WAY ONE CAN.
I KNOW HOW YOU FEEL, KORO. I ALSO JUST LOST A BROTHER.
HE WAS... HE WAS **NOT** MY BROTHER. HE WAS MY MASTER, MY DUTY. MY HONO--
YOU SPOKE OF DENYING YOUR DREAMS. DON'T ALSO DENY YOURSELF THE GRIEF OVER A LOVED ONE LOST.
AND A BLIND MAN COULD HAVE SEEN THE LOVE FOR AKI IN YOUR EYES.
BUT I SAW SOMETHING ELSE TOO...
...I SAW IN YOU A DESIRE TO GO YOUR OWN WAY.
IT'S ANOTHER FEELING I KNOW WELL. EVER SINCE THE FIRST TIME MY BROTHER SHOWED ME THE NIGHT SKY.
YOU DON'T BETRAY AKI'S MEMORY BY WISHING FOR A LIFE OF FREEDOM.
BUT YOU BETRAY HIS LOVE FOR YOU BY DENYING WHAT'S TRULY IN YOUR HEART.
AND AKI WOULD WANT YOU TO BE HAP--

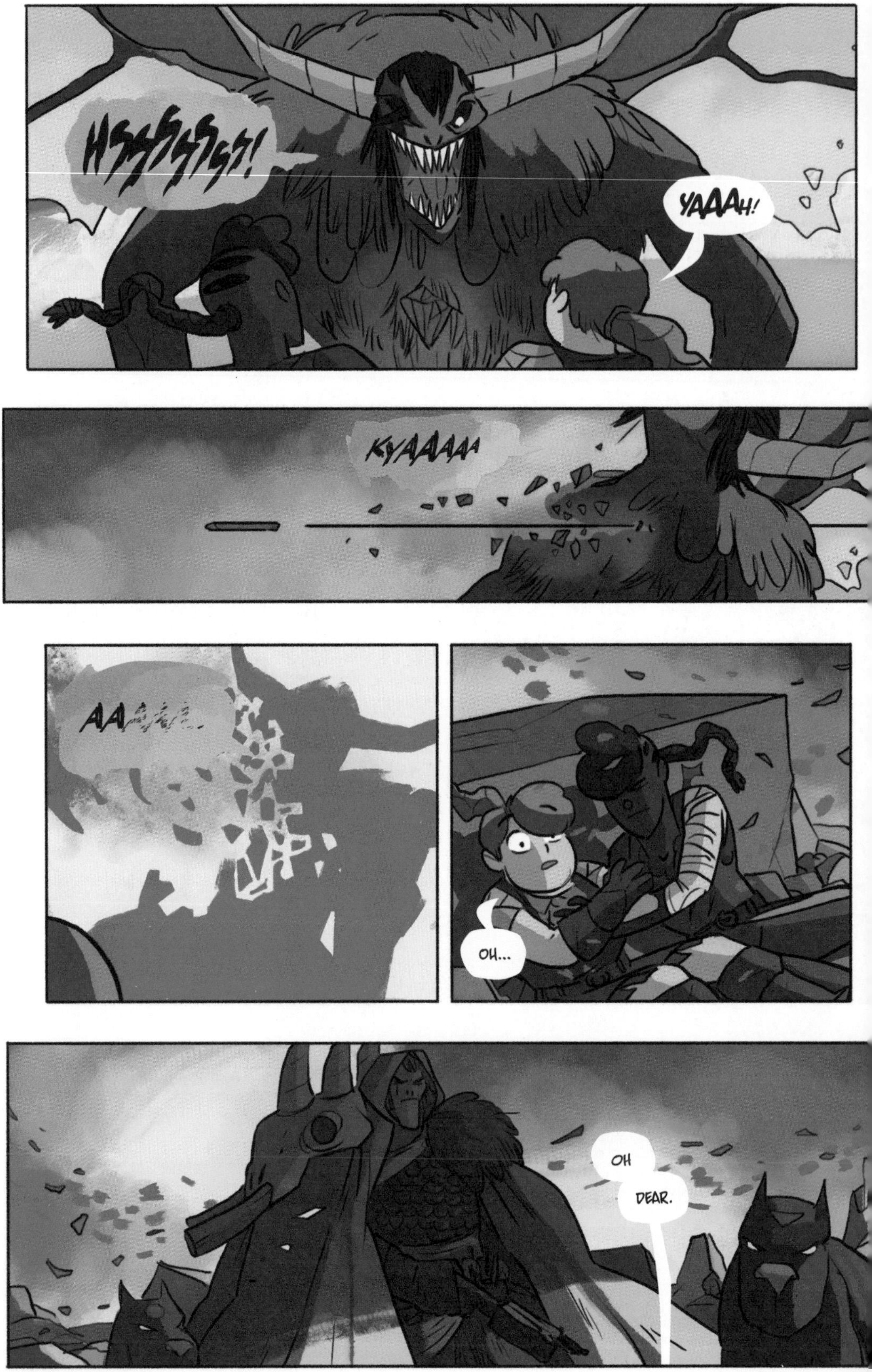
HSSSSSSSS!
YAAAH!
KYAAAAA
AAAAAA
OH...
OH
DEAR.

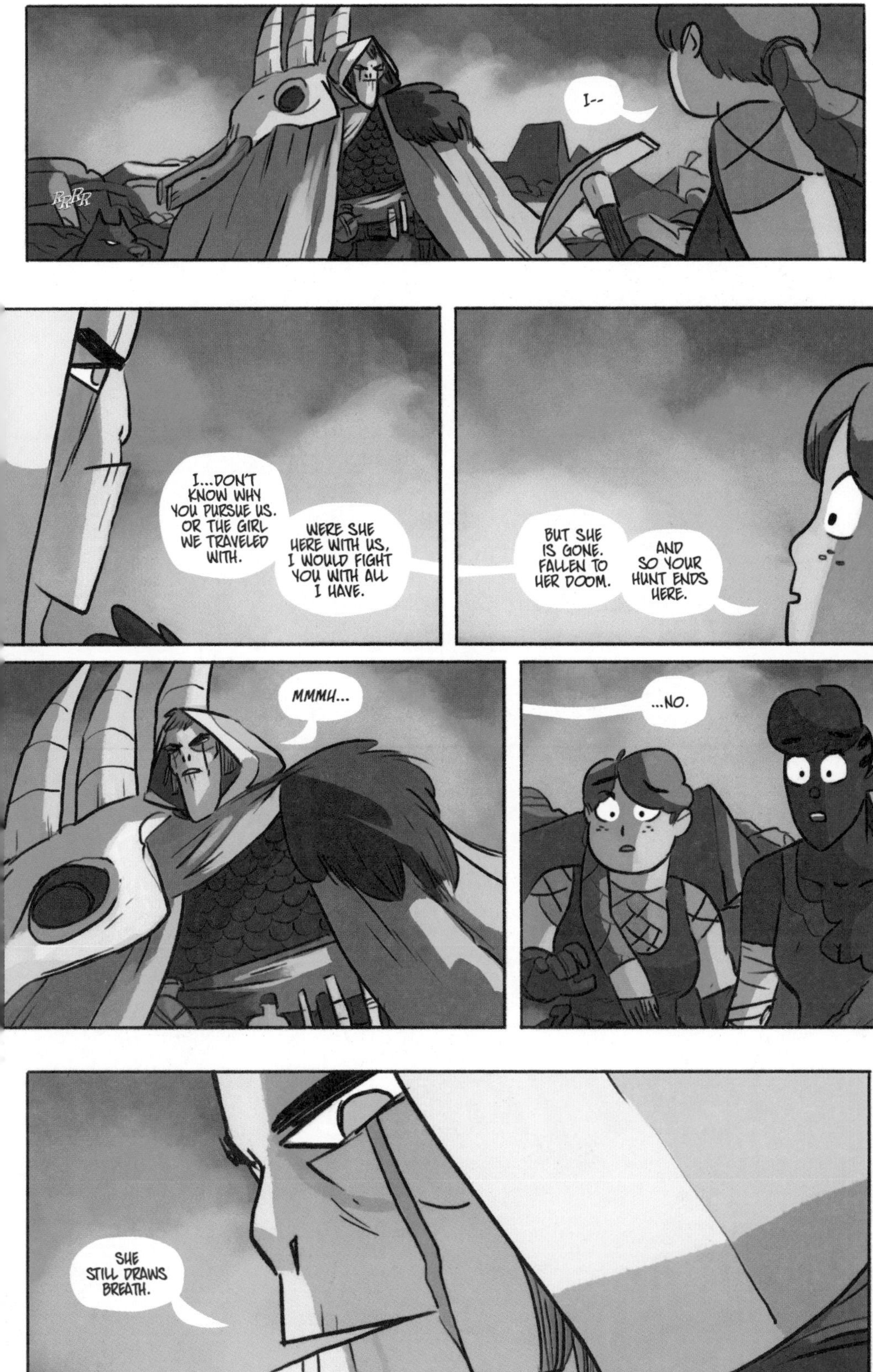
I--
RRRR
I...DON'T KNOW WHY YOU PURSUE US. OR THE GIRL WE TRAVELED WITH.
WERE SHE HERE WITH US, I WOULD FIGHT YOU WITH ALL I HAVE.
BUT SHE IS GONE. FALLEN TO HER DOOM.
AND SO YOUR HUNT ENDS HERE.
MMMH...
...NO.
SHE STILL DRAWS BREATH.

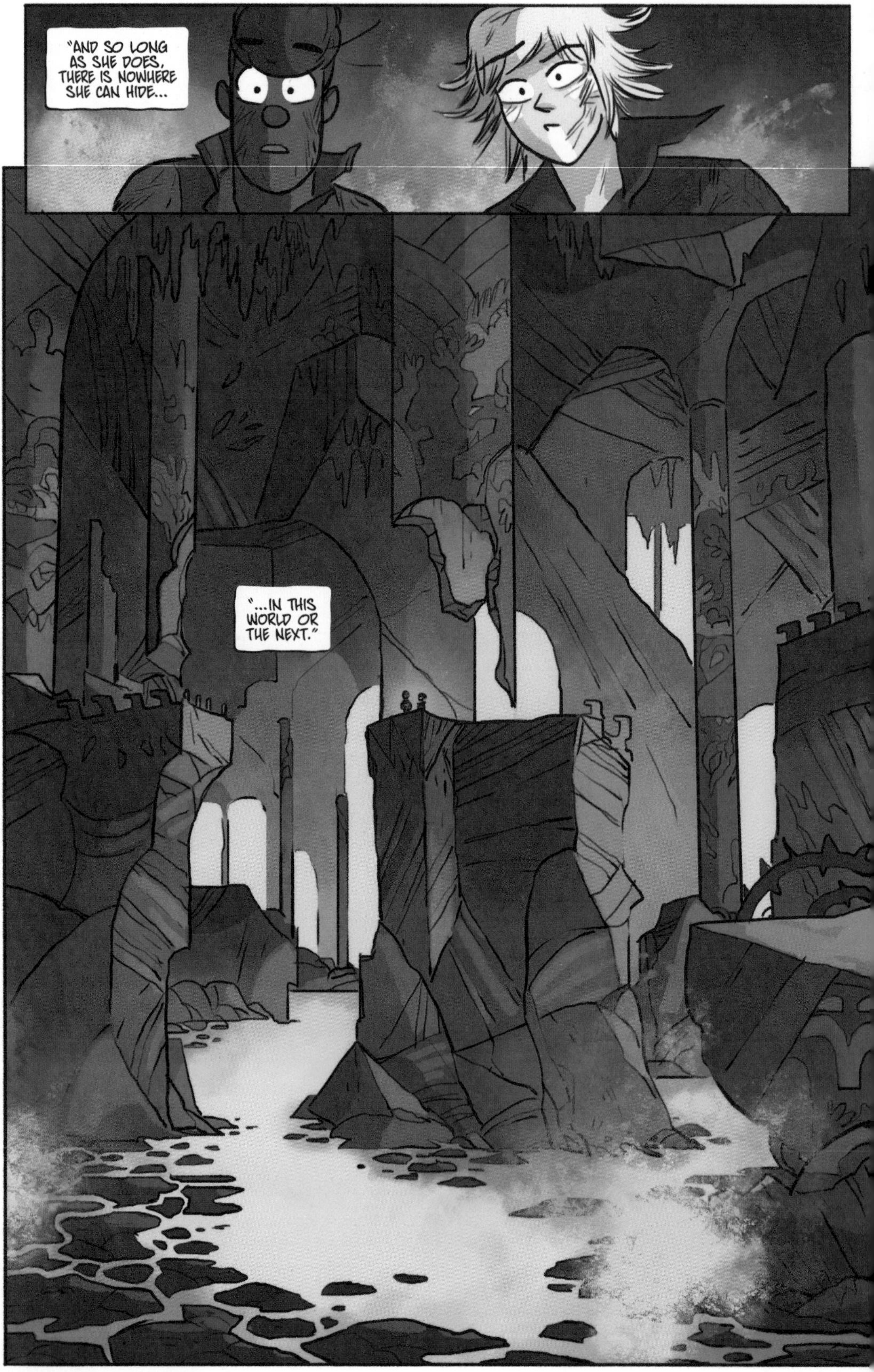
"AND SO LONG AS SHE DOES, THERE IS NOWHERE SHE CAN HIDE...
"...IN THIS WORLD OR THE NEXT."

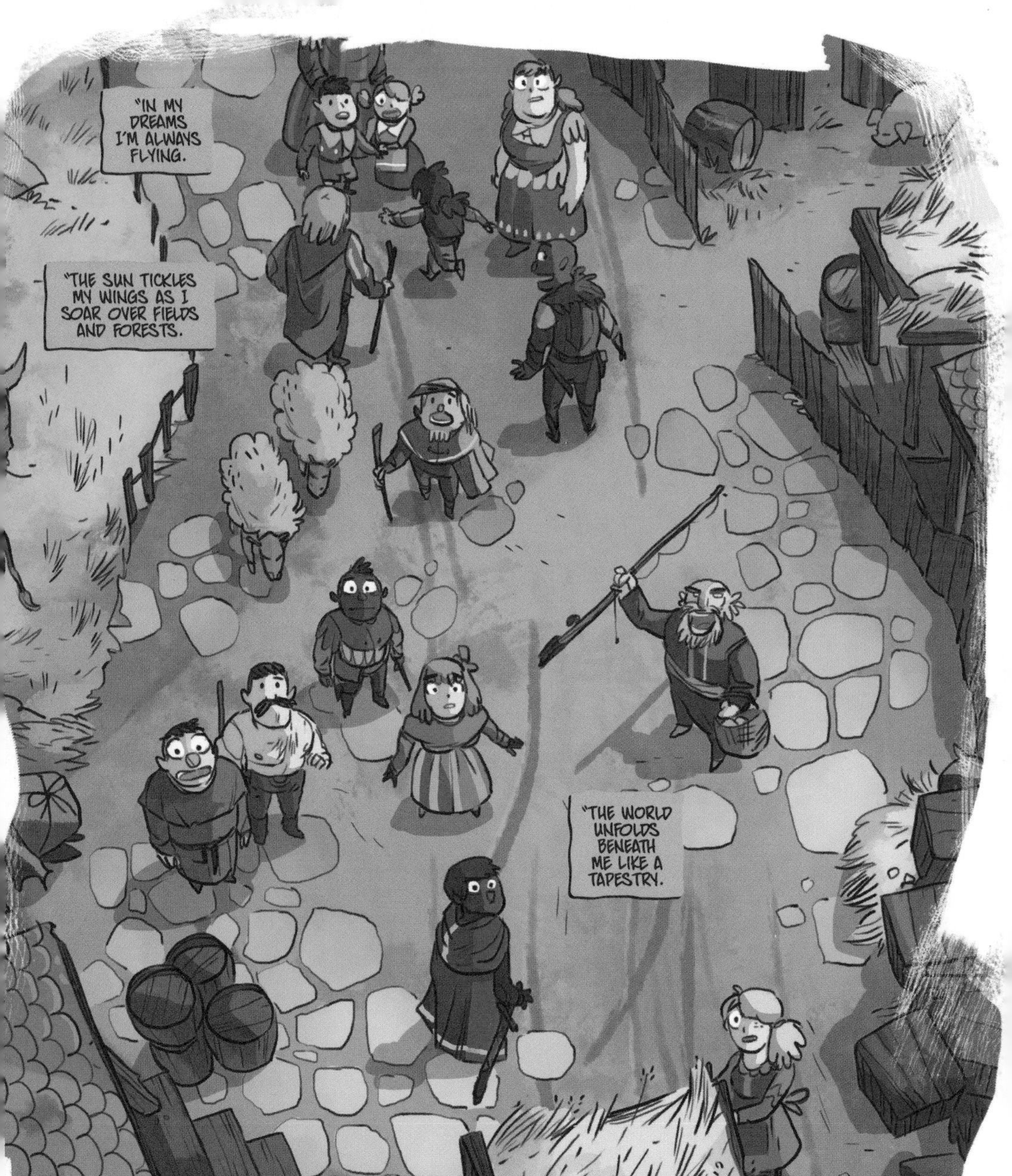
"IN MY DREAMS I'M ALWAYS FLYING.
"THE SUN TICKLES MY WINGS AS I SOAR OVER FIELDS AND FORESTS.
"THE WORLD UNFOLDS BENEATH ME LIKE A TAPESTRY.

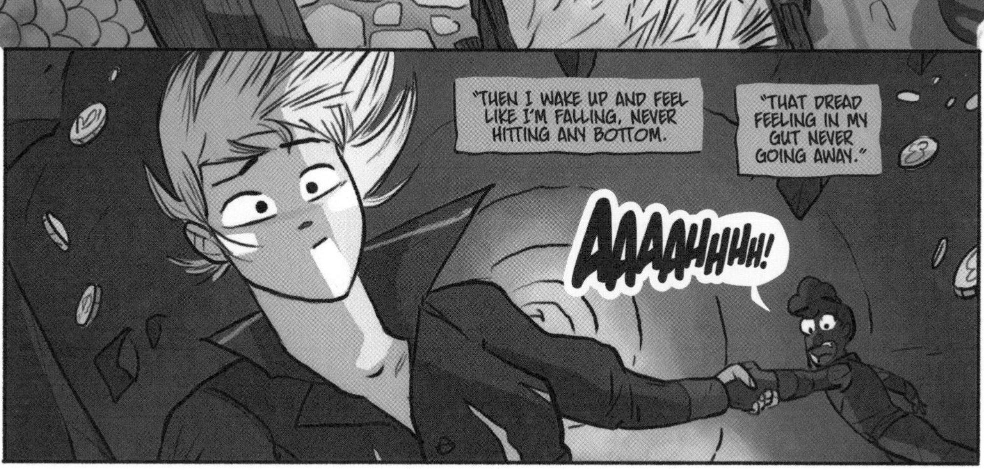
"THEN I WAKE UP AND FEEL LIKE I'M FALLING, NEVER HITTING ANY BOTTOM.
"THAT DREAD FEELING IN MY GUT NEVER GOING AWAY."
AAAAHHHH!

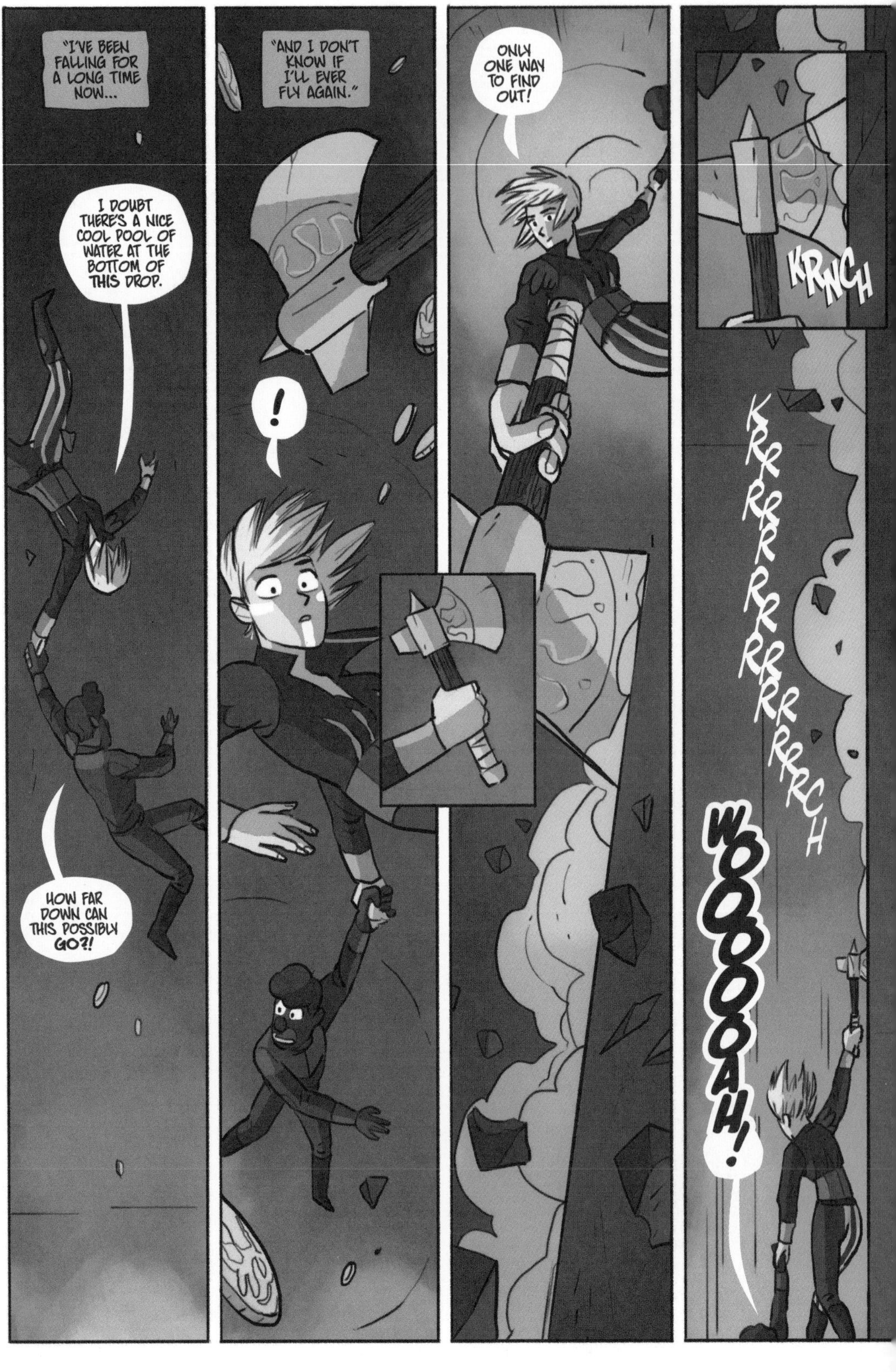
"I'VE BEEN FALLING FOR A LONG TIME NOW...
I DOUBT THERE'S A NICE COOL POOL OF WATER AT THE BOTTOM OF THIS DROP.
HOW FAR DOWN CAN THIS POSSIBLY GO?!
"AND I DON'T KNOW IF I'LL EVER FLY AGAIN."
!
ONLY ONE WAY TO FIND OUT!
KRNCH
KRRRRRRRRRRRRCH
WOOOOOOAH!

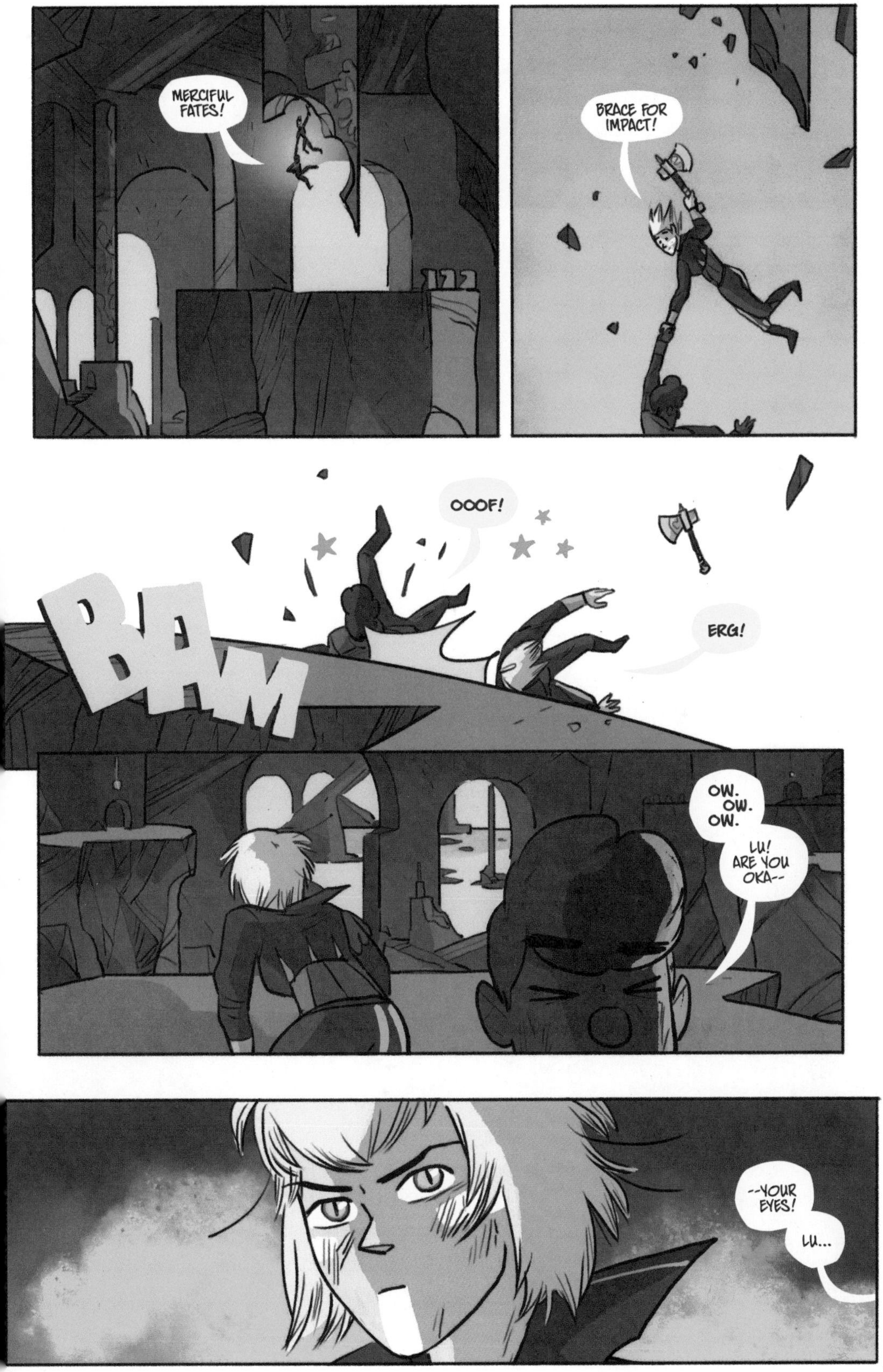
MERCIFUL FATES!
BRACE FOR IMPACT!
OOOF!
BAM
ERG!
OW. OW. OW.
LU! ARE YOU OKA--
--YOUR EYES!
LU...

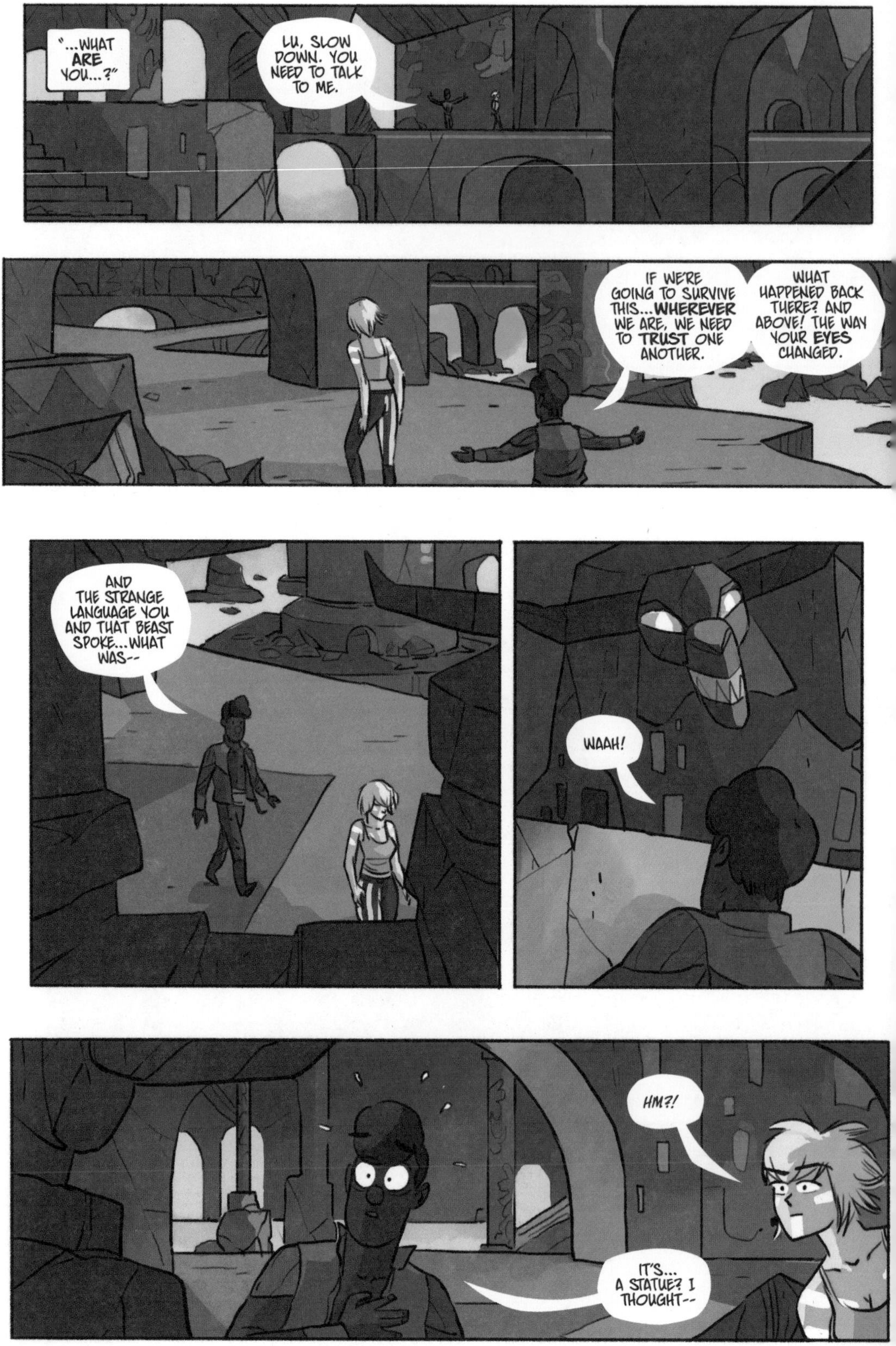
"...WHAT ARE YOU...?"
LU, SLOW DOWN. YOU NEED TO TALK TO ME.
IF WE'RE GOING TO SURVIVE THIS...WHEREVER WE ARE, WE NEED TO TRUST ONE ANOTHER.
WHAT HAPPENED BACK THERE? AND ABOVE! THE WAY YOUR EYES CHANGED.
AND THE STRANGE LANGUAGE YOU AND THAT BEAST SPOKE...WHAT WAS--
WAAH!
HM?!
IT'S... A STATUE? I THOUGHT--

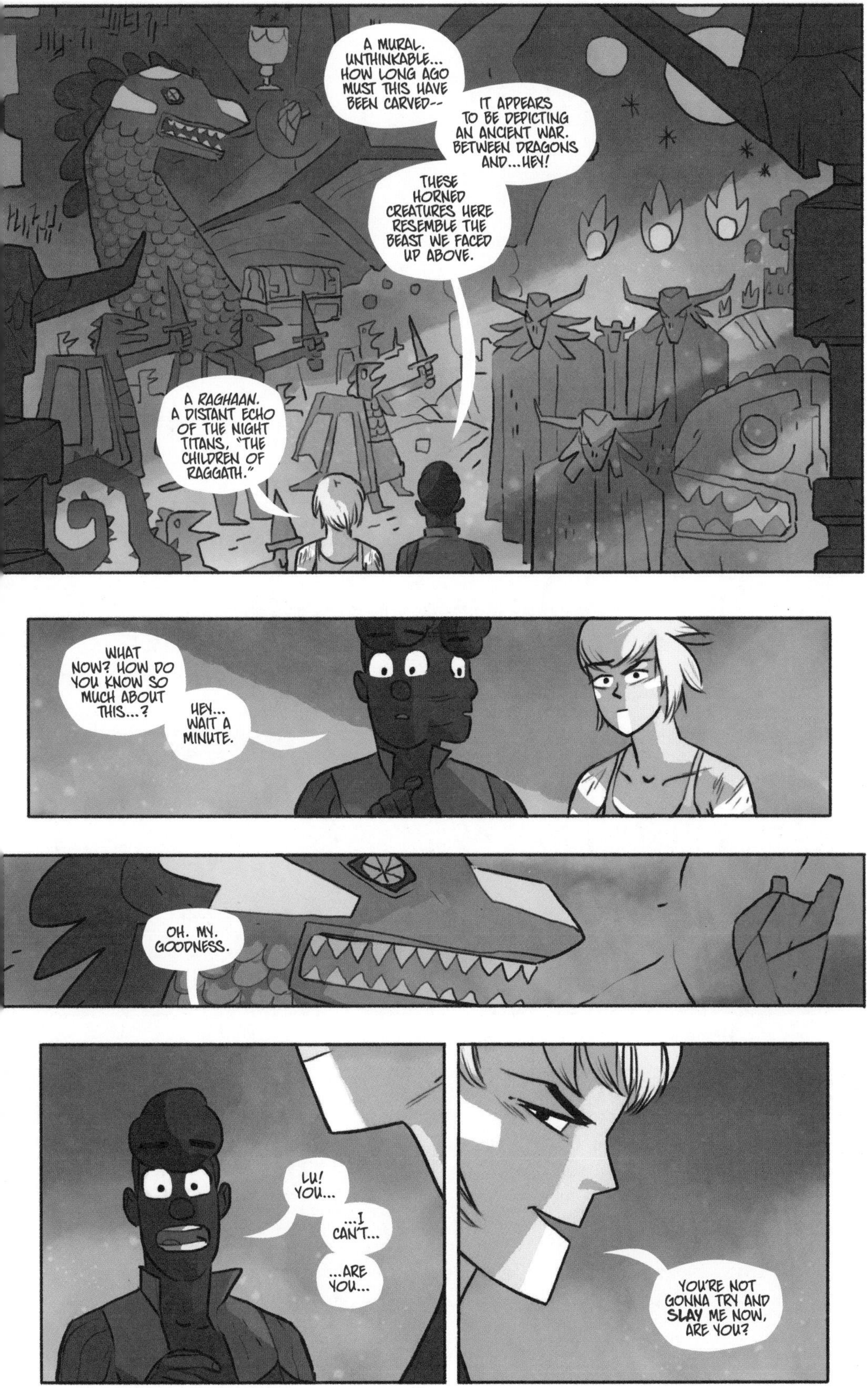
A MURAL. UNTHINKABLE... HOW LONG AGO MUST THIS HAVE BEEN CARVED--
IT APPEARS TO BE DEPICTING AN ANCIENT WAR. BETWEEN DRAGONS AND...HEY!
THESE HORNED CREATURES HERE RESEMBLE THE BEAST WE FACED UP ABOVE.
A RAGHAAN. A DISTANT ECHO OF THE NIGHT TITANS, "THE CHILDREN OF RAGGATH."
WHAT NOW? HOW DO YOU KNOW SO MUCH ABOUT THIS...?
HEY... WAIT A MINUTE.
OH. MY. GOODNESS.
LU! YOU...
...I CAN'T...
...ARE YOU...
YOU'RE NOT GONNA TRY AND SLAY ME NOW, ARE YOU?

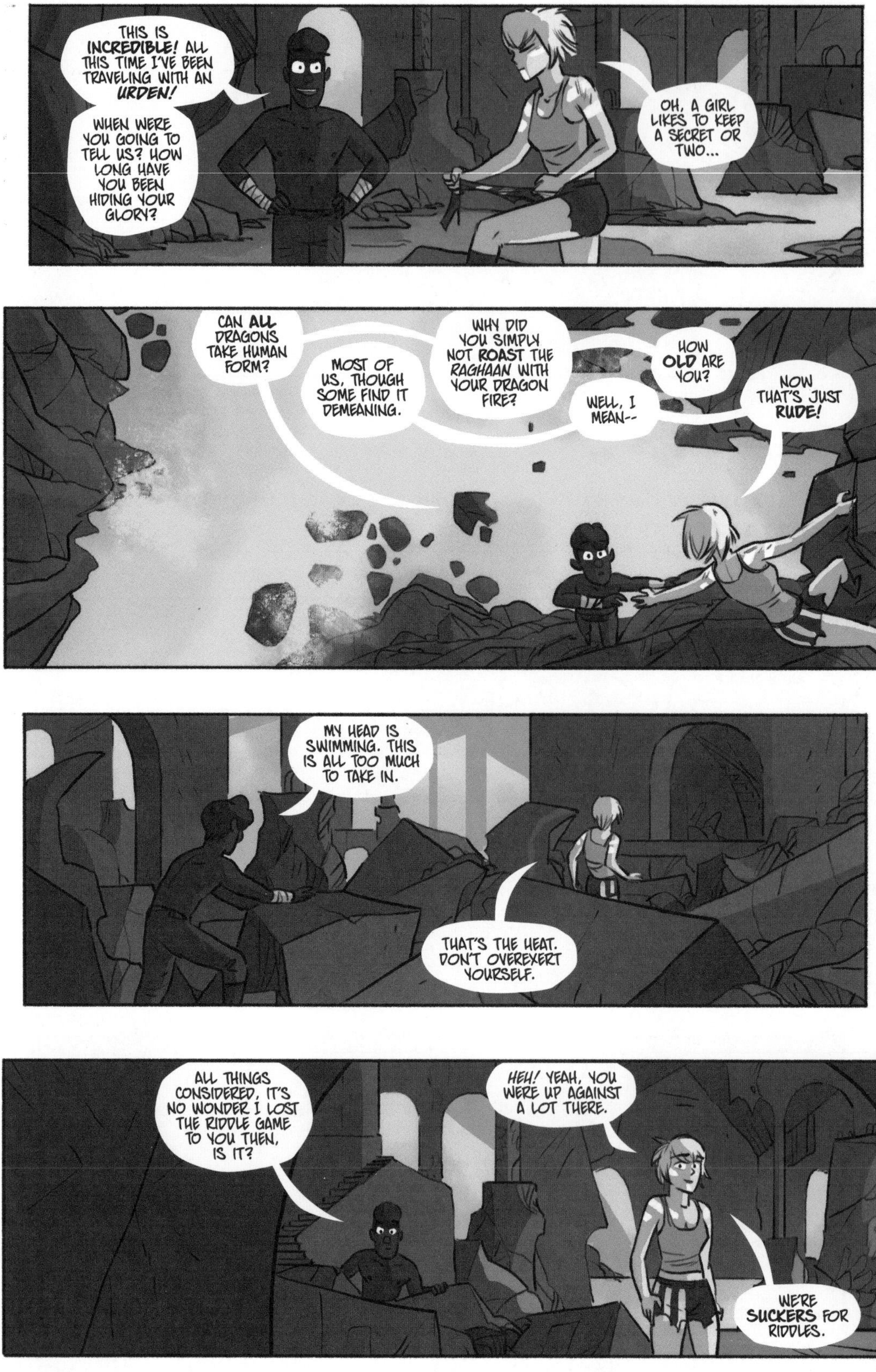
THIS IS **INCREDIBLE!** ALL THIS TIME I'VE BEEN TRAVELING WITH AN ***URDEN!***
WHEN WERE YOU GOING TO TELL US? HOW LONG HAVE YOU BEEN HIDING YOUR GLORY?
OH, A GIRL LIKES TO KEEP A SECRET OR TWO...
CAN **ALL** DRAGONS TAKE HUMAN FORM?
MOST OF US, THOUGH SOME FIND IT DEMEANING.
WHY DID YOU SIMPLY NOT **ROAST** THE RAGHAAN WITH YOUR DRAGON FIRE?
WELL, I MEAN--
HOW **OLD** ARE YOU?
NOW THAT'S JUST **RUDE!**
MY HEAD IS SWIMMING. THIS IS ALL TOO MUCH TO TAKE IN.
THAT'S THE HEAT. DON'T OVEREXERT YOURSELF.
ALL THINGS CONSIDERED, IT'S NO WONDER I LOST THE RIDDLE GAME TO YOU THEN, IS IT?
HEH! YEAH, YOU WERE UP AGAINST A LOT THERE.
WE'RE **SUCKERS** FOR RIDDLES.

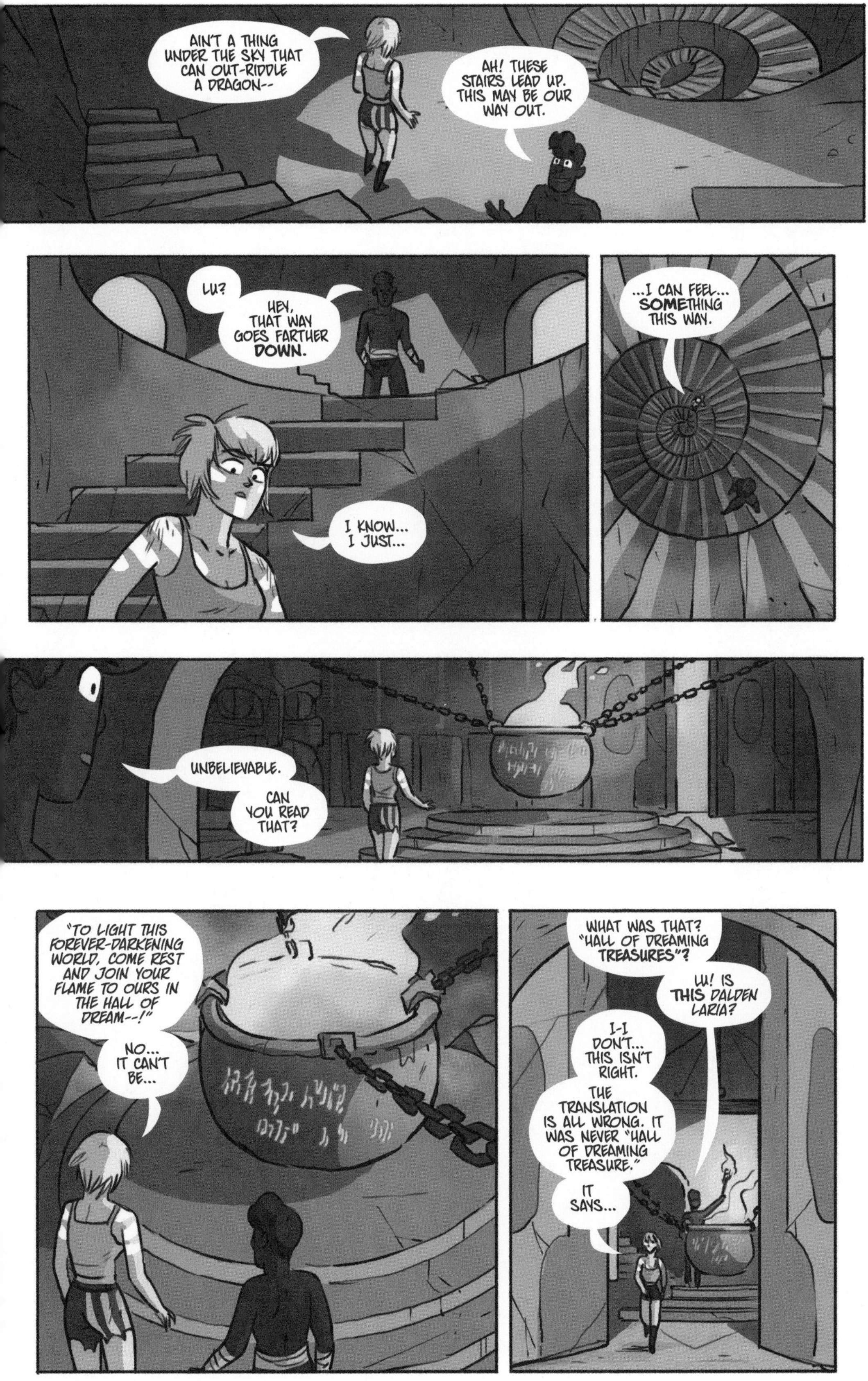
AIN'T A THING UNDER THE SKY THAT CAN OUT-RIDDLE A DRAGON--
AH! THESE STAIRS LEAD UP. THIS MAY BE OUR WAY OUT.
LU?
HEY, THAT WAY GOES FARTHER DOWN.
I KNOW... I JUST...
...I CAN FEEL... SOMETHING THIS WAY.
UNBELIEVABLE.
CAN YOU READ THAT?
"TO LIGHT THIS FOREVER-DARKENING WORLD, COME REST AND JOIN YOUR FLAME TO OURS IN THE HALL OF DREAM--!"
NO... IT CAN'T BE...
WHAT WAS THAT? "HALL OF DREAMING TREASURES"?
LU! IS THIS DALDEN LARIA?
I-I DON'T... THIS ISN'T RIGHT.
THE TRANSLATION IS ALL WRONG. IT WAS NEVER "HALL OF DREAMING TREASURE."
IT SAYS...

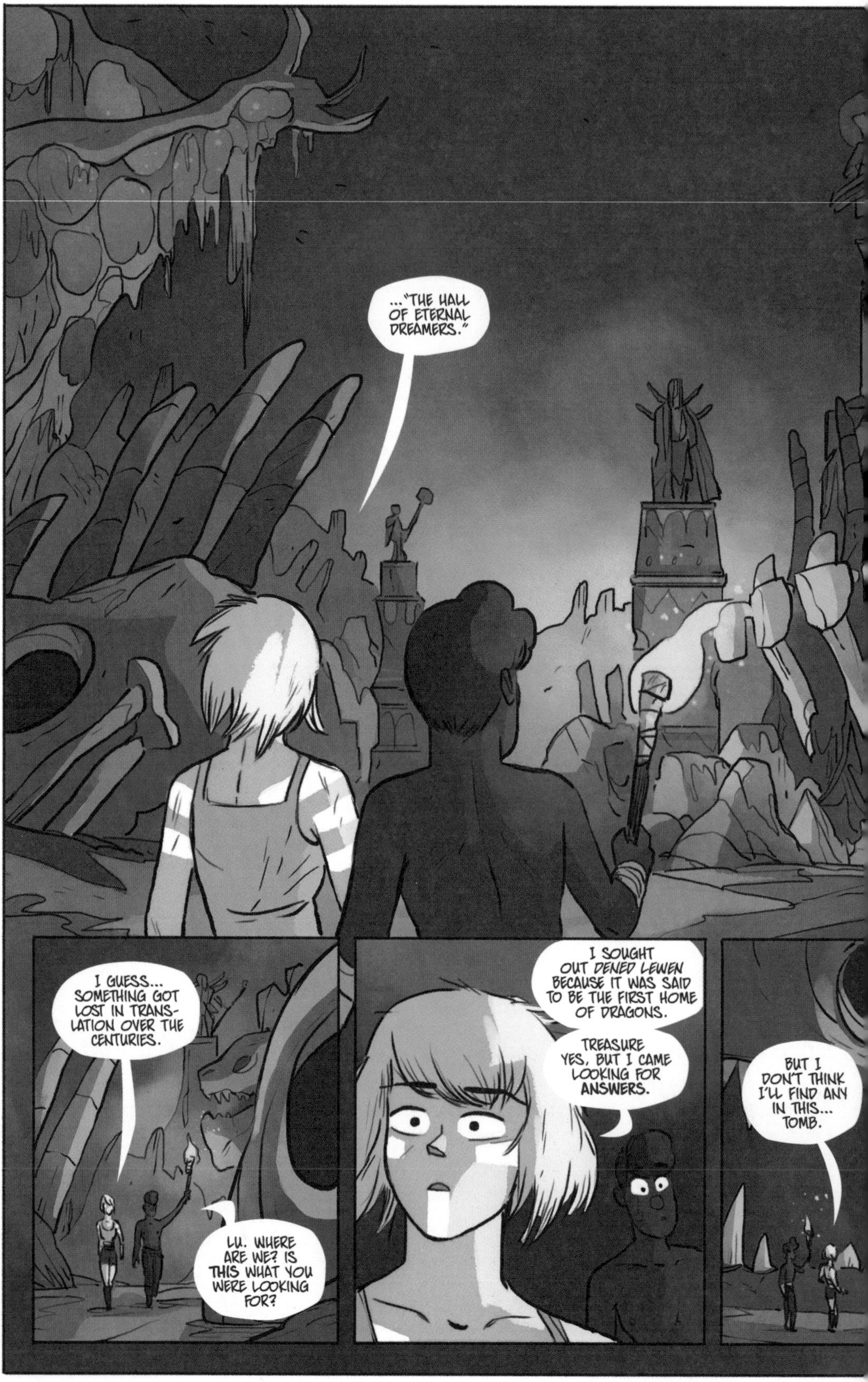

..."THE HALL OF ETERNAL DREAMERS."
I GUESS... SOMETHING GOT LOST IN TRANS-LATION OVER THE CENTURIES.
LU. WHERE ARE WE? IS THIS WHAT YOU WERE LOOKING FOR?
I SOUGHT OUT DENED LEWEN BECAUSE IT WAS SAID TO BE THE FIRST HOME OF DRAGONS.
TREASURE YES, BUT I CAME LOOKING FOR ANSWERS.
BUT I DON'T THINK I'LL FIND ANY IN THIS... TOMB.

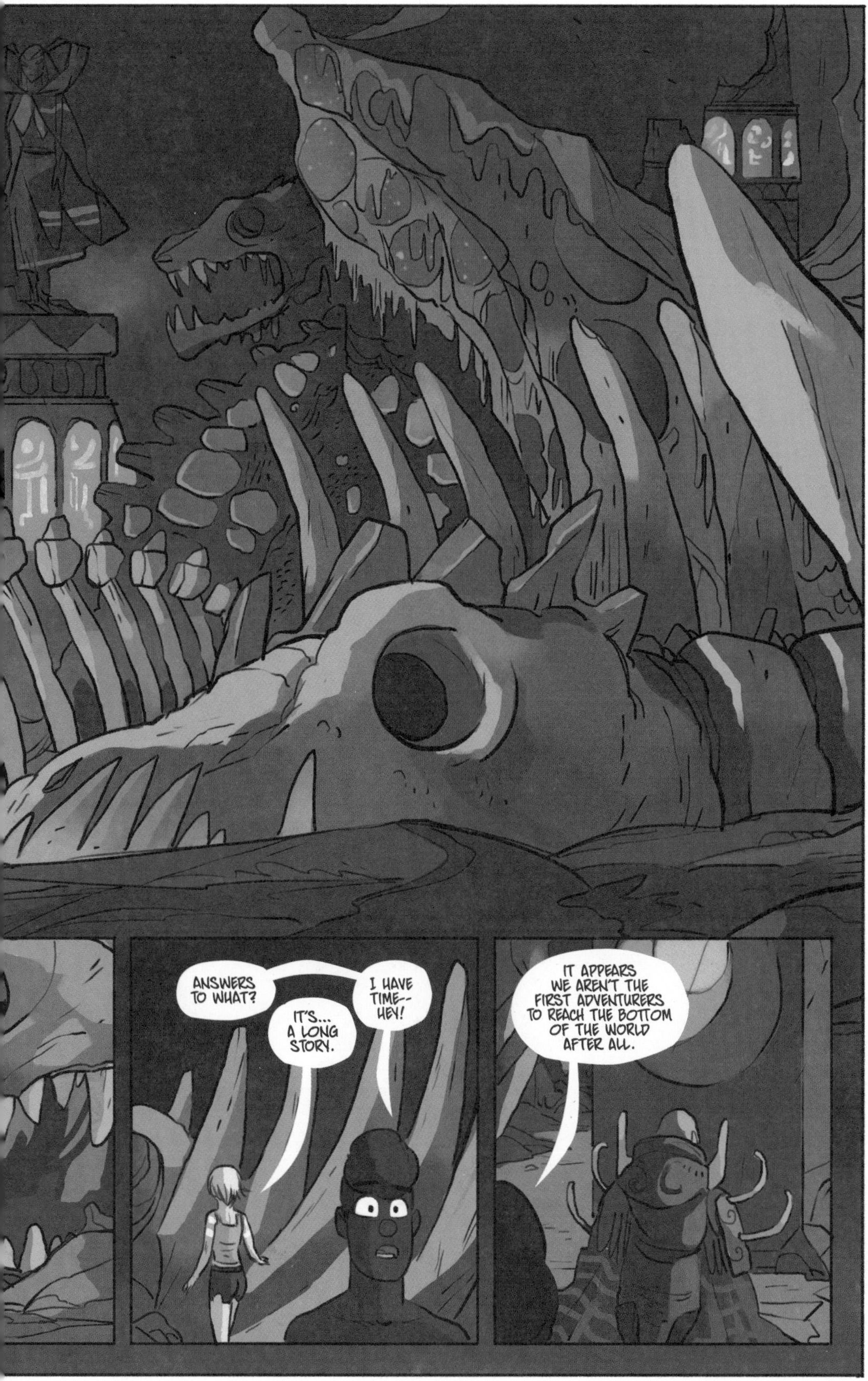
ANSWERS TO WHAT?
IT'S... A LONG STORY.
I HAVE TIME-- HEY!
IT APPEARS WE AREN'T THE FIRST ADVENTURERS TO REACH THE BOTTOM OF THE WORLD AFTER ALL.

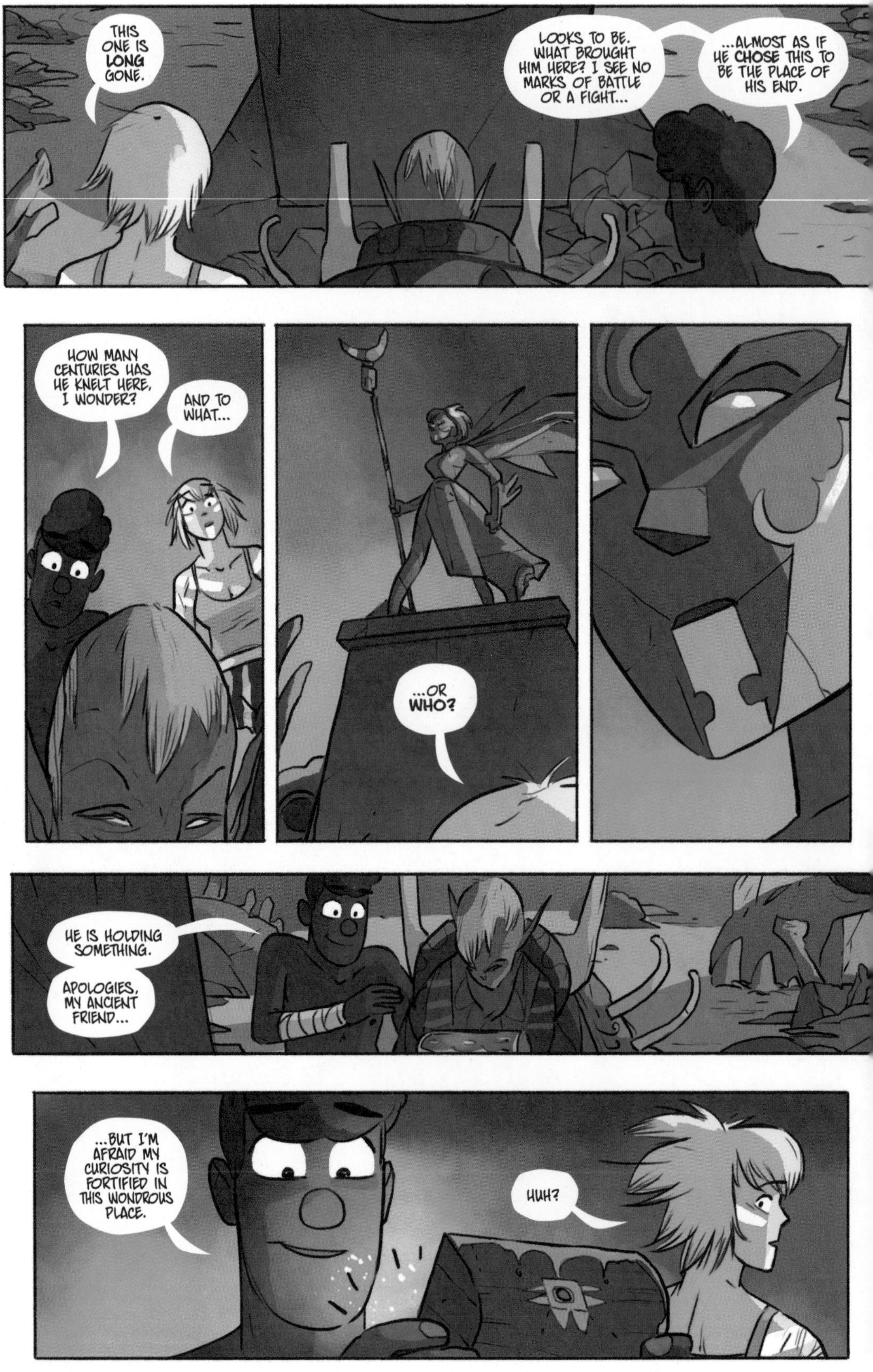
THIS ONE IS LONG GONE.
LOOKS TO BE. WHAT BROUGHT HIM HERE? I SEE NO MARKS OF BATTLE OR A FIGHT...
...ALMOST AS IF HE CHOSE THIS TO BE THE PLACE OF HIS END.
HOW MANY CENTURIES HAS HE KNELT HERE, I WONDER?
AND TO WHAT...
...OR WHO?
HE IS HOLDING SOMETHING.
APOLOGIES, MY ANCIENT FRIEND...
...BUT I'M AFRAID MY CURIOSITY IS FORTIFIED IN THIS WONDROUS PLACE.
HUH?

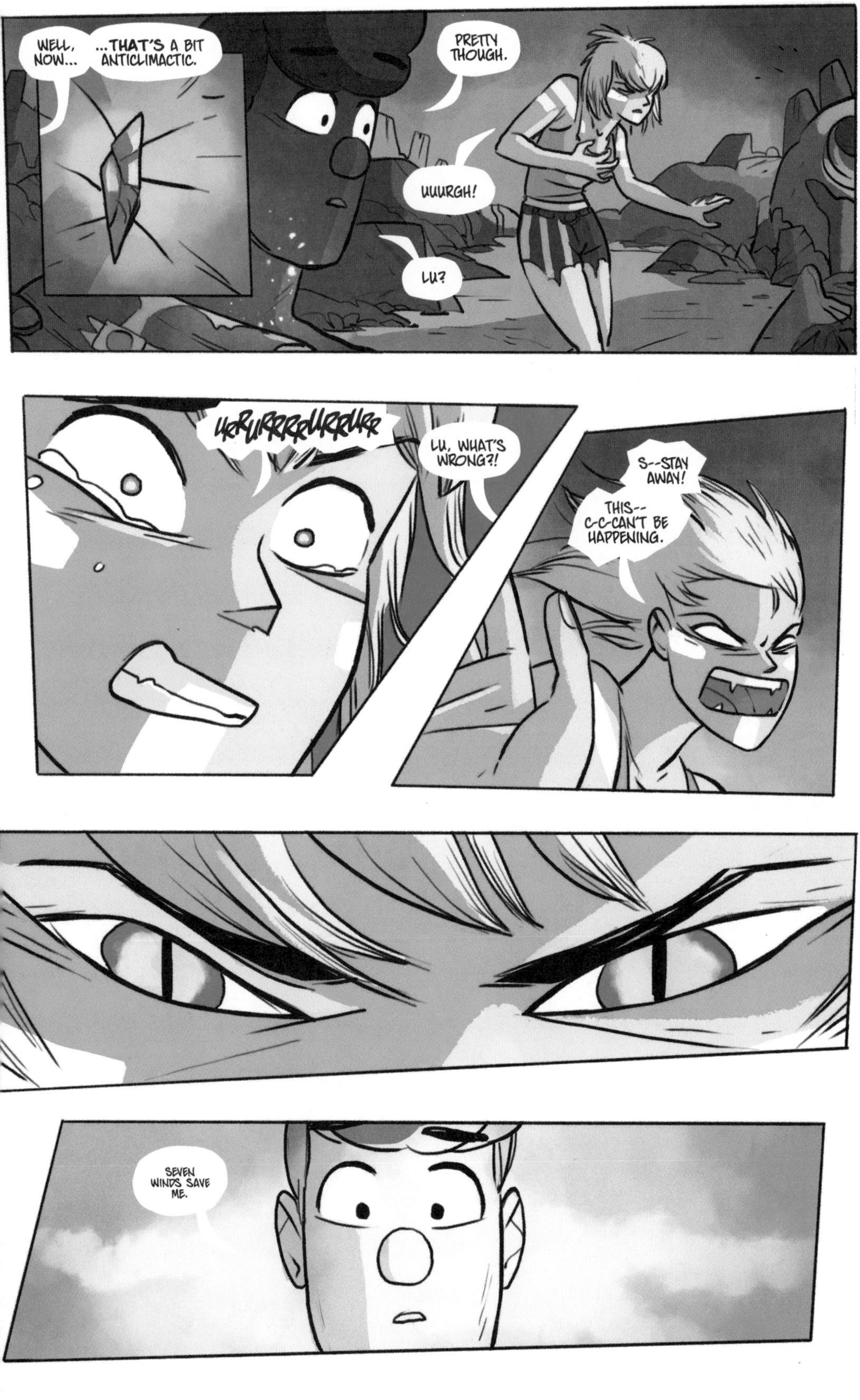
WELL, NOW...
...THAT'S A BIT ANTICLIMACTIC.
PRETTY THOUGH.
UUURGH!
LU?
URRURRRRURRURR
LU, WHAT'S WRONG?!
S--STAY AWAY!
THIS-- C-C-CAN'T BE HAPPENING.
SEVEN WINDS SAVE ME.

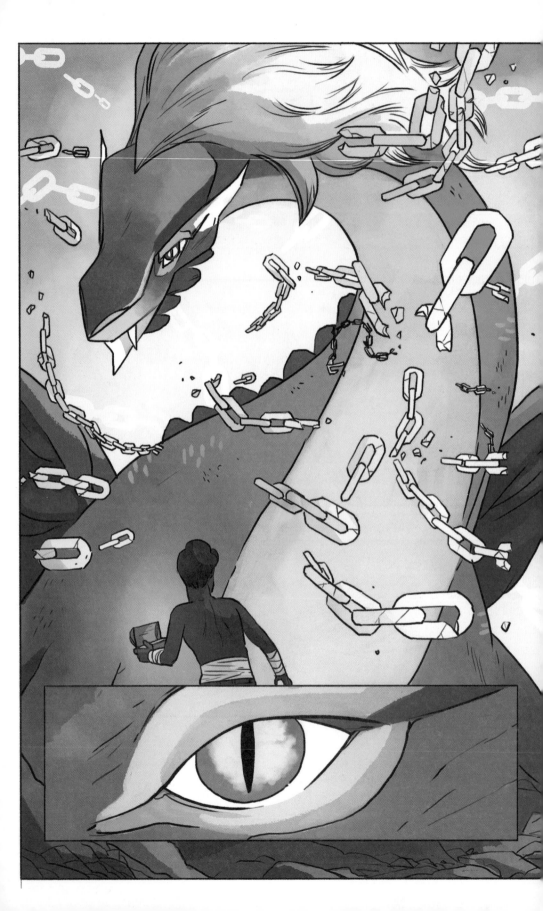

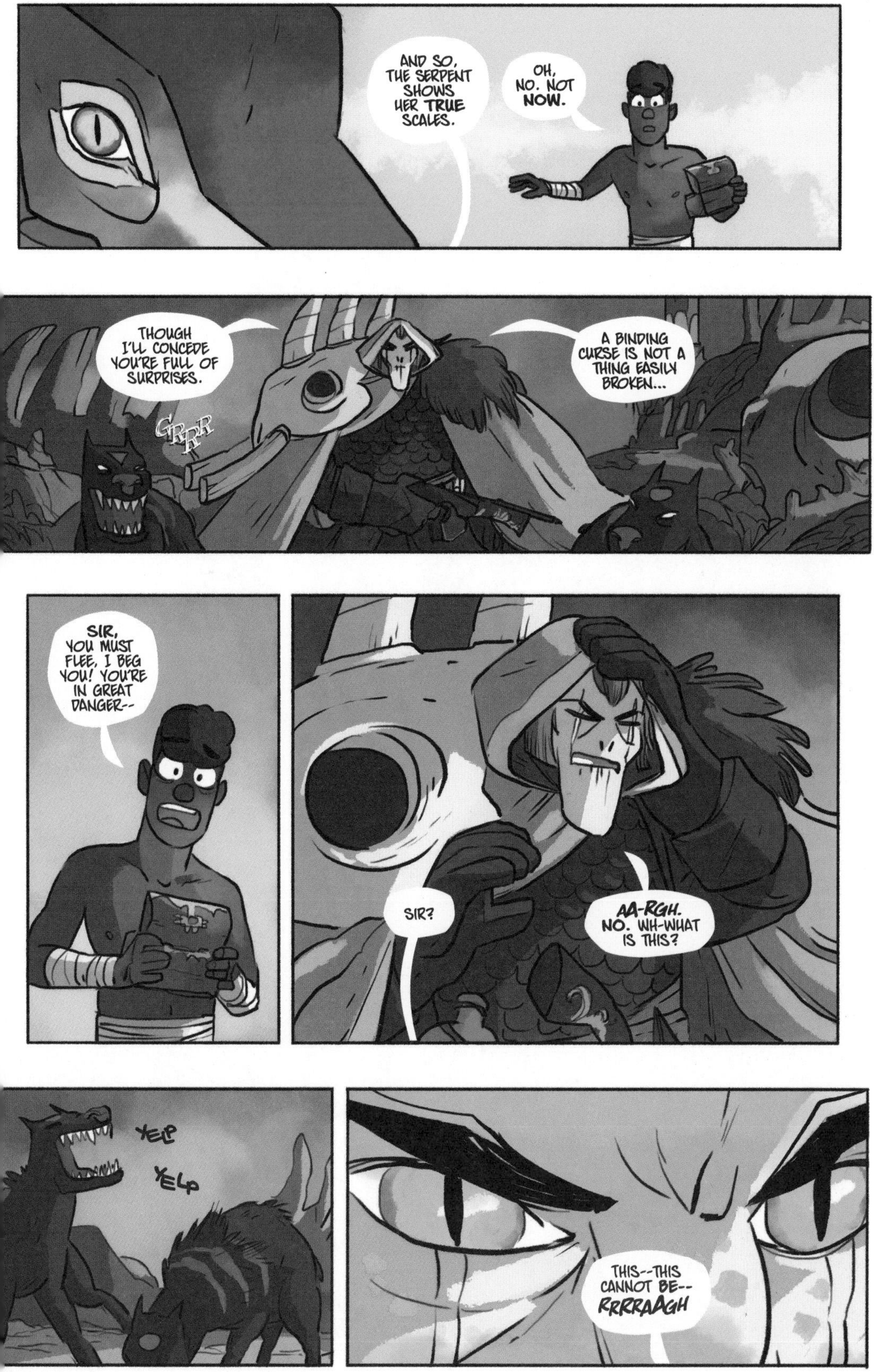
AND SO, THE SERPENT SHOWS HER TRUE SCALES.
OH, NO. NOT NOW.
THOUGH I'LL CONCEDE YOU'RE FULL OF SURPRISES.
A BINDING CURSE IS NOT A THING EASILY BROKEN...
GRRR
SIR, YOU MUST FLEE, I BEG YOU! YOU'RE IN GREAT DANGER--
SIR?
AA-RGH. NO. WH-WHAT IS THIS?
YELP
YELP
THIS--THIS CANNOT BE-- RRRRAAGH

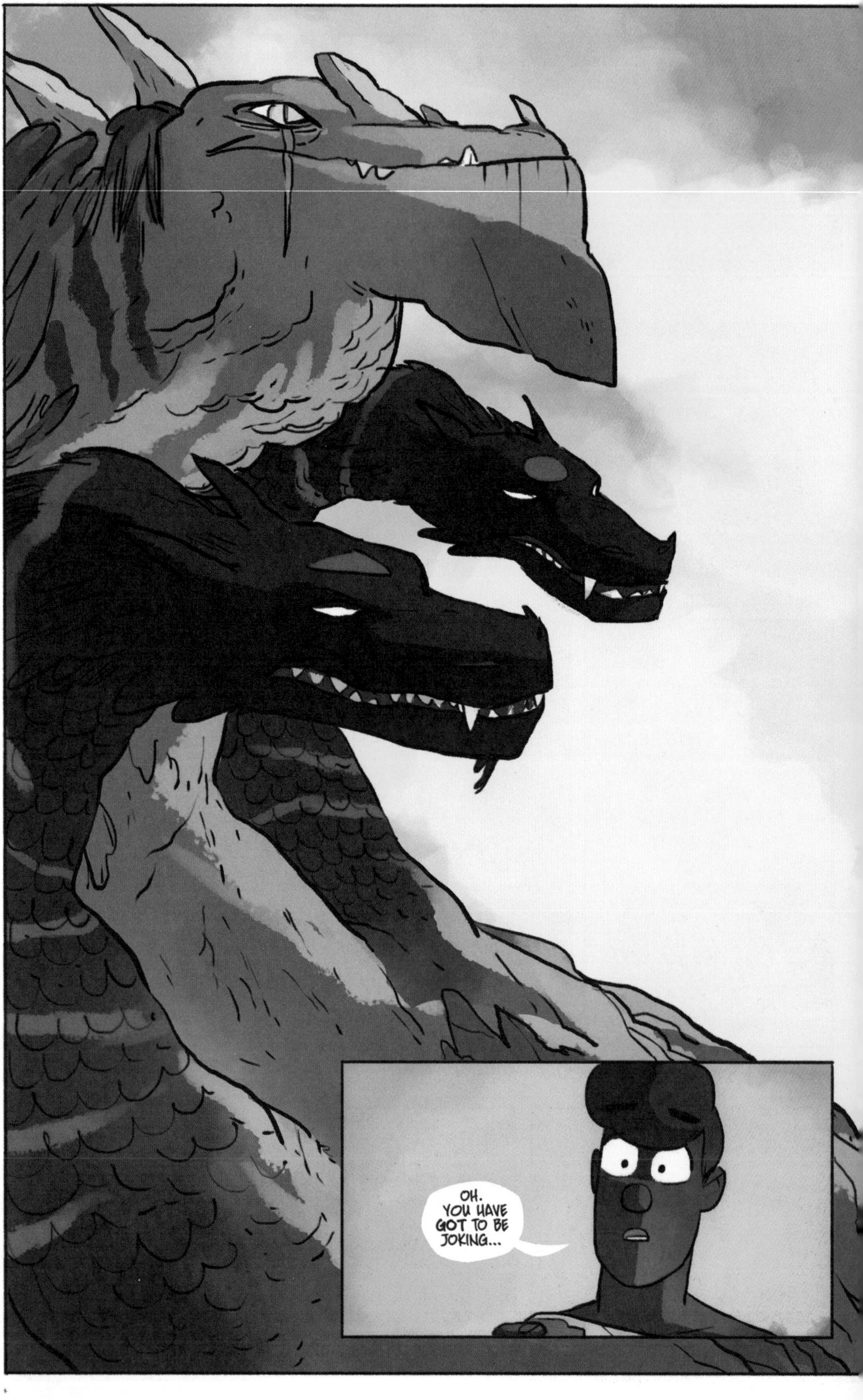
OH. YOU HAVE GOT TO BE JOKING...

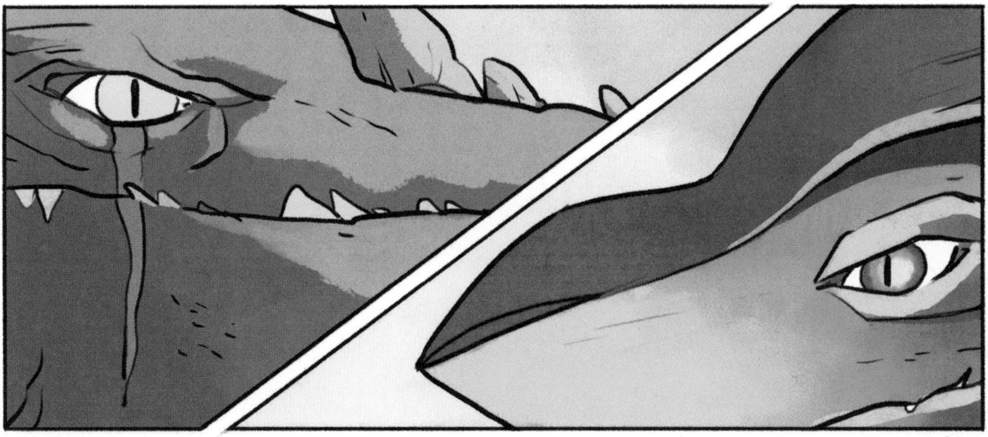

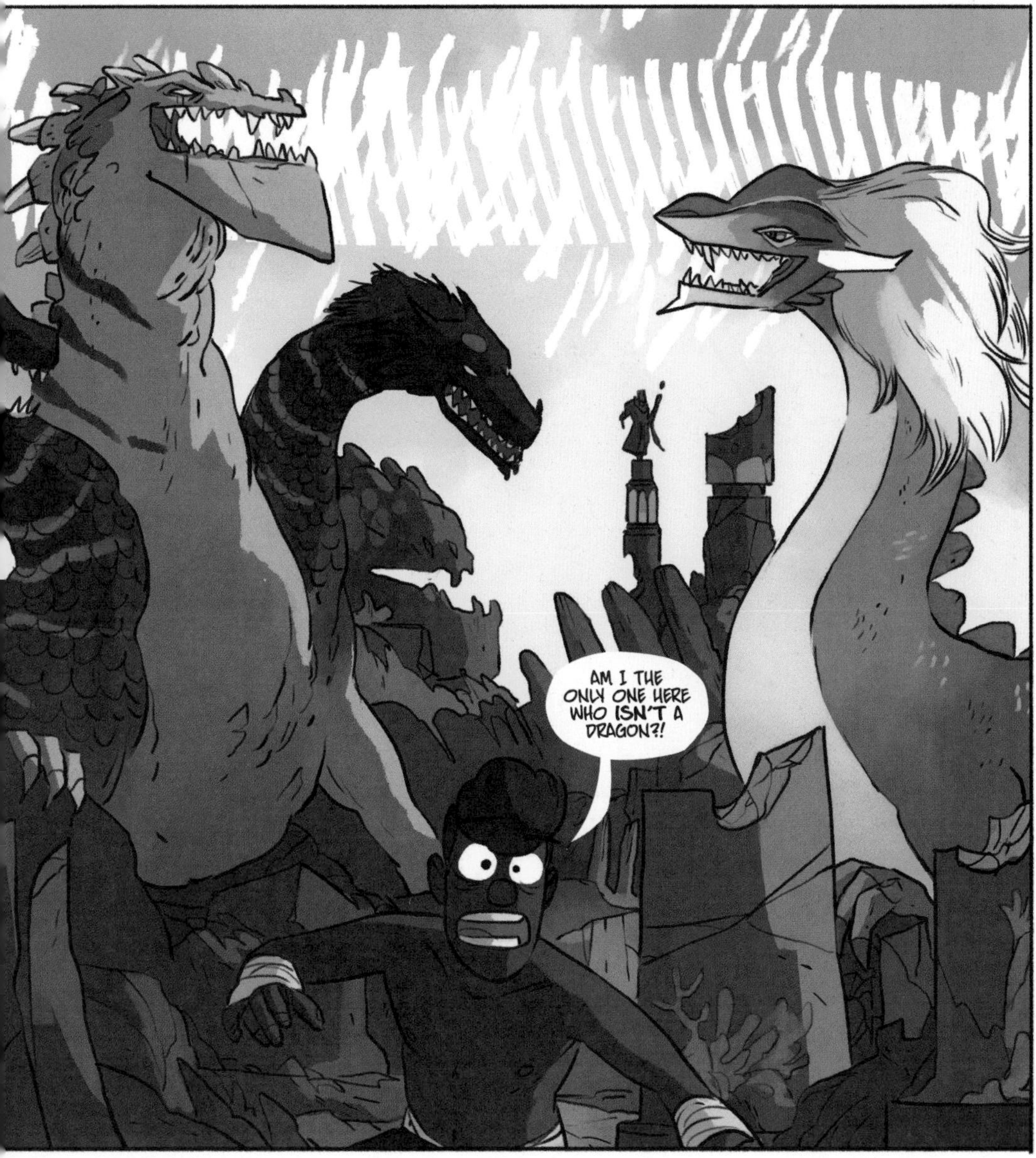
AM I THE ONLY ONE HERE WHO ISN'T A DRAGON?!

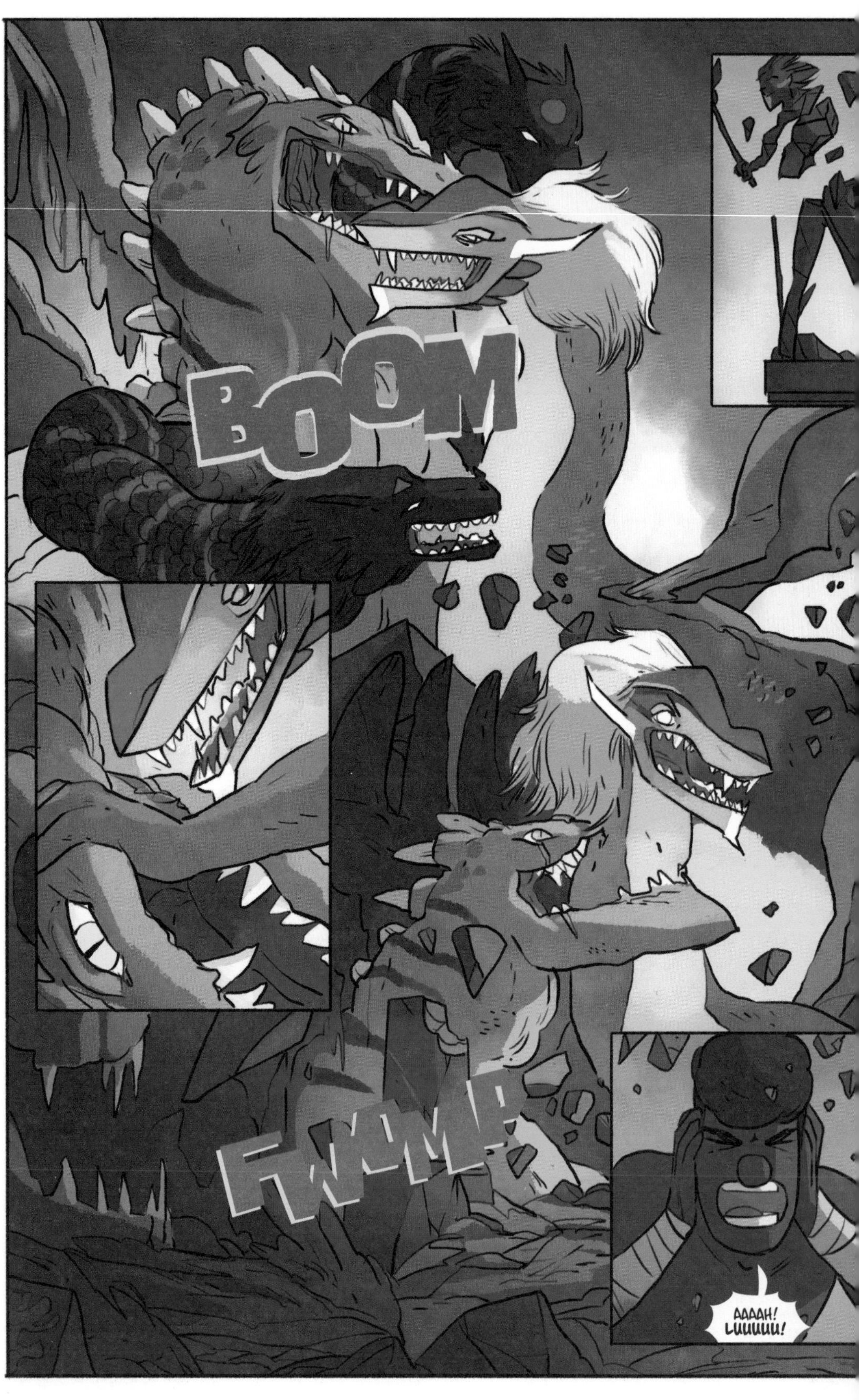
BOOM
FWOMP
AAAAH! LUUUUU!

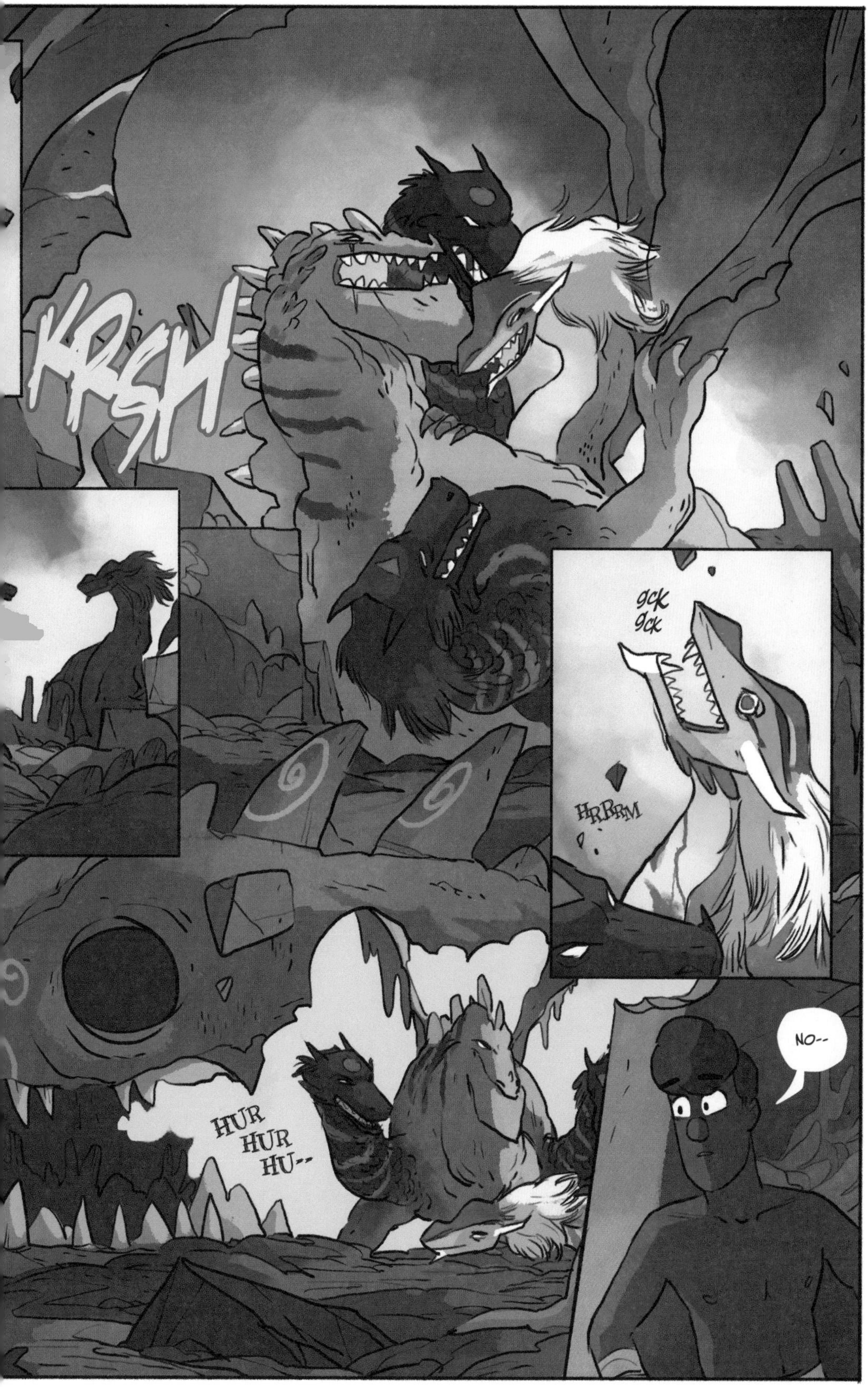
KRSH
gck
gck
HRRRM
HUR
HUR
HU--
NO--

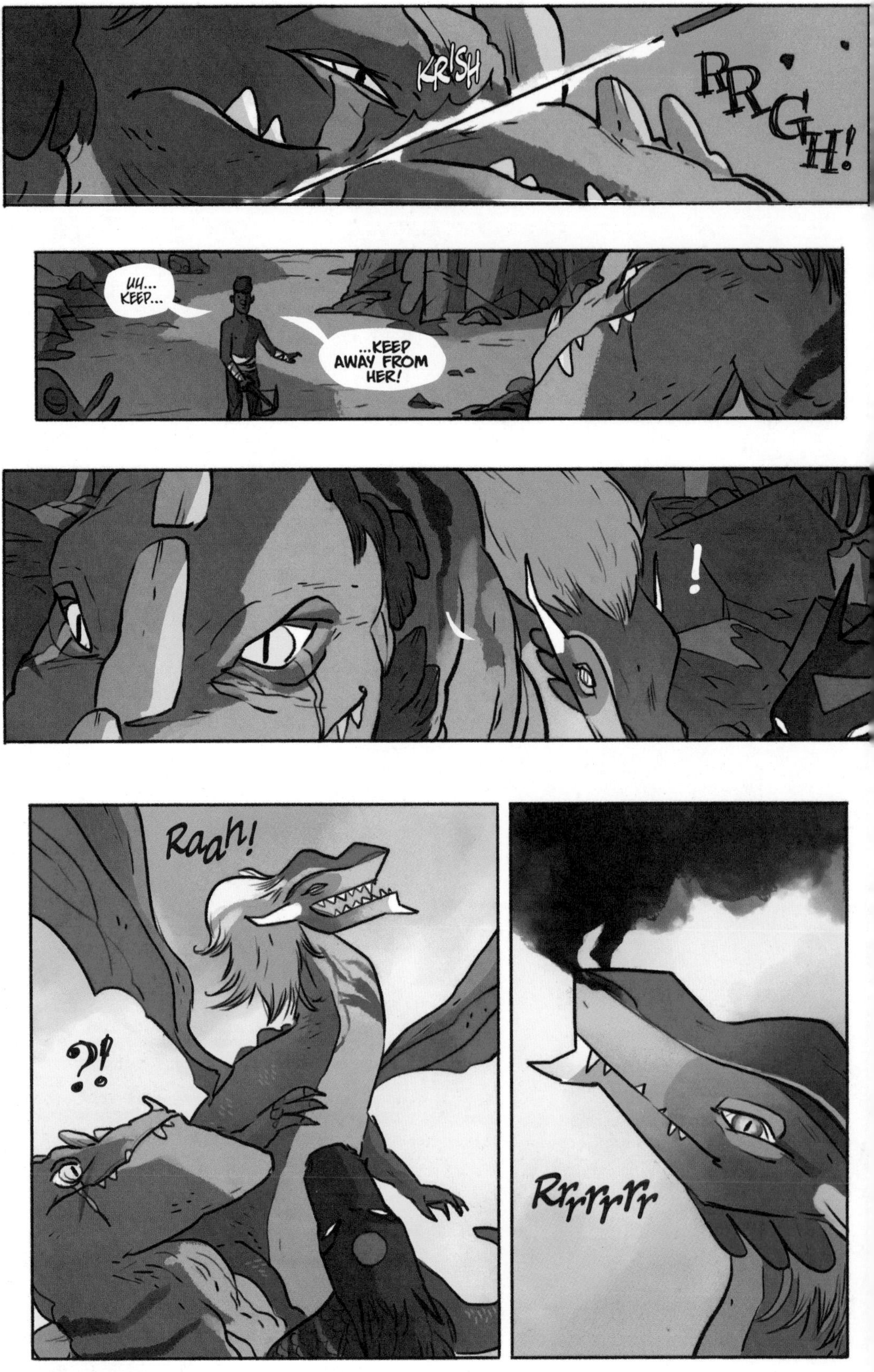
KRISH
RRRGH!
UH... KEEP...
...KEEP AWAY FROM HER!
!
Raah!
?!
Rrrrrr

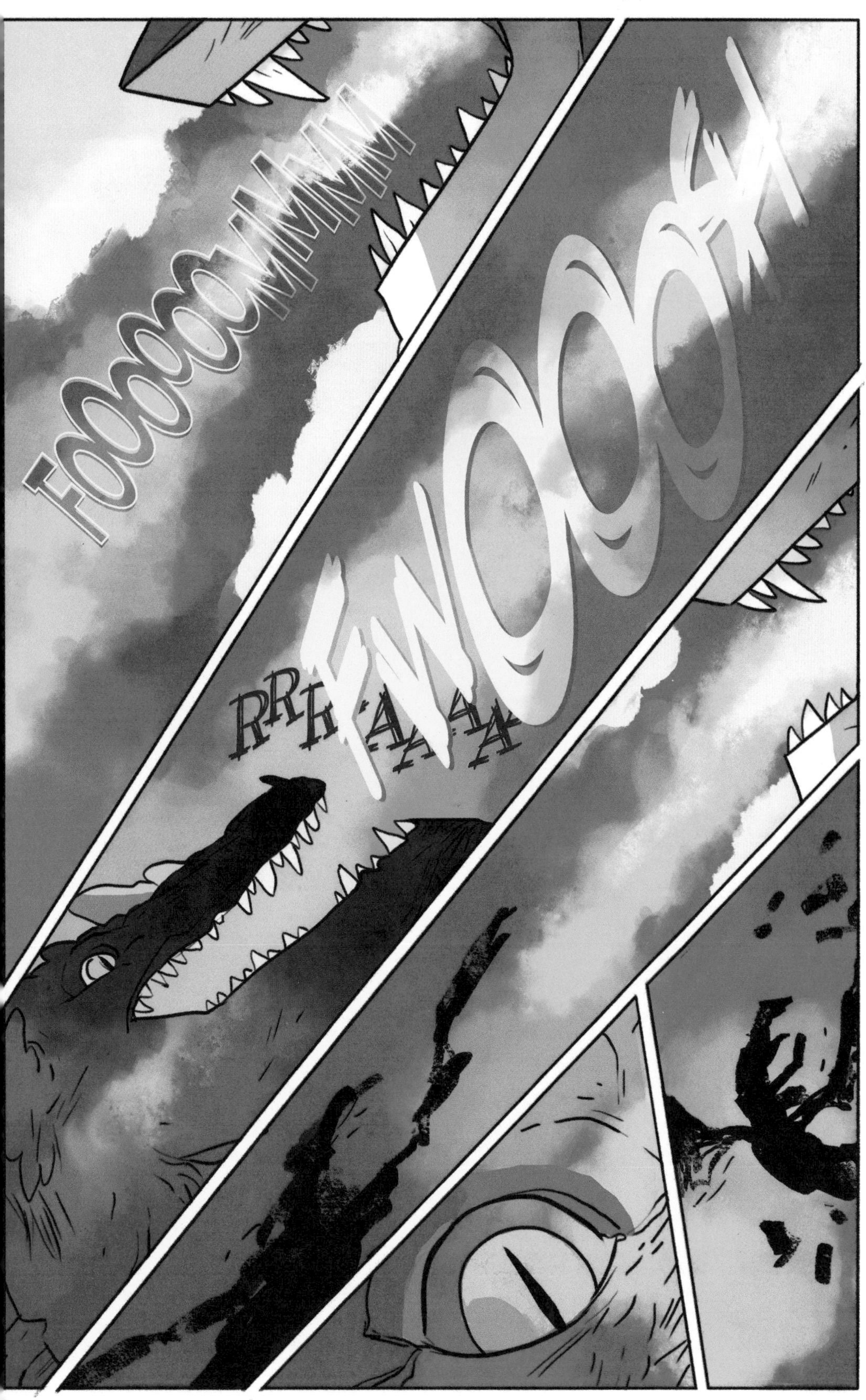

FOOOOOOMMMMM
FWOOOOSH
RRRAAAA

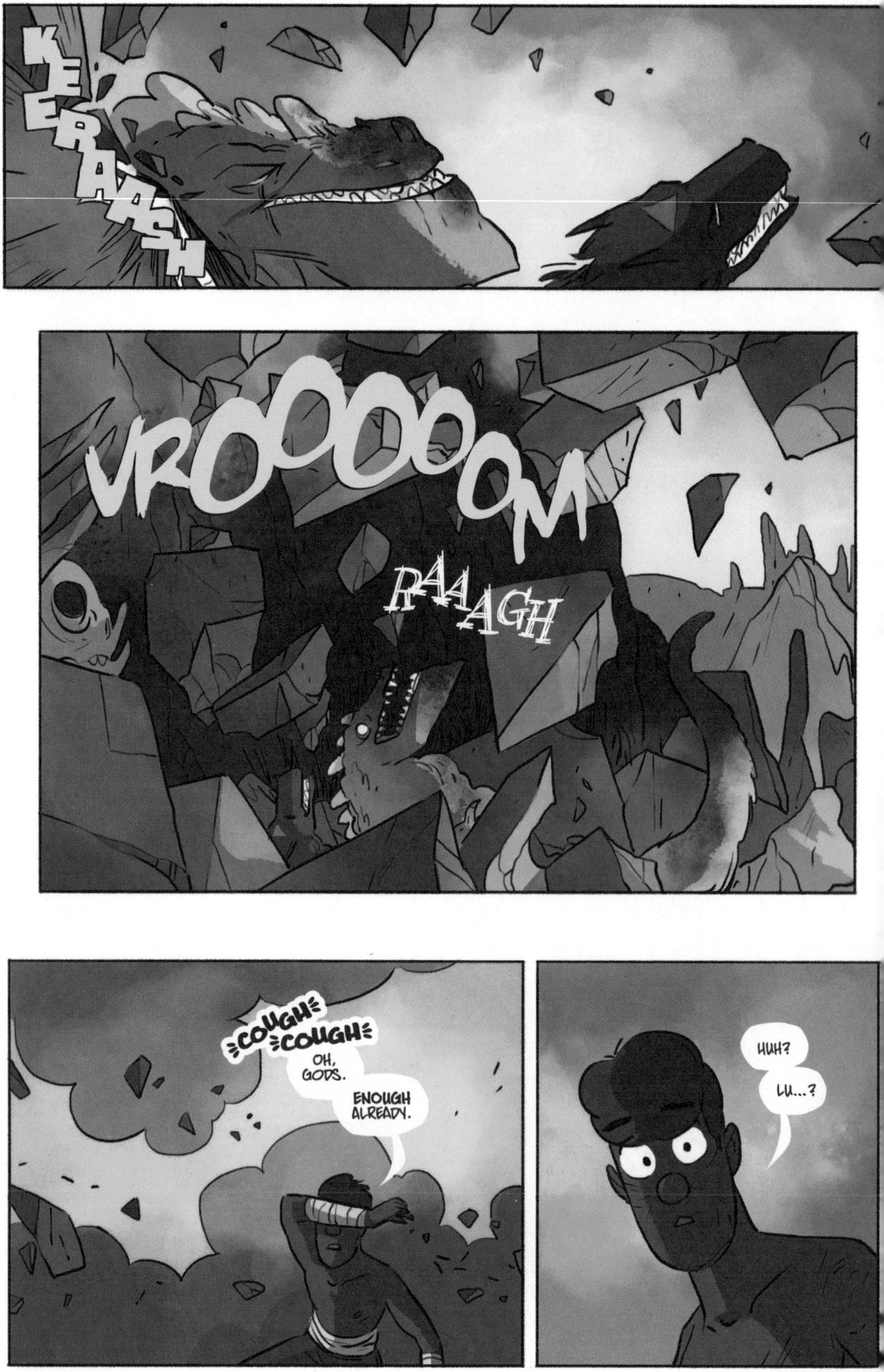
KEERRAASH
VROOOOOM
RAAAGH
COUGH COUGH
OH, GODS.
ENOUGH ALREADY.
HUH?
LU...?

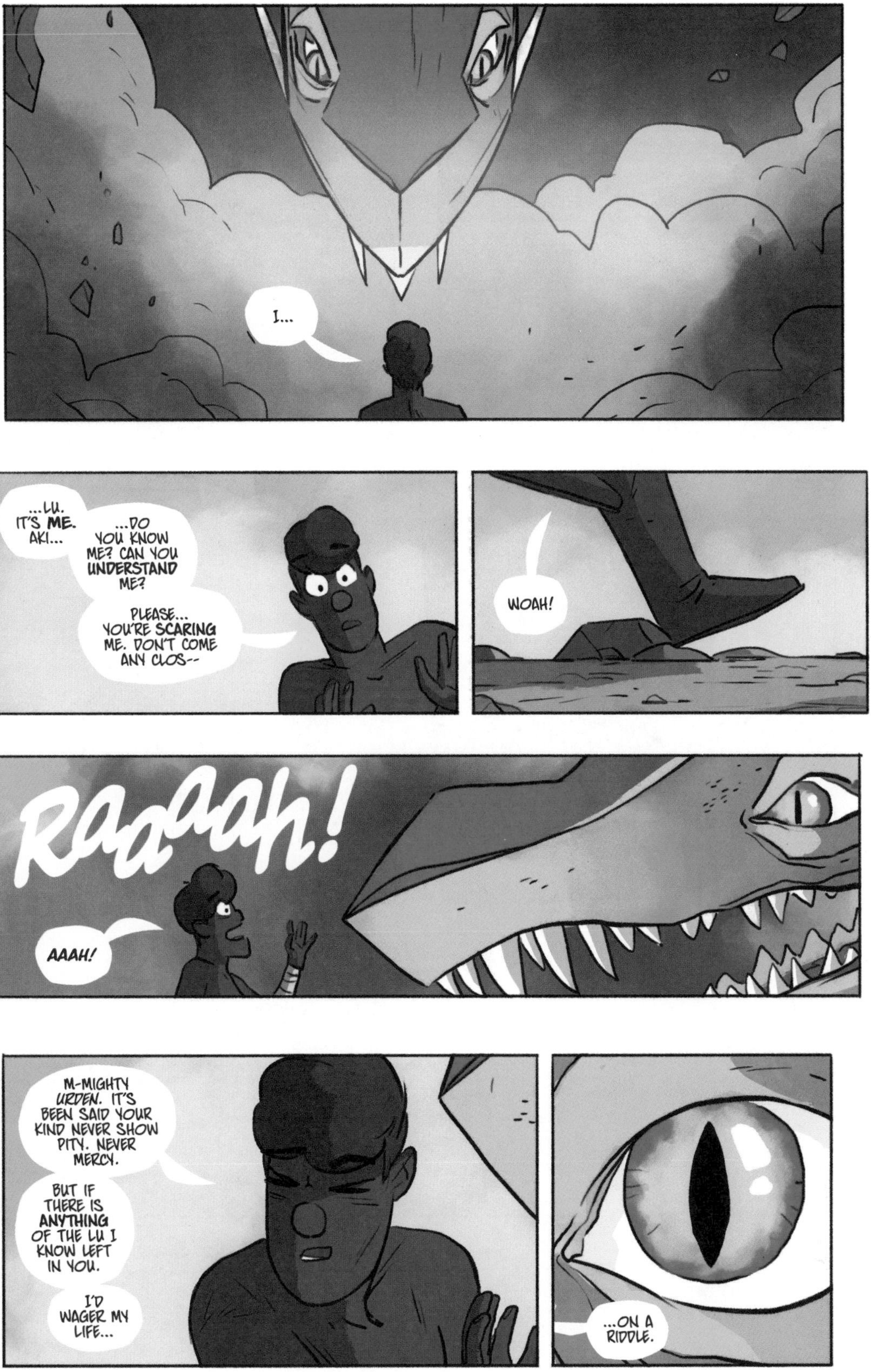
I...
...LU. IT'S ME. AKI...
...DO YOU KNOW ME? CAN YOU UNDERSTAND ME?
PLEASE... YOU'RE SCARING ME. DON'T COME ANY CLOS--
WOAH!
RAAAAH!
AAAH!
M-MIGHTY URDEN. IT'S BEEN SAID YOUR KIND NEVER SHOW PITY. NEVER MERCY.
BUT IF THERE IS ANYTHING OF THE LU I KNOW LEFT IN YOU.
I'D WAGER MY LIFE...
...ON A RIDDLE.

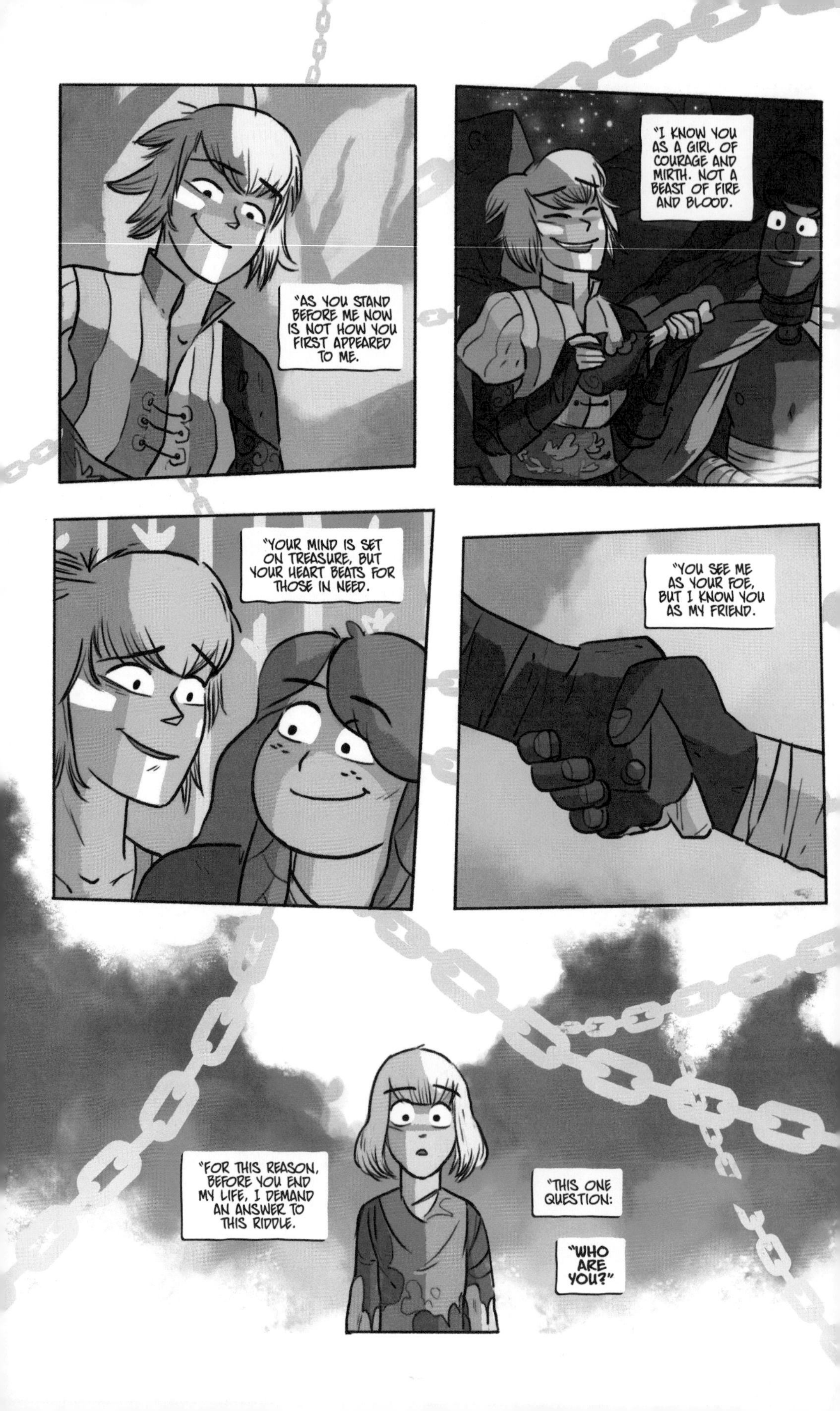
"AS YOU STAND BEFORE ME NOW IS NOT HOW YOU FIRST APPEARED TO ME.
"I KNOW YOU AS A GIRL OF COURAGE AND MIRTH. NOT A BEAST OF FIRE AND BLOOD.
"YOUR MIND IS SET ON TREASURE, BUT YOUR HEART BEATS FOR THOSE IN NEED.
"YOU SEE ME AS YOUR FOE, BUT I KNOW YOU AS MY FRIEND.
"FOR THIS REASON, BEFORE YOU END MY LIFE, I DEMAND AN ANSWER TO THIS RIDDLE.
"THIS ONE QUESTION:
"WHO ARE YOU?"

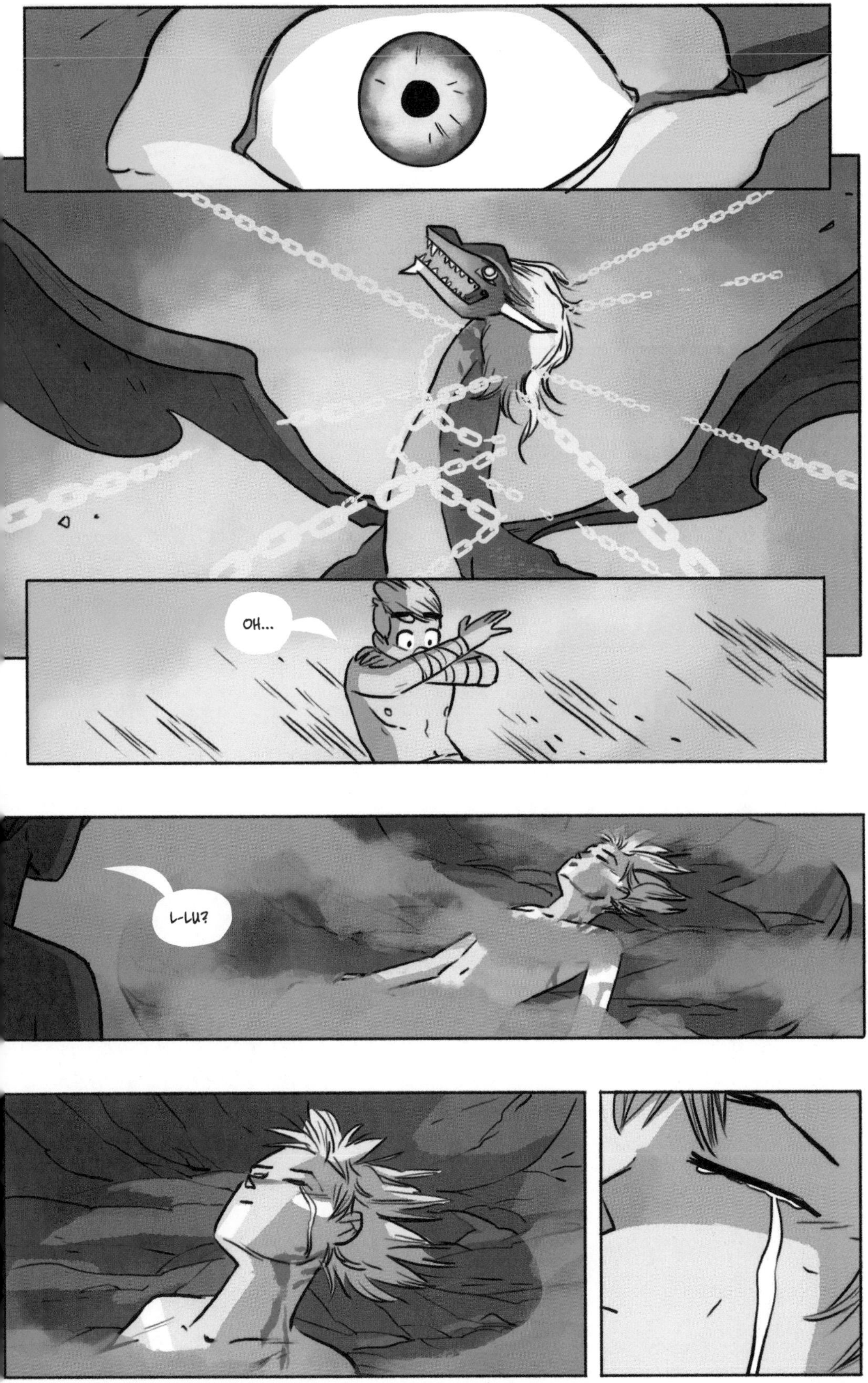
OH...
L-LU?

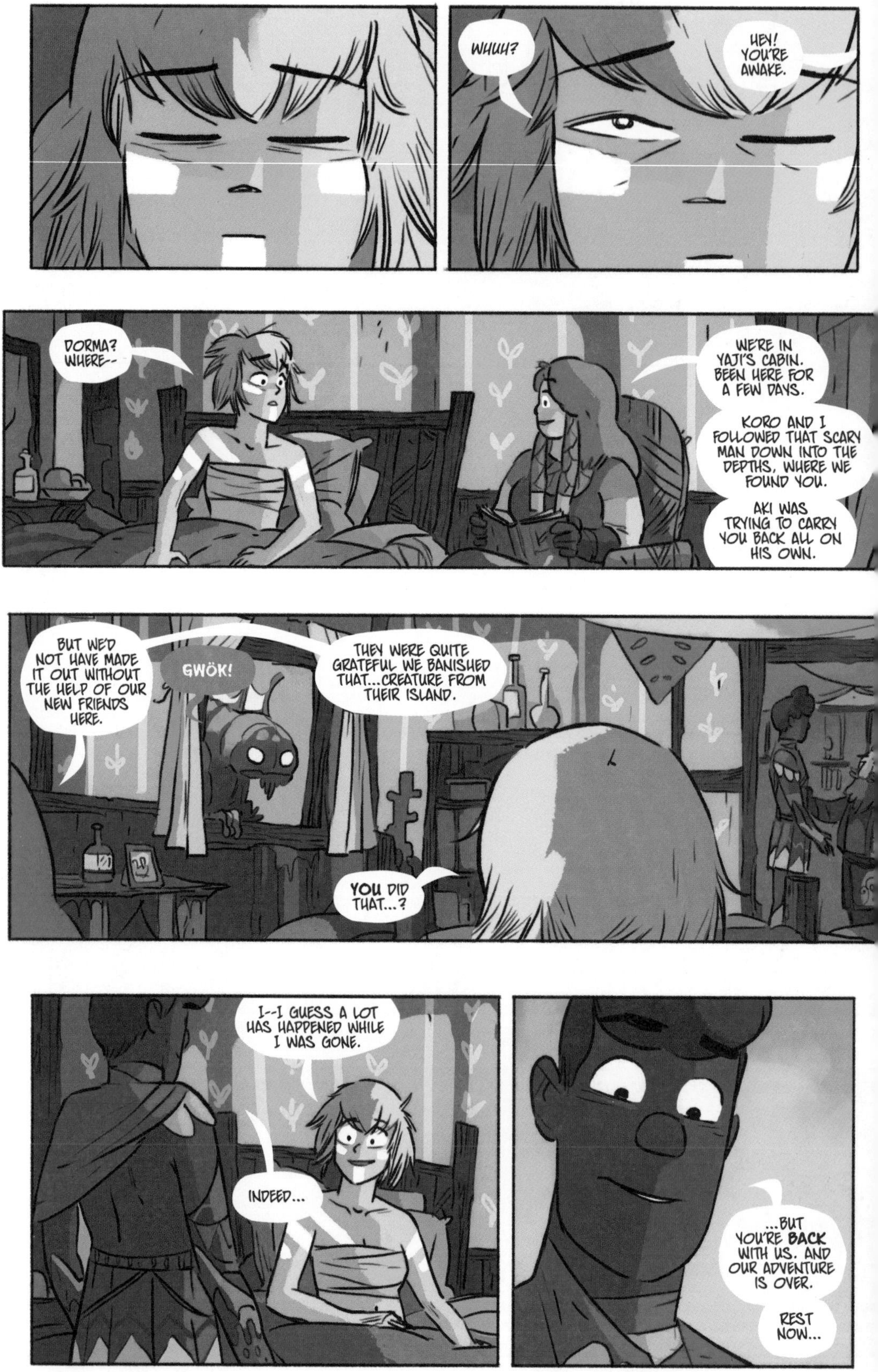
WHUH?
HEY! YOU'RE AWAKE.
DORMA? WHERE--
WE'RE IN YAJI'S CABIN. BEEN HERE FOR A FEW DAYS.
KORO AND I FOLLOWED THAT SCARY MAN DOWN INTO THE DEPTHS, WHERE WE FOUND YOU.
AKI WAS TRYING TO CARRY YOU BACK ALL ON HIS OWN.
BUT WE'D NOT HAVE MADE IT OUT WITHOUT THE HELP OF OUR NEW FRIENDS HERE.
GWÖK!
THEY WERE QUITE GRATEFUL WE BANISHED THAT...CREATURE FROM THEIR ISLAND.
YOU DID THAT...?
I--I GUESS A LOT HAS HAPPENED WHILE I WAS GONE.
INDEED...
...BUT YOU'RE **BACK** WITH US. AND OUR ADVENTURE IS OVER.
REST NOW...

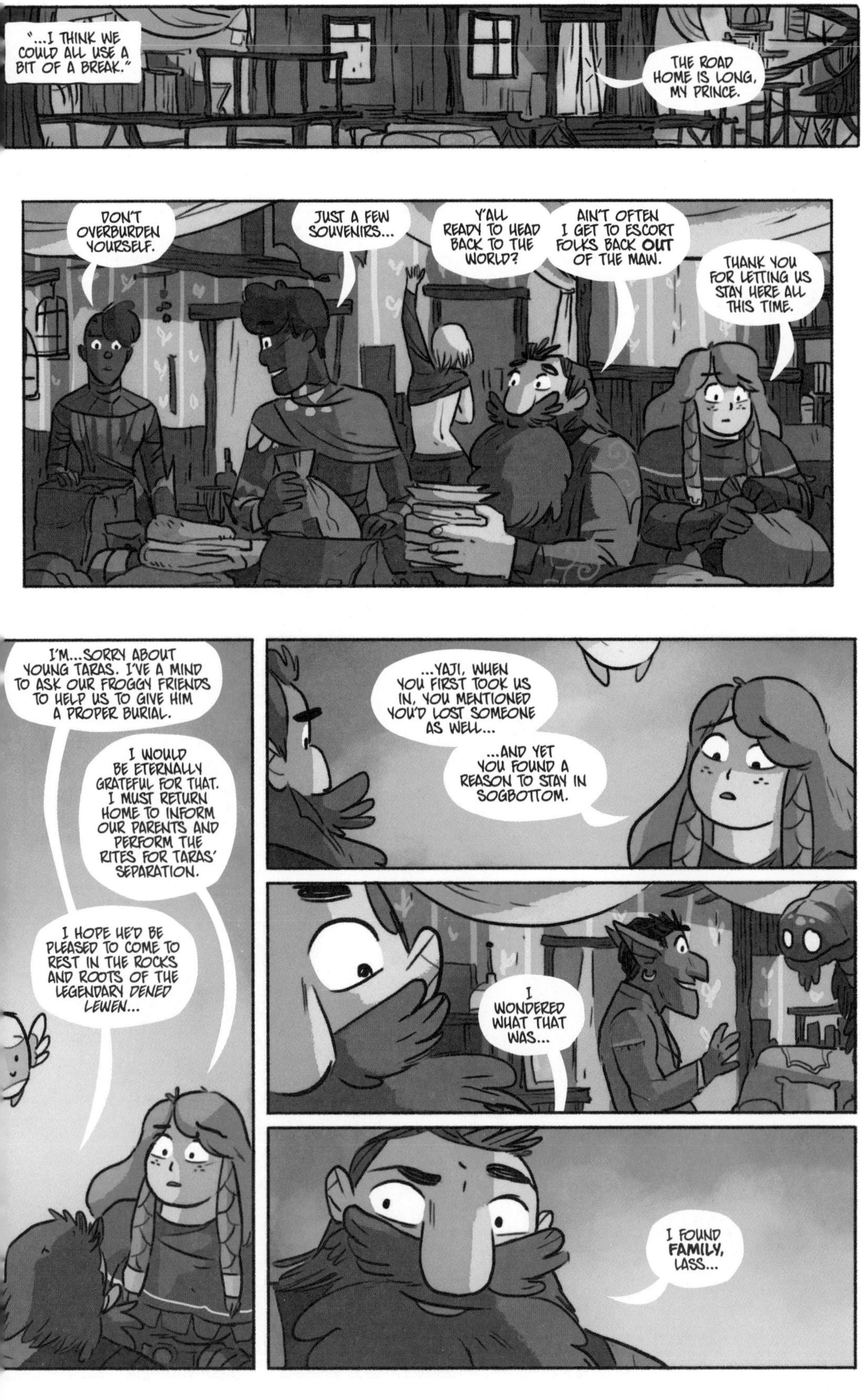
"...I THINK WE COULD ALL USE A BIT OF A BREAK."
THE ROAD HOME IS LONG, MY PRINCE.
DON'T OVERBURDEN YOURSELF.
JUST A FEW SOUVENIRS...
Y'ALL READY TO HEAD BACK TO THE WORLD?
AIN'T OFTEN I GET TO ESCORT FOLKS BACK **OUT** OF THE MAW.
THANK YOU FOR LETTING US STAY HERE ALL THIS TIME.
I'M...SORRY ABOUT YOUNG TARAS. I'VE A MIND TO ASK OUR FROGGY FRIENDS TO HELP US TO GIVE HIM A PROPER BURIAL.
I WOULD BE ETERNALLY GRATEFUL FOR THAT. I MUST RETURN HOME TO INFORM OUR PARENTS AND PERFORM THE RITES FOR TARAS' SEPARATION.
I HOPE HE'D BE PLEASED TO COME TO REST IN THE ROCKS AND ROOTS OF THE LEGENDARY DENED LEWEN...
...YAJI, WHEN YOU FIRST TOOK US IN, YOU MENTIONED YOU'D LOST SOMEONE AS WELL...
...AND YET YOU FOUND A REASON TO STAY IN SOGBOTTOM.
I WONDERED WHAT THAT WAS...
I FOUND **FAMILY,** LASS...

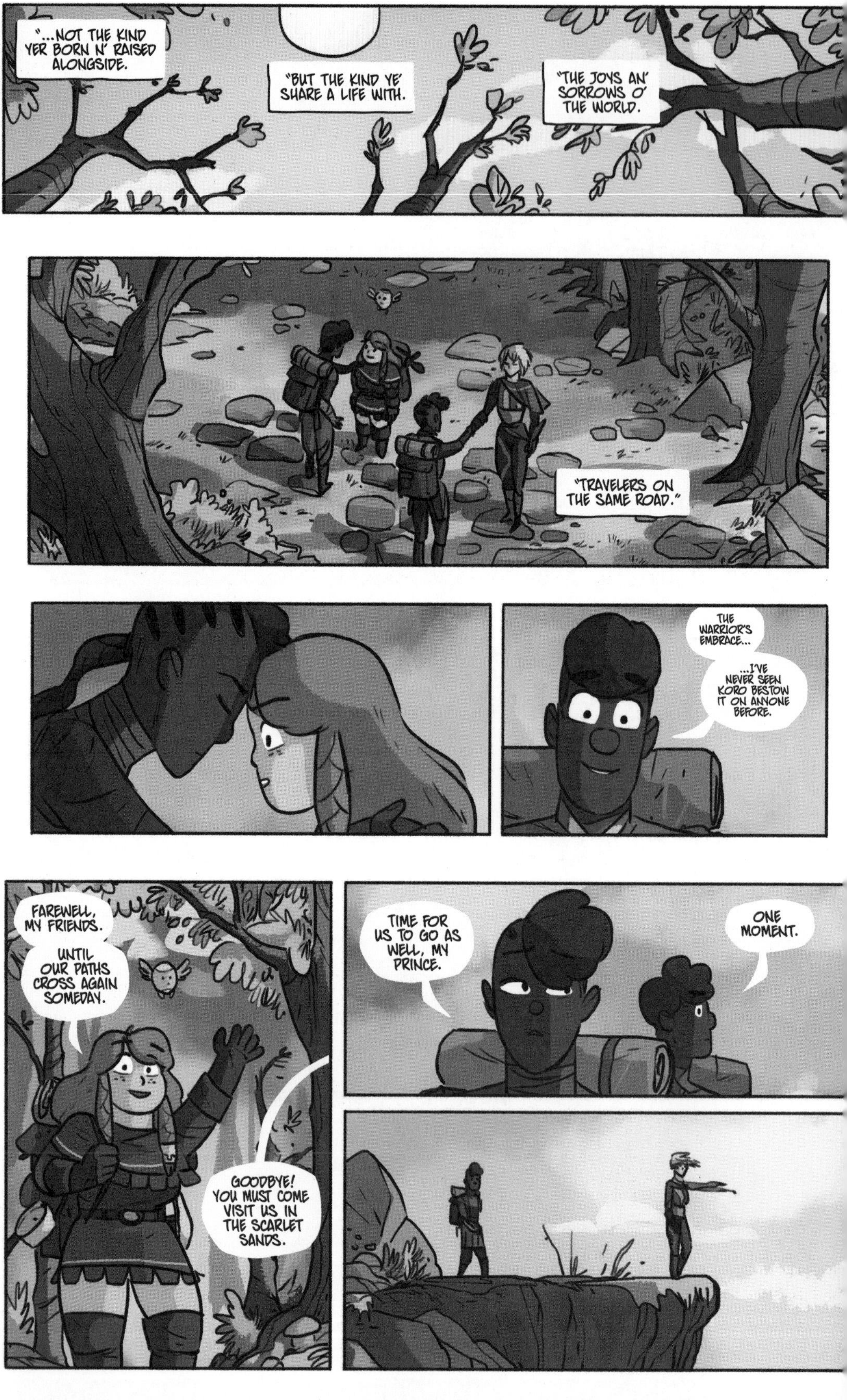
"...NOT THE KIND YER BORN N' RAISED ALONGSIDE.
"BUT THE KIND YE' SHARE A LIFE WITH.
"THE JOYS AN' SORROWS O' THE WORLD.
"TRAVELERS ON THE SAME ROAD."
THE WARRIOR'S EMBRACE...
...I'VE NEVER SEEN KORO BESTOW IT ON ANYONE BEFORE.
FAREWELL, MY FRIENDS.
UNTIL OUR PATHS CROSS AGAIN SOMEDAY.
GOODBYE! YOU MUST COME VISIT US IN THE SCARLET SANDS.
TIME FOR US TO GO AS WELL, MY PRINCE.
ONE MOMENT.

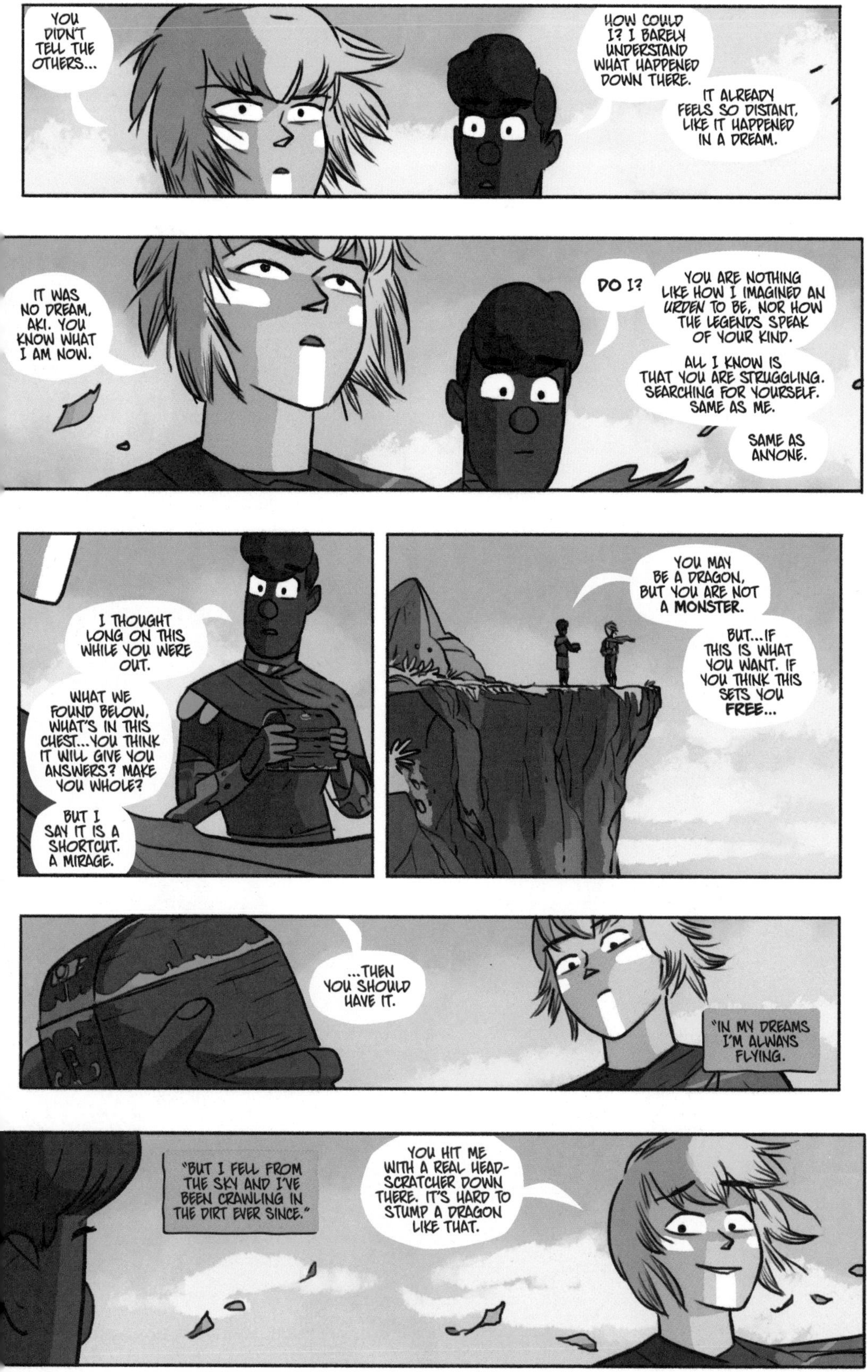

YOU DIDN'T TELL THE OTHERS...
HOW COULD I? I BARELY UNDERSTAND WHAT HAPPENED DOWN THERE.
IT ALREADY FEELS SO DISTANT, LIKE IT HAPPENED IN A DREAM.
IT WAS NO DREAM, AKI. YOU KNOW WHAT I AM NOW.
DO I?
YOU ARE NOTHING LIKE HOW I IMAGINED AN URDEN TO BE, NOR HOW THE LEGENDS SPEAK OF YOUR KIND.
ALL I KNOW IS THAT YOU ARE STRUGGLING. SEARCHING FOR YOURSELF. SAME AS ME.
SAME AS ANYONE.
I THOUGHT LONG ON THIS WHILE YOU WERE OUT.
WHAT WE FOUND BELOW, WHAT'S IN THIS CHEST...YOU THINK IT WILL GIVE YOU ANSWERS? MAKE YOU WHOLE?
BUT I SAY IT IS A SHORTCUT. A MIRAGE.
YOU MAY BE A DRAGON, BUT YOU ARE NOT A **MONSTER**.
BUT...IF THIS IS WHAT YOU WANT. IF YOU THINK THIS SETS YOU **FREE**...
...THEN YOU SHOULD HAVE IT.
"IN MY DREAMS I'M ALWAYS FLYING.
"BUT I FELL FROM THE SKY AND I'VE BEEN CRAWLING IN THE DIRT EVER SINCE."
YOU HIT ME WITH A REAL HEAD-SCRATCHER DOWN THERE. IT'S HARD TO STUMP A DRAGON LIKE THAT.

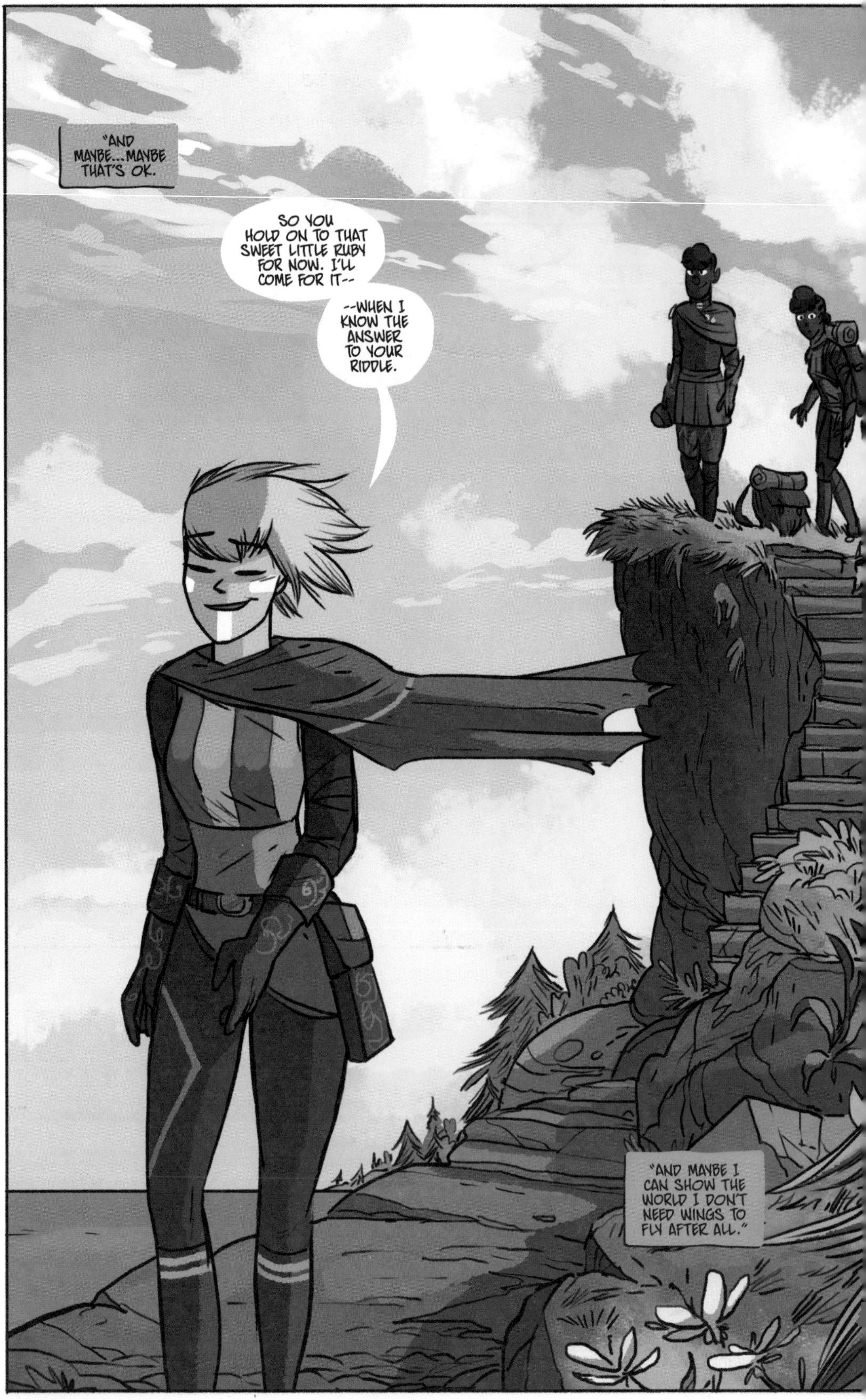
"AND MAYBE... MAYBE THAT'S OK.
SO YOU HOLD ON TO THAT SWEET LITTLE RUBY FOR NOW. I'LL COME FOR IT--
--WHEN I KNOW THE ANSWER TO YOUR RIDDLE.
"AND MAYBE I CAN SHOW THE WORLD I DON'T NEED WINGS TO FLY AFTER ALL."

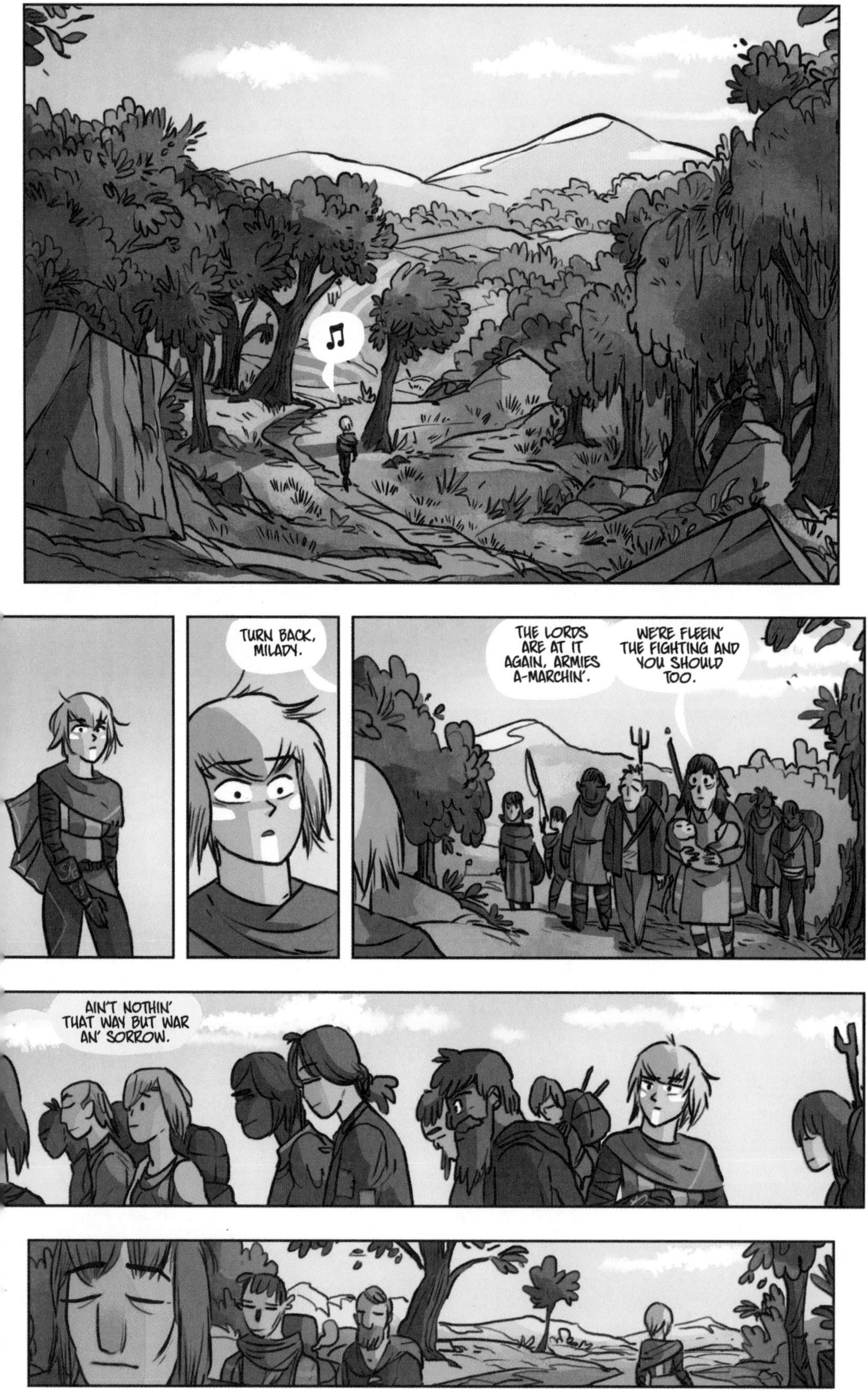
TURN BACK, MILADY.
THE LORDS ARE AT IT AGAIN, ARMIES A-MARCHIN'.
WE'RE FLEEIN' THE FIGHTING AND YOU SHOULD TOO.
AIN'T NOTHIN' THAT WAY BUT WAR AN' SORROW.

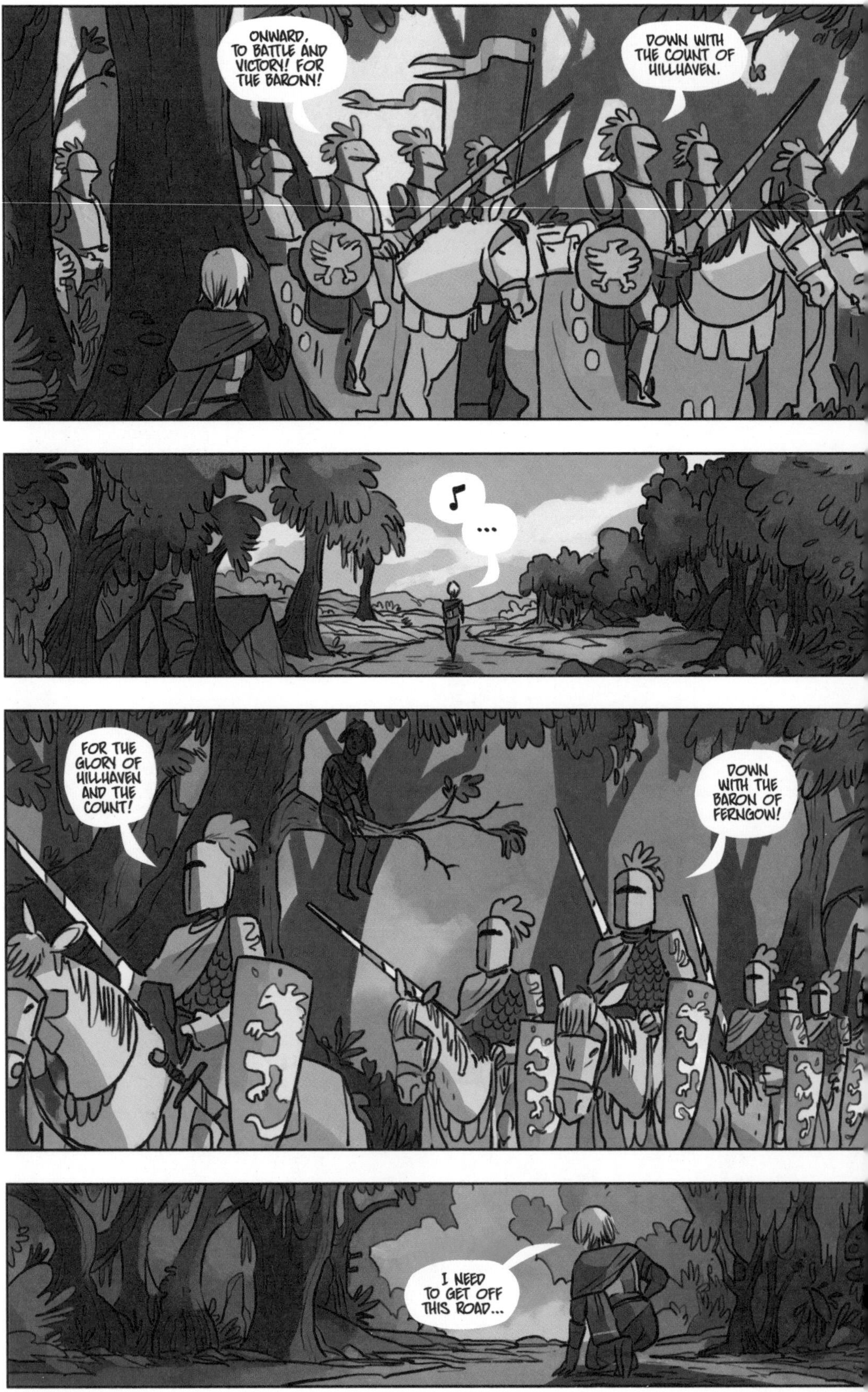
ONWARD, TO BATTLE AND VICTORY! FOR THE BARONY!
DOWN WITH THE COUNT OF HILLHAVEN.
♪
...
FOR THE GLORY OF HILLHAVEN AND THE COUNT!
DOWN WITH THE BARON OF FERNGOW!
I NEED TO GET OFF THIS ROAD...

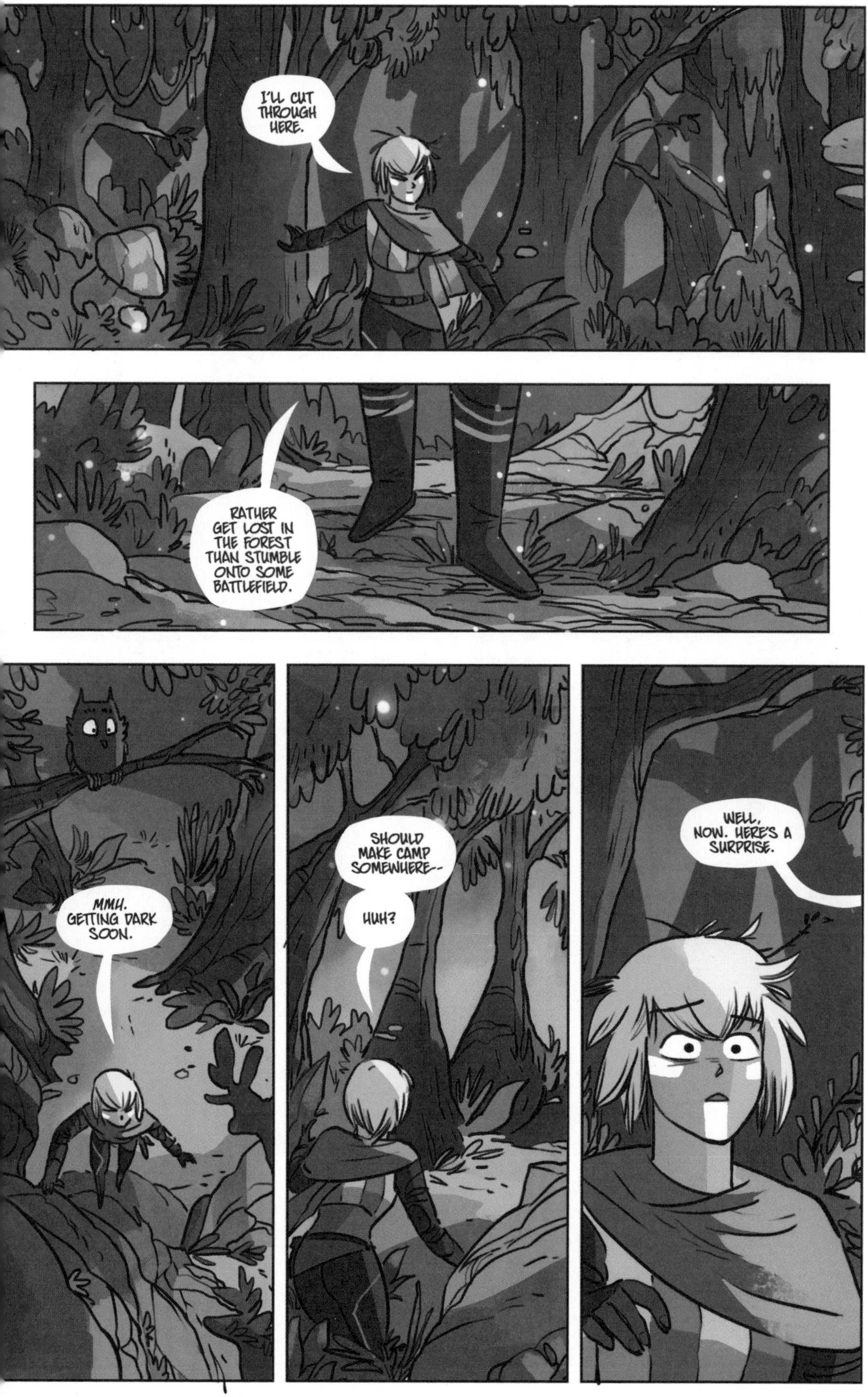
I'LL CUT THROUGH HERE.
RATHER GET LOST IN THE FOREST THAN STUMBLE ONTO SOME BATTLEFIELD.
MMH. GETTING DARK SOON.
SHOULD MAKE CAMP SOMEWHERE--
HUH?
WELL, NOW. HERE'S A SURPRISE.

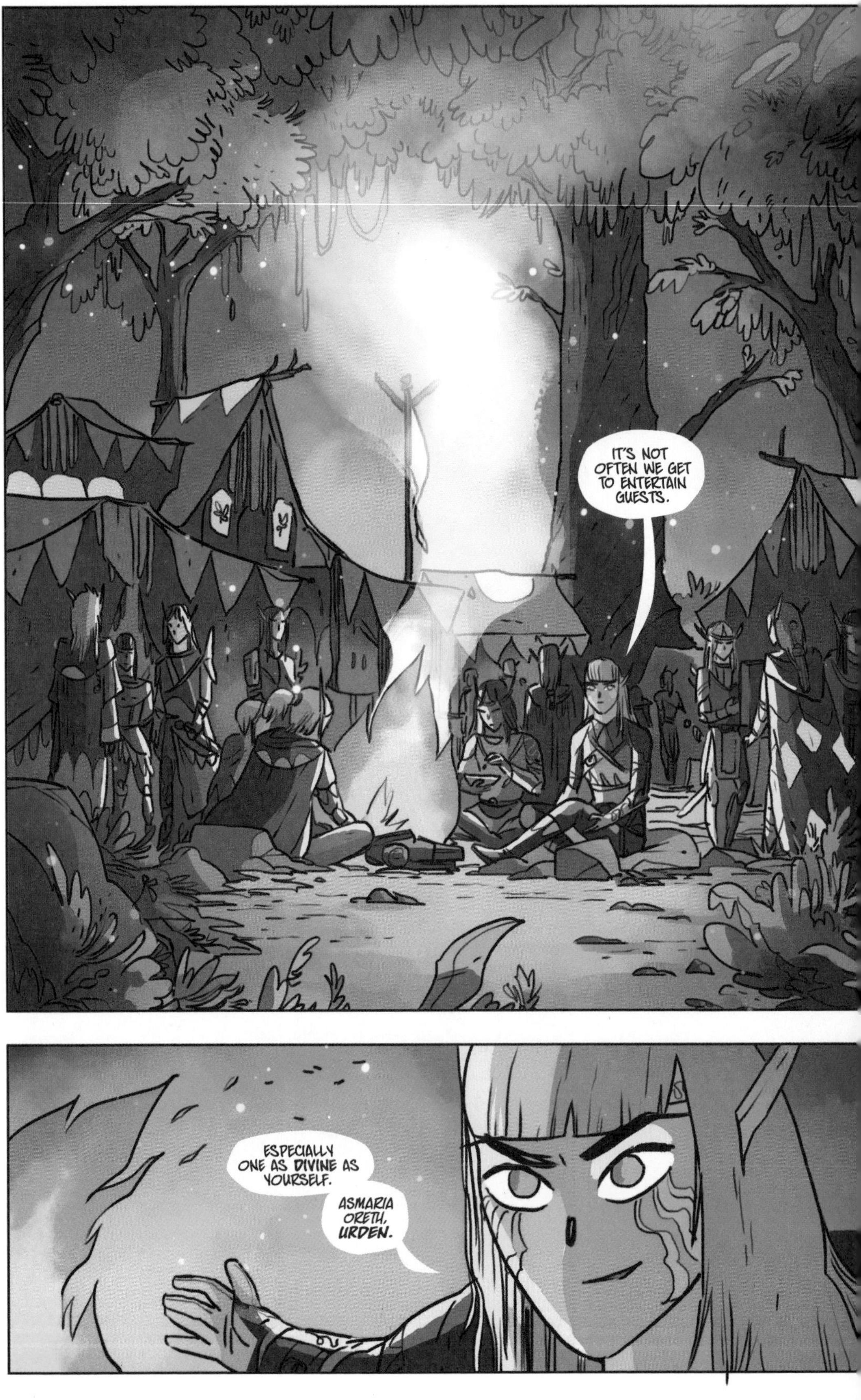

IT'S NOT OFTEN WE GET TO ENTERTAIN GUESTS.
ESPECIALLY ONE AS DIVINE AS YOURSELF.
ASMARIA ORETH, URDEN.

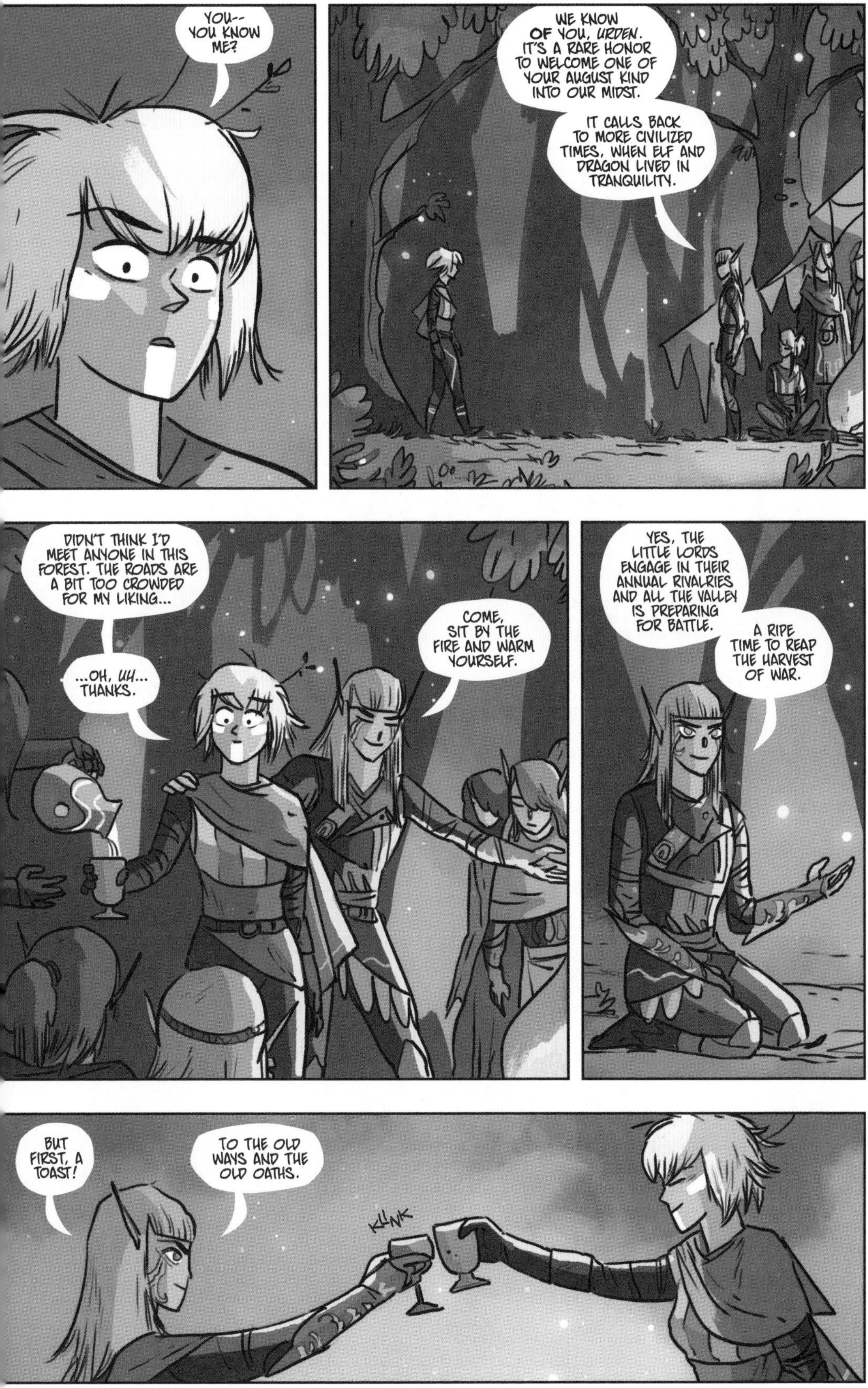
YOU-- YOU KNOW ME?
WE KNOW OF YOU, URDEN. IT'S A RARE HONOR TO WELCOME ONE OF YOUR AUGUST KIND INTO OUR MIDST.
IT CALLS BACK TO MORE CIVILIZED TIMES, WHEN ELF AND DRAGON LIVED IN TRANQUILITY.
DIDN'T THINK I'D MEET ANYONE IN THIS FOREST. THE ROADS ARE A BIT TOO CROWDED FOR MY LIKING...
...OH, UH... THANKS.
COME, SIT BY THE FIRE AND WARM YOURSELF.
YES, THE LITTLE LORDS ENGAGE IN THEIR ANNUAL RIVALRIES AND ALL THE VALLEY IS PREPARING FOR BATTLE.
A RIPE TIME TO REAP THE HARVEST OF WAR.
BUT FIRST, A TOAST!
TO THE OLD WAYS AND THE OLD OATHS.
KLINK

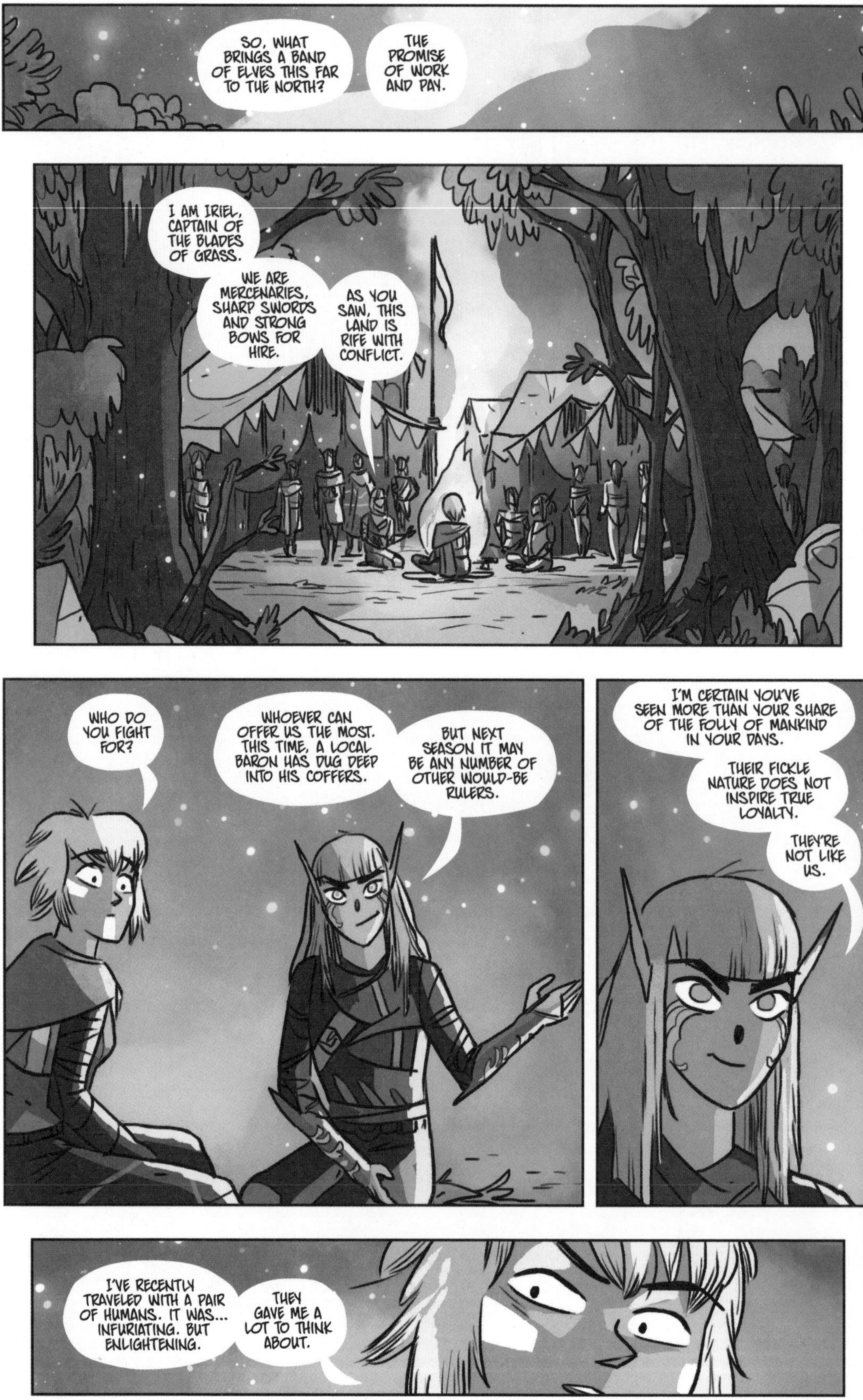
SO, WHAT BRINGS A BAND OF ELVES THIS FAR TO THE NORTH?
THE PROMISE OF WORK AND PAY.
I AM IRIEL, CAPTAIN OF THE BLADES OF GRASS.
WE ARE MERCENARIES, SHARP SWORDS AND STRONG BOWS FOR HIRE.
AS YOU SAW, THIS LAND IS RIFE WITH CONFLICT.
WHO DO YOU FIGHT FOR?
WHOEVER CAN OFFER US THE MOST. THIS TIME, A LOCAL BARON HAS DUG DEEP INTO HIS COFFERS.
BUT NEXT SEASON IT MAY BE ANY NUMBER OF OTHER WOULD-BE RULERS.
I'M CERTAIN YOU'VE SEEN MORE THAN YOUR SHARE OF THE FOLLY OF MANKIND IN YOUR DAYS.
THEIR FICKLE NATURE DOES NOT INSPIRE TRUE LOYALTY.
THEY'RE NOT LIKE US.
I'VE RECENTLY TRAVELED WITH A PAIR OF HUMANS. IT WAS... INFURIATING. BUT ENLIGHTENING.
THEY GAVE ME A LOT TO THINK ABOUT.

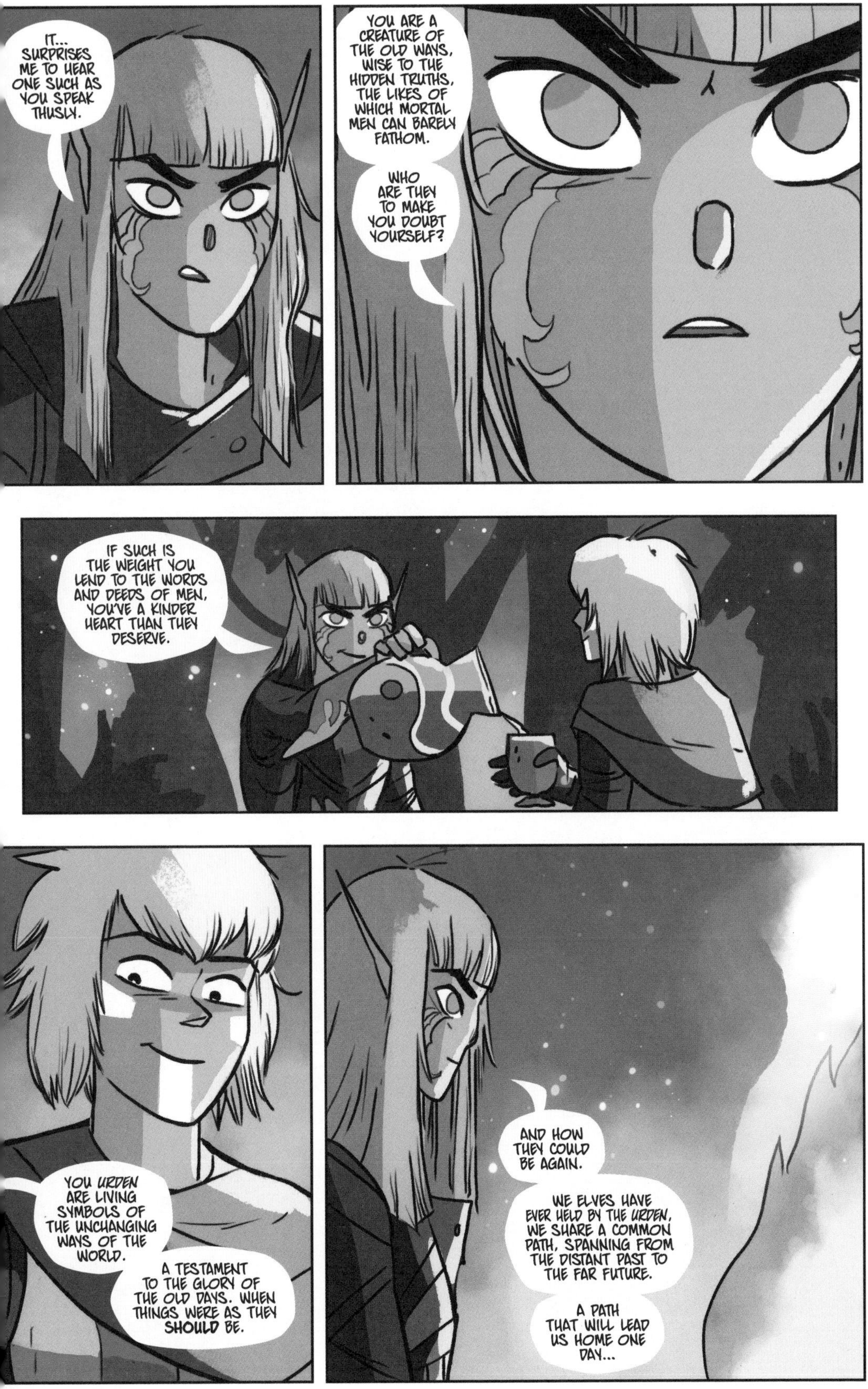
IT... SURPRISES ME TO HEAR ONE SUCH AS YOU SPEAK THUSLY.
YOU ARE A CREATURE OF THE OLD WAYS, WISE TO THE HIDDEN TRUTHS, THE LIKES OF WHICH MORTAL MEN CAN BARELY FATHOM.
WHO ARE THEY TO MAKE YOU DOUBT YOURSELF?
IF SUCH IS THE WEIGHT YOU LEND TO THE WORDS AND DEEDS OF MEN, YOU'VE A KINDER HEART THAN THEY DESERVE.
YOU URDEN ARE LIVING SYMBOLS OF THE UNCHANGING WAYS OF THE WORLD.
A TESTAMENT TO THE GLORY OF THE OLD DAYS. WHEN THINGS WERE AS THEY SHOULD BE.
AND HOW THEY COULD BE AGAIN.
WE ELVES HAVE EVER HELD BY THE URDEN, WE SHARE A COMMON PATH, SPANNING FROM THE DISTANT PAST TO THE FAR FUTURE.
A PATH THAT WILL LEAD US HOME ONE DAY...

"...TO FABLED IRILESH, HIDDEN IN LEAVES. THE ONLY PARADISE THE GODS EVER ALLOWED TO EXIST IN DIRA.

"WHEN THE CALAMITY STRUCK AND THE THRONES OF THE WORLD CRUMBLED, IRILESH STOOD STRONG, A TREE UNBENT BY THE FURIOUS TEMPESTS OF FATE.

"AND WHEN THE STORM OF NATIONS FOLLOWED, OUR ANCESTORS WOVE SPELLS OF ILLUSION, TO HIDE IRILESH FROM GREEDY EYES AND RAVENOUS HEARTS.

"BUT SO EXPERTLY DID THEY CRAFT THEIR MAGICS THAT EVEN THE MEMORY OF IRILESH'S LOCATION WAS WIPED FROM THE WORLD.

"CENTURIES LATER, WE BLADES OF GRASS ARE STILL SEARCHING.

"WE ARE LEAVES CAST ON THE WIND, YEARNING FOR A HOME WE'VE NEVER KNOWN."

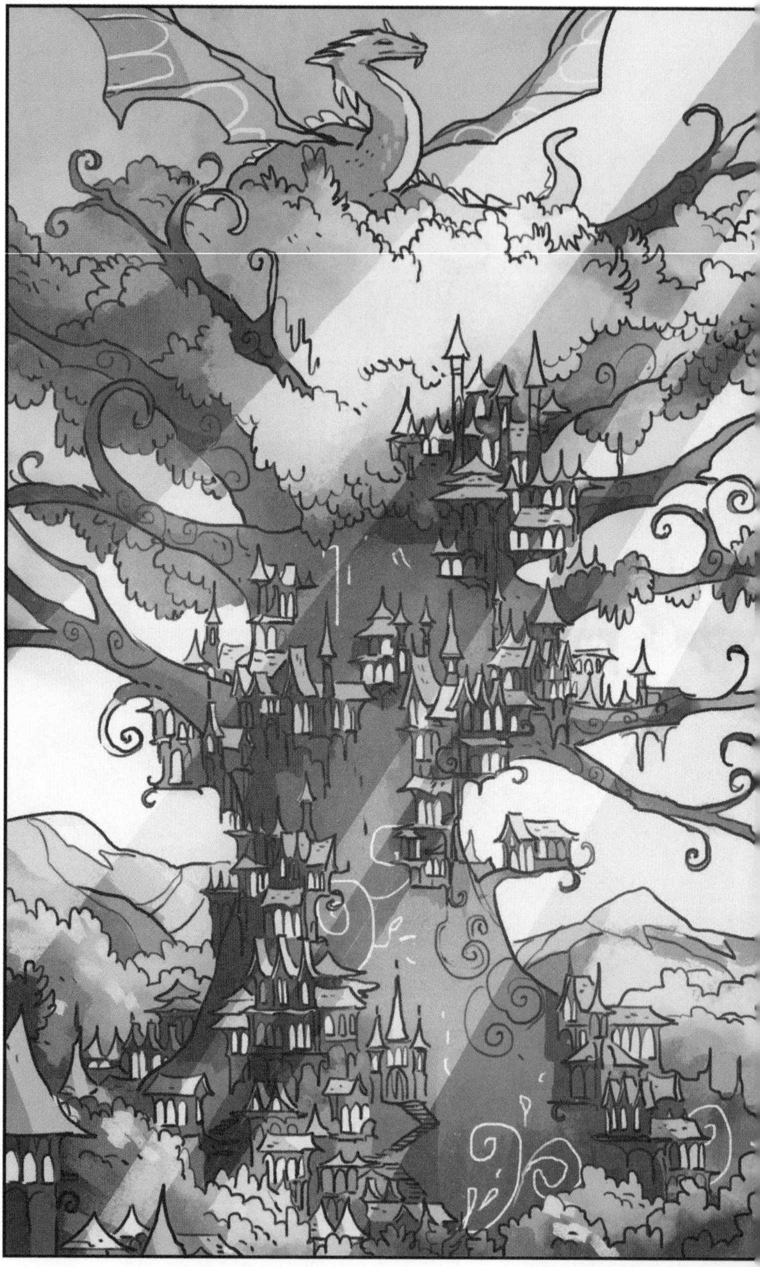

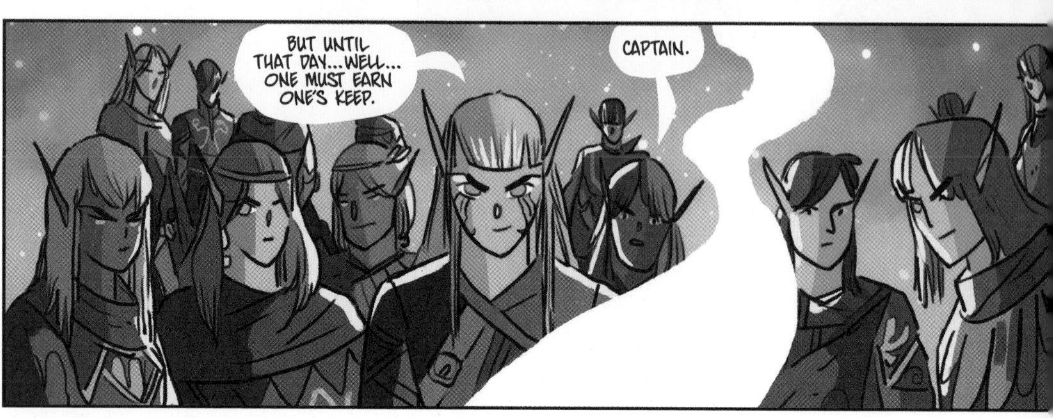
BUT UNTIL THAT DAY...WELL... ONE MUST EARN ONE'S KEEP.
CAPTAIN.

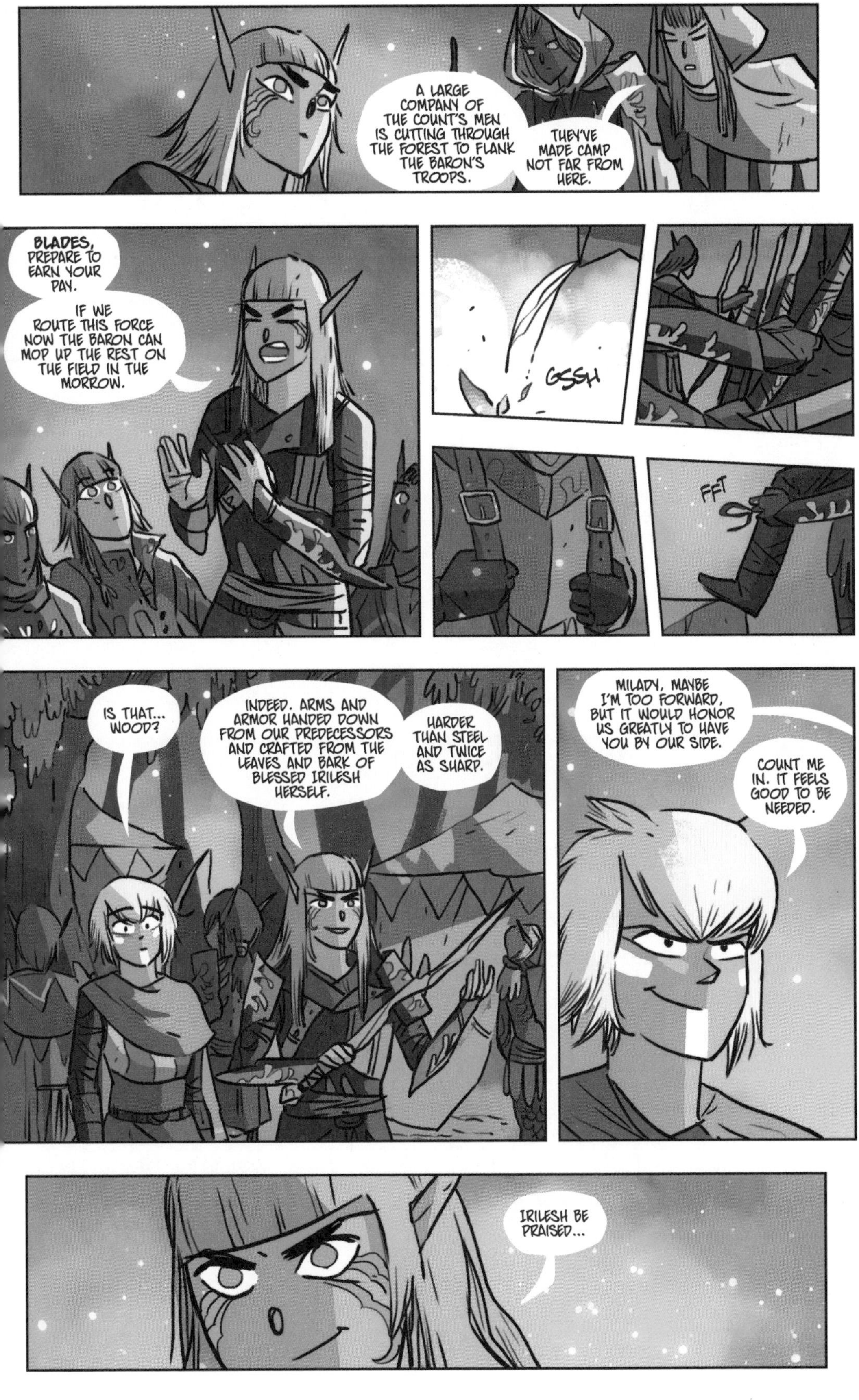
A LARGE COMPANY OF THE COUNT'S MEN IS CUTTING THROUGH THE FOREST TO FLANK THE BARON'S TROOPS.
THEY'VE MADE CAMP NOT FAR FROM HERE.
BLADES, PREPARE TO EARN YOUR PAY.
IF WE ROUTE THIS FORCE NOW THE BARON CAN MOP UP THE REST ON THE FIELD IN THE MORROW.
GSSH
FFT
IS THAT... WOOD?
INDEED. ARMS AND ARMOR HANDED DOWN FROM OUR PREDECESSORS AND CRAFTED FROM THE LEAVES AND BARK OF BLESSED IRILESH HERSELF.
HARDER THAN STEEL AND TWICE AS SHARP.
MILADY, MAYBE I'M TOO FORWARD, BUT IT WOULD HONOR US GREATLY TO HAVE YOU BY OUR SIDE.
COUNT ME IN. IT FEELS GOOD TO BE NEEDED.
IRILESH BE PRAISED...

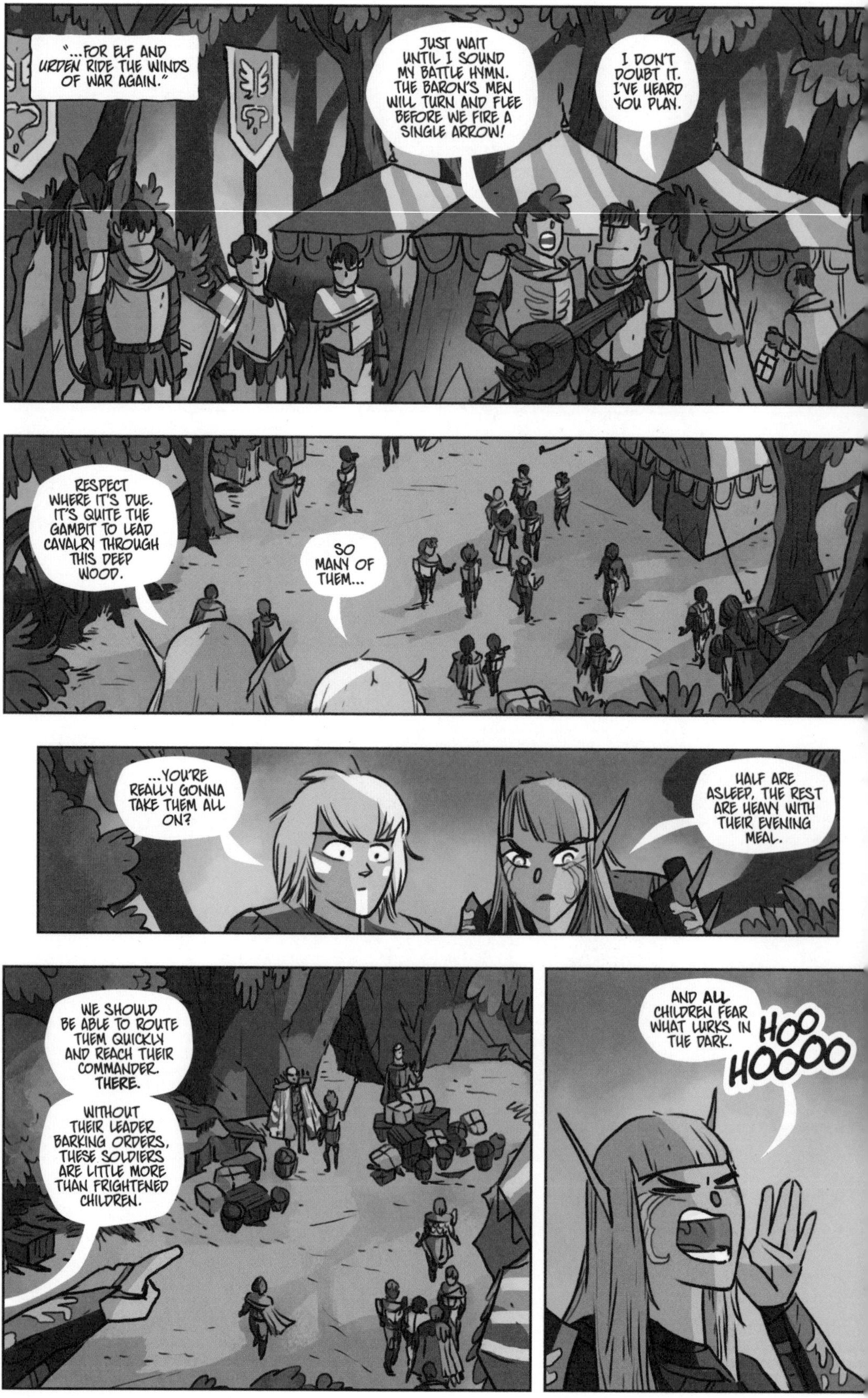
"...FOR ELF AND URDEN RIDE THE WINDS OF WAR AGAIN."
JUST WAIT UNTIL I SOUND MY BATTLE HYMN. THE BARON'S MEN WILL TURN AND FLEE BEFORE WE FIRE A SINGLE ARROW!
I DON'T DOUBT IT. I'VE HEARD YOU PLAY.
RESPECT WHERE IT'S DUE. IT'S QUITE THE GAMBIT TO LEAD CAVALRY THROUGH THIS DEEP WOOD.
SO MANY OF THEM...
...YOU'RE REALLY GONNA TAKE THEM ALL ON?
HALF ARE ASLEEP, THE REST ARE HEAVY WITH THEIR EVENING MEAL.
WE SHOULD BE ABLE TO ROUTE THEM QUICKLY AND REACH THEIR COMMANDER. THERE.
WITHOUT THEIR LEADER BARKING ORDERS, THESE SOLDIERS ARE LITTLE MORE THAN FRIGHTENED CHILDREN.
AND ALL CHILDREN FEAR WHAT LURKS IN THE DARK.
HOO HOOOO

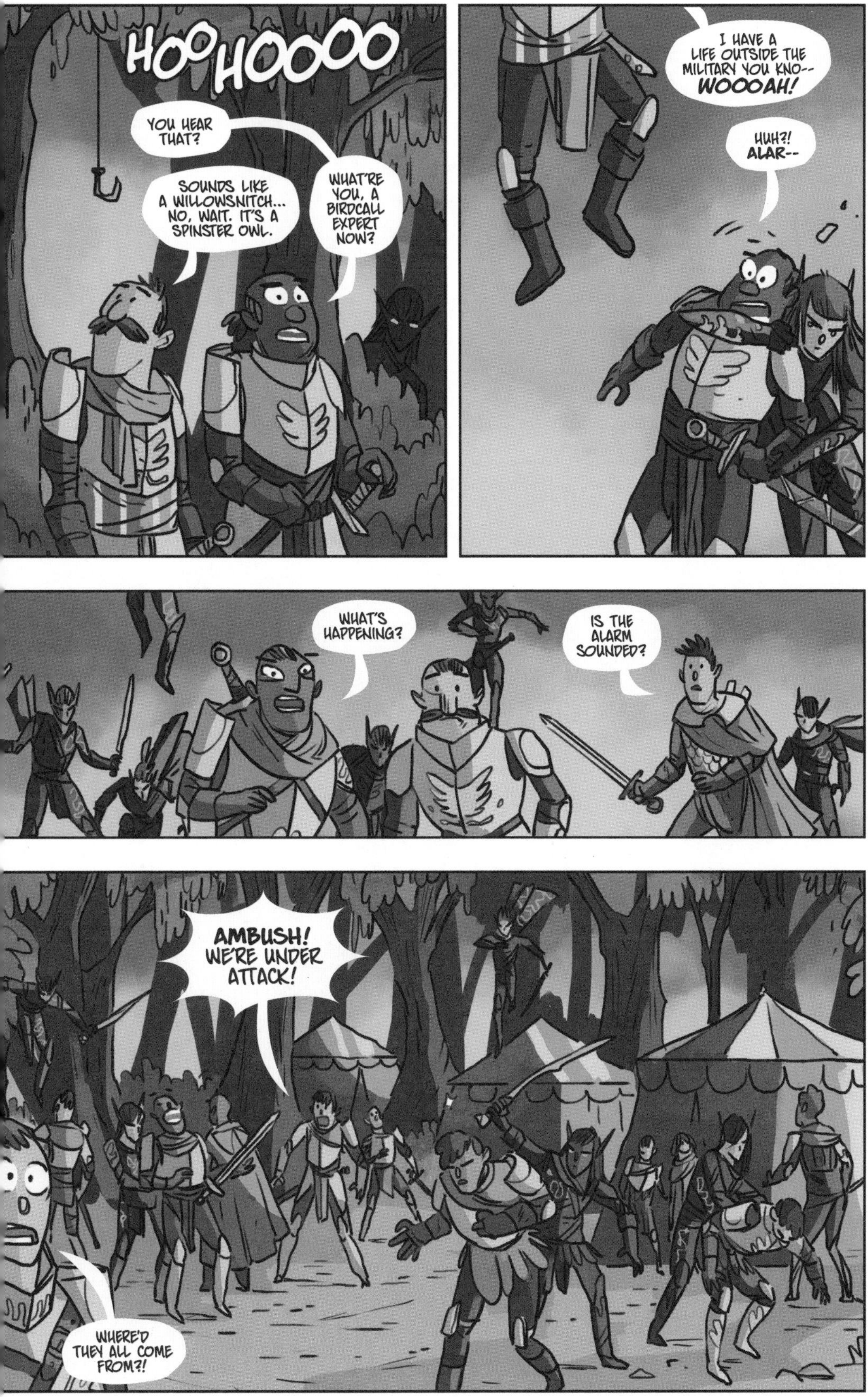

HOO HOOOO
YOU HEAR THAT?
SOUNDS LIKE A WILLOWSNITCH... NO, WAIT. IT'S A SPINSTER OWL.
WHAT'RE YOU, A BIRDCALL EXPERT NOW?
I HAVE A LIFE OUTSIDE THE MILITARY YOU KNO-- WOOOAH!
HUH?! ALAR--
WHAT'S HAPPENING?
IS THE ALARM SOUNDED?
AMBUSH! WE'RE UNDER ATTACK!
WHERE'D THEY ALL COME FROM?!

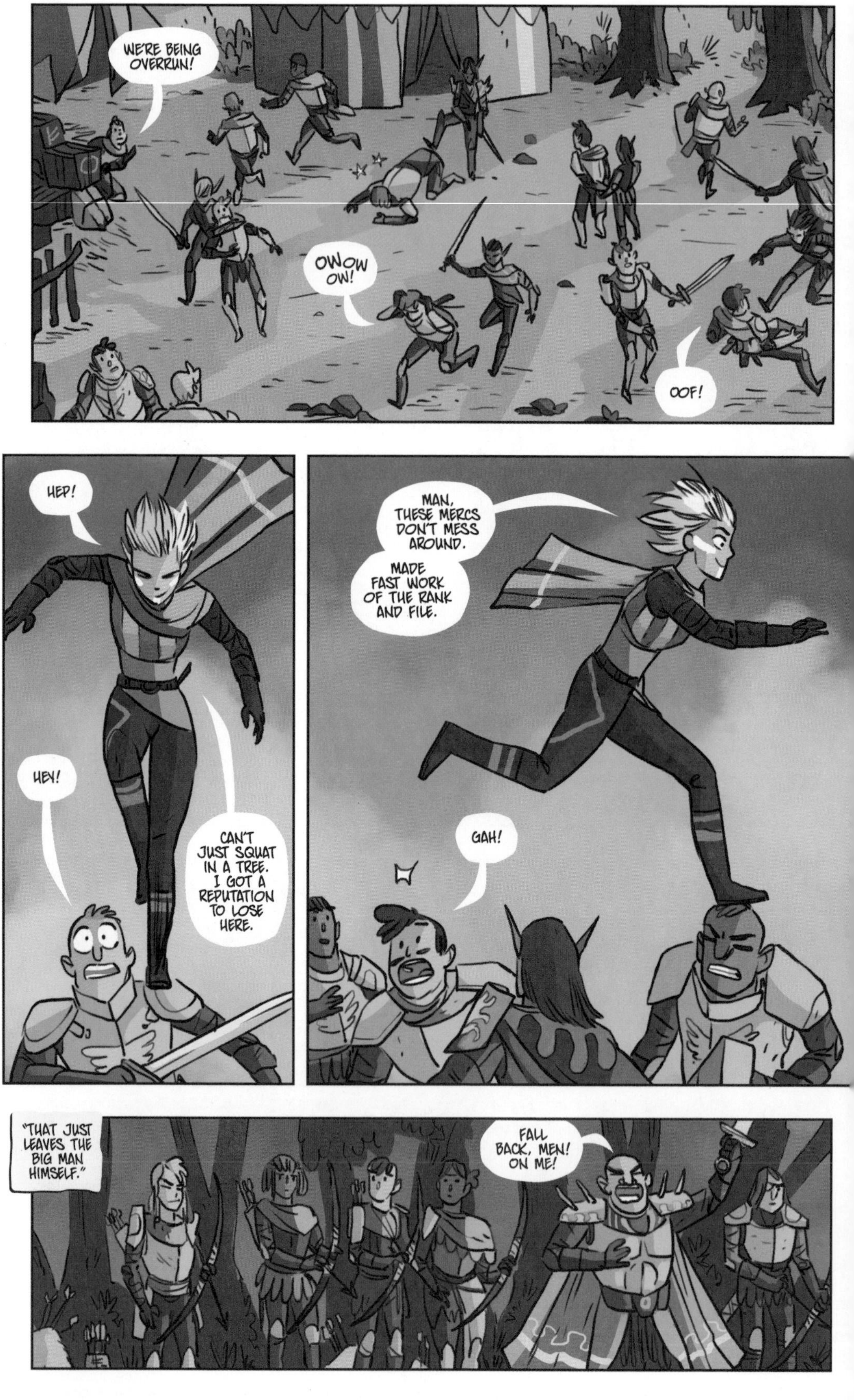

WE'RE BEING OVERRUN!
OWOW OW!
OOF!
HEP!
HEY!
CAN'T JUST SQUAT IN A TREE. I GOT A REPUTATION TO LOSE HERE.
MAN, THESE MERCS DON'T MESS AROUND.
MADE FAST WORK OF THE RANK AND FILE.
GAH!
"THAT JUST LEAVES THE BIG MAN HIMSELF."
FALL BACK, MEN! ON ME!

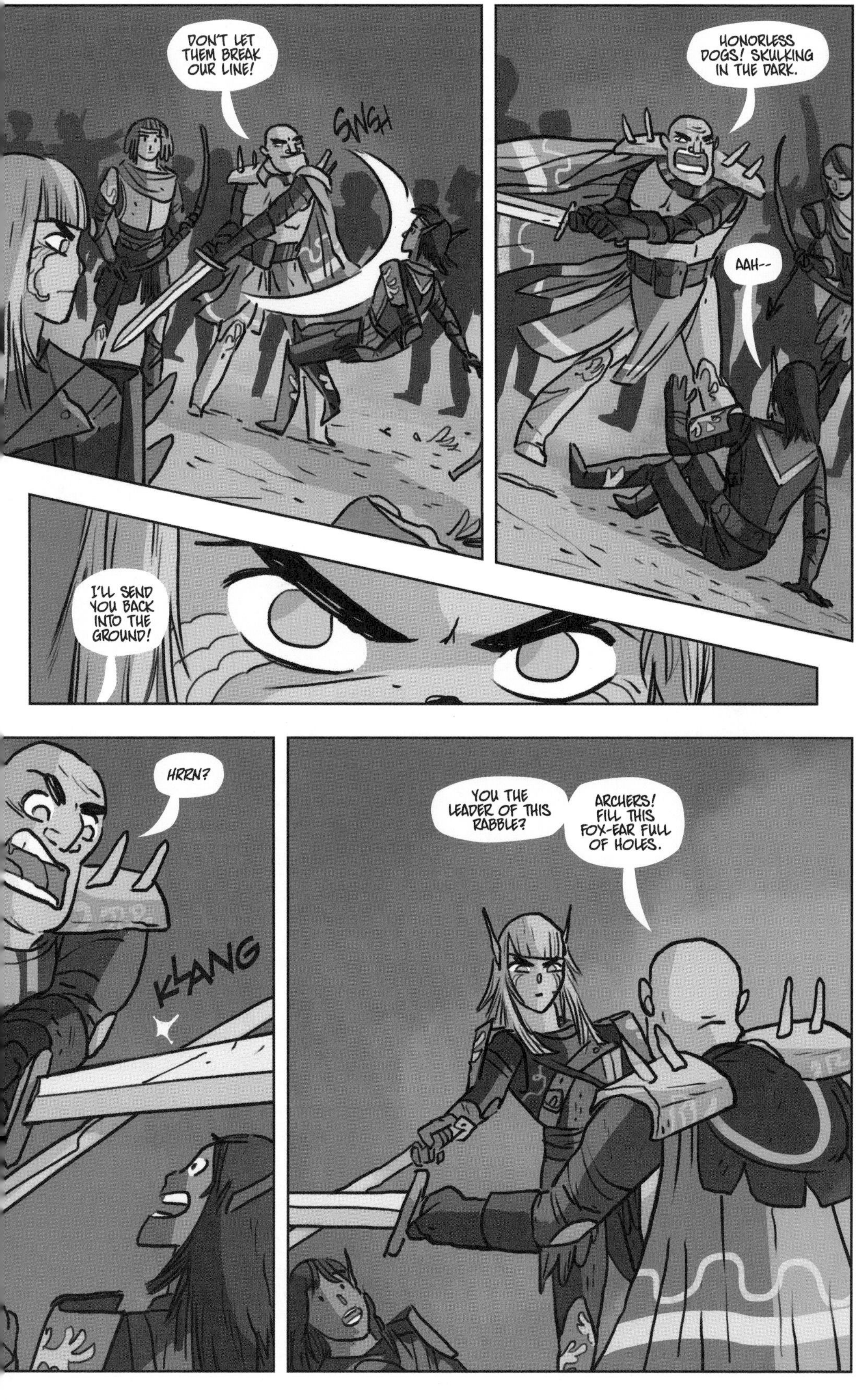
DON'T LET THEM BREAK OUR LINE!
SNSH
HONORLESS DOGS! SKULKING IN THE DARK.
AAH--
I'LL SEND YOU BACK INTO THE GROUND!
HRRN?
KLANG
YOU THE LEADER OF THIS RABBLE?
ARCHERS! FILL THIS FOX-EAR FULL OF HOLES.

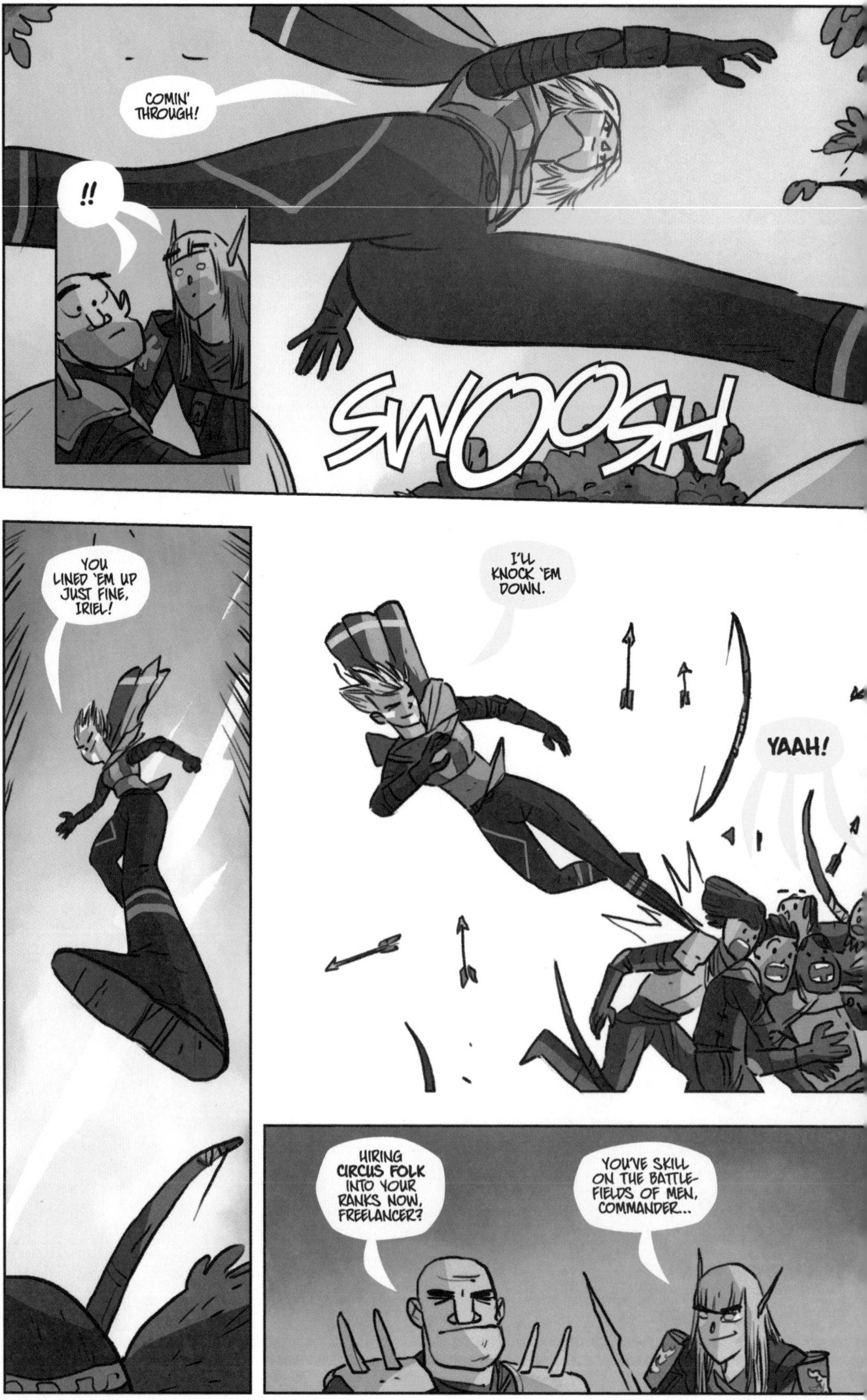
COMIN' THROUGH!
!!
SWOOSH
YOU LINED 'EM UP JUST FINE, IRIEL!
I'LL KNOCK 'EM DOWN.
YAAH!
HIRING CIRCUS FOLK INTO YOUR RANKS NOW, FREELANCER?
YOU'VE SKILL ON THE BATTLE-FIELDS OF MEN, COMMANDER...

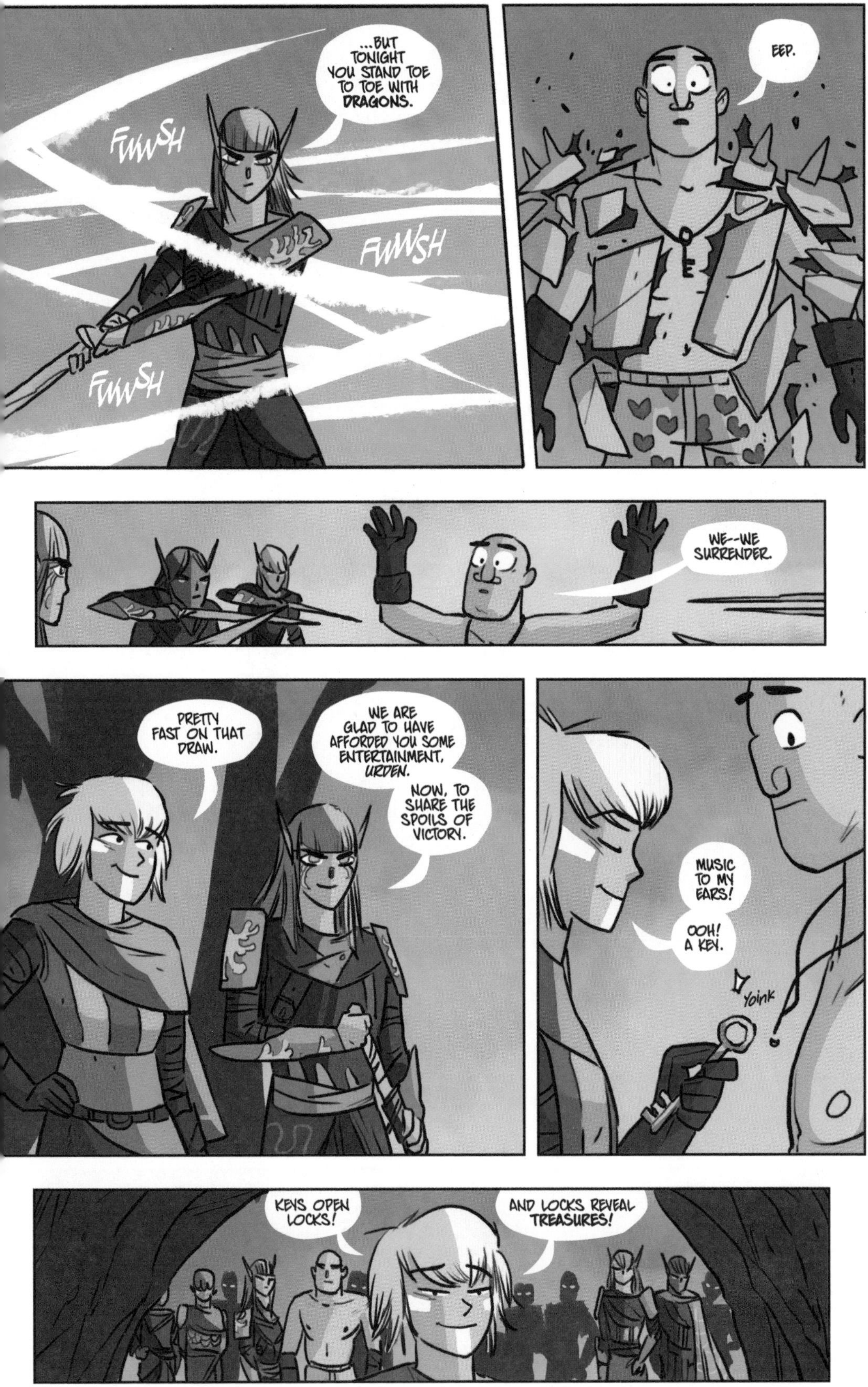
...BUT TONIGHT YOU STAND TOE TO TOE WITH DRAGONS.
FWWSH
FWWSH
FWWSH
EEP.
WE--WE SURRENDER.
PRETTY FAST ON THAT DRAW.
WE ARE GLAD TO HAVE AFFORDED YOU SOME ENTERTAINMENT, URDEN.
NOW, TO SHARE THE SPOILS OF VICTORY.
MUSIC TO MY EARS!
OOH! A KEY.
Yoink
KEYS OPEN LOCKS!
AND LOCKS REVEAL TREASURES!

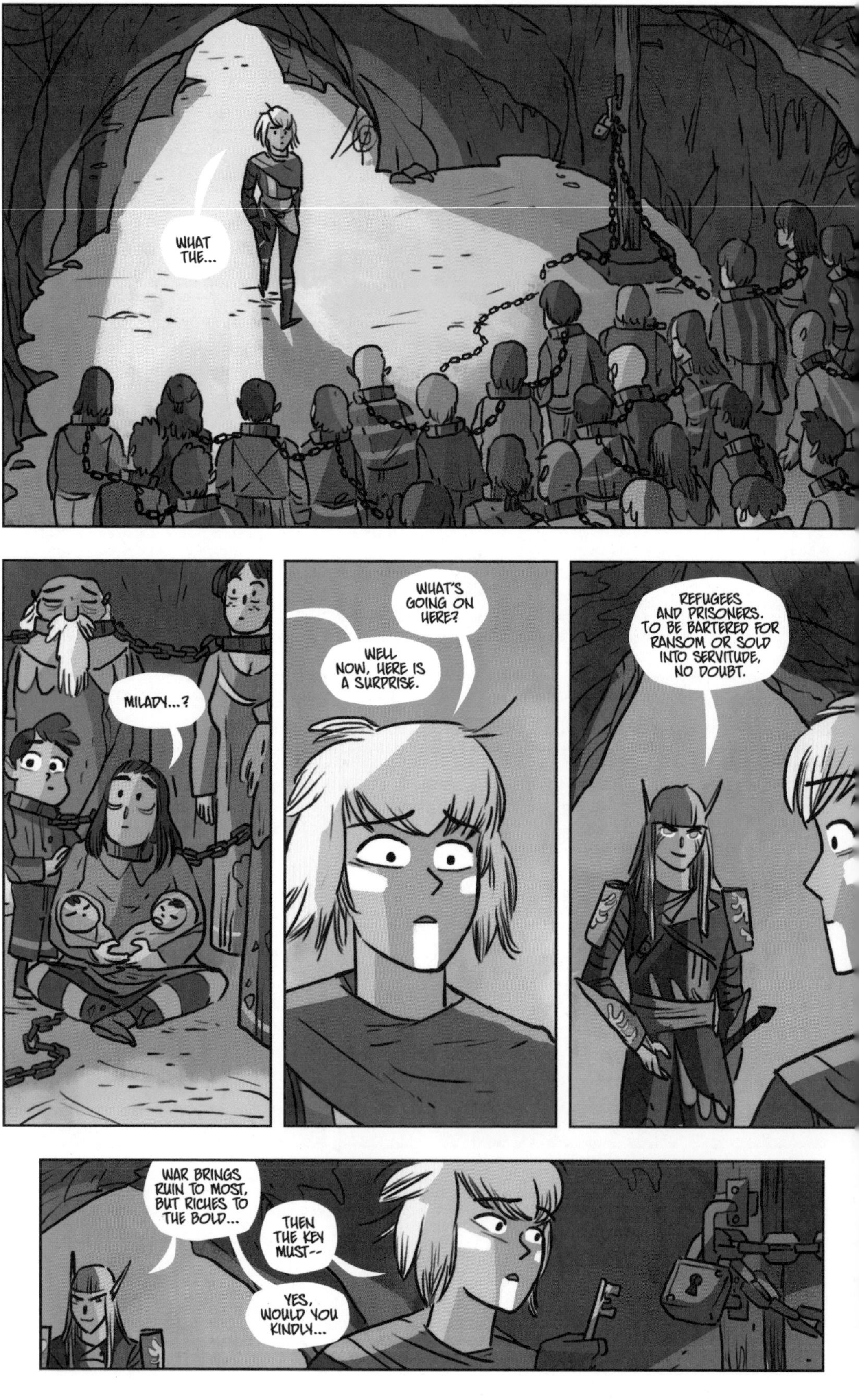
WHAT THE...
MILADY...?
WHAT'S GOING ON HERE?
WELL NOW, HERE IS A SURPRISE.
REFUGEES AND PRISONERS. TO BE BARTERED FOR RANSOM OR SOLD INTO SERVITUDE, NO DOUBT.
WAR BRINGS RUIN TO MOST, BUT RICHES TO THE BOLD...
THEN THE KEY MUST--
YES, WOULD YOU KINDLY...

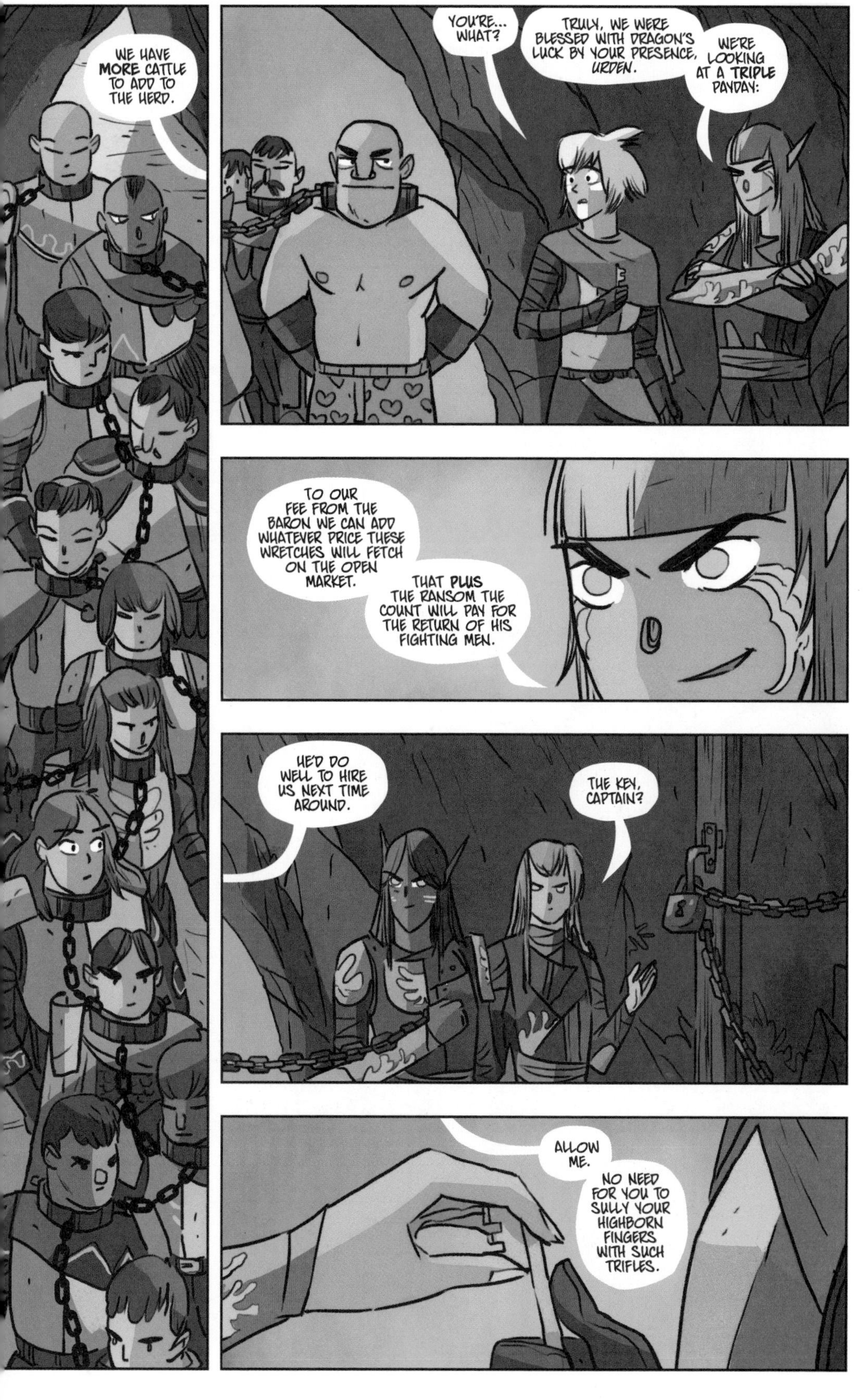
WE HAVE MORE CATTLE TO ADD TO THE HERD.
YOU'RE... WHAT?
TRULY, WE WERE BLESSED WITH DRAGON'S LUCK BY YOUR PRESENCE, URDEN.
WE'RE LOOKING AT A TRIPLE PAYDAY:
TO OUR FEE FROM THE BARON WE CAN ADD WHATEVER PRICE THESE WRETCHES WILL FETCH ON THE OPEN MARKET.
THAT PLUS THE RANSOM THE COUNT WILL PAY FOR THE RETURN OF HIS FIGHTING MEN.
HE'D DO WELL TO HIRE US NEXT TIME AROUND.
THE KEY, CAPTAIN?
ALLOW ME.
NO NEED FOR YOU TO SULLY YOUR HIGHBORN FINGERS WITH SUCH TRIFLES.

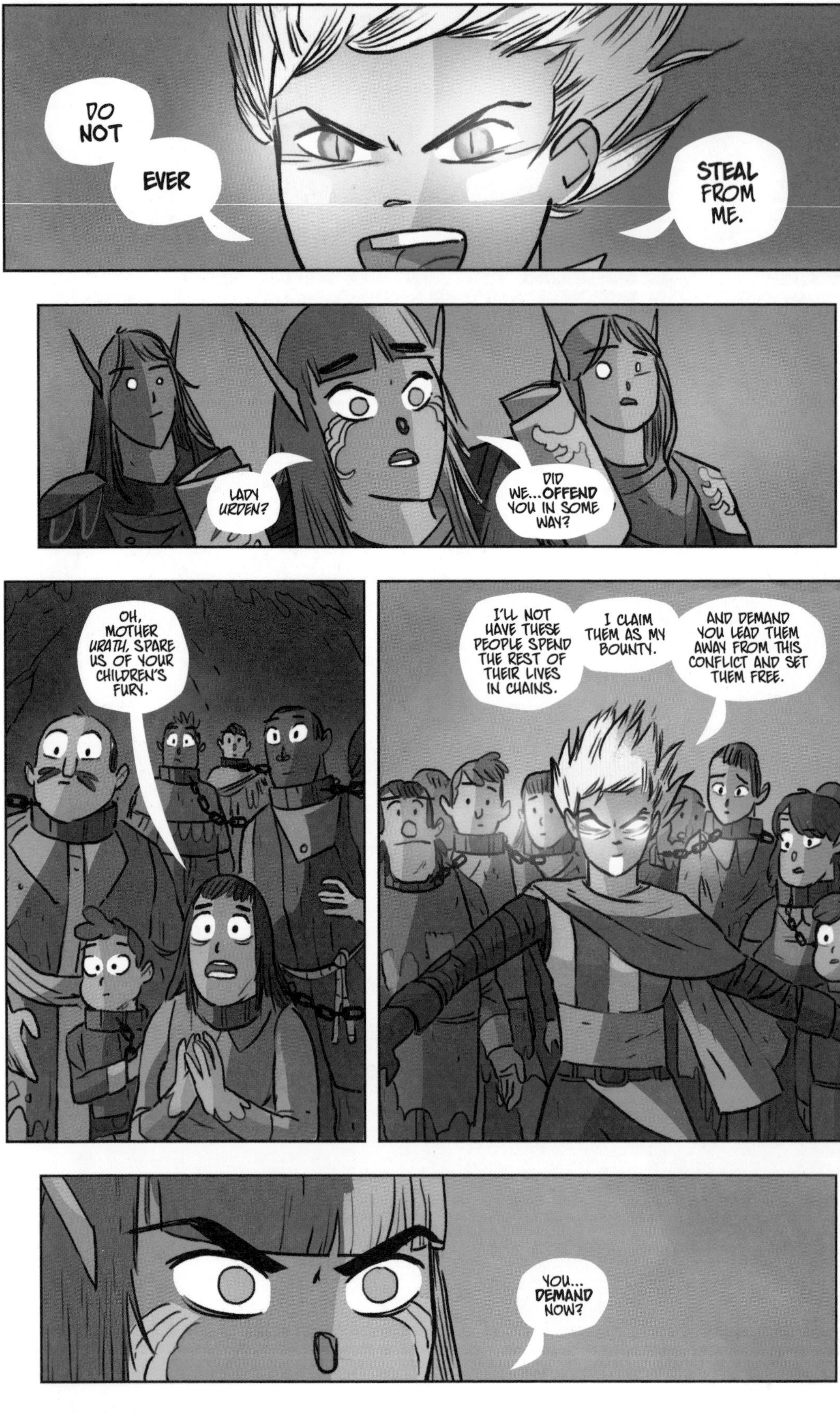
DO NOT
EVER
STEAL FROM ME.
LADY URDEN?
DID WE...OFFEND YOU IN SOME WAY?
OH, MOTHER URATH, SPARE US OF YOUR CHILDREN'S FURY.
I'LL NOT HAVE THESE PEOPLE SPEND THE REST OF THEIR LIVES IN CHAINS.
I CLAIM THEM AS MY BOUNTY.
AND DEMAND YOU LEAD THEM AWAY FROM THIS CONFLICT AND SET THEM FREE.
YOU... DEMAND NOW?

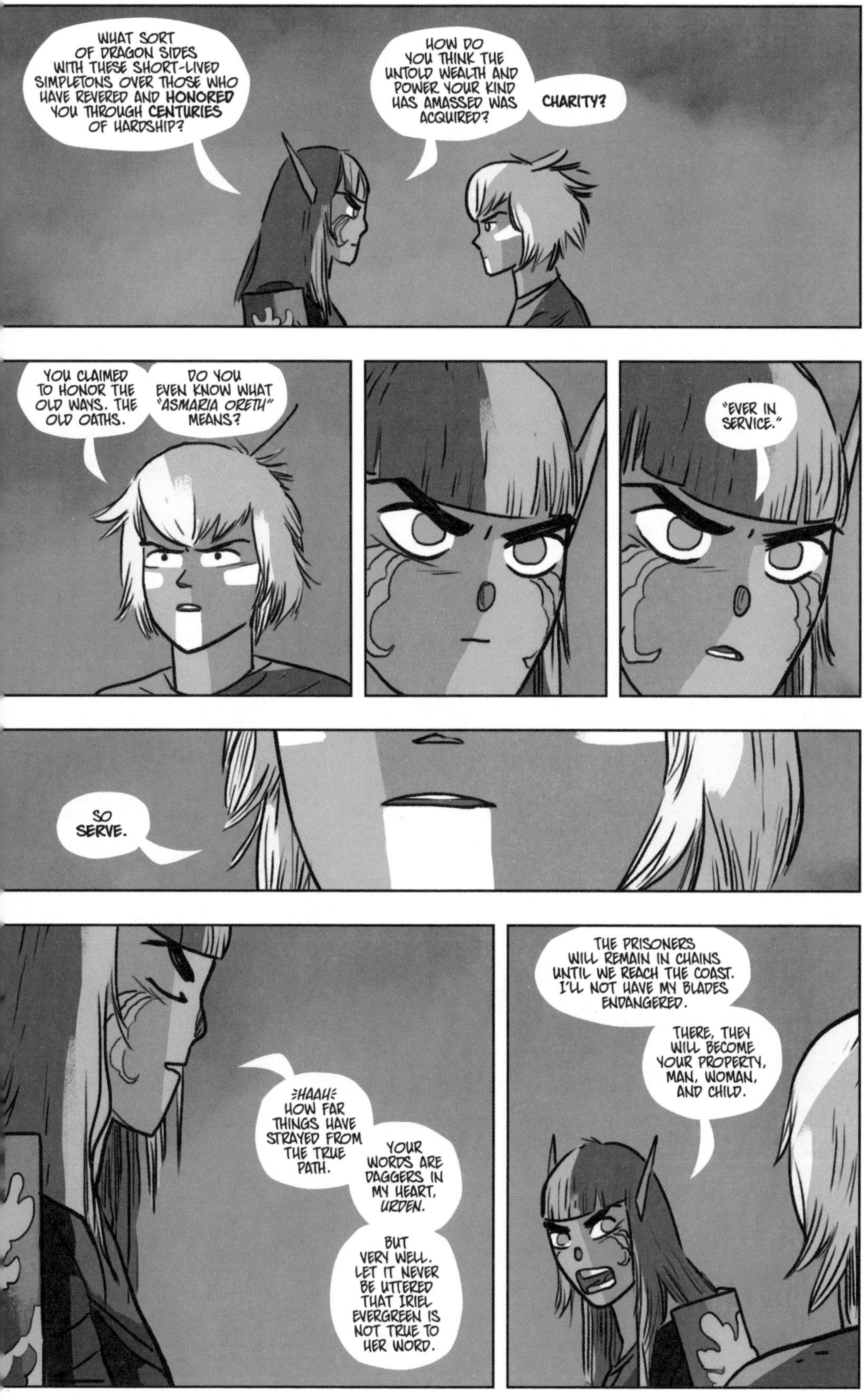

WHAT SORT OF DRAGON SIDES WITH THESE SHORT-LIVED SIMPLETONS OVER THOSE WHO HAVE REVERED AND **HONORED** YOU THROUGH **CENTURIES** OF HARDSHIP?
HOW DO YOU THINK THE UNTOLD WEALTH AND POWER YOUR KIND HAS AMASSED WAS ACQUIRED?
CHARITY?
YOU CLAIMED TO HONOR THE OLD WAYS. THE OLD OATHS.
DO YOU EVEN KNOW WHAT *"ASMARIA ORETH"* MEANS?
"EVER IN SERVICE."
SO **SERVE.**
HAAH HOW FAR THINGS HAVE STRAYED FROM THE TRUE PATH.
YOUR WORDS ARE DAGGERS IN MY HEART, *URDEN.*
BUT VERY WELL. LET IT NEVER BE UTTERED THAT IRIEL EVERGREEN IS NOT TRUE TO HER WORD.
THE PRISONERS WILL REMAIN IN CHAINS UNTIL WE REACH THE COAST. I'LL NOT HAVE MY BLADES ENDANGERED.
THERE, THEY WILL BECOME YOUR PROPERTY, MAN, WOMAN, AND CHILD.

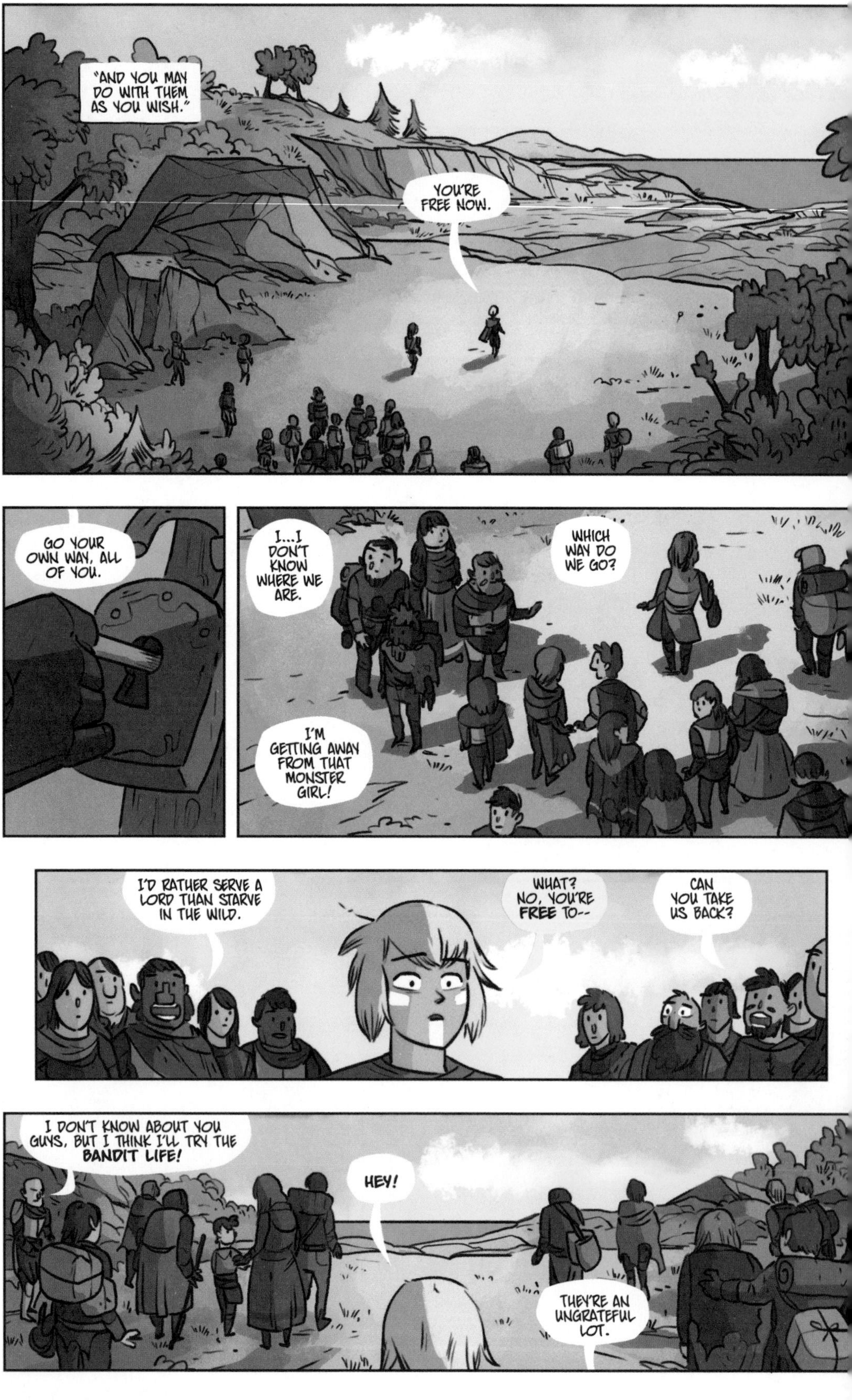
"AND YOU MAY DO WITH THEM AS YOU WISH."
YOU'RE FREE NOW.
GO YOUR OWN WAY, ALL OF YOU.
I...I DON'T KNOW WHERE WE ARE.
WHICH WAY DO WE GO?
I'M GETTING AWAY FROM THAT MONSTER GIRL!
I'D RATHER SERVE A LORD THAN STARVE IN THE WILD.
WHAT? NO, YOU'RE FREE TO--
CAN YOU TAKE US BACK?
I DON'T KNOW ABOUT YOU GUYS, BUT I THINK I'LL TRY THE BANDIT LIFE!
HEY!
THEY'RE AN UNGRATEFUL LOT.

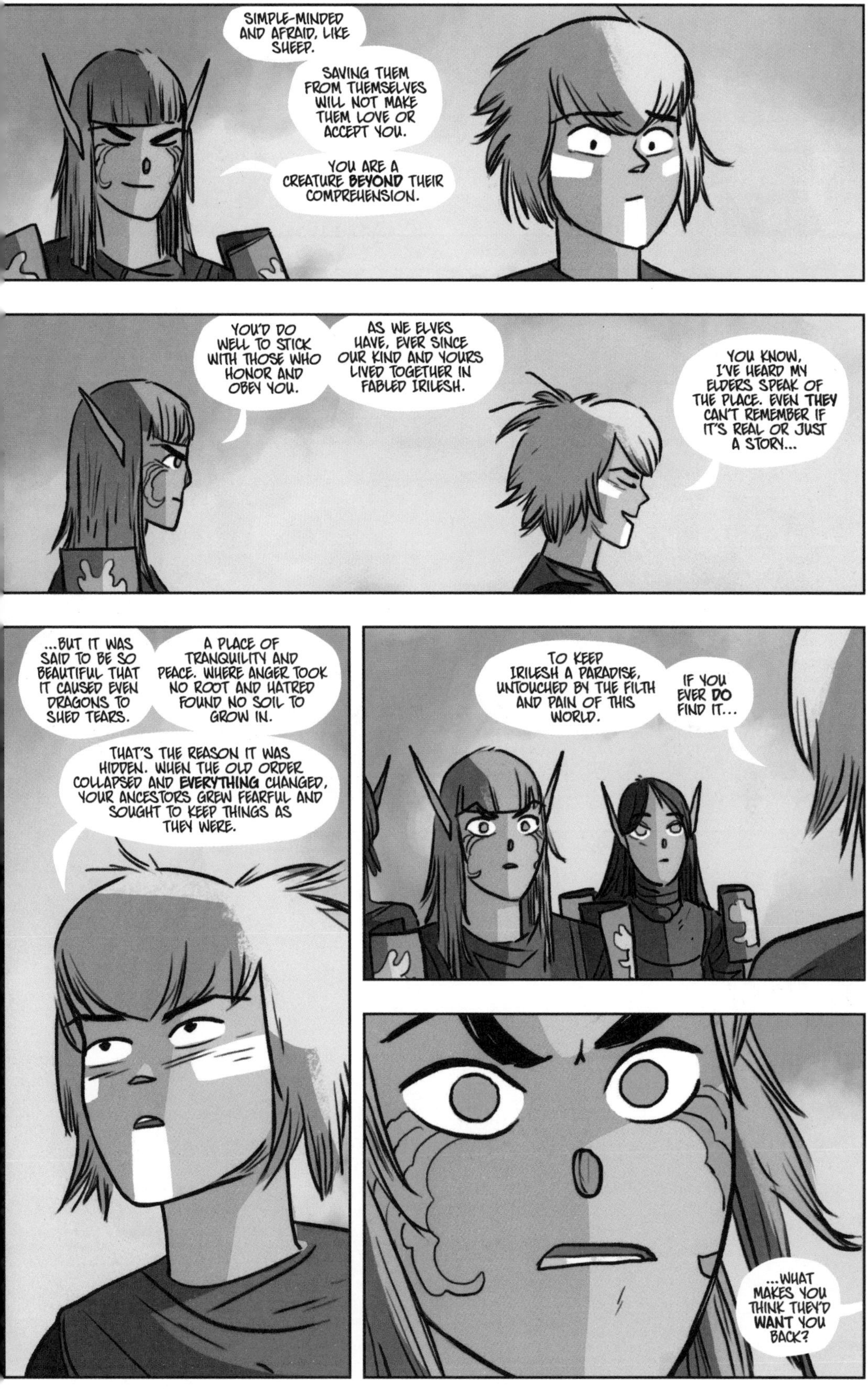
SIMPLE-MINDED AND AFRAID, LIKE SHEEP.
SAVING THEM FROM THEMSELVES WILL NOT MAKE THEM LOVE OR ACCEPT YOU.
YOU ARE A CREATURE **BEYOND** THEIR COMPREHENSION.
YOU'D DO WELL TO STICK WITH THOSE WHO HONOR AND OBEY YOU.
AS WE ELVES HAVE, EVER SINCE OUR KIND AND YOURS LIVED TOGETHER IN FABLED IRILESH.
YOU KNOW, I'VE HEARD MY ELDERS SPEAK OF THE PLACE. EVEN **THEY** CAN'T REMEMBER IF IT'S REAL OR JUST A STORY...
...BUT IT WAS SAID TO BE SO BEAUTIFUL THAT IT CAUSED EVEN DRAGONS TO SHED TEARS.
A PLACE OF TRANQUILITY AND PEACE. WHERE ANGER TOOK NO ROOT AND HATRED FOUND NO SOIL TO GROW IN.
THAT'S THE REASON IT WAS HIDDEN. WHEN THE OLD ORDER COLLAPSED AND **EVERYTHING** CHANGED, YOUR ANCESTORS GREW FEARFUL AND SOUGHT TO KEEP THINGS AS THEY WERE.
TO KEEP IRILESH A PARADISE, UNTOUCHED BY THE FILTH AND PAIN OF THIS WORLD.
IF YOU EVER **DO** FIND IT...
...WHAT MAKES YOU THINK THEY'D **WANT** YOU BACK?

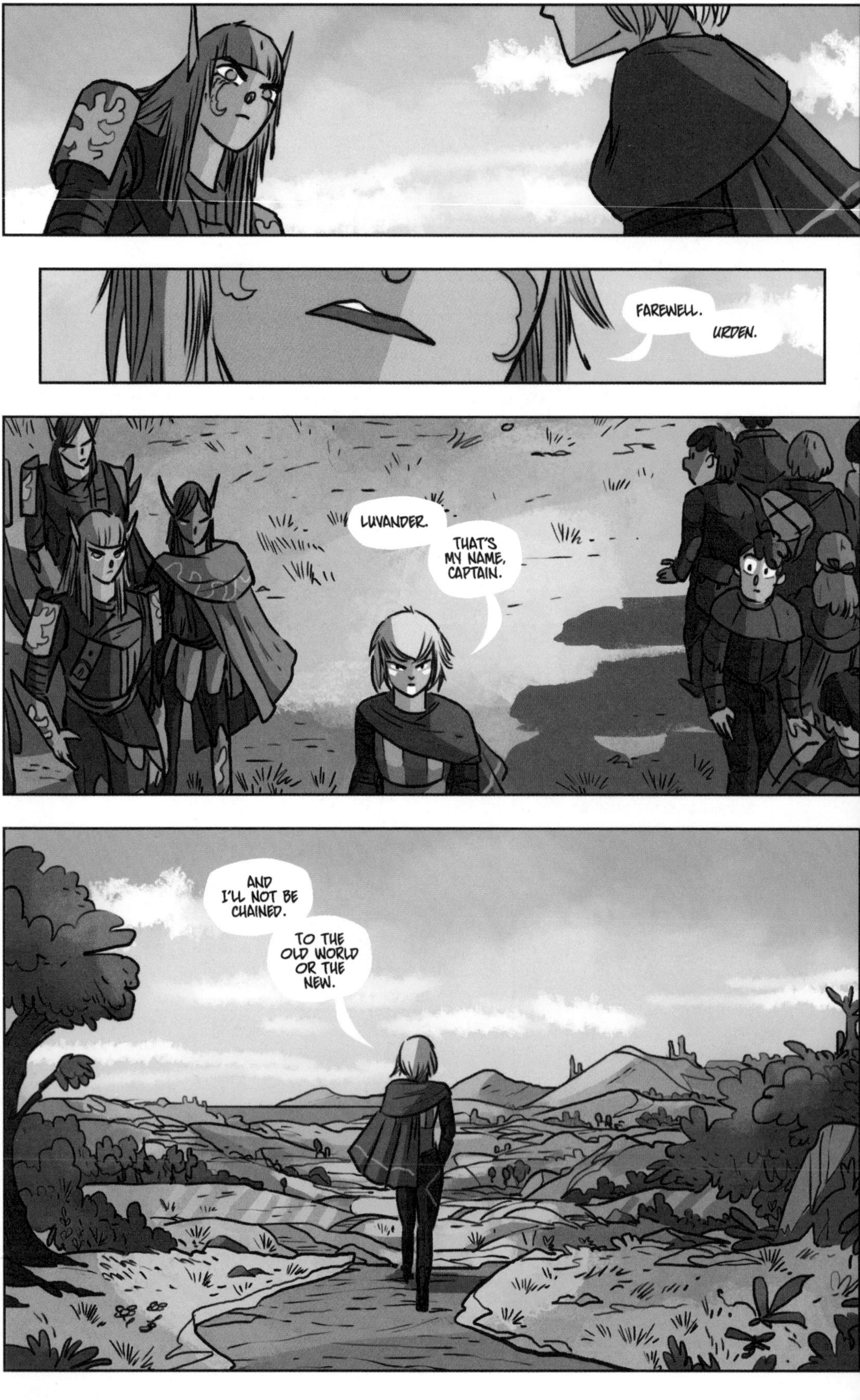
FAREWELL.
URDEN.
LUVANDER.
THAT'S MY NAME, CAPTAIN.
AND I'LL NOT BE CHAINED.
TO THE OLD WORLD OR THE NEW.

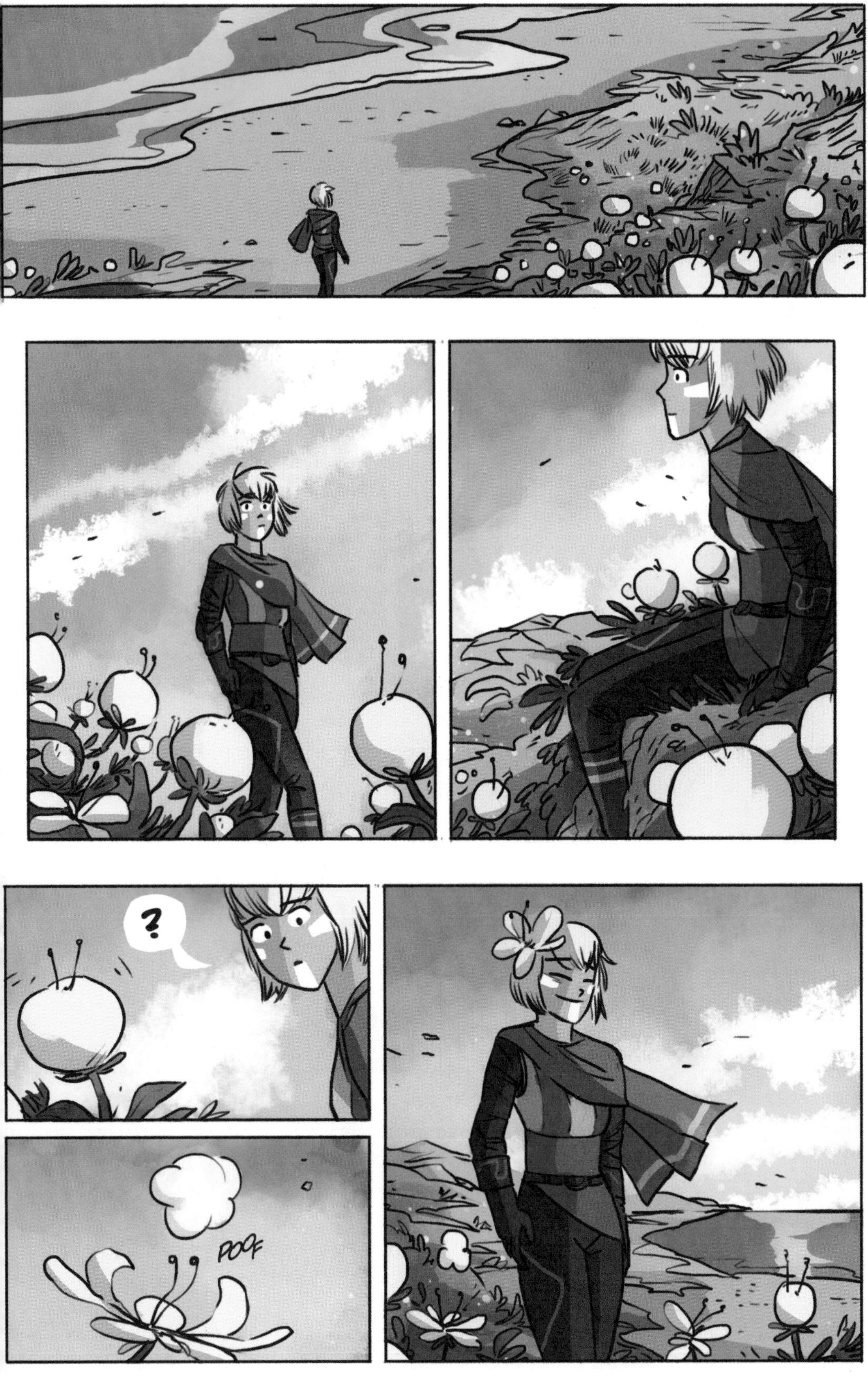
?
POOF

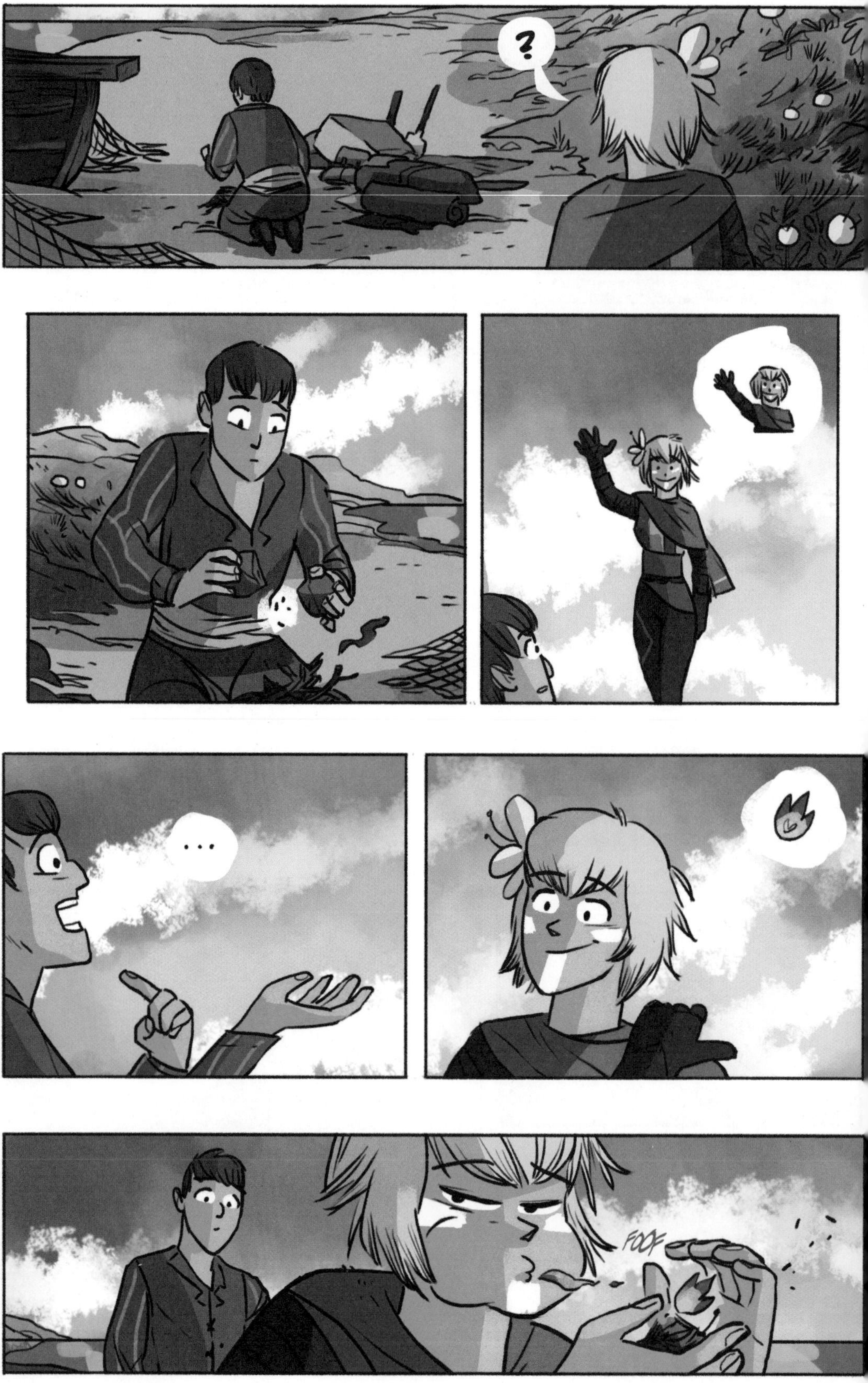
?
...
FOOF

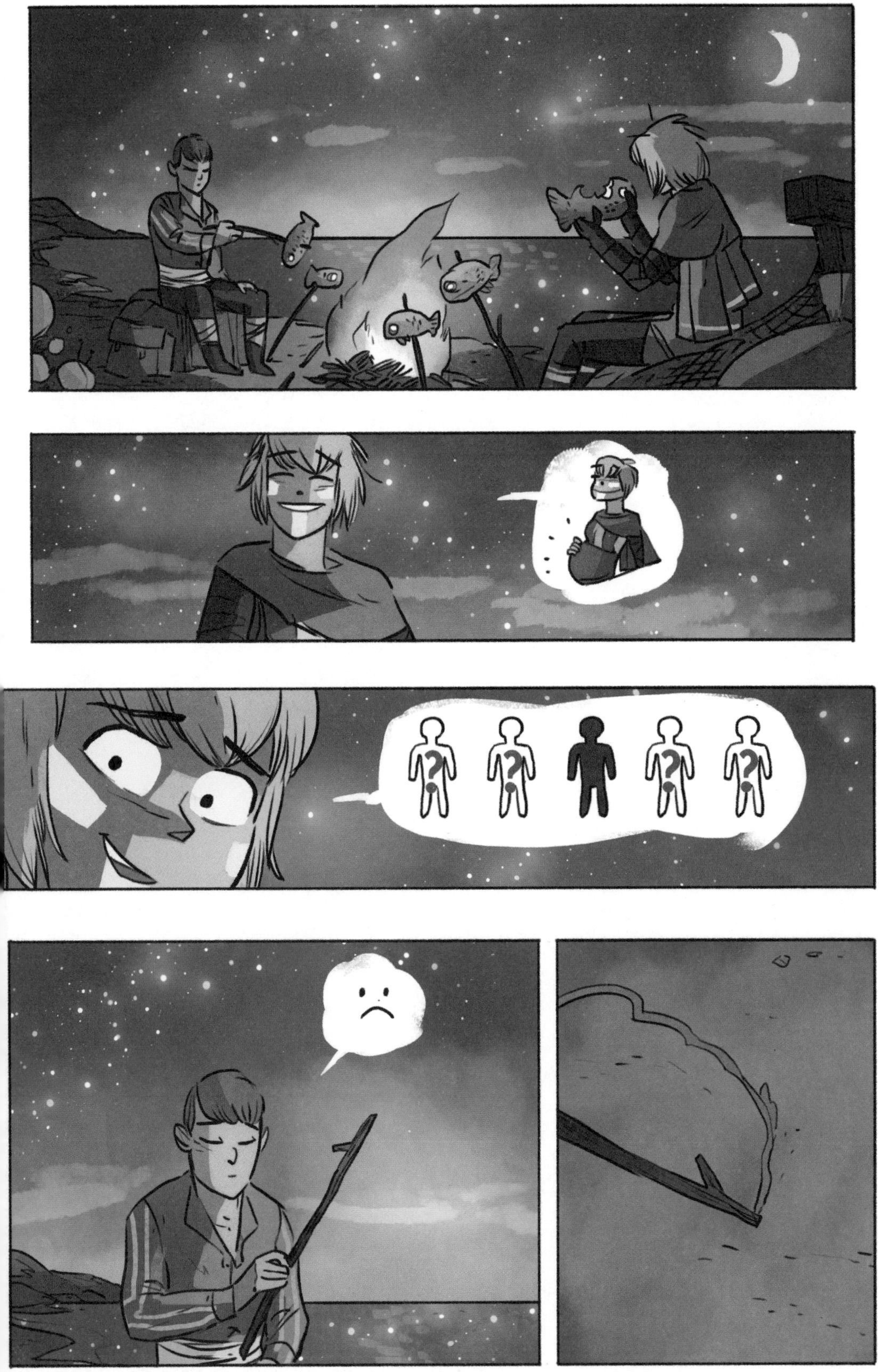

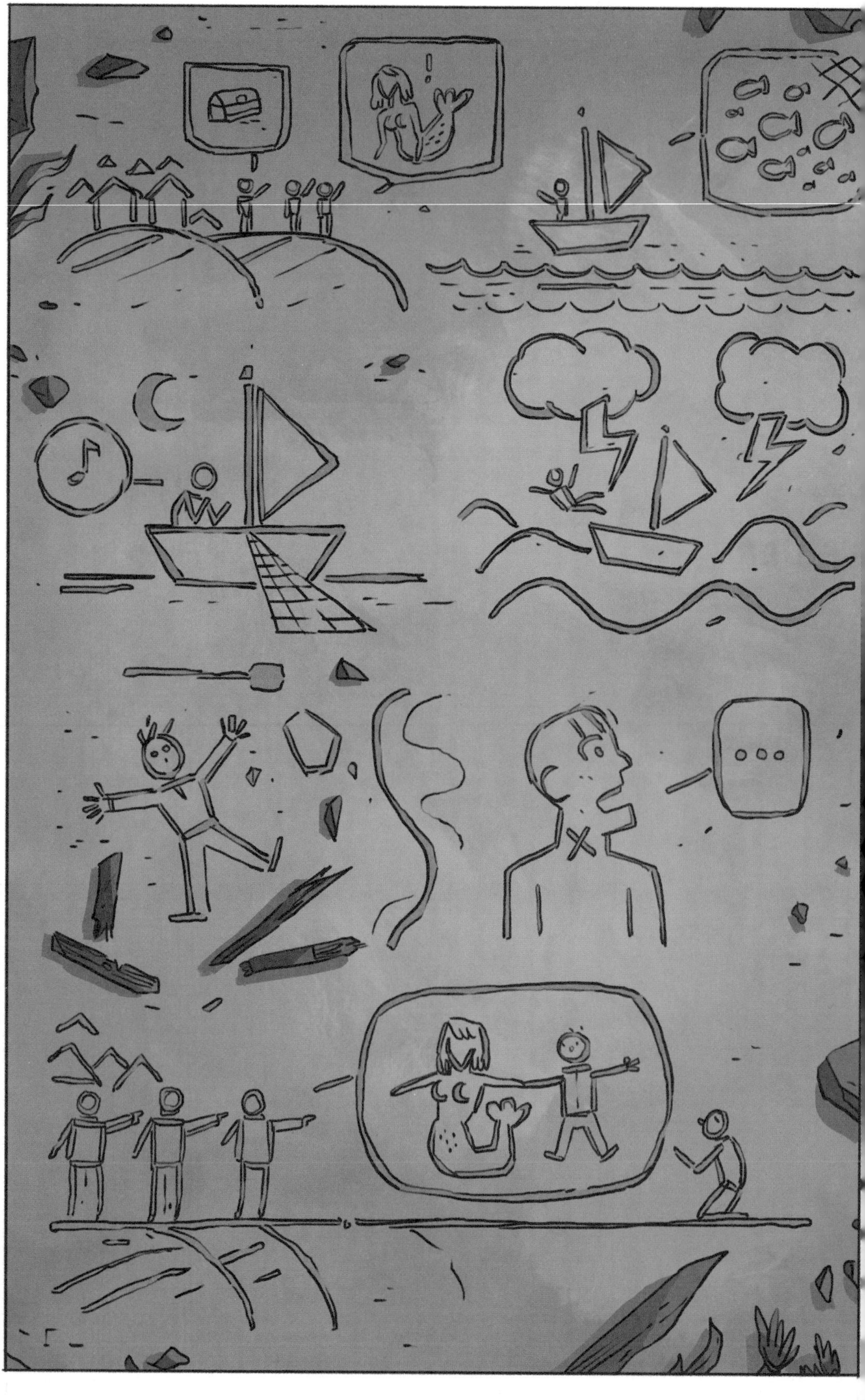

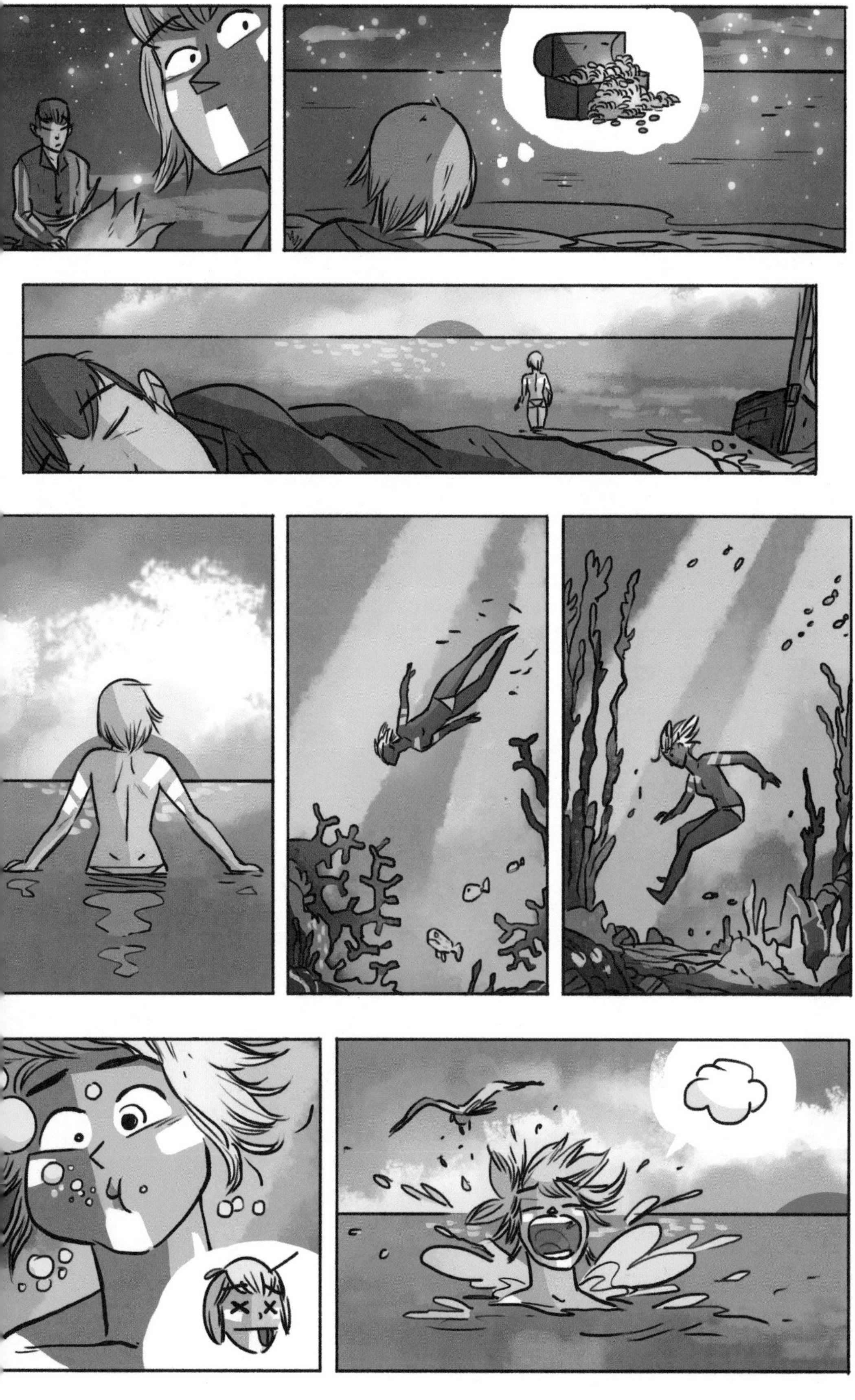

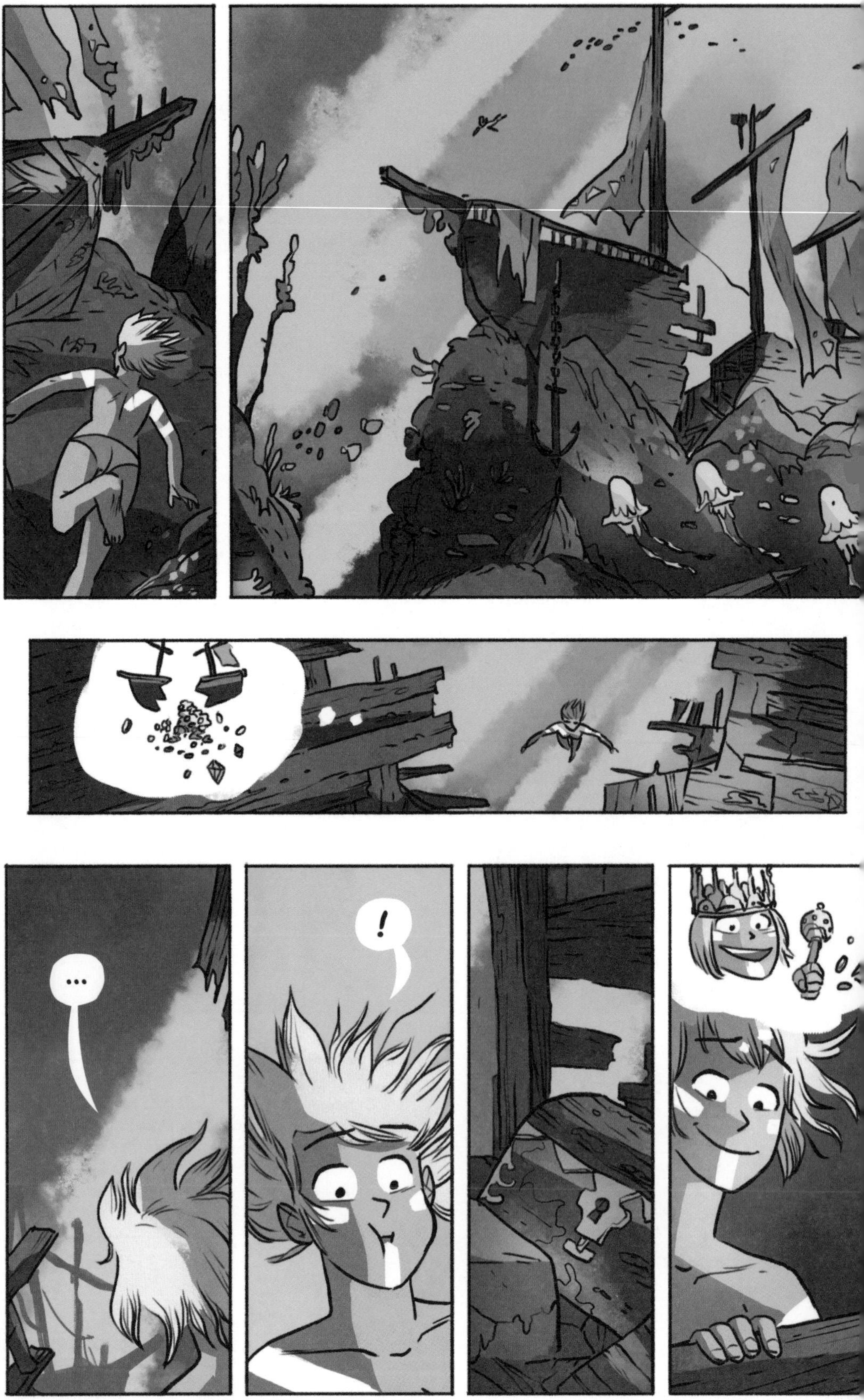
...
!

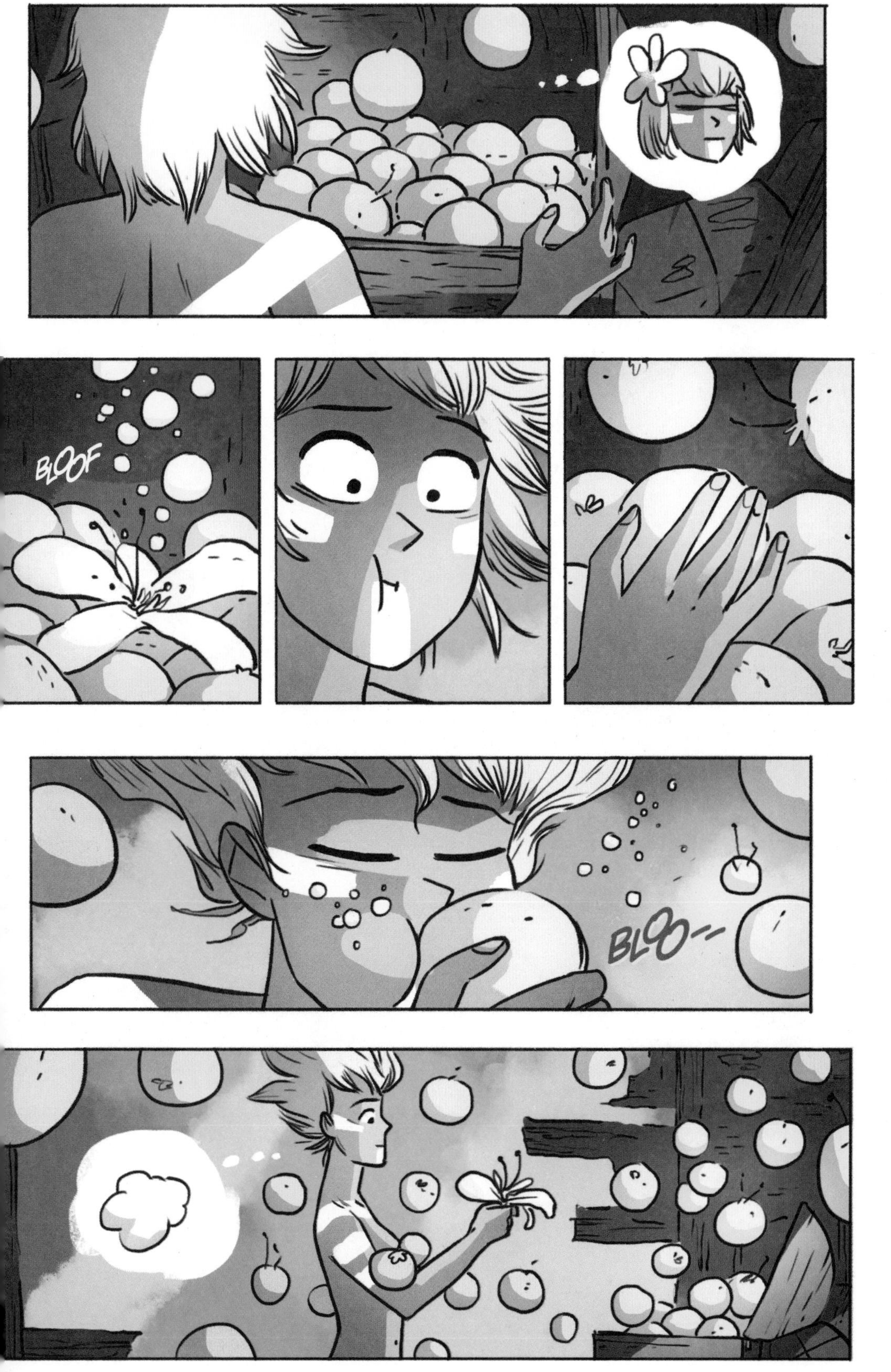
BLOOF
BLOO--

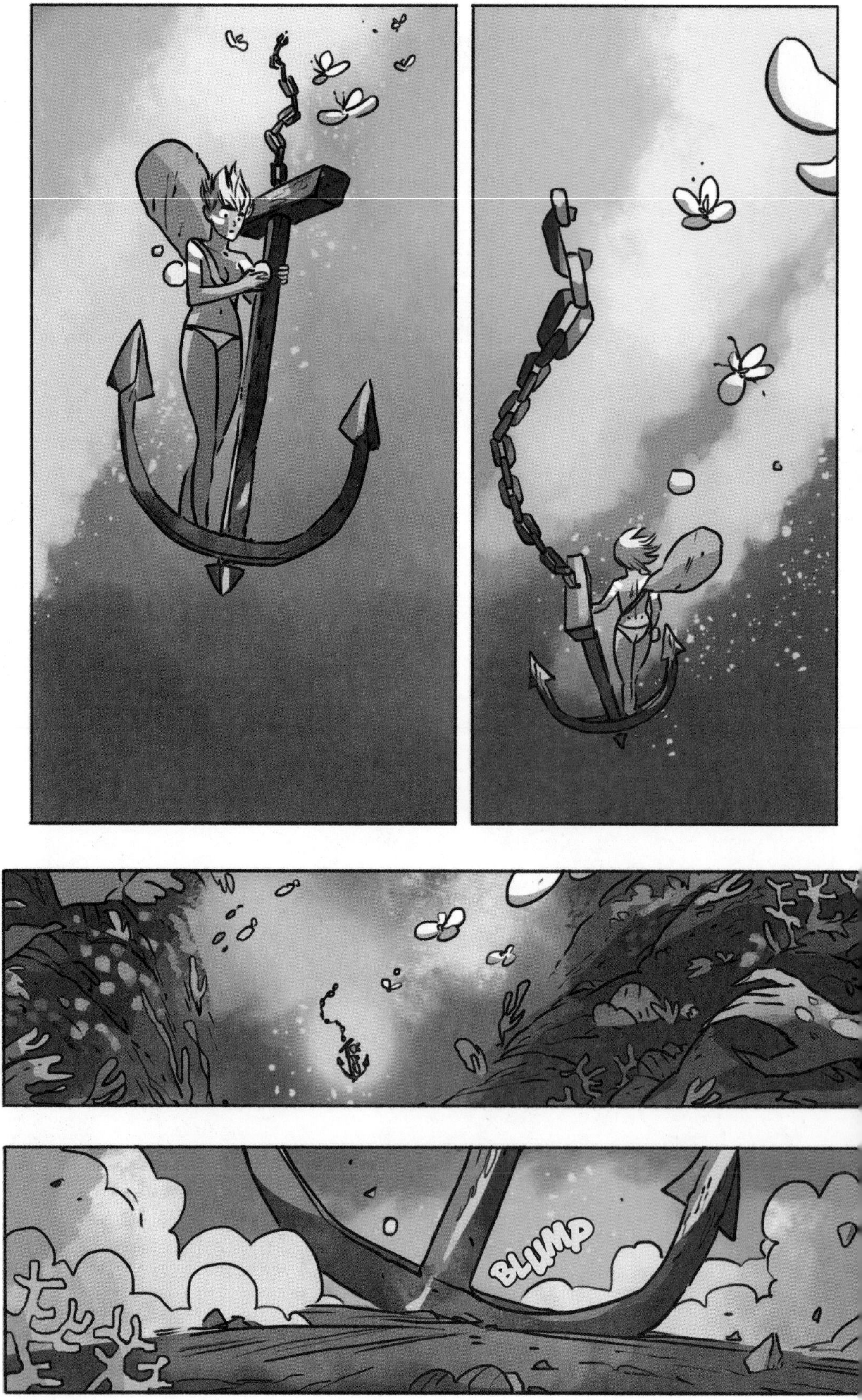
BLUMP

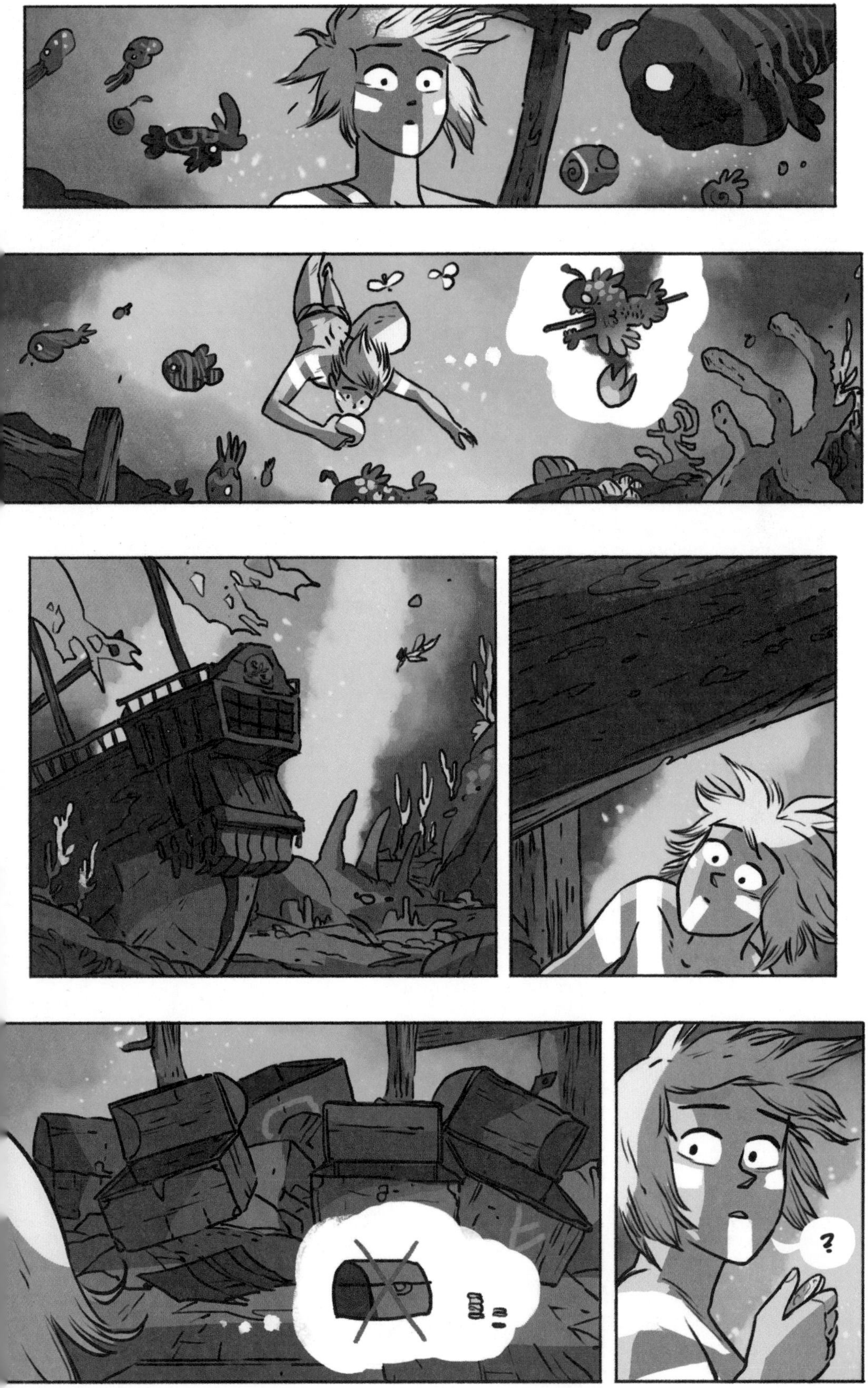
?

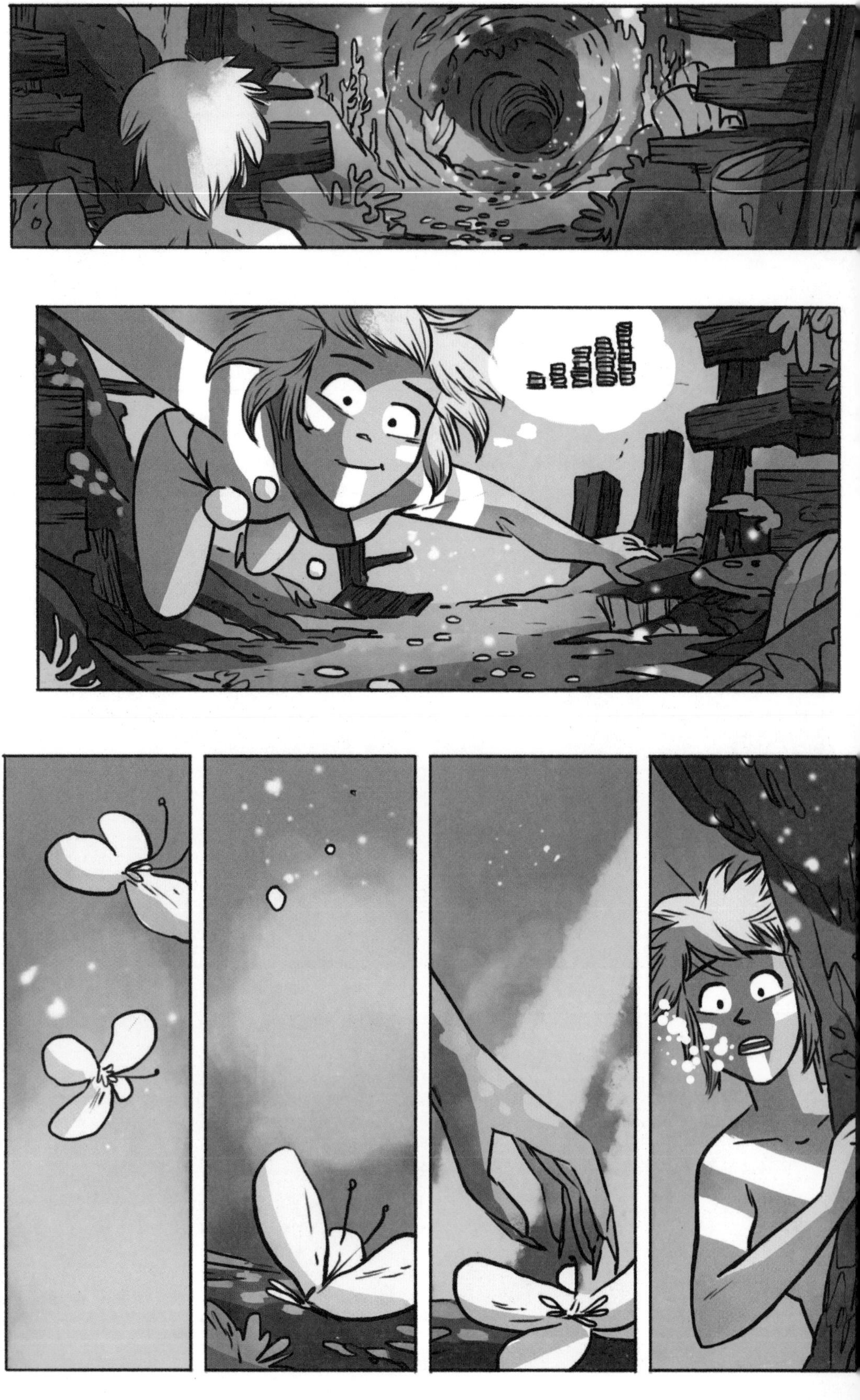

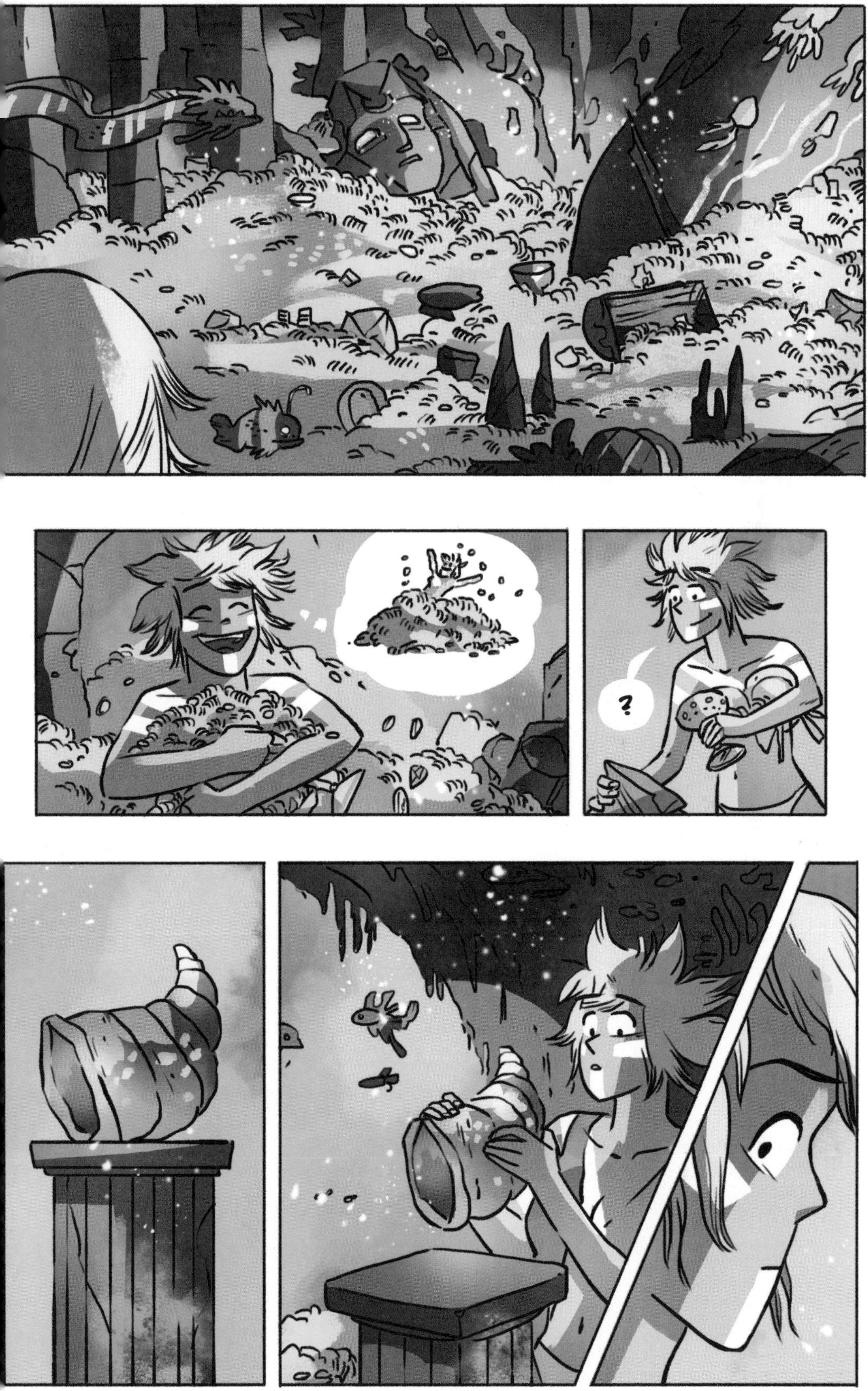
?

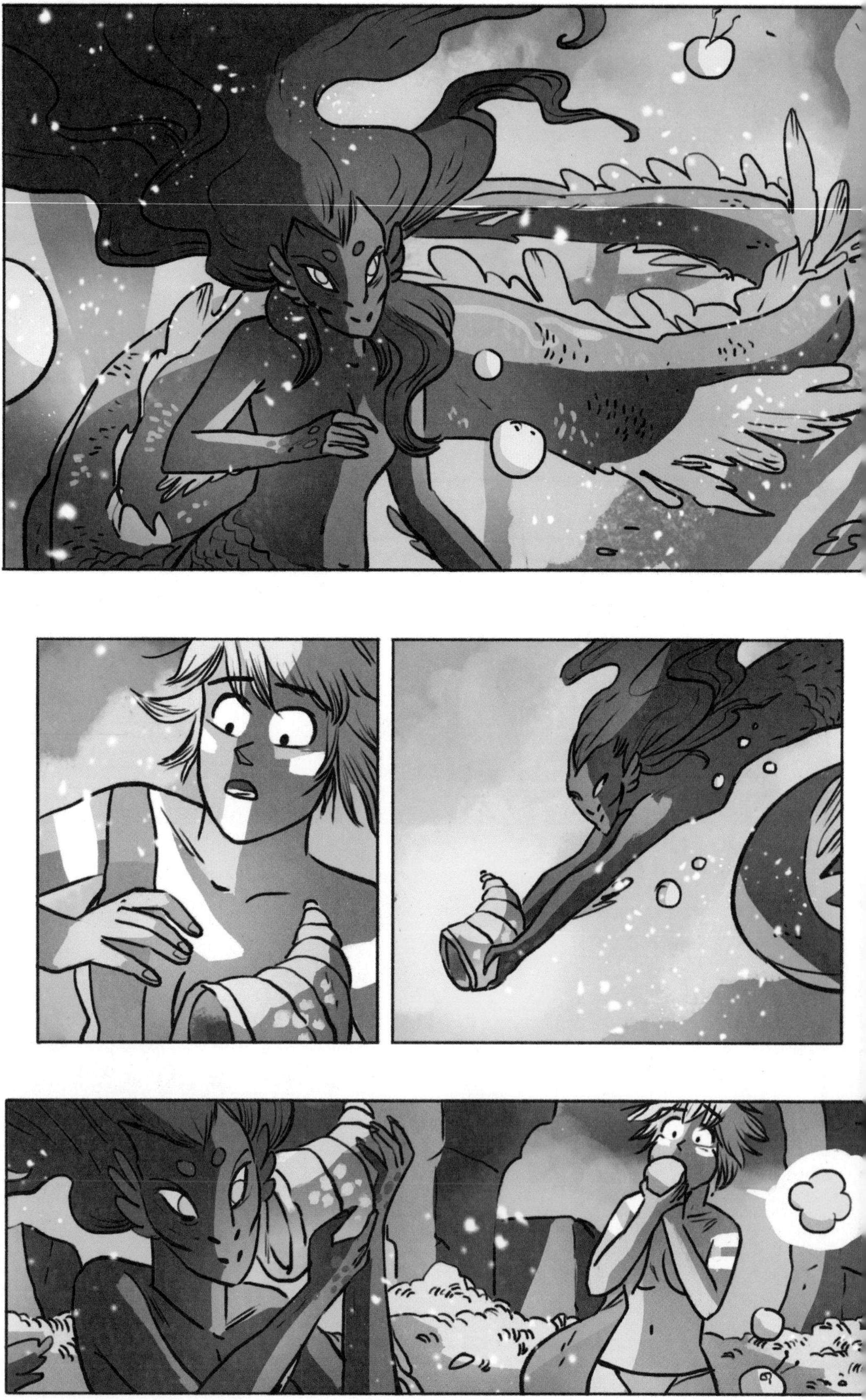

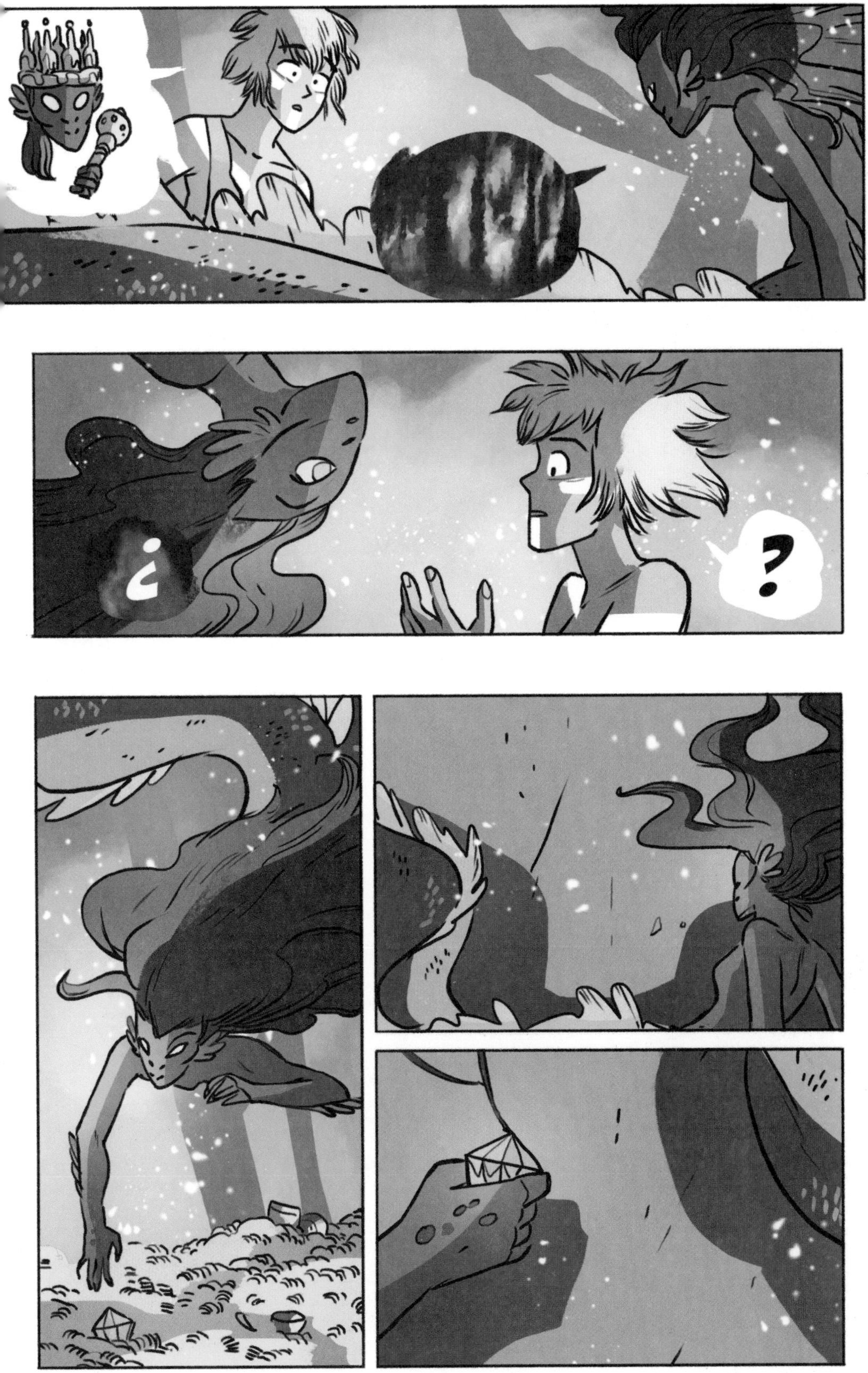
¿
?

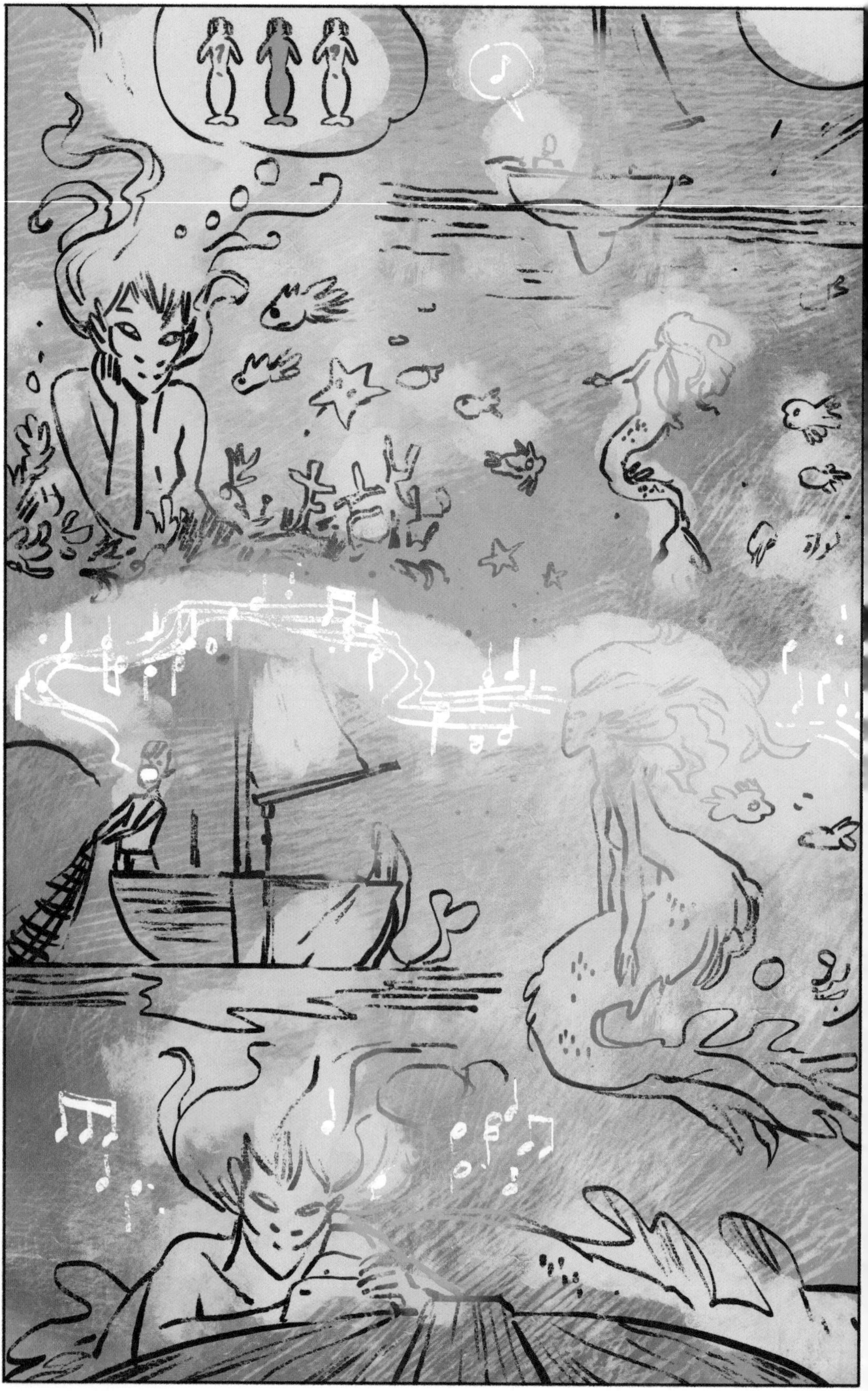

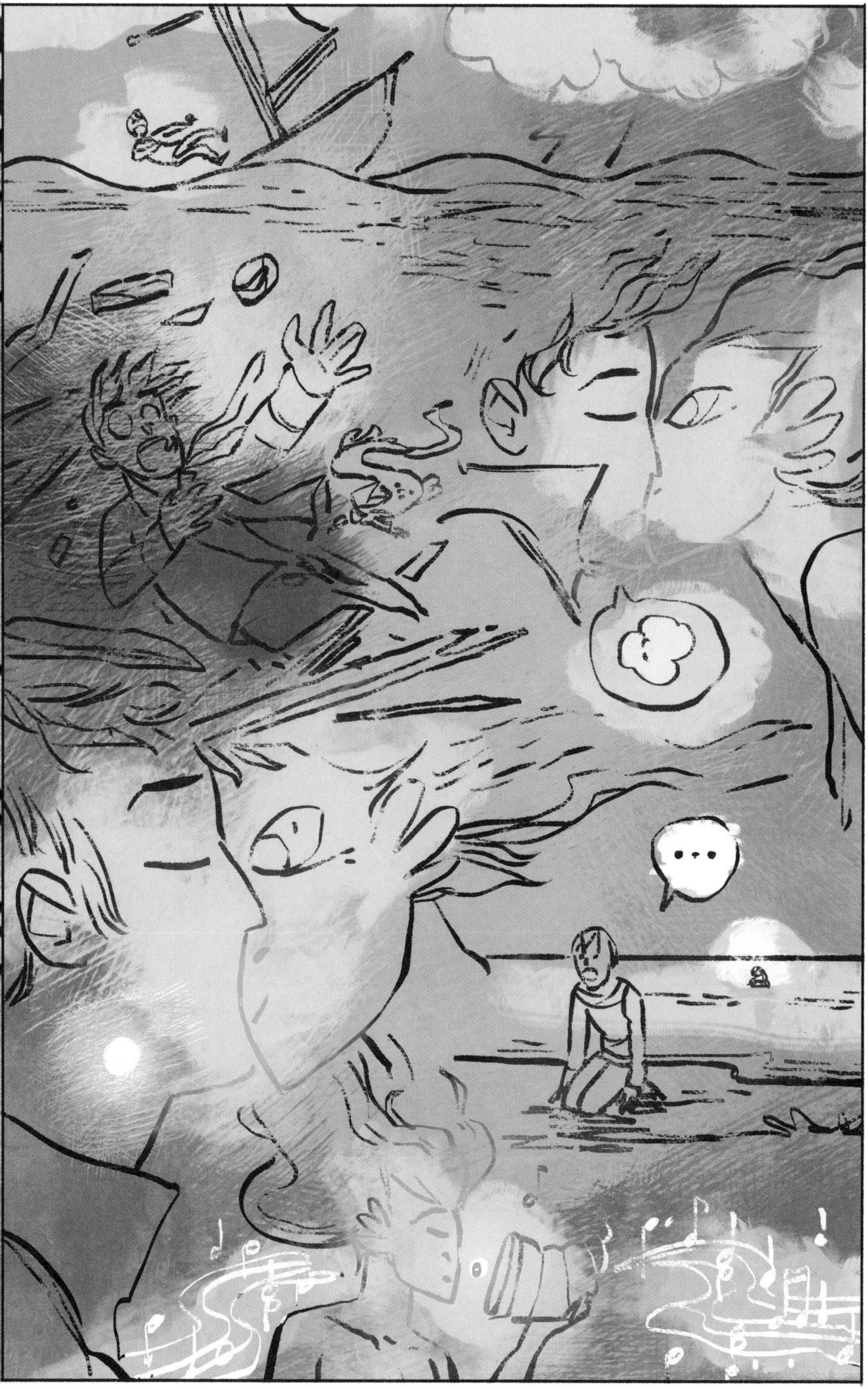
...

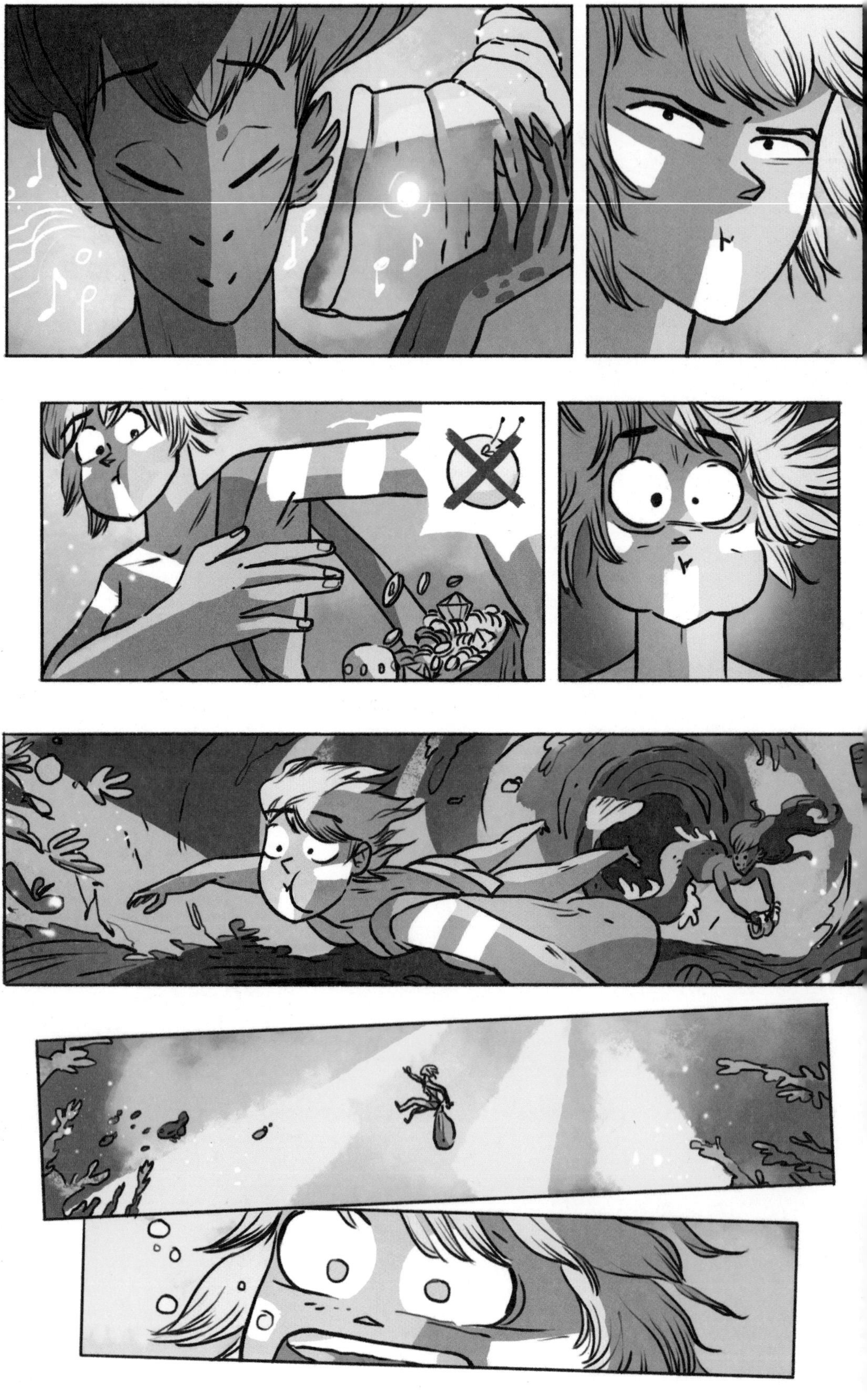

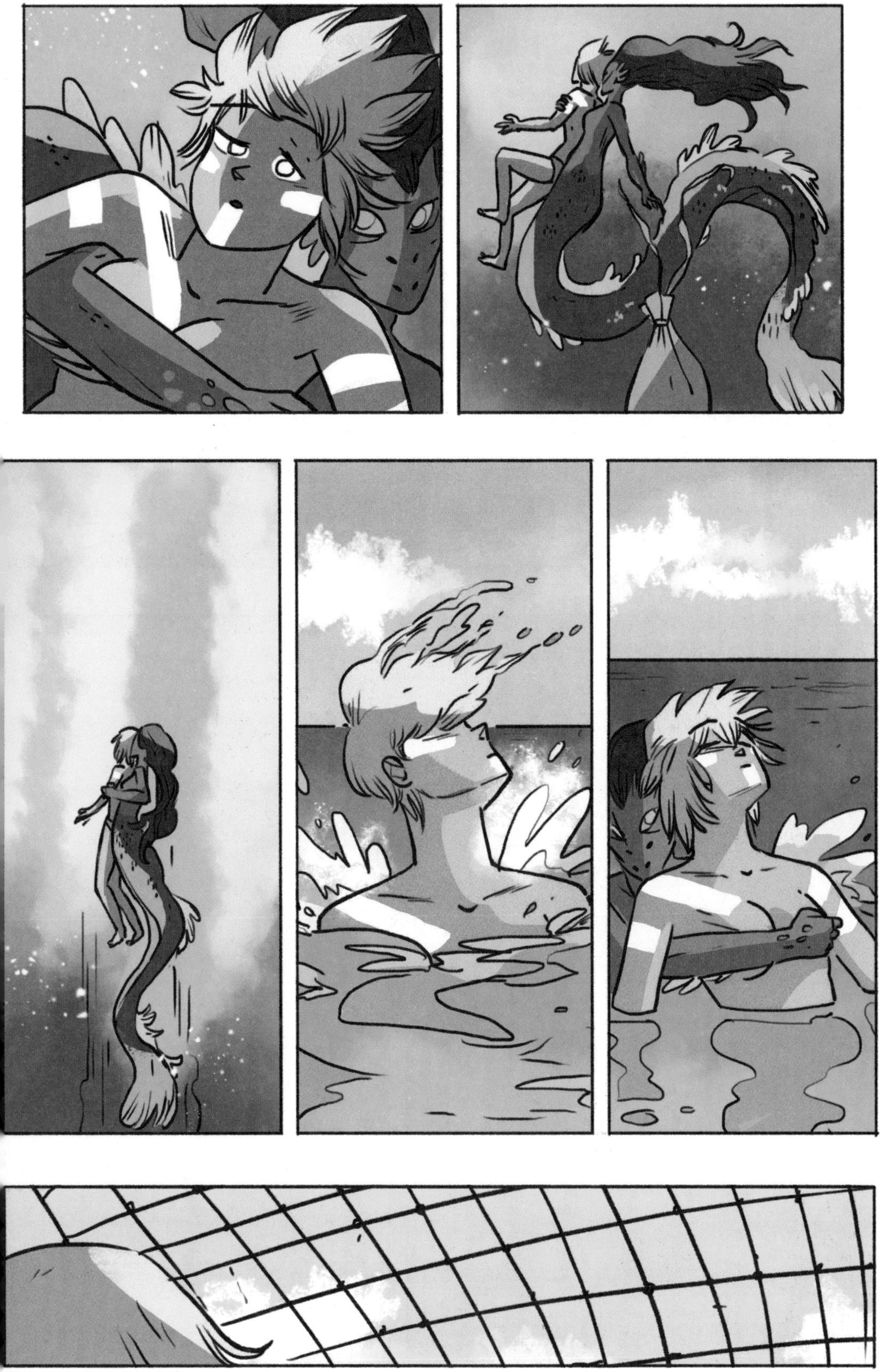

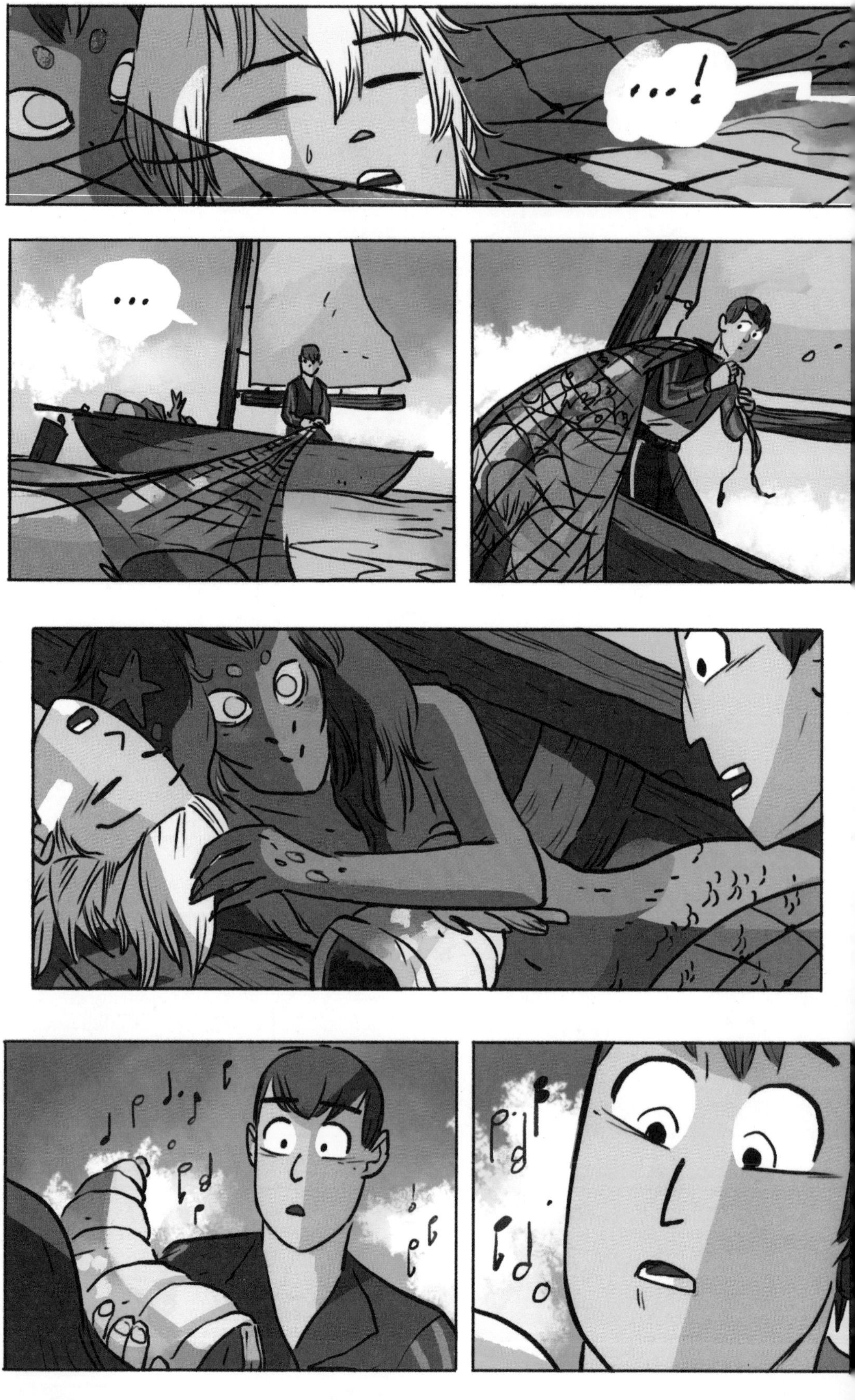

...!
...

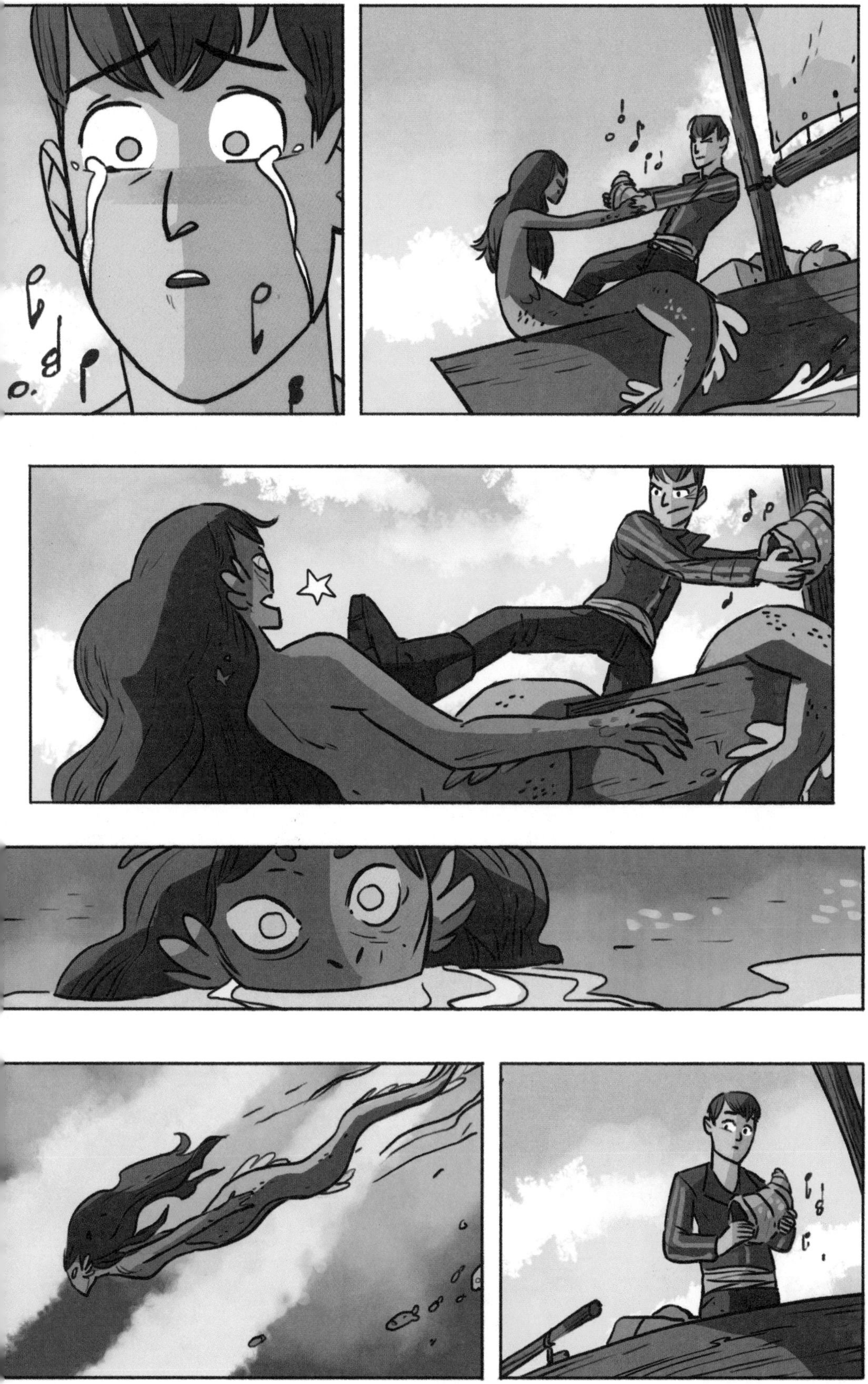

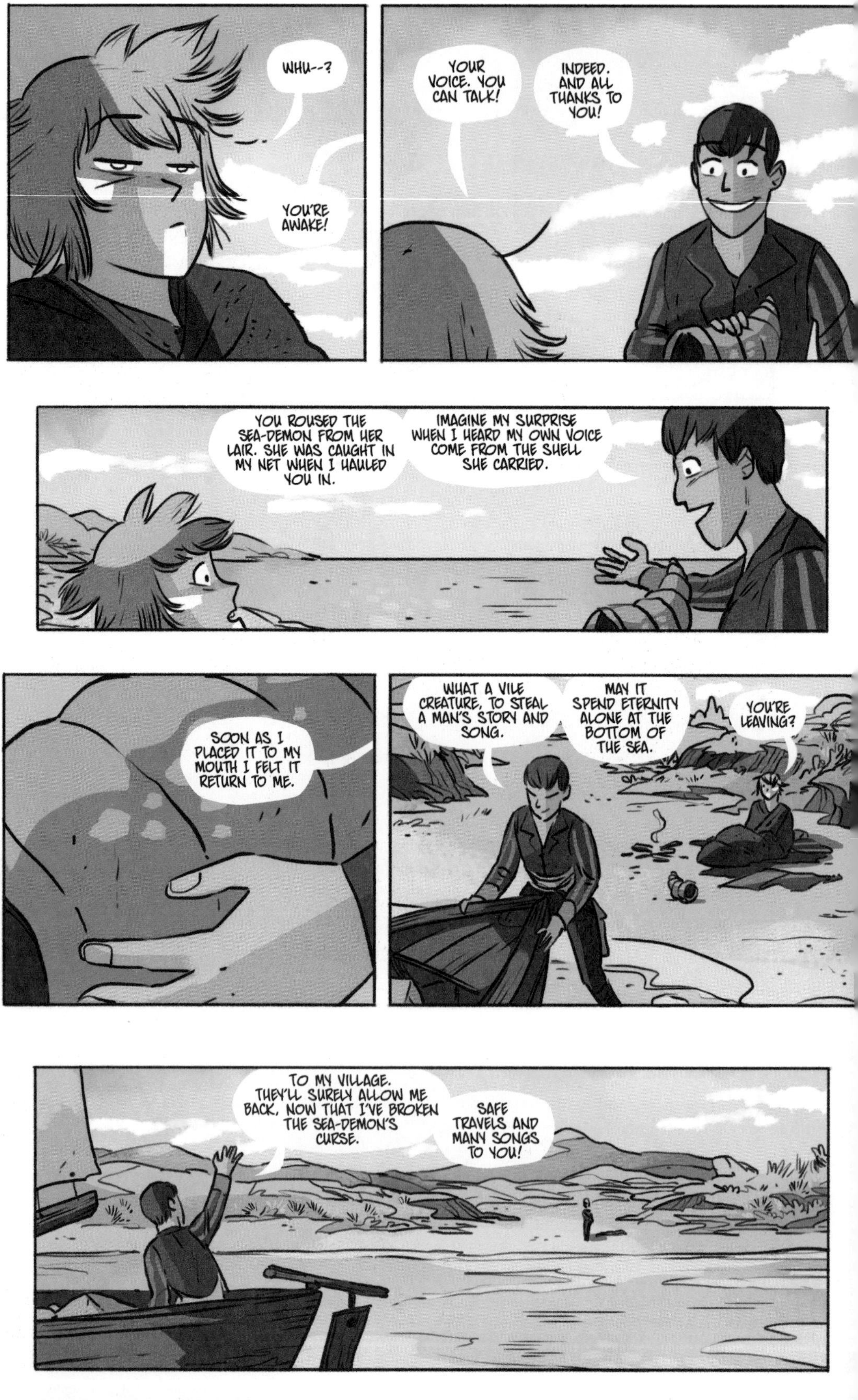

WHU--?
YOU'RE AWAKE!
YOUR VOICE. YOU CAN TALK!
INDEED. AND ALL THANKS TO YOU!
YOU ROUSED THE SEA-DEMON FROM HER LAIR. SHE WAS CAUGHT IN MY NET WHEN I HAULED YOU IN.
IMAGINE MY SURPRISE WHEN I HEARD MY OWN VOICE COME FROM THE SHELL SHE CARRIED.
SOON AS I PLACED IT TO MY MOUTH I FELT IT RETURN TO ME.
WHAT A VILE CREATURE, TO STEAL A MAN'S STORY AND SONG.
MAY IT SPEND ETERNITY ALONE AT THE BOTTOM OF THE SEA.
YOU'RE LEAVING?
TO MY VILLAGE. THEY'LL SURELY ALLOW ME BACK, NOW THAT I'VE BROKEN THE SEA-DEMON'S CURSE.
SAFE TRAVELS AND MANY SONGS TO YOU!

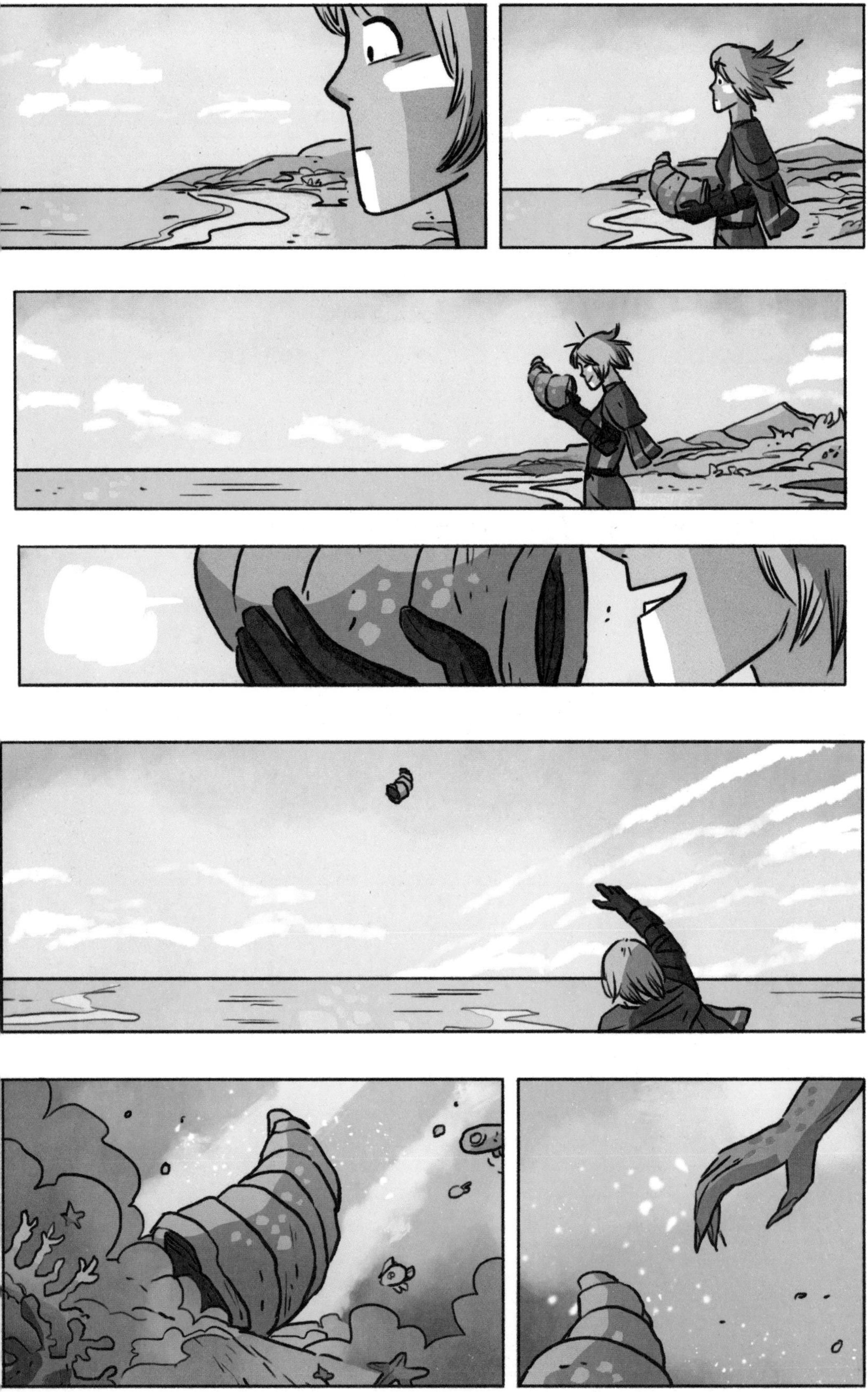

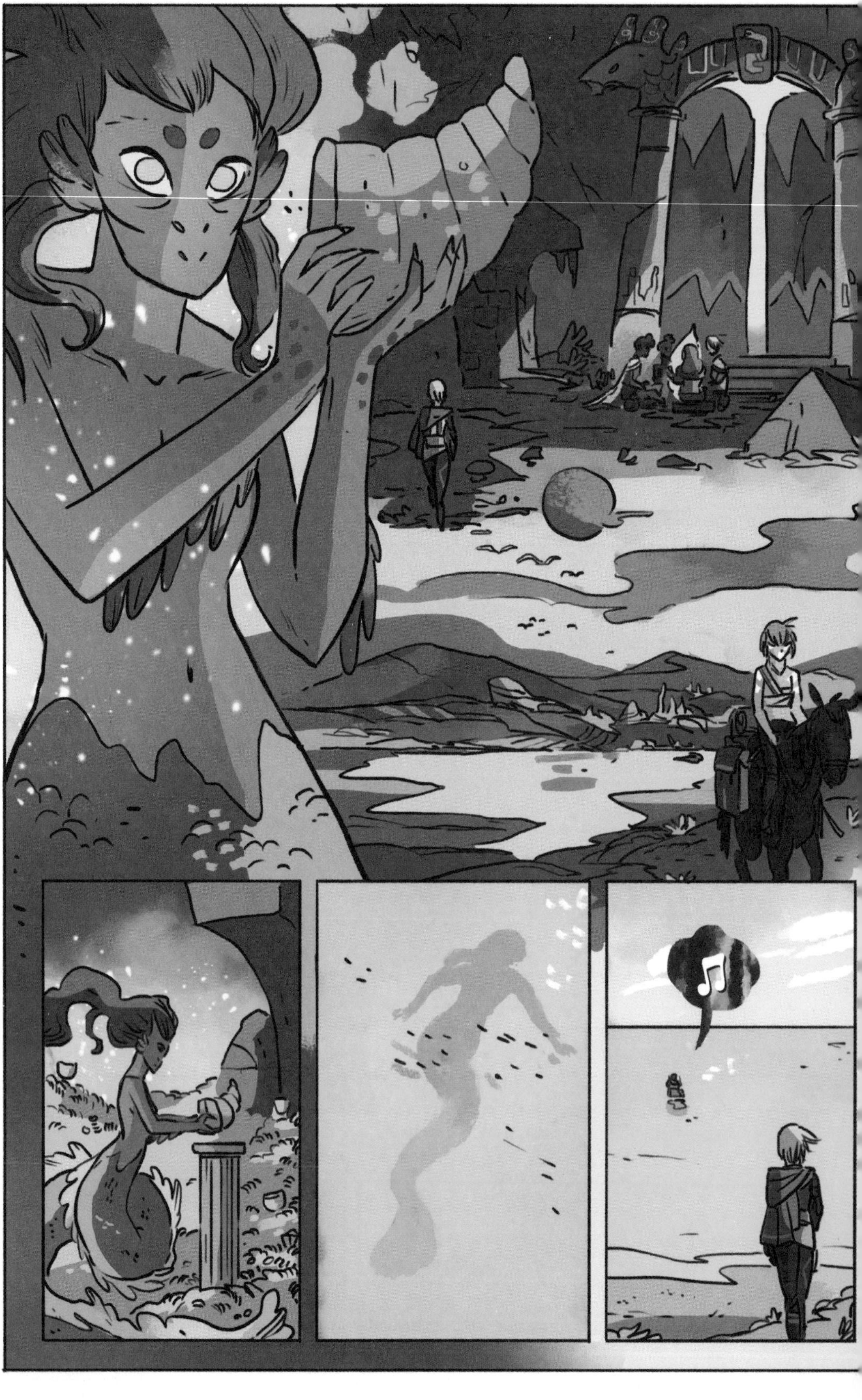

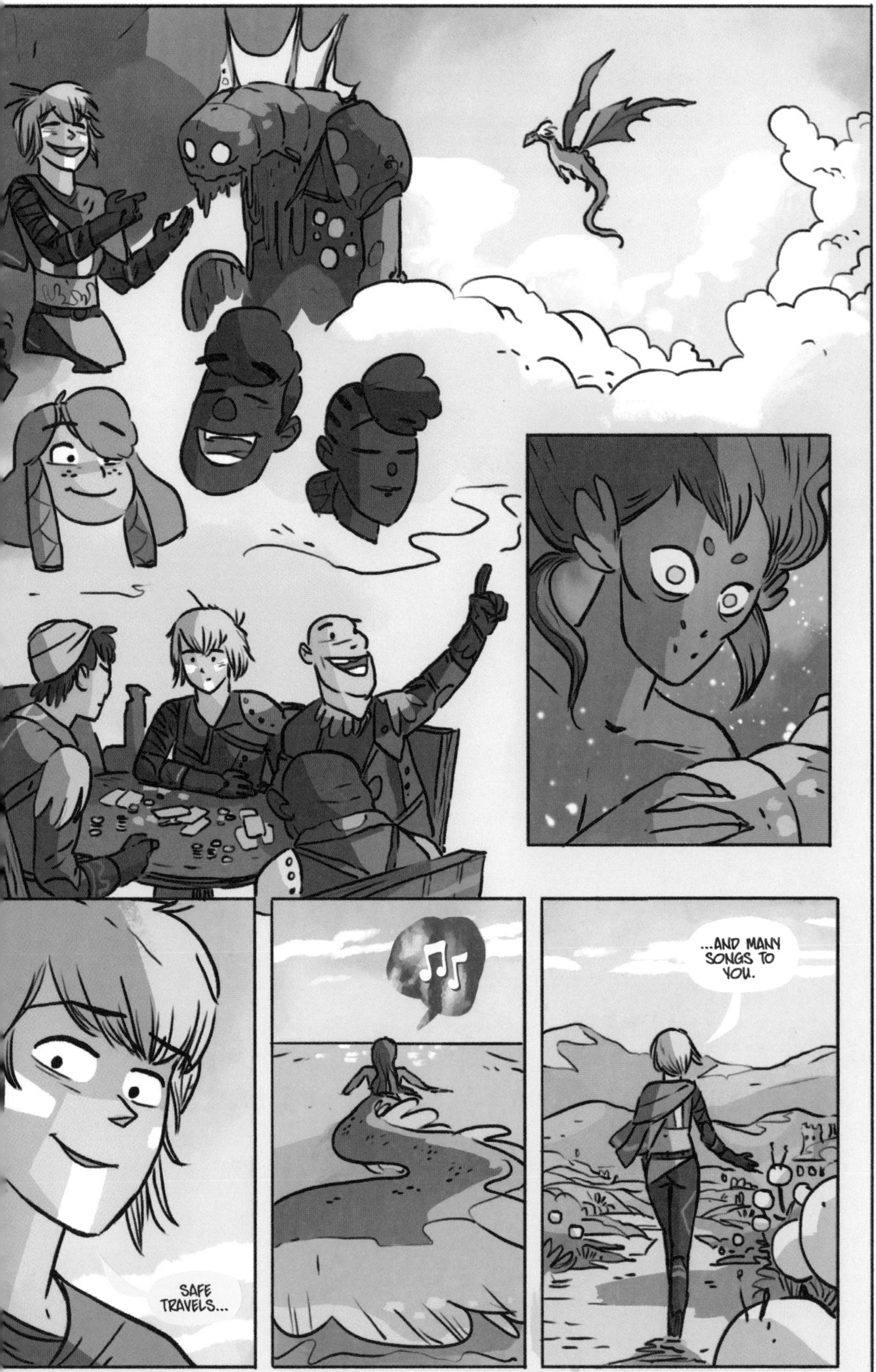
SAFE TRAVELS...
...AND MANY SONGS TO YOU.

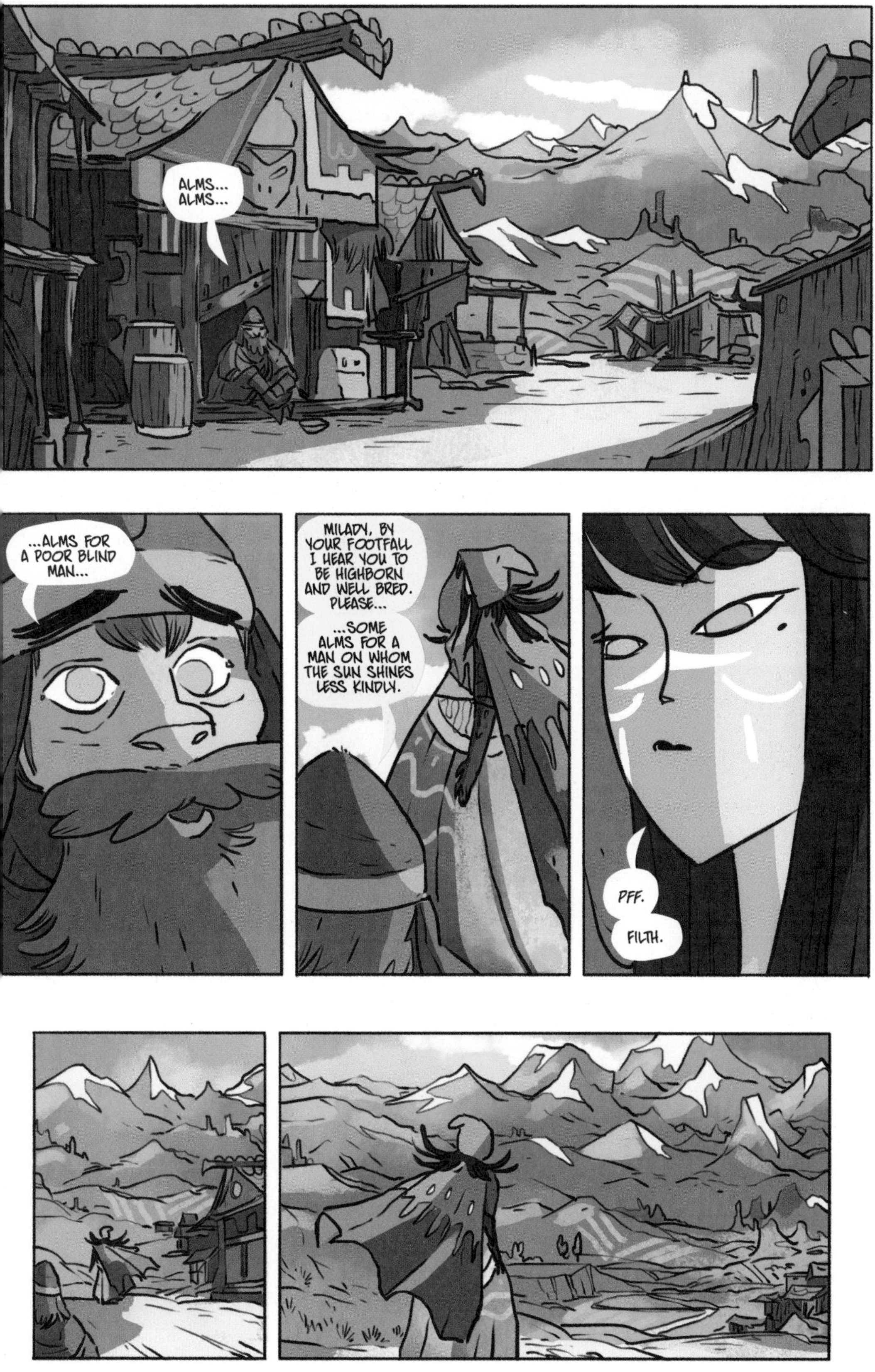
ALMS... ALMS...
...ALMS FOR A POOR BLIND MAN...
MILADY, BY YOUR FOOTFALL I HEAR YOU TO BE HIGHBORN AND WELL BRED. PLEASE...
...SOME ALMS FOR A MAN ON WHOM THE SUN SHINES LESS KINDLY.
PFF.
FILTH.

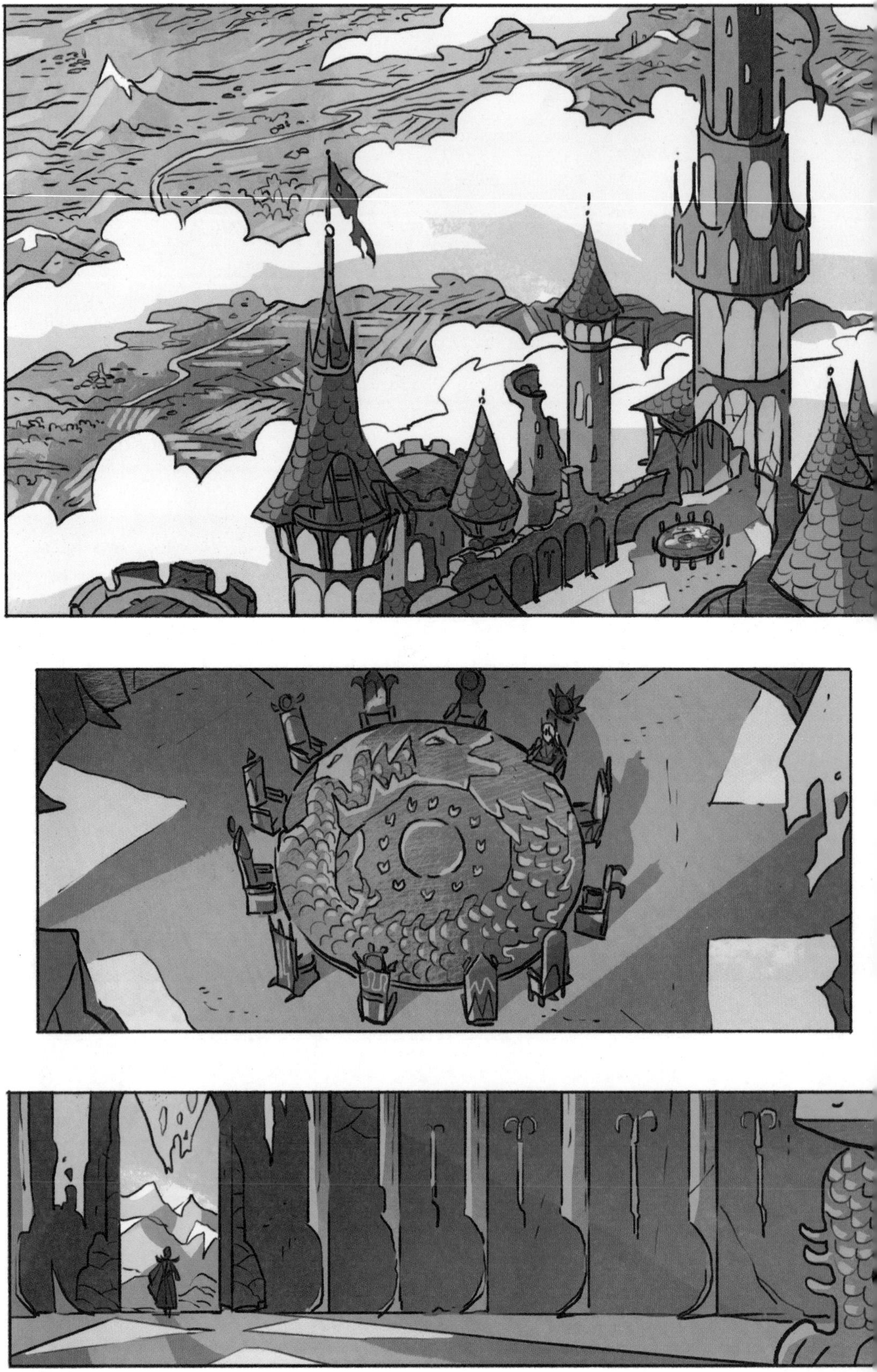

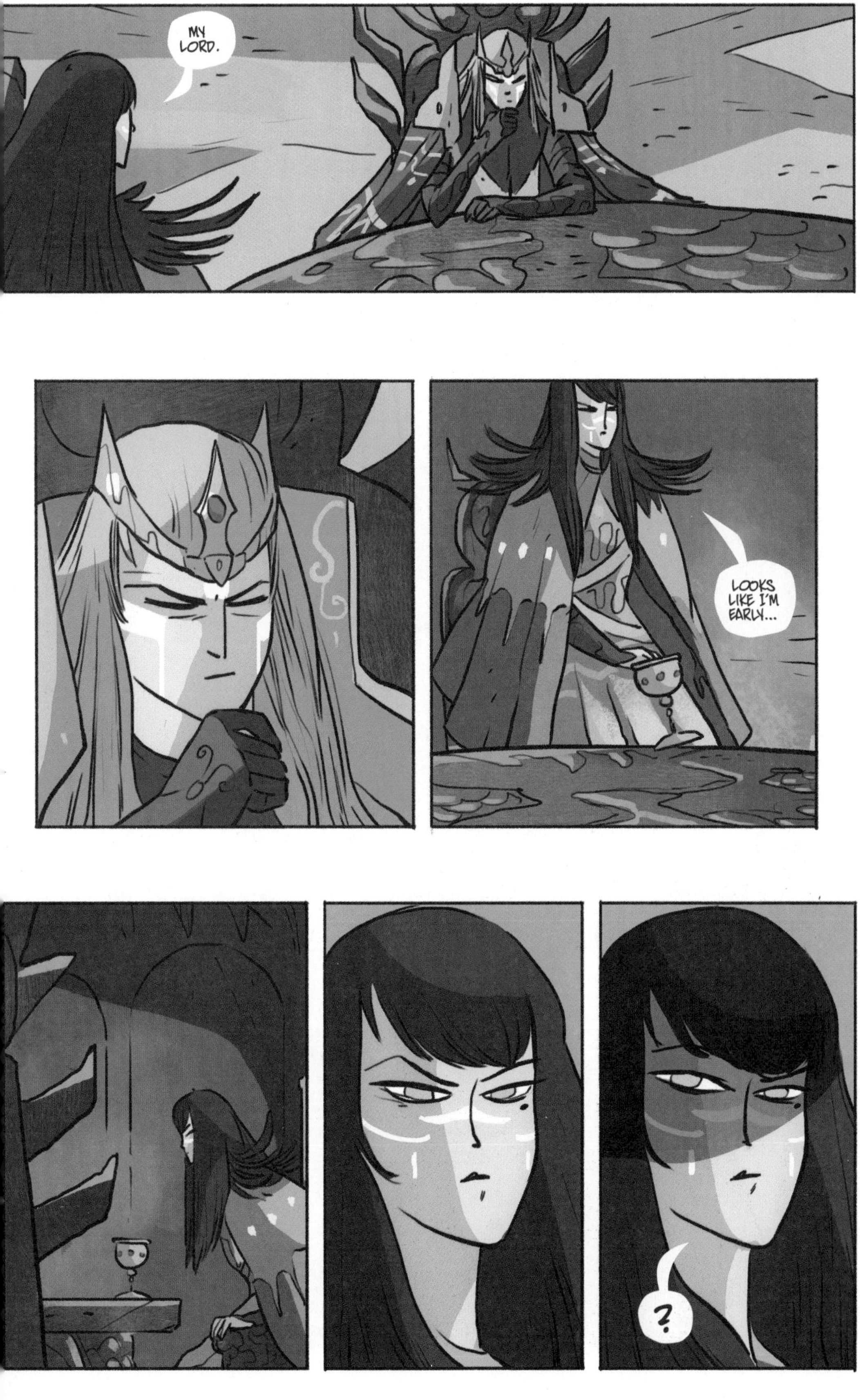
MY LORD.
LOOKS LIKE I'M EARLY...
?

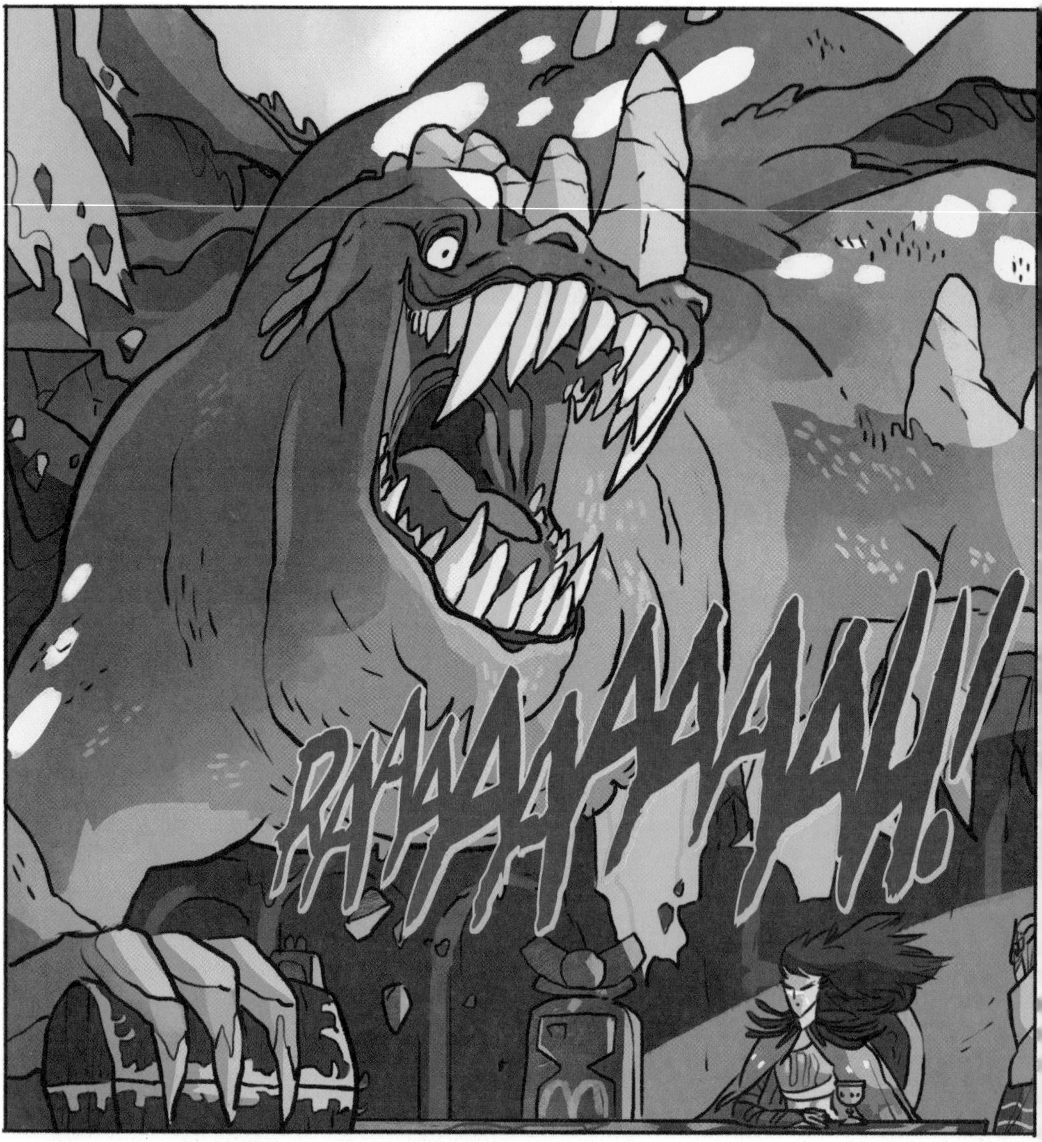
RAAAAAAAAAH!!

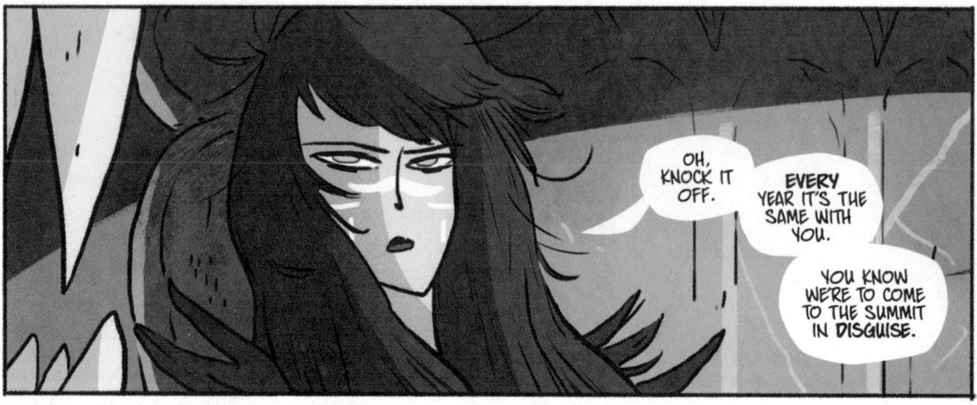
OH, KNOCK IT OFF.
EVERY YEAR IT'S THE SAME WITH YOU.
YOU KNOW WE'RE TO COME TO THE SUMMIT IN DISGUISE.

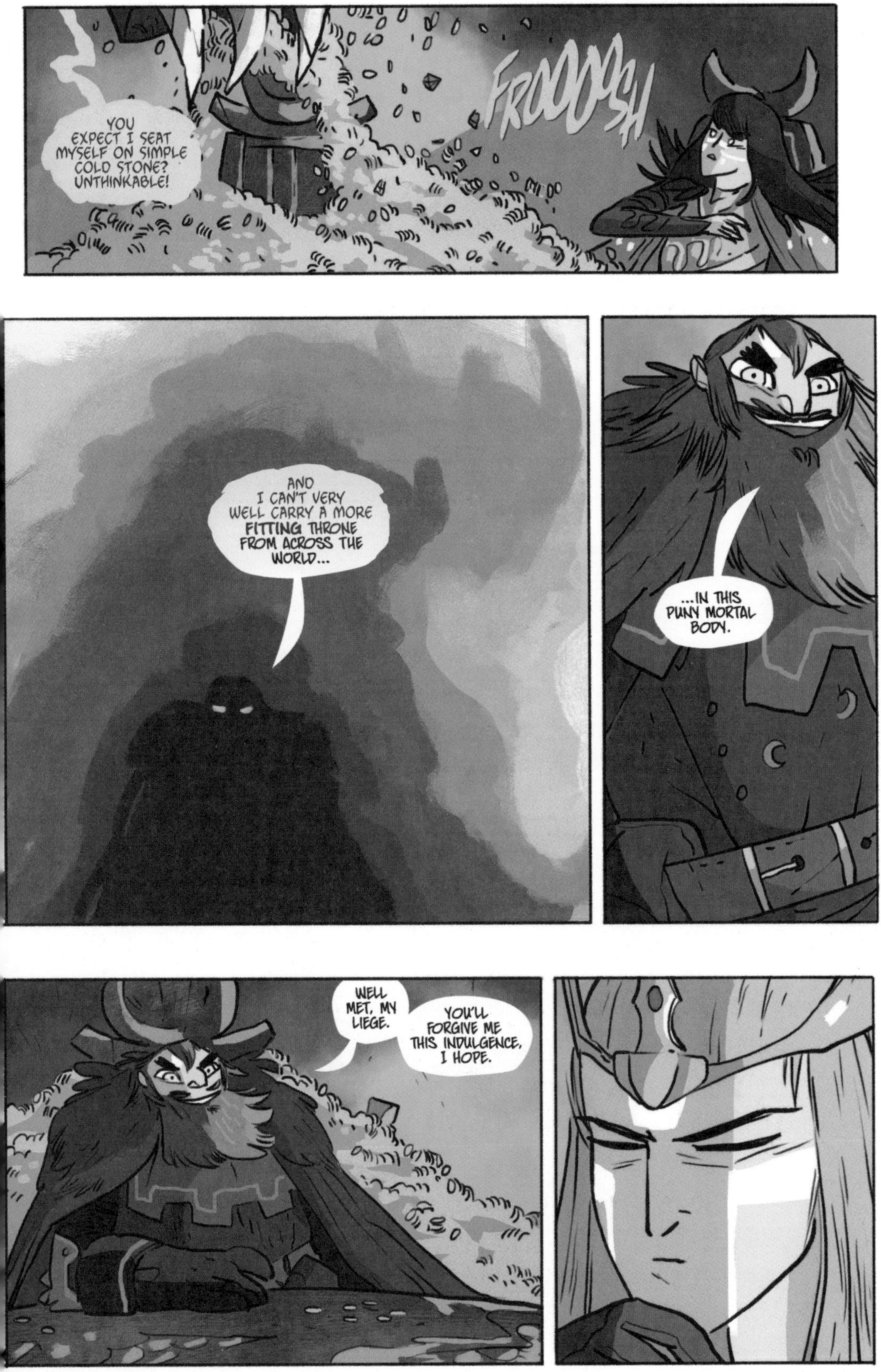
FROOOOSH
YOU EXPECT I SEAT MYSELF ON SIMPLE COLD STONE? UNTHINKABLE!
AND I CAN'T VERY WELL CARRY A MORE FITTING THRONE FROM ACROSS THE WORLD...
...IN THIS PUNY MORTAL BODY.
WELL MET, MY LIEGE.
YOU'LL FORGIVE ME THIS INDULGENCE, I HOPE.

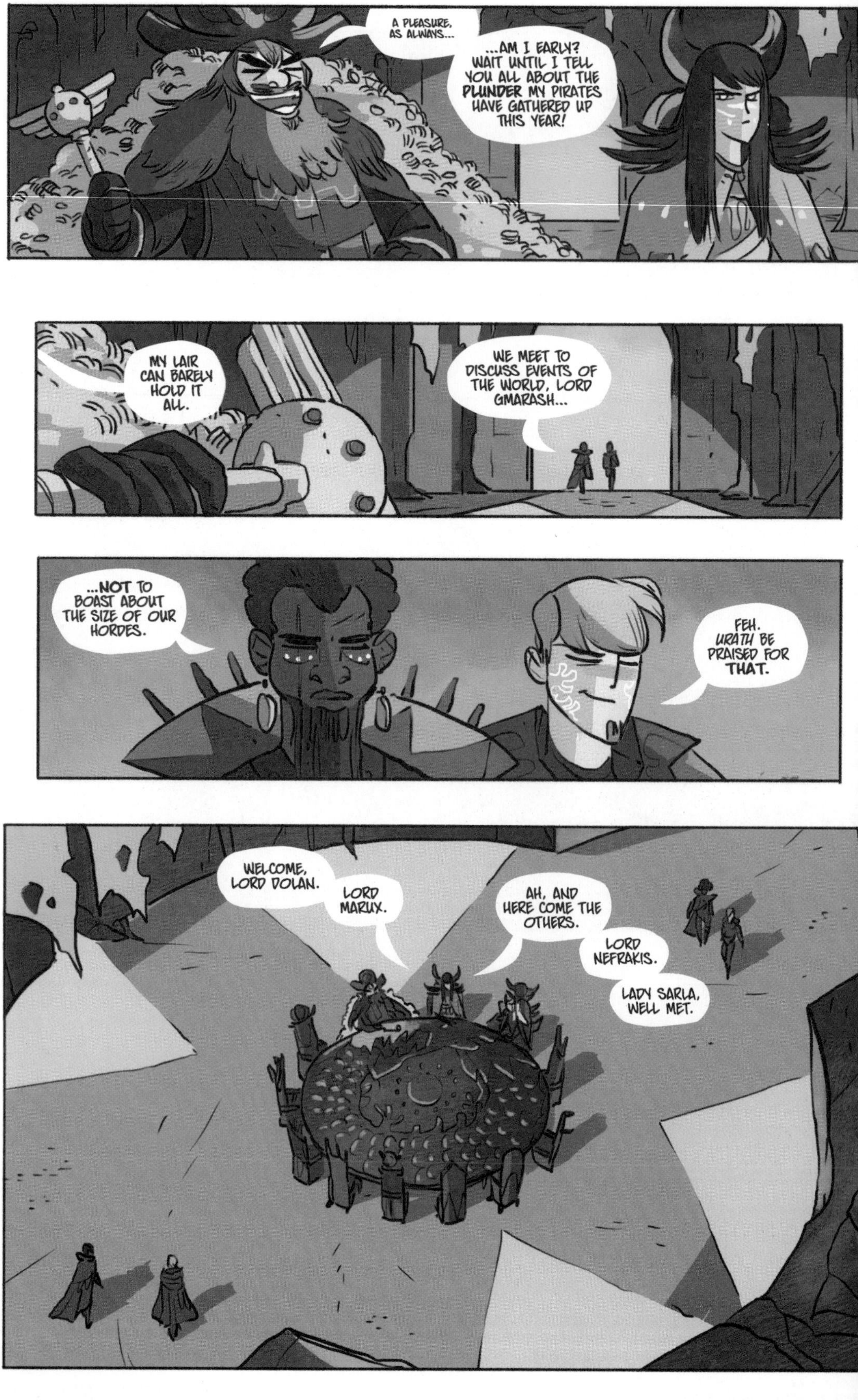
A PLEASURE, AS ALWAYS...
...AM I EARLY? WAIT UNTIL I TELL YOU ALL ABOUT THE PLUNDER MY PIRATES HAVE GATHERED UP THIS YEAR!
MY LAIR CAN BARELY HOLD IT ALL.
WE MEET TO DISCUSS EVENTS OF THE WORLD, LORD GMARASH...
...NOT TO BOAST ABOUT THE SIZE OF OUR HORDES.
FEH. URATH BE PRAISED FOR THAT.
WELCOME, LORD DOLAN.
LORD MARUX.
AH, AND HERE COME THE OTHERS.
LORD NEFRAKIS.
LADY SARLA, WELL MET.

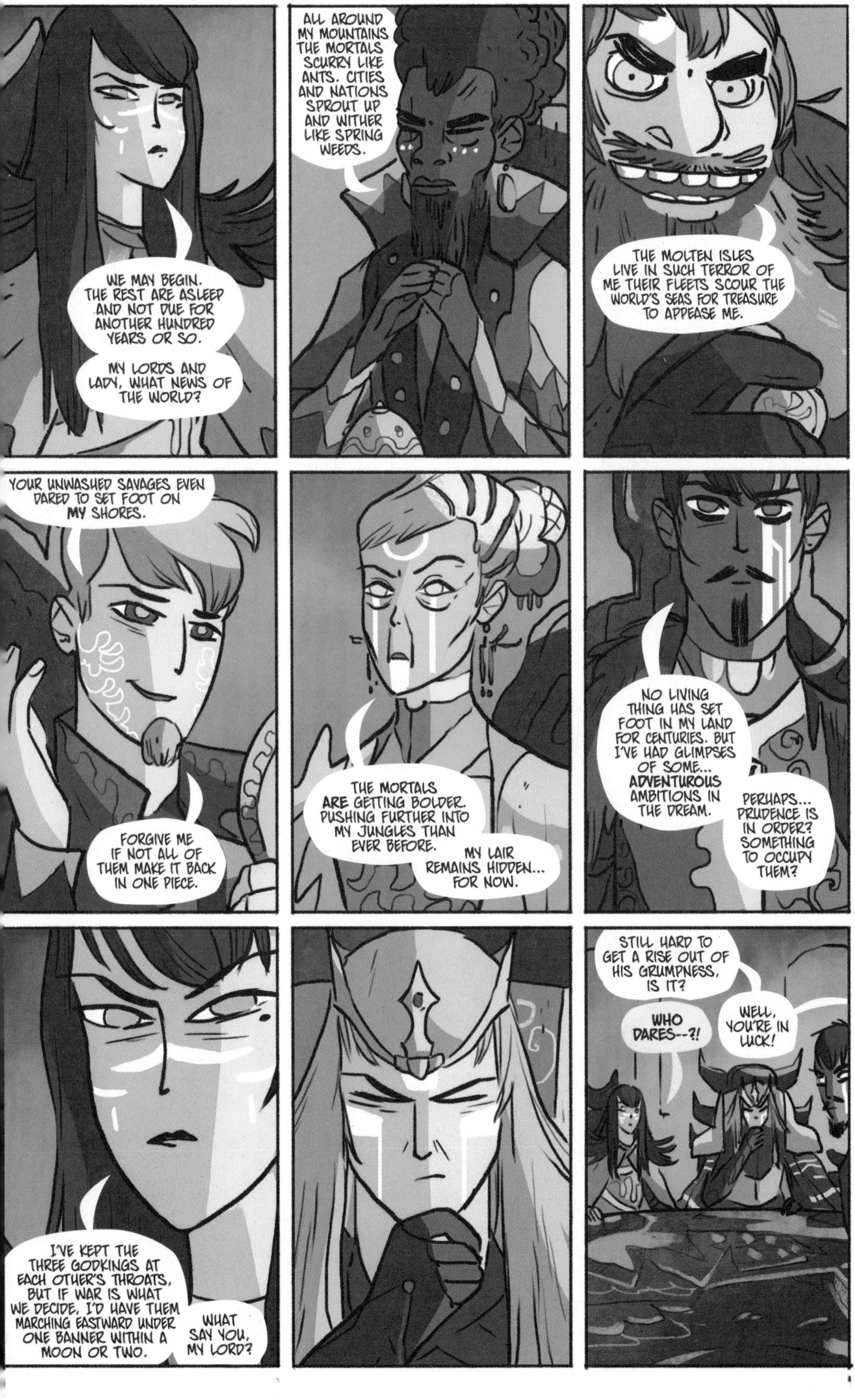

WE MAY BEGIN. THE REST ARE ASLEEP AND NOT DUE FOR ANOTHER HUNDRED YEARS OR SO.
MY LORDS AND LADY, WHAT NEWS OF THE WORLD?
ALL AROUND MY MOUNTAINS THE MORTALS SCURRY LIKE ANTS. CITIES AND NATIONS SPROUT UP AND WITHER LIKE SPRING WEEDS.
THE MOLTEN ISLES LIVE IN SUCH TERROR OF ME THEIR FLEETS SCOUR THE WORLD'S SEAS FOR TREASURE TO APPEASE ME.
YOUR UNWASHED SAVAGES EVEN DARED TO SET FOOT ON **MY** SHORES.
FORGIVE ME IF NOT ALL OF THEM MAKE IT BACK IN ONE PIECE.
THE MORTALS **ARE** GETTING BOLDER. PUSHING FURTHER INTO MY JUNGLES THAN EVER BEFORE.
MY LAIR REMAINS HIDDEN... FOR NOW.
NO LIVING THING HAS SET FOOT IN MY LAND FOR CENTURIES. BUT I'VE HAD GLIMPSES OF SOME... **ADVENTUROUS** AMBITIONS IN THE DREAM.
PERHAPS... PRUDENCE IS IN ORDER? SOMETHING TO OCCUPY THEM?
I'VE KEPT THE THREE GODKINGS AT EACH OTHER'S THROATS, BUT IF WAR IS WHAT WE DECIDE, I'D HAVE THEM MARCHING EASTWARD UNDER ONE BANNER WITHIN A MOON OR TWO.
WHAT SAY YOU, MY LORD?
STILL HARD TO GET A RISE OUT OF HIS GRUMPNESS, IS IT?
WHO DARES--?!
WELL, YOU'RE IN LUCK!

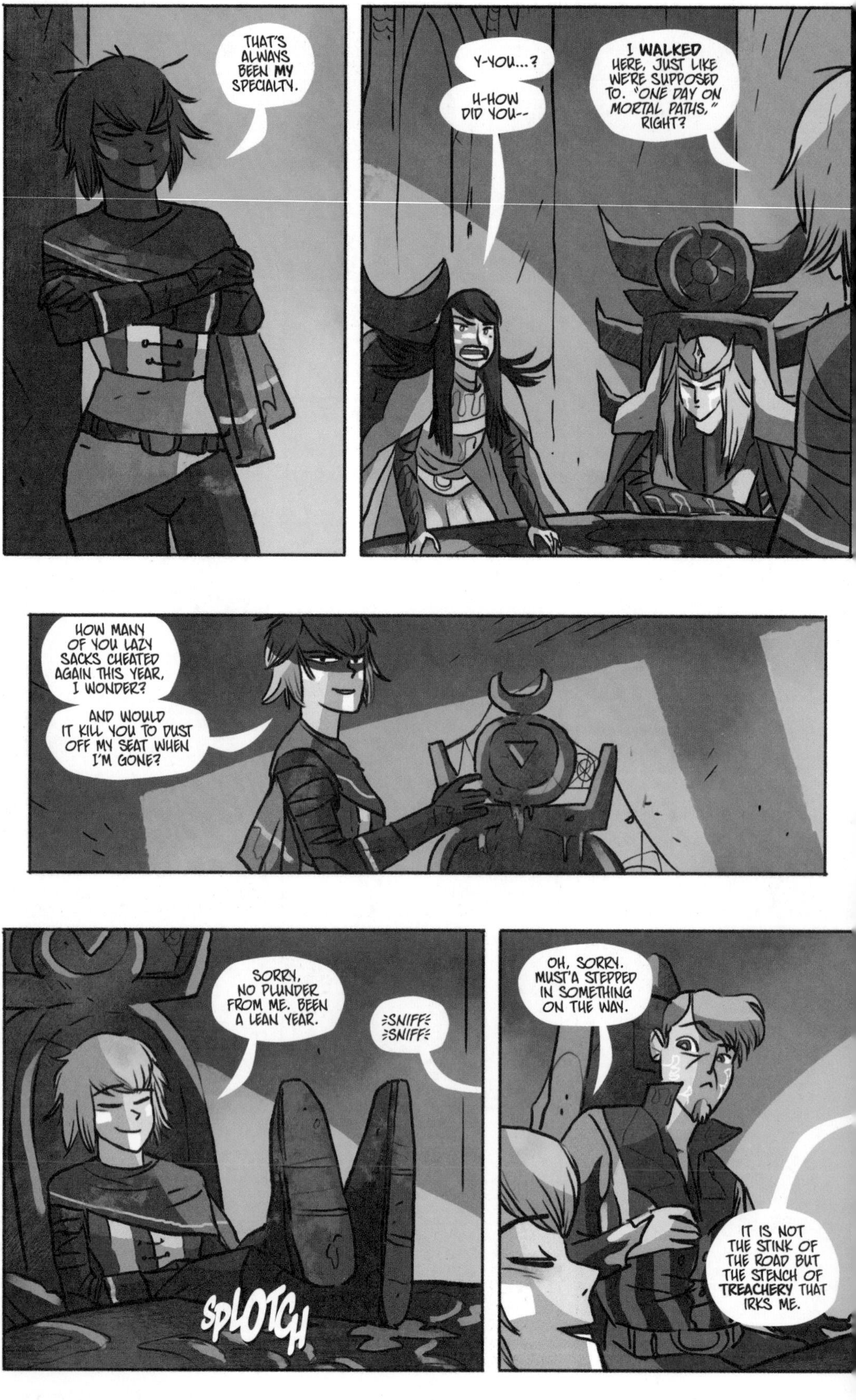
THAT'S ALWAYS BEEN MY SPECIALTY.
Y-YOU...?
H-HOW DID YOU--
I WALKED HERE, JUST LIKE WE'RE SUPPOSED TO. "ONE DAY ON MORTAL PATHS," RIGHT?
HOW MANY OF YOU LAZY SACKS CHEATED AGAIN THIS YEAR, I WONDER?
AND WOULD IT KILL YOU TO DUST OFF MY SEAT WHEN I'M GONE?
SORRY, NO PLUNDER FROM ME. BEEN A LEAN YEAR.
SNIFF SNIFF
SPLOTCH
OH, SORRY. MUST'A STEPPED IN SOMETHING ON THE WAY.
IT IS NOT THE STINK OF THE ROAD BUT THE STENCH OF TREACHERY THAT IRKS ME.

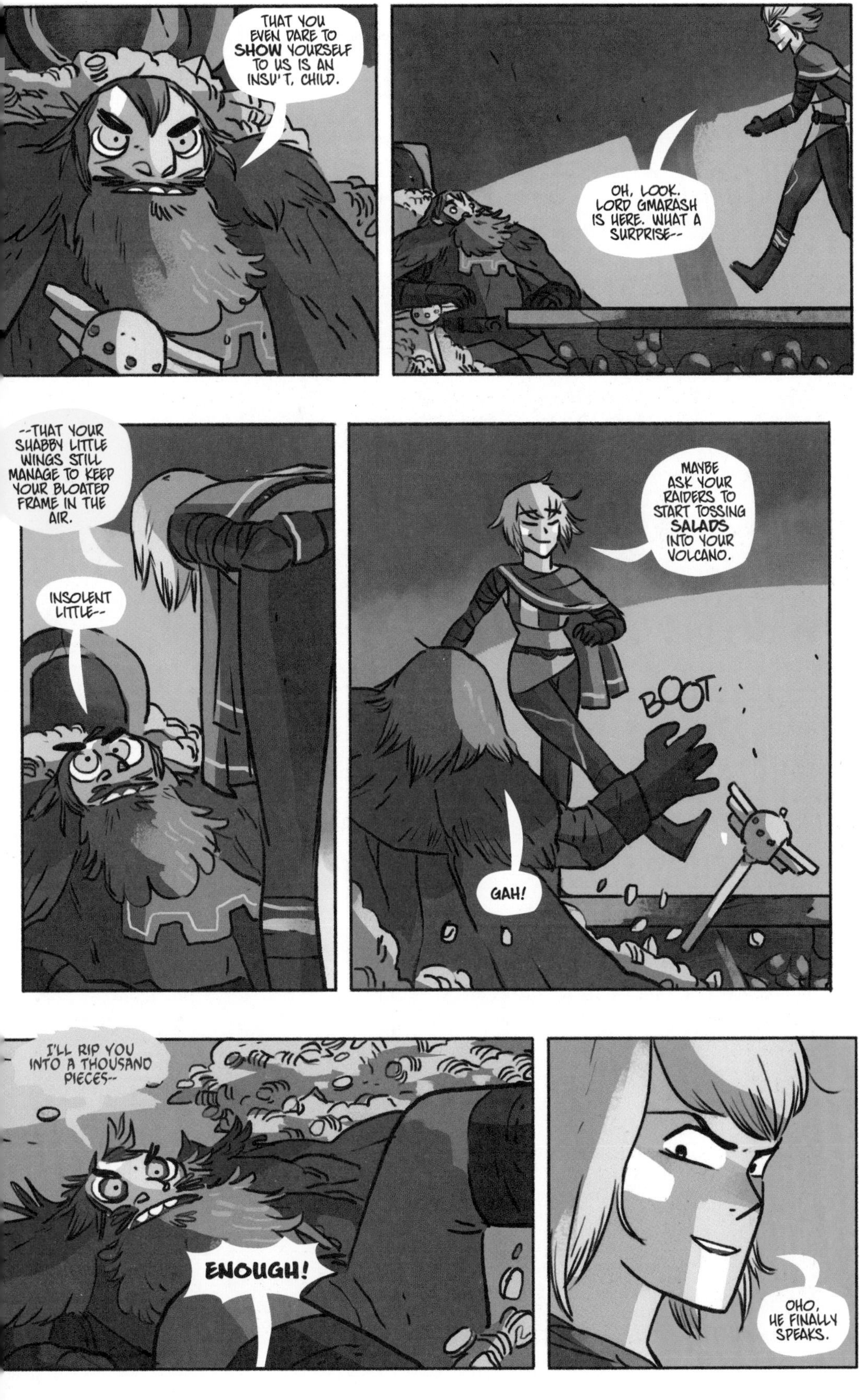
THAT YOU EVEN DARE TO **SHOW** YOURSELF TO US IS AN INSULT, CHILD.
OH, LOOK. LORD GMARASH IS HERE. WHAT A SURPRISE--
--THAT YOUR SHABBY LITTLE WINGS STILL MANAGE TO KEEP YOUR BLOATED FRAME IN THE AIR.
INSOLENT LITTLE--
MAYBE ASK YOUR RAIDERS TO START TOSSING **SALADS** INTO YOUR VOLCANO.
BOOT
GAH!
I'LL RIP YOU INTO A THOUSAND PIECES--
ENOUGH!
OHO, HE FINALLY SPEAKS.

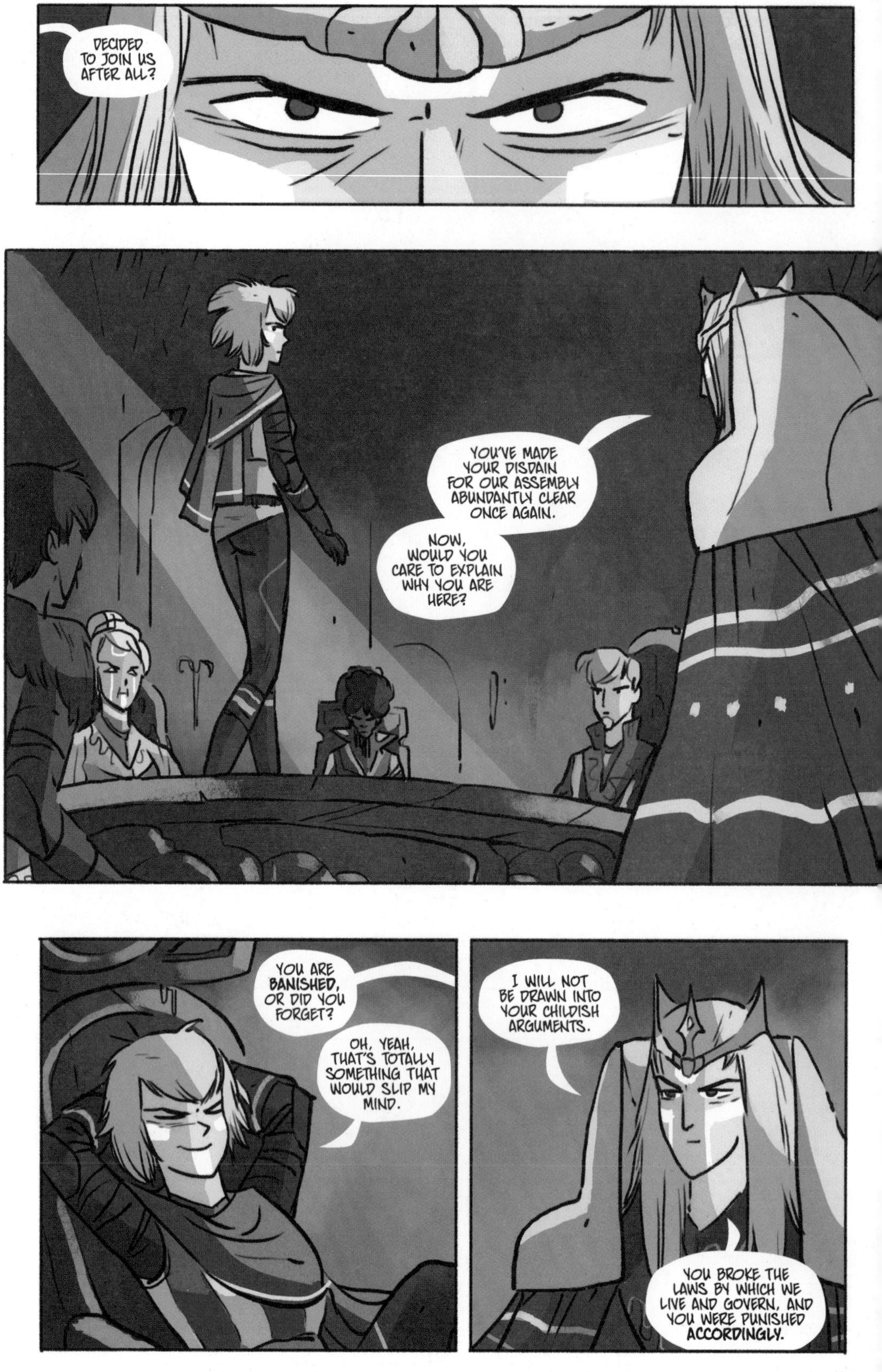
DECIDED TO JOIN US AFTER ALL?
YOU'VE MADE YOUR DISDAIN FOR OUR ASSEMBLY ABUNDANTLY CLEAR ONCE AGAIN.
NOW, WOULD YOU CARE TO EXPLAIN WHY YOU ARE HERE?
YOU ARE BANISHED, OR DID YOU FORGET?
OH, YEAH, THAT'S TOTALLY SOMETHING THAT WOULD SLIP MY MIND.
I WILL NOT BE DRAWN INTO YOUR CHILDISH ARGUMENTS.
YOU BROKE THE LAWS BY WHICH WE LIVE AND GOVERN, AND YOU WERE PUNISHED ACCORDINGLY.

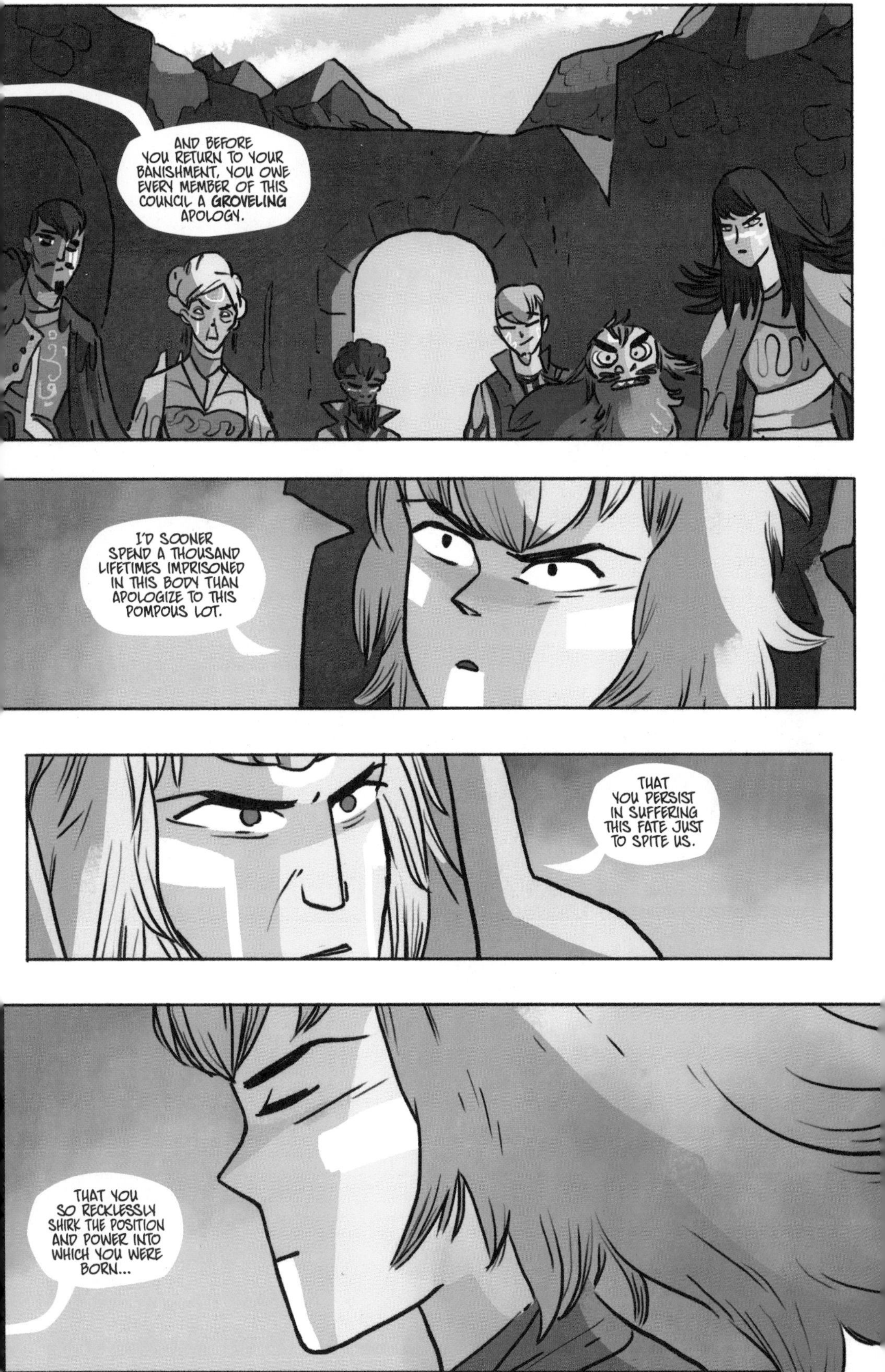
AND BEFORE YOU RETURN TO YOUR BANISHMENT, YOU OWE EVERY MEMBER OF THIS COUNCIL A GROVELING APOLOGY.
I'D SOONER SPEND A THOUSAND LIFETIMES IMPRISONED IN THIS BODY THAN APOLOGIZE TO THIS POMPOUS LOT.
THAT YOU PERSIST IN SUFFERING THIS FATE JUST TO SPITE US.
THAT YOU SO RECKLESSLY SHIRK THE POSITION AND POWER INTO WHICH YOU WERE BORN...

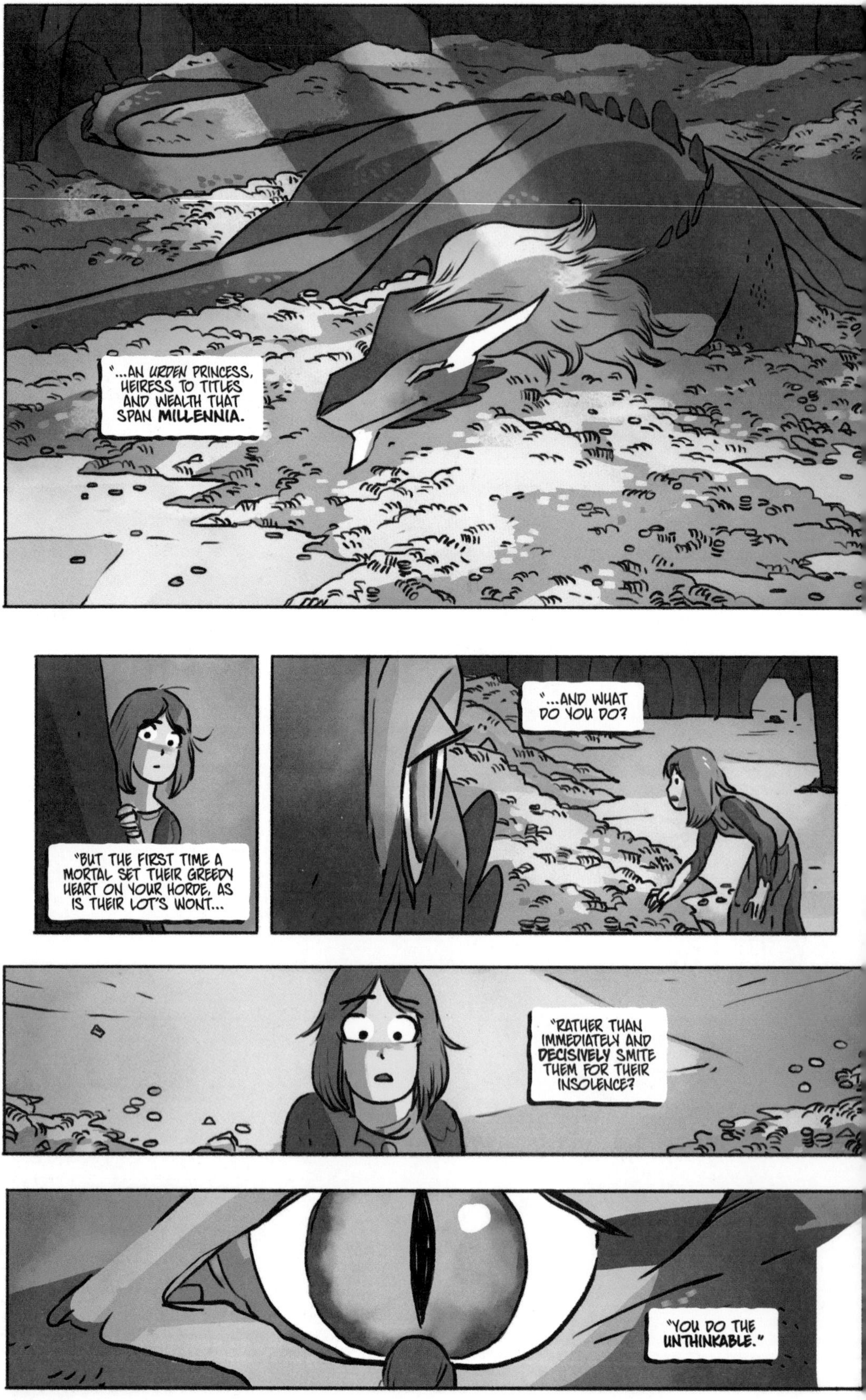
"...AN URDEN PRINCESS, HEIRESS TO TITLES AND WEALTH THAT SPAN MILLENNIA.
"BUT THE FIRST TIME A MORTAL SET THEIR GREEDY HEART ON YOUR HORDE, AS IS THEIR LOT'S WONT...
"...AND WHAT DO YOU DO?
"RATHER THAN IMMEDIATELY AND DECISIVELY SMITE THEM FOR THEIR INSOLENCE?
"YOU DO THE UNTHINKABLE."

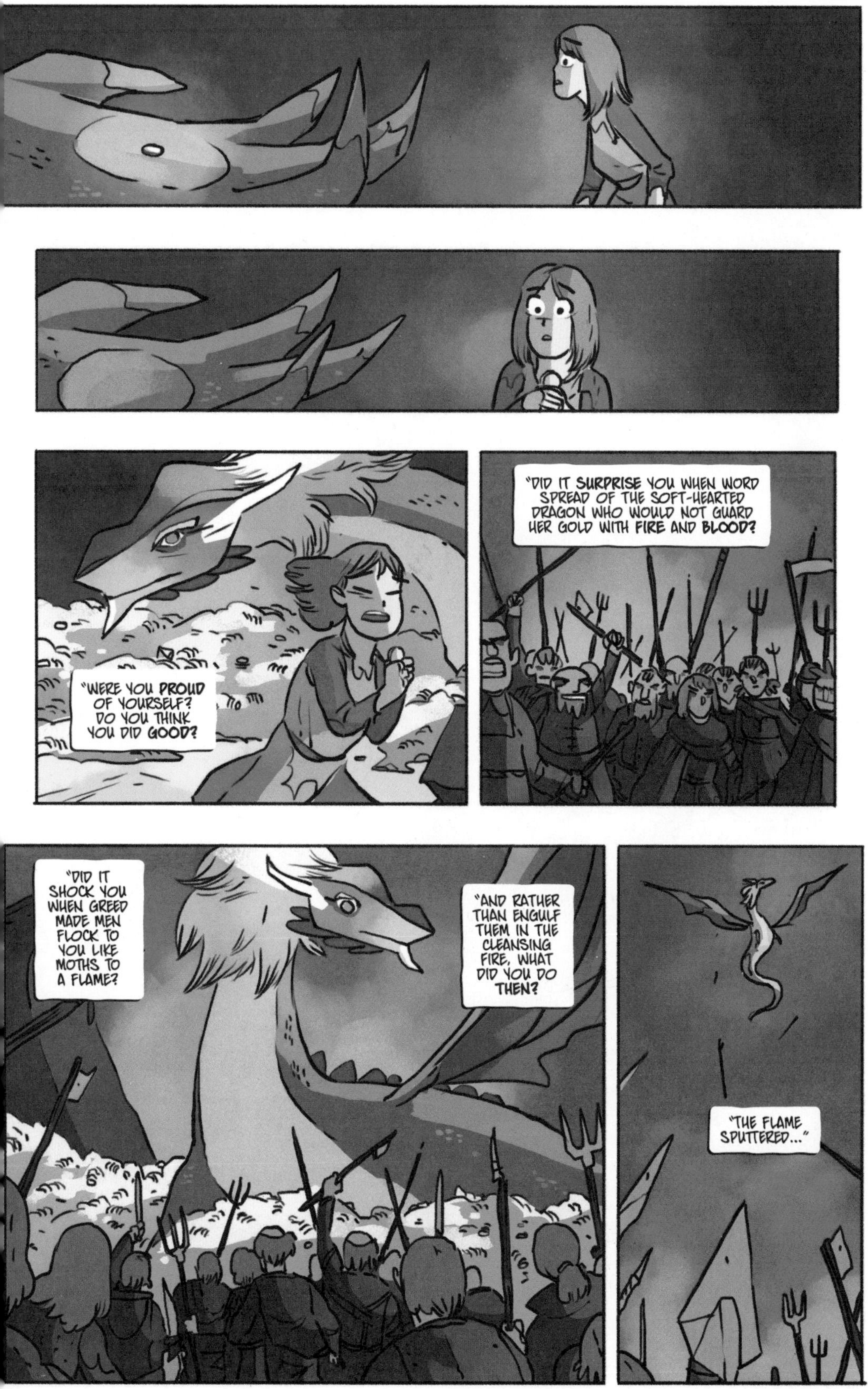
"WERE YOU PROUD OF YOURSELF? DO YOU THINK YOU DID GOOD?
"DID IT SURPRISE YOU WHEN WORD SPREAD OF THE SOFT-HEARTED DRAGON WHO WOULD NOT GUARD HER GOLD WITH FIRE AND BLOOD?
"DID IT SHOCK YOU WHEN GREED MADE MEN FLOCK TO YOU LIKE MOTHS TO A FLAME?
"AND RATHER THAN ENGULF THEM IN THE CLEANSING FIRE, WHAT DID YOU DO THEN?
"THE FLAME SPUTTERED..."

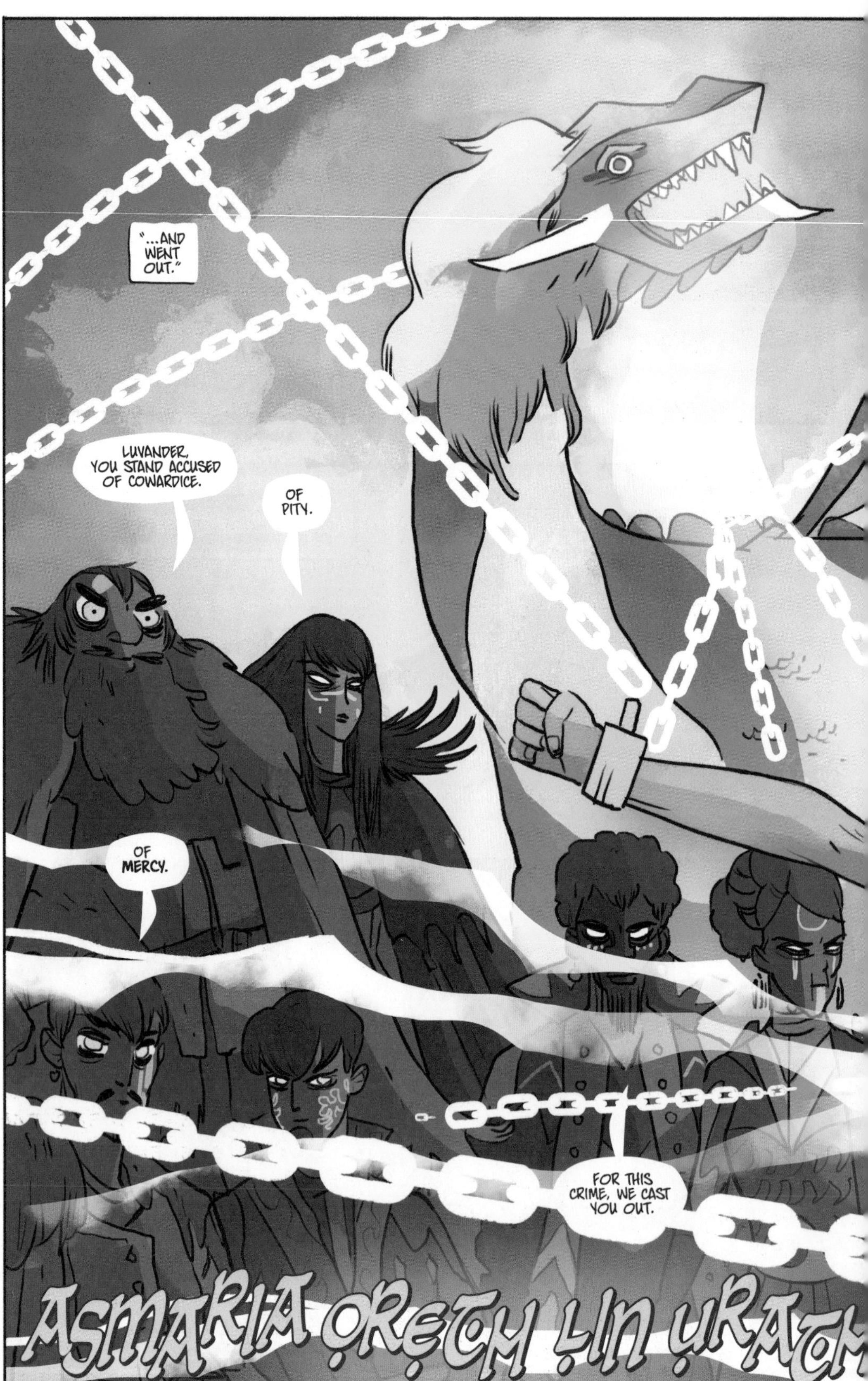
"...AND WENT OUT."
LUVANDER, YOU STAND ACCUSED OF COWARDICE.
OF PITY.
OF MERCY.
FOR THIS CRIME, WE CAST YOU OUT.
ASMARIA ỌRẸTM ḶIN ỤRATM

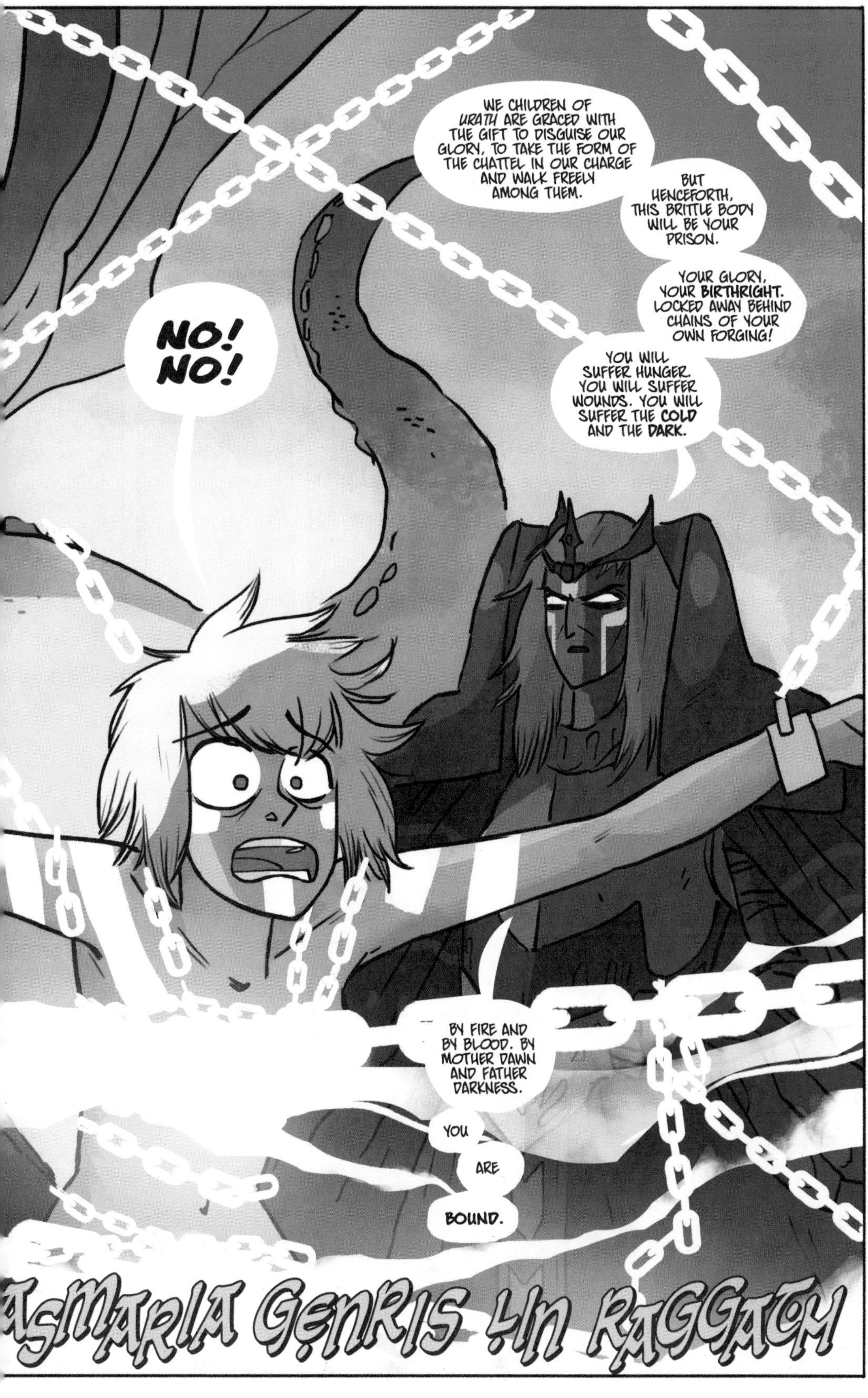
WE CHILDREN OF URATH ARE GRACED WITH THE GIFT TO DISGUISE OUR GLORY, TO TAKE THE FORM OF THE CHATTEL IN OUR CHARGE AND WALK FREELY AMONG THEM.
BUT HENCEFORTH, THIS BRITTLE BODY WILL BE YOUR PRISON.
YOUR GLORY, YOUR **BIRTHRIGHT**. LOCKED AWAY BEHIND CHAINS OF YOUR OWN FORGING!
NO! NO!
YOU WILL SUFFER HUNGER. YOU WILL SUFFER WOUNDS. YOU WILL SUFFER THE **COLD** AND THE **DARK**.
BY FIRE AND BY BLOOD. BY MOTHER DAWN AND FATHER DARKNESS.
YOU
ARE
BOUND.
ASMARIA GENRIS LIN RAGGATH

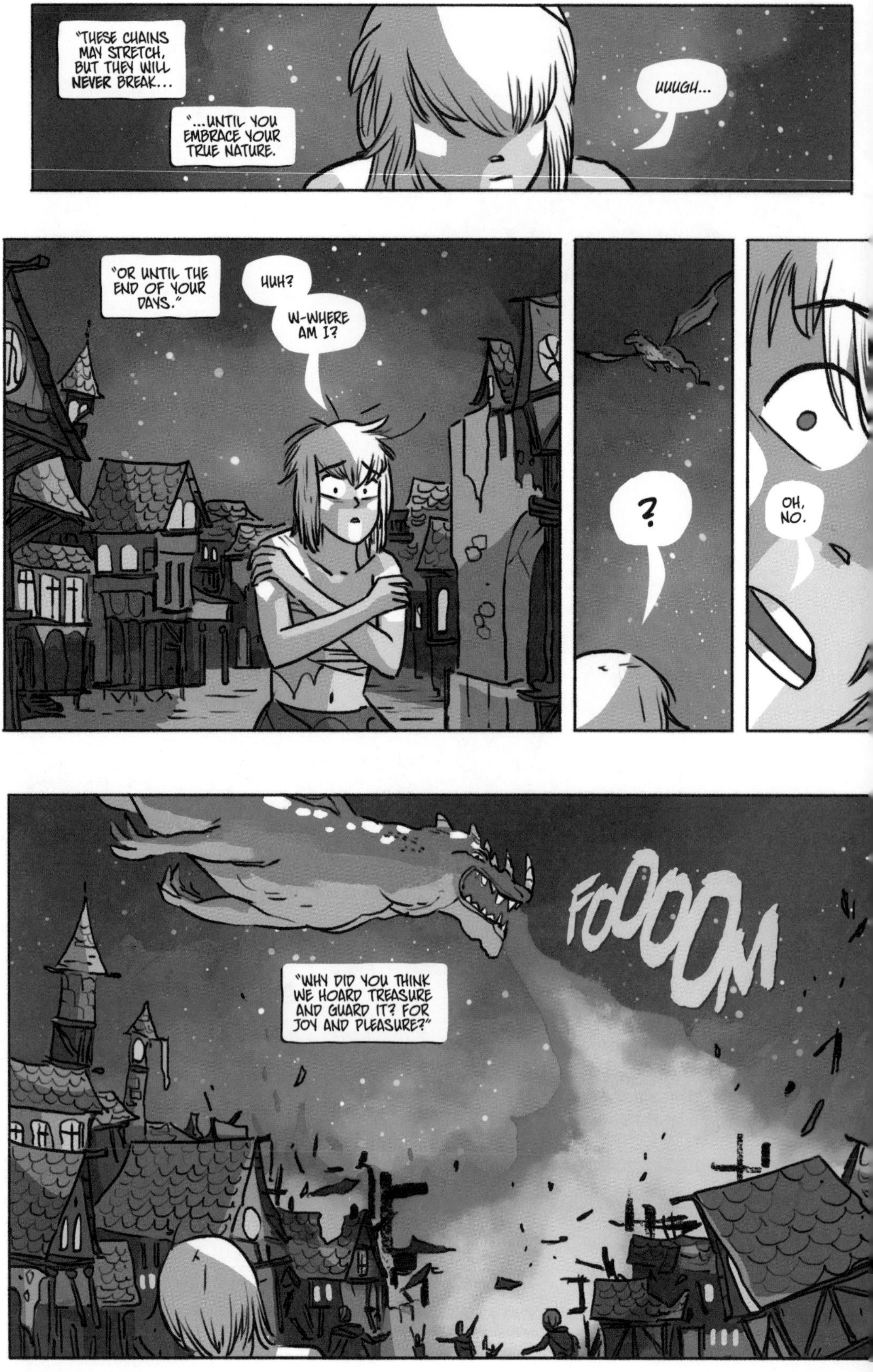
"THESE CHAINS MAY STRETCH, BUT THEY WILL NEVER BREAK...
"...UNTIL YOU EMBRACE YOUR TRUE NATURE.
UUUGH...
"OR UNTIL THE END OF YOUR DAYS."
HUH?
W-WHERE AM I?
?
OH, NO.
FOOOOM
"WHY DID YOU THINK WE HOARD TREASURE AND GUARD IT? FOR JOY AND PLEASURE?"

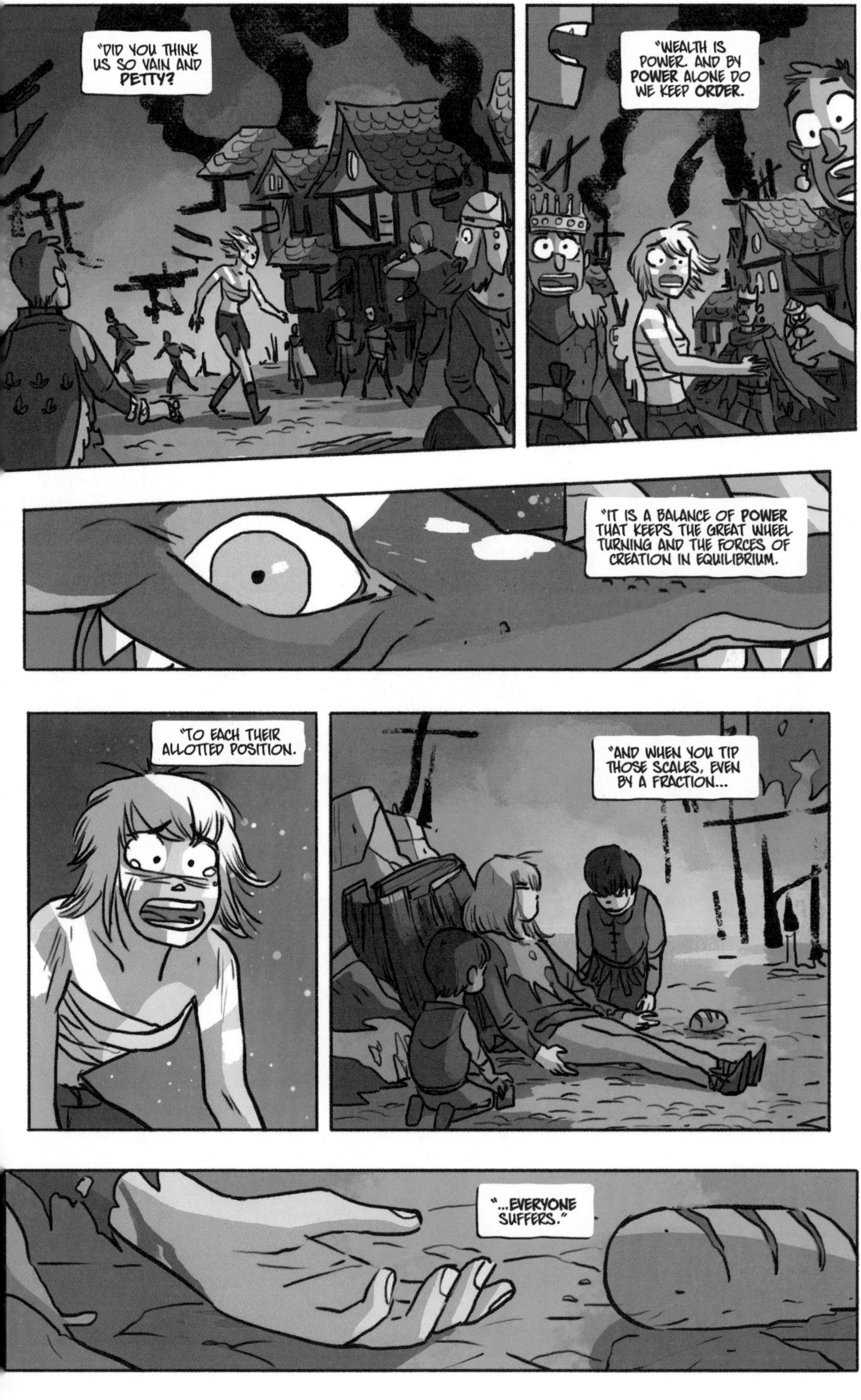
"DID YOU THINK US SO VAIN AND PETTY?
"WEALTH IS POWER. AND BY POWER ALONE DO WE KEEP ORDER.
"IT IS A BALANCE OF POWER THAT KEEPS THE GREAT WHEEL TURNING AND THE FORCES OF CREATION IN EQUILIBRIUM.
"TO EACH THEIR ALLOTTED POSITION.
"AND WHEN YOU TIP THOSE SCALES, EVEN BY A FRACTION...
"...EVERYONE SUFFERS."

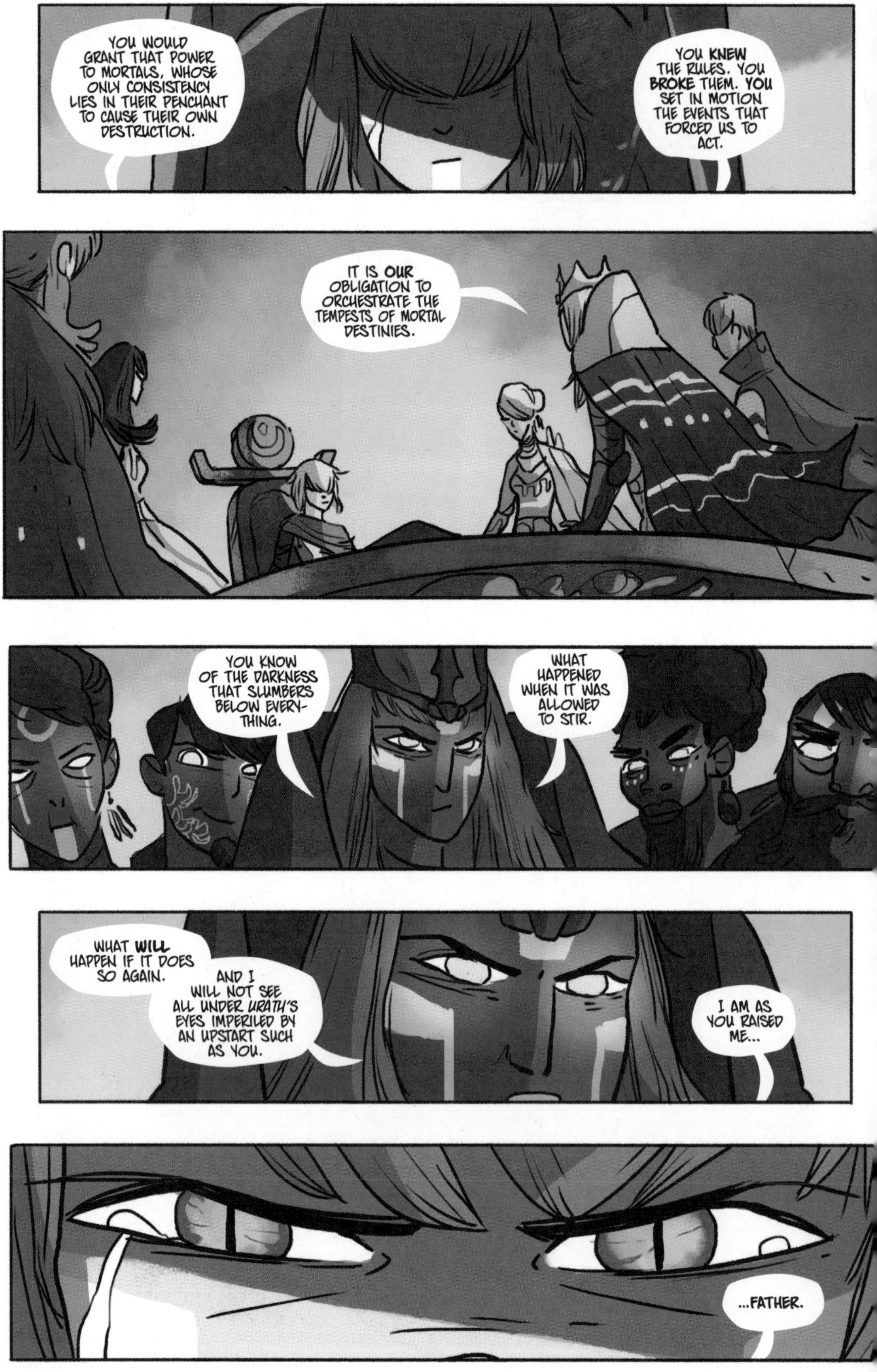

YOU WOULD GRANT THAT POWER TO MORTALS, WHOSE ONLY CONSISTENCY LIES IN THEIR PENCHANT TO CAUSE THEIR OWN DESTRUCTION.
YOU **KNEW** THE RULES. YOU **BROKE** THEM. **YOU** SET IN MOTION THE EVENTS THAT FORCED US TO ACT.
IT IS **OUR** OBLIGATION TO ORCHESTRATE THE TEMPESTS OF MORTAL DESTINIES.
YOU KNOW OF THE DARKNESS THAT SLUMBERS BELOW EVERY-THING.
WHAT HAPPENED WHEN IT WAS ALLOWED TO STIR.
WHAT **WILL** HAPPEN IF IT DOES SO AGAIN.
AND I WILL NOT SEE ALL UNDER *URATH'S* EYES IMPERILED BY AN UPSTART SUCH AS YOU.
I AM AS YOU RAISED ME...
...FATHER.

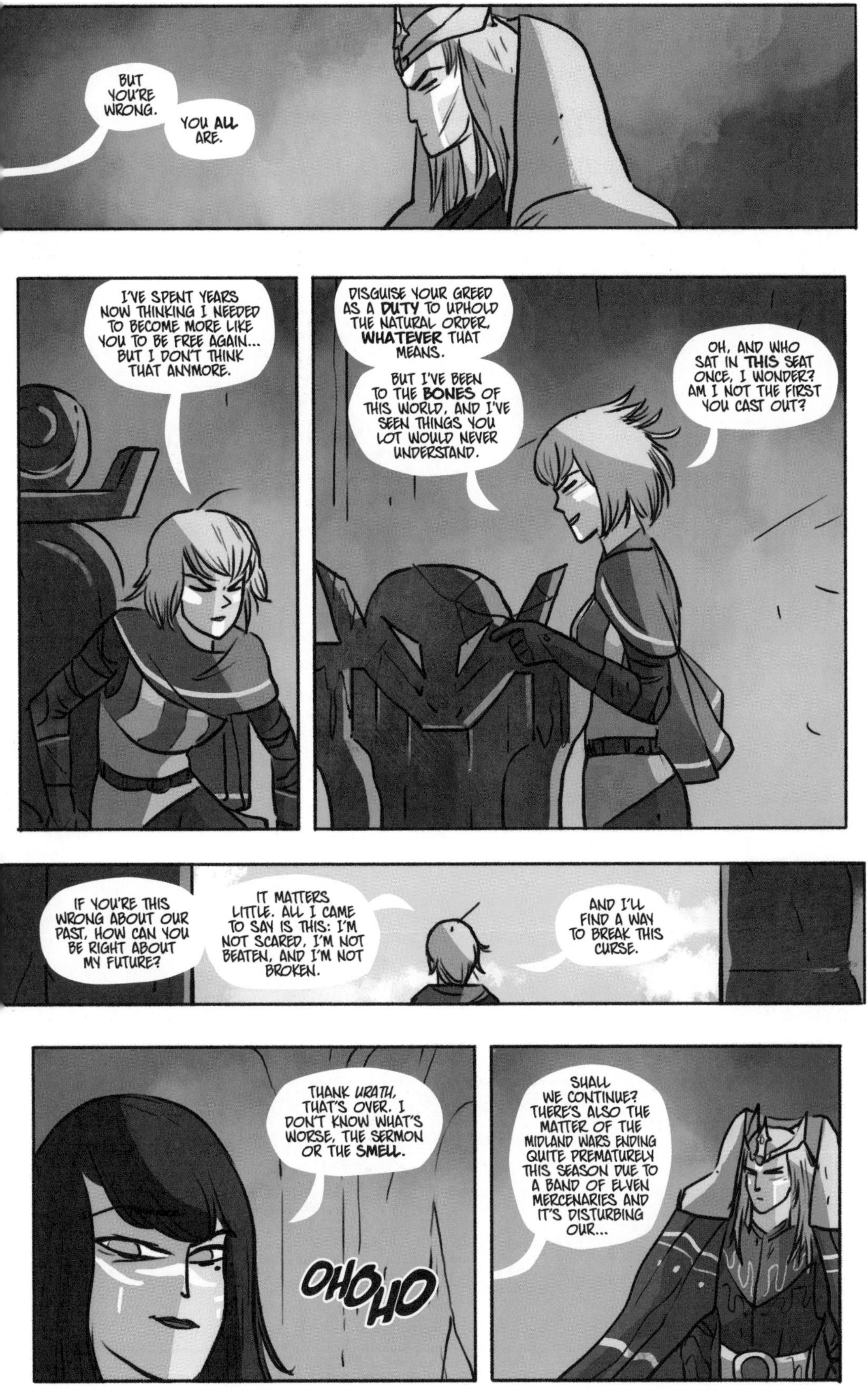
BUT YOU'RE WRONG.
YOU ALL ARE.
I'VE SPENT YEARS NOW THINKING I NEEDED TO BECOME MORE LIKE YOU TO BE FREE AGAIN... BUT I DON'T THINK THAT ANYMORE.
DISGUISE YOUR GREED AS A DUTY TO UPHOLD THE NATURAL ORDER, WHATEVER THAT MEANS.
BUT I'VE BEEN TO THE BONES OF THIS WORLD, AND I'VE SEEN THINGS YOU LOT WOULD NEVER UNDERSTAND.
OH, AND WHO SAT IN THIS SEAT ONCE, I WONDER? AM I NOT THE FIRST YOU CAST OUT?
IF YOU'RE THIS WRONG ABOUT OUR PAST, HOW CAN YOU BE RIGHT ABOUT MY FUTURE?
IT MATTERS LITTLE. ALL I CAME TO SAY IS THIS: I'M NOT SCARED, I'M NOT BEATEN, AND I'M NOT BROKEN.
AND I'LL FIND A WAY TO BREAK THIS CURSE.
THANK URATH, THAT'S OVER. I DON'T KNOW WHAT'S WORSE, THE SERMON OR THE SMELL.
OHOHO
SHALL WE CONTINUE? THERE'S ALSO THE MATTER OF THE MIDLAND WARS ENDING QUITE PREMATURELY THIS SEASON DUE TO A BAND OF ELVEN MERCENARIES AND IT'S DISTURBING OUR...

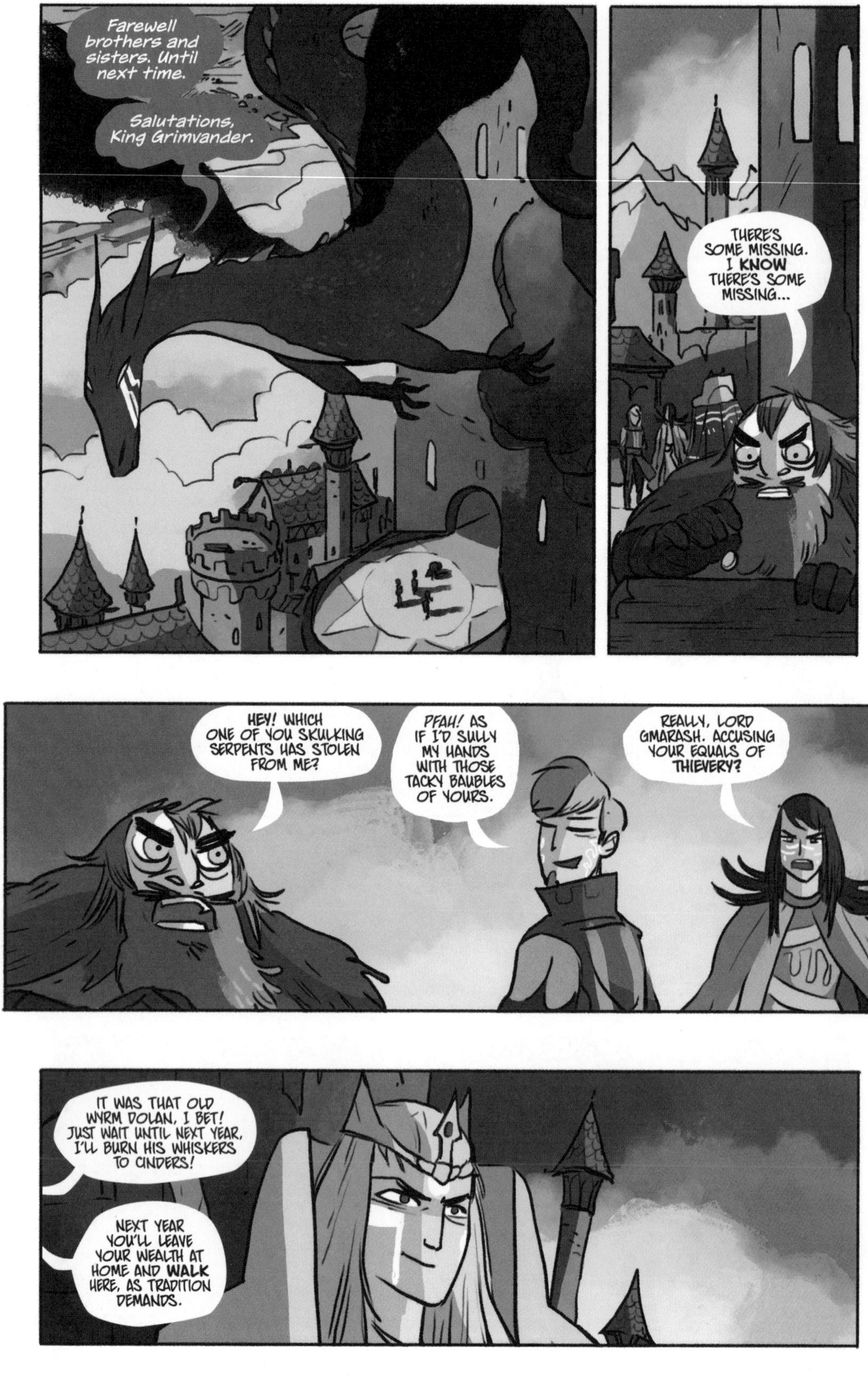

Farewell brothers and sisters. Until next time.
Salutations, King Grimvander.
THERE'S SOME MISSING. I **KNOW** THERE'S SOME MISSING...
HEY! WHICH ONE OF YOU SKULKING SERPENTS HAS STOLEN FROM ME?
PFAH! AS IF I'D SULLY MY HANDS WITH THOSE TACKY BAUBLES OF YOURS.
REALLY, LORD GMARASH. ACCUSING YOUR EQUALS OF **THIEVERY**?
IT WAS THAT OLD WYRM DOLAN, I BET! JUST WAIT UNTIL NEXT YEAR, I'LL BURN HIS WHISKERS TO CINDERS!
NEXT YEAR YOU'LL LEAVE YOUR WEALTH AT HOME AND **WALK** HERE, AS TRADITION DEMANDS.

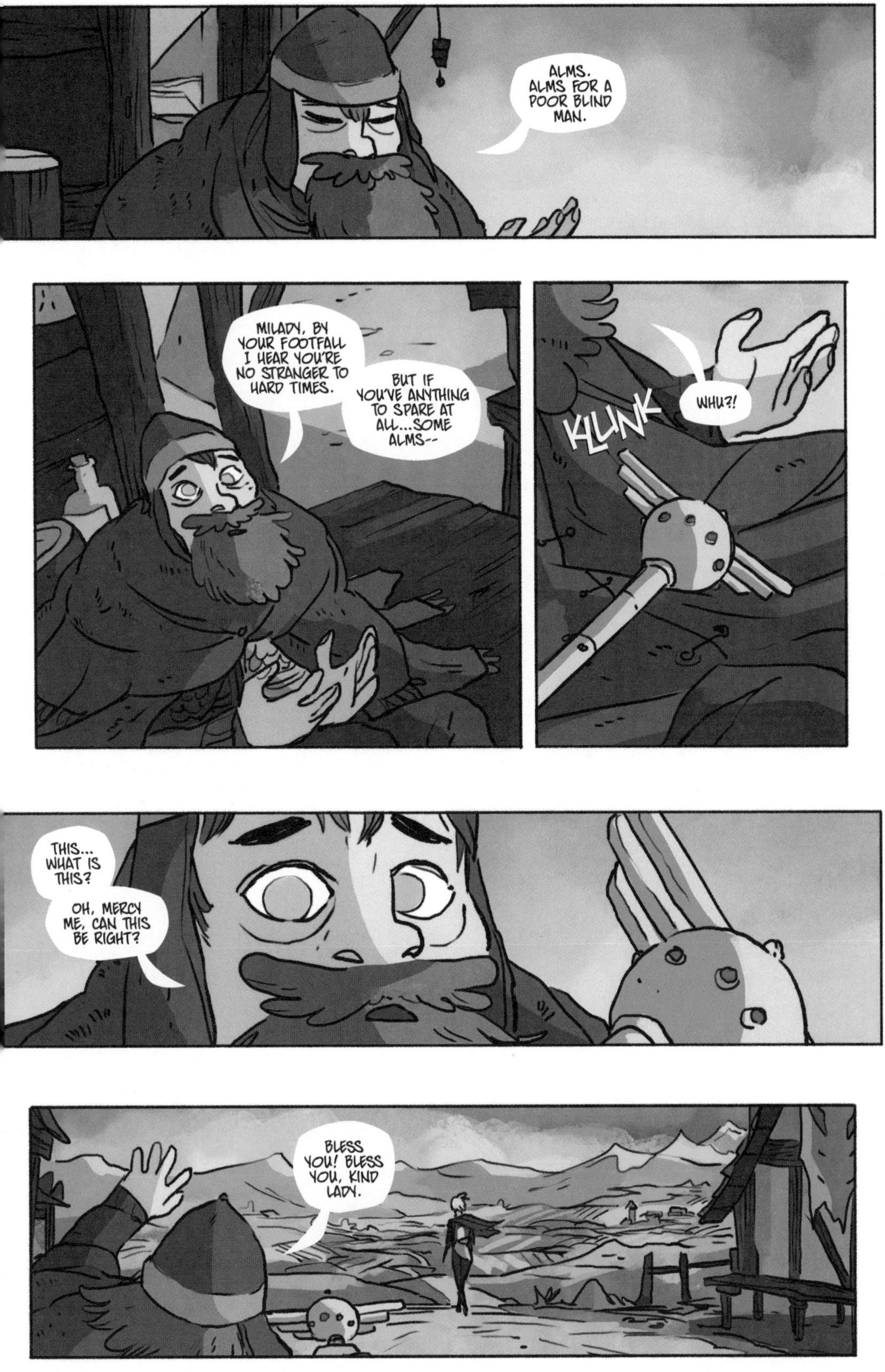
ALMS. ALMS FOR A POOR BLIND MAN.
MILADY, BY YOUR FOOTFALL I HEAR YOU'RE NO STRANGER TO HARD TIMES.
BUT IF YOU'VE ANYTHING TO SPARE AT ALL...SOME ALMS--
KLUNK
WHU?!
THIS... WHAT IS THIS?
OH, MERCY ME, CAN THIS BE RIGHT?
BLESS YOU! BLESS YOU, KIND LADY.

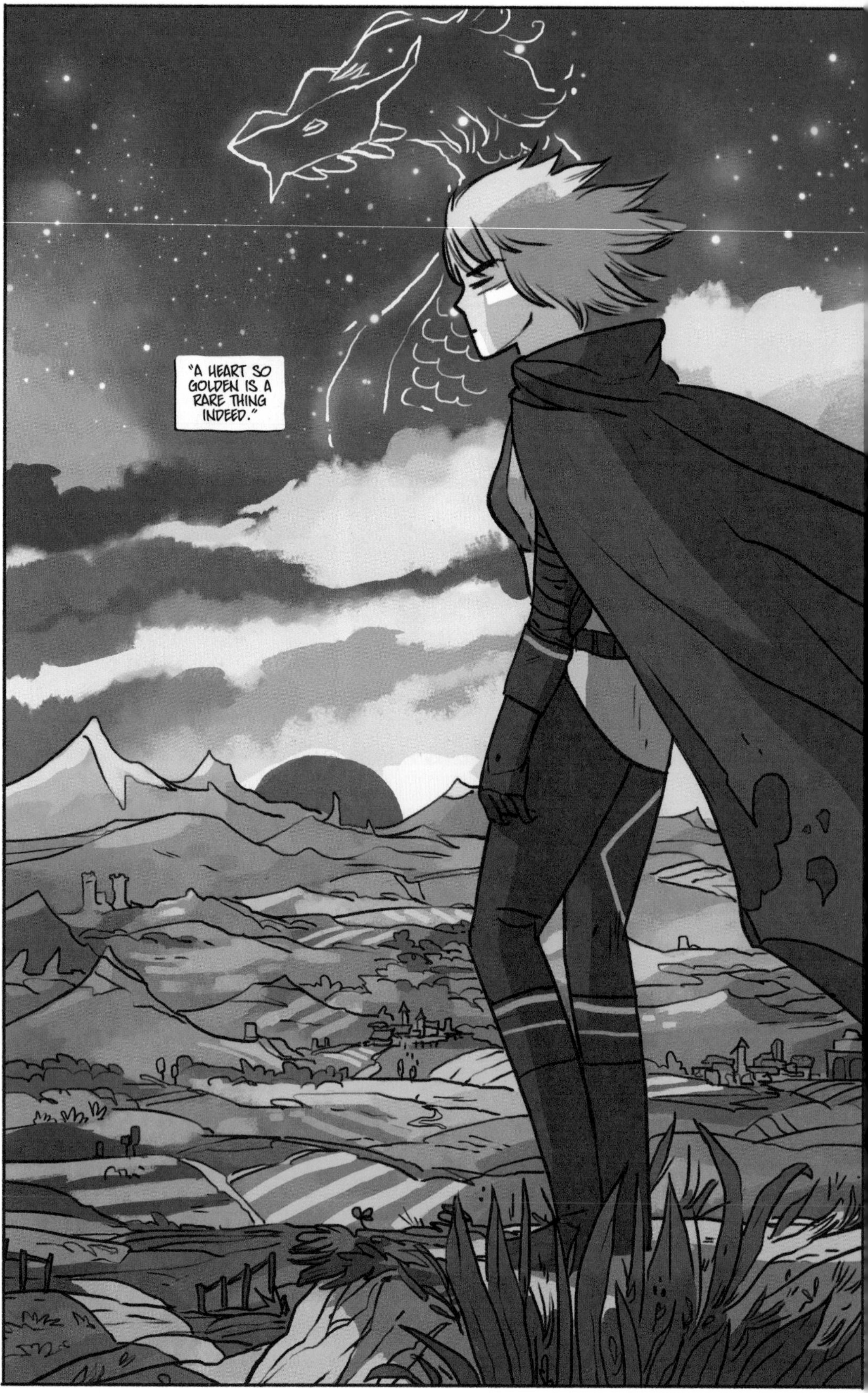
"A HEART SO GOLDEN IS A RARE THING INDEED."

END OF BOOK 1

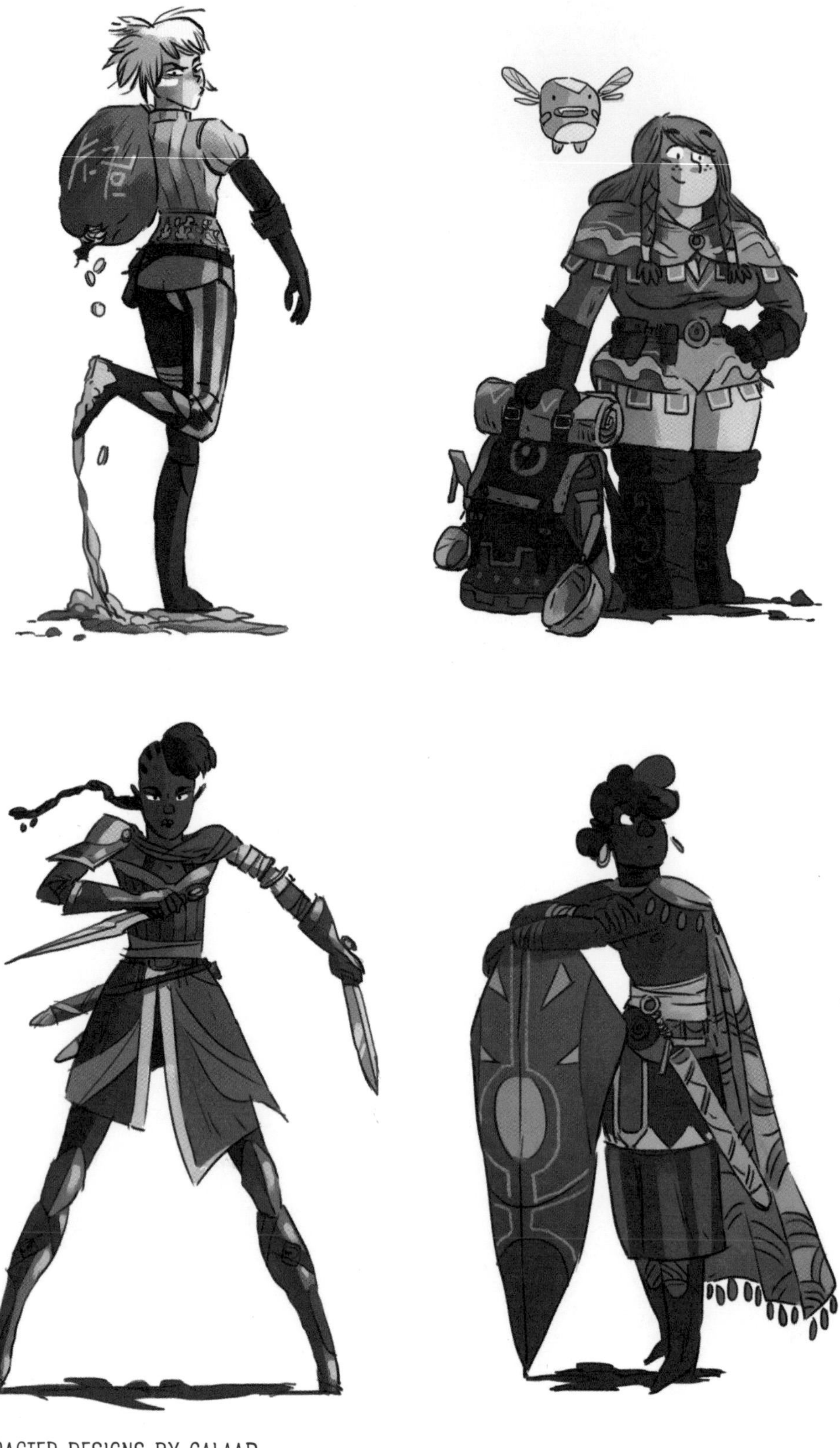

CHARACTER DESIGNS BY GALAAD

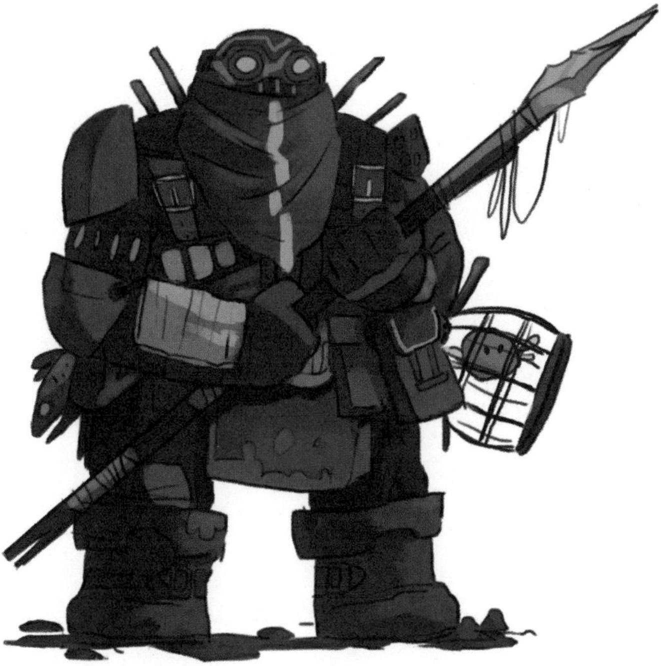

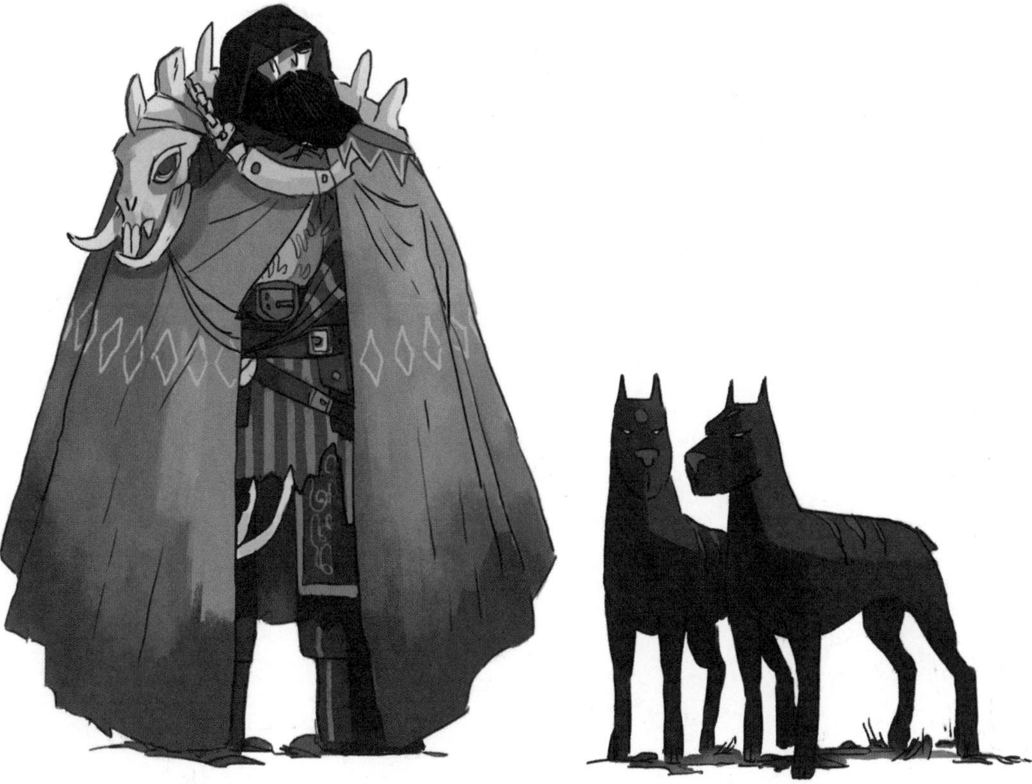

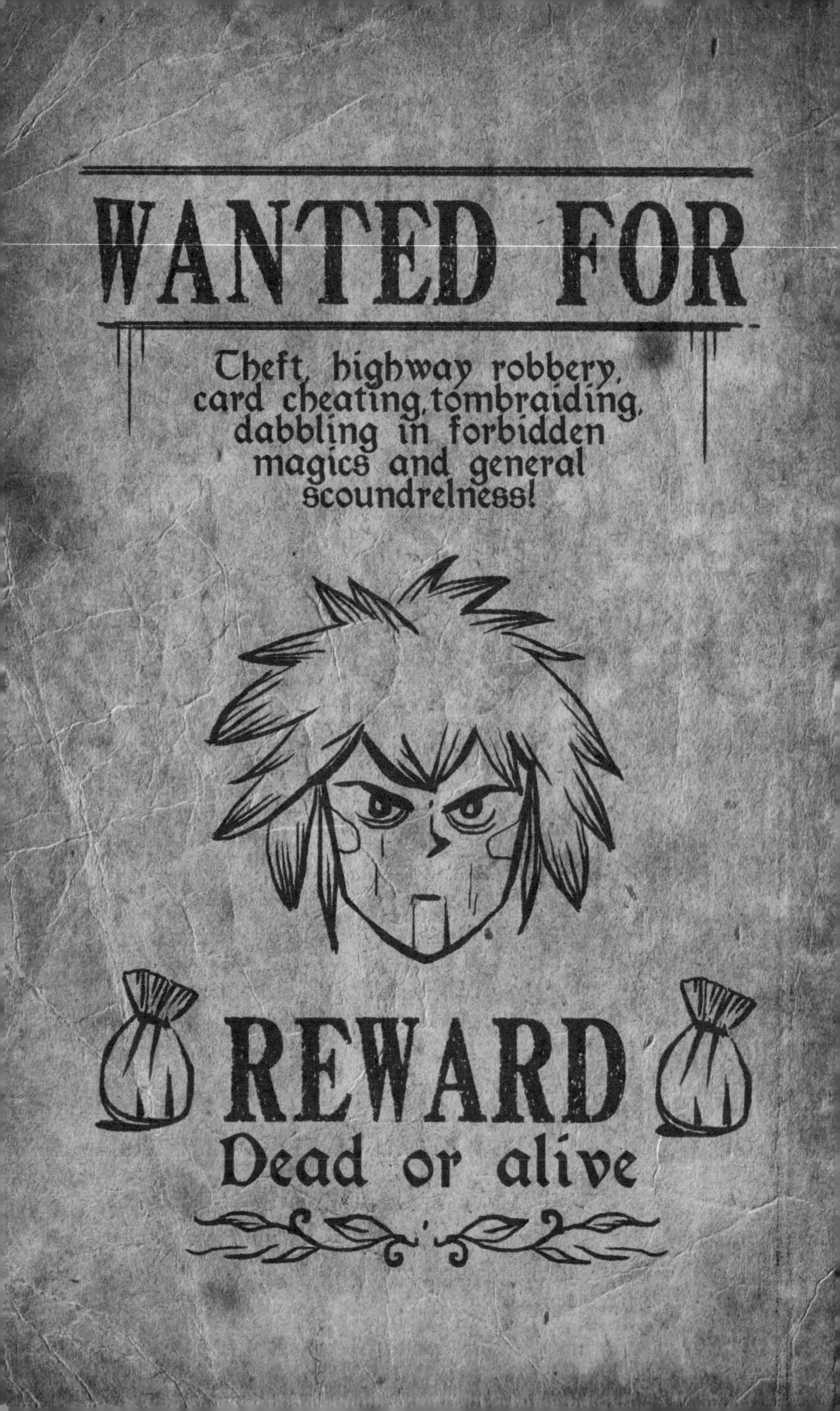
WANTED FOR
Theft, highway robbery, card cheating, tombraiding, dabbling in forbidden magics and general scoundrelness!
REWARD
Dead or alive

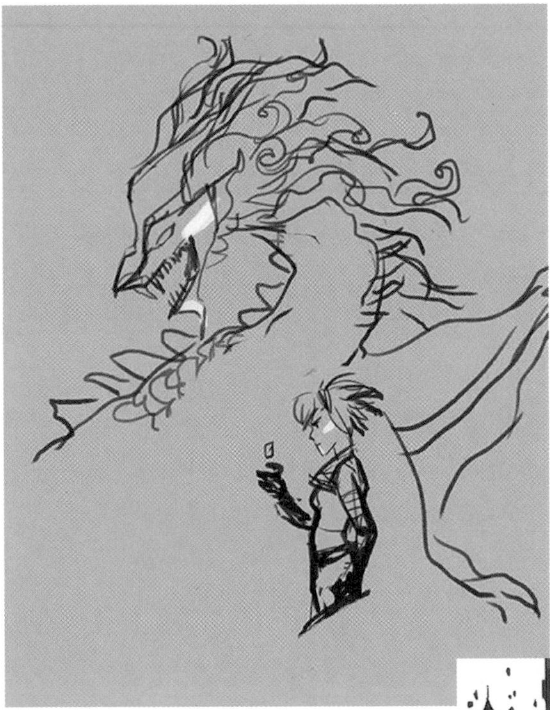

COVER SKETCH

FINAL COVER

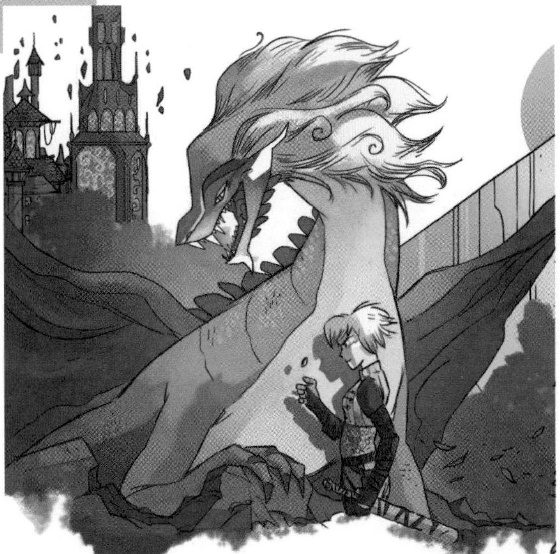

THANK YOU FOR READING!

GET AN EXCLUSIVE BEHIND-THE-SCENES LOOK AT THE CREATION OF SCALES & SCOUNDRELS BY VISITING TKOPRESENTS.COM/SCALES-BONUS

TKO STUDIOS

MEET THE SCOUNDRELS

SEBASTIAN GIRNER is a German-born, American-raised comic editor and writer. Since its launch in 2018 he has served as Editor-in-Chief for TKO STUDIOS. His comic book writing includes *Shirtless Bear-Fighter!* and *The Devil's Red Bride*. He lives and works in Brooklyn.

GALAAD is a French comic book artist and a former freelance illustrator, animator, concept artist and storyboard artist for video games and animation. A child of the 80s, his art style was heavily influenced by the Japanese animation of this era, among them *Neon Genesis Evangelion*, *Princess Mononoke*, *Nausicca of the Valley of the Wind* and *Dragon Ball*.

JEFF POWELL has lettered a variety of titles in his long career including *Teenage Mutant Ninja Turtles*, *Sonic the Hedgehog* and the award-nominated *Atomic Robo*. He has designed books, logos and trade dress for Marvel, Archie, IDW, Image Comics and others. He is neither German nor French.

TO BE CONTINUED IN...

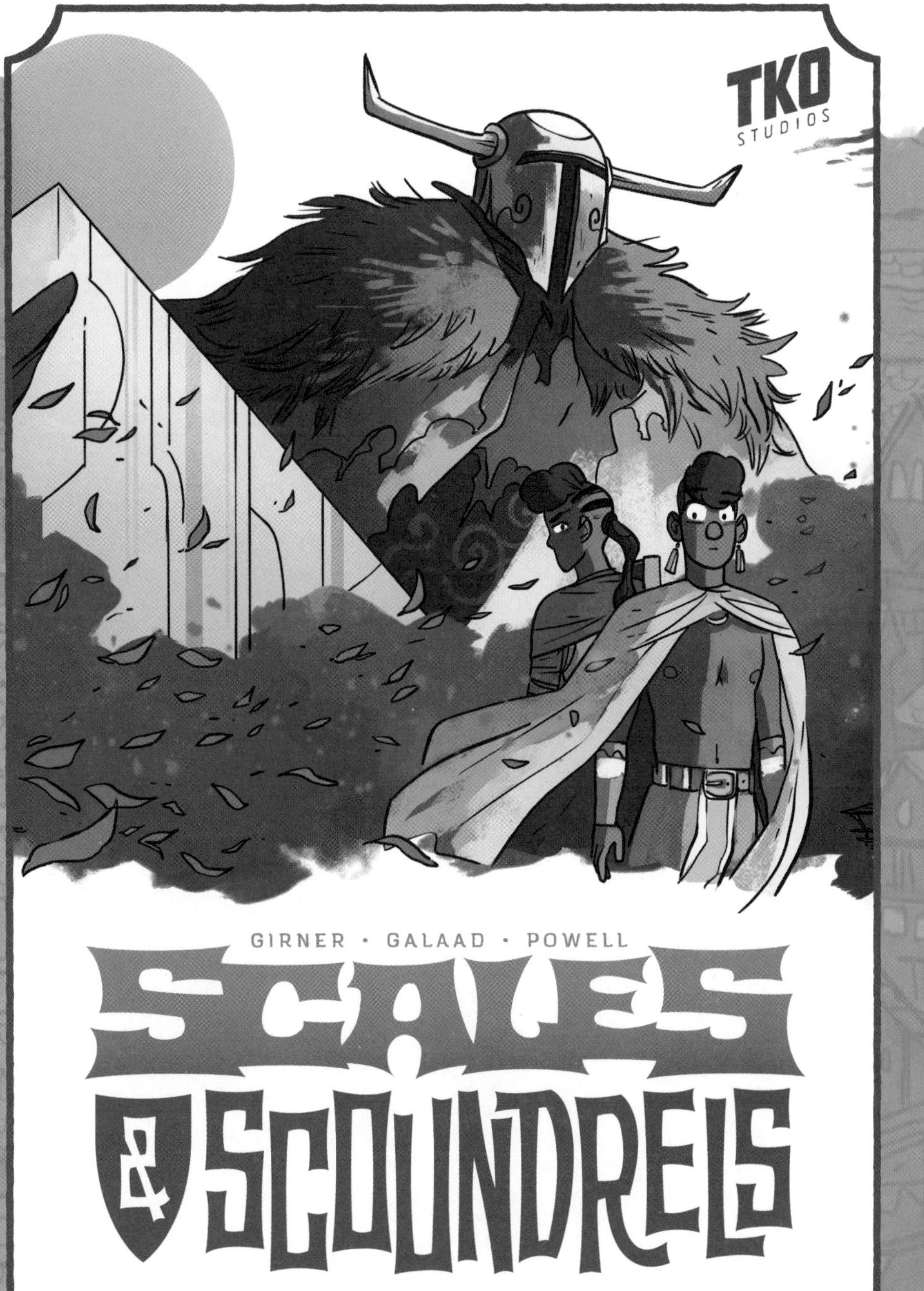
TKO
STUDIOS
GIRNER · GALAAD · POWELL
SCALES & SCOUNDRELS
BOOK 2: THE FESTIVAL OF LIFE

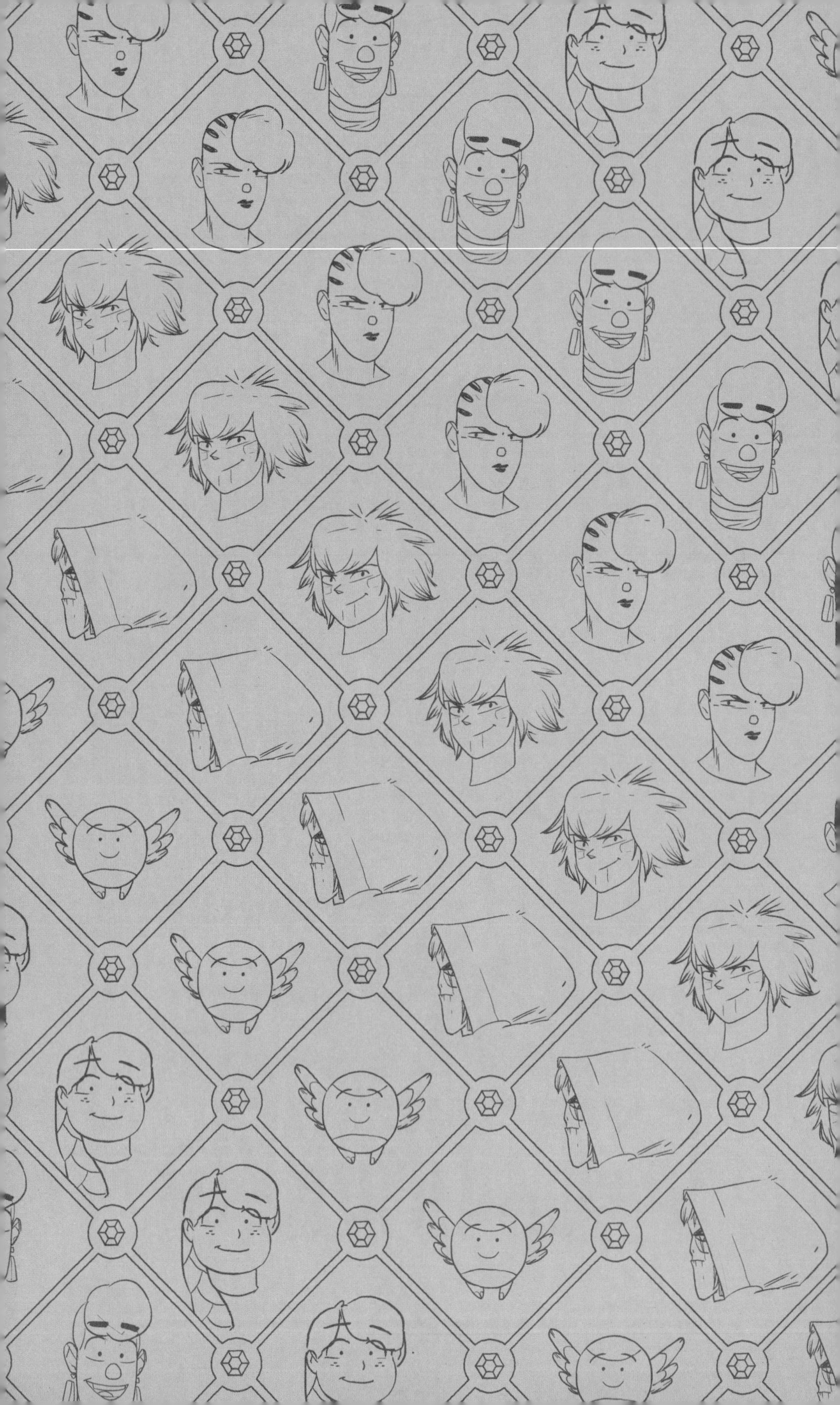